STEPHEN JONES lives in Lond[...]
three World Fantasy Awards, fou[...]
Stoker Awards and three Internat[...]
as being a seventeen-time recipien[...]
Hugo Award nominee. A former television p[...]
genre movie publicist and consultant (the first three *Hellraiser* movies,
Night Life, Nightbreed, Split Second, Mind Ripper, Last Gasp etc.),
he is the co-editor of *Horror: 100 Best Books, Horror: Another 100
Best Books, The Best Horror from Fantasy Tales, Gaslight & Ghosts,
Now We Are Sick, H. P. Lovecraft's Book of Horror, The Anthology
of Fantasy & the Supernatural, Secret City: Strange Tales of London,
Great Ghost Stories, Tales to Freeze the Blood: More Great Ghost
Stories* and the *Dark Terrors, Dark Voices* and *Fantasy Tales* series.
He has written *Stardust: The Visual Companion, Creepshows: The
Illustrated Stephen King Movie Guide, The Essential Monster Movie
Guide, The Illustrated Vampire Movie Guide, The Illustrated Dino-
saur Movie Guide, The Illustrated Frankenstein Movie Guide* and
The Illustrated Werewolf Movie Guide, and compiled *The Mammoth
Book of Best New Horror* series, *The Mammoth Book of Terror, The
Mammoth Book of Vampires, The Mammoth Book of Zombies, The
Mammoth Book of Werewolves, The Mammoth Book of Franken-
stein, The Mammoth Book of Dracula, The Mammoth Book of
Vampire Stories By Women, The Mammoth Book of New Terror,
The Mammoth Book of Monsters, Shadows Over Innsmouth, Weird
Shadows Over Innsmouth, Dark Detectives, Dancing with the Dark,
Dark of the Night, White of the Moon, Keep Out the Night, By
Moonlight Only, Don't Turn Out the Light, H. P. Lovecraft's Book
of the Supernatural, Travellers in Darkness, Summer Chills, Exor-
cisms and Ecstasies* by Karl Edward Wagner, *The Vampire Stories of
R. Chetwynd-Hayes, Phantoms and Fiends* and *Frights and Fancies*
by R. Chetwynd-Hayes, *James Herbert: By Horror Haunted, The
Complete Chronicles of Conan* by Robert E. Howard, *The Emperor
of Dreams: The Lost Worlds of Clark Ashton Smith, Sea-Kings of
Mars and Otherworldly Stories* by Leigh Brackett, *The Mark of the
Beast and Other Fantastical Tales* by Rudyard Kipling, *Clive Barker's
A–Z of Horror, Clive Barker's Shadows in Eden, Clive Barker's The
Nightbreed Chronicles* and the *Hellraiser Chronicles*. He was a Guest
of Honour at the 2002 World Fantasy Convention in Minneapolis,
Minnesota, and the 2004 World Horror Convention in Phoenix,
Arizona. You can visit his web site at www.herebedragons.co.uk/
jones

THE
MAMMOTH BOOK OF
BEST NEW
HORROR

VOLUME EIGHTEEN

Edited and with an Introduction by
STEPHEN JONES

ROBINSON
London

Constable & Robinson Ltd
3 The Lanchesters
162 Fulham Palace Road
London W6 9ER
www.constablerobinson.com

First published in the UK by Robinson,
an imprint of Constable & Robinson Ltd 2007

A copy of the British Library Cataloguing in
Publication Data is available from the British Library.

ISBN-13: 978-1-84529-481-6

Printed and bound in the EU

1 3 5 7 9 10 8 6 4 2

CONTENTS

ACKNOWLEDGMENTS

I would like to thank David Barraclough, Kim Newman, Michael Marshall Smith, Sara and Randy Broecker, Val and Les Edwards, Max Burnell, Rodger Turner and Wayne MacLaurin (*www.sfsite. com*), Gordon Van Gelder, Peter Crowther, Mandy Slater, Pamela Brooks, Hugh Lamb, Claudia Dyer, Tim Lucas, Brian Mooney, Violet Jones, Amanda Foubister, Christopher Wicking and, especially, Pete Duncan and Dorothy Lumley for all their help and support. Special thanks are also due to *Locus*, *Variety*, *Ansible* and all the other sources that were used for reference in the Introduction and the Necrology.

POL POT'S BEAUTIFUL DAUGHTER (FANTASY) copyright ©
Geoff Ryman 2006. Originally published in *The Magazine of Fantasy & Science Fiction* No.655, October/November 2006. Reprinted
by permission of the author and the author's agent.

DEVIL'S SMILE copyright © Glen Hirshberg 2006. Originally
published in *American Morons*. Reprinted by permission of the
author and the author's agent, Anderson Grinberg Literary Management, Inc.

THE MAN WHO GOT OFF THE GHOST TRAIN copyright ©
Kim Newman 2006. Originally published in *The Man from the
Diogenes Club*. Reprinted by permission of the author.

NECROLOGY: 2006 copyright © Stephen Jones and Kim Newman 2007.

USEFUL ADDRESSES copyright © Stephen Jones 2007.

Congratulations to
Paul *and* Marie
on the occasion of their wedding.

INTRODUCTION

Horror in 2006

IN FEBRUARY 2006, French conglomerate Lagardere bought the Time Warner Book Group for $537.5 million and became the third largest book publisher in the world (after Pearson and McGraw Hill). Lagardere is the parent company of publisher Hachette Livre, which already owned Orion/Gollancz and Hodder Headline in the UK. The acquisition meant that they also took control of the Warner Books, Warner Aspect, Little Brown and Mysterious Press imprints in the US, and Orbit and Atom in the UK. The various imprints were subsequently renamed Hachette Book Group USA and Little Brown Book Group.

Following the death of their founder in 2005, Byron Preiss Visual Publications and iBooks, Inc. voluntarily filed for Chapter 7 bankruptcy and closed down all operations at the end of February. It was announced that the companies did not have sufficient resources to continue operations. They were subsequently put up for public auction, with the back catalogue, copyrights and author agreements included amongst the assets. The companies were acquired by J. Boylston & Company, who placed an initial bid of $125,000 and planned to continue publishing titles under the Byron Preiss imprints.

American Marketing Services, which owned Publishers Group West, declared Chapter 11 bankruptcy on December 26th with debts of $200 million. AMS was the largest book distributor in America, with more than 150 clients including Carroll & Graf, Dark Horse Comics, McSweeney's, RE/Search, Thunder's Mouth Press and Underwood Books.

HMV acquired Britain's Ottakar's bookshop chain for £62.9 million, and pulped several million pounds of stock in the process. The 141 stores were subsequently rebranded as Waterstone's.

Mr Alton Verm of Conroe, Texas, was outraged when he saw the book his fifteen-year-old daughter brought home from the local high school. "It's just all kinds of filth," Verm complained. "I want to get the book taken out of the class." To that end, he filed a "Request for Reconsideration of Instructional Materials" with the Conroe Independent School District. The book he so vehemently objected to was Ray Bradbury's classic *Fahrenheit 451*, which is all about a near-future society where books are banned. Of course, Verm didn't know that – he admitted that he hadn't actually read it.

In September, the Rt Reverend David Gillett, the Bishop of Bolton, accused retailers of creating a "climate of fear" by selling traditional Halloween merchandise. Writing to Britain's five biggest supermarket chains, he urged them to rethink the way they marketed the pagan holiday: "I share the view of many Christians that large retailers are increasingly keen to commercialise Halloween celebrations in a way that pressurises parents to purchase goods that promote the dark, negative side of Halloween and could encourage anti-social behaviour," he said. "I am worried that Halloween has the potential to trivialise the realities of evil in the world and that occult practices should not be condoned, even if they are only being presented in a caricatured, light-hearted form."

It was estimated that Britain now spends $120 million on Halloween. Analysts say that the UK is fast catching up with America, where it costs the average family around $120.00 to buy Halloween accessories, in an industry that is worth nearly $9 billion a year. Although some critics decried the growing "Americanisation" of Halloween, in the UK it is the third most profitable event for retailers after Christmas and Easter, with the seven days before October 31st now the second busiest shopping week of the year.

In June, author J. K. Rowling was voted Britain's greatest living writer in an online survey for *The Book Magazine*. She received almost three times as many votes as the second-placed author, Terry Pratchett. Also down the list were Phillip Pullman (#6), Iain Banks (#14), Alasdair Gray (#19), Neil Gaiman (joint #21), J.G. Ballard (joint #28), Peter Ackroyd (joint #28), Diana Wynne Jones (#36) and Michael Moorcock (#44).

By the end of 2006, Rowling's *Harry Potter and the Deadly Hallows* was already topping the Amazon best-seller list, despite not being published for another six months. Not content with that, the "adult edition" of Rowling's latest magical opus was firmly established in the #2 slot. However, that did not stop shares in Rowling's British publisher, Bloomsbury, crashing after a shock profits warning that wiped £73 million off the company's value. Bloomsbury blamed poor retail sales during the run-up to Christmas.

According to the American Library Association, Rowling's *Harry Potter* series topped the list of the "most-challenged" books in the 21st century with the highest number of written complaints to US schools and libraries asking for them to be removed. *Of Mice and Men* by John Steinbeck only made #4 on that particular Top 10 of shame.

J. K. Rowling teamed up with fellow authors Stephen King and John Irving over August 1st and 2nd at New York City's Radio City Music Hall for a benefit appearance in aid of The Haven Foundation and Doctors Without Borders. The trio read from their work and answered questions in front of the 6,000-strong audiences.

In Stephen King's novel *Cell*, which the author dedicated to Richard Matheson and George Romero, people using their cell phones were turned into rampaging zombies by a mysterious electronic virus known as the Pulse. With 1.8 million copies in circulation in America, Scribner promoted the book with downloadable ringtones featuring King's voice and a mass text-messaging campaign. The first two chapters were excerpted in the January 27th issue of *Entertainment Weekly*, and when the book was released in the UK in February, *The Times* newspaper included an extract from the novel in the format of a newsprint supplement.

King's second novel of the year, *Lisey's Story*, explored many of the author's familiar themes as widow Lisey Landon discovered that she may have been receiving messages from her murdered author husband while strangers attempted to force her to hand over his papers. The novel debuted at #1 in the US and, for the first time in a decade, King made a promotional visit to the UK in November to promote the book.

In his occasional "The Pop of King" column in *Entertainment Weekly*, King discussed such diverse subjects as network morning TV, the Oscars, *United 93*, Britney Spears, dieting, HBO's *The Wire* and audio books. The author also listed *Dispatch* as one of the Top 10 Books of 2006 and described its author Bentley Little as "the horror poet of ordinary things".

Little's *The Burning* was an original mass-market novel about four disparate people across American whose lives converged in a series of ever weirder supernatural manifestations.

A landscape gardener set out to rescue his kidnapped wife and learn about his own dysfunctional past in *The Husband*, a psychological thriller by Dean Koontz. Also from Koontz, *Brother Odd* was the third in the "Odd Thomas" series with an initial US print-run of 650,000 copies.

James Herbert's *The Secret of Crickley Hall* was a haunted house tale about a couple who moved into a remote building after the strange disappearance of their young son.

With a first printing of 1.5 million copies from Bantam, Thomas Harris' lazy prequel *Hannibal Rising* took the reader back to Hannibal Lecter's roots as a war orphan in Eastern Europe. The book was written simultaneously with the screenplay for the 2007 film version.

Farewell Summer, Ray Bradbury's long-awaited sequel to *Dandelion Wine*, was once again set in Green Town, Illinois, during an idyllic summer that refused to end. Much of the book had been part of the earlier title's original manuscript.

The Southern Gothic *Candles Burning*, about a strange girl with acute hearing and a supernatural family mystery, was begun by Michael McDowell before his untimely death in 1999 and completed by Tabitha King.

When an ancient Egyptian tomb went on display in New York, people started eviscerating each other and only framed FBI agent Aloysius Pendergast could solve the mystery in *The Book of the Dead* by Douglas Preston and Lincoln Child.

Robin Cook's latest medical thriller, *Crisis*, featured Dr Laurie Montgomery and Dr Jack Stapleton investigating the dangers of "concierge medicine".

Parish vicar Merrily Watkins aided her daughter's investigation of the spirit of a dead drug-dealer and help protect the local ley lines in *The Remains of an Altar* by Phil Rickman, while Caitlín R. Kiernan's *Daughter of Hounds* involved a strange, yellow-eyed child and a woman who worked for a race of subterranean creatures.

A new communicator with the dead confronted invading aliens in Brian Lumley's *Necroscope: The Touch*, and a number of broken objects found in a summer house exerted a strange influence in John Saul's *In the Dark of the Night*.

After coming out of a period of writer's block, Shaun Hutson's latest was titled *Dying Words* and involved a contemporary murder mystery linked with a 13th-century philosopher reputed to have travelled to Hell.

The first volume in the "Sissy Sawyer" series, Graham Masterton's *Touchy and Feely* was about a fortune-teller with psychic powers.

Cowboys for Christ was Robin Hardy's sequel-of-sorts to *The Wicker Man*, set in another pagan Scottish community.

The UK's Headline imprint reissued the late Richard Laymon's novels in "Richard Laymon Collection" omnibus paperback editions, with *The Beast House Trilogy*, *The Woods Are Dark/Out Are the Lights*, *Beware!/Dark Mountain*, *Flesh/Resurrection Dreams*, *Funland/The Stake*, *Tell Us/One Rainy Night*, *Night Show/Allhallows Eve* and *Alarums/Blood Games*.

A new independent paperback imprint, Abaddon Books, was launched in Britain in August 2006. Simon Spurrier's *The Culled* was the first volume in "The Afterblight Chronicles", set in a world ravaged by a biological apocalypse, while *Sniper Elite: Spear of Destiny* by Jaspre Bark was inspired by the World War II video game. The "Tombs of the Dead" series was devoted to zombie fiction and kicked off with Matthew Sprange's *Death Hulk*, an historical nautical adventure involving a warship crewed by the walking dead.

On the eve of his wedding, a reluctant attorney teamed up with Jack Frost to prevent two realities encroaching on each other in Christopher Golden's *The Myth Hunters*, the first volume in "The Veil" trilogy. Golden also teamed up with actress Amber Benson for *Ghosts of Albion: Witchery*, based on the BBC animated Internet serial.

A serial killer apparently had a change of heart in Tom Piccirilli's *The Dead Letters*, and a former convict returned home to face his past and make peace with the dead in the same author's *Headstone City*.

A town remembered for a series of serial killings thirty years earlier was forced to confront a new evil in Jonathan Maberry's *Ghost Road Blues*, the first book in a trilogy.

In Scott Nicholson's lively horror novel *The Farm*, a North Carolina town was menaced by the ghost of a murdered preacher and beset with blood-drinking goats, while a dead family didn't like their home being renovated in Deborah LeBlanc's *A House Divided*.

Simon Clark's *The Tower* was about five young people house-sitting an empty edifice, and *London Under Midnight* involved a reporter investigating a vampiric menace that emerged from the River Thames. The author also made a short film, *Secret Realms, Haunted Places*, about locations around England that had inspired his work.

While the crumbling building was being renovated after standing empty for forty years, the ghosts of Pittsburgh's George Washington High School refused to stay buried in *The Night School*, and the refurbishment of an old opera house resulted in the haunting of a theatre company in *Stage Fright*, both by Michael Paine (John Michael Curlovich).

Jeff VanderMeer's *Shriek: An Afterword* was once again set in Ambergris and looked at the world of publishing in that legendary city.

A widow and her small child moved into a haunted house in Gayle Wilson's *Bogeyman*, and yet another small town was consumed by an ancient evil in Joseph Laudati's *In Darkness It Dwells*.

A murder in a remote village was linked to another committed in the summer of 1969 in *Piece of My Heart*, Peter Robinson's 16th novel featuring Chief Inspector Banks.

The cast of a reality TV show was deposited on an island with real demons in *Surviving Demon Island* by Jaci Burton, Mexican vegetation turned lethal in Scott Smith's *The Ruins*, and an investigator discovered an underground world in *The Water Wolf* by Thomas Sullivan.

A woman's search for her daughter's killer became a self-destructive obsession in *The Mother* by Australian musician Brett McBean.

The nightmares of a number of murder victims were linked in *In Dreams* by Shane Christopher (Matthew J. Costello), and a reporter shared a psychic link with her murdered twin in *Kindred Spirit* by John Passarella.

T. J. MacGregor's *Cold as Death* was the fifth book in the "Tango Key" series, featuring psychic Mira Morales. A diver was warned of evil by the image of a dead woman in Heather Graham's *The Vision*, while an investigation into missing tourists led to rumours of vampires in the same author's paranormal romance *Kiss of Darkness*.

Near-future necromancer Dante Valentine found she was *Working for the Devil* in Lilith Saintcrow's dark fantasy. The character returned in *Dead Man Walking*.

A man who disappeared during World War II reappeared thirty years later looking exactly the same in Frank Cavallo's *The Lucifer Messiah*.

A woman suspected that her boyfriend was evil in *The Boyfriend from Hell* by Avery Corman, and another woman's boyfriend wouldn't stay dead in D. V. Bernard's humorous *How to Kill Your Boyfriend (In Ten Easy Steps)*.

A book had the power to release a great evil in *Mr Twilight* by Michael Reaves and Maya Kaathryn Bohnhoff. Robert Masello's *Bestiary* was about a cursed manuscript and was a sequel to the author's *The Vigil*, while *Alhazred: Author of the Necronomicon* by

Donald Tyson was an "autobiography" of the mad Arab created by H. P. Lovecraft.

A mystical rock caused terrifying visions in Pete Earley's supernatural thriller *The Apocalypse Stone*.

Max Brooks' *World War Z: An Oral History of the Zombie War* was a post-holocaust novel presented in the form of a non-fiction book.

A hypochondriac San Francisco storeowner discovered that he had been given the job of Death's assistant in Christopher Moore's adult comedy *A Dirty Job*. The same author's vampire comedy, *You Suck: A Love Story*, was a sequel to *Bloodsucking Fiends* and included characters from other works.

Dorchester Publishing's Leisure imprint continued to churn out numerous paperback originals as apocalyptic flood waters awakened a breed of monstrous worms in Brian Keene's fun disaster novel *The Conqueror Worms*.

Tim Lebbon's *Berserk* was about zombies, and women in a sleepy Buckinghamshire village gave birth to spidery monsters in Sarah Pinborough's third novel, *Breeding Ground*.

A woman had the power to make other people's dreams and fears corporeal in Tim Waggoner's *Pandora Drive*, and something nasty arrived in the small town of Ptolemy in the same author's *Darkness Wakes*.

Al Sarrantonio's *Horrorween* was part of the author's ongoing "Orangefield" series, the reanimated dead were used as servants in Simon Clark's *Death's Domain*, and the Five Night Warriors entered the nightmares of expectant mothers in *Night Wars*, the fourth volume in the series by Graham Masterton.

Something hungry and evil waited in a subterranean well beneath the cellar of an old house in *Shelter* by L. H. Maynard and M. P. N. Sims, and other titles from the imprint included *The Loveliest Dead* by Ray Garton, *Smiling Wolf* by Philip Carlo, and *Deathbringer* by Brian Smith.

Leisure reissued Jack Ketchum's *Off Season* in "The Author's Uncut, Uncensored Version!", along with "Winter Child", a cut section from the novel *She Wakes*. J. F. Gonzalez's *Survivor* and *The Beloved* were other reissues, as were *The Immaculate* by Mark Morris, *Wolf Trap* by W. D. Gagliani, *Live Girls* by Ray Garton and *Slither* by Edward Lee. Douglas Clegg's *The Attraction* was an omnibus of two previously-published novels.

From Harlequin Books/Silhouette's Nocturne imprint, a woman who could talk to ghosts was stalked by a witch-hunting killer in Lisa Childs' *Haunted*, a paranormal romance in the "Witch Hunt" series.

The Daughter of the Flames and *The Daughter of the Blood* were the first two paranormal romances in "The Gifted" trilogy by Nancy Holder, featuring psychic Isabella "Izzy" DeMarco, while *Dangerous Tides* was the latest volume in the "Drake Sisters" paranormal romance series by the prolific Christine Feehan.

With reportedly six million copies of her "Anita Blake" books in print, *Micah*, the 13th volume and first mass-market original in Laurell K. Hamilton's vampire series since 1998, went straight to #1 in the US with a first printing of more than 400,000 copies. The next volume in the series, *Danse Macabre*, returned to the hardcover format as Anita thought she might be pregnant. It also went to #1 with a 250,000-copy first printing that quickly sold out.

Set in third century Rome, Chelsea Quinn Yarbro's 19th century historical novel about vampire Ragoczy Germain Sanctus-Franciscus was entitled *Roman Dusk*.

Proven Guilty was the eighth volume in Jim Butcher's "Dresden Files" and involved wizard PI Harry Dresden in a war between the Faeries and the vampires of the Red Court.

TV director Tony Foster had to halt a Demonic Convergence with the help of his friend, vampire Henry Fitzroy, in Tanya Huff's *Smoke and Ashes*, the third in the humorous dark fantasy series. Meanwhile, Huff's earlier "Vicki Nelson" books were repackaged by DAW Books as a three-volume series, *The Blood Books*, each containing two novels apiece.

No Dominion was the second volume in Charlie Huston's series about hardboiled vampire PI Joe Pitt. A private investigator who was half-human, half-elf had a vampire as her first client in *Even Vampires Get the Blues* by Katie MacAlister (aka Katie Maxwell), and a series of murders in a small town were blamed on vampires in *Pale Immortal* by Anne Frasier.

Navajo Nightwalker police officer Lee Nez returned in David Thurlo and Aimée Thurlo's *Surrogate Evil*, the fourth volume in the vampire mystery series.

B. H. Fingerman's *Bottomfeeder* was about a loser vampire in a dead-end job, and a man was recruited to hunt vampires in Graham Masterton's *Descendant*.

Barbara Hambly's *Renfield: Slave of Dracula* retold the story of the Count's fly-eating servant.

Whereas once vampires were used as figures of fear in literature, they are now more likely to be depicted as humorous characters or, even worse, potential romantic partners in numerous paperback originals ("vampromcoms"?) apparently aimed at middle-class housewives and undiscerning supermarket shoppers.

Reminiscent of the boom-and-bust horror cycle of the 1980s, vampire romances and – even more bizarrely – vampire/werewolf romances swamped the market in 2006. Not only were these volumes mostly aimed at people who read outside the horror genre, but the majority were written by authors (often under multiple pseudonyms) who had no other interest in horror. However, there was no denying that there was a huge audience for these types of books.

Telepathic waitress Sookie Stackhouse had to recover a bracelet belonging to the vampire Queen of Louisiana in *Definitely Dead*, the sixth in the humorous Southern Gothic series by Charlaine Harris.

An undead woman opened a vampire dating agency in Manhattan in Kimberly Raye's *Dead End Dating*, while *Undead and Unpopular* was the fifth book in MaryJanice Davidson's humorous "Betsy the Vampire Queen" series.

The Damned was the latest volume in the "Vampire Huntress Legends" series by L. A. Banks (Leslie Esdale Banks) and included a limited edition poster inside the back cover of the hardback edition. Banks also edited *Vegas Bites*, an anthology of four stories by J. M. Jeffries, Seressia Glass, Natalie Dunbar and the editor, set in a casino run by vampires, werewolves and other creatures.

An undead casino owner became involved in politics in Erin McCarthy's *High Stakes*, the latest volume in the humorous "Vegas Vampires" series, while a female security guard at a Las Vegas concert encountered her former vampire boyfriend in Cameron Dean's *Passionate Thirst*, the first book in the "Candace Steele Vampire Killer" series. It was followed by *Luscious Craving* and *Eternal Hunger*.

In Kerrelyn Sparks' *Vamps and the City*, two CIA vampire hunters became involved in a reality TV show, and a female FBI agent had a vampire lover in Caridad Piniero's *Death Calls*.

Mario Acevedo's comedy debut novel, *The Nymphos of Rocky Flats* introduced Latino vampire investigator Felix Gomez, while *Happy Hour at Casa Dracula* by Marta Acosta involved a Latina finding love amongst a family of bloodsuckers.

Traitor to the Blood was the fourth volume in Barb Hendee and J. C. Hendee's "Noble Dead" series, while both *Desire Calls* and *Death Calls* by Caridad Piñeiro featured women involved with vampires.

In *Touch the Dark*, the first in a new series by newcomer Karen Chance, necroscope Cassie Palmer was forced to rely on the protection of a dangerously seductive master vampire.

A bounty hunter became involved with vampires in *Hunting the Hunter*, the first in a series by Shiloh Walker, and after being left for dead, bounty hunter Anna Strong tracked down the vampires that transformed her in *The Becoming* by Jeanne C. Stein.

Blood Ties Book One: The Turning was the first in a new series by Jennifer Armintrout about a vampire doctor.

A woman discovered that she had a new destiny in Alexandra Ivy's vampire romance *When Darkness Comes*, the first book in the "Guardians of Eternity" trilogy, and a succubus worked as an exotic dancer in Jackie Kessler's *Hell's Belles*, the first in another trilogy.

Lover Eternal and *Lover Awakened* were the first two volumes in the "Black Dagger Brotherhood" vampire romance series by J. R. Ward (Jessica Bird).

A biochemist pursued by the undead was helped by a vampire hunter in *Seduced by the Night*, the second book in the "Night Slayer" series by Robin T. Popp, while *Past Redemption* by Savannah Russe (Charles Trantino) was the second book in "The Darkwing Chronicles".

The Devil's Knight and *Dark Angel* were the second and third volumes, respectively, in the "Bound in Darkness" Medieval vampire romance series by Lucy Blue (Jayel Wylie).

Nora Roberts' *Dance of the Gods* and *Valley of Silence* were the second and third books in the author's vampire "Circle" trilogy, and *I Only Have Fangs for You* by Kathy Love was the third in the series about vampire brothers.

Prince of Twilight was the latest title in the "Wings in the Night" series by Maggie Shayne, and *Dark Demon* and *Dark Celebration* were the next two novels in the "Carpathian" series by Christine Feehan, whose *Conspiracy Game* was the fourth in the "GhostWalkers" series.

Tall Dark & Dead was a humorous novel by Tate Hallaway (Lyda Morehouse) which involved a witch attracted to a vampire alchemist. Kathryn Smith's *Be Mine Tonight* combined vampires with the legend of the Holy Grail, while *The Vampire's Seduction* by Raven Hart featured a playboy bloodsucker confronting an ancient enemy.

A female PI discovered that her former fiancé had become a vampire and was accused of murder in Jenna Black's *Watchers in the Night*. Stolen computer files were at the heart of Susan Sizemore's vampire romance *Master of Darkness*, and a bloodsucker fell in love with a police officer in the same author's *Primal Heat*.

Just One Sip featured three vampire romance stories by Katie MacAlister, Jennifer Ashley and Minda Webber, while *Love at First*

Bite contained original tales from Sherrilyn Kenyon, Susan Squires, Ronda Thompson and L. A. Barks.

Originally published in different form as an e-book in 2001, *The Hunter's Prey: Erotic Tales of Texas Vampires* contained eleven stories by Diane Whiteside. From the same author, *Bond of Blood* was the first novel in the "Texas Vampires" trilogy.

Blood Red was an erotic Regency vampire romance by Sharon Page, and *The Burning* by Susan Squires was an erotic vampire novel set in early 19th-century England that featured psychic Ann Van Helsing.

Meanwhile, Dracula found himself in a lesbian Europe in Wendy Swanscombe's erotic novel *Fresh Flesh*. Edited by Bianca de Moss, *Blood Sisters: Lesbian Vampire Stories* contained eighteen original stories.

Michael Schiefelbein's *Vampire Transgression* was the third book in the gay "Victor Decimus" series, while David Thomas Lord's *Bound in Flesh* was another erotic gay vampire novel, the sequel to *Bound in Blood*.

Dark Side of the Moon was the ninth volume and first hardcover in Sherrilyn Kenyon's series about vampiric Dark-Hunters and shape-changing Were-Hunters. Seattle reporter Susan Michaels adopted a cat that turned out to be an immortal hybrid, being hunted by both supernatural factions.

A vampire fell in love with another werecat in Nina Bangs' *A Taste of Darkness*. Michele Bardsley's humorous *I'm the Vampire, That's Why* featured a vampiric single mother and a crazed werewolf, and Riley Jenson was a hybrid vampire/werewolf working for a government investigation agency in Keri Arthur's *Full Moon Rising*.

Kresley Cole's *A Hunger Like No Other* and *No Rest for the Wicked* were the first two volumes in the "Immortals After Dark" series about a valkyrie assassin's romantic trysts with werewolves and vampires.

Touch of Evil by C. T. Adams and Cathy Clamp was the first volume in a new dark fantasy romance series involving vampires, werewolves and a psychic heroine.

Jan Underwood's *Day Shift Werewolf* won the 28th Annual International 3-Day Novel Contest and also featured other image-challenged monsters.

Lori Handeland's *Crescent Moon*, *Midnight Moon* and *Rising Moon* were all werewolf or other monster romances in the "Night-creatures" series, set in and around New Orleans.

Through a letter reputedly written by Jack the Ripper, pregnant werewolf Elena Michaels unwittingly unleashed a Victorian serial killer and a pair of zombie thugs into the modern world in *Broken* by Kelley Armstrong.

Late night radio host and celebrity werewolf Kitty Norville took on a Senate committee investigating the paranormal in *Kitty Goes to Washington* by Carrie Vaughn. The book also included a related story.

A werewolf and a werefox teamed up in Christine Warren's *Wolf at the Door*, first in the "Others" series, while Gina Farago's *Ivy Cole and the Moon*, about the eponymous female werewolf vigilante, was also the first in a series.

A new governess discovered the secret of Wolfram Castle in Donna Lea Simpson's *Awaiting the Moon*, and a deadly legend had to be prevented from coming true in the sequel, *Awaiting the Night*.

A werewolf helped a woman who was turned into a were-jaguar by a serial killer in *Howling Moon* by C. T. Adams and Cathy Clamp. A Native American shape-changer was unable to kill his victim in Lindsay McKenna's *Unforgiven*, and witchy PI Rachel had to deal with a werewolf problem in *A Fistful of Charms*, the latest book in the humorous series by Kim Harrison (Dawn Cook).

A werewolf pretended to be a dog while investigating a murder in *Master of Wolves*, the third book in the romantic trilogy by Angela Knight.

Ronda Thompson's *The Untamed One* and *The Cursed One* were the second and third books, respectively, in the "Wild Wulfs of London" Regency romance series.

Shadow of the Moon was yet another werewolf romance, written by Rebecca York (Ruth Glick), whose earlier novels *Witching Moon* and *Crimson Moon* were reprinted in the omnibus *Moon Swept*.

Wolf Tales III was the third volume in the erotic werewolf series about the "Chanku" by Kate Douglas, and *Dead and Loving It* collected four humorous werewolf romances by MaryJane Davidson, including one related to the author's "Betsy the Vampire Queen" series. Three of the stories were originally published as e-books.

Diane Setterfield's debut novel, *The Thirteenth Tale*, sparked an international bidding war amongst publishers. Days after the teacher-turned-first-time-novelist submitted the manuscript to an agent, it sold for £800,000 in the UK and a further $1 million in the US.

A literary ghost story-within-a-story, the book went straight to #1 in America as the result of a major marketing campaign.

Following a global disaster, New York City was overrun by cannibal zombies in David Wellington's debut *Monster Island*. The first in a trilogy about the walking dead, originally serialised on the author's web site, it was followed by *Monster Nation*, which was set in California and looked back to when the dead first began to rise.

Sarah Langan's debut novel *The Keeper* came with glowing quotes from Ramsey Campbell, Douglas E. Winter, Tim Lebbon, Kelly Link and Jack Ketchum. It was about yet another haunted house in Maine.

The Harrowing by screenwriter Alexandra Sokoloff was set in a college over Thanksgiving break and involved the discovery of an old Ouija board and a tragedy that happened more than eighty-five years earlier.

Set in an alternate London, Mike Carey's first novel *The Devil You Know* introduced hardboiled exorcist Felix Castor. After dying for two minutes, small-time private investigator Harper Blaine returned to life with the power to see beyond the veil in Kat Richardson's *Greywalker*.

Dead City by Joe McKinney was about a virus that reanimated the dead of Texas as cannibal zombies.

Gordon Dahlquist's heavily promoted first novel, *The Glass Books of the Dream Eaters*, bought by its US publisher for a seven-figure sum, was a Victorian murder mystery set in a world where magic worked. Paul Malmont's *The Chinese Death Cloud Peril* was a tribute to the old pulp magazine heroes as authors Walter Gibson, Lester Dent and L. Ron Hubbard investigated the horrifying poisoning of H. P. Lovecraft.

A boy who thought he had superpowers was actually possessed by a demon in Sam Enthoven's YA debut, *The Black Tattoo*.

Michael Cox's Victorian murder mystery, *The Meaning of Night*, was written in just over a year while the author suffered a severe illness and the threat of blindness. The book followed the exploits of murderer Edward Glyver, who set out to convince himself that his acts of vengeance were justified.

Paul Magrs' comedic novel *Never the Bride* was set in a seaside town full of monsters.

Actor and scriptwriter Mark Gatiss' *The Devil in Amber* was a Boy's Own pastiche novel that involved the search by two-fisted hero Lucifer Box for the final fragment of an ancient papyrus that could raise Beelzebub. Tess Gerritsen's *The Mephisto Club* was about a

detective investigating a group who were attempting to prove that
Satan walked the Earth.

Matthew Pearl's *The Poe Shadow* dealt with the mystery of Edgar
Allan Poe's lost final hours before his death in 1849. Meanwhile,
Louis Bayard's thriller *The Pale Blue Eye* explored Poe's life as a
cadet at West Point in the 1830s.

A Shot in the Dark, from Hesperus Press' classy Classics series,
collected fifteen stories by "Saki" (H. H. Munro), along with a
Foreword by Jeremy Dyson and an historical Introduction by Adam
Newell.

From Strider Nolan Media, the first volume of *Horror's Classic
Masters Remastered* edited by Kurt S. Michaels featured twenty-one
tales by W. W. Jacobs, William Hope Hodgson, M. R. James, Ambrose
Bierce, Edgar Allan Poe, Bram Stoker, Robert Louis Stevenson,
Washington Irving, Nathaniel Hawthorne and H. G. Wells, along with
a very brief Foreword by Hollywood film producer J. C. Spink.

Dover Publications reissued *Gaslit Nightmares* edited by Hugh
Lamb, first published in 1988, with sixteen selected stories by Barry
Pain, Bernard Capes, Robert W. Chambers, Charles Dickens, Mary
E. Wilkins-Freeman, Richard Marsh and Jerome K. Jerome, amongst
others.

Tales to Freeze the Blood: More Great Ghost Stories, selected by
R. Chetwynd-Hayes and Stephen Jones, contained a further twenty-
four stories culled from *The Fontana Book of Great Ghost Stories*.
Authors included Ambrose Bierce, Sydney J. Bounds, Guy de Mau-
passant, F. Marion Crawford, J. Sheridan Le Fanu, M. R. James,
Tony Richards, Steve Rasnic Tem and Chetwynd-Hayes himself.

Also edited by Jones, *H. P. Lovecraft's Book of the Supernatural: 20
Classic Tales of the Macabre Chosen by the Master of Horror Himself*
featured Washington Irving, Robert Louis Stevenson, Guy de Mau-
passant, Edgar Allan Poe, Ambrose Bierce, Henry James, F. Marion
Crawford, Rudyard Kipling, Lafcadio Hearn, Bram Stoker, H. R.
Wakefield, Sir Arthur Conan Doyle, William Hope Hodgson, Arthur
Machen and many others, along with a Foreword on writing weird
fiction by Lovecraft and original illustrations by Randy Broecker.

The Complete Chronicles of Conan: Centenary Edition collected
all Robert E. Howard's stories about the mighty barbarian in a
single, leather-bound hardcover. Edited with an extensive Afterword
by Stephen Jones, the more than 900-page volume was illustrated
throughout by Les Edwards. Continuing the series originally started
by Wandering Star, *Kull: Exile of Atlantis* from Del Rey contained

twelve stories and fragments by Howard, all taken from the author's original manuscripts. The trade paperback was illustrated by Justin Sweet, who also supplied the Foreword.

September 13th was designated "Roald Dahl Day" for children in the UK. It would have been the author's 90th birthday.

Lemony Snicket (Daniel Handler) finally wrapped up his "Series of Unfortunate Events" after thirteen volumes with the aptly-titled *The End*, in which the Baudelaire siblings and evil Count Olaf encountered a group of white-robed islanders named after nautical literary figures.

Christopher Golden and Ford Lytle Gilmore's *The Hollow: Mischief* was the third volume about teenagers living in a cursed town. It was followed by *The Hollow: Enemies*.

In Scott Westerfield's *Midnighters 3: Blue Moon*, the final volume in the trilogy, the five members of the eponymous group had to prevent the secret hour spilling over into the real world.

Graham Joyce's *Do the Creepy Thing* was about a teenage girl's decision to live with a cursed bracelet. A boy who could talk to ghosts made contact with a missing cheerleader in *Dead Connection* by Charlie Price, and a group of college students tried to stop a demon that fed on emotions in Nina Kiriki Hoffman's *Spirits That Walk in Shadow*.

Nancy Holder's *Pretty Little Devils* was a young adult novel about a clique of girls, while cheerleaders found themselves being stalked at summer camp in Laura Kasischke's *Boy Heaven*.

Dead teenagers were trapped in the eponymous world of Neal Shusterman's *Everlost*, a boy kept receiving strange calls on his *Hell Phone* by William Sleator, and a monstrous dog terrorised a village for centuries in Janet Lee Carey's *The Beast of Noor*.

Slawter and *Bec* were the third and forth books, respectively, in "The Demonata" series by Darren Shan (Darren O'Shaughnessy). A stand-alone novel, *Koyasan*, was written by Shan for World Book Day 2006.

A trio of Victorian teenagers discovered that a factory owner was reanimating the dead in Justin Richards' *The Death Collector*, while the same author's *The Invisible Detective: Ghost Soldiers* was the third in the series set in the 1930s. A ghost led a teenager back to the 1940 bombing on London in Edward Bloor's *London Calling*.

Three children became lost in an attic of universe proportions in Garry Kilworth's *Attica*, a teenager killed in a steamship tragedy returned as a ghost in T. K. Welsh's *The Unresolved*, and David

Levithan's novella *Marly's Ghost* was a contemporary Valentine's Day retelling of Charles Dickens' *A Christmas Carol*.

Mirroring their popularity amongst romance readers, vampire novels also continued to do well with the young adult audience.

The Last Days was a loose sequel to Scott Westerfield's *Peeps*, set in a world ravaged by a vampire-parasite plague, while *Vampirates: Tide of Terror* was the second book in Justin Somper's post-apocalyptic series.

Vampire Plagues: Outbreak and *Vampire Plagues: Extermination* were the latest titles in the series published under the byline "Sebastian Rook". *Vampire Beach: Bloodlust* and *Vampire Beach: Initiation* were the first two volumes in a new YA series published by the pseudonymous "Alex Duval".

A sixteen-year-old college student discovered that she was living with some odd housemates in *Glass House*, the first volume in "The Morganville Vampires" series by Rachel Caine (Roxanne Longstreet Conrad).

A popular girl at school was turned into a vampire in Serena Robar's *Braced2Bite* and *Fangs4Freaks*, the first two books in a new series.

Teenage vampire twins wanted revenge on a girl's undead boyfriend in *Vampireville*, the third in the series by Ellen Schreiber. A girl was accidentally bitten by her twin's vampire boyfriend in Mari Mancusi's *Boys That Bite*. The sequel, *Stake That!*, was about a vampire slayer who would rather be undead herself.

A teenager discovered vampires living amongst New York high society in Melissa de la Cruz's *Blue Bloods*, *New Moon* was the second book in the trilogy by Stephanie Meyer, and mass-murderer Countess Bathory was the subject of Alisa M. Libby's *The Blood Confession*.

Issued as a handsome-looking hardcover by Californian imprint Medusa Press, with a Foreword by publisher Frank Chigas, *Left in the Dark: The Supernatural Tales of John Gordon* collected a career-spanning thirty stories (one original) by the acclaimed British author. It was published in a limited edition of 450 copies and a deluxe signed edition of 50 copies.

All Hallows' Eve: 13 Stories was an impressive collection of all-new tales by Edgar Award-winning author Vivian Vande Velde, each set on Halloween night and aimed at ages twelve and up.

Fragile Things: Short Fictions and Wonders contained twenty-seven previously uncollected stories and poems (one original) by Neil Gaiman. The contents of the US and UK editions differed slightly.

Collected Stories contained fifty-one previously published tales for adults by Roald Dahl.

From Serpent's Tail, *Mortality* collected twenty short stories (one original and two only previously available electronically) by Nicholas Royle.

Laurell K. Hamilton's *Strange Candy* collected fourteen stories, including a new "Anita Blake, Vampire Hunter" tale, while *Saffron and Brimstone: Strange Stories* contained eight stories (one original) by Elizabeth Hand, along with an Afterword by the author.

Twisted Tales presented fourteen original stories by Brandon Massey.

Alone on the Darkside: Echoes from the Shadows of Horror was the fourth in the series of original paperback anthologies edited by John Pelan. It featured sixteen all-new stories by Brian Hodge, Eddy C. Bertin, Mark Samuels, Glen Hirshberg, David Riley, Gerard Houarner, Lucy Taylor and Paul Finch, amongst others.

Edited by Iain Sinclair, *London: City of Disappearances* was a literary anthology that featured contributions from J. G. Ballard, Michael Moorcock, Will Self, Marina Warner and Nicholas Royle.

Ghosts in Baker Street edited by Martin H. Greenberg, Jon Lellenberg and Daniel Stashower included ten supernatural mystery stories featuring Sherlock Holmes. There was also an Introduction by "Dr Watson" and non-fiction pieces from Barbara Roden, Loren D. Estleman and Caleb Carr.

Edited by Brandon Massey, *Dark Dreams II: Voices from the Other Side* was an original anthology of seventeen stories by black authors.

Despite any publisher and author's profits being donated to the Save the Children Tsunami Relief Fund, *Elemental*, edited by Steven Savile and Alethea Kontis, was published almost a year-and-a-half after the tragedy in the Indian Ocean and appeared woefully redundant. Among those authors who donated their work for free were Brian Aldiss, David Drake, Joe Haldeman, Nina Kiriki Hoffman, Larry Niven and Michael Marshall Smith.

Edited by P. N. Elrod, *My Big Fat Supernatural Wedding* contained nine stories by such writers as Charlene Harris, Jim Butcher, Esther Friesner, Sherrilyn Kenyon and the editor herself.

Mysteria presented four paranormal romances set in a demon-haunted town in Colorado by MaryJanice Davidson, Susan Grant, P. C. Cast and Gena Showalter. *Hell With the Ladies* collected three linked stories about the sons of Satan by Julie Kenner, Kathleen O'Reilly and Dee Davis.

Dates from Hell contained four otherworldly tales of paranormal trysts by Kim Harrison (Dawn Cook), Lynsay Sands, Kelley Armstrong and Lori Handeland featuring werewolves, demon lovers and the romantically challenged undead. Yet another paranormal romance volume, *Dark Dreamers* featured a reprint "Carpathian" story by Christine Feehan and a new "Dirk & Steele" novella by Marjorie M. Liu.

Triptych of Terror included three gay horror stories by Michael Rowe, David Thomas Lord and John Michael Curlovich.

The Year's Best Fantasy & Horror: Nineteenth Annual Collection edited by Ellen Datlow and Kelly Link & Gavin J. Grant contained thirty-five stories, five poems and various end-of-the-year essays by the two sets of editors, Edward Bryant, Charles Vess, Joan D. Vinge, Charles de Lint and James Frenkel.

Edited by Stephen Jones, *The Mammoth Book of Best New Horror Volume Seventeen* contained twenty-two stories and novellas, along with the usual overview of the year, Necrology and list of Useful Addresses.

The two volumes overlapped with a number of authors but by just three stories, from Glen Hirshberg, Adam L. G. Nevill, and China Miéville, Emma Bircham and Max Schäfer.

2006 saw an explosion of "Year's Best" anthologies, with the busy Jason Strahan editing two titles from Night Shade Books and another for The Science Fiction Book Club. There were also at least five different titles from Prime Books/Wildside Press. The latter's output included *Horror: The Best of the Year: 2006 Edition* edited by John Gregory Betancourt and Sean Wallace. It contained fifteen stories and a short Introduction by the editors, along with contributions from Clive Barker, Ramsey Campbell, Joe R. Lansdale, Jack Cady, Michael Marshall Smith, Caitlín R. Kiernan, Joe Hill, Jeff VanderMeer, Laird Barron, Holly Philips, M. Rickert and David Niall Wilson.

From Wildside's new romance imprint, Juno Books, *Best New Paranormal Romance* edited by Paula Guran featured twelve stories by Jane Yolen, Elizabeth Hand, Elizabeth Bear and others.

Dark Corners was the first collection from scriptwriter Stephen Volk (TV's *Ghostwatch* and *Afterlife*). Available through print-on-demand imprint Gray Friar Press, it contained fifteen stories (three new) and an original screenplay, along with an Introduction by Tim Lebbon and an Afterword by the author.

From the same publisher, John Llewellyn Probert's linked collection *The Faculty of Terror* was a homage to the old Amicus anthology movies with an Introduction by Paul Finch and an interview with the author by Gary McMahon.

T. M. Wright's short novel *A Spider on My Tongue*, a sequel to *A*

Manhattan Ghost Story, was available as a print-on-demand volume from Nyx Books.

Midnight Library/Eibon Books' *Book of Legion* by "Victor Heck" (David Nordhaus) was a print-on-demand novel about the eponymous body-hopping demon's attempts to create a Hell on Earth.

When Darkness Falls from Midnight Library collected fourteen stories (one original) by J. F. Gonzalez with an Introduction and notes by the author. Ten original linked stories by Angeline Hawkes were collected in *The Commandments*, an on-demand trade paperback from Nocturne Press.

The Fungal Stain and Other Dreams from Hippocampus Press collected fifteen Lovecraftian stories (eight original) by W. H. Pugmire, while *Straight to Darkness: Lairs of the Hidden Gods Volume Three* from Kurodahan Press, was a Lovecraftian anthology of seven stories and one article edited by Ken Asamatsu and originally published in Japan in 2002. Robert M. Price supplied a new Introduction.

Time Intertwined released by Kerlak Publishing was an anthology of fourteen stories (one reprint) edited with a Forward [sic] by Mark Fitzgerald. From the same imprint, *Dark Chances* was the second book in Allan Gilbreath's vampire "Galen Saga".

Aegri Somnia was an on-demand anthology of twelve stories dealing with nightmares from Apex Publications. It was edited by Jason Sizemore and Gill Ainsworth and included contributions from Scott Nicholson, Christopher Rowe and Lavie Tidhar, amongst others.

Edited by Kevin L. Donihe, *Bare Bone #9* from Raw Dog Screaming Press contained fiction and poetry by Gary Fry, Andrew Humphrey, Paul Finch, Tim Curran, C. J. Henderson, James S. Dorr, Amy Grech and others.

Although its quarterly schedule was reportedly cut in half by Cosmos Books/Wildside Press, the twelfth volume of Philip Harbottle's *Fantasy Adventures* did finally appear with cover art by Sydney Jordan and new stories from veterans Sydney J. Bounds, Brian Ball, Eric Brown, John Glasby and Philip E. High. The remainder of the issue was filled out with John Russell Fearn's "I Spy", a short SF novel from 1954, and a reprint story by E. C. Tubb.

From Paul Miller's Earthling Publications, *American Morons* collected seven superior stories (two original) by Glen Hirshberg. There was also a signed edition of 150 copies and a twenty-six-copy traycased lettered edition.

World of Hurt was a 50,000-word short novel about the battle between Good and Evil by Brian Hodge, handsomely presented in hardcover by Earthling with a Foreword by Stephen Jones and an Introduction by Brian Keene. It was available in a 500-copy signed numbered edition.

Set in the Kansas Dust Bowl during the 1930s Depression, a young girl and an escaped convict battled a plague of vampiric creatures in *Bloodstained Oz*, a short novel by Christopher Golden and James A. Moore. With an Introduction by Ray Garton and illustrations by Glenn Chadbourne, the book was also available in both numbered and lettered editions.

Conrad Williams' novel *The Unblemished* was the second book in Earthling's Halloween series. With an Introduction by Jeff VanderMeer and an Afterword by the author, it was published in 500 numbered and 15 lettered hardcover copies.

Fine Cuts from Peter Crowther's prolific PS Publishing imprint collected twelve superior reprint stories by Dennis Etchison set in and around Hollywood, along with a new Preface by the author and an Introduction by Peter Atkins.

Fourteen stories (two original) by Steven Utley, along with an Introduction by Howard Waldrop, were collected in *Where or When*, and Jack Dann provided the Introduction to *Past Magic*, which contained eleven stories (including an excised chapter from *The House of Storms*) and a new Preface by Ian R. MacLeod.

Moby Jack and Other Tall Tales collected twenty-one reprint stories spanning all genres by Garry Kilworth, with an Introduction by Robert Holdstock. *Impossible Stories* assembled five of Yugoslavian writer Zoran Živković's linked narrative cycles, totalling twenty-nine stories in all. Paul Di Filippo provided the Introduction, and there was an Afterword by Tamar Yellin.

A young woman travelled through a dream landscape in Richard Calder's novel *Babylon*, introduced by K. J. Bishop.

Each PS hardcover was published in a 500-copy numbered trade edition signed by the author and a 200-copy slipcased edition signed by all contributors.

With an Introduction by Mark Morris, Mark Samuels' *The Face of Twilight* from PS Publishing was a bizarre novella set in London that blurred the living with the dead.

Two individuals apparently shared the same apartment with a highly intelligent parrot in T. M. Wright's *I Am the Bird*, introduced by Ramsey Campbell, and David Herter's novella *On the Overgrown Path* involved real-life opera composer Leoš Janáček investigating a mysterious murder in an obscure mountain village. John

Clute supplied the Introduction.

PS novellas were published in 500 numbered paperback editions signed by the author, and 300 numbered hardcover copies signed by all the contributors.

Produced as a "special publication for *PostScripts* subscribers", *Christmas Inn* by Gene Wolfe was an odd holiday fable about a group of enigmatic strangers that involved seances, ghosts and a mysterious child. A signed hardcover was sent by PS to all hardcover subscribers to its magazine, with an additional 200 copies available for sale.

Fifteen years after the previous volume appeared, Gauntlet Press published *Masques V* as a handsome signed and numbered hard-cover limited to 500 copies. Edited by the late J. N. Williamson with Gary A. Braunbeck, the anthology featured twenty-nine stories (one reprint), along with an Introduction and overly-enthusiastic story notes by Williamson and dust-jacket artwork by Clive Barker. The impressive line-up of contributors included Poppy Z. Brite, Richard Matheson, Ray Russell, Mort Castle, Barry Hoffman, Tom Piccirilli, John Maclay, Thomas F. Monteleone, Richard Christian Matheson, William F. Nolan, Ed Gorman, Ray Bradbury, and both editors. The lettered edition only also featured original drafts of the Bradbury and R. C. Matheson stories while, as a premium for those who ordered the book directly from the publisher, *Masques V: Further Stories* was an attractive chapbook with cover art by Barker. It contained more new fiction from Braunbeck, Hoffman, Castle and Tim Waggoner, and was limited to just 552 copies.

Bloodlines: Richard Matheson's Dracula, I Am Legend and Other Vampire Stories was edited by Mark Dawidziak and included appre-ciations by Ray Bradbury, John Carpenter, Mick Garris, Richard Christian Matheson, Steve Niles, Rockne S. O'Bannon and Frank Spotnitz. It was published in a signed edition of 500 copies.

Also from Gauntlet, *Harbingers* was the tenth volume in F. Paul Wilson's "Repairman Jack" series.

The Lost District and Other Stories was a major retrospective collection of twenty-four stories (five original) by Joel Lane, pub-lished by Night Shade Books in trade paperback. *Dark Mondays* contained nine offbeat tales (six original) by Californian writer Kage Baker. It was published in both trade and limited hardcover editions, the latter containing an extra new story.

The Ghost Pirates and Other Revenants of the Sea was the third volume in Night Shade's "The Collected Stories of William Hope Hodgson".

A West Virginia town found itself cut off from the rest of the world and invaded by creatures from another dimension in Stephen Mark Rainey's novel *The Nightmare Frontier*. It was available for Halloween from Sarob Press in a limited hardcover edition and as a deluxe signed and slipcased edition signed by the author and cover artist Chad Savage.

In Lee Thomas' novel *Damage*, something evil emerged into the suburban community of Pierce Valley. It was also published in hardcover by Sarob in a limited edition and a deluxe slipcased edition signed by Thomas and artist Paul Lowe.

Edited by Alison L. R. Davies with a Foreword by Stephen Jones and a frontispiece illustration by Clive Barker, *Shrouded in Darkness: Tales of Terror* was an anthology produced by Telos Publishing to raise money for DebRA, a British charity working on behalf of people with the genetic skin blistering condition Epidermolysis Bullosa (EB). The attractive trade paperback contained twenty-three stories by Neil Gaiman, Ramsey Campbell, Michael Marshall Smith, Poppy Z. Brite, Christopher Fowler, Tim Lebbon, Charles de Lint, Graham Masterton, Mark Samuels and Peter Crowther, amongst others, along with original tales from Justina Robson, Darren Shan, Paul Finch, James Lovegrove, Dawn Knox, Steve Lockley and Paul Lewis, Debbie Bennett, Simon Clark, publisher David J. Howe, and the editor herself. A signed, limited edition was also announced.

In Dominic McDonagh's debut novella *Pretty Young Things*, one of a group of predatory lesbian vampires set out to rescue a former boyfriend from her fellow bloodsuckers. Joseph Nassie's novella *More Than Life Itself* was about choice and consequences, as one desperate man was prepared to do anything to save his dying four-year-old daughter.

Also from Telos, *A Manhattan Ghost Story* was a reprint of T. M. Wright's superior 1984 supernatural novel.

Available from Cemetery Dance Publications, Stephen King's *The Secretary of Dreams* was a collection of six classic stories illustrated in varying styles by Glenn Chadbourne.

Dark Harvest was a short novel by Norman Partridge set on Halloween night in 1963, when the boys of a Midwestern town were pitted against the October Boy, a legendary creature with a Jack O'Lantern face.

Basic Black: Tales of Appropriate Fear was a twenty-year retrospective of Terry Dowling's work from CD Publications, while *Destination Unknown* contained two stories and a novella about automobiles by Gary A. Braunbeck.

Havoc Swims Jaded collected thirteen short stories by David J.

Schow (including a collaboration with Craig Spector), along with an Introduction by Bertrand Nightenhelser and a usual idiosyncratic Afterword by the author. Published by Subterranean Press, the special numbered edition was limited to 150 copies signed by Schow and artist Frank Dietz. *Water Music* was a special chapbook produced to accompany the limited edition. It contained Schow's eponymous "Hellboy" story, a brief Afterword, and a fascinating article on the author's Creature from the Black Lagoon fanzine, *The Black Lagoon Bugle*.

Made Ready & Cupboard Love collected two stories by Terry Lamsley, illustrated by Glenn Chadbourne. It was limited to a 500-copy signed edition and a twenty-six copy lettered edition.

Reassuring Tales contained ten stories, including a film treatment, by T. E. D. Klein, along with an Introduction by the author. There was also a signed edition of 600 copies and a twenty-six-copy lettered, leather-bound and slipcased edition.

Published by Subterranean as an attractive hardcover illustrated by Ted Naifeh, *Alabaster* collected all five stories featuring Caitlín R. Kiernan's albino heroine Dancy Flammarion, including the original tale "Bainbridge" and a new Author's Preface.

Joe R. Lansdale edited *Retro-Pulp Tales*, an anthology of pre-1960s style stories by such authors as F. Paul Wilson, Chet Williamson, Tim Lebbon, Kim Newman, Al Sarrantonio, Norman Partridge and Alex Irvine. A 1985 short story by Lansdale was the inspiration for *Joe R. Lansdale's Lords of the Razor* edited by Bill Sheehan and William Schafer. The titular tale kicked off the anthology, followed by twelve contributions from Chet Williamson, Thomas Tessier, Bradley Denton, Gary A. Braunbeck and Elizabeth Massie, amongst others, including an original story from Lansdale to also close the book. It was limited to a 500-copy signed and slipcased edition, and a leatherbound, lettered and traycased edition of twenty-six copies.

Edited by Kealan Patrick Burke, *Night Visions 12* was the latest volume in the long-running anthology series and included a total of eight stories by Simon Clark, Mark Morris and P. D. Cacek. It was also available in a signed edition of 250 copies.

The twentieth anniversary edition of Brian Lumley's vampire novel *Necroscope* included an original Introduction by the author plus five full-colour and multiple black and white interior illustrations by Bob Eggleton. The book was available in both signed hardcover and deluxe slipcased editions. Lumley's *Screaming Science Fiction: Horrors from Outer Space*, also from Subterranean, collected nine stories (one original) along with a new Foreword by the author and more interior illustrations from Eggleton. A 1,500-copy signed edition was available, along with a twenty-six lettered tray-cased edition.

Kim Newman's *The Man from the Diogenes Club* was an attractive trade paperback from MonkeyBrain Books that collected eight tales (including an original novella) about outlandish psychic investigator Richard Jeperson and the secret organisation he answered to. For American readers, there was a very useful guide to the names and terms used in the stories.

Co-published by MonkeyBrain and the Fandom Association of Central Texas (FACT) to tie-in with the 2006 World Fantasy Convention, *Cross Plains Universe: Texans Celebrate Robert E. Howard* was edited by Scott A. Cupp and Joe R. Lansdale. The trade paperback collected twenty-one original stories by Ardath Mayhar, Bradley Denton, Gene Wolfe, Howard Waldrop, Chris Roberson, Neil Barrett, Jr, Michael Moorcock and others.

From Golden Gryphon Press with a Foreword by Howard Waldrop, *Black Pockets and Other Dark Thoughts* collected nineteen horror stories (one original) by George Zebrowski, who also contributed an Afterword. All the stories differed from their original appearances, and two were significantly revised.

From the same imprint, Charles Stross' Lovecraftian spy novel *The Jennifer Morgue* was a sequel to *The Atrocity Archives* and featured nerdy CIA demon expert Bob Howard.

Jack Ketchum's 1991 novel *Offspring*, the sequel to *Off Season*, was reissued by The Overlook Connection Press in a trade paperback edition, a 1,000-copy signed edition, a 100-copy slipcased edition, and a fifty-two-copy boxed and leather-bound lettered edition. This "definitive" version contained the author's preferred text, a revised Afterword and a reprint article.

And Hell Followed With Them was an attractive hardcover anthology from Solitude Publications featuring a novella each by Geoff Cooper, Brian Knight, Tim Lebbon and Brian Keene, with impressive cover art by Chad Savage. It was available in signed hardcover editions of 500 numbered copies and twenty-six lettered.

Michael Cadnum's *Can't Catch Me and Other Twice-Told Tales* from San Francisco's Tachyon Publications collected eighteen stories (two original) that were described as "fairy tales for the tough-minded". From the same imprint, *Feeling Very Strange: The Slipstream Anthology* edited by James Patrick Kelly and John Kessel contained fifteen mostly reprint stories by Carol Emshwiller, Bruce Sterling, Kelly Link, Jonathan Lethem, Jeff VanderMeer, Karen Joy

Fowler, Jeffrey Ford, Michael Chadbon, Howard Waldrop and others.

Available from Sean Wright's Crowswing Books, *Clinically Dead and Other Tales of the Supernatural* was a hardcover collection of ten stories (two original) by David A. Sutton with an Introduction by Stephen Jones and an Afterword by Joel Lane. It was limited to 250 signed copies and a thirty-copy slipcased edition. Also from Crowswing, *The Impelled and Other Head Trips* collected eighteen stories (six original) by Gary Fry, along with an Introduction by Ramsey Campbell and an Afterword by the author.

She Loves Monsters was an impressive novella from Simon Clark about the search for a legendary lost movie. Featuring an Introduction by Paul Finch, it was published by Necessary Evil Press in a hardcover edition of 450 signed and numbered copies and twenty-six signed and lettered copies.

Gary McMahon's *Rough Cut*, a short novel about another fabled lost film and one man's journey into his own family's darkness, was published by Pendragon Press. From the same imprint, *At the Molehills of Madness* was a collection of twenty-five previously published stories by Rhys Hughes, dating from 1991-2003. The book also included a very brief Foreword and Afterword by the author, and a signed stickered edition was available of the first 100 pre-ordered copies.

Edited by Christopher C. Teague, *Choices* was an anthology of six novellas by Andrew Humphrey, Stephen Volk, Paul Finch, Gary Fry, Eric Brown and Richard Wright, also available from Pendragon Press.

Mirror Mere collected seventeen stories (five original) by Marie O'Regan. Published by Rainfall Books, it had an Introduction by Paul Kane, whose own collection of two novellas and a story, *Signs of Life*, was reissued by the same imprint with an Introduction by Stephen Gallagher and illustrations by Ian Simmons.

Also from Rainfall, *Terror Tales Issue #3* edited by John B. Ford and Paul Kane collected sixteen stories (seven original) from Stephen Laws, Richard Christian Matheson, Simon Clark, Peter Straub, Chaz Brenchley, Joel Lane, Conrad Williams, Mark Samuels, Allen Ashley and others.

Jon Farmer's iconoclastic study of history and popular culture from Savoy, *Sieg Heil: Iconographers*, was packed with photographs and artwork.

"Hosted" by Ramsey Campbell, *Read by Dawn Volume 1* was the first in an annual new anthology series published by Adèle Hartley's Bloody Books imprint from Beautiful Books. Along with a reprint by Campbell, it contained twenty-six original stories by David McGillveray, Lavie Tidhar, Andrew J. Wilson, Stephanie Bedwell-Grime, David Turnbull, John Llewellyn Probert and others. From the same imprint, *Classic Tales of Horror Volume 1* contained stories by M. R. James, Edgar Allan Poe, Ambrose Bierce, Mary Shelley and Charles Dickens.

Ramsey Campbell's classic 1979 serial killer novel *The Face That Must Die* was reissued as a trade paperback by Millipede Press with an original Introduction by Poppy Z. Bright, a new Afterword by the author, and the J. K. Potter illustrations from the 1983 Scream/Press edition. A 300-copy signed hardcover was also available.

From the same imprint, Theodore Sturgeon's *Some of Your Blood* contained the short 1961 novel, an associated story and a new Introduction by Steve Rasnic Tem, who signed the limited edition along with cover artist Harry O. Morris. Fredric Brown's *Here Comes a Candle* was originally published in 1950. Millipede's new edition included an extra story and essay by Brown, plus an Introduction by Bill Pronzini, who signed the limited hardcover.

Thomas Ligotti introduced Roland Topor's surreal 1964 novel *The Tenant*, which included four related stories and a gallery of art by the author. Ridley Scott supplied a Foreword to William Hjortsberg's *Falling Angel*, which also included an Introduction by James Crumley, and Jonathan Lethem introduced John Franklin Bardin's obscure crime thriller *The Deadly Percheron*, also featuring the first chapters of a previously unpublished novel by Bardin. As with the other titles from Millipede Press, it was released in both trade paperback and signed hardcover editions.

From Chicago's Twilight Tales, *My Lolita Complex and Other Tales of Sex and Violence* reprinted nine collaborations (including "Buffy" and "Hellboy" stories) between Max Allan Collins and Matthew V. Clemens, while *Ex Cathedra* collected eleven stories (four original) by Rebecca Maines (aka "Pamela D. Hodgson") in an edition of 200 copies.

Edited by Myna Wallin and Halli Villegas, *In the Dark: Stories from the Supernatural* was an anthology of twenty-five stories (three reprints) and five poems (one reprint) from Canada's Tightrope Books. Authors included Gemma Files and Brett Alexander Savory.

Produced by Spectre Library in a 200-copy limited edition, *The Surgeon of Souls* collected twelve stories about Dr Ivan Brodsky by Victor Rousseau. All but one was previously published in *Weird Tales*, but Mike Ashley's well-researched Introduction revealed prior publication details about several of them.

From Ash-Tree Press, Jessie Douglas Kerruish's classic 1922 werewolf mystery *The Undying Monster* was available in a new edition with an Introduction by Jack Adrian, limited to 500 copies.

Gothic Press founder Gary William Crawford was the author of *Mysteries of Von Domarus and Other Stories*, a collection of five tales.

Small Beer Press reissued Howard Waldrop's 1986 collection *Howard Who?* as a square paperback with the original Introduction by George R. R. Martin. From the same imprint, Alan DeNiro's debut collection *Skinny Dipping in the Lake of the Dead* contained sixteen offbeat stories (three original).

Edited by James Ambuehl for Elder Signs Press/Dimensions Books, *Hardboiled Cthulhu* was an anthology of twenty-one Lovecraftian mystery stories (five reprints) and a poem from Richard A. Lupoff, Robert M. Price, J. F. Gonzalez and others. *Arkham Tales: Legends of the Haunted City* edited by William Jones featured seventeen stories based on the Lovecraftian *Call of Cthulhu* role-playing game.

Government bio-engineered ticks got loose in the Ozark Mountains and started killing people in the humorous novel *Tick Hill* by Billy (William R.) Eakin, published by Yard Dog Press.

Available from Dark Arts Books, *Candy in the Dumpster: New and Used Stories* featured twelve stories (six reprints) by Martin Mundt, John Everson, Bill Breedlove and Jay Bonansinga, with an Introduction by Mort Castle.

Edited by Ron Shiflet, *Hell's Hangman: Horror in the Old West* was an original anthology from Tenoka Press featuring twenty-two "weird Western" stories, including one by the editor.

Then Comes the Child by husband and wife team Christopher Fulbright and Angeline Hawkes was a voodoo novella from Florida's Carnifax Press.

Steve Deighan's *A Dead Calmness* was a self-published collection of fourteen stories (six reprints) with an Introduction by the author. From the same writer, *Things from the Past* collected five stories and was available from Hadesgate Publications.

Also from Hadesgate, *Tiny Terrors Volume 1* was a small volume of five stories, some of which were introduced by Guy N. Smith. Garry Charles' *Heaven's Falling: Redemption* was the second volume in the author's Biblical fantasy series, from the same imprint.

Afterlife Battlefield was the third novel from "Johnny Ostentatious", about what really happened to people who committed suicide. It was published in trade paperback by Active Bladder.

New Wyrd: A Wyrdsmith's Anthology collected nine stories (one reprint) from the Minneapolis/St Paul writers' group with an Introduction by Naomi Kritzer. It was limited to 250 numbered copies. Selected from the Horror World website by editor Nanci Kalanta,

Eulogies: A Horror World Yearbook 2005 featured thirteen stories by Tom Piccirilli, Elizabeth Massie, Michael Laimo, Christopher Golden, Gary Braunbeck, Rick Hautala, Jack Ketchum and others. It also included six essays by Matthew Warner, interviews with Piccirilli, Golden, F. Paul Wilson, Douglas Clegg, John Skipp and David Morrell, plus brief Q&As with the contributors.

Horror Library Volume 1 from Texas' Cutting Block Press was edited with a Foreword by R. J. Cavender and contained thirty stories, including one by the editor. From the same imprint and edited by Frank J. Hutton, *Butcher Shop Quartet: Four Bold Stories to Disturb the Adventurous Mind* featured original tales by Boyd E. Harris, Clinton Green, Michael Stone and A. T. Andreas.

Bruce Boston's writings were collected in *Flashing in the Dark: Forty Short Fictions*, a thin volume from Sam's Dot Publishing, while *Shades Fantastic* was a volume of poetry from the same author, issued by Gromagon Press.

Twilight's Last Gleaming was the first volume in Mike Philbin's self-published and uncensored "Writing as Hertzan Chimera" series, from Chimericana Books. For Christmas, Philbin also edited *Chimeraworld #4: Twenty Three Tales of Traffic Mayhem*.

A paperback original from Hellbound Books Publishing, *Damned Nation* edited by Robert N. Lee and David T. Wilbanks contained twenty-two stories about "Hell on Earth" by Weston Ochse, Tom Piccirilli, Poppy Z. Brite, William F. Nolan, Gerard Houarner, James S. Dorr, Bev Vincent and others.

As a Christmas "present" for subscribers, Hill House Publishers produced a special signed and numbered edition of Ray Bradbury's 1973 story "The Wish", limited to 250 copies with a new Afterword by the author. A lettered edition of the small hardcover book was also available in a fifty-two-copy edition. As an added "thank you" to subscribers of the forthcoming *The Martian Chronicles: The Definitive Edition*, a signed fifty-copy edition of Bradbury's 1950 memoir "How I Wrote My Book" was produced by Hill House in matching format. The book included both a clean text version of the work as well as reproductions of the actual manuscript pages.

The Rolling Darkness Revue once again toured a number of bookstores in southern California during the run-up to Halloween, entertaining audiences with its unique blend of music and fiction. Joining founding members Peter Atkins and Glen Hirshberg in guest spots were Clay McLeod Chapman, Dennis Etchison, Aimee Bender, Lisa Morton and Norman Partridge. All but Bender had stories in the chapbook *At the Sign of the Snowman's Skull* (Etchison's contribution was the only reprint), issued by Earthling Publications to tie in with the 2006 performances. Other merchandising available at the various venues included a signed, limited edition CD of readings and music from the 2005 tour, a new T-shirt design, and a special "Snowman's Skull" shot glass.

From Gauntlet Press' Edge Books imprint, *Love Hurts and Other Short Stories* collected seven original tales and an Introduction by Barry Hoffman, with a cover illustration by Harry O. Morris.

Attractively produced by DreamHaven Books, *Strange Birds* included two original stories by Gene Wolfe, inspired by the paintings and sculptures of Lisa Snellings-Clark. It was limited to 1,000 copies, and was the first in a projected series by various authors based on Snellings-Clark's artwork.

Down in the Fog-Shrouded City by Alex Irvine was the tenth volume in the Wormhole Contemporary Chapbooks series. With an Introduction by James Patrick Kelly and cover and interior art by Steve Rasnic Tem, it was limited to 750 numbered booklets, 250 numbered hardcovers and fifty-two lettered editions signed by the author.

Absinthe was a stylish-looking chapbook from Bloodletting Press that contained an original story each by Jack Ketchum and Tim Lebbon. It was limited to 500 signed and numbered copies along with a fifty-two copy deluxe lettered edition.

From California's Tropism Press, *Show and Tell and Other Stories* was a collection of six offbeat stories (one original) by Greg van Eekhout. Jenn Reese' *Tales of the Chinese Zodiac* appeared from the same imprint.

Foreigners and Other Familiar Faces was a chapbook collection of nine unusual stories (three original) by Mark Rich, published by Small Beer Press.

Edited with an Introduction by Jonathan Reitan and James R. Beach, *Northwest Horrors: Stories Presented by the Northwest Horror Professionals* was a slim anthology of ten stories (three original) by Elizabeth Engstrom, Bruce Holland Rogers, John Pelan, W. H. Pugmire and others.

Tales from the Black Dog was published by the Minneapolis/St Paul writers' critique group The Wyrdsmiths. It contained eight stories (one reprint) from various members and an Introduction by founder Lyda Morehouse. Also hailing from St Paul, Velocity Press' *Rabid Transit: Long Voyages Great Lies* edited by Christopher Barzak, Alan DeNiro and Kristin Livdahl featured six original travel stories from F. Brett Cox, Geoffrey H. Goodwin, Alice Kim, Meghan McCarron, David J. Schwartz and Heather Shaw.

Poems That Go Splat from Naked Snake Press showcased the work of Brian Rosenberger.

With its sixth issue, PS Publishing's *PostScripts: The A to Z of Fantastic Fiction* changed to illustrated boards for its 150-copy signed hardcover edition. As usual, the title published four quarterly issues in 2006 with stories by Rhys Hughes, Stephen Baxter, Garry Kilworth, Conrad Williams, Stephen Volk, Jack Dann, T. M. Wright, Jay Lake, Michael Swanwick, Gene Wolfe, Darrell Schweitzer, Tony Richards, K. W. Jeter, Darren Speegle, Lavie Tidhar and John Grant, amongst others, interviews with Elizabeth Hand and Howard Waldrop, and guest editorials from Steven Erikson, Lucius Shepard, Terry Bisson and Jeff VanderMeer. Issue #6 also featured a fascinating article by Mike Ashley about stage magician Harry Houdini (Ehrich Weiss).

The three issues of Richard Chizmar and Robert Morrish's *Cemetery Dance Magazine* included contributions from Eric Brown, Tony Richards, Tim Waggoner, Lisa Morton, Simon R. Green, Ed Gorman, Darren Speegle, Gene O'Neill, Peter Atkins, Stephen Mark Rainey, Scott Nicholson, and Michael A. Arnzen and Mark McLaughlin. Neil Gaiman and Tim Lebbon were among those interviewed, and there were the usual columns by Bev Vincent, Thomas F. Monteleone, Paula Guran, Michael Marano and John Pelan. Issue #56 of *Cemetery Dance* was billed as a "Glen Hirshberg Special" and included a new short story, a novel excerpt and a fun article by Hirshberg, along with an interview with the author and an extended review of his latest collection, *American Morons*.

Possibly the best-looking of the "publisher's magazines", William Schafer's *Subterranean* featured fiction by Norman Partridge, Poppy Z. Brite, David Prill, David J. Schow, Jay Lake, Lewis Shiner, Orson Scott Card, Stephen Gallagher and Tad Williams, amongst others.

Another publisher to launch its own magazine title was Prime Books, an imprint of Wildside Press. Edited by Nick Mamatas and limited to 1,500 copies given away at World Fantasy convention 2006, the dull-looking "issue zero" of *Phantom* featured fiction from F. Brett Cox, Darren Speegle, Sarah Langan and Laird Barron, along with an interview with Stewart O'Nan.

Also now published by Wildside Press in association with Terminus Publishing Co., *Weird Tales* benefited from some excellent cover art by Rowena Morrell and Les Edwards. Fiction and verse was supplied by Parke Godwin, Nina Kiriki Hoffman, William F. Nolan, Gregory Frost, Tony Richards, Fitz-James O'Brien, Tanith Lee, Holly Phillips, Jay Lake, Brian Stableford, Richard Lupoff, Tina and Tony Rath, Robert Weinberg, George Barr, Jill Bauman, Darrell Schweitzer and Bruce Boston. Issue #341 featured an article celebrating Robert E. Howard's centenary, while a John Shirley "special author feature" in #342 included an interview with the writer.

In December, Wildside publisher John Betancourt fired the entire editorial team of *Weird Tales*. Stephen H. Segal was brought in to handle day-to-day operations while the magazine looked for a new fiction editor. Betancourt also announced that the magazine would be getting a new logo and interior design in 2007.

Also from Wildside, the third issue of *H. P. Lovecraft's Magazine of Horror* finally made a much-belated appearance. It featured a "Spotlight on Brian Lumley" that included two stories (one original), an interview by Darrell Schweitzer and an overview of the author's career by Stephen Jones. More decidedly non-Lovecraftian fiction was supplied by Chelsea Quinn Yarbro, Andrew J. Wilson, Lynne Jamneck and the late Earl Godwin, amongst others, along with review and opinion columns by editor Marvin Kaye, Craig Shaw Gardner, Peter Cannon and Ian McDowell.

Meanwhile, the second issue of the magazine was released as a "collector's edition" trade paperback with extra fiction not included in the newsprint version.

Although Gordon Van Gelder's *The Magazine of Fantasy & Science Fiction* tended to rely on too many of the same names, there were still some very fine stories by Terry Bisson, Claudia O'Keefe, Gene Wolfe, Charles Coleman Finlay, Steven Utley, Laird Barron, Gardner Dozois, Christopher Rowe, Peter S. Beagle, Geoff Ryman, Carol Emshwiller, Scott Bradfield and Susanna Clarke, amongst others. Harlan Ellison set a challenge in the September issue with a story outline about Lady Luck that was picked up by Tananarive Due, Michael Kandel and Michael Libling. The same issue also reprinted a selection of letters between the late James Tiptree Jr (Alice B. Sheldon) and Ursula K. Le Guin.

As usual, regular *FSF* columnists included Charles de Lint, Elizabeth Hand, Kathi Maio, Michelle West, Paul Di Filippo, Robert K. J. Killheffer, James Sallis and Lucius Shepard, while the "Curiosities" page, recommending obscure books, featured contributions from Bud Webster, F. Gwynplaine MacIntyre, Gregory J. Coster, Michael Swanwick, Dennis Lien, Bud Webster, Thomas Marcinko, Paul Di Filippo and David Langford.

Fourteen months after going "on hiatus", *Amazing Stories* was finally cancelled by Paizo Publishing after it was unable to increase circulation and attract media advertising. As a result, rights in the title reverted to Wizards of the Coast.

The third issue of *Allen K's Inhuman Magazine* expanded the rota of artists working on the title and included new and reprint fiction from Michael Shea, Gerard Houarner, Melanie Tem, Tina L. Jens, Edward Bryant Jr., Kevin J. Anderson, Michael Resnick and others.

James R. Beach's *Dark Discoveries* featured interviews with Elizabeth Massie, Douglas Winter, J. F. Gonzalez, Stephen Mark Rainey and Brian Knight, along with fiction from Gerard Houarner, Kealan Patrick Burke and Ken Goldman, plus a tribute to J. N. Williamson.

The four issues of Jason B. Sizemore's impressive-looking magazine *Apex Science Fiction & Horror Digest* included fiction from Ben Bova, Robert Dunbar, Amy Grech, William F. Nolan, Michael Laimo, Tom Piccirilli and Lavie Tidhar, interviews with Neil Gaiman, Robert Rankin, Sherrilyn Kenyon, Poppy Z. Brite, Kage Baker, Michael Laimo, Tim Powers, Tom Piccirilli and Kelly Link, plus various articles and reviews.

Patrick and Honna Swenson's *Talebones: Fiction on the Dark Edge* got a reprieve after the editors decided to close it down after almost eleven years due to financial difficulties and a dwindling subscriber base. Following an online plea, the magazine added 120 new subscribers, with more promised, and several extra pages of paid advertising. As a result, the title would survive for at least another year. The two issues published in 2006 contained stories and poetry by Charles Coleman Finlay, James Van Pelt, Nina Kiriki Hoffman, Don D'Ammassa and Mark Rich. The editors decided to drop the interview section following Ken Rand's talk with Louise Marley in issue #32.

Christopher M. Cevasco's twice-yearly *Paradox: The Magazine of Historical and Speculative Fiction* featured fiction and poetry by Lisa Jensen, Adam Stemple, Jane Yolen, Darrell Schweitzer and Sarah Monette, amongst others.

Published bi-monthly by TTA Press, *Interzone: Science Fiction & Fantasy* included fiction by F. Gwynplaine MacIntyre, Richard Calder, Paul Di Filippo and Jay Lake, plus interviews with Terry Pratchett (twice!), Gerry Anderson, K. J. Bishop, Steven Erickson and Christopher Priest, along with all the regular news and review columns. Also from TTA, *Crimewave Nine: Transgressions* contained twelve new stories by Scott Nicholson, John Shirley and others.

Despite still advertising subscriptions, TTA Press' previously announced horror magazine *Black Static* (formerly *The 3rd Alternative*) failed once again to appear in 2006.

Edited by Trevor Denyer, *Midnight Street: Journeys Into Darkness* included fiction by Paul Finch, Gary Couzens, Rhys Hughes and Peter Tennant, along with interviews with authors Deborah LeBlanc, Ralph Robert Moore and "B" movie actress Lilith Stabs. Tony Richards was the featured author in issue #6, Gary Fry in #7, and L. H. Maynard and M. P. N. Sims were showcased in #8.

The fourth annual issue of Adam Golaski and Jeff Paris' perfect-bound *New Genre* contained four stories by Jan Wildt, Paul A. Gilster, Christopher Harman and Don Tumasonis.

The December issue of *Realms of Fantasy* featured an exclusive interview with Laurell K. Hamilton, while the Winter issue of Joseph W. Dickerson's *Aberrant Dreams* included fiction by, and an interview with, Gerald W. Page.

Dave Lindschmidt's glossy *City Slab* included stories by Jack Ketchum and Sonya Taffe, interviews with Ketchum, Bill Moseley and Ray Garton, and articles about film directors Dario Argento and Takashi Miike.

Edited by Doyle Eldon Wilmoth Jr. and published by SpecFic-World, *Rogue Worlds* was another magazine featuring horror fiction and poetry, while the twentieth anniversary issue of Eric M. Heideman's perfect-bound *Tales of the Unanticipated* #27 was a special "Monsters Issue".

From Elder Sign Press, William Jones' *Dark Wisdom: The Magazine of Dark Fiction* took on a more professional appearance with full colour covers and fiction and poetry from John Shirley, Paul Finch, Gerard Houarner, Bruce Boston, Jay Caselberg, Scott Nicholson, James S. Dorr, William C. Dietz, Stephen Mark Rainey, Gene O'Neill and others. Each issue also featured a graphic tale and a serial.

Issue #23 of *Cthulhu Sex Magazine*, described as "the magazine for connoisseurs of sensual horror", included a portfolio of illustrators featured on the www.spookyART.com website, including co-founders Chad Savage and Alan M. Clark, Jill Bauman, Alex McVey, Jason Beam, Dan Ouellette, Robert Morris and John Schwegel.

With still no sign of their long-promised tome on Italian director Mario Bava, Tim and Donna Lucas managed to get just five issues of *Video Watchdog* out in 2006. Despite too much obvious "filler" material, there were still interesting articles on the making of *Amity-*

ville 3-D, Edgar Wallace's involvement in the original *King Kong*, and a look at the films of low budget director Del Tenney. While Joe Dante bowed out with his long-running review column, Ramsey Campbell joined the magazine with "Ramsey's Rambles".

Canada's *Rue Morgue* magazine turned out eleven glossy issues in 2006. Along with all the usual movie, DVD, book and music coverage, issues also featured interviews with Roger Corman, Clive Barker, Wes Craven, Jean Rollin, Lina Romay, Stuart Gordon, Jeffrey Combs, Basil Gogos, David Seltzer, Richard Donner, Peter Straub, Adrienne Barbeau, Takashi Miike, Pete Walker, R. Lee Ermey, Ingrid Pitt, Ramsey Campbell, the late Billy Van, Elvira, Bob Clark and John Saxon. The 9th Anniversary Halloween Issue was a tribute to late Italian director Lucio Fulci and also included "The Connoisseur's Guide to 50 Alternative Horror Books".

The annual Rue Morgue Festival of Fear, held over three days in September in Toronto included special guests Alice Cooper, Guillermo del Toro, Jeffrey Combs, Linda Blair, Roddy Piper, Ben Chapman, Michael Berryman and others.

HorrorHound was a new glossy magazine out of Cincinnati, Ohio, which was devoted to movies, comic books, video games, model kits, DVDs and gore.

Charles N. Brown's newszine *Locus* entered its 40th year of publication with interviews with, amongst others, Geoff Ryman, S. M. Stirling, Dave Duncan, the inevitable Neil Gaiman and Terry Pratchett, Jay Lake, Betsy Wollheim, Peter Straub, China Miéville, and Joe Hill (who was outed by *Variety* in early 2006 as Joseph Hillström King, the son of Stephen and Tabitha King). The May issue looked at "Young Adult Fiction" with essays by Ursula K. Le Guin, Garth Nix, Graham Joyce and others, while the July issue's "Special Horror Section" featured commentary from Edward Bryant, Ellen Datlow and bookseller Alan Beatts.

Prism: The Newsletter of the British Fantasy Society had an erratic schedule under the editorship of Jenny Barber. Despite this, each issue was packed with publishing and media news, and there was a brief interview with David Sutton.

Under editors Marie O'Regan and the busy Barber, the BFS' journal *Dark Horizons* was a messy mixture of short stories and non-fiction, including book and media reviews that would have been better suited in *Prism*. The two issues published in 2006 featured new and reprint fiction from Mark Chadbourn, Debbie Bennett, John Howard, Lavie Tidhar, Mark Morris, Ramsey Campbell, Tim Lebbon and others, along with interviews with Neil Gaiman and independent film-maker Jeff Brookshire.

Edited with an Afterword by the ubiquitous Paul Kane and Marie O'Regan, and featuring a "heartfelt" Introduction by Stephen Jones, *The British Fantasy Society: A Celebration* was an attractive trade paperback anthology of twenty horror, fantasy and SF stories (six original) with contributions from Christopher Fowler, Clive Barker, Michael Marshall Smith, John Connolly, Ramsey Campbell, Kim Newman, Peter Straub, Neil Gaiman, Brian Aldiss, Richard Christian Matheson, Robert Silverberg, Stephen Gallagher and others. All profits from the book went to the Society and the "Black Dust" Nqabakazula Charity Project in South Africa.

BFS members were also treated to a special edition of *Cinema Macabre* edited by Mark Morris. This trade paperback version replaced the J. K. Potter cover art on the PS Publishing edition with a new painting by Les Edwards, and Jonathan Ross' Introduction was dropped in favour of one by Marie O'Regan and Paul Kane.

From the Ghost Story Society, *All Hallows* contained fiction by Stephen Volk and others along with an interview with Australian author John Harwood, plus the usual reviews, columns and articles by Ramsey Campbell, Roger Dobson, Reggie Oliver and Gary McMahon.

Edited by Gwilym Games, *Machenalia* was the newsletter of The Friends of Arthur Machen. Along with plenty of Machen-related news, each issue also contained reviews of other genre material.

The tenth issue of David Longhorn's annual *Supernatural Tales* was another bumper volume featuring contributions from Don Tumasonis, Gary McMahon, Andrew Darlington, Lynda E. Rucker, Tina Rath and Michael Chislett, amongst others. *Whispers of Wickedness* included an interview with author Steven Pirie.

The two issues of John Benson's *Not One of Us* contained stories and poems by Sonya Taaffe and others. *Change* was the latest in a series of annual, variously-titled publications from the same publisher. A trade paperback anthology edited by Benson, *The Best of Not One of Us*, was published by Prime Books/Wildside Press and included fifteen stories that originally appeared in the magazine.

Gavin J. Grant and Kelly Link's *Lady Churchill's Rosebud Wristlet* and Heather Shaw and Tim Pratt's *Flytrap* featured the usual mixture of slipstream fiction, poetry and articles.

The October issue of *The New York Review of Science Fiction* included interviews with Thomas Ligotti and Peter Straub, and the Winter issue of *The Bulletin of the Science Fiction and Fantasy Writers of America* featured an introductory essay by Bud Webster on Donald A. Wollheim's classic horror anthologies *The Macabre Reader* and *More Macabre*.

Published by Writer's Digest in association with "The Horror Writers of America" [sic], Mort Castle's guide *On Writing Horror: Revised Edition* contained forty-four essays (twenty-four original and the others mostly revised) on how to write horror with a Foreword by Stanley Wiater and an Afterword by Harlan Ellison.

Dorothy Hoobler and Thomas Hoobler's *The Monsters: Mary Shelley & the Curse of Frankenstein* looked at the origins of Mary Shelley's influential novel.

Edited by Scott Connors for print-on-demand publisher Hippocampus Press, *The Freedom of Fantastic Things: Selected Criticism on the Writings of Clark Ashton Smith* collected twenty-six critical essays (five original) by Brian Stableford, S. T. Joshi, James Blish, Donald Sidney-Fryer and others on the author's work, along with a gathering of contemporary reviews.

H. P. Lovecraft's *Collected Essays Volume 3: Science* and *Collected Essays Volume 4: Travel* were also available from Hippocampus, edited with notes and an Introduction by S. T. Joshi. From the same imprint came *Lovecraft's New York Circle: The Kalem Club 1924-1927*, edited by Kirk Mara Hart and Joshi, with a Preface by Peter Cannon and an Introduction by Mara Kirk Hart.

In December, a number of original Lovecraft letters and manuscripts were auctioned at Sotheby's. Among the items was an autographed manuscript of "The Shunned House" that sold for $45,000.

Charles Addams: A Cartoonist's Life was a biography by Linda H. Davis.

From McFarland Publishing, Allen A. Debus' *Dinosaurs in Fantastic Fiction: A Thematic Survey* included Forewords by Donald F. Glut and Mark F. Berry.

Published by Greenwood Press/Praeger, *Legends of Blood: The Vampire in History and Myth* by Wayne Bartlett and Flavia Idriceanu looked at the undead in myths, literature and film.

Don D'Ammassa's *Encyclopedia of Fantasy and Horror Fiction* was a guide to the major authors and their works.

Published in a signed edition limited to 500 copies, John Clute's *The Darkening Garden: A Short Lexicon of Horror* contained a selection of terms defined for a proposed encyclopaedia on horror fiction, illustrated by thirty artists. The artwork was also available as thirty postcards, limited to 300 sets.

*   *   *

Translated from the Russian by Adam Bromfield and published in a movie tie-in edition, Sergei Lukyanenko's 1998 novel *Night Watch* (*Nochnol Dozor*) was the first in a trilogy about the epic battle between the creatures of Light and Dark.

Other tie-in novels of the year included *V for Vendetta* by Steve Moore, *Superman Returns* by Marv Wolfman and *Snakes on a Plane* by Christa Faust.

From BL Publishing/Black Flame, *Final Destination 3* was also written by Faust. It was joined by novelisations for *Final Destination* by Natasha Rhodes and *Final Destination 2* by Nancy A. Collins and Rhodes, while the spin-off title *Final Destination: Looks Could Kill* was written by Collins alone.

Dark Horse Comics' DH Press launched its paperback series of licensed Universal Monsters novels with *Dracula: Asylum* by Paul Witcover, *Frankenstein: The Shadow of Frankenstein* by Stefan Petrucha and *Creature from the Black Lagoon: Time's Black Lagoon* by Paul Di Filippo.

Other tie-in books based on older film properties included *The Toxic Avenger* by Lloyd Kaufman and Adam Jahnke, *Jason X: To the Third Power* by Nancy Kilpatrick, *Friday the 13th: The Jason Strain* by the busy Christa Faust, *Friday the 13th: Carnival of Maniacs* by Stephen Hand, *A Nightmare on Elm Street: The Dream Dealers* by Jeffrey Thomas, *A Nightmare on Elm Street: Perchance to Dream* by Natasha Rhodes, *Predator: Forever Midnight* by John Shirley and *Aliens: DNA War* by Diane Carey.

Although *Buffy the Vampire the Slayer* only lived on in TV re-runs, the novelisations continued apace with *Buffy the Vampire Slayer: After Image* by Pierce Askegren, *Carnival of Souls* by Nancy Holder, *Blackout* by Keith R. A. deCandido, *Portal Through Time* by Alice Henderson, *Bad Bargain* by Diana G. Gallagher and *Go Ask Malice*, which was told in diary form by Joseph Robert Levy.

The Power of Three may also have reached the end of its television run, but the Halliwell sisters continued their witchy ways in *Charmed: As Puck Would Have It* by Paul Ruditis and *Charmed: Light of the World* by Scott Ciencin.

At least *Lost: Signs of Life* by Frank Thompson was based on a show that was still running, and BBC Books issued new novelisations to tie in to the exploits of David Tennant's *Doctor Who* and his companion, Rose. The ghosts from a sunken navy ship flooded London in *The Feast of the Drowned* by Stephen Cole. A 2,000-year-old statue of Rose led to an adventure in Ancient Rome in Jac Rayner's *The Stone Rose*, and the duo searched for a key to eternal life on another planet in *The Resurrection Casket* by Justin Richards.

The exploits of the tenth Doctor and Rose continued in *The Price of Paradise*, *The Art of Destruction* and *The Nightmare of Black Island*, while the seventh Doctor and Ace were featured in Andrew Cartmel's *Doctor Who: Atom Bomb Blues*.

Based on the classic Gothic daytime soap opera, *Dark Shadows: The Salem Branch* was written by actress Lara Parker.

Games Workshop issued a profit warning following the end of the *Lord of the Rings* sales boom. Sales for the six months to November 2006 were down by £2.3 million and full year profits were expected to be below forecasts.

World of Darkness: Chicago: Three Shades of Darkness collected three novellas based on White Wolf's role-playing game, and Nick Kyme's *Necromunda: Back from the Dead* was based on another role-playing game.

30 Days of Night: Rumors of the Undead by Steve Niles and Jeff Mariotte was a novel based on the vampire graphic series created by Niles.

John Shirley was busy novelising *John Constantine: Hellblazer* with *War Lord* and *Subterranean*, and he still found time to turn out *Batman: Dead White*. Alex Irvine took over with *Batman: Inferno*, while *Infinite Crisis* by Greg Cox was based on the acclaimed DC Comics graphic serial.

Tim Lebbon's *Hellboy: Unnatural Selection* and young adult writer Thomas E. Sniegoski's *Hellboy: The God Machine* were both based on the comic series created by Mike Mignola.

Wolverine: Road of Bones was an X-Men spin-off by David Alan Mack, and *Durham Red: Black Dawn* by Peter J. Evans was based on the vampire character from *2000 AD* comic.

Editor Mark Morris asked fifty contributors to write about their favourite horror films in *Cinema Macabre*, from PS Publishing. The results ranged from *Nosferatu* (1922) to *The Sixth Sense* (1999) and included essays by Basil Copper, Stephen Jones, Neil Gaiman, Peter Atkins, Jo Fletcher, Stephen Gallagher, Lisa Tuttle, Mark Samuels, Thomas Tessier, Christopher Fowler, Kim Newman, Joel Lane, Simon Pegg, Michael Marshall Smith, Tim Lebbon, Muriel Gray, Peter Crowther, Paul McAuley, Terry Lamsley, Ramsey Campbell, Douglas E. Winter and the editor, along with an Introduction by UK TV personality Jonathan Ross. It was published in an edition of 500 trade hardcovers signed by Morris and a 200-copy slipcased edition signed by all fifty-two contributors.

Although *Monsters: A Celebration of the Classics from Universal Studios* featured a "Fearword" by Forrest J. Ackerman and contributions from a number of luminaries including John Landis, Stephen Sommers, Gloria Stuart and Ben Chapman, the minimalist text and unimaginative photo layouts didn't do their subjects justice.

Published by Telos as a hefty trade paperback, *Zombiemania: 80 Movies to Die For* included in-depth reviews by Dr Arnold T. Blumberg and Andrew Hershberger, along with a brief history of zombie cinema, a title index of more than 500 films, and a Afterword by zombie actor Mark Donovan.

Night Shade Books reissued Andrew Migliore and John Strysik's wide-ranging 1995 study *Lurker in the Lobby: A Guide to the Cinema of H. P. Lovecraft* in a handsomely redesigned and updated edition with a Preface by S. T. Joshi.

Andy Murray's *Into the Unknown: The Fantastic Life of Nigel Kneale* from Headpress was the first full biography of the British author and screenwriter (who died a few months after it was published).

The Winston Effect: The Art and History of Stan Winston Studio by Jody Duncan was a huge volume from Titan Books detailing the behind-the-scenes secrets of the make-up maestro's extensive work in the cinema. James Cameron contributed a brief Foreword, and there was also a short notation from the late Fay Wray. Equally hefty was Titan's *Crystal Lake Memories: The Complete History of Friday the 13th* by Peter M. Bracke, which included everything any fan of Jason Voorhees needed to know about the "slasher" film series.

From the same publisher, Denis Meikle's *The Ring Companion* looked at the Japanese film cycle about a cursed videotape and the novels that inspired it.

Celebrating its subject's 80th birthday, Alan Silver and James Ursini's *Roger Corman: Metaphysics on a Shoestring* looked at each of the director's films, with commentary by Corman himself.

Terry Pratchett's Hogfather: The Illustrated Screenplay included the shooting script by director Vadim Jean and Pratchett, who also contributed separate Forewords.

From Baylor University Press, Kim Paffenroth's study *Gospel of the Living Dead: George Romero's Visions of Hell on Earth* looked at the Christian imagery in the director's series of zombie movies.

In *Irwin Allen Television Productions, 1964-1970: A Critical History* from McFarland, Jon Abbott discussed the disaster movie producer's successful TV output, including such shows as *Voyage to the Bottom of the Sea*, *Lost in Space*, *The Time Tunnel* and *Land of the Giants*.

The Hellraiser Films and Their Legacy by Paul Kane covered Clive Barker's seminal 1980s movie and its sequels and spin-offs, with a Foreword by Pinhead himself, actor Doug Bradley.

Also from McFarland, Michael Klossner's *Prehistoric Humans in Film and Television* looked at nearly 600 dramas, comedies and documentaries made between 1905 and 2004.

Vampire fans could choose from Matthew Pateman's study *The Aesthetics of Culture in Buffy the Vampire Slayer*, Tim Kane's *The Changing Vampire of Film and Television* and Lyndon W. Joslin's updated 1999 study *Count Dracula Goes to the Movies: Stoker's Novel Adapted, 1922-2003*. Also of interest was *James Bernard, Composer to Count Dracula: A Critical Biography* by David Huckvale.

Cover Story: The Art of John Picacio was an impressive full-colour showcase of the award-winning artist's work, published in hardcover by MonkeyBrain Books with an Introduction by Michael Moorcock and an interview with Picacio by Joseph McCabe.

Best known for his many *Doc Savage* paperback covers, *James Bama: American Realist* looked at these and much more of the artist's work. Brian M. Kane wrote the text, and there was an Introduction by Harlan Ellison and a Foreword by Len Leone.

The subtitle of Steve Starger and J. David Spurlock's *Wally's World: The Brilliant Life and Tragic Death of Wally Wood, the World's Second-Best Comic Book Artist* pretty much summed up the life of its subject. A deluxe hardcover edition included an extra sixteen-page portfolio.

Amphigorey Again collected a number of previously unpublished illustrations and unfinished work by the late Edward Gorey.

Origins: The Art of John Jude Palencar featured more than 100 paintings and drawings by the artist with a Foreword by Christopher Paolini and an Afterword by Arnie Fenner, who edited the volume with his wife Cathy.

As usual, the Fenners also edited *Spectrum 13: The Best in Contemporary Fantastic Art*, which contained more than 400 pieces of art by some 300 different artists. Among those represented were Michael Whelan, Bob Eggleton, Brom, Leo and Diane Dillon, Donato Giancola, Adam Rex, Todd Lockwood and Thomas S. Kuebler, along with a profile of Grand Master Award winner Jeffrey Jones.

Ray Bradbury's classic story *The Homecoming* was issued as a picture book, profusely illustrated by Dave McKean.

The Illustrated Dracula featured artwork by Jae Lee, and included Bram Stoker's missing chapter, "Dracula's Guest", plus various non-fiction appendices by Marvin Kaye.

Frankenstein Makes a Sandwich and Other Stories You're Sure to Like, Because They're All About Monsters, and Some of Them Are Also About Food. You Like Food, Don't You? Well, All Right Then was the full title of Adam Rex's beautifully illustrated children's book featuring poems about all the classic creatures.

Mommy?, written by Arthur Yorinks with art by Maurice Sendak, was a pop-up picture book about a little boy searching for his missing mother who encountered many of the classic monsters.

Poet Laura Leuck teamed up with artist Gris Grimly for *Santa Claws*, a frighteningly festive tale about two boys at Christmas.

From Fantagraphics Books, *Beasts!* was subtitled *A Pictorial Schedule of Traditional Hidden Creatures*. Conceived, designed and edited by Jacob Covey, the attractively-produced hardcover volume collected artwork from ninety of the best visual artists from the worlds of comics, skate graphics, rock posters, animation, children's books, and commercial and fine art.

London's Great Ormond Street Hospital for Sick Children, which still holds the copyright to J. M. Barrie's *Peter Pan* in the EU, protested at the publication of *Lost Girls*, an erotic graphic novel by Alan Moore and artist Melinda Gebbie featuring the sexually explicit adventures of Alice from *Alice in Wonderland*, Wendy from *Peter Pan* and Dorothy from *The Wizard of Oz* on the eve of the First World War.

The hospital, which was bequeathed the rights to his books by Barrie, claimed that Moore's title would need their permission or license to publish. In response, the author told the BBC that "It wasn't our intention to try to provoke a ban". *Lost Girls* was subsequently issued as a three-volume deluxe hardcover set in the US by Top Shelf Productions. When pre-orders exceeded the 10,000-copy first printing, the book went into a second edition before publication. However, following discussions between the publisher and Great Ormond Street Hospital, publication of the book in the European Union was delayed until 2008, when the *Peter Pan* copyright expires.

Avatar's *George A. Romero's Night of the Living Dead* comics series launched with a special introductory issue, "Back from the Grave", written by original creators Romero and John Russo and set in 1968, prior to events in the first movie. The launch edition was

available in six variant editions with alternate covers by artists Jacen
Burrows ("Regular" and "Splatter"), Sebastian Fiumara ("Rotting"), Juan Jose Ryp ("Terror") and Tim Vigil ("Gore"). A special
"Foil" edition came packaged with a poster signed by Romero and
was limited to just 600 copies.

Many of Marvel's superheroes turned up as the walking dead in
writer Robert Kirkman's *Marvel Zombies* five-issue series, with
gruesome covers echoing classic comic book images of old.

Dark Horse Comics' *Universal Monsters: Cavalcade of Horror*
contained reprint graphic versions of *Dracula*, *Frankenstein*, *The
Mummy* and *The Creature from the Black Lagoon*, along with a new
painted cover by Eric Powell.

The Dark Horse Book of Monsters featured a new "Hellboy"
story by Mike Mignola, Kurt Busiek and Keith Giffen presented a
tribute to Jack Kirby's creature comics of the 1960s, while Garry
Gianni illustrated William Hope Hodgson's "A Tropical Terror".

IDW Publishing adapted Clive Barker's *The Great and Secret
Show* as a twelve-part series. Designed as a homage to the old
Warren comics magazines, IDW's *Doomed* featured graphic adapta-
tions of stories by, amongst others, David J. Schow, Robert Bloch,
Richard Matheson and F. Paul Wilson.

Reprinted by Headpress as a large format paperback, *The Complete Saga of the Victims* by "Archaic" Alan Heweston and Suso
Rego originally appeared in the early 1970s in the Skyward horror
comic *Scream*. A tale of two sexy women kidnapped and tortured by
all kinds of monsters, the graphic novel included the previously
unpublished sixth episode.

The "Best Sellers Illustrated" series featured Bram Stoker's *Dracula's Guest* illustrated by Dick Giordano and Edgar Allan Poe's *The
Murders in the Rue Morgue* illustrated by Frank Brunner.

Also available was a young adult graphic adaptation of *Dracula*,
written by Gary Reed and illustrated by Becky Cloonan.

Disney's exuberant if self-indulgent sequel *Pirates of the Caribbean:
Dead Man's Chest* smashed *Spider-Man 2*'s opening record of
$114.8 million in America with a three-day take of $132 million.
It went straight to the #1 slot on both sides of the Atlantic, became
the second-fastest movie to ever pass the $400 million mark (forty-
five days) and was the top-grossing film of the year in the UK with a
box-office take of almost £52 million. The film also became the
fastest-selling DVD ever in the UK as, during the run-up to Christmas, one in four DVDs sold was a copy of *Dead Man's Chest*.

Despite their success with the *Pirates* sequel, Walt Disney announced that they would cut 650 studio jobs to concentrate on creating blockbuster franchises over more adult subjects. Film output would be reduced from around eighteen titles a year to a dozen, with about ten being released under the Disney name and those under the Touchstone banner being cut back to two or three releases a year.

James Wong's silly but stylish *Final Destination 3* was held off the top spot by the long-delayed remake of *The Pink Panther* in America and Disney's animated *Chicken Little* in the UK. Following the premise of the earlier entries, a group of teens who survived a roller-coaster disaster discovered in various gruesome ways that they couldn't cheat Death (the voice of Tony Todd). The DVD release included a new interactive feature that let the viewer change the course of the plot. (So much for the *auteur* theory.)

Jonathan Liebesman's *The Texas Chainsaw Massacre: The Beginning* (from a story co-written by David J. Schow) was a pointless 1960s-set prequel to the equally misguided 2003 remake, in which audiences learned how young Thomas Hewitt (Andrew Bryniarski) ended up as the chainsaw-wielding cannibal called "Leatherface".

Co-scripted by Wes Craven and starring Kristen Bell (TV's *Veronica Mars*), Jim Sonzero's *Pulse* was another J-horror remake (*Kairo*) about a cursed website that released ghosts. Original *Ju-On* director Takashi Shimizu continued to recycle the same old tired J-horror clichés in *The Grudge 2*, which was once again irritatingly related out of sequence. As a local journalist, Edison Chen easily acted his American co-stars, the bland Amber Tamblyn and a returning Sarah Michelle Gellar, off the screen.

Gellar also turned up as the star of *The Return*, in which she travelled to a small Texas town that seemed to hold the key to her strange hallucinations.

Although a remake of John Carpenter's *The Fog* (1979) would seem redundant to most people, director Rupert Wainwright at least managed to include some atmospherically ghostly sequences in a tame tale of a cursed town and its murderous history.

Another unnecessary remake was *Black Christmas*, based on the superior and innovative 1975 slasher film of the same name. At least French director Alexandre Aja's reworking of *The Hills Have Eyes* brought some social commentary and a stylish veneer to producer Wes Craven's 1977 shocker about a murderous mutant family preying on tourists in the New Mexico desert. The film opened at #1 in the UK.

Simon West's remake of the 1979 film *When a Stranger Calls* opened at #1 in the US. Camilla Belle played the babysitter who realised that a series of threatening phone calls were coming from inside the house she was in.

Starring Liev Schreiber and Julia Stiles as the concerned parents, John Moore's *The Omen* was a pointless remake of the 1976 box-office smash and opened in the US on 6.6.06. Mia Farrow played the sinister nanny who hanged herself in front of Devil-child Damien (Seamus Davey-Fitzpatrick). The DVD included unrated extended scenes and an alternate ending.

Nicolas Cage starred as the duped cop in Neil LaBute's totally unnecessary remake of the 1973 classic *The Wicker Man*, which was relocated from Scotland to America, with Christopher Lee's pagan worshippers replaced by Ellen Burstyn's feminist beekeepers.

With its troubled production profiled in detail on HBO's hugely entertaining *Project Greenlight* more than a year earlier, John Gulager's monster-fest *Feast* finally received a three-week limited run at midnight showings in September before being dumped by Dimension onto DVD.

Another group of luckless victims were put through a series of gory tests by Tobin Bell's dying madman in Lionsgate's *Saw III*, which enjoyed the biggest opening of the series to date, debuting in the #1 slot with $33.6 million.

"Presented by" Quentin Tarantino, Eli Roth's gratuitous and un-pleasant *Hostel* had the interesting premise of a pair of American backpackers who discovered that an entire Slovakian town was involved in torturing and mutilating unsuspecting tourists. Apparently the Slovakian authorities were outraged at the film, along with more-discerning movie-goers. An "unrated" version released on DVD included no less than four commentary tracks featuring the director.

Fledgling distributor Fox Atomic's similarly-themed *Turistas* (aka *Paradise Lost*), directed by John Stockwell, in which Brazilian party-goers were sliced and diced by a mad surgeon (Miguel Lunardi), barely managed to register at the box-office with a $3.6 million opening weekend.

Jeroen Krabbe's eccentric film-maker assembled a group of dis-posable actors in Bernard Rose's *Snuff Movie*, while Brett Leonard's *Feed* was a pseudo-snuff film about a cyber investigator (Patrick Thompson) who uncovered a S&M world where men obsessed with overweight women bet on whether they could feed them to death.

World Wrestling Entertainment presented Gregory Dark's *See No Evil*, starring WWE wrestler "Kane" (Glen Jacobs) as a bald-headed psycho gruesomely dispatching teenagers in a creepy old hotel.

David Slade's *Hard Candy* played with audience perceptions of predator and victim when teenager Hayley (Ellen Page) hooked up with an older fashion photographer (Patrick Wilson) she met on the Internet.

Taking the splatter genre to its obvious comedy conclusion, Christopher Smith's *Severance* had a group of sales executives from a multinational weapons corporation being butchered one-by-one during a team-building exercise in the Eastern European backwoods.

Kate Beckinsale returned as leather-clad vampire werewolf-hunter Selene in her husband Len Wiseman's stylish-looking but confusing adventure *Underworld: Evolution*. Although not screened for US critics, it opened at #1 for a week before quickly dropping out of the box-office charts on both sides of the Atlantic. At least Sir Derek Jacobi and Bill Nighy added a touch of class to the cast. Along similar lines, Milla Jovovich donned a rubber suit to save mankind from a bio-engineered virus that turned humans into vampires in Kurt Wimmer's *Ultraviolet*.

Kristanna Loken played a half-human, half-vampire "dhampir" in Uwe Boll's third video game adaptation *BloodRayne*, which also starred Billy Zane, Michael Madsen, Meatloaf, Udo Kier, Michelle Rodriguez and Sir Ben Kingsley. It opened in the US with a gross of just $1.6 million.

In Ti West's low budget *The Roost*, a group of teens on their way to a wedding were attacked by vampire bats whose bite transformed their victims into bloodsuckers, while *Frostbite* was a Swedish vampire movie set in a hospital.

The creepy Countess Elizabeth Bathory used a bootleg version of a video game to select her victims in the surprisingly effective *Stay Alive*, featuring Frankie Muniz (TV's *Malcolm in the Middle*). The "unrated director's cut" on DVD was fifteen minutes longer than the soft PG-13 version briefly released in movie theatres.

A woman (Radha Mitchell) searched for her sick daughter in the zombie-haunted town of *Silent Hill*. Christophe Gans' confusing adaptation of the video game opened at #1 in the US. Sean Bean played hapless husbands in both *Silent Hill* and *The Dark*, John Fawcett's low budget chiller in which another mother (Maria Bello) searched for her missing daughter after staying at a creepy Welsh house, where a religious cult once committed mass suicide.

Jeff Broadstreet's *Night of the Living Dead 3D*, featuring Sid Haig, was a long way from George Romero's original series.

Demi Moore played a successful novelist who moved to a remote Scottish village where she was apparently haunted by the ghost of her recently-deceased young son in Craig Rosenberg's curiously old-

fashioned British thriller *Half Light*. In Hadi Hajaig's overly ambi-
tious *Puritan*, Nick Moran starred as a washed-up paranormal
investigator involved in a Gothic mystery in modern Whitechapel.

David Payne's *Reeker* was about a group of students in a creepily
deserted desert motel menaced by mutilated ghosts and the titular
monster, while Renny Harlin's *The Covenant* was based on Aron
Coleite's graphic novel about teenage warlocks and flopped at the
box-office.

Lucky McKee's long-delayed second feature *The Woods*, featuring
Bruce Campbell, finally saw the light of day, and something nasty lurked
on a deserted island in Michael J. Bassett's survivalist horror *Wilderness*, featuring ubiquitous Brit actor Sean Pertwee overseeing a group
of violent young offenders who were killed off by a crazed psycho.

David Zucker's uneven comedy *Scary Movie 4* spoofed *The
Grudge*, *Saw*, *The Village* and, er . . . *Brokeback Mountain*. Pamela
Anderson, Charlie Sheen, Cloris Leachman, Shaquille O'Neal and
Dr. Phil turned up in embarrassing cameos. Incredibly, it opened at
#1 in the US and #2 in the UK in April.

Despite a huge, Internet-fuelled publicity build-up, David R. Ellis'
entertaining *Snakes on a Plane* didn't quite live up to the pre-release
hype as Samuel L. Jackson's tough-talking FBI agent had to contend
with . . . a plane full of 400 deadly snakes. Although it opened in
both the US and UK at #1, not screening the film for critics prior to
release apparently harmed its chances at the box-office.

Director Joon-ho Bong's clever and amusing *The Host* (*Gwoemul*)
had a giant mutant fish creature created by toxic waste storing its
human victims in Seoul's sewers. It was a huge box-office hit in its
native Korea. Su-chang Kong's *R-Point* was a Korean production
about a cursed island and the spirits of the dead soldiers who were
trapped there.

In Marc Forster's clever metaphysical fantasy *Stranger Than
Fiction*, Will Ferrell's lonely tax inspector Harold Crick discovered
that he was a character about to be killed off in author Emma
Thompson's latest novel. Ewan McGregor's psychiatrist found his
life beginning to merge with Ryan Gosling's suicidal art student in
Forster's other release of the year, the hopelessly pretentious *Stay*.

Rival Victorian illusionists Christian Bale and Hugh Jackman
attempted to destroy each other with real magic in Christopher
Nolan's flashback-driven *The Prestige*, based on the novel by Christopher Priest. Meanwhile, Edward Norton's turn-of-the-century
magician used his powers to free the woman he loved in Neil Burger's
The Illusionist, which also starred Paul Giamatti.

M. Night Shyamalan's overly complicated fable *Lady in the Water* featured Giamatti's apartment complex loner protecting Bryce Dallas Howard's mysterious mermaid from toothy creatures from another dimension.

Guillermo del Toro had far more success creating an alternate reality in his sumptuous *Pan's Labyrinth*. Set in Franco's civil war-ravaged Spain of 1944, the young Ofelia (Ivana Baquero) discovered that she was really a princess and must complete three tasks to return to her magical underground kingdom.

Despite being directed by Dave McKean and scripted by Neil Gaiman, *MirrorMask* was a dull combination of live action and digital animation as sulky young circus girl Helena (Stephanie Leonidas) found herself transported into a bizarre fantasy world. Meanwhile, the Brothers Quay looked at the links between creativity and madness in their surreal feature *The Piano Tuner of Earthquakes*.

Filmed during a break in the making of *The Brothers Grimm*, Terry Gilliam's *Tideland* was an odd Southern Gothic about a lonely little girl (Jodelle Ferland) growing up in an old derelict house and her encounters with the bizarre locals.

Darren Aronofsky's long-in-development *The Fountain*, which starred Hugh Jackman as three different characters in history searching for immortality and love with the writer-director's real-life partner Rachel Weisz, died at the box-office, despite wasting $18 million before it was ever made.

Hans Horn's *Adrift* was about a group of old friends on a luxury yacht who all dived overboard before they realised that they had forgotten to lower the ladder, leaving them stranded in open sea. A toxic terrorist attack on Los Angeles looked at the human fallout in a city under siege in Chris Gorak's impressive directorial debut *Right at Your Door*.

Sissy Spacek and Donald Sutherland starred in Courtney Solomon's *An American Haunting*, a not-really ghost story set in the early 19th century and "based on true events", while a student (Sandra Hüller) thought she was possessed by the Devil in *Requiem*.

Rock musicians Jack Black and Kyle Gass were on the trail of a mythical Satanic guitar plectrum in the uneven comedy *Tenacious D in The Pick of Destiny*.

For film-goers who thought they had seen it all before, Denzel Washington's ATF agent used advanced digital surveillance to "travel back through time" to prevent a terrorist bombing in Tony Scott's high-concept SF thriller *Déjà Vu*, which also featured Val

Kilmer and Jim Caviezel. Keanu Reeves' architect and Sandra Bullock's doctor exchanged letters through time in Alejandro Agresti's romantic drama *The Lake House*.

Nathan Fillion was the likeable small town sheriff who had to contend with a killer alien plague that turned the townsfolk into zombies in *Slither*, writer/director James Gunn's inventive and entertaining tribute to 1950s SF movies. Made on a pathetically low budget, Jake West's dire SF/comedy *Evil Aliens*, about extraterrestrial rapists in Wales, somehow managed to get a (mercifully brief) theatrical release in the UK.

Alfonso Cuarón's impressive *Children of Men*, based on a novel by P. D. James, was set in a dystopian near-future where women could no longer give birth. Clive Owen's reluctant hero had to deliver the last pregnant woman to safety with the help of Michael Caine's aging hippie. The film opened at #1 in the UK in September.

Utilising a rotoscoped animation process, Richard Linklater's *A Scanner Darkly* was based on the novel by Philip K. Dick and starred two-dimensional representations of Keanu Reeves, Robert Downey Jr., Woody Harrelson and Winona Ryder. Along the same lines, Christian Volckman's animated French film *Renaissance* was shot in motion-captured black and white and featured a tough detective (voiced by Daniel Craig) searching for a missing geneticist in a dystopian Paris of the near-future.

Scripted by Larry and Andy Wachowski and based on Alan Moore's cult graphic novel (he asked for his name to be taken off the credits, as usual), Natalie Portman and Hugo Weaving starred as the political revolutionaries in James McTeigue's delayed *V for Vendetta*, set in a near-future Britain controlled by John Hurt's totalitarian dictator. It opened at #1 in the US with a lower-than-expected gross.

When Bryan Singer pulled out to revive another comic book franchise, Brett Ratner took over at the helm of the third and possibly final entry in the mutant superhero franchise, *X-Men: The Last Stand*. With a war between the mutants triggered by the discovery of a "cure" for their powers, this flashy but bland sequel featured former footballer Vinnie Jones as the brutish Juggernaut and a surprisingly good Kelsey Grammer as Beast.

Despite technically being a semi-sequel to Richard Donner's 1978 film, Singer's *Superman Returns* was unable to match the heights of that movie, with newcomer Brandon Routh failing to fill Christopher Reeve's tights as the Man of Steel and Kevin Spacey apparently content to simply channel Gene Hackman's Lex Luthor. The less said about Kate Bosworth's insipid Lois Lane the better, but at least the late Marlon Brando was back as Jor-El in an extended cameo. In the US, the film dropped 58% at the box-office in its second week.

Shown theatrically in Beverly Hills for one night only in November to benefit The Christopher Reeve Foundation, original director Donner's cut of *Superman II* (1980) was finally destined for DVD release.

Ben Affleck portrayed former *Superman* actor George Reeves, found dead under suspicious circumstances in 1959, in Allen Coulter's period mystery *Hollywoodland*.

Ivan Reitman's harmless chick-flick comedy, *My Super Ex-Girlfriend*, starred Uma Thurman as the jealous superhero girlfriend unwisely dumped by Luke Wilson. Meanwhile, Bollywood's own superhero adventure, *Krrish*, earned an Indian record of £8.3 million in its first week of release. Featuring a masked singing and dancing hero (Hrithik Roshan) saving the world from a mad scientist, around one-third of the film's takings came from overseas, mostly in the UK and US.

Based on Patrick Süskind's best-selling novel, Ben Whishaw played the Parisian serial killer with heightened olfactory sense in German director Tom Tykwer's *Perfume: The Story of a Murderer*.

Olivia Bonamy and Michaël Cohen were the married couple menaced by feral schoolchildren in their remote Romanian mansion in the French production *Ils* (*Them*), supposedly based on a true story.

A blonde angel (Rie Rasmussen) gave a man (Jamel Debbouze) contemplating suicide his life back in Luc Besson's pretentious *Angel-A*, while Virginia Madsen played a mysterious blonde who may or may not have been the Angel of Death in Robert Altman's final film, *A Prairie Home Companion*. Penelope Cruz was haunted by the ghost of her dead mother (Carmen Maura) in Pedro Almodóvar's offbeat family drama *Volver*.

Over a weekend in November, Freestyle Releasing/After Dark Films offered a "horror fest" of independent films under the umbrella title *8 Films to Die For*, plus *Snoop Dogg's Hood of Horror*, starring Snoop Dog, Danny Trejo and Jason Alexander, which quickly came and went.

The same month, cinemagoers got a sneak preview of *Harry Potter and the Order of the Phoenix* when the first trailer was released with the animated *Happy Feet*.

Gerard Butler, Sarah Polley and Stellan Skarsgård starred in the mythological saga of *Beowulf & Grendel*, while *Eragon* was based on the successful young adult fantasy book series and featured some nice-looking CGI dragons and shameless scene-stealing by Jeremy Irons and John Malkovich, who obviously realised how terrible the script was.

Based on the popular series of YA novels by Anthony Horowitz, *Stormbreaker* (aka *Alex Rider: Operation Stormbreaker*) introduced the teenage super-spy (Alex Pettyfer) battling Mickey Rourke's crazed computer genius, and two thirteen-year-old friends discovered a teen mermaid (Sara Paxton) in *Aquamarine*.

Veterans Dick Van Dyke and Mickey Rooney added a much-needed touch of class to the Ben Stiller fantasy/comedy *Night at the Museum*, also featuring Robin Williams, Owen Wilson and Ricky Gervais. It stayed in the #1 slot for two weeks at Christmas.

Adam Sandler's office workaholic discovered that he could take control of his life with a universal remote invented by Christopher Walken's crazy scientist in Frank Coraci's crass comedy *Click*.

John Favreau's children's adventure *Zathura: A Space Adventure* was a SF follow-up to *Jumanji* and also based on a book by Chris Van Allsburg, while *Charlotte's Web* was based on E. B. White's classic children's novel and starred Dakota Fanning as the girl befriended by the titular spider (voiced by Julia Roberts).

Tim Allen's deputy DA found himself transforming into a were-pooch in Brian Robbins' contemporary remake of Walt Disney's *The Shaggy Dog*, while Allen's Santa had to prevent Jack Frost (a mugging Martin Short) from hijacking Christmas in Michael Lembeck's *The Santa Clause 3: The Escape Clause*, also from Disney. The busy Allen also turned up as Captain Zoom, who (along with Chevy Chase and Courtney Cox) instructed four children with special powers how to be accepted in the dire superhero comedy *Zoom*.

Britain's Aardman Studios eschewed its usual claymation technique for computer graphics with DreamWorks' derivative mouse-out-of-water adventure *Flushed Away*, featuring the voices of Hugh Jackman, Kate Winslet and Sir Ian McKellen, and the likeable rodent Scrat and his prehistoric friends from the original were forced to flee the melting polar ice caps in the cartoon comedy sequel *Ice Age 2: The Meltdown*. *Garfield: A Tale of Two Kitties* was a reworking of *The Prince and the Pauper* as the fat ginger cat (a CGI creation voiced by Bill Murray) was accidentally switched with an upper-crust British feline.

Featuring the voices of Julia Roberts, Nicolas Cage and Meryl Streep, John A. Davis' children's animated adventure *The Ant Bully* was produced by Tom Hanks and released in some Imax theatres in very impressive 3-D. Ricardo Montalban replaced the late Marlon Brando as the voice of the Head of the Ant Council, while genre artist Bob Eggleton worked on the film's designs.

Also shown in selected venues in 3-D, Gil Kenan's *Monster House* was a disappointing motion-capture animated children's adventure in which a trio of children found themselves trapped in a living house that ate anyone who ventured inside. Robert Zemeckis and Steven Spielberg were executive producers.

Tim Burton's classic *The Nightmare Before Christmas* was re-issued for the Holiday Season in Disney Digital 3-D.

Although the original *King Kong* (1933) never won a single Oscar, Peter Jackson's overlong and self-indulgent remake picked up no less than three (Visual Effects, Sound Mixing and Sound Editing) at the 78th Academy Awards, presented on March 5th in Hollywood. It was mostly a night for independent films, although *Wallace & Gromit: The Curse of the Were-Rabbit* collected the award for Animated Feature, and *The Chronicles of Narnia: The Lion, The Witch and The Wardrobe* won for Make-up.

2006 became the year that we finally said "goodbye" to the VHS ("Vertical Helical Scan") cassette. The revolutionary home entertainment format went the way of Sony's Betamax tapes and laser-discs when DVD, new high-definition formats and the emerging video game consoles finally replaced it after thirty years. When the studios stopped manufacturing the tapes, retailers were left with no choice but to pull the plug on the format.

Peter Jackson's overblown *King Kong* remake became even more bloated with a three-disc "Deluxe Extended Edition" on DVD that included nearly forty minutes of deleted scenes, 230 new visual effects and a mind-numbing six hours of original special features. Thankfully, it was only available for a limited time.

Meanwhile, Jackson's ongoing lawsuit against New Line Cinema over revenue disclosure from *The Fellowship of the Ring* resulted in further delays in green lighting the studio's *Lord of the Rings* prequel, *The Hobbit*.

Warner Bros' *Hollywood Legends of Horror Collection* was a three-disc DVD compilation of classic 1930s MGM horrors. *Mark of the Vampire, The Mask of Fu Manchu, Doctor X, The Return of Doctor X, Mad Love* and *The Devil Doll* featured commentaries by Kim Newman and Stephen Jones, Greg Mank, Scott McQueen, director Vincent Sherman and Steve Haberman.

Sony Pictures' *Icons of Horror: Boris Karloff* was a two-disc collection containing Columbia Pictures' *The Black Room*, *The Man They Could Not Hang*, *Before I Hang* and *The Boogie Man Will Get You*, all making their DVD debut. If that wasn't enough, then Universal's three-disc *The Boris Karloff Collection* bought together such disparate titles as *Night Key*, *Tower of London* (1939), *The Climax* (in Technicolor), *The Strange Door* and *The Black Castle*, all featuring the screen's "Master of Horror". Disappointingly, both sets were extremely light on extras.

The two-disc 75th Anniversary editions of Universal's *Frankenstein* and *Dracula* contained all the familiar bonus features, along with two new documentaries about stars Boris Karloff and Bela Lugosi and audio commentaries by Rudy Behlmer, Sir Christopher Frayling, David J. Skal and Steve Haberman.

Universal also finally released a long-awaited two-disc set of *Inner Sanctum Mysteries: The Complete Collection*, featuring all six films in the "B" movie series (1943-45) based on the old radio series and starring Lon Chaney, Jr.

Fox's *The Mr Moto Collection Vol.1* starred Peter Lorre as the inscrutable Japanese investigator in *Thank You Mr Moto*, *Think Fast Mr Moto*, *Mr Moto Takes a Chance* and *Mysterious Mr Moto*. Meanwhile, *The Charlie Chan Collection Vol.1* featured Earl Derr Biggers' Honolulu-based detective in *Charlie Chan in London*, *Charlie Chan in Paris*, *Charlie Chan in Egypt* and *Charlie Chan in Shanghai*, all starring Warner Oland. The set also included *Eran Trece*, the Spanish-language version of the "lost" entry in the series, *Charlie Chan Carries On*.

Anchor Bay Entertainment's six-disc "Ultimate Collection of Video Nasties", *Box of the Banned 2*, contained five hardcore horror films from the 1970s and '80s (*The Witch Who Came from the Sea*, *Contamination*, *Tenebrae*, *Don't Go Near the Park* and *Evilspeak*) along with David Gregory's documentary *Ban the Sadist Videos 2* and various other extras.

From Britain's DD Home Entertainment, *Hammer Horror: The Early Classics* was a box set featuring *The Quatermass Experiment*, *Quatermass 2*, *X The Unknown* and *Four Sided Triangle*. *Hammer House of Mystery and Suspense: The Complete Collection* collected all thirteen feature-length episodes of the 1970s TV series, and *The Peter Cushing Collection* brought together *The Abominable Snowman*, *Island of Terror*, *The Blood Beast Terror* and *Frankenstein and the Monster from Hell*.

Released under the distributor's "Classic Horror" label, *Blood of the Vampire*, *Corridors of Blood* and the obscure *Daughter of*

Darkness all featured informative booklets written by Jonathan Rigby and Marcus Hearn.

Kim Newman and Stephen Jones contributed the booklets to the Network DVD releases of James Whale's *The Old Dark House*, *The Medusa Touch*, and Hammer's *Countess Dracula*, *Hands of the Ripper* and *Twins of Evil*, along with audio commentaries that also featured director Jack Gold and actresses Ingrid Pitt and Angharad Rees.

A two-disc special edition of *What Ever Happened to Baby Jane?*, starring Bette Davis and Joan Crawford, included three documentaries, a vintage featurette and an excerpt from *The Andy Williams Show* featuring Davis singing the title song.

The two-disc special edition of *The Green Mile* featured more than two hours of bonus material, including a new half-hour documentary, *Stephen King: Storyteller*, that included interviews with Frank Darabont, William Goldman, Tom Hanks, Stephen Jones, Lawrence Kasdan, Kim Newman, David J. Schow, Peter Straub, Bernie Wrightson and King himself.

Original cast members Anne Francis, Earl Holliman, Richard Anderson, Warren Stevens and Robby the Robot reunited in mid-November for a 50th Anniversary screening of MGM's 1956 classic *Forbidden Planet* at the American Cinematheque's Egyptian Theater in Hollywood. The remastered DVD also featured three documentary supplements plus outtakes and test scenes. Additionally, the two-disc tin set included *The Invisible Boy* and a 1958 episode of TV's *The Thin Man* featuring Robby, along with collector's cards and a 3.5-inch tall model of the screen's most iconic robot.

New label Casa Negra Entertainment began releasing classic Mexican horror films in restored subtitled versions on DVD. Remastered and uncut, *The Brainiac* had never officially been released on DVD before, while "The Vampire Collection" showcased the classic *El Vampiro* and its sequel *El Ataúd del Vampiro* on a two-disc set. A bonus on *Black Pit of Dr M/Misterios de Ultratumba* was the original English continuity script, while *The Witch's Mirror* and *The Curse of the Crying Woman* both included the English-language dub tracks.

The first direct-to-DVD release from Warner Bros' specialty horror division Raw Feed, John Shiban's *Rest Stop* featured Jaimie Alexander menaced by yet another backwoods psycho.

Set in a world of murderous children, *Clive Barker's The Plague* was actually co-written and directed by Hal Masonberg.

I'll Always Know What You Did Last Summer was released directly to DVD, while the similarly-distributed *The Tooth Fairy* was scripted by TV veteran Stephen J. Cannell, amongst others.

From Retro Shock-O-Rama Cinema, Joe Sarno's cult 1974 vampire film *The Devil's Plaything* was released in a widescreen version with a new mini-documentary about the director and an insert booklet by Michael J. Bowen.

Bill Moseley, Tim Thomerson, Phil Fondacarro and Tommy Chong all made special appearances in Charles Band's *Evil Bong*, and *Monarch of the Moon/Destination Mars!*, released on the Dark Horse Indie label, was a two-disc DVD set spoofing 1950s sci-fi films.

The Munsters Two-Movie Fright Fest paired *Munster Go Home!* with the TV movie *The Munsters' Revenge*. From Paramount came a three-disc set, *The Wild Wild West: The Complete First Season (1965-66)*, and a second volume of *The Time Tunnel (1966-67)* featuring fifteen episodes over four discs.

Superman: The 1948 and 1950 Theatrical Serial Collection from Warner Bros. was a four-disc DVD set that included all the chapters from both *The Adventures of Superman* and *Atom Man vs. Superman* (both starring Kirk Alyn as The Man of Steel).

When released on DVD in the UK, *Point Pleasant: The Complete Series* included five previously unaired episodes of the disappointing Fox series.

I Was a Teenage Movie Maker collected all forty-one 16mm amateur movies made by Don Glut between 1953-69.

Anchor Bay's *Halloween: 25 Years of Terror* was a two-disc tribute to the "slasher" movie franchise, featuring interviews with more than eighty celebrities, including John Carpenter, Jamie Lee Curtis, Clive Barker, Rob Zombie and many others.

Made without a grain of talent or humour, A. Susan Svehla's dire *Terror in the Tropics* incorporated plenty of copyright-free footage of Bela Lugosi, Boris Karloff and Lon Chaney, Jr into a distinctly amateur production about the reading of a will on eerie Fog Island. Many of the characters were named after old actors, and this even included dinosaur footage from the silent *Lost World*.

Fans of the old horror stars were much better served by *The Witch's Dungeon: 40 Years of Chills*. Directed by Dennis Vincent and hosted by Zacherley the "Cool Ghoul", the documentary traced the history of Cortlandt Hull's Connecticut-based horror museum and the films and actors who inspired it with the help on-screen appearances by Christopher Lee, Sara Karloff, Ron Chaney, Bela Lugosi Jr, Dick Smith, Tom Savini, Caroline Munro, Forrest J Ackerman, Bob Burns, Ben Chapman, Ricou Browning and a host of others.

Written, produced and directed by Paul Davids, *The Sci-Fi Boys* was anothr feature-length documentary about many of the film-makers and other creative people who were inspired and cham-pioned by Forrest J Ackerman's *Famous Monsters of Filmland* magazine. Along with Ackerman himself, those interviewed included Rick Baker, Ray Bradbury, Bob Burns, Roger Corman, Donald F. Glut, Ray Harryhausen, Peter Jackson and John Landis.

In November, Forry Ackerman celebrated his 90th birthday with a party in Los Angeles. Among those attending were Ray Bradbury, Carla Laemmle, Anne Robinson, James Karen, Bobbi Bresse, George Clayton Johnson, David J. Skal, Peter Atkins and Dennis Etchison. Guests received a copy of *Famous Monster of Filmland #90*, a facsimile magazine of the original manuscript pages of *FM #1*.

Jonathan English's mythological fantasy adventure *Minotaur* fea-tured guest turns by Tony Todd, Rutger Hauer and an unrecogni-sable Ingrid Pitt and was released directly to the Sci Fi Channel.

Also from those purveyors of fine flicks, Yancy Butler starred in *Basilisk: The Serpent King*, a reanimated Dean Cain battled infec-tious giant beetles carrying a zombie virus in *Dead and Deader*, and Michael Paré witnessed the battle between *Komodo vs. Cobra* on a desert island.

Tom Skerritt turned up in the self-descriptive *Mammoth*, about an alien-possessed museum exhibit (no, really), while *Kraken: Tentacles of the Deep* (aka *Deadly Water*), starring Victoria Pratt, Charlie O'Con-nell, Jack Scalia and a giant squid, won its title from an online publicity stunt. Spelunkers Christopher Atkins and Colm Meaney faced Roma-nian rock-eating rhinoceros beetles in *Caved In: Prehistoric Terror*.

Casper Van Dien and Lynda Carter found themselves up against some scary Latin American vampires in *Slayer*, and a prison guard (Jennifer Wiggins) battled a monster assassin working for the Rus-sian mafia in *Shapeshifter*.

Room 6 was set in a creepy hospital and starred Jerry O'Connell, while Stacy Keach confronted evil ghosts on a deserted island penitentiary in *Haunted Prison*. Lance Henriksen encountered a big bloodthirsty backwoods creature in *Abominable*, and he reprised his role from the original film as a ghost in *Pumpkinhead III: Ashes to Ashes* (filmed back-to-back with a third sequel).

Tobe Hooper directed *Mortuary*, about an undertaker (Denise Crosby) who took over a creepy funeral home, and Emmanualle Vaugier's special ops team blew flesh-eating zombies away in *House of the Dead 2*. Meanwhile, psychic siblings Charisma Carpenter and

Eric Mabius wanted revenge on the evil that destroyed their home-town twenty years earlier in *Voodoo Moon*.

A slumming Ben Cross' mad Nazi scientist created a device that transformed a World War II German soldier into a monstrous killing machine in David Flores' cheap and cheerful *SS Doomtrooper*.

A scientific expedition to an unknown world encountered hungry mutants in *Savage Planet* starring Sean Patrick Flanery, and Jason Connery was the fleet-footed superhero of the Sci Fi Channel's *Stan Lee's Lightspeed*, which was gone in a Flash.

Dark Kingdom: The Dragon King starred Alicia Witt, Julian Sands and Max Von Sydow and was shown in two parts on Sci Fi Channel.

Directed by Mick Garris and scripted by the author himself, *Stephen King's Desperation* found a group of typical King characters trapped in the eponymous Nevada desert town controlled by a demonic spirit and Ron Perlman's psychotic cop. Unfortunately, ABC-TV scheduled its three-hour "movie event" opposite the pen-ultimate episode of that season's *American Idol*, with predictable results.

Noah Wyle returned as nerdy bookworm Flynn Carsen, protecting the world's most treasured supernatural artefacts, in Jonathan Frakes' *The Librarian: Return to King Solomon's Mines* on TNT. This time he teamed up with a spirited archaeologist (Gabrielle Anwar) to find a stolen scroll that was said to reveal the location of the legendary diamond mines.

Casper Van Dien's roguish archaeologist and Leonor Varela's museum curator tried to beat Malcolm McDowell's secret Hellfire Council to a collection of Ancient Egyptian tablets with supernatural powers in Hallmark's *The Curse of King Tut's Tomb*.

A widow's daughter claimed she was murdered in a former life in the Lifetime Movie Network's *Past Tense* starring Paula Trickey, and Julie Delpy and Justin Theroux discovered that their new home came with its own 250-year-old ghost in the same network's *The Legend of Lucy Keyes*, which was "based on a true story".

Peter Krause played homicide detective Joe Miller, searching for his missing daughter (Elle Fanning) through a mysterious motel room that was a gateway in time and space, in the three-part Sci Fi mini-series *The Lost Room*. Miller soon found himself embroiled in a secret war over long-lost objects that possessed extraordinary powers that dated back to a fateful day in May 1961. Julianna Margulies, Dennis Christopher and Kevin Pollak also starred.

Daryl Hannah played an unlikely insectoid alien queen planning world domination in Robert Leiberman's ludicrous mini-series *Final Days of Planet Earth*, also from the Sci Fi Channel.

Created by Stephen Gallagher, who soon left the project due to ubiquitous "creative differences", Granada's *Eleventh Hour* was shown as four self-contained TV movies based around the concept of "science-gone-wrong". Patrick Stewart starred as government trouble-shooter Professor Ian Hood who, with his Special Branch minder Rachel Young (Ashley Jensen), investigated such things as a European cloning conspiracy, a flesh-eating virus, a formula to predict the weather and spring water that could apparently cure cancer.

Gallagher was also set to script a TV movie of *Dracula* before the BBC announced its own version, shown at Christmas. Writer Stewart Harcourt's attempt to do something different with Bram Stoker's much-filmed novel resulted in Marc Warren's laughably effeminate Count and David Suchet's clearly potty Abraham Van Helsing.

As Las Vegas, the Hoover Dam and Mount Rushmore were destroyed over two nights, the North American continent was split in two by a massive earthquake in NBC's by-the-numbers sequel *10.5: Apocalypse*, starring Kim Delaney, Dean Cain and a slumming Frank Langella.

Ray Winstone did little more than walk through his performance as the sympathetic barber who cut the throats of his customers in David Moore's BBC film of *Sweeney Todd*, shot on nicely atmospheric Romanian locations. Essie Davis was a nymphomaniac Mrs Lovett who turned the victims into pies, and David Warner played a blind policeman investigating the mysterious disappearances. The "Director's Cut" was subsequently released on DVD with exclusive unseen footage.

Based on a story by Dennis Wheatley, *The Haunted Airman* was a short BBC film about a recuperating RAF pilot (Robert Pattinson) who was tormented by terrifying flashbacks. Julian Sands played his sinister doctor.

Number 13 was the latest M. R. James ghost story for Christmas. Greg Wise starred as the academic who discovered that his lodging house contained a ghostly room next to his own.

In Stuart Orme's two-part *Ghostboat*, based on the novel by George E. Simpson, David Jason played the only survivor of a World War II submarine disaster who found he was still linked with the past when the haunted vessel mysteriously reappeared thirty-eight years later.

Ian Richardson provided the voice of Death who, with his reluctant assistant Albert (David Jason), had to save Christmas from Marc Warren's psychotic Mr Teatime and the mysterious "Auditors" in Vadim Jean's all-star holiday treat *Terry Pratchett's Hogfather*, which was shown over two nights on Sky Television. Based on Pratchett's 20th "Discworld" novel, the author contributed to the script and turned up in a cameo as a Toymaker.

For younger viewers, Pratchett's time-travel adventure *Johnny and the Bomb* was adapted as a three-part children's series starring Zoë Wanamaker, Frank Finlay and Keith Barron.

In *Return to Halloweentown*, the fourth instalment in the Disney franchise, Sara Paxton starred as teenage witch Marnie, who was on her way to Witch College with a little help from Grandma Aggie (Debbie Reynolds).

John Goodman starred as Saint Nick in NBC's live-action remake of *The Year Without a Santa Claus*, based on the 1974 Rankin/Bass claymation original.

Re-Animated, the Cartoon Network's first live-action movie, was about a young boy who received a brain transplant from the founder of a theme park. Fred Willard played the Walt Disney-like entrepreneur.

The animated *Superman: Brainiac Attacks* on the Cartoon Network pitted the Man of Steel against his two greatest enemies, Brainiac and Lex Luthor. The network also aired the superhero movies *Teen Titans in Tokyo*, *Ultimate Avengers II* and the Japan-set *Hellboy: Sword of Storms* (featuring the voices of Ron Perlman and Selma Blair).

BBC-TV's revived *Doctor Who* series continued to be one of Britain's most popular programmes. For the second, thirteen-part series, Scottish actor David Tennant took over as a dynamic incarnation of the Time Lord, who shared a more romantic relationship with his companion, Rose Tyler (Billie Piper). The better episodes involved a werewolf murder mystery surrounding Queen Victoria (Pauline Collins), the poignant return of former companions Sarah Jane Smith (Elisabeth Sladen) and the robot dog K-9, a two-part Cyberman invasion of London, a soul-sucking 1950s TV entity (Maureen Lipman) and a Satanic creature trapped by the power of a black hole. In the epic two-part finale, an Earth besieged by ghosts and the destruction of the mysterious Torchwood Institute were only a prelude to an apocalyptic confrontation between the Cybermen and the Daleks as Rose made a decision that would change her life forever.

For the show's Christmas special, "The Runaway Bride", the Doctor teamed up with comedian Catherine Tate as a sarcastic bride who vanished from her wedding ceremony and ended up on the Tardis. Together they battled Sarah Parish's impressive giant spider-queen.

Although the first episode of the "adult" *Doctor Who* spin-off series *Torchwood* broke the record for the biggest audience for a UK digital TV channel, Captain Jack Harkness (John Barrowman) and his Cardiff team of ludicrously bisexual paranormal investigators were never as entertaining as the show that spawned them.

Modern Manchester police detective Sam Tyler (John Simm) was knocked down by a car and apparently found himself transported back to a surprisingly un-PC 1973 in the BBC's enjoyable and amusing eight-part series *Life on Mars* (named after the David Bowie song). While Tyler (and the viewers) tried to work out if he had actually travelled back in time or if it was all in his head, he also had to contend with his no-nonsense boss Gene Hunt (the excellent Philip Glenister) and a particularly creepy young girl off the television test card.

Less successful was the BBC's feature-length remake of Fred Hoyle and James Elliot's 1961 SF series *A for Andromeda*, shot on HD video and shown in March. Kelly Reilly starred as the eponymous new biological life form.

Also disappointing, *Random Quest* was an hour-long adaptation of the John Wyndham story (previously filmed for TV in 1969 and as *Quest for Love* in 1971). Following a laboratory accident, research scientist Colin Trafford (Samuel West) found himself in a parallel universe inhabiting the body of his namesake and living a very different life.

For those fans still missing *Buffy* and *Angel*, rapper Kirk "Sticky" Jones starred as the vengeance-seeking half-human, half-vampire "daywalker", who teamed up with Jill Wagner's undercover blood-sucker to defeat the sinister House of Chthon in Spike TV's surprisingly engaging *Blade: The Series*, created by David Goyer and based on the Marvel Comics character.

The second, thirteen-episode season of Showtime Network's anthology series *Masters of Horror* kicked off in October with Richard Christian Matheson's loose adaptation of Ambrose Bierce's "The Damned Thing", directed by Tobe Hooper and starring Sean Patrick Flanery. The series also included hour-long episodes directed by John Landis, Ernest Dickerson, Brad Anderson, John Carpenter, Dario Argento, Joe Dante and creator Mick Garris, and featured George

Wendt, Michael Ironside, Ron Perlman, Meat Loaf, Elliot Gould and Tony Todd among the guest stars.

Richard Christian Matheson also scripted "Battle Ground", the first and probably best episode of TNT's *Nightmares & Dreamscapes*, an hour-long anthology show filmed in Australia and based on eight of Stephen King's lesser-known stories. The series continued through the Lovecraftian "Crouch End" (set in a *very* peculiar depiction of London), "Umney's Last Case", "The End of the Whole Mess", "The Road Virus Heads North", "The Fifth Quarter", "Autopsy Room Four" and "You Know They've Got a Hell of a Band". Guest stars included William Hurt, William H. Macy, Henry Thomas, Tom Berenger, Samantha Mathis, Richard Thomas and Steven Weber.

In Showtime Network's blackly humorous *Dexter*, Miami police forensic expert and secret serial killer Dexter Morgan (Michael C. Hall) discovered that his sister's new boyfriend was the Ice Truck Killer and that he had a familial connection to the mixed-up murderer. Although the season finale marginally failed to live up to the promise of the rest of the series, *Dexter* was still one of the best new shows on TV, based on Jeff Lindsay's 2004 novel *Darkly Dreaming Dexter*.

In America, The CW was the network that was created out of the merger of The WB and UPN. Co-owners CBS and Time Warner launched the new channel in September with a $50 million promotional campaign.

In The CW's *Supernatural*, Dean (Jensen Ackles) and Sam (Jared Padalecki) finally teamed up with their missing father John Winchester (Jeffrey Dean Morgan) to confront vampires and obtain a mystical gun that could destroy the demon that killed their mother. Not only did the boys have to deal with Reapers, a flesh-eating clown and the death of their father, but they also battled the ghost of America's first serial killer, H. H. Holmes and encountered a seriously homicidal vampire-hunter. In a clever piece of stunt-casting that was guaranteed to turn heads, Linda Blair turned up as a sympathetic cop in an episode entitled "The Usual Suspects".

In NBC's *Medium*, the show's executive producer, Kelsey Grammer, showed up as an urbane Death, Molly Ringwald played the victim of a stalker, and psychic Alison (Patricia Arquette) had an *It's a Wonderful Life* moment in the second season finale when she discovered what her life would have been like if things had worked out differently. The show was back with a two-hour premiere in November, in which Alison's dead ex-boyfriend (Arquette's real-life husband Thomas Jane) turned up.

Following a near-fatal séance at the end of the first season, Lesley Sharp returned as morose medium Alison Mundy, haunted by the ghost of her dead mother (Amanda Lawrence) in a second, eight-part series of *Afterlife*, created by Stephen Volk.

Meanwhile, Melinda (Jennifer Love Hewitt) had to make peace with her mother to lay a ghost to rest in CBS-TV's *Ghost Whisperer*. The first season ended with a plane crash and the death of series regular Andrea (Aisha Tyler). However, the character was back in the first show of the second series. Camryn Manheim joined the cast as Delia, and Jay Mohr played Rick Payne, a professor studying the supernatural.

The Dead Zone returned for its fifth and supposedly final season, filmed back-to-back with series four. In the season finale, Johnny (Anthony Michael Hall) discovered that vice president Greg Stillson (Sean Patrick Flanery), who was being controlled by evil mastermind Janus (Martin Donovan), was the target of an assassin. In a surprise announcement in September, the USA Network picked up the show for a sixth season.

Bill Paterson's scientific investigator Douglas Monaghan was mostly missing from the six-part, third series of the BBC's *Sea of Souls*, and it was left to his assistants Craig Stevenson (Iain Robertson) and psychic Justine McManus (Dawn Steele) to debunk the supernatural manifestations that kept cropping up all over Scotland. In the penultimate episode they encountered a genuine succubus who drained her victims of their life-force.

A group of dull characters discovered that they possessed superpowers and had to "save the cheerleader (Hayden Panettiere), save the world" in NBC-TV's over-hyped *Heroes*. The show went on hiatus in December before returning with twenty-two new episodes in 2007.

CBS-TV's gloomy post-apocalyptic drama *Jericho*, starring Skeet Ulrich and Gerald McRaney as an estranged son and father among the inhabitants of a Kansas town cut off by a nuclear attack on America, also took a mid-season break in December.

In ABC-TV's meandering *Lost*, Ana Lucia (Michelle Rodriguez) and Libby (Cynthia Watros) were both shot dead before the two-hour second season finale in May and, when the series returned, the ruthless Mr Eko (Adewale Akinnuoye-Agbaje) was killed off by the show's mysterious monster. While everybody else was still trying to uncover the secret of the island, a dithering Kate (Evangeline Lily) still couldn't make up her mind between doctor Jack (Matthew Fox) and bad boy Sawyer (Josh Holloway). To avoid repeats, the show went on hiatus for two months in December to make way for the confusing *Day Break*, in which Taye Diggs' disgraced LAPD detective kept reliving the same bad day over and over again (now where have we seen that before?).

Meanwhile, Hurley's cursed lottery numbers from *Lost* turned up on a fortune cookie message in the January 25th episode of UPN's *Veronica Mars* and appeared *the same day* on the cover of DC Comics' *Catwoman* #51. Now that was *really* weird!

After five seasons, ABC's *Alias* finally came to a two-hour end in May, as secret agent Sydney Bristow (Jennifer Garner) confronted a group of old foes and attempted to make some sense of the "Rambaldi" prophecy.

The Sci Fi Channel's *Battlestar Galactica* continued to be the best SF show on television, as the remaining humans escaped from slavery on New Caprica and raced their humanoid enemies the Cylons to find the way to Earth in a two-part, mid-season, cliff-hanger.

USA Network's *The 4400* returned for a third season of thirteen episodes in June, as Tippi Hedren guest starred in the two-hour opener. Government investigators Tom Baldwin (Joel Gretsch) and Diana Skouris (Jacqueline McKenzie) tried to foil Jordan Collier's (Billy Campbell) plans for mankind, and baby Isabelle mysteriously transformed into a sexy twenty-year-old (Megalyn Echikunwoke).

Stargate SG-1 became TV's longest-running SF series with its tenth and final series, which also saw the show celebrate its 200th episode (with a *Wizard of Oz* spoof and numerous in-jokes). Richard Dean Anderson reprised his role as Jack O'Neill in a number of episodes, including a two-part crossover episode with *Stargate Atlantis*. MGM announced that it would be making two *Stargate SG-1* movies once the series was over.

Despite being an interesting variation on *Invasion of the Body Snatchers*, ABC's *Invasion* was cancelled after its first season, without ever resolving its human-hybrid conspiracy.

After being marooned with his rebellious teenage daughter Zoe (Jordan Hinson) in the eponymous town of the Sci Fi Channel's *Eureka* (aka *A Town Called Eureka*), Jack Carter (the likeable Colin Furguson) found himself the new sheriff of a top-secret community filled with geniuses. The first episode attracted an audience of 4.1 million in the US, the most for a series launch in the channel's history.

Series eight of The WB's *Charmed* saw the witchy Halliwell sisters working for Homeland Security with the help of teenage witch Billie (Kaley Cuoco). After 178 episodes, the series bowed out with an episode in which the Charmed Ones travelled back in time to save the world from the forces of evil and finally put their lives in order.

Paul Wesley's eighteen-year-old orphan discovered that he was a Nephilim, the offspring of an angel and a mortal in the ABC Family limited-run series *Fallen*, while Matt Dallas learned that he was a teenage clone without a past or any emotions in the ABC Family show *Kyle XY*.

Over on The CW's *Smallville*, which passed its 100th episode early in the year with the death of Clark's adoptive father Jonathan Kent (John Schneider) from a heart attack (he returned as a ghost), a pregnant Lana (Kristen Kreuk) finally married Lex Luthor (Michael Rosenbaum), while Clark (Tom Welling) rounded up a group of escapees from the Phantom Zone. Meanwhile, Jimmy Olsen (Aaron Ashmore) was introduced, the Martian Manhunter briefly turned up, and semi-regular Oliver Queen/Green Arrow (Justin Hartley) rounded up past guest stars The Flash, Cyborg and Aquaman to form a nascent Justice League to investigate LuthorCorp's mysterious "Project 33.1".

Hyperdrive was a six-part BBC comedy series set aboard the spaceship HMS Camden Lock, whose crew (led by Nick Frost) had a mission to promote British interests across the galaxy. In an attempt to impress a couple of Goth girls, Howard (Julian Barratt) and Vince (Noel Fielding) accidentally summoned the most evil demon known to man in a second season episode of the BBC comedy series *The Mighty Boosh*.

The team went searching for a woman who disappeared after an exorcism in an episode of CBS' *Without a Trace*. A series of bombings in Seattle were linked to a sci-fi novel set in an apocalyptic future controlled by robots in an episode of the same network's *Criminal Minds*, and Roger Daltrey guest-starred in an episode of *CSI: Crime Scene Investigation* that paid homage to the classic slasher films of the 1980s.

Not content with its usual lunacy, *Bad Girls: A Christmas Special* added the supernatural to the final episode of the long-running British women's prison drama, as the ghost of Larkhill's supposedly escaped inmate Natalie Buxton (Dannielle Brent) put the frights on G Wing while her rotting body blocked the prison sewers.

Fan-of-the-show Peter Straub played a blind retired police officer on the March 27th episode of the daytime soap opera *One Life to Live*.

Inspired by the book by Michael Lawrence, the BBC's *Young Dracula* was a fourteen-part children's comedy in which single father Count Dracula (Keith-Lee Castle) couldn't understand why his son Vlad (Gerran Howell) wanted to turn his back on blood-drinking and become a normal London teenager, much to the disgust of Vlad's older sister, Ingrid (Clare Thomas).

Filmed in New Zealand, *Maddigan's Quest* was based on Margaret Mahy's book and was set in a post-apocalyptic world.

The animated *Zombie Hotel* was about eight-year-old twins, Fungus and Maggot, and their dead parents Rictus and Funerella.

An episode of The CW's animated series *The Batman* featured new Superman actor Brandon Routh as the villainous Everywhere Man, who used quantum technology to duplicate himself.

Ghostly DC Comics characters Deadman, Mr Terrific, Stargirl and the Shining Knight all turned up in episodes of the animated *Justice League Unlimited*. After five seasons, the show ended with a two-part episode in which Lex Luthor and the Legion of Doom attempted to reanimate Brainiac.

Fox's seventeenth annual *The Simpsons: Treehouse of Horror* featured the guest voices of Dr Phil, Richard Lewis and Fran Drescher. The Halloween episode's three tales of terror included Homer being transformed into a man-eating blob by a meteorite, Springfield's own version of the Golem, and a spoof on Orson Welles' infamous *War of the Worlds* radio broadcast featuring aliens Kang and Kodos.

Mario Bava: Maestro of the Macabre was the title of a documentary that aired on IFC in September. John Carpenter, Joe Dante and Tim Burton were amongst those who paid tribute to the influential Italian director and cinematographer. Over on the History Channel, *Vampire Secrets* looked at vampire mythology and its influence on Bram Stoker's *Dracula*.

Going to Pieces: The Rise and Fall of the Slasher Film was a Starz documentary on Friday the 13th in October, and Bravo celebrated Halloween with the two-hour *Even Scarier Movie Moments*. Meanwhile, there was a two-day *Munsters Marathon* on TV Land, the Sci Fi Channel programmed *13 Days of Halloween*, ABC Family went with *13 Nights of Halloween*, and AMC offered up *Monsterfest X*, a ten-day non-stop monster movie marathon to celebrate the horror-day season.

Michael Sheen portrayed the author in the BBC dramatised profile *H. G. Wells: War with the World*, while Jonathan Ross, Lord Hattersley and astronomer Patrick Moore contributed to the documentary *H. G. Wells and Me*.

Dennis Wheatley: A Letter to Posterity was an hour-long documentary about the bestselling writer whose work has now fallen out of favour.

The Martians and Us was a three-part BBC series exploring the roots of British science fiction. Contributors included Brian W. Aldiss, Arthur C. Clarke, Doris Lessing, Ian M. Banks, Margaret Atwood, Will Self and Kim Newman. Over six episodes, *The Cult of . . .* looked at the history of cult TV shows *Adam Adamant Lives!*, *Doomwatch*, *Star Cops*, *Survivors*, *Blakes 7* and *Tripods*.

Transylvania Babylon presented an entertaining selection of clips of big and small screen Draculas from the past.

The third season finale of the Sci Fi Channel's "reality" show *Ghost Hunters* featured a visit to Colorado's Stanley Hotel, the real-life inspiration for Stephen King's Overlook in *The Shining*.

Spike TV broadcast the *Spike Scream Awards 2006* in October, "hosted by the women of *Grindhouse*" (Rosario Dawson, Rose McGowan and Marley Shelton). For some reason it also featured a special tribute to Ozzy Osbourne.

In early December, BBC Radio 3 broadcast *Weird Tales – The Strange Life of H. P. Lovecraft*. Geoff Ward, professor of literature at Dundee University presented the forty-five minute show about the influential author with contributions from Neil Gaiman, S. T. Joshi, Kelly Link, Peter Straub and China Miéville.

Playwright and poet Lemn Sissay traced *Poe the Poet* for Radio 3's *Twenty Minutes* programme, while actor Kerry Shale read from some of Edgar Allan's better-known verse.

BBC Radio 4's *Confessions of a Crap Artist* was a half-hour documentary about Philip K. Dick's reported encounter with God in 1974, while writer Francis Spufford looked at the history of British science fiction in the four-part series *Imagining Albion: The Great British Future*.

Terry Pratchett's "Discworld" novel *Small Gods* was dramatised in four parts on Radio 4. Thea von Harbou's classic SF novel *Metropolis* was adapted for the hour-long *Friday Play* in March, and Ian McKellen narrated a dramatisation of *Sir Gawain and the Green Knight* for the *Afternoon Play* at Christmas.

Toronto's Princess of Wales Theatre became the first venue in the world to mount the epic three-and-a-half hour stage production of *The Lord of the Rings*. Matthew Warchus and Shaun McKenna squeezed J. R. R. Tolkien's trilogy into a three-act structure with stunning special effects and a score by A. R. Rahman and the Finnish musical group Vårttinå. Touted as the most expensive production in theatre history, the show reportedly cost more than $23 million.

Despite being nominated for two Tony Awards, Elton John and Bernie Taupin's lavish stage musical of Anne Rice's *Lestat* closed on Broadway in May, after just thirty-three preview and thirty-nine regular performances. Directed by Robert Jess Roth, Hugh Panaro was cast as the titular vampire.

It was announced in February that Andrew Lloyd Webber's stage musical *The Woman in White*, based on the Gothic novel by Wilkie Collins, was to end its Broadway run after only two months at New York's Marquis Theatre. Although it was playing to less than capacity audiences, producers blamed illness amongst the cast. Meanwhile, the original production in London's West End starring Ruthie Henshall closed after nineteen months to make way for the Monty Python musical *Spamalot*.

There was more success for Sir Lloyd Webber's *The Phantom of the Opera* which, in the previous month, became the longest-running show in Broadway history when it notched up performance #7,486. Since the show opened in London in 1986, it had been seen by more than 80 million people worldwide.

Having started out in a small club in Toronto in 2003, *Evil Dead: The Musical* finally arrived in New York City as an Off Broadway show in time for Halloween. Inspired by Sam Raimi's 1980s cult horror films, audience members in the front two rows of the theatre at the World Stages complex ended up nightly drenched in fake blood.

In Los Angeles, the Gangbusters Theatre Company presented the official world stage premiere of George A. Romero's *Night of the Living Dead*. Running from October through December at The Stella Adler Theatre on Hollywood Boulevard, the poorly-reviewed production starred Mancini Graves as the zombie-battling Ben and was produced and directed by Christian Levatino. Free beer was offered to all adult patrons.

A short drive across town at the Lex Theatre, Theatre East's *They're Not Zombies*, written and directed by Leif Gantvoort, covered much the same ground with more humour. Many of the characters were named after people connected with the original Romero movie. Adding to the LA zombiefest, *Zombies!* was an improv show put on by The Acme Comedy Theatre.

Over April and May, South Pasadena's Freemont Centre Theatre presented a limited engagement of *Ray Bradbury's The Machineries of Joy*. Directed by Alan Neal Hubbs and presented by Ray Bradbury's Pandemonium Theatre Company, the production featured stage versions of "I Will Arise and Go Now", "The Machineries of

Joy", "The Finnegan" and "The Parrot Who Met Papa", the latter three being world premieres.

The Dorothy Chandler Pavilion hosted the world premiere in May of the LAOpera's production of *Grendel*, directed by Julie Taylor. A darkly comic exploration of the Beowulf legend told from the monster's point of view, the production ran for just seven performances and used projections, puppetry and masks to tell the epic tale.

Presented by the Improbable theatre company and the National Theatre of Scotland, *The Wolves in the Walls: A Musical Pandemonium*, based on the illustrated children's book by Neil Gaiman and Dave McKean, enjoyed limited runs in Glasgow and London in April.

The Children's Society's 125th Anniversary was celebrated at London's Royal Albert Hall on October 22nd with two fundraising performances of Stephen Sondheim and James Lapine's musical *Into the Woods*, featuring Anita Dobson, Vinnie Jones and many others stars of stage and screen.

For the first time ever, Jeff Wayne performed his *Musical Version of War of the Worlds* with a live orchestra across the UK in April. The shows also included special guest Justin Hayward and the long-dead Richard Burton in both sight and sound as "The Journalist".

Jonathan Kent's Glyndebourne on Tour's production of *The Turn of the Screw* updated Benjamin Britten's opera to the 1950s and introduced a suggestion of paedophilia to the classic ghost story.

Nintendo's Wii console was the new must-have gadget of 2006, especially after Sony delayed the European launch of its new PlayStation 3 until the following spring. The Wii controller, shaped like a television remote, interacted with a sensor bar placed in front of the TV that translated the player's motion into movement on the screen.

Meanwhile, Johnny Depp voiced the disappointing *Pirates of the Caribbean: Legend of Jack Sparrow* spin-off video game, and *Monster House* was based on the animated film and obviously aimed at younger children.

At least *Stubbs the Zombie in Rebel Without a Pulse* allowed the player to actually become a zombie and turn the inhabitants of a small American town into an army of the walking dead.

Although the film was not due for release until 2007, Gentle Giant offered six-inch busts of "Harry Potter", "Draco Malfoy" and "Cho

Chang", based on the characters in *Harry Potter and the Order of the Phoenix*.

The third "Now Playing" series included a seven-inch figure of the Werewolf from *Dog Soldiers*, while Shaun (from *Shaun of the Dead*), Chucky (from *Child's Play*) and Sebastian "The King" Haff (from *Bubba Ho-Tep*) were all part of the fourth "Cult Classics" series.

NECA's "The Cult Classics Hall of Fame" included limited edition figures of The Crow, Freddy Krueger, Jason Vorhees and the ever-popular Pinhead.

McFarlane Toys acquired the licensing rights to the 1992 movie *Bram Stoker's Dracula* and issued a two-pack of deluxe action figures depicting Dracula in his incarnations as a bat and a wolf as part of the "Movie Maniacs" series.

From Factory X, the replica of Rupert Giles' *Vampyr Book* from *Buffy the Vampire Slayer* opened up to reveal a hidden storage area. The six-inch tall *Buffy the Vampire Slayer: Übervamp Bust* was sculpted by Gabriel Marquez and limited to 2,000 hand-numbered pieces.

"Black Widow" and "Bonejangles" statues from *Tim Burton's Corpse Bride* were each available with certificates of authenticity.

Fantastik Plastiks' *Mad Monster Party Vinyl Figures* depicted Dracula, Frankenstein's Monster, Werewolf and the Zombie Bellhop from the 1966 Rankin/Bass animated puppet movie. Each figure, based on the original design by Jack Harris, was packaged in a colourful tube and limited to 1,500 pieces each.

"Herman Munster" and "Grandpa Munster" were caricatured in Electric Tiki's *Tooned-Up Television Series*, based on original designs by Tracy Mark Lee. The eleven-inch high polystone maquettes came with hand-numbered certificates of authenticity.

Hawthorne Village offered *The Munsters Halloween Village* with sculptures of "1313 Mockingbird Lane" (with a free Herman Munster figurine), "Lily's Inn" and "Grandpa's Touch of Transylvania Hotel".

Artbox's set of 72 *Frankenstein Cards* featured images from the 1931 Universal movie. "Monster Sketch" cards, depicting Frankenstein's creation through the eyes of various artists, and "Monster-Glo" cards were randomly inserted into packs.

Comic Images' *Godzilla King of the Monsters Cards* were released to celebrate the Big G's 50th anniversary, and included randomly inserted sketch cards illustrated by Bob Eggleton, Matt Harris and others.

Fay Wray, in a classic pose from *King Kong*, was one of four famous "Canadians in Hollywood" (the others being Mary Pickford,

Lorne Greene and John Candy) who were immortalised on a stamp by Canada Post.

San Francisco was the popular location for World Horror Convention 2006, held over May 11th-14th. Despite an impressive line-up of guests that included international authors Kim Newman and Koji Suzuki, publisher John Pelan, artist Brom, actor Bill Moseley and Toastmaster Peter Straub, mismanagement led to some problems after the event. Ray Garton was announced as the somewhat premature recipient of the Grand Master Award.

The 19th annual Horror Writers Association Bram Stoker Awards were presented at a banquet at an airport hotel in Newark, New Jersey, on June 17th.

The Novel award was a tie between David Morrell's *Creepers* and Charlee Jacob's *Dread of the Beast*. First Novel went to Weston Ochse's *Scarecrow Gods*, Short Fiction was awarded to Gary A. Braunbeck's "We Now Pause for Station Identification", and Joe Hill's "Best New Horror" was awarded Long Fiction. Del Howison and Jeff Gelb's *Dark Delicacies* won the anthology award, and Hill made it a popular double when he also received the Collection award for *20th Century Ghosts*. *Horror: Another 100 Best Books* edited by Stephen Jones and Kim Newman won in the Non-Fiction category, and Michael A. Arnzen's *Freakcidents* and Charlee Jacob's *Sineater* tied for the Poetry award. The HWA Life Achievement Award went to Peter Straub, Necessary Evil Press was the recipient of the Specialty Press Award, and the Richard Laymon President's Award went to Lisa Morton for her services to the HWA.

British FantasyCon XXX was held in Nottingham over September 22nd-24th. The impressive line-up of Guests of Honour included Clive Barker, Ramsey Campbell, Neil Gaiman, Raymond E. Feist and Juliet E. McKenna, while David J. Howe was Master of Ceremonies.

The August Derleth Award for Best Novel went to Neil Gaiman's *Anansi Boys*. Best Novella was Stuart Young's "The Mask Behind the Face", and Joe Hill's "Best New Horror" repeated its Stoker success, collecting the award for Best Short Fiction. The author also continued his winning streak by picking up the Best Collection award for *20th Century Ghosts*. *The Elastic Book of Numbers* edited by Allan Ashley won for Best Anthology, Peter Crowther's PS Publishing picked up the Best Small Press award, and Les Edwards was once again voted Best Artist. Clive Barker presented The Karl Edward Wagner Award for Special Achievement to Stephen Jones, and all the winners were present to accept their statuettes. A Special BFS Committee Founders Award was given to Keith Walker, Rosemary Pardoe, Phil Spencer and David A. Sutton.

World Fantasy Convention 2006, celebrating the "Robert E. Howard Centennial", was held in Austin, Texas, over November 2nd-5th. Authors Glen Cook, Dave Duncan and "Robin Hobb" (Megan Lindholm) were Guests of Honor. Editor GoH was the legendary Glenn Lord, Artist GoH was John Jude Palencar, and Gary Gianni was billed as Robert E. Howard Artist Guest.

The eleventh International Horror Guild Awards (now apparently referred to as the "Iggys") were presented on the Thursday evening at World Fantasy, hosted by artist John Picacio.

Chelsea Quinn Yarbro became the first woman honoured with the IHG Living Legend Award, which was presented by Suzy McKee Charnas. Brett Easton Ellis' *Lunar Park* won the Novel award, Short Fiction went to "There's a Hole in the Sky" by Rick Bowes (*SciFiction*), Mid-Length Fiction went to "La Peau Verte" by Caitlín R. Kiernan (*To Charles Fort, with Love*) and Long Fiction was awarded to "Kiss of the Mudman" by Gary Braunbeck (*Home Before Dark*). PS Publishing had a double success when Joe Hill's *20th Century Ghosts* received the award for Collection and Peter Crowther's *PostScripts* won for Periodical. *Memories* by Enki Bilal received the Illustrated Narrative award, Non-Fiction went to editors S. T. Joshi and Stefan Dziemianowicz's comprehensive three-volume *Supernatural Literature of the World: An Encyclopedia*, and Clive Barker's "Exhibition: Visions of Heaven and Hell (and Then Some)" at Los Angeles' Bert Green Fine Art gallery was the somewhat odd choice for the Art award.

In fact, the 2006 IHG Awards were surrounded by controversy, but we will return to that a little later . . .

Three days later in Austin, Toastmaster Bradley Denton hosted the 2006 World Fantasy Awards presentation following a crowded banquet on the Sunday afternoon. The Special Award, Non-Professional went to David J. Howe and Stephen Walker for their publishing imprint Telos Books, and the Special Award, Professional was somewhat controversially presented to Sean Wallace for Prime Books. James Jean won for Artist, Bruce Holland Rogers' *The Keyhole Opera* was awarded Collection, and *The Fair Folk* edited by Marvin Kaye collected Anthology. George Saunders' story "CommComm" (from *The New Yorker*) collected the award for Short Fiction, Joe Hill rounded out an incredible year when his "Voluntary Committal" won for Novella, and Haruki Murakami's

Kafka on the Shore was deemed the winner in the Novel category. Life Achievement Awards were announced for artist Stephen Fabian and writer John Crowley. Only one of the winners was actually present.

More observant readers may have noticed that no anthology winner was listed in the International Horror Guild Awards above. This was not an oversight.

I've talked about awards in these pages before, and they continue to be a thorny subject. Although most general readers will be unaware of the situation, in 2006 there was a brief flurry of controversy in the horror field over a decision by the IHG judges to not even *nominate* the minimum three titles required in the "Anthology" category.

For a year that produced many new and notable anthologies, not to mention the two annual "Year's Best" horror volumes, it seemed inexplicable to many people working in the genre that the panel of IHG judges were apparently unable to come up with at least three titles first published in the year 2005 worthy of a nomination. Obviously, this did not seem to have been a problem for any other major awards in the field.

As a result, around seventy people (including myself and other previous and multiple IHG winners) put our names to an "Open Letter" to the administrators condemning their decision and pointing out that their failure to acknowledge *any* anthology titles was not only blinkered, but sent entirely the wrong message to not only readers of the genre, but also to publishers.

The anthologies market is already depressed enough. Why should any publisher support future anthology projects if one of the major awards in the field could not find anything even worthwhile to nominate out of a year's worth of titles? Arguably, 2005 may not have been the best of years, but it was certainly far from the worst . . .

As we had intended, our open letter stirred up discussion within the field. However, what none of us who put our names to the statement expected was the vehemence that it would provoke.

Within hours of its posting, message boards were buzzing with people discussing the pros and cons of the letter. I soon started receiving e-mails attacking me personally. Over the following weeks I was threatened and insulted, and I know that others received similar treatment.

However, I'm delighted to say that these kinds of bullying tactics ultimately failed. Only one person who signed the letter subsequently asked to have his name removed. Many more contacted us and asked if they could have their names *added*.

In the end, the IHG judges claimed that they didn't really consider "reprint" anthologies (an odd statement, given that such information appears nowhere in their rules and, in the past, I have won the IHG Award for this very anthology series). Perhaps even more telling was the excuse by another judge that the panel did not receive enough *free* copies of anthologies to make an informed decision.

What the IHG judges and administrator had failed to take into account was that it is the job of the panel to track down individual titles and then discuss the subjective merits of those books amongst themselves.

Even more importantly, it is not in the judges' remit to compare one year's output of books with that of any earlier years. In this particular case, they should have nominated whichever anthology titles they collectively felt were the best of those published in 2005. If they then decided that none of these titles ultimately deserved the final award, then so be it. But to simply say that not one single book – and the genuine contributions made by the authors, editors and publishers involved – was worth acknowledging not only harmed people's perception of the genre, but it is also diminished an award that is supposed to be all about recognising "achievement" in the field of horror and dark fantasy.

At the very least, our protest raised some important issues, and I hope that such a decision will not be taken so lightly again.

For me, personally, it was a nasty, spiteful and disheartening time that exposed the dark and malicious underbelly of the genre I love and work in. Am I glad I got involved? Sure. Given the harassment that I had to put up with, would I do it again? You betcha!

The Editor
May, 2007

AL SARRANTONIO

Summer

AL SARRANTONIO IS THE AUTHOR of more than forty books. He is a winner of the Bram Stoker Award and has been a finalist for the World Fantasy Award, the British Fantasy Award, the International Horror Guild Award, the Locus Award and the Private Eye Writers of America Shamus Award.

His novels, spanning the horror, science fiction, fantasy, mystery and Western genres, include *Moonbane*, *Skeletons*, *House Haunted*, *The Five Worlds Trilogy*, *Masters of Mars*, *West Texas Orangefield* and *Hallows Eve*, the last two part of his Halloween cycle of stories. Hailed as "a master anthologist" by *Booklist*, he has edited such high-profile volumes as *999: New Stories of Horror and Suspense*, *Redshift: Extreme Visions of Speculative Fiction* and *Flights: Extreme Visions of Fantasy*.

The author's short stories have appeared in magazines such as *Heavy Metal*, *Twilight Zone*, *Isaac Asimov's Science Fiction Magazine*, *Realms of Fantasy*, *Analog* and *Amazing*, as well as in anthologies such as *The Year's Best Horror Stories*, *Visions of Fantasy: Tales from the Masters*, *Great Ghost Stories* and *The Best of Shadows*.

Upcoming publications include a new horror collection, *Halloween and Other Seasons*, a limited edition of *Moonbane*, and a new "Orangefield" novel, *Halloweenland*, all from Cemetery Dance Publications, as well as a paperback edition of *Halloweenland* from Leisure Books. He currently lives in New York's historic Hudson Valley region with his family.

"Unless I'm mistaken," reveals Sarrantonio, "'Summer', an unabashed homage to Ray Bradbury, presents one of the very few ideas that Bradbury never covered in his *Weird Tales* and *Thrilling*

Wonder Stories days: Namely, what if the glorious season of summer came but never ended?

"Not to say that he's never touched on the season: His 'Rocket Summer' and 'All Summer in a Day' (you may notice my clumsy and roundabout paraphrase of that title in the first line of my story) are wonderful evocations of the warm months.

"Regardless, I'd like to think there's a little salt and pepper of the Old Master in my tale. Perhaps if Ray had had that idea before me, it would have looked a little bit like my story."

IT WAS A SUMMER DAY that was all of summer. Dry heat rose from the cracks in the sidewalks, brushing the brown grass that grew there as it shimmered by. There was a hush in the stilted air, high and hanging, the sun like a burnt coin frozen in the pale and cloudless sky, the trees still, green leaves dried and baked, panting for a breeze.

Rotating window fans moved hot air from outside to inside. Newspapers rustled on kitchen tables, their pages waving until the artificial breeze moved on, then settling hot and desultory back into unread place. The breakfast plates sat unstacked, forgotten; lunch plates with uneaten lunch – curling pumpernickel, wilted lettuce, an inkblot of mustard dry as paper – sat nearby. Morning coffee milled in two mugs, still tepid from the afternoon warmth.

"My Gosh, Mabel, has it ever been this hot before?" George Meadows said from his easy chair; he sat arranged like a man who had eaten a great meal, with his shirt and trousers loosened, but only against the heat.

His wife Mabel, prostrate on the nearby couch, the faded sunflowers of her house dress clashing and merging in a wilted riot with the worn daisies of the sofa print, tried to say something but failed. Her right hand continued to weakly fan herself with its magazine and she tried again.

"Hot as it's . . . ever been," she managed to get out in a croak, and then closed her eyes and ears, discouraging further comment.

"Yep," George managed to answer before closing his own eyes. He couldn't resist, he never could, getting the last word in. He rallied to add, even though Mabel was already perfectly aware: "Man on the radio said it might get hotter still."

Three twelve-year-old boys hated Summer.

They hadn't always. At one time, Summer had belonged to them. From the first day of school letting out, until the dreaded bell sounded again, they had ruled summer as if they owned it. There had been baseball and bad tennis, and miniature golf and marbles in the hot dust. There had been butterfly hunts with orange black monarchs big as pterodactyls and just as difficult to catch. Trips to the secret pond with jars, and pondwater drops under Lem's microscope to watch the amoebas within. And their own swimming, from dawn to dusk some days, emerging at the end waterlogged beings, raisin boys, to dry and unwilt in the setting sun. And Monk's telescope at night, the fat dry cold moon sliding across the eyepiece like a pockmarked balloon; Saturn hanging silent and majestic with its golden split ring. Backyard campouts, the walls of Shep's pup tent lit from within not with fireflies but with the flashlights of boys with comic books, the smell of Sterno and pancake batter the next morning, the metal taste of warm water in boy scout canteens.

Summer had been their time – the time away from schoolbooks and parents' waggling fingers, the time to be boys. And this year it had started the same – the banishment of black-and-white marble notebooks, pencils thrown under beds spearing dust bunnies, school clothes in the backs of closets.

And out with the baseball glove! Oiled, smelling like new wet leather, sneakers that smelled of dirt, short pants, the dewy morning giving way to a fresh hot feeling and late afternoon thunderstorms scattering the ballplayers with warm wet drops big as knuckles and the temperature dropping and making them shiver. And swimming, and more swimming, and more swimming still, and the cool-warm nights, the sharp cold taste of ice cream, of a bottle of cola drawn from an iced bucket, of a hot dog steaming, hiding under hot sauerkraut. A drive-in movie in Uncle Jed's pickup truck: two hiding under the tarp until they were in.

Morning noon and night it was summer.

Real summer.

Until:

Something . . .

. . . began to change.

It was Shep who noticed it first: in the dangerous treehouse on a mid-August afternoon. They had finished trading baseball cards, arguing over how many cards (always doubles!) to attach to bicycle spokes to make them clack and were halfway through another argument about who was prettier, Margaret O'Hearn or Angie Bernstein, when Shep's head went up and he sniffed, just like a hound dog might. His leg, swinging through one of the hut's many floor holes, pendulumed to a frozen stop.

"What's wrong?" Lem asked, and Monk looked up from his new copy of *Vault of Horror* with a frown.

"Turn off your brain, Shep," Monk growled. "It's summer."

"Just because you don't want to talk about girls or leg hair or B.O.—" Lem began, but he stopped dead at the look on Shep's face.

"Something's different," Shep said, and he still held that pointer-at-a-bird look.

Lem tried to laugh, but stopped abruptly, a hiccup of seriousness at the look in Shep's eyes.

A whisper: "What do you mean: different?"

Shep spoke without breaking his concentration. "Don't you *feel* it?"

Monk shook his head with finality and went back to his comic, but Lem's face had taken on a worried look.

Shep was never wrong about these kinds of things.

"I . . . don't feel anything . . ." Lem offered mildly.

Idly, still scanning his *Vault of Horror*, Monk kicked out his sneaker and caught Lem on the shin. A scatter of orange infield dust, dislodged from the sculpted sole, trickled down the other boy's bare leg.

"You feel *that*, Lemnick?"

"Be quiet—" Shep said abruptly, and it was not a request.

The other two boys were silent – and now Monk sat up, his butt easily finding the structure's largest hole, which they inevitably called "the crapper."

Something like a faint hiss, something like the eerie castanet sound cicadas make, passed by his ears and brushed him on one cheek, but there was not so much as a breeze in the early hot afternoon.

"What was—?"

"It's getting hotter," Shep said simply.

"Maybe it's because of Hell's Cave," Monk laughed, but nobody joined him.

That afternoon it was too hot to swim. It stayed that way the next three days. They abandoned the treehouse, leaving its lopsided openwork collection of mismatched boards and tattooed, badly nailed orange crates, and moved into Monk's cellar, which was damp but cool.

It had never been too hot to swim before:

Never.

They perused Monk's comic book collection, which after banishment to the basement was on the verge of mold. Monk had built, from boards too useless even for the treehouse, a lab table in one corner, and they fiddled with the chemistry set, trying to make things that were yellow and then turned red, others that made smoke. They toyed with the rabbit-ear antenna on the ancient television, a huge wooden box with a tiny black and white screen the size of a TV dinner tin – for a while they brought in the monster movie channel, and watched, in a snowy and line-infested picture, the Man from Planet X rampage through the Scottish moors. Monk brought down a bowl of grapes, and they ate some of them, and spit the rest at each other out of their mouths, pressing their cheeks for cannonade.

But their eyes kept drifting to the cellar windows, and the heat and light outside.

"Maybe we should go swimming anyway," Monk said, finally, on the second day.

They made it halfway to the secret pond, and turned around, dripping and panting.

Overhead, the sun looked hotter, if not larger.

They played darts in the cellar, and set up plastic army men and knocked them down with marbles and rubber bands.

Lem and Shep talked about body odor and shaving their upper lips while Monk scowled.

And always, for three days, they kept looking to the cellar windows, up high, filled with light, and closed against the summer heat.

That night they took Monk's telescope to the secret pond, and Shep's pup tent, and Lem's dad's battery radio.

The radio played music, and talked about the heat. The air was dry as the inside of an oven. There was a cloudless sky, and a smile of moon tilted at an amused angle, and, after a while, there were stars in the dark but they looked faraway and dim through the hot air. The telescope went unused. They swam for a while, but the water, over the last three days, had taken on the temperature and feel of warm tea. Inside the tent it was as hot as outside, and they shifted uncomfortably as they tried to sleep. When they tried to read comics by flashlight, the flashlights dimmed and then went out.

In the dark, Lem tried to talk again about Margaret O'Hearn and Amy Bernstein, and about Shep joining the track team when they all started Junior High in the fall, but Monk told them to shut up.

Later Shep said, out of the blue, "What do you think about Hell's Cave?"

"What about it?" Monk sneered. "You think it leads down to Hell?"

"That's what they say."

Lem was silent, and then he said, "You think that's why the heat won't end . . . ?"

"I wonder," Shep replied.

"You really think—?" Lem began.

"Go to sleep!" Monk demanded.

In the morning it was even hotter.

The sun came up over the trees the color of melted butter. Monk set up the griddle over two Sterno cans, but no one was hungry so he didn't even start breakfast. They spit out the water in their canteens, which tasted like warm aluminum.

It was getting even hotter.

"Ninety-nine today," the radio chirped, "and who knows how hot tomorrow. It only went down to eighty-nine last night, folks. Hope you've got those fans on high, or your head in the fridge!"

He went on to say the weather bureau had no idea why it was so hot.

"What does that mean?" Shep said. "Isn't it their job to know?"

As if in answer the chirpy radio voice said, "Apparently, folks, this heat has little to do with the weather! According to meteorological indications, it should be in the middle eighties, with moderate humidity! Fancy that!"

"Fancy *that*!" Monk nearly spat, in mocking imitation.

The radio voice, again as if in answer, chirped just before a commercial came on: "Hey, folks! Maybe it'll *never* be cool again!"

Shep looked at his friends, and there was a suddenly grim look on his face.

"Maybe he's right," he said.

It didn't rain over the next ten days. Thunder heads would gather in the West, dark mushrooming promises of cool and wet, and then break apart as they came overhead, dissipating like pipe smoke into the blue high air. The grasses turned from moist green to brown; postage stamp lawns changed color overnight and died. In town, the few places with air conditioning – Ferber's Department Store, the Five and Dime with its brand new machine perched over the front door, dripping warm condenser water from its badly installed drain onto entering customers – were packed with customers who didn't buy anything, only wandered the isles like zombies seeking cool relief. The temperature rose into the low hundreds, dropping into the nineties at night. On the roads, automobiles like ancient reptiles sat deserted at angles against curbs, their hoods up, radiators hissing angrily. Buses, looking like brontosauruses, passengerless, stood unmoving, their front and middle doors accordianed open, yawning lazily at empty white bus stop benches.

Birds stopped singing in trees; the morning dawned as hot as midday. Dogs panted in their doghouses. There were no mosquitoes, and houseflies hung motionless to window screens. Spiders crawled into shadows and stayed there.

Cold water came out of taps almost steaming.

It was getting even hotter.

Three twelve-year-old boys made one more pilgrimage to the secret pond. They were sick of Monk's cellar, had done every experiment in the chemistry manual, had recklessly mixed chemicals on their own until one produced in a beaker a roiling cloud of orange choking gas that drove them upstairs. It had become too hot in the cellar anyway, with the windows closed or open. In Monk's kitchen the refrigerator whirred like an unhappy robot, its doors permanently open to provide a tiny measure of coolness to the kitchen. Milk had spoiled, its odor battling with the sour stench of rotting vegetables. Dishes, unwashed, were piled in the sink. The radio was on, a background insect buzz. Monk's parents had gone to the five and dime for the air conditioning.

"And even hotter, with record temperatures reported now not only around the United States but in Europe and Asia as well, in a widening area . . ." the radio said, though the announcer sounded less chirpy, almost tired. "Locally, state authorities are warning anyone prone to heat stroke . . ."

Monk and Shep and Lem took whatever dry food was left, found Shep's pup tent, inexpertly rolled and abandoned in a corner, and set out for the pond.

". . . forty deaths reported in . . ." the radio voice reported unhappily as the screen door banged behind them.

It was like walking through a bakery oven. The heat was not only in the ground and in the air, but all around them. They felt it through their sneakers, on their knees, their eyelids. Their hair felt hot. The air was dry as a firecracker.

Shep looked up into the sun, and his eyes hurt.

"I don't care how hot the water is," Monk said, "it can't be worse than this."

It was. When they got to the pond and stripped, there was vapor

rising from the surface of the water, and fish floated dead, like flat
plastic toys.

"I don't care," Monk said, and stepped in, and yelped.

He looked back at his friends in awe, and showed his retracted
foot, which was red.

"It's actually *hot*!" Monk said.

Lem sat on the ground and put his head in his hands.

Monk was putting his clothes back on, his hands shaking.

Shep said with certainty, "Someone stole summer, and we're going
to Hell's Cave to get it back."

"Ungh?" a weak voice said from the kitchen table. George Meadows
sat staring at his half empty coffee cup, watching the coffee in it
steam. He had poured it an hour and a half ago, and it was still hot.

He lifted his hand toward it, looked at the sweat stain it left in the
shape of a hand on the table and lowered it again.

"Mabel?" he called in a raspy, whispery voice. The sound of
fanning had stopped and when George Meadows made the extreme
effort to turn his head he saw that his wife's house dress looked as if it
was melting, with her in it, into the sofa. Her right hand, unmoving,
still gripped her magazine and her eyes held a fixed, glazed look. Her
chest barely moved up and down.

"Oh, Lord . . ." he breathed, closing his eyes, getting the last word
in though she hadn't said anything. "Gettin' hotter still . . ."

Three twelve-year-old boys stood in front of a cave opening but-
tressed with rotting timbers. With them was Monk's rusting Radio
Flyer, bursting like a Conestoga wagon with their supplies: the
battery radio, two new-batteried flashlights (one of them worked);
three boxes of cereal; six comic books, no doubles; a large thermos of
hot ice tea; four cans of warm cream soda; a length of clothesline
pilfered from Lem's mother's backyard; a mousetrap, over which
they had bantered incessantly ("What if we meet up with rats?" Lem
debated; "Why not a gorilla?" Shep shot back; in the end Shep got
tired of the argument and threw it on the pile), a B-B gun, a kitchen
knife with a broken handle, a crucifix, a Bible. The last two had been
added by Shep, because, he said, "We're heading down *there*," and
would listen to no argument.

They headed in.

It was dim, and, compared to outside, almost cool in the cave. But
as they moved farther in it got even dimmer and hot and stuffy. Their
bodies were covered with sweat, but they didn't notice. There was a

twist to the left, and then a climb that disappointed them, and then a suddenly drop which brought them real darkness and a halt.

Lem, who was pulling the wagon, rummaged through the pile and pulled out the bad flashlight, and then the good one, which he handed to Shep.

Shep switched it on and played the light over their faces.

"You look scared," he said.

"Can we stop here for the night?" Lem asked.

Shep consulted his watch with the light beam. "It's two in the afternoon!"

Behind them, they saw how steeply the floor had dropped; there was a circle of light leading out that looked hot and far away.

"I'm hungry," Monk said.

"Later," Shep answered, and turned the flashlight beam ahead of them.

There was darkness, and a steep descent, and Monk and Lem followed as the beam pointed down into it.

After twenty minutes that seemed like a day, the black wagon handle slipped out of Lem's sweaty hand and the wagon clattered past him.

"Look out!" he called, and Monk and Shep jumped aside as the wagon roared down the steep incline ahead of them.

They heard it rattle off into the bowels of the earth, then they heard nothing.

"Why did you tell us to get out of the way?" Shep asked angrily. "We could have stopped it!"

"We'll catch up to it," Monk shot back.

"Sorry . . ." Lem said.

"No matter. Monk's right." The flashlight beam pointed ahead, and down they went.

Two real hours went by. Lem was thirsty, and Monk wanted to stop, but Shep kept going. If anything it was hotter than above now, and Lem finally panted timidly, "You think we're almost . . . there?"

"You mean *Hell*?" Shep replied, and then added, "If we are, we don't have the crucifix anymore to protect us. It's in the wagon."

Monk snorted, and Shep spun angrily toward him with the flashlight, which at that exact moment went out.

"*Ohhh*," Lem mewled.

"Be quiet," Shep ordered, "it's just stuck." They heard him shaking the flashlight in the dark, but the beam didn't come on.

"Maybe the cover's loose—"

There was the rattle of loosened metal, a *twang*, and they heard flashlight parts hitting the floor of the cave.

"Uh oh," Monk said.

"Help me find them—" Shep ordered, but now there was a note of desperation in his voice.

"I hear rats!" Lem cried, and they all went silent.

Something was skittering in the dark ahead of them.

"Get down and help me find the parts!" Shep said, and for a few minutes there was only the sound of frightened breathing and the pat and slide of hands on the floor of the cave.

"I've got the lens!" Shep cried suddenly.

"And here's the reflector!" Monk added.

"What if there are *rats* on the *floor*!" Lem said, but Shep ignored him.

"All we need is the cover, and one of the batteries. The other one is still in the body."

"I've got the battery!" Monk exulted a moment later.

"I can't find the cover!" Shep said desperately.

"I'm telling you there are rats!" Lem whimpered.

"I can't find the cover either!" Monk.

There was fumbling in the dark, heavy breathing.

A bolt of light blinded them, went out, blinded them.

"I don't need the cover – I'll hold it on," Shep said.

He pointed the flashlight, clutched together by the pressure of his hand, at his friends, Monk on the cave floor, still probing, Lem with his back against the wall, eyes closed.

The beam shot to the floor, moved crazily this way and that, then froze on a round red piece of plastic.

"The cover!" Monk yelled, and pounced on it.

"Give it to me!" Shep said.

There was more fumbling, darkness, then bright light again.

They stood huffing and puffing at their exertion.

Their breaths quieted.

The scrabbling sound was still ahead of them.

"*Rats!*" Lem cried, and then let out a wail.

The flashlight beam swung down and ahead of them, and caught the crashed remains of the red wagon on its side, a chewed-open box of cereal, and the long fat grey-brown length of a rat as it put its whiskered, sniffing nose into the mouse trap.

There was a loud *snap!* which made the light beam shiver, and then, in the darkness behind Shep, he heard Lem laugh nervously and say, "See?"

*   *   *

They stopped two hours later for the night. By Shep's watch it was ten o'clock. The flashlight had gone out again, and this time it was the batteries but Shep took the batteries from the other unworking one. They were tired and hungry, thirsty and hot. The wagon was serviceable but now made a loud squeak with each turn of the front wheels. The handle had been bent, but Lem forced it back into shape. They'd found everything but one can of pop, which Monk promptly stepped on when they set out. He smelled like cream soda, and his friends didn't let him forget it.

"We'll need the batteries for tomorrow," Shep said solemnly. He had found a flat wide place to stop, a kind of hitch in the slope. Ahead of them was only darkness.

It was hot and close and sticky, and they felt a vague heat drifting up at them from below.

"What happens when the batteries run out?" Lem asked.

"We'll have to conserve them," Shep said.

"But what happens—?"

"Be quiet," Shep said, at the same moment Monk snapped, "Shut up, Lem."

They ate in darkness, and drank warm soda and un-iced tea, and listened, but there was nothing to hear. No rats, no nearby roasting fires, no dripping water, no sound of any kind. Just the silent sound of heat getting hotter.

"I hope we're close," Lem said. "I want to go home."

"Home to what?" Shep answered. "If we don't find something down here . . ."

The rest went unsaid.

They sat in a circle, and moved closer, the flashlight in the midst of them like a doused campfire.

Shep laughed and said, "We never finished talking about Angie Bernstein, did we?"

Lem laughed too. "Or how your pits smell!"

"Or your mustache!" Shep shot back.

Monk was silent.

"Hey, Monk," Shep said, "you shaving your lip yet?"

"And using '*B*-Oderant'? You smell like cream soda, but do you also smell like a *horse*?"

Monk feigned snoring.

"Hey Monk—"

The snoring ceased. "Leave me alone."

Lem hooted: "Cream soda boy!"

"Horse pit boy!" Shep laughed.

Monk said nothing, and soon he was snoring for real.

Shep woke them up at seven o'clock by his watch.

At first he couldn't move; it was hard to breathe and so hot he felt as if he was under a steam iron. He knew it was growing impossibly warmer. He could feel and smell and taste it, just like he had in the tree house.

"We have to find the end today," he said, grimly.

They ate and drank in the dark, just like the night before. Now there was no talking. Lem was having trouble breathing, taking shallow ragged huffs at the air.

"Feels . . . like . . . we're . . . in a . . . barbecue . . ." he rasped. "Hard . . . to . . . breathe . . ."

They turned on the battery radio and there was hiss up and down the dial until the one strong local channel came on. It was the same announcer, only now all of the chirp had gone out of his voice.

". . . hundred and ten here this morning, folks," he said. "And it's September first! Local ponds are steamed dry, and the electricity was out for three hours yesterday. Same all over, now. Ice caps are melting, and in Australia, where it's the end of wintertime, the temperature hit ninety-nine yesterday . . ."

They snapped off the radio.

"Let's go," Shep said.

Lem began to cry after a half-hour.

"I can't *do* this!" he said. "Let's go home! I want to swim in the pond, and get ready for school, and look at the fall catalogs and feel it get chilly at night!"

"It's not much farther," Shep said evenly. He was having trouble breathing himself. "This is something we've got to do, Lem. If we do it maybe we can have all that again."

Shep pointed the flashlight at Monk, who was trudging silently, straight ahead.

The flashlight began to fail as they reached a wall of fallen rocks. Ignoring the impediment for the moment, Shep used the remaining light to rip the battery cover off the back of the radio and pull the batteries out.

They were a different size, so he put the radio on and let it stay on, a droning buzz in the background.

The flashlight went out, then flickered on again.

"Quick!" Shep shouted. "Check to either side and see if there's a way around!"

Lem shuffled off to the left, and Monk stood unmoving where he was.

Shep pushed impatiently past him, flicking the flash on and off to pull precious weak yellow beams out of it.

"There's no way around here," Lem called out laconically from the left.

Shep blinked the light on, off, punched desperately around the edge of the barrier, looking for a hole, a rift, a way through.

"Nothing . . ." he huffed weakly.

He turned with a last thought, flaring the flash into life so that the beam played across Monk.

"Maybe there's a crack! Maybe we can pull the wall down!"

"There is no crack," Monk said dully, "and we can't pull it down." His legs abruptly folded underneath him and he sat on the cave floor.

Shep turned the light off, on again; the beam was dull, pumpkin colored but he played it all over the rock barrier.

"Got to be—"

"There is no 'Hell's Cave'," Monk said dully. "It's just a myth. My father told me about it when I was seven. This is just an old mine that played out and then caved in."

"But—"

"*I* made it all happen," Monk said hoarsely, without energy. "The heat, the endless summer. It was me."

"What?" Shep said, moving closer. On the other side, Lem sank to the floor.

"It was me . . ." Monk repeated.

Lem began to cry, mewling like a hurt kitten, and the flashlight beam died again. In the dark, Shep flicked it on, off, on, off.

"*Me*," Monk said fiercely.

Shep hit the button one more time on the flashlight, and it flared like a dying candle, haloing Monk's haunted face, and then faded out again.

"I didn't want it to end." In the darkness Monk spoke in a whispered, monotone. "I didn't want it *ever* to end."

"Didn't want *what* to end?" Shep asked, confused.

"This summer," Monk answered, sighing. "The three of us. I wanted it to last forever. I didn't want us to . . . change. Which is what we were doing. Talking about girls instead of baseball cards, hairy legs instead of monster comics, body odor instead of swimming and telescopes. We used to do everything together and now that was going to change. When we went to Junior High Lem was going to try to date Angie Bernstein and you were going out for track. Then you would go out with Margaret O'Hearn, and the baseball cards and comics would go in the back of the closet, along with the marbles and the pup tent and the canteen and butterfly net. The chemistry set would collect dust in the corner of the basement. I could see it coming. It was all changing, and I didn't want it to."

"But how . . . ?" Shep asked.

In the dark, he could almost hear Monk shrug and heard him hitch a sob. "I don't *know* how I did it. I just wanted it, I fell asleep crying for it at night, I prayed for it every day. Every time you and Lem started talking about girls and body hair and growing up, I prayed for it louder. And then, suddenly, it happened. And then I couldn't make it go away . . ."

Lem cried out hoarsely, then settled into low rasping sobs.

It had become even hotter, and then hotter still. The radio, still on, blurted out a stifled cry of static and then was silent.

In the sweaty, close, unbearably hot cave, the flashlight went on with one final smudge of sick light, illuminating Monk's crying face.

"I'm so sorry . . ." he whispered.

"Mabel?" George Meadows croaked. He could barely talk, his words fighting through the heat, which had intensified. His wife lay unmoving on the sofa, her desiccated arm hanging over the side, fingers brushing her dropped magazine. Her house dress was now completely part of the couch's pattern, melded into it like an iron transfer. The window fan had given up. The sky was very bright. Puffs of steam rose from the floor, up from the cellar, from the ground below. Somewhere in the back of his nostrils, George smelled smoke, and fire.

"Mabel?" he called again, although now he could not feel the easy chair beneath him. He felt light as a flake of ash rising from a campfire.

His eyes were so hot he could no longer see.

He took in one final, rasping, burning breath as the world turned to fire and roaring flame around him.

And, even now, he could not resist getting in the last word, letting his final breath out in a cracked whisper even though there was no one to listen: "Yep. Hottest ever."

RAMSEY CAMPBELL

Digging Deep

RAMSEY CAMPBELL'S LATEST NOVEL is titled *Thieving Fear*, and that will be followed by *The Creatures of the Pool*.

Along with his columns in *Video Watchdog* and *All Hallows* magazines, Campbell also now writes a column for the critical magazine *Dead Reckonings* as well.

"The following story came out of the air or rather the airwaves," explains the author. "BBC Radio 4 reported that a significant number of people do indeed take their mobiles with them as my protagonist does.

"It seems to prove that one of the seminal images of horror fiction has yet to be driven underground by technology. Sometimes the old ideas are best, eh? But I hope I've brought it up to date."

IT MUST HAVE BEEN QUITE a nightmare. It was apparently enough to make Coe drag the quilt around him, since he feels more than a sheeted mattress beneath him, and to leave a sense of suffocating helplessness, of being worse than alone in the dark. He isn't helpless. Even if his fit of rage blotted out his senses, it must have persuaded the family. They've brought him home. There wasn't a quilt on his hospital bed.

Who's in the house with him? Perhaps they all are, to impress on him how much they care about him, but he knows how recently they started. There was barely space for all of them around his bed in the private room. Whenever they thought he was asleep some of them would begin whispering. He's sure he overheard plans for his funeral. Now they appear to have left him by himself, and yet he feels hemmed in. Is the dark oppressing him? He has never seen it so dark.

It doesn't feel like his bedroom. He has always been able to distinguish the familiar surroundings when any of his fears jerked him awake. He could think that someone – his daughter Simone or son Daniel, most likely – has denied him light to pay him back for having spent too much of their legacy on the private room. However much he widens his eyes, they remain coated with blackness. He parts his dry lips to call someone to open the curtains, and then his tongue retreats behind his teeth. He should deal with the bedclothes first. Nobody ought to see him laid out as if he's awaiting examination. In the throes of the nightmare he has pulled the entire quilt under him.

He grasps a handful and plants his other hand against the padded headboard to lift his body while he snatches the quilt from beneath him. That's the plan, but he's unable to take hold of the material. It's more slippery than it ought to be, and doesn't budge. Did his last bout of rage leave him so enfeebled, or is his weight pinning down the quilt? He stretches out his arms to find the edges, and his knuckles bump into cushions on both sides of him. But they aren't cushions, they're walls.

He's in some kind of outsize cot. The walls must be cutting off the light. Presumably the idea is to prevent him from rolling out of bed. He's furious at being treated like this, especially when he wasn't consulted. He flings up his hands to grab the tops of the walls and heave himself up to shout for whoever's in the house, and his fingertips collide with a padded surface.

The sides of the cot must bend inwards at the top, that's all. His trembling hands have flinched and bruised his sunken cheeks, but he lifts them. His elbows are still pressed against the bottom of the container when his hands blunder against an obstruction above his face. It's plump and slippery, and scrabbling at it only loosens his nails from the quick. His knees rear up, knocking together before they bump into the obstacle, and then his feet deal it a few shaky kicks. Far too soon his fury is exhausted, and he lies inert as though the blackness is earth that's weighing on him. It isn't far removed. His family cared about him even less than he suspected. They've consigned him to his last and worst fear.

Can't this be another nightmare? How can it make sense? However prematurely eager Simone's husband may have been to sign the death certificate, Daniel would have had to be less than professional too. Could he have saved on the embalming and had the funeral at once? At least he has dressed his father in a suit, but the pockets feel empty as death.

Coe can't be sure until he tries them all. His quivering fists are clenched next to his face, but he forces them open and gropes over his ribs. His inside breast pocket is flat as a card, and so are the others in the jacket. When he fumbles at his trousers pockets he's dismayed to find how thin he is – so scrawny that he's afraid the protrusion on his right hip is a broken bone. But it's in the pocket, and in his haste to carry it to his face he almost shies it out of reach. Somebody cared after all. He pokes at the keypad, and before his heart has time to beat, the mobile phone lights up.

He could almost wish the glow it sheds were dimmer. It shows him how closely he's boxed in by the quilted surface. It's less than a hand's breadth from his shoulders, and when he tilts his face up to judge the extent of his prison the pudgy lid bumps his forehead. Around the phone the silky padding glimmers green, while farther down the box it's whitish like another species of mould, and beyond his feet it's black as soil. He lets his head sink onto the pillow that's the entire floor and does his desperate best to be aware of nothing but the mobile. It's his lifeline, and he needn't panic because he can't remember a single number. The phone will remember for him.

His knuckles dig into the underside of the lid as he holds the mobile away from his face. It's still too close; the digits merge into a watery blur. He only has to locate the key for the stored numbers, and he jabs it hard enough to bruise his fingertip. The symbol that appears in the illuminated window looks shapeless as a blob of mud, but he knows it represents an address book. He pokes the topmost left-hand key of the numeric pad, although he has begun to regret making Daniel number one, and holds the mobile against his ear.

There's silence except for a hiss of static that sounds too much like a trickle of earth. Though his prison seems oppressively hot, he shivers at the possibility that he may be too far underground for the phone to work. He wriggles onto his side to bring the mobile a few inches closer to the surface, but before his shoulder is anything like vertical it thumps the lid. As he strives to maintain his position, the distant phone starts to ring.

It continues when he risks sinking back, but that's all. He's close to pleading, although he doesn't know with whom, by the time the shrill insistent pulse is interrupted. The voice isn't Daniel's. It's entirely anonymous, and informs Coe that the person he's calling isn't available. It confirms Daniel's number in a different voice that sounds less than human, an assemblage of digits pronounced by a computer, and invites him to leave a message.

"It's your father. That's right, I'm alive. You've buried me alive. Are you there? Can you hear me? Answer the phone, you – Just answer. Tell me that you're coming. Ring when you get this. Come and let me out. Come now."

Was it his breath that made the glow flicker? He's desperately tempted to keep talking until this chivvies out a response, but he mustn't waste the battery. He ends the call and thumbs the key next to Daniel's. It's supposed to contact Simone, but it triggers the same recorded voice.

He could almost imagine that it's a cruel joke, even when the voice composed of fragments reads out her number. At first he doesn't speak when the message concludes with a beep, and then he's afraid of losing the connection. "It's me," he babbles. "Yes, your father. Someone was a bit too happy to see me off. Aren't you there either, or are you scared to speak up? Are you all out celebrating? Don't let me spoil the party. Just send someone who can dig me up."

He's growing hysterical. These aren't the sorts of comments he should leave; he can't afford to antagonise his family just now. His unwieldy fingers have already terminated the call – surely the mobile hasn't lost contact by itself. Should he ring his son and daughter back? Alternatively there are friends he could phone, if he can remember their numbers – and then he realises there's only one call he should make. Why did he spend so long in trying to reach his family? He uses a finger to count down the blurred keypad and jabs the ninth key thrice.

He has scarcely lowered the phone to his ear when an operator cuts off the bell. "Emergency," she declares.

Coe can be as fast as that. "Police," he says while she's enquiring which service he requires, but she carries on with her script. "Police," he says louder and harsher.

This earns him a silence that feels stuffed with padding. She can't expect callers who are in danger to be polite, but he's anxious to apologise in case she can hear. Before he can take a breath a male voice says "Gloucestershire Constabulary."

"Can you help me? You may have trouble believing this, but I'm buried alive."

He sounds altogether too contrite. He nearly emits a wild laugh at the idea of seeking the appropriate tone for the situation, but the policeman is asking "What is your name, sir?"

"Alan Coe," says Coe and is pinioned by realising that it must be carved on a stone at least six feet above him.

"And where are you calling from?"

The question seems to emphasise the sickly greenish glimmer of the fattened walls and lid. Does the policeman want the mobile number? That's the answer Coe gives him. "And what is your location, sir?" the voice crackles in his ear.

Coe has the sudden ghastly notion that his children haven't simply rushed the funeral – that for reasons he's afraid to contemplate, they've laid him to rest somewhere other than with his wife. Surely some of the family would have opposed them. "Mercy Hill," he has to believe.

"I didn't catch that, sir."

Is the mobile running out of power? "Mercy Hill," he shouts so loud that the dim glow appears to quiver.

"Whereabouts on Mercy Hill?"

Every question renders his surroundings more substantial, and the replies he has to give are worse. "Down in front of the church," he's barely able to acknowledge. "Eighth row, no, ninth, I think. Left of the avenue."

There's no audible response. The policeman must be typing the details, unless he's writing them down. "How long will you be?" Coe is more than concerned to learn. "I don't know how much air I've got. Not much."

"You're telling us you're buried alive in a graveyard."

Has the policeman raised his voice because the connection is weak? "That's what I said," Coe says as loud.

"I suggest you get off the phone now, sir."

"You haven't told me how soon you can be here."

"You'd better hope we haven't time to be. We've had enough Halloween pranks for one year."

Coe feels faint and breathless, which is dismayingly like suffocation, but he manages to articulate "You think I'm playing a joke."

"I'd use another word for it. I advise you to give it up immediately, and that voice you're putting on as well."

"I'm putting nothing on. Can't you hear I'm deadly serious? You're using up my air, you – Just do your job or let me speak to your superior."

"I warn you, sir, we can trace this call."

"Do so. Come and get me," Coe almost screams, but his voice grows flat. He's haranguing nobody except himself.

Has the connection failed, or did the policeman cut him off? Did he say enough to make them trace him? Perhaps he should switch off the mobile to conserve the battery, but he has no idea whether this would leave the phone impossible to trace. The thought of waiting in the dark without knowing whether help is on the way brings the walls and lid closer to rob him of breath. As he holds the phone at a cramped arm's length to poke the redial button, he sees the greenish light appear to tug the swollen ceiling down. When he snatches the mobile back to his ear the action seems to draw the lid closer still.

An operator responds at once. "Police," he begs as she finishes her first word. "Police."

Has she recognised him? The silence isn't telling. It emits a burst of static so fragmented that he's afraid the connection is breaking up, and then a voice says "Gloucestershire Constabulary."

For a distracted moment he thinks she's the operator. Surely a policewoman will be more sympathetic than her colleague. "It's Alan Coe again," Coe says with all the authority he can summon up. "I promise you this is no joke. They've buried me because they must have thought I'd passed on. I've already called you once but I wasn't informed what's happening. May I assume somebody is on their way?"

How much air has all that taken? He's holding his breath as if this may compensate, although it makes the walls and lid appear to bulge towards him, when the policewoman says in the distance "He's back. I see what you meant about the voice."

"What's wrong with it?" Coe says through his bared teeth, then tries a shout, which sounds flattened by padding. "What's the matter with my voice?"

"He wants to know what's wrong with his voice."

"So you heard me the first time." Perhaps he shouldn't address her as if she's a child, but he's unable to moderate his tone. "What are you saying about my voice?"

"I don't know how old you're trying to sound, but nobody's that old and still alive."

"I'm old enough to be your father, so do as you're told." She either doesn't hear this or ignores it, but he ensures she hears "I'm old enough for them to pass me off as dead."

"And bury you."

"That's what I've already told you and your colleague."

"In a grave."

"On Mercy Hill below the church. Halfway along the ninth row down, to the left of the avenue."

He can almost see the trench and his own hand dropping a fistful of earth into the depths that harboured his wife's coffin. All at once he's intensely aware that it must be under him. He might have wanted to be reunited with her at the end – at least, with her as she was before she stopped recognising him and grew unrecognisable, little more than a skeleton with an infant's mind – but not like this. He remembers the spadefuls of earth piling up on her coffin and realises that now they're on top of him. "And you're expecting us to have it dug up," the policewoman says.

"Can't you do it yourselves?" Since this is hardly the best time to criticise their methods, he adds "Have you got someone?"

"How long do you plan to carry on with this? Do you honestly think you're taking us in?"

"I'm not trying to. For the love of God, it's the truth." Coe's free hand claws at the wall as if this may communicate his plight somehow, and his fingers wince as though they've scratched a blackboard. "Why won't you believe me?" he pleads.

"You really expect us to believe a phone would work down there."

"Yes, because it is."

"I an't hea ou."

The connection is faltering. He nearly accuses her of having wished this on him. "I said it is," he cries.

"Very unny." Yet more distantly she says "Now he's aking it ound a if it's aking up."

Is the light growing unreliable too? For a blink the darkness seems to surge at him – just darkness, not soil spilling into his prison. Or has his consciousness begun to gutter for lack of air? "It is," he gasps. "Tell me they're coming to find me."

"You won't like it if they do."

At least her voice is whole again, and surely his must be. "You still think I'm joking. Why would I joke about something like this at my age, for God's sake? I didn't even know it was Halloween."

"You're saying you don't know what you just said you know."

"Because your colleague told me. I don't know how long I've been here," he realises aloud, and the light dims as if to suggest how much air he may have unconsciously used up.

"Long enough. We'd have to give you full marks for persistence. Are you in a cupboard, by the way? It sounds like one. Your trick nearly worked."

"It's a coffin, God help me. Can't you hear that?" Coe cries and scrapes his nails across the underside of the lid.

Perhaps the squealing is more tangible than audible. He's holding the mobile towards it, but when he returns the phone to his ear the policewoman says "I've heard all I want to, I think."

"Are you still calling me a liar?" He should have demanded to speak to whoever's in charge. He's about to do so when a thought ambushes him. "If you really think I am," he blurts, "why are you talking to me?"

At once he knows. However demeaning it is to be taken for a criminal, that's unimportant if they're locating him. He'll talk for as long as she needs to keep him talking. He's opening his mouth to rant when he hears a man say "No joy, I'm afraid. Can't trace it."

If Coe is too far underground, how is he able to phone? The policewoman brings him to the edge of panic. "Count yourself lucky," she tells him, "and don't dare play a trick like this again. Don't you realise you may be tying up a line while someone genuinely needs our help?"

He mustn't let her go. He's terrified that if she rings off they won't accept his calls. It doesn't matter what he says so long as it makes the police come for him. Before she has finished lecturing him he shouts "Don't you speak to me like that, you stupid cow."

"I'm war ing ou, ir—"

"Do the work we're paying you to do, and that means the whole shiftless lot of you. You're too fond of finding excuses not to help the public, you damned lazy swine." He's no longer shouting just to be heard. "You weren't much help with my wife, were you? You were worse than useless when she was wandering the streets not knowing where she was. And you were a joke when she started chasing me round the house because she'd forgotten who I was and thought I'd broken in. That's right, you're the bloody joke, not me. She nearly killed me with a kitchen knife. Now get on with your job for a change, you pathetic wretched—"

Without bothering to flicker the light goes out, and he hears nothing but death in his ear. He clutches the mobile and shakes it and pokes blindly at the keys, none of which brings him a sound except for the lifeless clacking of plastic or provides the least relief from the unutterable blackness. At last he's overcome by exhaustion or despair or both. His arms drop to his sides, and the phone slips out of his hand.

Perhaps it's the lack of air, but he feels as if he may soon be resigned to lying where he is. Shutting his eyes takes him closer to sleep. The surface beneath him is comfortable enough, after all. He could fancy he's in bed, or is that mere fancy? Can't he have dreamed he wakened in his coffin and everything that followed? Why, he has managed to drag the quilt under himself, which is how the nightmare began. He's vowing that it won't recur when a huge buzzing insect crawls against his hand.

He jerks away from it, and his scalp collides with the headboa
which is too plump. The insect isn't only buzzing, it's glowing feebly.
It's the mobile, which has regained sufficient energy to vibrate. As he
grabs it, the decaying light seems to fatten the interior of the coffin.
He jabs the key to take the call and fumbles the mobile against his
ear. "Hello?" he pleads.

"Coming."

It's barely a voice. It sounds as unnatural as the numbers in the
answering messages did, and at least as close to falling to bits. Surely
that's the fault of the connection. Before he can speak again the
darkness caves in on him, and he's holding an inert lump of plastic
against his ear.

There's a sound, however. It's muffled but growing more audible.
He prays that he's recognising it, and then he's sure he does.
Someone is digging towards him.

"I'm here," he cries and claps a bony hand against his withered
lips. He shouldn't waste whatever air is left, especially when he's
beginning to feel it's as scarce as light down here. It seems unlikely
that he would even have been heard. Why is he wishing he'd kept
silent? He listens breathlessly to the scraping in the earth. How did
the rescuers manage to dig down so far without his noticing? The
activity inches closer – the sound of the shifting of earth – and all at
once he's frantically jabbing at the keypad in the blackness. Any
response from the world overhead might be welcome, any voice
other than the one that called him. The digging is beneath him.

JOHN GORDON

The Night Watch

JOHN GORDON WAS BORN in Jarrow-on-Tyne and now lives in
Norwich with his wife, Sylvia. As a child he moved with his family
to Wisbech in the Fens of Cambridgeshire, where he went to school.
After serving in the Royal Navy on minesweepers and destroyers
during World War II he became a journalist on various local newspapers.

His first book for young adults, *The Giant Under the Snow*, was
published by Hutchinson in 1968 and gained praise from Alan
Garner, among others. It was reissued in 2006 by Orion, with
editions in Italy and Lithuania and as a talking book. Since then
Gordon has published a number of fantasy and horror novels
including *The House on the Brink*, *The Ghost on the Hill*, *The
Quelling Eye*, *The Grasshopper*, *Ride the Wind*, *Blood Brothers*,
Gilray's Ghost, *The Flesh Eater*, *The Midwinter Watch*, *Skinners*
and *The Ghosts of Blacklode*.

Gordon's short stories are collected in *The Spitfire Grave and
Other Stories*, *Catch Your Death and Other Stories*, *The Burning
Baby and Other Stories* and *Left in the Dark*. He was one of five
authors who contributed to the Oxrun Station "mosaic novel"
Horror at Halloween, edited by Jo Fletcher, and his autobiography
Ordinary Seaman appeared from Walker Books in 1992.

"Museums are potent places for storytellers," reveals the author,
"none more so than Norwich Castle, which is the setting for 'The Night
Watch'. It stands on Castle Mound overlooking the heart of the city as
it has done for eight centuries, but internally its bright and intriguing
exhibits and showcases disguise a dark period of its history.

"It was once a prison, and I was standing in the corner of a picture
gallery one day when one of the attendants told me that I had my feet

on the spot where felons were hanged. Where once a trapdoor had let go under the feet of quite minor wrongdoers there was now smooth parquet flooring.

"There is also a deep well at the centre of the Castle's main hall where children drop coins and count the seconds before the ripples spread. It is all so innocent . . ."

I T HAD BEEN A HARD DAY in the dungeons. Now, as the summer sun dipped to the horizon, Martin Glover stood on the Castle battlements and gazed out over the city. The golden cockerel at the tip of the of the Cathedral's thin spire glinted in the setting sun and urged him to lean out through the crenellations as if he was about to fly to it across the rooftops. He tested the notion by opening his mouth as if to feel the rush of air.

"We want none of that, young sir." There was a harsh rasp to the voice that made him start and look over his shoulder. "We wouldn't want to have to scrape you up off of the street, would we, son?"

Dr Martin Glover, the scholar, was amused to be addressed as son. He was young, but not young enough for that. But he was aware he had just been spotted leaning too far over the parapet like a schoolboy showing off to a girl. "I was just enjoying the view," he said.

"They all say that, son – but they go for the long drop just the same."

"Do they, indeed?" Martin had not been aware that any suicides had chosen to leap from the battlements. He said so.

The man merely grinned. "There's several been for the high jump hereabouts."

"But surely not recently?" Martin had not seen the man before but he was obviously an attendant at the Castle. He had an air of authority, and at this hour all visitors had long since gone.

"Maybe not recently, but we do keep a record of all of them who come here to end it all."

"That's bizarre . . . I had no idea."

"We keep a book." The man was thin and his shaved head and hollow cheeks were frosted with a grey stubble. "We make a note of the names, and someone has to sign to say it happened. It's our duty, *Mister* Glover." The emphasis was deliberate and his smile seemed to invite Dr Glover, the scholar, to correct him, but Martin merely smiled back. It was too late in the day to stand on his dignity, and maybe he did look too young to hold a doctorate.

As a historian, he had been granted the freedom of the records kept in the Castle museum and he had been given space to work in what must have been the dungeons long ago. He had climbed to the battlements for a breath of fresh air before leaving. Now he glanced at his watch. It was later than he thought. "The Castle must have closed long ago!" he exclaimed.

"Locked and bolted some time back. Maybe you didn't want to hear us making the last rounds . . . had your hands over your ears, maybe." The man's smile was watchful.

"Why should I not want to hear?"

"Matter of opinion, son. Some don't want to hear me coming."

Martin laughed. "People like me, you mean – too busy with their lives to want to stop work."

"If that's the way you want to think of it, son."

The man's dark clothes were slightly shabby, and not what Martin expected of a museum attendant, particularly the loose leather jacket, sleeveless and rubbed smooth with wear. Dress regulations were plainly relaxed for night staff.

Martin, suddenly embarrassed by his own silence as he studied the man's clothes, said, "I have to apologise. You must have stayed on late to let me out."

The attendant was amused. "That's no problem at all, son. We keep a night watch hereabouts."

"Nevertheless . . ." Martin began, then changed his tack. "Well I must be on my way and let you get on with your night's work . . . your patrols, or whatever you have to do." He nodded towards the large bunch of keys in the man's hand, "Locking up, and that sort of thing."

"Locking up . . ." The thin smile pushed up wrinkles that turned his eyes into watery slits that glinted in the last of the sun. "Plenty of that, oh yes."

Martin grinned a shade uncomfortably with the golden glint of the eyes on him. "I hope you can *unlock* doors as well as lock them or I shan't get home tonight."

"Enjoy the fresh air while you have the chance, *Mr Glover*." The man still mocked his name, as if to deprive him of his title.

Martin made a mild attempt to correct him. "You haven't chased me off the roof," he said, "so I imagine my name is on a list of people allowed behind the scenes."

It had no effect. "There's always a list, Mr Glover, always a list."

"Well I'm very pleased to be on the right one." Suicides were still on Martin's mind. "But I'm afraid I don't know your name, Mr . . ."

"Me name is Jack, but that don't matter . . . you won't be around when I'm here next."

That could be true. Martin, the historian, had almost finished his work among the records kept in the old dungeons, but it rankled that the nightwatchman was dismissing him so curtly.

The man had turned away and the sunlight no longer showed his face. "We've had our glimpse of daylight," he said, "so now it's time to go." Another order, but Martin had no reason to disobey. He had had a profitable day and his laptop held many files that would fill out the detail of his research.

He crossed the roof and began descending the stair into the heart of the Castle. Above him keys rattled as the door to the roof was locked. It seemed an unnecessary precaution. No thief could possibly scale the Castle walls to make an entry, but perhaps locking up was a measure to prevent people coming out onto the roof from below . . .

"Suicide . . ." The nightwatchman's voice broke into his thoughts. "You'd be surprised at how often it's in their minds when I bring 'em up here."

Martin turned and looked up. A skylight at the top of the steep stair framed the foreshortened figure of the nightwatchman as he came down. He was as squat as a frog.

"As you work nights," said Martin, "you don't take tour parties up here so I suppose it's only the odd person like me who is allowed on the roof alone."

"That's right. People just like you . . . but the ones you've got to watch is them who've got out of the habit of daylight, if you know what I mean." No, Martin did not understand him, but the descending figure was pressing him and he had to turn and continue going down. "I take 'em up as a kindness, so as they can see the world spread out on every side, but it's then I've got to watch 'em most of all . . . talk about trying to cheat the hangman!"

The nightwatchman was laughing as they came down to the open floor that had once been the Great Hall of the Castle. Martin pushed thoughts of suicide out of his mind, but for a moment he trembled and felt very small at the edge of the huge emptiness. Without its daytime visitors the Castle brooded on too many secrets, and even though the museum exhibits in their glass cases were still illuminated and shed a familiar and friendly glow, the ceiling high overhead was a shroud of darkness.

He turned to the watchman. "I wouldn't blame you if you kept these lights on all night."

"Not up to me, son. They go off all by theirselves."

"Then I imagine you are pretty lonely, Jack." It was the first time he had used the man's name, but it sounded ingratiating as if he sought companionship in facing a childish fear of the dark.

"I wouldn't say lonely. I've always enjoyed my work."

"I mean there are so many strange things here to work on the imagination." Martin turned and marched swiftly to where an iron grating was set in the centre of the floor. "Take this, for example."

They stood on each side of the grating and looked down. A vertical shaft had been cut through the rock and they gazed down through the long funnel that had been rigged with lights but nevertheless ended in darkness far below.

"I know it's only a well, but it's dark down there at the bottom. Gives me the creeps." Martin shuddered. The well had always made him uneasy even when, feeling like a child himself, he had stood among crowds of children kneeling on the grating to let pennies fall into the darkness. He stepped back. "Too big a drop for me," he said.

The watchman did not appear to have heard him. He stood with head bent, contemplating the depth of the pit, and the light from below emphasised his heavy brow, the spread of his nostrils, and the severe line of his mouth as he concentrated. "Yes," he said, and blew out his breath in a grim chuckle. "I've seen men sprung apart in a drop not half so big as that."

"Sprung apart? What does that mean?"

"Don't ask . . . or I might tell you." The watchman lifted his head and the shadows flung up from the light below distorted his smile. He was gloating at the thoughts he had put into Martin's mind. "It's not something a young feller would want to know about – not in your situation."

"What situation is that?" Martin was angry and expected an answer, but none came. Instead, the watchman motioned him to step ahead and lead the way across the Great Hall. Martin, on the verge of defying him, hesitated. And then it was too late. There was a hint of malice in the watchman's steady stare that persuaded him to swallow his pride and obey. He went ahead, but it was a mistake. He felt like a schoolboy . . . or worse. The faint jangle of keys at his back compelled him to think of the watchman as his jailer which, in effect, he was. There was no way out of the Castle without him.

The lights in the exhibition cases suddenly went out and he stumbled. It betrayed his nervousness, and he felt foolish because there was enough pale greyness in the air from the arrow slits in the Castle wall to show him the way to the next chamber. He apologised for the stumble.

"And they call *me* clumsy!" There was a bitter edge to the watchman's voice. "Some of 'em reckon I'm a bungler, but not one of 'em would do the job I do. Never. They haven't the nerve."

"I suppose it's the night work they don't like." Martin was sympathetic, but the response was a laugh so harsh he felt the back of his neck crawl.

"It's not the night they don't like – it's the morning! It's what has to be done when the sun comes up – that's what makes 'em go all lily-white."

Martin manoeuvred so that the watchman was no longer completely behind him but alongside. "What is it they have to do . . . in the morning?"

"They have to open up the place, don't they? But there's one door in particular they don't want to open, ain't there?" The bristled head turned towards him. "And you know what door that is, I reckon."

Martin did know. It was suddenly obvious what was happening. The nightwatchman had detected his anxiety and was putting him through something that happened several times every day. The old Castle, in more recent times, had been a prison and parties were conducted through what little remained intact of those brutal days. It was an entertainment. The guides made the prison tour as gruesome as they could, and there was one place in particular where to be told of the unlocking of a door at dawn gave tourists a ghastly thrill.

"It's the door of the execution chamber," said Martin.

"You got nerve, son. A lot of people in your shoes don't want to know about it."

"In my shoes?"

"You're standing there talking about it when you know what's coming."

Martin was ignorant of what came next. It was his guide who knew what would happen.

"I can open that door and I don't feel a thing," said the watchman, "but some o' them others always jib at it."

The man loved his work. His grim pleasure was to make people fear him. Dread at being alone in the Castle with such a man must have shown in Martin's face. Jack the watchman detected it.

"There's nothing to worry about, son," he said. "I'm good at me job." His chuckle was a rasp as if he was clearing phlegm. "None of me clients ever complained . . . yet."

Too much talk of death. Martin was caught up in the night-watchman's world. He was losing himself, as if he was a scared child.

Too much like a child. He wanted to be safe at home . . . with his mother and father, as if they were still alive.

He and the watchman had entered part of the Castle where each room led into others in a confusing honeycomb. "It's very late." His mouth was dry and, like the terrified boy he had become, he had to lick his lips before he went on. "I don't need to fetch my papers from down below, I'll just leave straight away."

He had begun to cross the room before he realised he did not know which way to go. The honeycomb was a maze and he was not sure which archway led to the foyer and the outer door. To take the wrong one would make confusion even worse.

He paused, and turned. The watchman had not budged.

"Lost your way, son?"

"If you could just point me in the right direction . . ."

"And even then you wouldn't get far without these." The watchman, smiling, held up his bunch of keys and jangled them softly.

The room was a picture gallery lit only by the blue glow of the emergency lights close to the floor. Martin felt its dimness close around him. He was trapped. Then the watchman spoke.

"Nothing to worry about, son. You'll be out and away in just a few minutes. I can guarantee you that."

And Martin's head sagged with relief. Jack the watchman was playing a game with him. He was still acting out the daytime tour to give him an idea of what the Castle meant to those who were not allowed the privileges of scholars.

"I'm tired." He yawned and his eyes were closed as he listened. The watchman was still playing his part. He had the voice for it; harsh and without pity.

"Some of them tell me they'll be glad when it's all over. After all that time down in them dark dungeons they come up here as quiet as lambs. They don't even want to go for that little walk on the roof that we just had. Everyone knows I always offer – but some just don't want me to take 'em."

There was silence. Martin kept his eyes closed. The nightwatchman would see that he was not afraid. The game was over.

"You know where you are, son."

He did know. More than a hundred years ago this picture gallery had not existed. It had been part of the prison.

He felt a hand on his arm. Jack the watchman changed his tone. He gave orders. "You've had your walk, lad. Now it's time to go."

The grip tightened, and Martin opened his eyes.

The light in the room had changed, but that could only be the effect of having had his eyes closed. The light was yellow, like the pale glow of candles, and the walls were dull and seemed to have closed in. The ceiling, too, was lower, and in the centre of the room was something he had not noticed. At first he took it for an open doorway until he realised it was no more than a doorframe, free-standing in the middle of the floor.

He opened his mouth to ask a question when, from one side of the room, what seemed to be a group of people entered in single file, gliding silently until they stood behind the open doorway. It was then he saw that the framework was no door. It was a gallows. A noose hung from the centre beam.

It was all a trick. The figures were no more than a shadow show, a projection on the wall to entertain visitors. And only the nightwatch-man could have switched it on. Martin moved to tell him so, but before he could even look over his shoulder his arms were forced together behind his back and his wrists were bound.

He opened his mouth to cry out but the cord at his wrists was twisted and bit into his flesh with a spasm that arched him backwards.

"It's no good, lad." The watchman's voice rasped in his ear. "You know you got to go through with it."

He gritted his teeth. "Go through with what!"

"You should never have done what you done," said Jack. "You knew this was coming."

And in that moment Martin did know what lay ahead. Every sinew in his body tautened and he twisted. He felt his shirt sleeve rip, and he backed away. But he got no further than a single step. He stood against a stone wall. Cold stone. And the floor was stone. Except for the wooden flap of the trap in the centre, under the noose.

"It ain't no use." It was Jack's voice.

There was no way out. He had slipped from century to century. Even his clothes were different. His prison shirt had been torn in his struggle. His feet were clammy in the cold leather of his shoes. The gallows were in front of him and there was nowhere to go.

"You know you got to go through with it, lad. You was a naughty boy, wasn't you?"

Martin shrank from the voice. It spoke the truth. He was a boy. He was wicked. He had put his skinny fingers into a purse and pulled out a coin.

"You done it, so you knew this was coming. I give you a walk on the roof, didn't I? Like I do to everyone I has to deal with. I give you a breath of fresh air and let you see the countryside, but then I bring you down here and you got to face it."

There were tears on his face, but there was no chance to cry out. He was choked to silence by heavy fingers across his face.

"You don't want to be gagged now, do you, son?"

The fingers relaxed and as they did so Martin ceased to struggle.

"That's more like it, boy. Now I want you to step forward."

He heard himself whimper. Then the voice of the hangman. "Three steps . . . that's all it takes."

He was gripped and pushed. He saw the outline of the trap in the floor, and his feet were kicked until he stood on it.

His legs were bound. The rope brushed his head, but there was no hood. He felt the knot of the noose tighten under his ear. The rope was rough on his neck. He struggled, silently, lithe as a cat, writhing like a dangling man but with his feet still scuffling the solid trapdoor. And now came the hood, and blackness. The cloth was against his mouth and his last breath was muffled as the trap fell away beneath him, and he dropped.

Then nothing . . .

blankness . . .

darkness . . .

Pain flashed white in his brain, and a voice was saying something.

The hangman had bungled. His neck was not broken. He struggled to free his arms from the cords. There were no cords.

The voice again: "Dr Glover . . . can you hear me? We've been looking for you. You weren't in your office and we found you here . . ."

He lay on a hard floor. He moved an arm. He was not shackled. A flashlight blinded him, and he shielded his eyes.

"We thought you must've gone onto the roof for a breath of air, but there was no sign of you."

Suddenly he was sitting up. There were two men. "Who are you!"

"Night staff. We've just found you."

He looked around wildly. He was in the picture gallery. The light was dim except for the beam stabbing into his eyes. No gallows. He slid his hand over the polished floor. No sign of a trapdoor.

"Where is he?" he said

The men were crouched beside him. Who did he mean, they asked.

"Jack," he said. He scrambled to his feet. "Where's the one they call Jack?"

The men were silent for a moment. Then one of them said, "There's only us two, Dr Glover – Maurice and Fred, we do the night watch together."

Silence. He looked from one to the other. Maurice and Fred. He opened his mouth but no words came.

"You must have fainted, Doctor. Did you hurt yourself?"

"No . . . no, there's nothing wrong with me." He looked around the gallery. He got to his feet without help, and after a moment turned cautiously to face them. "Long ago," he said, knowing that he spoke slyly, "I believe this room had another purpose. Is that so?"

Both men smiled. "You mean when it was a prison?" said Maurice, the leader. "Someone's been telling you the old story." He nodded towards the corner. "It's true enough. The gallows used to be over there, in the execution chamber."

Martin's mouth was too dry to speak. He was unsteady, and Maurice noticed. "Let's go down to your room, Dr Glover, and we'll get you a drink."

Sitting at his desk with the companionship of two others he began to recover. "I didn't know anything about the gallows but I certainly felt strange in that room," he said.

They both nodded. "Fred and I can tell you that something lingers in places like that, and if you weren't feeling too good, well . . ." Maurice shrugged.

Martin had only hinted at his nightmare, but he had to test what had happened. "I was told . . ." he began and then corrected himself. "People say there have been a lot of suicides here . . . people leaping from the Castle walls."

"I've never heard of any," said Maurice, and Fred agreed.

"But there's a list," Martin insisted.

Both men looked blank and shook their heads and in his exasperation Martin suddenly burst out, "Jack told me the Castle kept a record!" Jack again, and there was no Jack. He looked away. "I'm sorry."

It was Fred, the quieter of the two, who shuffled for a moment before he stood up and went to a filing cabinet in the corner of the tiny room that had at one time been a dungeon. He had to rummage before he took out what looked like an old account book and laid it on Martin's desk. "I don't know about suicides," he said, "but I reckon this is a sort of register."

Martin opened it. In fact it was an account book with columns marked in red ink. There was a list of dates and against each was a person's name, and beneath that another name and then a sum of money. In each case the amount was one guinea.

Martin looked up. "They can't be suicides."

"No, Doctor. Not suicides, but they all died here in the Castle. They were executed here. Murderers mostly."

He looked again at the columns. The names of hanged men, their age, and against each one the name of his trade. On the line beneath every one was written: *Paid J. Ketch, one guinea.*

"That was for a job well done, Doctor Glover." Both watchmen were smiling. "Jack Ketch was the name this city used to give to the public hangman – so as no one knew who he really was."

"And they do say that Jack made all his clients suffer," said Maurice. "Kind of played with them before he turned them off. And he never got the drop right so they suffered a lot more than they had to – more strangled than hanged."

Martin nodded. His eyes dipped again to the page, the column of names and, at the bottom of the list, one in particular: Martin Jones, aged twelve, thief, and then the trade he was apprenticed to . . . *glover.*

CHRISTOPHER FOWLER

The Luxury of Harm

CHRISTOPHER FOWLER HAS WRITTEN many award-winning novels and collections of short stories. His 2003 book *Full Dark House* won the British Fantasy "August Derleth" Award for Best Novel and was also a finalist for the Crime Writer Association's Dagger Award. *The Water Room* was short-listed for the CWA's People's Choice Award in 2004, and he won British Fantasy Awards for his short story "American Waitress" the same year and for his novella "Breathe" in 2005.

When he's not writing horror or dark comedy, he's creating new adventures for Bryant & May, his elderly detectives of the sinister. He lives in King's Cross, London, with a very nice view of St Paul's Cathedral. His latest novel is *White Corridor*, and his upcoming collection of twenty-one new short stories is titled *Old Devil Moon*.

As Fowler admits: "'The Luxury of Harm' is a mean-spirited blend of real-life events that included being Best Man at an old friend's wedding and going to a horror festival in an English coastal town. I don't think I'll be invited back after they read this."

WHEN I WAS ELEVEN, I was warned to stay away from a new classmate with freckles and an insolent tie, so naturally we became inseparable partners in disruption, reducing our educators to tears of frustration.

For the next eight years our friendship proved mystifying to all. Simon horrified our teachers by illegally racing his Easy Rider motorbike across the football field. We took the deputy headmaster's car to pieces, laying it out in the school car park as neatly as a

stemmed Airfix kit. We produced a libellous school magazine with
jokes filched from TV programmes, and created radio shows mocking everyone we knew. When you find yourself bullied, it's best to
team up with someone frightening. Simon perverted me from learning, and I made his soul appear salvageable whenever he super-glued
the school cat or made prank phone-calls. I fretted that we would get
into trouble, and he worked out how we could burn down the school
without being caught.

Boys never tire of bad behaviour. Through the principals of
economics and the theory of gravity, the Wars of the Roses and
Shakespeare's symbolism, we cut open golf balls and tied pupils up in
the elastic, carved rocket-ships into desks and forged each others'
parental signatures on sick notes.

During puberty, Simon bought a mean leather jacket. I opted for
an orange nylon polo-neck shirt with Velcro fastenings. He looked
like James Dean. I looked like Simon Dee. In order to meet girls, we
signed up for the school opera. Simon met a blue-eyed blonde
backstage while I appeared as a dancing villager in a shrill, off-
key production of *The Bartered Bride*. We double-dated. I got the
blonde's best friend, who had legs like a bentwood chair and a
complexion like woodchip wallpaper, but her father owned a sweet
shop so we got free chocolate. I rang Simon's girlfriends for him
because he was inarticulate, and hung around his house so much that
his mother thought I'd been orphaned. Our friendship survived
because he gave me visibility, confidence and a filtered charisma
that reached me like secondary smoking. He stopped me from
believing there was no one else in the world who understood me.
And there he remained in my mind and heart, comfortable and
constant, throughout the years, like Peter Pan's shadow, ready to be
reattached if ever I needed it, long after his wasteful, tragic death.

But before that end came, we shared a special moment. By the time
this happened, we had gone our separate ways; he became the
conformist, with a country home and family, and I turned into
the strange one, living alone in town. Recontacting Simon, I persuaded him to come to a horror convention with me, in a tiny
Somerset town called Silburton, where the narrow streets were
steeped in mist that settled across the river estuary, and fishing boats
lay on their sides in the mud like discarded toys. The place reeked of
dead fish, tar and rotting shells, and the locals were so taciturn it
seemed that conversation had been bred out of them.

The hotel, a modern brick block that looked like a caravan site
outhouse, had no record of our booking, and was full because of the

convention. In search of a guesthouse, we found a Bed & Breakfast place down beside the river ramps and lugged bags up three flights through narrow corridors, watching by the landlady in case we scratched her Indian-restaurant wallpaper. The beds felt wet and smelled of seaweed.

By the time we returned to the convention hotel, the opening night party was in full swing. A yellow-furred alien was hovering uncertainly in the reception area, struggling to hold a pint mug in his rubber claws, and a pair of local Goth girls clung to the counter, continually looking around as though they were afraid that their parents might wander in and spot them, raising their arms to point and scream like characters from *Invasion of the Body Snatchers*.

Every year the convention had a theme, and this year it was "Murderers on Page and Screen", so there were a few Hannibal Lecters standing around, including a grinning lad with the top of his head sawn off. The bar staff took turns to stare at him through the serving hatch.

"Is this really what you do for fun?" Simon asked me, amazed that I could take pleasure from hanging out with guys dressed as Jason and Freddy, films no one even watched any more. "Who comes to these things?"

"Book people, lonely people," I said simply, gesturing at the filling room. "Give it a chance," I told him. "There's no attitude here, and it gets to be fun around midnight, when everyone's drunk. Come on, you said your life was very straight. This is something new."

Simon looked unsure; he hardly ever read, so the dealers' rooms, the panels and the literary conversation held no interest for him. He talked about his kids a lot, which was boring. I wanted him to be the kid I'd admired at school. He could relate to drinking, though, and relaxed after a couple of powerful local beers that swirled like dark sandstorms in their glasses. Simon could drink for England. "So," he asked, "are they all writers looking for tips?"

"In a way. Take this year's theme. We're intrigued by motivation, method, character development. How do you create a realistic murderer? Who would make a good victim?" I tried to think of a way of involving Simon in my world. "Take the pair of us, for example. I'm on my home turf here. People know me. If I went missing, there would be questions asked. For once, you're the outsider. You were once the tough guy, the bike-riding loner nobody knew, and you're unknown here. That would make you the perfect victim."

"Why?" Simon wasn't the sort to let something beat him. His interest was piqued, and he wanted to understand.

"Because taking you out would require an act of bravery, and would be a show of strength. Killers seek notoriety to cover their inadequacies. But they also enjoy the remorse of loss."

Simon snorted. "How the hell does that work?"

"There's a strange pleasure to be taken in melancholy matters, don't you think? A kind of tainted sweetness. Look at the Goths and their fascination with death and decay."

"Okay, that's the victim sorted, so who's the killer?"

"Look around. Who would you choose?"

Simon scoped out the bar area. "Not the Jason or Freddy look-alikes. They're geeks who would pass out at the sight of a paper cut. They'd be happy to watch, but they wouldn't act."

"Good, keep going."

"And the Goths couldn't kill, even though they're professional mourners. They look tough but play gentle."

"Excellent."

"But him, over there." He tapped his forefinger against the palm of his hand, indicating behind him. "He looks like he's here to buy books about guys who murder their mothers. It wouldn't be such a big step to committing a murder."

"Yeah, we get a few of those at conventions. They sit in the front row at the Q&As, and are always the first to raise their hands with a question. There's one guy, a retired doctor, who even gives me the creeps. Over there." I pointed out the cadaverous Mr Henry, with his greasy comb-over and skin like the pages of a book left in the sun. He never missed a convention, even though he wasn't a writer or publisher, or even a reader. "He once told me he owns one of the country's largest collections of car crash photographs, and collects pictures of skin diseases."

"That's gross. I knew there would be freaks here."

"Relax, he's too obvious. If there's one trick to serial killer stories, it's making sure that the murderer is never someone you suspect. Have you noticed there are some very cute girls hanging around the bar?"

"You're right about that," Simon grudgingly admitted, watching two of them over the top of his glass.

"You should go and make their acquaintance," I suggested. "I'll just be here talking weird books with old friends, or the other way around."

I got into a long discussion/argument about the merits of *Psycho II* and *III*, about Thomas M. Disch and William Hope Hodgson and what makes a good story, and lost all track of the time. I only checked my watch when the waiter started pulling shutters over the bar. Bidding farewell to my fellow conventioneers, I staggered off through the damp river air toward the guest-house.

Somehow I managed to overshoot the path, and ended up on the seaweed-slick ramp to the harbour. The only sounds were the lapping of the water and the tinging of masts. The tide was coming in, and the boats were being raised from their graves like reanimating corpses. Drunk and happy and suddenly tired, I sat down on the wet brown sand and allowed the sea-mist to slowly reveal its secrets. It formed a visible circle around me, like the kind of fog in a video game that always stays the same distance no matter how hard you run. A discarded shovel someone had used to dig for lugworms stood propped against the harbour wall. Orange nylon fishing nets, covered with stinking algae, were strung out like sirens' shawls.

And through the mist I gradually discerned a slender figure, his head lolling slightly to one side, one arm lower than the other, like the skeleton in Aurora's "Forgotten Prisoner" model kit, or the one that features on my cover of *The Seventh Pan Book of Horror Stories*. It was standing so still that it seemed to be more like the unearthed figurehead of a boat than a man.

There was a strong smell of ozone and rotting fish. The figure raised a ragged, dripping sleeve to its skull, rubbing skin to bone. It seemed as though it had ascended from the black bed of the sea.

"I fell off the fucking dock and tore my jacket. I am so incredibly slaughtered," said Simon, before tipping over and landing on his back in the sand with a thump.

The next morning, screaming seagulls hovered so close to my bedroom window that I could see inside their mouths. Shafts of ocean sunlight bounced through the window, punching holes in my brain. My tongue tasted of old duvet. I needed air.

I knocked on Simon's door, but there was no answer. Breakfast had finished, and the landlady had gone. The Easy Rider motorbike still stood in the car park behind the guest house.

The tide was out and the mist had blown away, leaving the foreshore covered in silvery razor-clams and arabesques of green weed. On the stone walkway above the harbour, an elderly lady in a tea-cosy hat marched past with a shopping bag. There was no one else about. The gulls shrieked and wheeled.

Carefully, I walked across the beach to the spot where Simon had fallen, and knelt down. It took a moment to locate the exact place. Rubbing gently at a patch of soft sand, I revealed his sand-filled mouth, his blocked nostrils, one open shell-scratched eye that stared bloodily up into the sky. I rose and stood hard on his face, rocking back and forth until I had forced his head deeper into the beach. I carefully covered him over with more sand, smoothing it flat and adding some curlicues of seaweed and a couple of cockleshells for effect. Finally I threw the shovel I had used on his neck as far as I could into the stagnant water of the harbour.

As I headed back to the convention hotel, ready to deliver my lecture on "Random Death: The Luxury of Harm", a heartbreaking happiness descended upon me. I knew that there would be plenty of time to savour the full delicious loss of my old friend in the days, the months, the years to come.

MARK SAMUELS

Sentinels

MARK SAMUELS WAS BORN in Clapham, London. He is the author of two collections, *The White Hands and Other Weird Tales* and *Black Altars*, as well as the novella *The Face of Twilight*. His third collection of short stories is provisionally titled *Glyphotech and Other Macabre Processes* and is scheduled to be published by Midnight House.

His stories have appeared in both *The Mammoth Book of Best New Horror* and *The Year's Best Fantasy and Horror* series, along with such recent anthologies as *Summer Chills*, *Inferno* and *Alone on the Darkside*. He has been nominated twice for the British Fantasy Award.

"When my friend Adam Clayton brought out his non-fiction book *Subterranean City* in 2000," Samuels recalls, "its publication reawakened in me an interest in the abandoned 'ghost' stations of the London Underground tube network, which I then began to research in more detail.

"This research somehow got mixed up in my imagination with a 1970s film called *Deathline* starring one of my favourite actors, Donald Pleasance. His portrayal of a seedy police inspector, in turn, got mixed up with 'Death and the Compass' by Jorge Luis Borges. This story is the final result."

INSPECTOR GRAY'S INVOLVEMENT in the affair was due to a combination of ill fortune and the photographic cover of a London "urban legends" paperback called *The Secret Underground*. He should not really have been in that part of London at the time, but had been forced to stay late in the office and complete a batch of gruelling paperwork required by his superior the following morning. Had he driven past a matter of seconds before, he would have seen nothing. After all, he was off-duty and his main concern was to get back to his dingy flat in Tufnell Park, sink a few glasses of whiskey and forget about that day.

He planned to lose himself in some cheap and trashy horror paperback from his little collection. The TV had broken down months ago and instead of replacing it he found that he had got into the habit of reading musty book relics from the '60s and '70s, with their yellowing, brittle pages and lurid covers. Gray fancied himself something of a connoisseur when it came to the covers; in fact he felt himself in opposition with the old maxim about never judging a book by them. He harboured the conviction that those featuring a weird photographic composition were invariably superior to those that had artwork depicting the tired cliché-symbols of horror; skulls, snakes or gothic castles for example.

In fact, he had come in for some jokes at his expense back at the Yard over his choice of reading matter. Most of his colleagues talked about little except what they watched on TV the night before, often sleazy porn videos that they'd "loaned" from the Obscene Publications division. They'd taken to calling him "The Weird Detective" behind his back and on one occasion he'd turned around sharply to find a group of constables miming having vampire fangs by putting their index fingers at the corners of their mouths. Gray made sure thereafter that he wasn't seen reading any of his books during the little time he had for lunch. Instead he read one of the broadsheet papers as he consumed his sandwiches at his desk. His alienation from his colleagues caused him pain and he suspected that the department would run more smoothly were he not there.

What Gray saw as he passed by in his car appeared to be some sort of stunted, emaciated creature peering through the trellis gates of Kentish Town Underground Station. The thing was only around four or five feet tall and dressed in black ragged overalls. Its face was obscured by a mass of dusty shoulder-length hair.

It was gone 1:00 a.m. when Gray passed the Underground Station, and it had been closed for only a short time. He had pulled over to the side of the road and looked back in order to see whether the apparition was still there, but there was no sign of it at all. Doubtless, he thought, his colleagues back at the Yard would have laughed at what he thought he saw; too many of those damn books he read. But Gray felt his heart racing in his chest. He could not dismiss the thing that easily from his mind. What he'd seen was no product of the imagination. It had really been there.

Although the station was closed, it might not yet be deserted. Once the train service finished there were still staff working on the platforms and in the tunnels. An army of cleaners called "Fluffers" made their way along the lines and scoured them for debris. All manner of litter had to be cleared away, beer-cans, half-eaten junk food, newspapers, even tumbleweeds composed of skin and human hair. There was also the "Gangers"; the engineers who checked track safety. Perhaps Gray had simply glimpsed one of those overnight workers having a break, one whose similarity to the uncanny thing on the front cover of *The Secret Underground* was nothing more than a trick of the light.

Nevertheless, what he had observed remained in his thoughts, causing uneasy dreams when he finally slept: dreams of endless subterranean tunnels and of a gaunt silence punctuated by a distant rustling or whispering noise. Had he not seen whatever it was at the station (or whatever *he thought* it was) the case that came to his attention afterwards might not have seemed significant and worth pursuit.

As he sat at his desk the next morning, sipping at a cup of vile instant coffee, Gray flicked through the case files in his in-box. He had a feeling that had become increasingly commonplace during the course of the last few months. It was that the investigations to which he had been assigned were effectively a waste of effort. The assault that he'd suffered months ago during the arrest of Montrose the serial rapist had left him hospitalised for weeks and resulted in internal ruptures that would, he had been advised by the surgeon, require a much more sedate lifestyle. The Yard had done the best they could under the circumstances and found him a role, albeit desk bound, but although his initial assignments had been current Gray discovered that as time passed he was being asked to examine cases that had little chance of being solved. The bulk of these were missing persons.

Scarcely sociable before, Gray had turned further inwards after the beating. It had affected his mind just as much as his body. Somehow he had allowed his old friends to drift away and found excuses not to keep in touch with them. He felt himself to be little more than an empty shell and contact with others only served to reinforce the impression. The Yard offered Gray counselling to help him come to terms with the trauma caused by the Montrose incident, but he found the idea even more repellent than his doctor's suggestion that he take

a course of anti-depressants. When fate worked upon him he
intended to adapt to it and not resist. Even so, he felt like a missing
person who had himself been assigned to trace other missing persons.

Gray ran his tongue over his scalded lips, again cursing the too-hot
and foul-tasting coffee, when his attention was taken up by a
communiqué that had come in only a few hours earlier. Although
a missing persons report is not usually filed until some days after a
disappearance (except where children are involved), this one had
been "fast-tracked" due to there being no question of the subject
having absented himself deliberately. The missing individual was a
tube train driver (or "operator" as they were now called). His name
was Adam Drayton. The curious thing was this: he had abandoned
his train between the Camden Town and Kentish Town stations on
the Northern Line. It had been the very last service of the night, due
to terminate at High Barnet at 1:30 a m. Moreover, if there had been
any passengers in the carriages then they too had vanished.

Early in the morning a replacement driver had shunted the train
into a siding. On the front of the case file a joker in the office had
scrawled the words "Mary Celeste Tube? A Case for the Weird
Detective?" with a marker pen.

But Inspector Gray, through some bizarre coincidence, was one of
the few people who would recognise the name "Adam Drayton" in
another connection. For it was also the name of the author/editor of
that outré book of urban legends published under the title *The Secret
Underground*, whose cover preyed upon his mind.

Gray spent the afternoon interviewing Drayton's colleagues in the
staff mess room of the train depot just outside Finchley Central
Station. This was where the tube drivers spent their time between
shifts, sitting around drinking coffee, smoking their cigarettes and
reading newspapers. They were a talkative bunch although the
inspector could not help noticing their mistrust and fear of him as
a representative from an outside authority. Some of them even
seemed to believe that Drayton's disappearance was an internal
matter and should be left to the union to investigate. Outside
interference, whether from the law or elsewhere, was certainly not
welcome. Still, there were one or two who retained a sense of
individuality and were able to realise that Gray had not come in
order to apportion any blame, merely to discover what may have led
Drayton to act in the manner that he did.

One of the drivers, Carlos Miguel, a Castilian, was particularly
communicative. He had settled in this country after leaving Madrid

in the early 1990s. He had been almost alone in befriending Drayton, who had been regarded by the others as an oddball whose political views were not sufficiently radical. Miguel was a tall, distinguished man in his forties with a shock of jet-black hair and a neatly trimmed moustache. He had shared Drayton's enthusiasm for the recondite and whilst the others talked of union activities or the football results, the two men had retreated to a corner and held their own discussions.

Had Gray not been aware of Drayton's editorship of that paperback *The Secret Underground* he doubted that he would have achieved quite the same rapport with Carlos Miguel.

"So," the Spaniard declared, "you know of *el libro de Drayton*?"

"Yes," Gray replied, "I think it's a bit garish but the cover's particularly . . ."

Miguel cut in.

"*Señor*, you know that Drayton only applied to become a train operator so that he could travel the tunnels of the Northern Line and examine their mysteries?"

Gray looked blank and shook his head.

"Well," Miguel went on, "you must understand that it would not be mistaken to say that he was obsessed with them. Drayton told me that the Northern Line has the longest continuous Yerkes tunnel on the network, over seventeen miles long. The stretch between East Finchley and Morden. Also it has the deepest. At Hampstead 900 feet below ground. He had numerous theories about what was down there; *fantástico, ¿no?*"

"Speculations, rumour, hearsay," Gray responded, "amounting to nothing more than fiction. He was just an editor of a horrible series of urban legends. I confess that the parallel between his disappearance and obsession is striking but . . ."

"*Perdón, señor*, but it is more than that simple fact. Drayton was my friend; it was in me that he felt he could confide. *Las estaciones fantasmas*, you know of them? In English: the ghost stations? North End, City Road, South Kentish Town and King William Street? These were what obsessed Drayton."

"The abandoned stations?"

"*Sí*, abandoned. *Pero* in Drayton's eyes, *no*. Taken over he would have replied. No longer safe to use. *Señor*, if you are operating the last train on the line it is easier to slow down when you wish, no? Perhaps while travelling through one of those stations and even bringing trains to a complete stop. There are not so many passengers and they are too drunk or sleepy to complain at that time of night, *¿tú comprendes?*"

"Are you suggesting that Adam Drayton stopped his train and got out at one of these ghost stations?"

"*Como una palomilla atraída por la llama . . .*"

"I don't understand."

". . . like a moth drawn to a flame."

That evening, once Gray had got back to his cramped flat in Tufnell Park, he sat down in his easy chair with his copy of *The Secret Underground*. He flicked back and forth through its yellowed brittle pages, glancing at them over and over again. The book was divided into several chapters, each specialising in a subterranean urban legend: (1) Cases of Posthumous Mutation in London Cemeteries (2) Derelict reverse Skyscrapers 1936–57 (3) Mass disappearance of Persons sheltering in the Underground during the Blitz (4) Graffiti or Occult Symbolism? (5) Suppressed Eyewitness accounts during the Construction of the Underground Railways 1860–1976 (6) The Fleet Line extension to Fenchurch Street must be Halted (7) Secret Bunkers or Extermination Centres? (8) The deep level Platforms of the proposed Express Tube: Why they caused Insanity (9) The Hidden Shafts that connect Subterranean London.

There was one paragraph in the final chapter that seemed to be the inspiration for the uneasy dreams Gray had experienced. It ran as follows:

"*Most of the city is now underground and not above the surface, and I scarcely need list its innumerable tunnels, subterranean car parks, cellars, crypts, bunkers, basements, vaults, passageways, and sewers. Every building in London has an underside buried deep in the earth. Beneath our feet are the ruins of Anglo-Saxon Lundenwic and of Roman Londinium. The contemporary city will, in time, be swallowed up. This neon and concrete labyrinth will become an Atlantis of catacombs. The higher we build up, the deeper it is necessary to build down in order to support the structures above. All the nightmare sewage that we pump into the depths, all the foulness and corruption, the abortions, the faeces and scum, the blood and diseased mucus, but mostly the hair: what a feast for those underground beings that exist in darkness, and shun the sunlight! Those things below hate us and have every reason to do so.*"

His attention kept jumping from the text to the series of bizarre black and white photographs throughout the book. Quite where Drayton had obtained them from was not made clear; they were not credited. They may even have come from his personal collection. What they showed was this:

(Front cover) A blurred humanoid figure seen from a passing tube train whose face is almost completely covered by its hair. Between the strands there seems to be a mouth lined with shark-like fangs. The haggard creature is backing into a siding, away from the light.

(pg.18) A photographic record of a series of exhumed graves with empty coffins whose bases had been torn apart.

(pg.33) A blueprint of a subterranean reverse-tower with forty-five storeys and access shafts radiating from it in all directions, some leading to burial grounds, others to sewers etc. bearing the legend "North End (Hampstead)".

(pg.49) What appears to be a series of bloody, smeared handprints on the white wall tiles of British Museum Station during its use as an air-raid shelter circa 1941.

(pg.87) Human bones, including a skull, photographed lying alongside the tracks of an Underground tunnel.

(pg.102) Graffiti scrawled (in charcoal?) on the side of 1972 Mk. 1 train stock that reads "THE HUNGRY CANNOT SLEEP", "WE CRAWL THROUGH GRAVES", "THE DARKNESS BEHIND YOUR EYES" and "BELOW THERE IS ONLY PAIN".

(pg.126) A sewer chamber choked by vast quantities of hair hanging from a curved ceiling of Victorian brickwork.

It was relatively easy for Gray to obtain a search warrant in order to enter the disused South Kentish Town station. Although above ground the building was now occupied by a massage parlour where once the ticket hall had been, all the subterranean shafts, corridors and other passageways were still owned by London Underground. Since their abandonment there had been no reason to maintain them and parts of the former station were unsafe. In order to gain access Gray had to agree to be accompanied by a track maintenance engineer who worked on that stretch of the Northern Line and who was familiar with the site.

This engineer, John Heath, arranged to meet Gray outside the massage parlour at the corner of Kentish Town Road and Castle Place. The inspector parked his car directly in front of the building and was struck by the fact that its exterior still had the appearance of an Underground Station, lacking only the familiar sign displayed outside. Hanging around in front of the entrance to the newsagents was a small man in a yellow safety helmet and boiler suit. He carried a heavy bag with a sub-contractors' logo on it. His hands were entirely covered with a thick layer of soot. Doubtless it was the man who been assigned to assist Gray.

Heath looked just like a throwback to the 1960s. His hippie-length hair was brittle and grey as dust. Over his mouth and nose he wore a loose protective mask. He also wore a pair of John Lennon style glasses with thick lenses that made the eyes behind them look liquid. He was really quite horribly ridiculous.

After Gray had produced his police ID, the two went inside, and the Inspector explained their purpose to the owners of the massage parlour (who seemed relieved that the search was not connected with what went on at their premises). Then Heath, consulting a map of the structure, led Gray down into a storage cellar at the back of the establishment where access to the emergency stairs could be gained.

The old lift shafts were useless. Their cages and all the workings had been removed back when the station was closed in 1924, but the stairway to the upper lift landing and the emergency staircase to the lower lift landing were passable. The entry doors were padlocked and Heath sought and tried several keys drawn from his bag before he found the correct ones to use.

"They," Heath said, his voice muffled by the baggy mask covering his mouth and nose, "told me why you want to get down here. Anyway it's pointless. We already looked for Drayton. All you're doing is putting yourself in danger."

"I'll be the judge of that," replied Gray, "just get on with it. You do your job and I'll do mine, okay?"

"Watch your step as we go. These old passageways are treacherous. Even if you don't wind up falling into a ventilation shaft, you might stumble in front of a passing train. Hear the noise?"

As he unlocked the door there came from far below in the depths the sound of carriages rumbling along distant tracks, followed moments later by a powerful draught of musty air.

Heath chuckled. He turned on a powerful torch and aimed its beam along the stairway and around to the dark-green tiled walls at the turn ahead. The steps were littered with debris.

Gray was amazed at how familiar and yet how strange their surroundings appeared. Like any Londoner he had used the tube system on innumerable occasions and had passed through the subterranean mazes of many stations, though always when they were illuminated by overhead strip lighting, with hurried passengers making their way to or from a platform. But here the darkness was in control and every echoing footfall reinforced the grim feeling of total isolation. And yet it was only the withdrawal of light and of other people that created this feeling: actually it was just the same as any other tube station would be after the services had stopped running. Except that this was no temporary interruption to be resumed in the morning. This really was what Carlos Miguel called *Una estación fantasma.*

"Did you know Adam Drayton?" Gray asked in order to break the gaunt silence between the sound of passing trains.

He could only see the back of Heath. The engineer's slightly hunched form crept downwards along the steps, apparently intent solely upon what he was doing. But he finally responded after what seemed to be a considered pause.

"Oh yes," Heath said, "I knew *of* him all right. He was legendary on the Northern Line. Kept stopping his train at odd places and holding up the services. Only worked at night, when it didn't matter so much. The union stepped in to stop him getting the sack, said he was worried about safety."

"Safety?"

"The union said it was faulty signals that were to blame. And strange noises on the track. Made him cautious. Better to be safe than sorry. Go-slow is preferable to taking chances. That's what the union said."

They had reached the bottom of the stairway and emerged onto the upper lift landing. The tiles here were a grimy cream and red colour. In the circle of light cast by Heath's torch, he caught glimpses of advertising posters from the early 1920s that had been left up on the tiled walls of the corridor ahead; LIFEBUOY, BOVRIL, OXO, WRIGLEY'S and GUINNESS. Another tube train roared through one of the tunnels below and the accompanying blast of air flapped the torn parts of the posters.

"What do you know about the disused stations here on the Northern Line? Have you seen the others for yourself?" Gray asked.

"I know something. I've been in them all at one time or another. They have a bad reputation. The most significant is North End or the 'Bull & Bush' as the train operators like to call it." Heath responded.

"Why significant?"

"The floodgates, y'know," said Heath. "Instead of the tube station that was going to be there in 1906 they developed it into a central command centre. Certain stations on the network have the gates, but they're all controlled from North End. Reckon the building goes down more than a thousand feet, though only the higher levels were initially used. It was started in the 1940s so they could stop the entire Underground system being flooded. Most of the gates were individually controlled before then."

"How could the whole system be flooded?"

"If the Nazis had dropped a bomb in the Thames the tunnels under the river could have collapsed. Within ten minutes the Underground system would have been completely filled with water and submerged, y'know. Well, that's what they said. Later on, in the early 1970s, they built a second zone of gates just outside stations like Shepherds Bush, Aldgate East and Bounds Green, before where the tracks emerge overground."

"What have they got to do with flooding?"

"Nothing. But they thought people would go mental when the three-minute warnings went off and try to run along the tracks into the train tunnels to escape from Soviet atom bombs. Well, you get the idea . . ."

By now they'd reached the emergency spiral stairway, which led much further downward to the lower lift landing. It was considerably steeper than the previous stairway and Gray kept a hand against the wall as the two men descended. Their footfalls echoed as if ghosts were following close behind.

"Talking of weird stuff like that, you know about the Sentinel Train?" Heath asked. He didn't wait for an answer before continuing with his topic, "First stop King William Street station along the abandoned spur, runs down to Borough without halting, then reverses up the Bank branch of the Northern Line. Only stops at the ghost stations along the route; nowhere else, goes on to City Road, right here to South Kentish Town, then back via Camden, before terminating at the deepest of all: North End, under Hampstead Heath. Anyway, I told you about that one, didn't I? The Sentinel lets the inspection crews examine the stuff the public never sees. Company doesn't leave the traction current to the rails on overnight, so a diesel locomotive pulls the old F Stock carriages. The train has a free run on the deserted tracks. Happens once a week or thereabouts. Every tube line has its own Sentinel."

"Are you pulling my leg?" Gray replied testily. "That's straight out of Drayton's book. It seems to me you must have read it."

They'd reached the lower lift landing.

"This passageway leads to the north and southbound platforms," Heath said, "but they're long gone."

Were the idea not totally ridiculous Gray could have mistaken his companion for something dressed up in a boiler suit in order to pass as human. His colleagues at the Yard would have laughed at his suspicion. But he could not shake off the impression that, in the darkness, Heath's appearance was genuinely similar to the figure that Gray had glimpsed peering out of the trellised gates of Kentish

Town Station. That was only a few nights ago and one stop along the Northern Line from this ghost station. He'd seen it with his own eyes and the experience was not drawn from the pages of a crazy book like *The Secret Underground*. Gray could easily believe that this character Heath had not just read the volume but had stepped out from its pages into life.

"You didn't answer my question." Gray said. From his coat pocket he drew a packet of Benson & Hedges cigarettes.

"What one was that again?" Heath snuffled.

"The one about having read *The Secret Underground*." Gray responded as he jammed one of the smokes between his lips and touched the end with the flame from a battered old Zippo. A faint smell of petrol wafted from the lighter. He drew on the cigarette and exhaled, sending curling blue smoke across the beam of Heath's torch.

"Oh, that . . . look, you can't smoke down here. It's dangerous."

"Do you see any 'No Smoking' signs around? Anyway I'm sure your mask will protect you."

Heath paused and regarded the glowing tip of Gray's cigarette. He finally came back to the point.

"Yeah, I've read that book. I know it off by heart. It's a favourite of mine."

From further back along the passageways Gray thought he detected a rustling noise, like a pile of leaves dispersed by the wind. But, before he was able to tell from which direction it came, the racket of a passing northbound train drowned them out. Gray thought he heard Heath muttering.

It sounded like ". . . bigmouth . . . Miguel . . . he's sorted . . ." but most of these words were also lost in the roar.

It was obvious that Heath knew something about Drayton's disappearance and may even have had a hand in it. Perhaps he was also dangerously obsessed with all those ghost stations and had come to regard Drayton as his rival. In any case, the place to interview Heath was back at the Yard, not here and now. Gray's back and stomach ached; the old ruptures were playing up again. It was time to get back to the surface. There was nothing down here that was of any use to his investigation. Besides, although Heath was small, Gray feared that he was dealing with a lunatic.

There was that damn rustling again, like leaves! It sounded closer this time. Heath seemed not to notice it though and coldly regarded Gray smoking his cigarette, glaring through narrowed eyes that swam behind the thick lenses of his glasses.

"Well," said Gray, "I've seen everything I want to see here. Let's get back to the surface.

"All right," Heath replied, "but you ain't looked yet. To come all this way and not look at it would be a waste of my time and yours."

"Look at what exactly?"

"Over there in the corner. Thirty yards, right up against the wall." Heath flashed the torch's beam onto what appeared to be a large pile of rags. "Go and see. I already know what it is. I'll stay where I am. In case you're worried, like."

As he got nearer, Gray glanced back to make sure that Heath made no attempt to creep up on him. What he believed was a pile of rags was in fact a body slumped in the angle between wall and floor, its face turned towards the tiles. The back of its skull was smashed in. Dried blood caked the matted hair. As he turned the body over, Gray guessed that its face would be unfamiliar; he expected it to be Drayton, whom he'd never seen. But it was the Spaniard, Carlos Miguel. Heath had not moved an inch whilst Gray examined the corpse, but something living dropped from the darkness of the ceiling onto him and the impact drove the police inspector crashing to the floor.

His head struck the concrete and he blacked out.

Gray awoke in a tube train carriage. He felt nauseous with pain as consciousness returned. He ran his fingers over his head and found half a dozen scratches and wounds around his face and on the back of his skull. There was a stabbing pain in his stomach and he was aware of feeling wet around the seat of his trousers. The fall had reopened some of his old internal ruptures and blood was leaking out of his lower intestine.

Although racked with pain, he forced himself to take in the details of his surroundings. He was on a moving train, one that hurtled through the tunnels at breakneck speed.

The floor was littered with prostrate bodies. Some were hanging by their necks from knotted leather straps attached to the ceiling rails. All had been recently murdered and bore signs of mutilation. There were dozens of the corpses packed into the carriage. Their limbs protruded at misshapen angles from the humps of flesh and clothing. Extreme terror and pain marked their facial expressions. The body of Carlos Miguel lay amongst the charnel crowds. Like the Castilian, Gray had been left for dead.

Somehow he'd come to be a passenger in a carriage that appeared to date from, he guessed, the 1920s. The carriage lights were single bulbs housed in Art-Deco glass oysters with a very wide aisle running between the longitudinal seating. It must have been antiquated rolling stock, for there were advertisements from that far-off decade above the windows and the Underground map showed routes such as the Hampstead and Highgate Line, the City and South London Railway and the Central London Railway. Back then the Victoria and Jubilee lines had not even been thought of, let alone built. Moreover, the map was like a complicated tangle of spaghetti and not modelled on the famous Beck circuit-board design.

Struggling to his feet and clutching the pole at the end of the seats, Gray stood in a daze for a moment, rocking with the motion of the train. His wristwatch showed 1:20 a.m. He'd been out cold for well over eight hours. His left trouser leg stuck to the inside of his thigh, where the stream of blood oozing from his rectum had partially dried. He picked his way through the corpses and found that he was trapped in the last carriage of the train and the connecting door to the penultimate carriage had been welded shut.

Gray crept back to a seat and peered through the window to the tunnels outside. Suddenly the train entered a platform, without slowing, and he pressed his face to the glass in order to try and make out the station name as it flashed past. The light from the interior of the carriages projected enough illumination for him to see a faded sign reading NORTH END. It also just made visible the stunted, faceless forms that haunted the shadows of passageways further back – forms that shunned the light, but which welcomed the arrival of the Sentinel with malefic glee, chattering deafeningly in the semi-darkness.

Gray had no doubt that the inner and outer gates were closed right the way across the Underground network, now that the Sentinel had completed its journey. He harboured the notion that these gates served a purpose quite different from the official one and were used to prevent escape along the tracks to the surface. Drayton had described many pieces of the jigsaw in his book *The Secret Underground*. Gray had not fitted them together until it was too late and would finally solve the mystery in the labyrinthine reaches of an industrial Sheol.

In his mind's eye he saw a vision in which the disparate chapters of Drayton's book merged to form a coherent explanation of what was happening. It was an explanation involving a series of derelict reverse skyscrapers, one of which was beneath North End, whose ultimate depth was probably over a thousand feet; a structure populated by beings who were sometimes bored with the repast foraged by using the smaller tunnels that led to the cemeteries and burial grounds across London. Could it be possible that the feasters had absorbed some of the characteristics of the corpses upon which they preyed, as in cannibalistic folklore?

He thought of an abandoned train and its driver . . . *Como una palomilla* . . . of a man called Heath with thick eyeglasses, his face obscured, and who knew as much as Drayton himself . . .

As he thought about the ghost stations on the Piccadilly Line, the Central Line, the Metropolitan Line and all the others, he guessed that each doubtless had its own Sentinel operating that night as well.

Suddenly, the lights in all the carriages went out.

Acting on the signal, as they'd done so many times in the past, they surged up from the edifice's black abyss of corridors and debris-choked rooms in a ravenous tide.

As the stunted forms eagerly scrambled across the divide between them and the train, he finally realised that, in order to keep them down there in the dark, to prevent them overrunning London altogether, it was necessary for them to be fed.

Gray only had time to scream once in the darkness.

ELIZABETH HAND

The Saffron Gatherers

ELIZABETH HAND IS THE multiple-award-winning author of eight novels, including *Generation Loss* and *Mortal Love*, and three collections of short fiction, the most recent being *Saffron & Brimstone: Strange Stories*. She lives on the coast of Maine.

" 'The Saffron Gatherers' is the last tale in a four-story sequence titled 'The Lost Domain'," the author reveals, "which deals with the themes of creative and erotic obsession.

"All four tales are set in a post-9/11 world resembling our own; in the case of 'The Saffron Gatherers', a dark world that is just now being born."

H E HAD ALMOST BEEN as much a place to her as a person; the lost domain, the land of heart's desire. Alone at night she would think of him as others might imagine an empty beach, blue water; for years she had done this, and fallen into sleep.

She flew to Seattle to attend a symposium on the Future. It was a welcome trip – on the East Coast, where she lived, it had rained without stopping for thirty-four days. A meteorological record, now a tired joke: only six more days to go! Even Seattle was drier than that.

She was part of a panel discussion on natural disasters and global warming. Her first three novels had presented near-future visions of apocalypse; she had stopped writing them when it became less like fiction and too much like reportage. Since then she had produced a series of time-travel books, wish-fulfilment fantasies about visiting the ancient world. Many of her friends and colleagues in the field had turned to similar themes, retro, nostalgic, historical. Her academic background was in classical archeology; the research was joyous, if exhausting. She hated to fly, the constant round of threats and delay. The weather and concomitant poverty, starvation, drought, flooding, riots – it had all become so bad that it was like an extreme sport now, to visit places that had once unfolded from one's imagination in the brightly-colored panoramas of 1920s postal cards. Still she went, armed with eyeshade, earplugs, music and pills that put her to sleep. Behind her eyes, she saw Randall's arm flung above his head, his face half-turned from hers on the pillow. Fifteen minutes after the panel had ended she was in a cab on her way to SeaTac. Several hours later she was in San Francisco.

He met her at the airport. After the weeks of rain back East and Seattle's muted sheen, the sunlight felt like something alive, clawing at her eyes. They drove to her hotel, the same place she always stayed; like something from an old B-movie, the lobby with its ornate cast-iron stair-rail, the narrow front desk of polished walnut; clerks who all might have been played by the young Peter Lorre. The elevator with its illuminated dial like a clock that could never settle on the time; an espresso shop tucked into the back entrance, no bigger than a broom closet.

Randall always had to stoop to enter the elevator. He was very tall, not as thin as he had been when they first met, nearly twenty years earlier. His hair was still so straight and fine that it always felt wet, but the luster had faded from it: it was no longer dark-blonde but grey, a strange dusky color, almost blue in some lights, like pale damp slate. He had grey-blue eyes; a habit of looking up through downturned black lashes that at first had seemed coquettish. She had since learned it was part of a deep reticence, a detachment from the world that sometimes seemed to border on the pathological. You might call him an agoraphobe, if he had stayed indoors.

But he didn't. They had grown up in neighboring towns in New York, though they only met years later, in DC. When the time came to choose allegiance to a place, she fled to Maine, with all those other writers and artists seeking a retreat into the past; he chose Northern California. He was a journalist, a staff writer for a glossy magazine that only came out four times a year, each issue costing as much as a bottle of decent sémillon. He interviewed scientists engaged in paradigm-breaking research, Nobel Prize-winning writers; poets who wrote on their own skin and had expensive addictions to drugs that subtly altered their personalities, the tenor of their words, so that each new book or online publication seemed to have been written by another person. Multiple Poets' Disorder, Randall had tagged this, and the term stuck; he was the sort of writer who coined phrases. He had a curved mouth, beautiful long fingers. Each time he used a pen, she was surprised again to recall that he was left-handed. He collected incunabula – *Ars oratoria*, Jacobus Publicus's disquisition on the art of memory; the *Opera Philosophica* of Seneca, containing the first written account of an earthquake; Pico della Mirandola's *Hetaplus* – as well as manuscripts. His apartment was filled with quarter-sawn oaken barrister's bookcases, glass fronts bright as mirrors, holding manuscript binders, typescripts, wads of foolscap bound in leather. By the window overlooking the Bay, a beautiful old mapchest of letters written by Neruda, Beckett, Asaré. There were signed broadsheets on the walls, and drawings, most of them inscribed to Randall. He was two years younger than she was. Like her, he had no children. In the years since his divorce, she had never heard him mention his former wife by name

The hotel room was small and stuffy. There was a wooden ceiling fan that turned slowly, barely stirring the white curtain that covered the single window. It overlooked an airshaft. Directly across was another old building, a window that showed a family sitting at a kitchen table, eating beneath a fluorescent bulb.

"Come here, Suzanne," said Randall. "I have something for you."

She turned. He was sitting on the bed – a nice bed, good mattress and expensive white linens and duvet – reaching for the leather mailbag he always carried to remove a flat parcel.

"Here," he said. "For you."

It was a book. With Randall it was always books. Or expensive tea: tiny, neon-colored foil packets that hissed when she opened them and exuded fragrances she could not describe, dried leaves that looked like mouse droppings, or flower petals, or fur; leaves that, once infused, tasted of old leather and made her dream of complicated sex.

"Thank you," she said, unfolding the mauve tissue the book was wrapped in. Then, as she saw what it was, "Oh! *Thank* you!"

"Since you're going back to Thera. Something to read on the plane."

It was an oversized book in a slipcase: the classic edition of *The Thera Frescoes*, by Nicholas Spirotiadis, a volume that had been expensive when first published, twenty years earlier. Now it must be worth a fortune, with its glossy thick photographic paper and fold-out pages depicting the larger murals. The slipcase art was a detail from the site's most famous image, the painting known as "The Saffron Gatherers." It showed the profile of a beautiful young woman dressed in elaborately-patterned tiered skirt and blouse, her head shaven save for a serpentine coil of dark hair, her brow tattooed. She wore hoop earrings and bracelets, two on her right hand, one on her left. Bell-like tassels hung from her sleeves. She was plucking the stigma from a crocus blossom. Her fingernails were painted red.

Suzanne had seen the original painting a decade ago, when it was easier for American researchers to gain access to the restored ruins and the National Archaeological Museum in Athens. After two years of paperwork and bureaucratic wheedling, she had just received permission to return.

"It's beautiful," she said. It still took her breath away, how modern the girl looked, not just her clothes and jewelry and body art but her expression, lips parted, her gaze at once imploring and vacant: the 15-year-old who had inherited the earth,

"Well, don't drop it in the tub." Randall leaned over to kiss her head. "That was the only copy I could find on the net. It's become a very scarce book."

"Of course," said Suzanne, and smiled.

"Claude is going to meet us for dinner. But not till seven. Come here—"

They lay in the dark room. His skin tasted of salt and bitter lemon; his hair against her thighs felt warm, liquid. She shut her eyes and imagined him beside her, his long limbs and rueful mouth; opened her eyes and there he was, now, sleeping. She held her hand above his chest and felt heat radiating from him, a scent like honey. She began to cry silently.

His hands. That big rumpled bed. In two days she would be gone, the room would be cleaned. There would be nothing to show she had ever been here at all.

They drove to an Afghan restaurant in North Beach. Randall's car was older, a second-generation hybrid; even with the grants and tax breaks, a far more expensive vehicle than she or anyone she knew back east could ever afford. She had never gotten used to how quiet it was.

Outside, the sidewalks were filled with people, the early evening light silvery-blue and gold, like a sun shower. Couples arm-in-arm, children, groups of students waving their hands as they spoke on their cell phones, a skateboarder hustling to keep up with a pack of *parkeurs*.

"Everyone just seems so much more absorbed here," she said. Even the panhandlers were antic.

"It's the light. It makes everyone happy. Also the drugs they put in our drinking water." She laughed, and he put his arm around her.

Claude was sitting in the restaurant when they arrived. He was a poet who had gained notoriety and then prominence in the late 1980s with the "Hyacinthus Elegies," his response to the AIDS epidemic. Randall first interviewed him after Claude received his MacArthur Fellowship. They subsequently became good friends. On the wall of his flat, Randall had a handwritten copy of the second elegy, with one of the poet's signature drawings of a hyacinth at the bottom.

"Suzanne!" He jumped up to embrace her, shook hands with Randall then beckoned them both to sit. "I ordered some wine. A good cab I heard about from someone at the gym."

Suzanne adored Claude. The day before she left for Seattle, he'd sent flowers to her, a half-dozen delicate *narcissus serotinus*, with long white narrow petals and tiny yellow throats. Their sweet scent perfumed her entire small house. She'd emailed him profuse but also wistful thanks – they were such an extravagance, and so lovely; and she had to leave before she could enjoy them fully. He was a few years younger than she was, thin and muscular, his face and skull hairless save for a wispy black beard. He had lost his eyebrows during a round of chemo and had feathery lines, like antenna, tattooed in their place and threaded with gold beads. His chest and arms were heavily tattooed with stylized flowers, dolphins, octopi, the same iconography Suzanne had seen in Akrotiri and Crete; and also with the names of lovers and friends and colleagues who had died. Along the inside of his arms you could still see the stippled marks left by hypodermic needles – they looked like tiny black beads worked into the pattern of waves and swallows – and the faint white traces of an adolescent suicide attempt. His expression was gentle and melancholy, the face of a tired ascetic, or a benign Antonin Artaud.

"I should have brought the book!" Suzanne sat beside him, shaking her head in dismay. "This beautiful book that Randall gave me – Spirotiadis' Thera book?"

"No! I've heard of it, I could never find it. Is it wonderful?"

"It's gorgeous. You would love it, Claude."

They ate, and spoke of his collected poetry, forthcoming next winter; of Suzanne's trip to Akrotiri. Of Randall's next interview, with a woman on the House Committee on Bioethics who was rumored to be sympathetic to the pro-cloning lobby, but only in cases involving "only" children – no siblings, no twins or multiples – who died before age fourteen.

"Grim," said Claude. He shook his head and reached for the second bottle of wine. "I can't imagine it. Even pets . . ."

He shuddered, then turned to rest a hand on Suzanne's shoulder. "So: back to Santorini. Are you excited?"

"I am. Just seeing that book, it made me excited again. It's such an incredible place – you're there, and you think, What could this have been? If it had survived, if it all hadn't just gone *bam*, like that—"

"Well, then it would really have gone," said Randall. "I mean, it would have been lost. There would have been no volcanic ash to preserve it. All your paintings, we would never have known them. Just like we don't know anything else from back then."

"We know *some* things," said Suzanne. She tried not to sound annoyed – there was a lot of wine, and she was jet-lagged. "Plato. Homer . . ."

"Oh, *them*," said Claude, and they all laughed. "But he's right. It would all have turned to dust by now. All rotted away. All one with Baby Jesus, or Baby Zeus. Everything you love would be buried under a Tradewinds Resort. Or it would be like Athens, which would be even worse."

"Would it?" She sipped her wine. "We don't know that. We don't know what it would have become. This—"

She gestured at the room, the couple sitting beneath twinkling rose-colored lights, playing with a digital toy that left little chattering faces in the air as the woman switched it on and off. Outside, dusk and neon. "It might have become like this. "

"This." Randall leaned back in his chair, staring at her. "Is this so wonderful?"

"Oh yes," she said, staring back at him, the two of them unsmiling. "This is all a miracle."

He excused himself. Claude refilled his glass and turned back to Suzanne. "So. How are things?"

"With Randall?" She sighed. "It's good. I dunno. Maybe it's great. Tomorrow – we're going to look at houses."

Claude raised a tattooed eyebrow. "Really?"

She nodded. Randall had been looking at houses for three years now, ever since the divorce.

"Who knows?" she said. "Maybe this will be the charm. How hard can it be to buy a house?"

"In San Francisco? Doll, it's easier to win the stem cell lottery. But yes, Randall is a very discerning buyer. He's the last of the true idealists. He's looking for the *eidos* of the house. Plato's *eidos*; not Socrates'," he added. "Is this the first time you've gone looking with him?"

"Yup."

"Well. Maybe that *is* great," he said. "Or not. Would you move out here?"

"I don't know. Maybe. If he had a house. Probably not."

"Why?"

"I don't know. I guess I'm looking for the *eidos* of something else. Out here, it's just too . . ."

She opened her hands as though catching rain. Claude looked at her quizzically.

"Too sunny?" he said. "Too warm? Too beautiful?"

"I suppose. The land of the lotus-eaters. I love knowing it's here, but." She drank more wine. "Maybe if I had more job security."

"You're a writer. It's against Nature for you to have job security."

"Yeah, no kidding. What about you? You don't ever worry about that?"

He gave her his sweet sad smile and shook his head. "Never. The world will always need poets. We're like the lilies of the field."

"What about journalists?" Randall appeared behind them, slipping his cell phone back into his pocket. "What are we?"

"Quackgrass," said Claude.

"Cactus," said Suzanne.

"Oh, gee. I get it," said Randall. "Because we're all hard and spiny and no one loves us."

"Because you only bloom once a year," said Suzanne.

"When it rains," added Claude.

"That was my realtor." Randall sat and downed the rest of his wine. "Sunday's open house day. Two o'clock till four. Suzanne, we have a lot of ground to cover."

He gestured for the waiter. Suzanne leaned over to kiss Claude's cheek.

"When do you leave for Hydra?" she asked.

"Tomorrow."

"Tomorrow!" She looked crestfallen. "That's so soon!"

"'The beautiful life was brief,'" said Claude, and laughed. "You're only here till Monday. I have a reservation on the ferry from Piraeus, I couldn't change it."

"How long will you be there? I'll be in Athens Tuesday after next, then I go to Akrotiri."

Claude smiled. "That might work. Here—"

He copied out a phone number in his careful, calligraphic hand. "This is Zali's number on Hydra. A cell phone, I have no idea if it will even work. But I'll see you soon. Like you said—"

He lifted his thin hands and gestured at the room around them, his dark eyes wide. "This is a miracle."

Randall paid the check and they turned to go. At the door, Claude hugged Suzanne. "Don't miss your plane," he said.

"Don't wind her up!" said Randall.

"Don't miss yours," said Suzanne. Her eyes filled with tears as she pressed her face against Claude's. "It was so good to see you. If I miss you, have a wonderful time in Hydra."

"Oh, I will," said Claude. "I always do."

Randall dropped her off at her hotel. She knew better than to ask him to stay; besides, she was tired, and the wine was starting to give her a headache.

"Tomorrow," he said. "Nine o'clock. A leisurely breakfast, and then . . ."

He leaned over to open her door, then kissed her. "The exciting new world of California real estate."

Outside, the evening had grown cool, but the hotel room still felt close: it smelled of sex, and the sweetish dusty scent of old books. She opened the window by the airshaft and went to take a shower. Afterwards she got into bed, but found herself unable to sleep.

The wine, she thought; always a mistake. She considered taking one of the anti-anxiety drugs she carried for flying, but decided against it. Instead she picked up the book Randall had given her.

She knew all the images, from other books and websites, and the island itself. Nearly four thousand years ago, now; much of it might have been built yesterday. Beneath fifteen feet of volcanic ash and pumice, homes with ocean views and indoor plumbing, pipes that might have channeled steam from underground vents fed by the volcano the city was built upon. Fragments of glass that might have been windows, or lenses. The great pithoi that still held food when they were opened millennia later. Great containers of honey for trade, for embalming the Egyptian dead. Yellow grains of pollen. Wine.

But no human remains. No bones, no grimacing tormented figures as were found beneath the sand at Herculaneum, where the fishermen had fled and died. Not even animal remains, save for the charred vertebrae of a single donkey. They had all known to leave. And when they did, their city was not abandoned in frantic haste or fear. All was orderly, the pithoi still sealed, no metal utensils or weapons strewn upon the floor, no bolts of silk or linen; no jewelry.

Only the paintings, and they were everywhere; so lovely and

beautifully wrought that at first the excavators thought they had uncovered a temple complex.

But they weren't temples: they were homes. Someone had paid an artist, or teams of artists, to paint frescoes on the walls of room after room after room. Sea daffodils, swallows; dolphins and pleasure boats, the boats themselves decorated with more dolphins and flying seabirds, golden nautilus on their prows. Wreaths of flowers. A shipwreck. Always you saw the same colors, ochre-yellow and ferrous red; a pigment made by grinding glaucophane, a vitreous mineral that produced a grey-blue shimmer; a bright pure French blue. But of course it wasn't French blue but Egyptian blue – Pompeiian blue – one of the earliest pigments, used for thousands of years; you made it by combining a calcium compound with ground malachite and quartz, then heating it to extreme temperatures.

But no green. It was a blue and gold and red world. Not even the plants were green.

Otherwise, the paintings were so alive that, when she'd first seen them, she half-expected her finger would be wet if she touched them. The eyes of the boys who played at boxing were children's eyes. The antelopes had the mad topaz glare of wild goats. The monkeys had blue fur and looked like dancing cats. There were people walking in the streets. You could see what their houses looked like, red brick and yellow shutters.

She turned towards the back of the book, to the section on Xeste 3. It was the most famous building at the site. It contained the most famous paintings – the woman known as the "Mistress of Animals." "The Adorants," who appeared to be striding down a fashion runway. "The Lustral Basin."

The saffron gatherers.

She gazed at the image from the East Wall of Room Three, two women harvesting the stigma of the crocus blossoms. The flowers were like stylized yellow fireworks, growing from the rocks and also appearing in a repetitive motif on the wall above the figures, like the fleur-de-lis patterns on wallpaper. The fragments of painted plaster had been meticulously restored; there was no attempt to fill in what was missing, as had been done at Knossos under Sir Arthur Evans' supervision to sometimes cartoonish effect.

None of that had not been necessary here. The fresco was nearly intact. You could see how the older woman's eyebrow was slightly raised, with annoyance or perhaps just impatience, and count the number of stigmata the younger acolyte held in her outstretched palm.

How long would it have taken for them to fill those baskets? The crocuses bloomed only in autumn, and each small blossom contained just three tiny crimson threads, the female stigmata. It might take 100,000 flowers to produce a half-pound of the spice.

And what did they use the spice for? Cooking; painting; a pigment they traded to the Egyptians for dyeing mummy bandages.

She closed the book. She could hear distant sirens, and a soft hum from the ceiling fan. Tomorrow they would look at houses.

For breakfast they went to the Embarcadero, the huge indoor market inside the restored ferry building that had been damaged over a century before, in the 1906 earthquake. There was a shop with nothing but olive oil and infused vinegars; another that sold only mushrooms, great woven panniers and baskets filled with tree-ears, portobellos, fungus that looked like orange coral; black morels and matsutake and golden chanterelles.

They stuck with coffee and sweet rolls, and ate outside on a bench looking over the Bay. A man threw sticks into the water for a pair of black labs; another man swam along the embankment. The sunlight was strong and clear as gin, and nearly as potent: it made Suzanne feel lightheaded and slightly drowsy, even though she had just gotten up.

"Now," said Randall. He took out the newspaper, opened it to the real estate section, and handed it to her. He had circled eight listings. "The first two are in Oakland; then we'll hit Berkeley and Kensington. You ready?"

They drove in heavy traffic across the Oakland-Bay bridge. To either side, bronze water that looked as though it would be too hot to swim in; before them the Oakland Hills, where the houses were ranged in undulating lines like waves. Once in the city they began to climb in and out of pocket neighborhoods poised between the arid and the tropic. Bungalows nearly hidden beneath overhanging trees suddenly yielded to bright white stucco houses flanked by aloes and agaves. It looked at once wildly fanciful and comfortable, as though all urban planning had been left to Dr Seuss.

"They do something here called 'staging'," said Randall as they pulled behind a line of parked cars on a hillside. A phalanx of realtors' signs rose from a grassy mound beside them. "Homeowners pay thousands and thousands of dollars for a decorator to come in and tart up their houses with rented furniture and art and stuff. So, you know, it looks like it's worth three million dollars."

They walked to the first house, a Craftsman bungalow tucked

behind trees like prehistoric ferns. There was a fountain outside, filled with koi that stared up with engorged silvery eyes. Inside, exposed beams and dark hardwood floors so glossy they looked covered with maple syrup. There was a grand piano, and large framed posters from Parisian cafés – Suzanne was to note a lot of these as the afternoon wore on – and much heavy dark Mediterranean-style furniture, as well as a few early Mission pieces that might have been genuine. The kitchen floors were tiled. In the master bath, there were mosaics in the sink and sunken tub.

Randall barely glanced at these. He made a beeline for the deck. After wandering around for a few minutes, Suzanne followed him.

"It's beautiful," she said. Below, terraced gardens gave way to stepped hillsides, and then the city proper, and then the gilded expanse of San Francisco Bay, with sailboats like swans moving slowly beneath the bridge.

"For four million dollars, it better be," said Randall.

She looked at him. His expression was avid, but it was also sad, his pale eyes melancholy in the brilliant sunlight. He drew her to him and gazed out above the treetops, then pointed across the blue water.

"That's where we were. Your hotel, it's right there, somewhere." His voice grew soft. "At night it all looks like a fairy city. The lights, and the bridges . . . You can't believe that anyone could have built it."

He blinked, shading his eyes with his hand, then looked away. When he turned back his cheeks were damp.

"Come on," he said. He bent to kiss her forehead. "Got to keep moving."

They drove to the next house, and the next, and the one after that. The light and heat made her dizzy; and the scents of all the unfamiliar flowers, the play of water in fountains and a swimming pool like a great turquoise lozenge. She found herself wandering through expansive bedrooms with people she did not know, walking in and out of closets, bathrooms, a sauna. Every room seemed lavish, the air charged as though anticipating a wonderful party; tables set with beeswax candles and bottles of wine and crystal stemware. Countertops of hand-thrown Italian tiles; globular cobalt vases filled with sunflowers, another recurring motif.

But there was no sign of anyone who might actually live in one of these houses, only a series of well-dressed women with expensively restrained jewelry who would greet them, usually in the kitchen, and make sure they had a flyer listing the home's attributes. There were plates of cookies, banana bread warm from the oven. Bottles of sparkling water and organic lemonade.

And, always, a view. They didn't look at houses without views. To Suzanne, some were spectacular; others, merely glorious. All were more beautiful than anything she saw from her own windows or deck, where she looked out onto evergreens and grey rocks and, much of the year, snow.

It was all so dreamlike that it was nearly impossible for her to imagine real people living here. For her a house had always meant a refuge from the world; the place where you hid from whatever catastrophe was breaking that morning.

But now she saw that it could be different. She began to understand that, for Randall at least, a house wasn't a retreat. It was a way of engaging with the world; of opening himself to it. The view wasn't yours. You belonged to it, you were a tiny part of it, like the sailboats and the seagulls and the flowers in the garden; like the sunflowers on the highly polished tables.

You were part of what made it real. She had always thought it was the other way around.

"You ready?" Randall came up behind her and put his hand on her neck. "This is it. We're done. Let's go have a drink."

On the way out the door he stopped to talk to the agent.

"They'll be taking bids tomorrow," she said. "We'll let you know on Tuesday."

"Tuesday?' Suzanne said in amazement when they got back outside. "You can do all this in two days? Spend a million dollars on a house?"

"Four million," said Randall. "This is how it works out here. The race is to the quick."

She had assumed they would go to another restaurant for drinks and then dinner. Instead, to her surprise, he drove to his flat. He took a bottle of Pommery Louise from the refrigerator and opened it, and she wandered about examining his manuscripts as he made dinner. At the Embarcadero, without her knowing, he had bought chanterelles and morels, imported pasta colored like spring flowers, arugula and baby tatsoi. For dessert, orange-blossom custard. When they were finished, they remained out on the deck and looked at the Bay, the rented view. Lights shimmered through the dusk. In a flowering quince in the garden, dozens of hummingbirds droned and darted like bees, attacking each other with needle beaks.

"So." Randall's face was slightly flushed. They had finished the champagne, and he had poured them each some cognac. "If this happens – if I get the house. Will you move out here?"

She stared down at the hummingbirds. Her heart was racing. The quince had no smell, none that she could detect, anyway; yet still they swarmed around it. Because it was so large, and its thousands of blossoms were so red. She hesitated, then said, "Yes."

He nodded and took a quick sip of cognac. "Why don't you just stay, then? Till we find out on Tuesday? I have to go down to San Jose early tomorrow to interview this guy, you could come and we could go to that place for lunch."

"I can't." She bit her lip, thinking. "No . . . I wish I could, but I have to finish that piece before I leave for Greece."

"You can't just leave from here?"

"No." That would be impossible, to change her whole itinerary. "And I don't have any of my things – I need to pack, and get my notes . . . I'm sorry."

He took her hand and kissed it. "That's okay. When you get back."

That night she lay in his bed as Randall slept beside her, staring at the manuscripts on their shelves, the framed lines of poetry. His breathing was low, and she pressed her hand against his chest, feeling his ribs beneath the skin, his heartbeat. She thought of canceling her flight; of postponing the entire trip.

But it was impossible. She moved the pillow beneath her head, so that she could see past him, to the wide picture window. Even with the curtains drawn you could see the lights of the city, faraway as stars.

Very early next morning he drove her to the hotel to get her things and then to the airport.

"My cell will be on," he said as he got her bag from the car. "Call me down in San Jose, once you get in."

"I will."

He kissed her and for a long moment they stood at curbside, arms around each other.

"Book your ticket back here," he said at last, and drew away. "I'll talk to you tonight."

She watched him go, the nearly silent car lost among the taxis and limousines; then hurried to catch her flight. Once she had boarded she switched off her cell, then got out her eyemask, earplugs, book, water bottle; she took one of her pills. It took twenty minutes for the drug to kick in, but she had the timing down pat: the plane lifted into the air and she looked out her window, already feeling not so much calm as detached, mildly stoned. It was a beautiful day, cloudless; later it would be hot. As the plane banked above the city she looked down at the skein of roads, cars sliding along them like beads or raindrops on a string. The traffic crept along 280, the road Randall would take to San Jose. She turned her head to keep it in view as the plane leveled out and began to head inland.

Behind her a man gasped; then another. Someone shouted. Everyone turned to look out the windows.

Below, without a sound that she could hear above the jet's roar, the city fell away. Where it met the sea the water turned brown then white then turgid green. A long line of smoke arose – no, not smoke, Suzanne thought, starting to rise from her seat; dust. No flames, none that she could see; more like a burning fuse, though there was no fire, nothing but white and brown and black dust, a pall of dust that ran in a straight line from the city's tip north to south, roughly tracking along the interstate. The plane continued to pull away, she had to strain to see it now, a long green line in the water, the bridges trembling and shining like wires. One snapped then fell, another, miraculously, remained intact. She couldn't see the third bridge. Then everything was green crumpled hillsides, vineyards; distant mountains.

People began to scream. The pilot's voice came on, a blaze of static then silence. Then his voice again, not calm but ordering them to remain so. A few passengers tried to clamber into the aisles but flight attendants and other passengers pulled or pushed them back into their seats. She could hear someone getting sick in the front of the plane. A child crying. Weeping, the buzz and bleat of cell phones followed by repeated commands to put them all away.

Amazingly, everyone did. It wasn't a terrorist attack. The plane, apparently would not plummet from the sky; but everyone was too afraid that it might to turn their phones back on.

She took another pill, frantic, fumbling at the bottle and barely getting the cap back on. She opened it again, put two, no three, pills into her palm and pocketed them. Then she flagged down one of the flight attendants as she rushed down the aisle.

"Here," said Suzanne. The attendant's mouth was wide, as though she were screaming; but she was silent. "You can give these to them—"

Suzanne gestured towards the back of the plane, where a man was repeating the same name over and over and a woman was keening. "You can take one if you want, the dosage is pretty low. Keep them. Keep them."

The flight attendant stared at her. Finally she nodded as Suzanne pressed the pill bottle into her hand.

"Thank you," she said in a low voice. "Thank you so much, I will."

Suzanne watched her gulp one pink tablet, then walk to the rear of the plane. She continued to watch from her seat as the attendant went down the aisle, furtively doling out pills to those who seemed to need them most. After about twenty minutes, Suzanne took another pill. As she drifted into unconsciousness she heard the pilot's voice over the intercom, informing the passengers of what he knew of the disaster. She slept.

The plane touched down in Boston, greatly delayed by the weather, the ripple affect on air traffic from the catastrophe. It had been raining for thirty-seven days. Outside, glass-green sky, the flooded runways and orange cones blown over by the wind. In the plane's cabin the air chimed with the sound of countless cell phones. She called Randall, over and over again; his phone rang but she received no answer, not even his voicemail.

Inside the terminal, a crowd of reporters and television people awaited, shouting questions and turning cameras on them as they stumbled down the corridor. No one ran; everyone found a place to stand, alone, with a cell phone. Suzanne staggered past the news crews, striking at a man who tried to stop her. Inside the terminal there were crowds of people around the TV screens, covering their mouths at the destruction. A lingering smell of vomit, of disinfectant. She hurried past them all, lurching slightly, feeling as though she struggled through wet sand. She retrieved her car, joined the endless line of traffic and began the long drive back to that cold green place, trees with leaves that had yet to open though it was already almost June, apple and lilac blossoms rotted brown on their drooping branches.

It was past midnight when she arrived home. The answering machine was blinking. She scrolled through her messages, hands shaking. She listened to just a few words of each, until she reached the last one.

A blast of static, satellite interference; then a voice. It was unmistakably Randall's.

She couldn't make out what he was saying. Everything was garbled, the connection cut out then picked up again. She couldn't tell when he'd called. She played it over again, once, twice, seven times, trying to discern a single word, something in his tone, background noise, other voices: anything to hint when he had called, from where.

It was hopeless. She tried his cell phone again. Nothing.

She stood, exhausted, and crossed the room, touching table, chairs, countertops, like someone on a listing ship. She turned on the kitchen faucet and splashed cold water onto her face. She would go online and begin the process of finding numbers for hospitals, the Red Cross. He could be alive.

She went to her desk to turn on her computer. Beside it, in a vase, were the flowers Claude had sent her, a half-dozen dead narcissus smelling of rank water and slime. Their white petals were wilted, and the color had drained from the pale yellow cups.

All save one. A stem with a furled bloom no bigger than her pinkie, it had not yet opened when she'd left. Now the petals had spread like feathers, revealing its tiny yellow throat, three long crimson threads. She extended her hand to stroke first one stigma, then the next, until she had touched all three; lifted her hand to gaze at her fingertips, golden with pollen, and then at the darkened window. The empty sky, starless. Beneath blue water, the lost world.

MARK MORRIS

What Nature Abhors

MARK MORRIS BECAME a full-time writer in 1988 on the British government's Enterprise Allowance Scheme, and a year later saw the publication of his first novel, *Toady*.

His thirteenth novel, *Doctor Who: Forever Autumn*, was recently released, and his fourteenth, *The Deluge*, will be published by Leisure Books. The author's short stories, novellas, articles and reviews have appeared in a wide variety of anthologies and magazines, and he is editor of the HWA Bram Stoker Award-nominated *Cinema Macabre*, a book of fifty horror movie essays by genre luminaries.

Forthcoming titles includes a *Hellboy* novel, *The All-Seeing Eye*, and a novella entitled *It Sustains*, which will be published by Earthling in summer 2008.

"'What Nature Abhors' was inspired by an otherwise extremely pleasant visit to Hampton Court Palace with my wife, Nel," Morris explains. "It was a sunny day, and we were strolling through the gardens when we came across the statue of a figure, the upper half of which was tightly draped in black plastic.

"A sign explained that the statue had been damaged by the elements and was awaiting restoration, but the sight of it, like an upright, partially concealed murder victim, was arresting, incongruous and deliciously eerie, and it stayed with me."

W HEN MEACHER OPENED his eyes the train was empty, though he had thought it was the jolt of the brakes that had woken him. He stood up, the low-level anxiety of disorientation already beginning to grind in his belly. The carriage was old and grimy, and smelled musty, as if each threadbare seat had absorbed too much sweat over too many years. The upholstery and stained carpet was predominantly grey with overlapping flecks in two shades of bilious green that jittered like TV interference on the periphery of his vision.

Outside the window the stone walls of the station building looked smoke-blackened, except for pale oblongs where the station's name-plates had been removed, probably by vandals. As far as Meacher could see, it was not only the train that was deserted but the platform too – and so profoundly, it seemed to him, that he suppressed the urge to call out, oddly fearful of how intrusive, or worse insignif-icant, his voice might sound in the enveloping silence.

Stepping into the aisle, he automatically reached towards the luggage rack above his head, but found it empty. Had he had a bag, or even a jacket, at the outset of his journey? It would have been unusual for him to have travelled with neither, but his brain felt so dulled by fatigue that he honestly couldn't remember. He sat down again, intimidated by solitude and by his own aberrant memory. He had a notion that the merest glimpse of a guard or another passenger, or perhaps even the incomprehensible blare of a station announcer's voice, would be all that he would need to restore his sense of himself and his surroundings.

However when he realised, ten minutes later, that he was actually holding his breath in anticipation of a hint of life besides his own, he decided he could be passive no longer. He stood up with a decisive-ness that was for no one's benefit but his and lurched along the length of the carriage, his arms pumping like a cross-country skier's as he yanked at seats to maintain his momentum.

Once on the platform he paused only briefly, so that he would not have to consciously acknowledge the absence of life. The EXIT sign caused his spirits to flare with a disproportionate fierceness if only because, albeit impersonal, it was a form of communication, and hinted at more to come. He stumped through the arch beneath the sign and found himself in a ticket office containing back-to-back rows of red metal seats and an unmanned ticket window. From above this too a name-plate had been removed, and with such care that Meacher wondered whether the place was understaffed because it was on the verge of closure.

The station was certainly small enough for this theory to be feasible, or at least appeared too inconsequential to have been granted a car park, because a further exit door led down a flight of stone steps and thence to what appeared to be a town centre side-street. Even out here there was no indication of life, though Meacher felt optimistic that he would encounter some sooner rather than later. There were signs of human occupation – the stink of stale urine as he had descended the steps, discarded confectionery wrappers and food cartons emblazoned with comfortingly iconic logos: McDonalds, Kit Kat, KFC. On the far side of a pedestrian crossing a chalked sign in a pub window promised BIG SCREEN SKY SPORTS! Meacher might have ventured inside to freshen his dry mouth with something sweet and fizzy if the pub's wooden doors, so hefty they put him in mind of a dungeon, had not been firmly shut.

The pub's neighbours were equally inaccessible. Indeed, a grubby jeweller's and a shop which contained second-hand musical instruments had reinforced their unwillingness to attract trade via the employment of metal shutters. Meacher wondered what time it was. If the shops were closed and the pub not yet open he guessed it must be somewhere between six and seven p.m. Looking up afforded him no clue, because the greyness between the rooftops more closely resembled a thick net stretched between the buildings than a portion of sky.

He started to walk, though had no real idea in which direction the town centre lay. The silence was so unnerving that even the tiny crackle of grit beneath his soles made him wince. The narrow streets with their shuttered store-fronts all looked the same, and after a while he began to wonder whether he was walking in circles. His mind still felt oddly inactive, as though unable to form thoughts of any substance. Every so often he didn't so much stop to listen as stumble to a halt, as if he was a machine that periodically needed to conserve its energy to recharge. Unless his senses were as faulty as his memory, it seemed he was utterly alone. There was neither the distant rumble of traffic, nor even the faintest trill of birdsong.

Perhaps it was Sunday and everything was shut. The thought was less a comfort, and more an attempt to prevent his sense of disquiet escalating into fear. In truth he knew that no town centre was ever *this* devoid of life. Something had happened here, probably while he had been asleep on the train. The town had been abandoned or evacuated for some reason, and somehow he had been overlooked.

Blundering to yet another halt he nervously sniffed the air. The only reason he could think of for such a wide-scale evacuation was the presence of some kind of severe physical threat. Was the place about to be bombed by terrorists or could the attack already be underway? Perhaps he was wandering around, blithely inhaling toxic fumes; perhaps germ warfare had come to middle England and he was gulping down anthrax spores or worse. Or perhaps, he thought, as he examined his skin and tried to convince himself that the nausea and breathlessness he was feeling were psychosomatic, the attack had already happened. Perhaps a nuclear bomb had been dropped close by and the town's population had been evacuated to protect them from the approaching cloud of radioactive dust.

There were flaws in his thinking, he knew that. But one thing was certain: he had to get to a phone, had to find out what was going on. He started to run, telling himself it was only stress that was making his lungs hurt and his legs feel leaden. But if so, what was it that was affecting his memory? He couldn't even remember getting on the train, never mind where he had been going, or for what reason.

As if his desperation for answers had made it happen, he suddenly emerged from the stultifying maze of drab streets full of shuttered buildings and found himself in a pedestrianised precinct leading to what appeared to be a central square. There were comfortingly familiar chain-stores here – Woolworth, Gap, HMV – though they seemed to be more impoverished versions of the ones he was used to seeing back home.

Home. Where was that? The renewed surge of panic that accompanied his dawning realisation that he knew almost nothing about himself was so overwhelming that he stumbled and almost fell as the strength drained out of him. He staggered up to a Miss Selfridge's and put an outspread palm on the display window to steady himself. His head was pounding, his body slick with sweat, and he was finding it difficult to breathe.

His mind, however, was in overdrive. He thought of the air teeming with germs and chemicals, thought of toxins rushing through his body, disrupting and destroying it. He expected to start coughing up blood at any moment, expected blisters to erupt on his skin. He waited for the first searing pain in his gut or head, and hoped that when it came it would be intense enough to render him quickly unconscious. He'd rather pass out and die unknowing than writhe in agony as his innards dissolved into soup.

He was heartened to discover, however, that several minutes later, rather than deteriorating, his condition had actually improved. He felt well enough, at least, to push himself away from the window and stand unaided. He even managed a wry grin. *Panic attack*, he thought, *not gas attack. Now pull yourself together, Meacher.* It was at this point that he noticed that all the mannequins in the clothes shop window had plastic bags over their heads.

At first he thought it was some kind of *avant-garde* display, thought the store was simply using shock tactics to grab attention.

If so, he hoped it backfired on them. It was creepy, sick and irresponsible. He almost welcomed his sense of indignation. For the first time since waking up on the train he was responding emotionally to something that was not directly related to his own situation, and the respite, though brief, was welcoming. He looked around almost as if hoping to spot someone in authority he could complain to, as if momentarily forgetting he was alone. His eyes swept across the rows of shops, of which several more – River Island, Envy, Benetton – used mannequins to display the clothes they sold, and as he noticed each of them in turn his indignation gave way to a mounting unease.

There was not one mannequin he could see that did not have its face hidden in some way. Most had plastic bags over their heads, though in Envy they (whoever *they* were; the staff presumably) had simply draped articles of clothing over the figures. The sight put Meacher in mind of parrots whose cages are covered to simulate night and encourage them to sleep. He couldn't for the life of him imagine what the motives of the staff might have been in *this* instance, unless the gesture was somehow symbolic or perhaps even a form of black joke.

Whatever the reason, the sight of all those smothered heads gave him the creeps. He shuddered and turned his gaze purposefully towards the central square. As he did so, noticing that it contained a statue of what appeared to be a figure on horseback, which he thought might be able to give him an indication of where he was, he heard the first sound behind him that he hadn't made himself.

It was an odd sound, and brief, like someone liquidly clearing their throat or attempting to gargle with their own phlegm. It was also faint and muffled, as if he had heard it inside a house from several rooms away. He whirled round, but by the time he had spun ninety degrees all was quiet once more. Nevertheless, he hurried across to the door of River Island, which he had pinpointed in his mind as the source of the sound, and yanked the handle. Finding the door locked, he peered through one of its reinforced glass panels at the store interior.

The place was gloomy and apparently deserted. He was about to turn away when yet another mannequin caught his eye. This one was standing at the back of the shop, and like all the others had a plastic bag draped over its head. In this case, however, not only did the bag appear to be clinging tightly to the mannequin's face, but there seemed to be an oval-shaped indentation in the plastic that to Meacher resembled a gaping mouth desperate for air.

Recoiling with a cry, Meacher turned away. There was a part of him that instantly wanted to go back, if only to reassure himself that what he had seen had been nothing but the result of shadow-play and his own imagination. However his revulsion was too great, and propelled him towards the statue that dominated the central square. As he drew closer to it he noticed two things almost in unison. One was the presence of a quartet of telephone boxes – all Perspex and cold grey steel – on the pavement outside a darkened café called Petra's Pantry, and the other was that what appeared to be a hessian sack had been pulled down over the statue's head.

At least they left the horse alone, Meacher thought, and felt a sudden urge to giggle. He clapped a hand over his mouth and rushed towards the telephone boxes like a drunken man looking for somewhere to throw up.

Wrenching open the door almost pulled his arm out of its socket. He fell inside, snatched up the receiver and rammed it against his ear. The familiar hum of the dialling tone filled him with such joy that he *did* laugh out loud, and was immediately alarmed at how hysterical he sounded. The display screen informed him there was a minimum call charge of twenty pence. Meacher shoved his left hand into his pocket and felt nothing but lining. Tilting his head to trap the phone between shoulder and ear, he rooted through all his pockets increasingly feverishly with both hands. At some point during his snooze on the train he must have been robbed because his pockets were empty. Not only did he have no money, he had no wallet, no train tickets, not even a handkerchief. Had he once had a mobile phone? If so, it had gone now.

He was on the verge of taking out his frustration by smashing the receiver against the smugly indifferent display screen when he remembered that emergency calls were free. Unable to prevent the escape of a triumphant whoop that he found hard to equate to himself, he jabbed thrice at the nine, and was only able to quell his eagerness to do it again by clenching his fist.

A phone burred once, then was interrupted by a barely audible click. Meacher was framing his lips to say hello into the expectant pause that followed when the screaming began.

It was a child's voice, shrill and bubbling with terror. Its words were running together, to form a plea that it seemed would never end. *"Nodaddynodaddynopleasedon'tpleasestopdaddynopleaseno—* " Meacher slammed the phone into its cradle, then slid, as if boneless, to the floor. He wrapped his arms around his head and began to keen.

The child's voice had had a devastating effect on him, not only because it had been distressing to hear, but because it had awakened what felt like a memory he couldn't grasp. He *knew* the child, he was sure of that, but he couldn't put a name or face to it. He clenched his hands into fists and began to pound the top of his head, punishing his brain for failing to yield its secrets. With each blow he grew angrier at himself and his situation, until his rage reached such a peak that he scrambled to his feet, shoved open the door of the telephone box and charged, teeth bared, towards the hooded statue.

The base of the statue was a rectangular block of stone six feet high and inset with panels, each of which contained an elaborate carving of interweaving vines. Meacher threw himself at it, scraping a layer of skin off his arms as he hauled himself up beside the horse and its rider. The statue was slightly larger than life-size, the rider's covered head now eight or ten feet above him. As Meacher placed his left foot on the horse's raised foreleg and grasped a loop of stone rein to heave himself closer to the sack which he intended to tear from the rider's head in an act of manic defiance, he heard the rattling thump of a door opening on the opposite side of the square.

Excited, fearful, and even a little abashed at the prospect of being discovered in such an uncompromising position, Meacher strained to see which of the many doors had opened and who had opened it. However he hadn't raised himself quite high enough to lift his gaze above the horse's frozen mane, and so had to clamber down from his perch and peer between its motionlessly galloping legs, feeling not unlike a child engaged in a game of hide and seek.

What he saw bewildered him for no more than a second before cold, harsh fear stabbed at the base of his throat, then cascaded through his body, lodging in his stomach like broken glass. On the far side of the square, the door of a pub, the fleur-de-lis, had opened and four men had emerged from it. Dressed in jeans and shirts and boots, they looked perfectly normal except for one thing. Like the mannequins in the clothes stores and the stone rider atop its horse, each of them wore a sack-like hood over their head.

The two thoughts that sped through Meacher's mind were more like sharp, bright flashes of despair than anything else. The first thought was an instinctive one that Meacher would have found curious had he had time to ponder it. He thought that if only he had removed the sack from the statue's head and placed it over his own, he would have been safe. His second thought was perhaps equally intriguing, but more fundamental: he knew with absolute conviction that he had to get away before the men caught sight of him.

Even as he jumped sprawlingly from the statue's plinth and tried to use its blocky mass to cover his retreat, however, he knew he was already too late. The men did not cry out, but even through their makeshift hoods it was obvious they were aware of his presence. They moved towards him with a purpose both remorseless and terrifying, and when he began to run, his terror making him feel as though he was wearing lead boots, their pursuit became more purposeful still.

The subsequent chase through the unknown town's deserted streets was as surreally terrifying as any nightmare. Meacher's terror made him stumble and stagger and skid. Within moments his body was greasy with sweat, which flowed from his hair and into his eyes, blinding him. His heart hammered, his lungs toiled, and his breath felt like a length of barbed wire that he couldn't dislodge from his throat. Whenever he glanced back, his pursuers were the same distance behind him, which may have been encouraging if not for the fact that they appeared to be marching rather than running, their movements effortless, machine-like, full of deadly intent.

They were toying with him, Meacher knew. They were wearing him down prior to closing in for the kill. Meacher wished he could see their faces, and yet at the same time dreaded the disclosure of whatever might be concealed within those sack-cloth hoods. In fact, in some ways the prospect of finding out was what terrified him more than anything else.

The streets were getting narrower, danker. Sooner or later he would come to a dead end and then that would be that. If he couldn't outrun his pursuers he had to escape them in some other way. The only viable alternative was to evade them for long enough to find a hiding place. At best that would be a short-term solution, but at least it would give him time to think, to plan his next move.

He rounded a corner, his hand slapping the brick to steady himself as he changed direction, and – as though he had willed it to appear – saw an aperture between two buildings on his right, so narrow it could barely even be termed an alleyway. He plunged down it, and was immediately doused in a gloom cold enough to make him feel he was underwater. Above him the tops of the buildings on either side of the rat-run appeared to be craning to touch one another. Certainly they gave the impression that they were squeezing the thin white stripe of sky that separated them still thinner. So dark did this make the alleyway that from his present position Meacher couldn't see its end.

It was too late to change his mind, though. If he emerged from the alleyway now his pursuers would be on to him in an instant. He began to trot forward, stepping as lightly as he could in the hope that those behind him might plough straight past the slit-like entrance, oblivious. How much could they see through those hoods? How much could they hear? How much could they *smell*?

This last thought came unbidden, and disturbed him the most. He thought of sniffer dogs, attuned not to the scent of food or drugs, but to fear. He quickened his pace. Was the alleyway getting narrower still? If he stretched out both arms like a child pretending to fly, he reckoned he might just about be able to touch the buildings on either side.

As he passed them, he barely glanced at the individual establishments embedded within the grey stone edifices. On a subconscious level he registered that each of them was a cramped shop unit, comprising of a door and a narrow display window with a sign above it. However there was not one that wasn't coated in a layer of dust and grime so thick that it both obscured the name on the sign and made it impossible to tell what the shop sold, or once had. This, combined with a deepening murk that felt like twilight's closing fist, made him fail to notice that one of the shop doors was ajar until it creaked as it widened further.

Meacher's senses were so attuned to danger that his instinctive leftward spring was balletic. His landing, however, was not so graceful. His ankle turned on the pitted tarmac and he all but shoulder-charged the door opposite the one which had opened. As he fought to regain his senses and his balance, he saw a grey-shrouded figure materialise from the gloom beyond the open door and extend a beckoning hand. The figure's face was concealed within a triangle of shadow so black it seemed impenetrable, but its words were clear enough.

"In here, quickly, if you don't want them to find you."

Though Meacher hesitated, it still took him less than a second to make up his mind. The boom of his shoulder hitting the door was even now reverberating in the alleyway; in the otherwise total silence his pursuers would have to be deaf not to have heard it. Scrambling upright, he propelled himself towards the figure, that backed away at his approach.

Crossing the threshold felt like passing through a portal between this world and the next. The darkness into which Meacher plunged seemed so profound that for several seconds he was completely disorientated. Opening his eyes wide and finding nothing for his vision to latch on to, he flailed with his arms, and was rewarded or punished by a crack of pain across the knuckles of his left hand.

Undeterred, he groped again for the hard surface he had encountered
and found a thin ledge of some kind – possibly a shelf or the edge of a
desk. He clung to it like a shipwrecked man might cling to driftwood
until his eyes had adapted to the sudden absence of light.

It took perhaps a minute for the slowly emerging slatted shapes to
gain sufficient definition to reveal themselves as books. As soon as
they did, he acknowledged that the shop was full of them. Of course,
he would have known sooner if he had focused on any sense other
than his eyesight, because as soon as he *saw* the books he became
aware of their musty odour. In any other circumstance he would
have found the smell comforting, even homely, though he had hardly
read a book since his childhood. Hearing a *snick* behind him he
whirled, but it was only the sound of the catch sliding into place as
the shop door closed. So dingy was it, and so effectively did the shop
owner blend into his surroundings, that the cowled man's movement
from the door to the far side of the room seemed as soundless and
insubstantial as a drift of smoke.

"Thank you," Meacher said, his throat clogged by dust and
exertion, but the man's only response was a sharp upraising of
his left hand.

Though it was hard to make him out in the gloom, Meacher could
tell by his stance that he was listening. As though deferring to a
greater authority, Meacher too remained as still as he could, even
though his exhausted body longed to sag. He did his utmost to
contain his breath despite the attempts his racing heart and toiling
lungs were making to encourage him to pant and wheeze. The two of
them stood there for so long that Meacher began to wonder whether
the shop owner was once again waiting for him to speak, and he was
gathering the courage to do so when the man murmured, "Alas."

Before Meacher could ask him what was wrong, a pounding on
the door invalidated his question. Meacher instinctively scuttled
forward, then ducked, twisting his head to look wildly behind
him. Perhaps the most frightening aspect of the blows that seemed
to be making the books shiver on their shelves was that they were not
urgent but ponderous, relentless, evenly spaced. They sounded more
like the pounding of some vast machine piston than human fists on
wood. They suggested to Meacher that his pursuers would never give
up, that they would hunt him down remorselessly, that in their eyes
(if they *had* eyes beneath those hoods) the outcome of the chase was
inevitable. Still cowering, he looked from the door to the shop owner,
in the same way that a small child would look to a parent for
guidance.

"Go up the stairs," the man murmured, pointing to a shadowy patch of wall between two bookcases that on closer inspection Meacher realised was a door. "You'll find an unlocked room there. Go inside and lock yourself in."

Will I be safe? Meacher would have asked if fear had not denied him his voice, and if he had not been so terrified of the answer.

He blundered across the room, feeling as though the must and mould of ancient books was lining his lungs like silt, and scrabbled at the dark blot of shadow that was the handle to the door that led upstairs. It opened smoothly, devoid of the creak he was expecting. He caught a glimpse of the stairs – little more than bands of differently-hued shadow – before the door clicked shut behind him, taking the last vestige of light with it.

A part of him welcomed the blackness. He wished he could curl up and close his eyes and lose himself in its folds. It was almost with reluctance that he forced himself on, edging forward until his toe-end connected with the bottom stair. He began to climb, his body now incredibly weary, his joints grinding with glassy pain. He tried not to wonder where this would end, whether – by some miracle – he would escape the clutches of his pursuers, recover his memory and find his way home. Without knowing why, he had become a fugitive, and the purpose of a fugitive was to run, and to keep running until he either got away or was caught.

Maybe his new-found ally would help him. Maybe, when Meacher's pursuers had gone, the two of them would sit down together and the shop owner would answer all his questions. Meacher couldn't hear anything from downstairs, couldn't even hear the pounding. Was the shop owner talking to his pursuers at this moment? Or had they simply moved on? Had they knocked on the shop door not because they had known he was inside, but because they were knocking on every door, hoping to either rouse and question the occupants or simply to frighten him into bolting from wherever he might have chosen to hide?

He knew he had reached the upper landing only when his raised right foot failed to encounter another stair. He settled it gently next to his left and used his arms as antennae to probe the way ahead. Encountering no resistance, he shuffled forward, the soles of his feet scraping along a surface that felt like rough, gritty wood. After a few steps he moved to his right, and within seconds encountered a wall of what seemed to be cold, uneven plaster.

Feeling his way along, it only took him several seconds more to locate a door. His hands slithered over it until one of them found the knob, which was twisted in both directions several times before Meacher concluded that it was locked.

What was it the shop owner had said? Go upstairs and into the unlocked room? Something like that. Which meant, presumably, that of several rooms up here, only one was unlocked. He simply had to find it, that was all, simply had to be methodical.

Rather than move across to the other side of the landing, he decided to feel his way to the next door on this side, then there would be no chance of missing one. Blinking into the darkness and finding it unchanging, he probed the way cautiously forward with his feet, and almost immediately his left palm, caressing the wall, bumped against the jutting side of a second door frame.

Even without his sight, his hand moved unerringly to the door knob, and this time, with barely a twist, the door opened. Meacher stepped inside and quietly closed it behind him. Remembering what the shop owner had said about locking himself in, his searching fingers found a key, which rewarded him with a satisfying click when he twisted it clockwise.

Turning to face the room, he realised that it was not as dark as he had first thought. The faint, brownish illumination was provided by a meagre spill of light through a small window coated in grime and dust. Though the light was barely managing to establish itself, Meacher could just make out a bed with rumpled bedclothes and a tall blocky wardrobe. He did not notice the child, however, until it started whispering.

His head twisted so sharply that a hot thread of pain flared in his neck. The child was standing so closely to the wall furthest away from the door that until he focused on it fully it resembled nothing so much as a particular fall of shadow on an uneven patch of plaster. Thinking that his fumblings at the door may have caused the child to scuttle across the room and press itself against the wall in fear, Meacher moved closer to reassure it, more out of fear that it would give him away than because of a genuine urge to offer it comfort. However he had taken no more than four steps towards it when he stopped.

He had assumed the whispering to be a prayer, or an attempt by the child to find its voice, but now that he was close enough to hear it clearly he realised it was neither. What the child was whispering were the words that it, or some other child, had wailed in abject terror down the phone in the square at him. "*Nodaddynodaddynopleasedon'tpleasestopdaddynopleaseno.*"

It was as though, by repeating the words, the child was giving them the power of an incantation, was mocking or damning him with them. Meacher felt anger, or more than anger, boiling inside him and he took two further steps across the room. It was only at this point, some six or eight feet from the child, that the scant light finally enabled him to make out particular details that had been denied him from further away. It was these details that caused the strength to drain from his legs so abruptly that he thumped forward on to his knees.

The child did not have its back to the wall at all; it was *facing* the wall, presenting its back, almost insolently, to him. Furthermore, like the mannequins, like his pursuers, like the statue in the square, it was wearing a bag over its head.

It was the sight of the bag – black plastic wound round with masking tape – that triggered the memories in Meacher's mind. Now, finally, he was beginning to realise why he was here. He held out his hands in supplication.

"I'm sorry," he whispered. "I'm so sorry. *Please*. Have mercy."

Slowly the child turned to face him. "*Nodaddynodaddynoplease don't – pleasestopdaddynopleaseno*," it whispered.

As though relishing the moment, the child raised its hands, its fingertips resting on the black plastic, making it crackle. Then, still whispering, it hooked its fingers into the plastic and began to tear the bag from its face.

LYNDA E. RUCKER

The Last Reel

LYNDA E. RUCKER WAS BORN in Birmingham, Alabama, and currently lives in Portland, Oregon, but will be packing it in shortly to go vagabonding around other parts of the world, for as long as those other parts of the world will have her.

In the last few years she has taken time off from writing fiction to pursue a graduate degree and, as an inexplicable result, has several stories scheduled to appear this year.

Her fiction has been, or will be, published in *The Third Alternative*, *Black Static* and *Supernatural Tales*, among other periodicals. This is her second appearance in *The Mammoth Book of Best New Horror*.

"This story came from two places," she reveals: "an imagined dialogue – which practically wrote itself – between a film lover and his girlfriend playing a silly game (and friends who read this commented that I seemed to have written a story in which my partner was the main character); and my grandmother's house in rural Georgia, which I found spooky as a child.

"I once dreamed a witch lived behind that house – and to this day, as it falls further into dereliction and collapses into the woods surrounding it, it still feels like a terrifying, magical place to me."

"WAIT A MINUTE," Sophie said, "give me a clue, I know this one."

"If you know it, you don't need a clue, do you?" Kevin lit another cigarette and sank back against the seat.

She shot him a look. "Watch the road," he cautioned, and she reached over to punch him in the shoulder.

"Smartass," she said.

He sang softly, in a deep false bass. "Seven, seven, seven . . ."

"*The Magnificent Seven*," she finished for him. "I said give me a clue, not give it away."

"Well, if you didn't get the *Seven Samurai* reference what could I—"

Sophie hit the brakes. The car slewed to the right and skidded to a stop.

"That was the turn back there," she said. "Way to go, navigator."

"I know that one. Kiwi film about Black Death victims who time-travel to modern-day New Zealand. And there was a Buster Keaton flick with the same name. Either way, I am trouncing your ass!"

"That wasn't part of the game. Could you stop being a movie geek for five damn minutes?" Sophie asked rhetorically, dragging the gear stick into reverse.

"I'm a film critic. I know no other way."

"Well, next time we'll play some kind of – of *cooking* game or something and I will trounce your ass, as you so elegantly put it."

"A cooking game? Food geek."

"At least we eat well. You guys would live on popcorn and Junior Mints if it wasn't for people like me."

The missed turn was unsignposted and, he noted, not visible until you were upon it and saw the break in the trees and brush that grew right to the edge of the highway. He decided not to mount a self-defense at that particular moment.

"Great," Sophie murmured moments later as they bumped up the narrow gravel lane, rocks popping ominously against the underside of the car, branches scraping at the sides. "I wonder if the rental company has a 'back of beyond' clause absolving us from damages incurred in the actual middle of nowhere . . ."

She trailed off as they rounded a bend and the house was before them, all at once. It lurked in a clearing where all the grass had died and been dug up by the six dogs Sophie's Aunt Rose had kept. According to the animal control people they were all feral, and had to be destroyed.

The house itself was low and dark, all blank windows and weathered boards the color of old dishwater.

Kevin said, "It's haunted, right? I mean, it would have to be. Jesus, what a dump." He hated the way his voice went up at the end, losing control a little bit like the sight of the house had really shaken him. "Jesus," he said again.

"Well. It's not like we have to spend the night here or anything." Sophie was brisk, the way she always got when something made her uneasy.

"*House on Haunted Hill*," he said.

"What?"

"William Castle feature. Vincent Price offers ten thousand dollars to whoever will spend the entire night in a haunted house."

"Ah, but ten thousand dollars doesn't go nearly as far as it did back in those days, even if having Mr Vincent Price do the offering makes it a little more attractive. Did they up the going price in the remake?"

"In the what?"

"The remake."

"Blasphemer!" he said.

"Race you!" she answered. She was out the door before he knew it, her sandals clattering on the steps when he was only halfway across the yard.

"No fair," he said, "you tricked me." They were both laughing until she turned round to face the house, when it suddenly seemed rude to display too much levity as they prepared to survey the meager estate of poor deceased Aunt Rose.

Sophie's key stuck in the front door, and for a moment he hoped it wouldn't work at all, but then the lock turned easily. The dark spilled out.

They crossed the threshold into a foyer smelling of mold, and stale with the heat of a hot September day. Just a few feet ahead he could make out monstrous shapes that were revealed, once Sophie touched the light switch, to be a coat-rack bearing numerous heavy coats, and a hulking wardrobe. The hallway was short, a few steps across the worn grey carpet carrying him to the end.

Sophie had shown him photos late last night at her mother's condo back in Atlanta, the mutilated snapshots with sister Rose snipped from every one. It struck him as cruel and excessive, the way family inter-actions so often do to anyone on the outside, the story behind it all – for there always is one – too convoluted and painful to ever be properly recalled or recounted by the perceived injured party. *You have no idea what she did to me, you can't understand, you see she always.*

Already the estrangement made more sense, though, now that he'd seen the house. He tried to imagine two sisters more different than Sophie's bright, intimidating mother, vice-president of something-or-other at a big Atlanta bank, and this weird reclusive woman lost like a fairy tale witch in her spooky house in the woods. "Can you remember her at all?" he'd asked.

"Once," Sophie had told him; she'd been very young – she couldn't say for sure how young, but once, at some family gathering, maybe a funeral. "She scared me."

No, that wasn't right, her mother had insisted. Sophie and her Aunt Rose had never met. "I can't fathom any circumstance under which *that* would occur," her mother had told Kevin with a brittle laugh.

Sophie just shrugged. "She's lying. Aunt Rose taught me a weird little dance, like a jig or something, but then Mother made me stop doing it when she found out who I learned it from. So I used to do it in secret, in my bedroom." It was all, she said, that she did remember, and now scary Aunt Rose was dead and she was doing the responsible grown-up thing where her mother could not. *I'll go out there. I'll look the place over*, for crazy scary Aunt Rose had left the dump to Sophie in her will.

Sophie's mother had been opposed.

"I'm telling you, you don't even need to deal with it, honey. You stay right where you are. I'll have people take care of it – get some appraisers out there, get the place sold, have the money deposited straight into your account."

The harder her mother pushed, the more Sophie's resolve grew to handle matters her own way. Kevin stayed silent and stayed out of it.

The doors to either side of them leading out of the foyer were closed. "Well," Sophie said, and reached for the one on her right. Kevin had a moment of uneasiness as she passed into a darkness that swallowed her up. "Good God." A dim light went on and he joined her just at the doorway of the kitchen, where the rancid smell of spoiled food hit him full on. "Will you look at that," Sophie said, and he did. All three windows – one over the sink, and two at the front of the house – were covered with cardboard and held in place with black duct tape.

The rest of the room was unremarkable, old but standard appliances, rough wooden cabinets. The refrigerator door stood open, the bulb burned out, and unidentifiable bundles – perhaps packages of meat – littered the floor before it, some of them leaking thin rivulets of dark fluid. Scattered across the counter, lumps that had presumably been fruit or vegetables were grey and furry.

"I've worked in kitchens that were *almost* this unsanitary," Sophie said, but neither one of them smiled.

He wanted to tell her to stop then, not to go into any more rooms ahead of him. She'd laugh at him, or get annoyed. *This place is creepy enough, don't freak me out.*

"Enough seen," she said, pinching her nose, backing out, pulling the door shut after them. "How I hate to say this, but maybe my mother was right."

The other door, now. Blackness, but this time he was prepared for it. In the second before Sophie found the switch he heard her finger scrabbling along the wall. It reminded him of something dried out and dead.

"*Well*," said Sophie, "what have we here?"

"Wow," he said, struck stupid.

Even without the contrast of the squalid kitchen, the suffocating opulence of the living room would have been striking. Oriental rugs covered every inch of wall space, including, presumably, the windows. His knowledge of old furniture was confined to an occasional stroll through an antique mall back in Seattle, idly wondering what would possess people to pay hundreds of dollars for old Coca-Cola merchandise. But even his unpracticed eye spotted some value in the chaos of clashing eras and continents. A Chinese lacquer cabinet was wedged against one wall, next to it a couple of heavy ornate chairs, and a sleek Art Deco lamp. A mostly clear path meandered through the clutter to the opposite door, but you still had to make yourself compact to get through.

Sophie had already done so, fighting her way past a roll-top desk and tugging at an unremarkable looking occasional table that blocked the next door. He had a passing irrational urge to beg her not to open it. Too late anyway, as miraculous afternoon sunshine fell across her path.

"Auntie's bedroom," she said as she stepped through the doorway, and he hurried to join her with a growing anxiety that the first two rooms had left in him, a sense of being lost, buried alive.

The unblocked windows helped him to breathe easier. "I wish you'd stop going ahead of me," he said. Auntie's bedroom was as neat and bare as a nun's cell. A single iron bed, white pillows, white coverlet pulled up tight. One wooden nightstand, empty save for an overflowing ashtray and a crumpled cigarette package. The cigarette butts were ringed with bright red lipstick. They reminded him of how badly he wanted to smoke, and he fumbled for his lighter before remembering he'd left his pack in the car. He crossed to one of the windows.

"I can't see our car," he said.

"Of course not. You're looking out the back of the house."

But that was nonsense. He ought to be seeing the driveway, and the ruined front yard, but there was only a stretch of bare ground and then a line of trees thickening into forest. He had a sense then that they moved, like curtains fluttering when something stirred on the other side.

"Look," Sophie said. She lifted a shoebox from the other side of the bed and set it on the night table. He saw her flinch and jump back. The back of her hand caught the ashtray, and it smashed to the floor.

"Shit!" Sophie yelled.

"Are you okay?"

"I thought a spider ran out of the box. What an idiot."

He came round the side of the bed and saw beads of blood welling up on her legs and sandaled feet where the shattered glass had pierced her skin. "I'm okay," she said, "it just scared me. There's probably Band Aids in the bathroom." She pushed past him and opened the last door. He caught sight of a heavy porcelain sink and a bathtub on feet, then Sophie said, "Ew" and he went in after her. Brown water sputtered from the faucet.

"It's just because it hasn't been turned on in a while," he said, "it'll clear in a few minutes."

"No Band-Aids," she said, "no medicine cabinet, nothing. Apparently Aunt Rose didn't even use soap. Doesn't matter. They're shallow." Working in a kitchen had left her inured to minor cuts and burns. "Let's see what's in the box."

Let's not, he wanted to say, but what came out when he followed her back to the bed was, "Three movies featuring a head-in-a-box. Name them."

"God," she said, "do you have to be so morbid? *Se7en*." She lifted the lid.

"That's one," he said, so he wouldn't shout something stupid and hysterical like *Don't look inside!*

"It's filled with photographs," she said. "*Bring Me the Head of Alfredo Garcia*."

"That's head-in-a-bag, not head-in-a-box," he said desperately.

"Oh, for God's sake. Picky, aren't we?" Her voice changed. "That's weird."

"What?"

"I don't know how she got hold of these. It's all pictures of *me*."

So. What's the story with your mom and your Aunt Rose? he'd asked.

Mom always said she was a witch.

A witch . . . Like a Wicca-witch? New Agey, blessed be and white magic and all that? Like Teresa? Teresa was their neighbor back in Seattle.

No, I mean a bad old witch. Yeah, hard to believe, isn't it? It's the one subject guaranteed to make my rational mom completely irrational.

Then she said, *Also, something about my dad.*

Your dad . . . Sophie never talked about her father.

When they were young. I don't know; they fought over him. He was Rose's boyfriend and Mom stole him, I think. I don't remember him at all.

She said it so cleanly, so matter-of-factly, that he couldn't believe she wasn't masking her pain.

He disappeared before I was three. Who are you when you're that young? You're not even through becoming a person yet – you don't have memories, even, just bright flashes of moments here and there, and what people remember for you, what they've told you so many times you start to think it belongs to you. He went away before I could have any part of him to myself.

"*Barton Fink,*" she said. She was pulling out handfuls of photos and tossing them on the bed. Sophie as toddler in a birthday hat, Sophie grinning to expose missing teeth for an elementary school photo, Sophie wearing a strapless blue dress and holding hands with a skinny dark-haired boy at a high school dance.

"Check. That's two."

She grinned, waved snapshots at him in a less than menacing manner. "I'll show you the life of the mind!"

"You don't look a bit like John Goodman."

But she wasn't listening anymore. "What's this?"

He had a sinking feeling of inevitability, like the second or third time you watch a movie in which something terrible is going to happen, and even as you know it's coming, some part of you is hoping against hope that this time the film will magically find its path to a different fate. But this was not a movie, and it was nothing he'd seen before, so there was no reason for this sick feeling to engulf him when Sophie pulled a key out of the box.

"This is freaking me out," she said. "Where did she get all these pictures of me? And why'd she keep them?"

"Maybe your mom sent them to her." Families did weird stuff like that, mingling devotion and resentment, like his cousin Shelby who wouldn't speak to her dad but made her son write him a letter once a month.

"Sent a whole shoebox full of pictures?" she asked. He shrugged. "It looks like a door key," she went on. "I wonder . . . Kevin, do you have any idea how much that stuff in the other room is worth? What if this is the key to something even more valuable? Imagine if I came out of this with enough money to open my own restaurant?" Her eyes were shining when she looked at him. He wanted to take her hand and insist that they leave immediately, tell her that her mother was right and they should let other people deal with this.

Instead he said again, "This window ought to look out at the front yard. Why can't I see the car?"

"There's nothing *out* there." She was back at the doorway to the living room, tense and impatient. "There must be another room. Maybe she hung a rug over the doorway like she hid all the windows."

He lingered, not wanting to go back to the stuffy closed-in part of the house. On a whim he tried one of the windows; it seemed important to have another route of escape besides the front door, and anyway he was noticing a heavy flowery scent hanging about, the kind of sickly sweetness used to disguise the odor of something foul. He took a deep breath, but could find no hint to the source of the rottenness underneath. It was not the same as the spoiled food in the kitchen; this was something earthier and more intense.

Fresh air would do him good. He tugged at the window, and it did not budge. It appeared to be painted shut.

When he walked back into the living room, Sophie had vanished. A woman stood with her back to him, shoulders rigid, black-haired, wearing Sophie's sweater. She turned and smiled at him, Sophie's smile, Sophie's eyes.

"Check out this funky wig," she said. "Wouldn't it be great for Halloween? What do you think my batty old aunt was doing with something like this?"

"Take it off," he pleaded, but he must not have sounded serious at all because she laughed and flounced past him. "Head in a box," she said. "Are you sure it's not *Bring Me the Head of Alfredo Garcia*?"

"Of course I'm sure, it's my clue. I made it up," he said, but he could no longer remember what he'd had in mind for the third head-in-a-box film or why he'd started them on such a gruesome tack in the first place.

"Torso-in-a-box," she said. "*Boxing Helena*, ugh. You've got me. I need another clue." She had her back to him again, and her voice coming from the black-haired figure unnerved him. "Did I ever tell you what my Aunt Rose looked like?" she said. "She was beautiful once. Way more attractive than my mom. Mom got the brains, Rose got the beauty."

"How do you know that? That she was beautiful?"

"You know what?" She laughed. "I hid some pictures of her when I was little, before my mom got hold of all the rest and cut them to pieces. I still have them somewhere, I guess. When I was a kid and I'd get mad at my mom, I'd make up a story that an evil witch had taken her over, my real mom was actually Aunt Rose and that she and my dad were coming to rescue me. Isn't that stupid?"

"We should get going," he said. "There's nothing else out here, and it's a long drive back."

"That dance she taught me," Sophie said. "She called it the something reel. The witches' reel? Oh, I can't remember. Anyway, I just want to look around a little more. I want to see if we can find out what this key goes to."

He wanted to say that if it was truly concealing something so valuable, surely Aunt Rose would not make it so difficult to find and identify. Then again, Aunt Rose was at least a little bit crazy. Someone like Aunt Rose might think *I have to hide it, so no one finds it and steals it before she gets here.*

"I know," Sophie said. He followed her into the hallway, where she was tugging at the wardrobe.

"Be careful," he said, "you'll bring it down on yourself." He went forward to help her. "Take hold at the bottom here. We don't want to overbalance it." He had not noticed, when they first walked in, how much worse the smell was here. This place was sealed up so tightly, could the air go bad, like you heard about in caving collapses, mining disasters?

Between the two of them they heaved the wardrobe a couple of feet away from the wall. Sophie said, "Kevin, look. Come round on my side." She'd been right, after all; it had concealed a door, and she could twist the key in the lock and open the door just far enough to allow her to slip inside.

"Don't," he said, while she still stood on his side of the doorway, her hand on the knob.

She grinned at him. "Let's make a deal. You tell me the other head-in-a-box movie and I won't open it."

"I can't remember," he said. "I guess it was *Bring Me the Head*. Anyway, it wasn't even my turn just then."

"Not good enough," she said, and slipped into the darkness.

Long moments later she spoke. "I can't find a light switch. Maybe there's a string I can pull or something. Do you have your lighter?" She sounded as though she were speaking to him from the bottom of a well.

"It's in the car," he said. "Sophie, come out of there."

"Can't you just run out and get it for me? Come on, Kevin, five minutes and then we're gone."

He hesitated, then threw up his hands. "Fine." It was easier to get angry with her. He must have imagined the way the front door resisted him when he turned the knob; it was swollen from exposure, maybe, and that made it stick when he tugged at it. Then he was out on the porch again, where the day was still warm and sunny and their car waited just where he'd parked it. Halfway back to it he turned and searched for the bedroom windows he'd looked out from.

A movement on the roof caught his eye. Something scampered across the peak and out of his sight down the other side. Something blackened and low. *Just a squirrel.*

He snatched the lighter up from where he'd left it in the well between seats and sprinted back to the house. He called her name as he burst through the front door, and her voice came back to him, muffled.

"Oh, shit, Sophie, why'd you shut the door?" He slumped against the wardrobe, rattled the knob. "It's locked. Did you lock it?"

She sounded close – she must have been just on the other side of the door, but she might have been whispering against his ear. "There's nothing *in* here."

"Well, stay where you are. Don't go moving around in there when you can't see." But she was doing just that; he could hear her, thumping about. "Are you *dancing* in there?" *The something reel. The witches' reel.*

He'd once read somewhere that the best way to go about breaking down a door was to direct a blow near the lock.

"What are you *doing*?" Sophie said, as his foot smashed against it. His second kick splintered the wood; it was old and cheap and not made to keep anyone out. More than anything, he did not want to walk into that inky blackness. But he got the lighter out and struck at it once, twice, with the ball of his thumb. *Third time's the charm.*

As he stepped over the threshold, he was surprised at how much of the room it illuminated when he held it high over his head. He felt his shoulders sag, tension draining out of them as he asked himself what he'd been expecting to find in there; Sophie's father's head in a box, perhaps? She was right, it was a small, bare, perfectly square room, perhaps ten feet by ten.

Then he noticed the walls. He stepped forward, one, two paces. "Get up," he said. Sophie sat cross-legged in the middle of the room. The flame nipped at his thumb and he let the light go out.

He hoped that she had not seen what he had: every inch of wall space covered in thick black cursive writing or tattered pages torn from books, punctuated with photographs of Sophie. He thought that some of them had been hung upside down, perhaps defaced. He didn't want to look again to confirm it.

Sophie was silent. Then, "There's something painted on the floor here." She sounded different in the dark. They had been together for years; how could any nuance be unknown to him? He took a few more steps in. He felt swallowed by the blackness. "Bring the light over here."

His thumb was raw as he spun it against the wheel of the lighter. "Sophie," he said, and the little flame spewed; the room flickered once more in shades of grey. He squatted, and held the lighter down low and close between them. "Sophie, will you please take off that wig?"

She giggled, and that sounded wrong too. "If it's such a big deal to you," she said, and snatched it off, tossed it in a corner. He wished she hadn't done that, and almost asked her to pick it up. He hated the idea of it lying there like some furry dead thing, and he let the light go out once more.

"Your mother's going to get worried if we don't head back soon," he said.

"I wonder what's in the wardrobe?" she said.

"Your father's head?"

Silence again. Then, "That's not funny. Anyway, wouldn't be much left of it, would there?"

"I'm sorry. I was kidding. It was stupid." He could feel his shirt damp and stuck to his back, sweat trickling down his sides from his armpits. He became aware that his mouth hung open and he was breathing like he'd been running, heavy and ragged. "*Night Must Fall.*"

"What?"

"*Night Must Fall.* That's the other movie with a head in it. I just remembered."

"Oh. I never heard of it."

"Albert Finney with an axe and a yen for decapitation."

"Oh," she said again. "That was kind of a cheat, then, if you knew I couldn't possibly get it." The boards creaked beneath her feet as she made her way over to him. He resisted the urge to recoil, but jumped anyway when she touched him. Her hand was icy through the cloth of his shirt, her fingernails sharp and hard. "It's so dark in here. Like there never was any light." Her breath was on his cheek, warm and moist and stale-smelling. "You know?" she said, and then she pressed against him and fixed her mouth on his. Her tongue invaded, prying his lips apart.

He stumbled back away from her. "We have to go."

She coughed, a phlegmy sound like she was a longtime smoker. "You're right," she said. "There's nothing here anyway."

He was relieved when she pushed past him and continued down the hall. The wig had left her hair matted and stuck to the crown of her head. When she opened the front door and he saw how the light had changed he realized how much later it was than he'd thought. She commented that it seemed to be growing dark so early these days, it was hard to believe that it wasn't yet fall.

"Sophie, those cuts look terrible," he said, noticing her legs. They'd gone dry and puckered-looking, like tiny gaping mouths. But she was already crawling in on the passenger side, and didn't seem to hear him.

The engine failed to turn over the first time, then again and again, and sweat was dripping into his eyes. Sophie sat placid beside him, unmoved by the useless revving of the motor.

"What's the number for Triple A?" he said. "Where's your phone?"

"It's dead. I forgot to recharge it last night." She went on, "It's not such a bad place, really. I bet we could do something with it."

"I forgot my lighter," he said.

"What?"

"Nothing," he said, already willing to forget that for a split second he'd thought of sending her back inside on the pretense of fetching something, then driving away – no, running away, a mile or more back up to the highway where he'd flag down a car. It wasn't Sophie that stopped him—rather, the certainty that he might run as far as he could and would never find the highway, because it would no longer be there.

"Poor thing," she said, "you must be tired. You probably shouldn't drive anyway. There's a bed inside, you know, if you need to rest."

He steadied his foot on the accelerator and gunned the engine. He would feel better if only he would look at her, and she'd laugh, propose some calm and sensible plan for getting them out of this predicament. Someone will stop for us up on the highway, she'd say in a moment, out here in the country people still help you like that. But he could not do it. He found that a sort of numbness had taken him, rather than grief or any sense of loss, and he kept turning the key and pressing the gas long after it produced only a series of dry dead clicks, and still he could not bring himself to look into her eyes.

JAY LAKE

The American Dead

JAY LAKE LIVES IN PORTLAND, Oregon with his books and two inept cats, where he works on numerous writing and editing projects.

His current novels are *Trial of Flowers* from Night Shade Books and *Mainspring* from Tor Books, with sequels to both volumes due in 2008. His short fiction appears in numerous markets world-wide, most recently *The Mammoth Book of Monsters* and *Logorrhea*.

He is the winner of the 2004 John W. Campbell Award for Best New Writer and a multiple nominee for the Hugo and World Fantasy Awards.

"There are little markers that tells us things about the world," Lake explains, "so-called telling details. The airliner in the river in this story tells us the world has ended, because in our world we don't leave downed airliners where they fell. The policeman's notebook tells its own story. But the story that lasts the longest is the story of our dead.

"Someday the American dead will be the stuff of history. This is a story of one way that might have happened, and what it means to the people who remain standing puzzled in the ruins."

AMERICANS ARE ALL RICH, even their dead. Pobrecito knows this because he spends the hottest parts of the days in the old *Cementerio Americano* down by the river. The water is fat and lazy while the pipes in the *colonia* drip only rust brown as the eyes Santa Marguerite. Their graves are of the finest marble, carved with photographs in some manner he does not understand, or wrought with sculpted angels that put the churches up the hill to shame. Some of the American dead even have little houses, tight boxes with broken doors that must have once contained great riches.

He sits within a drooping tree which fights with life and watches the flies make dark, wiggling rafts out on the water. There are dogs which live in the broken-backed jet out in the middle of the current, eyes glowing from behind the dozens of little shattered oval windows. At night the dogs swim across the slow current and run the river banks, hunting in the *colonia* and up toward the city walls.

They are why he never sleeps in the *Cementerio*. That some of the dogs walk on two legs only makes them worse.

When he was very young, Pobrecito found a case of magazines, old ones with bright color pictures of men and women without their clothes. Whoever had made the magazines had an astonishing imagination, because in Pobrecito's experience most people who fucked seemed to do it either with booze or after a lot of screaming and fighting and being held down. There weren't very many ways he'd ever seen it gone after. The people in these pictures were smiling, mostly, and arranged themselves more carefully than priests arranging a corpse. And they lived in the most astonishing places.

Pobrecito clips or tears the pictures out a few at a time and sells them on the streets of the *colonia*. He knows the magazines themselves would just be taken from him, before or after a beating, but a kid with a few slips of paper clutched in his hand is nothing. As long as no one looks too closely. But even if he had a pass for the gates, he dares not take them within the walls, for the priests would hang him in the square.

What he loves most about the magazines is not the nudity or the fucking or the strange combinations and arrangements these people found themselves in. No, what he loves is that these are Americans. Beautiful people in beautiful places doing beautiful things together.

"I will be an American some day," he tells his friend Lucia. They are in the branches of the dying tree, sharing a bottle of *pulque* and a greasy bowl of fried plantains in the midday heat. Pobrecito has a secret place up there, a hollow in the trunk where he hides most of his treasures.

The magazines are stored elsewhere, in a place he has never even shown to Lucia.

"You are an idiot," she declares, glancing out at the airplane in the river. The American flag can still be seen on its tall tail, small and weathered. No one has gone out to paint it over, for fear of the dogs. "All Americans are dead," she adds with prim authority.

Lucia is smaller than Pobrecito, though older. She is one of the *menoriítas*, born to be little. Though she is of an age to have breasts and make her bleedings, her body is smooth and slick as any young child's. Pobrecito knows this because they often curl together to sleep, and she likes him to touch her as if she were a baby, rubbing his hand over her sides and back and pulling her to his chest. He has tried to use his fingers to do a few of the things seen in his pictures, but she is too small down there both before and behind, and complains of the hurt.

She has never offered to touch him.

Pobrecito shakes off that thought. "What is dead can be reborn. This is what the priests are always telling us." He grins, mottled teeth flashing even in shadow. "I shall bleach my skin and hair like they did, and have a fine house filled with swimming pools and bright furniture. My automobiles would be colorful and shiny and actually have petrol."

She laughs then and sets her shoulder against his chest, tucking her head into his neck, sucking on the *pulque* bottle in a way which makes him both warm and uncomfortable. He strokes her hair and dreams of distant, lost cities such as Los Angeles and Omaha.

That evening the folk of the *colonia* are upset. They surge through the muddy streets, even the day workers who should already be sleeping, and there is an angry mutter like bottle wasps swarming. He even sees some weapons, knives dangling from hands, a few pistols tucked into belts. These are offences of the worst order, to keep or carry weapons.

Pobrecito dodges booted feet and moves with the crowd, listening. He already knows he will sell no pictures tonight. Selling no pictures, he will not eat tomorrow. But he wants to understand what is wrong.

The crowd is speaking of priests.

"Girls, indeed."

". . . a scandal. And they use God's name!"

"They wear those black dresses. Let them lie with one another."

"Called them up there from a list. I tell you, I won't allow my . . ."

"Hush! Do you want to hang?"

"A tax. How is this a *tax*?"

"Their time is coming. Soon."

Pobrecito comes to understand. Girls are being taken away by the priests. To be used, he supposes, like the Americans in his pictures use each other. Will the girls of the *colonia* smile beneath the lusts of the priests? Surely they will be cleaned and fed and cared for. It is the priests in their walled city that hold all wealth, all power.

But eventually the anger melts into fatigue, and word comes that the *guardia* are on their way down to the *colonia*, and so the knives and pistols vanish and people trudge home, some of them weeping more than usual.

Over the weeks, a few more girls are called every few days, always the hale ones with good curves to their breasts. The *guardia* comes to collect them now, as the people are no longer willing to send their sisters and daughters up the hill simply because a summons has come. There are beatings and a few quiet murders in which no priest-advocate will take any interest.

None of the girls come back.

In a few month's time, some older women are called, and younger girls as well. They do not return, either. The *colonia* remains restless, but the crystallizing anger of the first night never quite reappears. There is always food to worry about, and the dogs from the river, and the clouds of flies and wasps which can strip a man's skin in minutes, and the sicknesses which prowl just as deadly if less visible.

And the heat.

It is always a little hotter. This has been the way of things all of Pobrecito's life.

The vanishing girls and women are good for Pobrecito's little business. Sad men and wild-eyed boys buy from him, paying him in dented cans of dog food or little bundles of yams or onions. Even a few of the old women seek him out, clucking and tutting like senile chickens draped in funeral black, wanting pictures "of a girl alone, none of your despicable filth, just something to remember her by."

But he is becoming too well known, too rich. He has more food than he and Lucia can eat in a day, and even a few metal tools and some old bits of gold, which he hides in his tree by the river.

Is he rich enough to be an American yet, Pobrecito wonders?

One day he makes his way into the *Cementerio Americano* carrying two books and an old bottle of wine he has been paid for a handful of pictures of three thin, yellow-haired women kissing each other. By habit Pobrecito keeps to the shadows, the edges of fences and tumbled walls, but also by habit he has made a path in and out of this place. He steps around the edge of a rotting shed which contains a flat-tired tractor and some large metal implements to find three of the *guardia*.

"Ah," says Pobrecito, and reflexively offers them the wine. Perhaps it will save him from whatever is next. He doubts that, though.

The leader, for he has more decoration on his buttoned shoulder tabs, strokes the bright leather of his pistol belt for a moment, then smiles. It is a horrid sort of smile, something a man remembering an old photo he is trying to imitate might offer up. The other two do not bother. Instead they merely cradle a machete each, staring corpse-eyed at Pobrecito. All three of them are fat, their bellies bigger than their hips, unlike anyone in the *colonia*, except a few who are dying of growths in their guts.

No one takes the wine.

"You are the guardian of Lucia Sandoz, is it not true?" the leader asks.

This is not what Pobrecito expected. "Ah . . . no. She comes here sometimes."

The leader consults a thin notebook, ragged with handling, pages nearly black with ink. "You are Pobrecito the street merchant, no address, of the *colonia*."

"Yes."

"Then you are the guardian of Lucia Sandoz. It says so here in my book, and so this must be a true thing." His smile asserts itself again. "We have a summons for her." All three *guardia* peer around, as if expecting her to fall from the sky. Pobrecito realizes this has become an old game for them already.

"She is not mine," he says to his feet. Not Lucia. "And besides," he adds, "she is a *menoriíta*. She cannot be used in the manner of a woman." Will this help?

They laugh, his tormentors, before one of the machete-carriers says, "How would you know if you hadn't had her?"

The leader leans close. "She is *clean*, boy. That is enough these days."

Then they beat him, using the flat of the machete blades and the rough toes of their boots. Pobrecito loses most of his left ear when a blade slips, and the palm of his hand is cut to the bone, but they stop before staving in his ribs or breaking any large bones.

"Find her," says the leader. Pobrecito can barely hear him through the pain and blood in his ear. The *guardia* tears the pages of the books from their bindings, unzips, and urinates on the paper. Taking the wine bottle, he turns to leave. "Before tomorrow."

Pobrecito does not waste time on crying. He stumbles to his tree, knowing there are some extra clothes there that he can use to bind his ear and his hand. There are so many sicknesses that come in through bloody cuts and sores – black rot, green rot, the red crust – and he fears them all.

Stumbling, eyes dark and head ringing, Pobrecito can barely climb his tree because his arms and legs hurt so much. When he reaches the branch, he sees that someone has been at his cache of riches and food. *Guardia*, dogs, it does not matter. The hollow in the trunk has been hacked open, made wide and ragged with an axe or a machete, and everything that is not gone is smashed or torn or broken. His riches are nothing but trash now.

"I will never be an American," Pobrecito whispers. He lays his mutilated ear against the slashed palm of his hand, pressing them together to slow the bleeding and protect the wounds from insects. Despite the pain, he lays that side of his head against the branch and stretches out to surrender to the ringing darkness.

"Wake up, fool!" It is Lucia's voice. She is slapping him.

Pobrecito feels strange. His skin is itchy, crawly, prickly.

More slaps.

"Stop it this instant!" Her voice is rising toward a frightening break.

He opens his mouth to answer her and flies tumble in.

He is covered in flies.

"Gaaah!" Pobrecito screams.

"Get them off before they bite," she says, her voice more under control.

Pobrecito stumbles to his feet, runs down the branch where it overhangs the water.

"Not the river . . ." she says behind him, but it is too late. The old branch narrows, is rotten, his legs are weak, his eyes not clear. In a crackling shower of wood, flies and blood, Pobrecito tumbles the five or six meters downward to slam into the slow, brown water, knocking the air from his body.

The river is blood warm, shocking him awake. He is under the surface, eyes open to a uniform brown with no way up. The water is sticky, strange, clinging to him, trying to draw him further down. Pobrecito kicks his legs, trying to come out, but there is still no up.

At least the flies are gone.

He begins to wonder if he could open his mouth and find something besides the burning in his empty lungs.

Something scrapes his legs. Something long, slow and powerful. Pobrecito throws his hands out and finds a stick. He pulls on it, but it does not come, so he pulls himself toward it.

A moment later he is gasping and muddy, clinging to a root sticking out from the river bank. Air is in his lungs, blessed air.

Behind him the water burbles as the long, slow, powerful thing circles back to test him again. Out in the middle of the river, the dogs are barking.

Lucia is scrambling down the tree trunk, sobbing. "Fool! Idiot!"

She helps him pull himself out before his legs are taken. He lies on the bank gasping and crying, blessedly free of flies. He does not want to think about what the river water might have done to his wounds. "They . . . they came . . . they came for you . . ." he spits out.

"No one wants me," she says fiercely.

"They said you were *clean*. That clean was enough for them these days."

She is quiet for a moment. "Fire-piss is killing the rich men up in the city, the old women say. The priests have heard from god that to fuck a clean woman takes the fire-piss from the man and gives it to her."

"How do you know? No one comes back."

"Some people pass in and out of the walls. Servants. Farmers. The word comes. And the cemetery is overflowing, up on the hill. With rich city men." She stares at him for a moment. "The *colonia* girls they dump down the old wells with some quicklime and gravel, and a prayer if they're feeling generous."

"Ahhh . . ." He weeps, eyes filling with hot tears as they hadn't for the beating, or for anything in his memory, really. "And they want you now."

"The cure does not work, but it does not stop them from trying over and over. The priests say it is so, that they are not faithful enough. Up in the city, they believe they can make the world however they want it." She stares at him for a while. "And perhaps they have a taste for new girls all the time."

Pobrecito thinks about his American pictures. Obviously many people had a taste for new girls all the time. Has he somehow been feeding this evil? But he doesn't sell his pictures in the city, or even to city men. Not directly. He has always wondered if some of his buyers did.

And if he could make the world the way he wanted it, he would wish away the heat and the insects and the sicknesses. He would make them all Americans like in his pictures, naked, happy, pale-skinned blondes with big houses and tables full of food and more water than any sane person could ever use. He would not wish for more girls to kill. Not even if God told him to.

"I want to show you something," he says.

"Show me soon. I think the dogs are coming over."

"In the day?"

"You got their attention, my friend."

Out at the airplane, dogs were gathering on the wing, their feet in the slow water. Some of them were casting sticks and stones out into the river, looking for that great predator that had touched Pobrecito for a moment. Others growl through pointed teeth, eyes glowing at him. Smoke curls from some of the shattered oval windows. Great red and blue letters, faded and worn as the tail's flag, loom along the rounded top of the airplane in some American prayer for the coming assault.

"It is over anyway," he says. "Come." He leads her deeper into the *Cementerio Americano*. Here Pobrecito has always been careful to hop from stone to stone, scramble along mortared kerbs, step on open ground, never making a path.

Here among the houses of the American dead is his greatest treasure.

He shows Lucia a squared-off vault, door wedged tightly shut. Grabbing a cornice, Pobrecito pulls himself to the roof though his body strains with the pain of the beating and the curious ache of his fall into the river. He then dangles his arm over to help her up. There are two windows in the roof, and he knows the secret of loosening one.

In a moment they are in the cool darkness of the vault. There are two marble coffins here, carved with wreaths and flowers, and Pobrecito's precious box of magazines at one end. He has left a few supplies, a can of drinkable water and some dried fruit, a homespun shirt without quite enough holes for it to disintegrate to ragged patches. And matches, his other great treasure.

"These people do not seem so wealthy," Lucia whispers. "This is a fine little house for them, but the only riches here are yours."

Pobrecito shrugs. "Perhaps they were robbed before I found them. Or perhaps their riches are within their coffins. This is a finer room than any you or I will ever live or die in." As soon as he says that last, he wishes he hadn't, as they may very well die in this room.

"So now what will you do?"

He pulls the magazines out of the their box, fans the pages open. Sleek American flesh in a hundred combinations flashes before his eyes, cocks, breasts, tongues, leather and plastic toys, sleek cars . . . all the world that was, once. The American world lost to the heat and the sicknesses. Pobrecito tosses the magazines into a pile, deliberately haphazard. After a few moments, Lucia begins to help, tearing a few apart, breaking their spines so they will lay flat. She ignores the pictures, though she is not so used to them as Pobrecito is.

Soon they have a glossy pile of images of the perfect past. Without another word, Pobrecito strikes a match and sets fire to a bright, curled edge. Cool faces, free of sweat and wounds, blacken and shrivel. He lights more matches, sets more edges of the pile on fire, until the flames take over.

The smoke stinks, filling the little vault, curling around the opening in the roof. He does not care, though Lucia is coughing. Pobrecito pulls off his wet, bloody clothes and pushes them into the base of the fire, then climbs atop one of the marble coffins. A few moments later, Lucia joins him.

She is naked as well.

They lie there on the bed of marble, smooth skinned as any Americans, kissing and touching, while the fire burns the pretty people in their pretty houses and the smoke rises through the roof. Outside dogs howl and *guardia* pistols crack.

When Lucia takes his cock in her mouth, Pobrecito knows he is as wealthy as any American. A while later he feels the hot rush of himself into her, even as the smoke makes him so dizzy his thoughts have spun off into the sky like so many airplanes rising from their river grave.

Soon he will be a true American, wealthy and dead.

PETER ATKINS

Between the Cold Moon and the Earth

PETER ATKINS IS A NATIVE of Liverpool, but has lived in Los Angeles for fifteen years with his wife Dana. He is the author of the novels *Morningstar* and *Big Thunder* and the collection *Wishmaster and Other Stories*.

His work has also appeared in *Weird Tales*, *The Magazine of Fantasy & Science Fiction*, *Cemetery Dance* and several award-winning anthologies. He has written for television and the stage, but is probably best known for his work in the cinema, where he has scripted three of the *Hellraiser* movies and created the *Wishmaster* franchise.

"Between the Cold Moon and the Earth" was written for the October 2006 tour of *The Rolling Darkness Revue*, the multi-media collective that Atkins founded with his friends and fellow-authors Glen Hirshberg and Dennis Etchison. It first appeared in *At the Sign of the Snowman's Skull*, a chapbook produced for the tour by Paul Miller's Earthling Publications.

"The story played very well on the reading tour," recalls Atkins, "but my American audiences were confused by the fact that some of the 16-year-old characters had spent the earlier part of the evening in a pub.

"In fact, such flouting of the drinking laws was common in the 1970s Liverpool where I grew up. Other parts of the story are from life also, including its lovely and foul-mouthed heroine."

T HEY ONLY BRUSHED his cheek for a second or two, but her lips were fucking *freezing*.

"Christ, Carol," he said. "Do you want my coat?"

She laughed. "What for?" she asked.

"Because it's one in the morning," he said. "And you're cold."

"It's summer," she pointed out, which was undeniably true but wasn't really the issue. "Are you going to walk me home then?"

Michael had left the others about forty minutes earlier. Kirk had apparently copped off with the girl from Woolworth's that they'd met inside the pub so Michael and Terry had tactfully peeled away before the bus stop and started walking the long way home around Sefton Park. He could've split a taxi fare with Terry but, given that they were still in the middle of their ongoing argument about the relative merits of T. Rex and Pink Floyd and that it was still a good six months before they'd find Roxy Music to agree on, they'd parted by unspoken consent and Michael had opted to cut across the park alone.

Carol had been standing on the path beside the huge park's large boating lake. He'd practically shit himself when he first saw the shadowed figure there, assuming the worst – a midnight skinhead parked on watch ready to whistle his mates out of hiding to give this handy glam-rock faggot a good kicking – but Carol had been doing nothing more threatening than staring out at the center of the lake and the motionless full moon reflected there.

"All right, Michael," she'd said, before he'd quite recognised her in the moonlight, and had kissed his cheek lightly in further greeting before he'd spoken her name. Now, he fell into step beside her and they began to walk the long slow curve around the lake.

"God, Carol. Where've you been?" he asked. "Nobody's seen you for months."

It was true. Her mum had remarried just before last Christmas and they'd moved. Not far away, still in the same city, but far enough for sixteen-year-olds to lose touch.

"I went to America," Carol said.

Michael turned his head to see if she was kidding. "You went to *America*?" he said. "What d'you mean, you went to America? When? Who with?"

Her eyes narrowed for a moment as if she were re-checking her facts or her memory. "I think it was America," she said.

"You *think* it was America?"

"It might have been an imaginary America," she said, her voice a little impatient. "Do you want to hear the fucking story or not?"

Oh. Michael didn't smile nor attempt to kiss her, but he felt like doing both. Telling stories – real, imagined, or some happy collision of the two – had been one of the bonds between them, one of the things he'd loved about her. Not the only thing of course. It's not like he hadn't shared Kirk and Terry's enthusiastic affection for her astonishingly perfect breasts and for the teasingly challenging way she had about her that managed to suggest two things simultaneously: that, were circumstances to somehow become magically right, she might, you know, actually *do it* with you; and that you were probably and permanently incapable of ever conjuring such circumstances. But her stories, and her delight in telling them, were what he'd loved most and what, he now realised, he'd most missed. So yes, he said, he wanted to hear the story.

There was some quick confusion about whether she'd got there by plane or by ship – Carol had never been a big fan of preamble – but apparently what mattered was that, after a few days, she found herself in a roadside diner with a bunch of people she hardly knew.

They were on a road trip and had stopped for lunch in this back-of-beyond and unpretentious diner – a place which, while perfectly clean and respectable, looked like it hadn't been painted or refurbished since about 1952. They were in a booth, eating pie and drinking coffee. Her companions were about her age – but could, you know, *drive* and everything. Turned out boys in America could be just as fucking rude as in Liverpool. One of them – Tommy, she thought his name was – was giving shit to the waitress. Hoisting his empty coffee mug, he was leaning out of the booth and looking pointedly down the length of the room.

"Yo! Still need a refill here!" he shouted to the counter.

Carol stood up and, announcing she was going to the ladies' room, slid her way out of the booth. Halfway down the room, she crossed paths with the waitress, who was hurrying toward their booth with a coffee pot. The woman's name tag said *Cindi*, a spelling Carol had never seen before and hoped could possibly be short for Cinderella because that'd be, you know, great. Carol spoke softly to her, nodding back towards Tommy, who was impatiently shaking his empty coffee mug in the air.

"Don't mind him, love," Carol said. "He's a bit of a prick, but I'll make sure he leaves a nice tip."

Cindi, who was harried-looking and appeared to be at least 30, gave her a quick smile of gratitude. "Little girls' room's out back, sweetheart," she said.

Carol exited the main building of the diner and saw that a separate

structure, little more than a shack really, housed the bathrooms. She
started across the gravelled parking lot, surrounded by scrub-grass
that was discoloured and overgrown, looking down the all-but-
deserted country road – the type of road, she'd been informed by
her new friends, which was known as a two-lane blacktop. The diner
and its shithouse annex were the only buildings for as far as her eye
could see, apart from a hulking grain silo a hundred yards or so
down the road. As Carol looked in that desolate direction, a cloud
drifted over the sun, dimming the summer daylight and shifting the
atmosphere into a kind of pre-storm dreariness. Carol shivered and
wondered, not without a certain pleasure in the mystery, just where
the hell she was.

Done peeing and alone in the bathroom, Carol washed her hands
and splashed her face at the pretty crappy single sink that was all the
place had to offer. The sound of the ancient cistern laboriously and
noisily re-filling after her flush played in the background. Carol
turned off the tap and looked for a moment at her reflection in the
pitted and stained mirror above the sink. As the cistern finally
creaked and whistled to a halt, the mirror suddenly cracked noisily
across its width as if it was just too tired to keep trying.

"Fuckin' 'ell!" said Carol, because it had made her jump and
because she didn't like the newly mismatched halves of her reflected
face. She turned around, ready to walk out of the bathroom, and
discovered she was no longer alone.

A little girl – what, six, seven years old? – was standing, silent and
perfectly still, outside one of the stall doors, looking up at her. Oddly,
the little girl was holding the palm of one hand over her right eye.

"Oh, shit," said Carol, remembering that she'd just said *fucking
hell* in front of a kid. "I didn't know you were –" She paused, smiled,
started over. "Hello, pet. D'you live around here?"

The little girl just kept looking at her.

"What's your name?" Carol asked her, still smiling but still getting
no response. Registering the hand-over-the-eye thing, she tried a new
tack. "Oh," she said. "Are we playing a game and nobody told me
the rules? All right then, here we go."

Raising her hand, Carol covered her own right eye with her palm.
The little girl remained still and silent. Carol lowered her hand from
her face. "Peek-a-boo," she said.

Finally, the little girl smiled shyly and lowered her own hand. She
had no right eye at all, just a smooth indented bank of flesh.

Carol was really good. She hardly jumped at all and her gasp was
as short-lived as could reasonably be expected.

The little girl's voice was very matter-of-fact. "Momma lost my eye-patch," she said.

"Oh. That's a shame," said Carol, trying to keep her own voice as equally everyday.

"She's gonna get me another one. When she goes to town."

"Oh, well, that's good. Will she get a nice colour? Do you have a favourite colour?"

The little girl shrugged. "What are you, retarded?" she said. "It's an eye-patch. Who cares what colour it is?"

Carol didn't know whether to laugh or slap her.

"You can go now, if you like," said the little girl. "I have to make water."

"Oh. All right. Sure. Well, look after yourself," Carol said and, raising her hand in a slightly awkward wave of farewell, headed for the exit door. The little girl called after her.

"You take care in those woods now, Carol," she said.

"I hadn't told her my name," said Carol.

"Well, that was weird," Michael said.

Carol smiled, pleased. "*That* wasn't weird," she said. "It *got* weird. Later. After I got lost in the woods."

"You got lost in the woods?"

Carol nodded.

"Why'd they let you go wandering off on your own?"

"Who?"

"Your new American friends. The people you were in the café with."

"Ha. Café. *Diner*, stupid. We were in America."

"Whatever. How could they let you get lost?"

"Oh, yeah." She thought about it for a second, looking out to their side at the boating lake and its ghost moon. "Well, p'raps they weren't there to begin with. Doesn't matter. Listen."

Turned out Carol *did* get lost in the woods. Quite deep in the woods, actually. Heart of the forest, Hansel and Gretel shit, where the sunlight, through the thickening trees, was dappled and spotty and where the reassuring blue sky of what was left of the afternoon could be glimpsed only occasionally through the increasingly oppressive canopy of high leafy branches.

Carol was tramping her way among the trees and the undergrowth on the mossy and leaf-strewn ground when she heard the sound for the first time. Faint and plaintive and too distant to be truly identifiable, it was nevertheless suggestive of something, something that Carol couldn't quite put her finger on. Only when it came again, a few moments later, did she place it. It was the sound of a lonely ship's horn in a midnight ocean, melancholy and eerie. Not quite as eerie, though, as the fact that once the horn had sounded this second time, all the other sounds stopped, all the other sounds of which Carol hadn't even been consciously aware until they disappeared: birdsong; the footsteps of unseen animals moving through the woods; the sigh of the breeze as it whistled through the branches.

The only sounds now were those she made herself: the rustle and sway of the living branches she was pushing her way through and the crackle and snap of the dead ones she was breaking beneath her. Carol began to wonder if moving on in the same direction she'd been going was that great of an idea. She turned around and started heading back and, within a few yards, stepping out from between two particularly close trees, she found herself in a small grove-like clearing that she didn't remember passing through earlier.

There was a downed and decaying tree-trunk lying in the leafy undergrowth that momentarily and ridiculously put Carol in mind of a park bench. But she really wasn't in the mood to sit and relax and it wasn't like there was, you know, a boating lake to look at the moon in or anything. So she kept moving, across the clearing, past the downed trunk, and stopped only when the voice spoke from behind her.

"What's your rush, sweetheart?"

Carol turned back. Sitting perched on the bench-like trunk was a sailor. He was dressed in a square-neck deck-shirt and bell-bottomed pants and Carol might have taken a moment to wonder if sailors still dressed like that if she hadn't been too busy being surprised just to see him at all. He was sitting in profile to her, one leg on the ground, the other arched up on the trunk and he didn't turn to face her fully, perhaps because he was concentrating on rolling a cigarette.

"Ready-mades are easier," the sailor said. "But I like the ritual – opening the paper, laying in the tobacco, rolling it up. Know what I mean?"

"I don't smoke," said Carol, which wasn't strictly true, but who the fuck was he to deserve the truth.

"You chew?" he asked.

"Chew what?"

"Tobacco."

"Eugh. No."

The sailor chanted something rhythmic in response, like he was singing her a song but knew his limitations when it came to carrying a tune:

"*Down in Nagasaki,*
Where the fellas chew tobaccy
And the women wicky-wacky-woo."

Carol stared at him. Confused. Not necessarily nervous. Not yet. She gestured out at the woods. "Where'd you come from?" she said.

"Dahlonega, Georgia. Little town northeast of Atlanta. Foot of the Appalachians."

That wasn't what she'd meant and she started to tell him so, but he interrupted.

"Ever been to Nagasaki, honeybun?"

"No."

"How about Shanghai?"

The sailor was still sitting in profile to her. Talking to her, but staring straight ahead into the woods and beyond. He didn't wait for a reply. "Docked there once," he said. "Didn't get shore-leave. Fellas who did told me I missed something, boy. Said there were whores there could practically tie themselves in knots. Real limber. Mmm. A man likes that. Likes 'em limber."

Carol was very careful not to say anything at all. Not to move. Not to breathe.

"Clean, too," said the sailor. "That's important to me. Well, who knows? Maybe I'll get back there one of these days. 'Course, once they get a good look at me, I might have to pay extra." He turned finally to face her. "Whaddaya think?"

Half of his face was bone-pale and bloated, as if it had drowned years ago and been underwater ever since. His hair hung dank like seaweed and something pearl-like glinted in the moist dripping blackness of what used to be an eye-socket.

"Jesus Christ!" Carol said, frozen in shock, watching helplessly as the sailor put his cigarette in his half-ruined mouth, lit it, and inhaled.

"Calling on the Lord for salvation," he said. "Good for you. Might help." Smoke oozed out from the pulpy white flesh that barely clung to the bone beneath his dead face. "Might not."

He rose to his feet and grinned at her. "Useta chase pigs through the Georgia pines, sweet thing," he said, flinging his cigarette aside. "Let's see if you're faster than them little squealers."

And then he came for her.

"I was a lot faster, though," said Carol. "But it still took me ten minutes to lose him."

"Fuck, Carol," said Michael. "That wasn't funny."

"I didn't say it was funny. I said it was weird. Remember?"

Michael turned to look at her and she tilted her face to look up at his, dark eyes glinting, adorably proud of herself. They'd walked nearly a full circuit of the lake now, neither of them even thinking to branch off in the direction of the park's northern gate and the way home.

"Well, it was weird, all right," Michael said. "Creepy ghost sailor. Pretty good."

"Yeah," she said. "Turns out there was a ship went down there in the Second World War. All hands lost."

"Went down in the woods. That was a good trick."

"It wasn't the *woods*. Didn't I tell you that? It was the beach. That's where it all happened."

"Was it Redondo?"

"The fuck's *Redondo*?" she said, genuinely puzzled.

"It's a beach. In America. I've heard of it. It's on that Patti Smith album."

"Oh, yeah. No. This wasn't in America. It was in Cornwall." She thought about it for a moment. "Yeah. Had to be Cornwall because of the rock pool."

"You didn't say anything about a rock pool."

"I haven't *told* you yet," she said, exasperated. "God, you're rubbish."

Michael laughed, even though something else had just hit him. He was walking on a moonlit night alone with a beautiful girl and it apparently wasn't occurring to him to try anything. He hadn't even put his arm around her, for Christ's sake. Terry and Kirk would give him such shit for this when he told them. He wondered for the first time if that was something Carol knew, if that was what had always been behind her stories, why she found them, why she told them, like some instinctive Scheherazade keeping would-be lovers at bay with narrative strategies. He felt something forming in him, a kind of sadness that he couldn't name and didn't understand.

"Is everything all right, Carol?" he asked, though he couldn't say why.

"Well, it is *now*," she said, deaf to the half-born subtext in his question. "I got away. I escaped. But that spoils the story, dickhead. You've got to hear what *happened* first."

The park was silver-grey in the light from the moon. He wondered what time it was. "The rock pool," he said.

"Exactly," she said, pleased that he was paying attention.

*   *   *

She hadn't seen it at first. Had kept moving along the deserted beach until the sandy shore gave way to rocky cave-strewn outcrops from the cliffs above the coastline. It was only when she clambered over an algae- and seaweed-coated rock wall that she found it. Orphaned from the sea and held within a natural basin formation, the pool was placid and still and ringed by several large boulders about its rim. It was about twenty feet across and looked to be fairly deep.

On one of the boulders, laid out as if waiting for their owner, were some items of clothing. A dress, a pair of stockings, some underwear. Carol looked from them out to the cool inviting water of the pool. A head broke surface as she looked, and a woman started swimming toward the rock where her clothes were. Catching sight of Carol, she stopped and trod water, looking at her suspiciously. "What are you doing?" she said. "Are you spying?" She was older than Carol, about her mum's age maybe, a good-looking thirty-five.

"No, I'm not," Carol said. "Why would I be spying?"

"You might be one of them," the woman said.

"One of who?"

The woman narrowed her eyes and looked at Carol appraisingly. "You know who," she said.

"No, I don't," Carol said. "And I'm not one of anybody. I was with some friends. We went to France. Just got back. The boat's down there on the beach."

"They've all got stories," the woman said. "That's how they get you."

"Who?! Stop talking shit, willya? I –" Carol bit her tongue.

For the first time, the woman smiled. "Are you moderating your language for me?" she said. "That's adorable."

Carol felt strangely flustered. Was this woman *flirting* with her?

"I understand," the woman said, still smiling, still staring straight into Carol's eyes. "I'm an older lady and you want to be polite. But, you know, I'm not really *that* much older." She stepped out of the pool and stood there right in front of Carol, glistening wet and naked. "See what I mean?" she said.

Carol felt funny. She swallowed. The woman kept her eyes fixed on Carol as she stepped very close to her. "I'm going to tell you a secret," she said, and leaned forward to whisper the secret in Carol's ear. "I'm real limber for my age."

Carol jumped back as the woman's voice began a familiar rhythmic chant.

"*Down in Nagasaki,*
Where the fellas chew tobaccy,

And the women wicky-wacky-woo."

Carol tried to run but the woman had already grabbed her by the throat. "What's your rush, sweetheart?" she said, and her voice was different now, guttural and amused. "Party's just getting started."

Carol was struggling in the choking grip. She tried to swing a fist at the woman's head but her punch was effortlessly blocked by the woman's other arm.

"Your eyes are so pretty," the woman said. "I'm going to have them for earrings."

Her mouth opened inhumanly wide. Her tongue flicked out with reptile speed. It was long and black and forked.

"But, like I said," said Carol, "I escaped."

"How?" said Michael, expecting another previously unmentioned element to be brought into play, like a knife or a gun or a really sharp stick or a last-minute rescue by her Francophile friends from the recently-invented boat. But Carol had a different ending in mind.

"I walked into the moon," she said.

Michael looked up to the night sky.

"No," said Carol. "Not that moon. This one."

She was pointing out towards the center of the utterly calm lake and the perfect moon reflected there. Looking at it with her, neither of them walking now, Michael felt the cold of the night as if for the first time. He waited in silence, afraid to speak, afraid to give voice to his questions, afraid that they would be answered.

She told another story then, the last, he knew, that his sweet lost friend would ever tell him, the tale of how the other moon had many ways into and out of this world: through placid lakes on summer evenings; through city streets on rain-slicked nights; from out of the ocean depths for the eyes of lonely night-watch sailors.

And when she was done, when Michael could no longer pretend not to know in whose company he truly was, she turned to him and smiled a heartbreaking smile of farewell.

She looked beautiful in monochrome, in the subtle tones of the moon that had claimed her for its own. Not drained of colour, but richly reimagined, painted in shades of silver and grey, of black and delicate lunar blue. She looked almost liquid, as if, were Michael to reach out a hand and even try to touch her, she might ripple into strange expansions of herself.

"Thanks, Michael," she said. "I can make it home from here."

Michael didn't say anything. Didn't know what he could possibly find to say that the tears in his young eyes weren't already saying.

The beautiful dead girl pointed a silver finger beyond him, in the direction of his life. "Go on," she said kindly. "Don't look back."

And he didn't look back, not even when he heard the impossible footsteps on the water, not even when he heard the shadow moon sigh in welcome, and the quiet lapping of the lake water as if something had slipped effortlessly beneath it.

He'd later hear the alternative versions, of course – the stories of how, one moonlit night, Carol had walked out of the third-floor window of her step-father's house and the vile rumors as to why – but he would prefer, for all his days, to believe the story that the lost girl herself had chosen to tell him.

He continued home through the park, not even breaking step as his fingers sought and found the numb spot on his cheek, the frozen place where her cold lips had blessed him, waiting for her frostbite kiss to bloom in tomorrow's mirror.

GENE WOLFE

Sob in the Silence

GENE WOLFE IS ACCLAIMED for his dense, allusion-rich prose. He is a prolific short story writer as well as a novelist, and has won two Nebula Awards and three World Fantasy Awards.

His latest books are *Pirate Freedom*, published by Tor, and *Severian of the Guild: The Book of the New Sun*, from Gollancz. The author has been described as being "simultaneously the Dickens and the Nabokov of the speculative genres". He lives in Barrington, Illinois.

" 'Sob in the Silence' is horror, I think," says Wolfe. "It originally appeared in *Strange Birds*, a chapbook published by Greg Ketter's DreamHaven Books. The art is Lisa Snelling-Clark's, and the stories are mine.

"In the booklet, the reproduction of Lisa's 'The Children's Hour' is too small and too dim to see the terrified faces of the children; they are peeping from the pocket of a tall figure with a puppet. The original art, in all its dark glory, comes pretty close to terrifying."

"THIS," THE HORROR WRITER told the family visiting him, "is beyond any question the least haunted house in the Midwest. No ghost, none at all, will come within miles of the place. So I am assured."

Robbie straightened his little glasses and mumbled, "Well, it looks haunted."

"It does, young man." After teetering between seven and eight, the horror writer decided that Robbie was about seven. "It's the filthy yellow stucco. No doubt it was a cheerful yellow once, but God only knows how long it's been up. I'm going to have it torn off, every scrap of it, and put up fresh, which I will paint white."

"Can't you just paint over?" Kiara asked. (Kiara of the all-conquering pout, of the golden hair and the tiny silver earrings.)

Looking very serious, the horror writer nodded. And licked his lips only mentally. "I've tried, believe me. That hideous color is the result of air pollution – of smoke, soot, and dirt, if you will – that has clung to the stucco. Paint over it, and it bleeds out through the new paint. Washing—"

"Water jets under high pressure." Dan was Robbie's father, and Kiara's. "You can rent the units, or buy one for a thousand or so."

"I own one," the horror writer told him. "With a strong cleaning agent added to the water, it will do the job." He paused to smile. "Unfortunately, the stucco's old and fragile. Here and there, a good jet breaks it."

"Ghosts," Charity said. Charity was Mrs Dan, a pudgy woman with a soft, not unattractive face and a remarkable talent for dowdy hats. "Please go back to your ghosts. I find ghosts far more interesting."

"As do I." The horror writer favored her with his most dazzling smile. "I've tried repeatedly to interest psychic researchers in the old place, which has a – may I call it fascinating? History. I've been persuasive and persistent, and no less than three teams have checked this old place out as a result. All three have reported that they found nothing. No evidence whatsoever. No spoor of spooks. No cooperative specters a struggling author might use for research purposes."

"And publicity," Kiara said. "Don't forget publicity. I plan to get into public relations when I graduate."

"And publicity, you're right. By the time you're well settled in public relations, I hope to be wealthy enough to engage you. If I am, I will. That's a promise."

Charity leveled a plump forefinger. "You, on the other hand, have clearly seen or heard or felt something. You had to have something more than this big dark living-room to get the psychics in, and you had it. Tell us."

The horror writer produced a sharply bent briar that showed signs of years of use. "Will this trouble anyone? I rarely smoke in here, but if we're going to have a good long chat – well, a pipe may make things go more smoothly. Would anyone care for a drink?"

Charity was quickly equipped with white wine, Dan with Johnnie-Walker-and-water, and Robbie with cola. "A lot of the kids drink beer at IVY Tech," Kiara announced in a tone that indicated she was one of them. "I don't, though."

"Not until you're twenty-one," Dan said firmly.

"You see?" She pouted.

The horror writer nodded. "I do indeed. One of the things I see is that you have good parents, parents who care about you and are zealous for your welfare." He slipped Kiara a scarcely perceptible wink. "What about a plain soda? I always find soda water over ice refreshing, myself."

Charity said, "That would be fine, if she wants it."

Kiara said she did, and he became busy behind the bar.

Robbie had been watching the dark upper corners of the old, high-ceilinged room. "I thought I saw one."

"A ghost?" The horror writer looked up, his blue eyes twinkling.

"A bat. Maybe we can catch it."

Dan said, "There's probably a belfry, too."

"I'm afraid not. Perhaps I'll add one once I get the new stucco on."

"You need one. As I've told my wife a dozen times, anybody who believes in ghosts has bats in his belfry."

"It's better, perhaps," Charity murmured, "if living things breathe and move up there. Better than just bells, rotting ropes, and dust. Tell us more about this place, please."

"It was a country house originally." With the air of one who performed a sacrament, the horror writer poured club soda into a tall frosted glass that already contained five ice cubes and (wholly concealed by his fingers) a generous two inches of vodka. "A quiet place in which a wealthy family could get away from the heat and stench of city summers. The family was ruined somehow – I don't recall the details. I know it's usually the man who kills in murder-suicides, but in this house it was the woman. She shot her husband and her stepdaughters, and killed herself."

Charity said, "I could never bring myself to do that. I could never kill Dan. Or his children. I suppose I might kill myself. That's conceivable. But not the rest."

Straight-faced, the horror writer handed his frosted glass to Kiara. "I couldn't kill myself," he told her. "I like myself too much. Other people? Who can say?"

Robbie banged down his cola. "You're trying to scare us!"

"Of course I am. It's my trade."

Dan asked, "They all died? That's good shooting."

The horror writer resumed his chair and picked up his briar. "No. As a matter of fact they didn't. One of the three stepdaughters survived. She had been shot in the head at close range, yet she lived."

Dan said, "Happens sometime."

"It does. It did in this case. Her name was Maude Parkhurst. Maude was a popular name back around 1900, which is when her parents and sisters died. Ever hear of her?"

Dan shook his head.

"She was left penniless and scarred for life. It seems to have disordered her thinking. Or perhaps the bullet did it. In any event, she founded her own church and was its pope and prophetess. It was called – maybe it's still called, since it may still be around for all I know – the Unionists of Heaven and Earth."

Charity said, "I've heard of it. It sounded innocent enough."

The horror writer shrugged. "Today? Perhaps it is. Back then, I would say no. Decidedly no. It was, in its own fantastic fashion, about as repellent as a cult can be. May I call it a cult?"

Kiara grinned prettily over her glass. "Go right ahead. I won't object."

"A friend of mine, another Dan, once defined a cult for me. He said that if the leader gets all the women, it's a cult."

Dan nodded. "Good man. There's a lot to that."

"There is, but in the case of the UHE, as it was called, it didn't apply. Maude Parkhurst didn't want the women, or the men either. The way to get to Heaven, she told her followers, was to live like angels here on earth."

Dan snorted.

"Exactly. Any sensible person would have told them that they were not angels. That it was natural and right for angels to live like angels, but that men and women should live like human beings."

"We really know almost nothing about angels." Charity looked pensive. "Just that they carry the Lord's messages. It's Saint Paul, I think, who says that each of us has an angel who acts as our advocate in Heaven. So we know that, too. But it's really very little."

"This is about sex," Kiara said. "I smell it coming."

The horror writer nodded. "You're exactly right, and I'm beginning to wonder if you're not the most intelligent person here. It is indeed. Members of the UHE were to refrain from all forms of sexual activity. If unmarried, they were not to marry. If married, they were to separate and remain separated."

"The University of Heaven at Elysium. On a T-shirt. I can see it now."

Charity coughed, the sound of it scarcely audible in the large, dark room. "Well, Kiara, I don't see anything wrong with that if it was voluntary."

"Neither do I," the horror writer said, "but there's more. Those wishing to join underwent an initiation period of a year. At the end of that time, there was a midnight ceremony. If they had children, those children had to attend, all of them. There they watched their parents commit suicide – or that's how it looked. I don't know the details, but I know that at the end of the service they were carried out of the church, apparently lifeless and covered with blood."

Charity whispered, "Good God . . ."

"When the congregation had gone home," the horror writer continued, "the children were brought here. They were told that it was an orphanage, and it was operated like one. Before long it actually was one. Apparently there was some sort of tax advantage, so it was registered with the state as a church-run foundation, and from time to time the authorities sent actual orphans here. It was the age of orphanages, as you may know. Few children, if any, were put in foster homes. Normally, it was the orphanage for any child without parents or close relatives."

Dan said, "There used to be a comic strip about it, *Little Orphan Annie*."

The horror writer nodded. "Based upon a popular poem of the nineteenth century.

> " 'Little Orphant Annie's come to our house to stay,
> An' wash the cups an' saucers up,
> an' brush the crumbs away,
> An' shoo the chickens off the porch,
> an' dust the hearth an' sweep,
> An' make the fire, an' bake the bread,
> an' earn her board an' keep.
> An' all us other children,
> when the supper things is done,
> We set around the kitchen fire an' has the mostest fun
> A-list'nin' to the witch tales 'at Annie tells about,
> An' the Gobble-uns 'at gets you
> > Ef you
> > > Don't
> > > > Watch
> > > > > Out!'

"You see," the horror writer finished, smiling, "in those days you could get an orphan girl from such an orphanage as this to be your maid of all work and baby-sitter. You fed and clothed her, gave her a place to sleep, and paid her nothing at all. Despite being showered with that sort of kindness, those girls picked up enough of the monstrosity and lonely emptiness of the universe to become the first practitioners of my art, the oral recounters of horrific tales whose efforts preceded all horror writing."

"Was it really so bad for them?" Kiara asked.

"Here? Worse. I haven't told you the worst yet, you see. Indeed, I haven't even touched upon it." The horror writer turned to Dan. "Perhaps you'd like to send Robbie out. That might be advisable."

Dan shrugged. "He watches TV. I doubt that anything you'll say will frighten him."

Charity pursed her lips but said nothing.

The horror writer had taken advantage of the pause to light his pipe. "You don't have to stay, Robbie." He puffed fragrant white smoke, and watched it begin its slow climb to the ceiling. "You know where your room is, and you may go anywhere in the house unless you meet with a locked door."

Kiara smiled. "Secrets! We're in Bluebeard's cashel – castle. I knew it!"

"No secrets," the horror writer told her, "just a very dangerous cellar stair – steep, shaky, and innocent of any sort of railing."

Robbie whispered, "I'm not going."

"So I see. From time to time, Robbie, one of the children would learn or guess that his parents were not in fact dead. When that happened, he or she might try to get away and return home. I've made every effort to learn just how often that happened, but the sources are contradictory on the point. Some say three and some five, and one says more than twenty. I should add that we who perform this type of research soon learn to be wary of the number three. It's the favorite of those who don't know the real number. There are several places on the grounds that may once of have been graves – unmarked graves long since emptied by the authorities. But . . ."

Charity leaned toward him, her face tense. "Do you mean to say that those children were killed?"

The horror writer nodded. "I do. Those who were returned here by their parents were. That is the most horrible fact attached to this really quite awful old house. Or at least, it is the worst we know of – perhaps the worst that occurred."

He drew on his pipe, letting smoke trickle from his nostrils. "A special midnight service was held here, in this room in which we sit. At that service the church members are said to have flown. To have fluttered about this room like so many strange birds. No doubt they ran and waved their arms, as children sometimes do. Very possibly they thought they flew. The members of medieval witch cults seem really to have believed that they flew to the gatherings of their covens, although no sane person supposes they actually did."

Charity asked, "But you say they killed the children?"

The horror writer nodded. "Yes, at the end of the ceremony. Call it the children's hour, a term that some authorities say they used themselves. They shot them as Maude Parkhurst's father and sisters had been shot. The executioner was chosen by lot. Maude is said to have hoped aloud that it would fall to her, as it seems to have done more than once. Twice at least."

Dan said, "It's hard to believe anybody would really do that."

"Perhaps it is, although news broadcasts have told me of things every bit as bad. Or worse."

The horror writer drew on his pipe again, and the room had grown dark enough that the red glow from its bowl lit his face from below. "The children were asleep by that time, as Maude, her father, and her sisters had been. The lucky winner crept into the child's bedroom, accompanied by at least one other member who carried a candle. The moment the shot was fired, the candle was blown out. The noise would've awakened any other children who had been sleeping in that room, of course; but they awakened only to darkness and the smell of gun smoke."

Dan said, "Angels!" There was a world of contempt in the word.

"There are angels in Hell," the horror writer told him, "not just in Heaven. Indeed, the angels of Hell may be the more numerous."

Charity pretended to yawn while nodding her reluctant agreement. "I think it's time we all went up bed. Don't you?"

Dan said, "I certainly do. I drove one hell of a long way today."

Kiara lingered when the others had gone. "Ish really nice meeting you." She swayed as she spoke, though only slightly. "Don' forget I get to be your public relations agent. You promised."

"You have my word." The horror writer smiled, knowing how much his word was worth.

For a lingering moment they clasped hands. "Ish hard to believe," she said, "that you were dad's roommate. You sheem – seem – so much younger."

He thanked her and watched her climb the wide curved staircase that had been the pride of the Parkhursts long ago, wondering all the while whether she knew that he was watching. Whether she knew or not, watching Kiara climb stairs was too great a pleasure to surrender.

*   *   *

On the floor above, Charity was getting Robbie ready for bed. "You're a brave boy, I know. Aren't you a brave boy, darling? Say it, please. It always helps to say it."

"I'm a brave boy," Robbie told her dutifully.

"You are. I know you are. You won't let that silly man downstairs fool you. You'll stay in your own bed, in your own room, and get a good night's sleep. We'll do some sight-seeing tomorrow, forests and lakes and rugged hills where the worked-out mines hide."

Charity hesitated, gnawing with small white teeth at her full lower lip. "There's no nightlight in here, I'm afraid, but I've got a little flashlight in my purse. I could lend you that. Would you like it?"

Robbie nodded, and clasped Charity's little plastic flashlight tightly as he watched her leave. Her hand – the one without rings – reached up to the light switch. Her fingers found it.

There was darkness.

He located the switch again with the watery beam of the disposable flashlight, knowing that he would be scolded (perhaps even spanked) if he switched the solitary overhead light back on but wanting to know exactly where that switch was, just in case.

At last he turned Charity's flashlight off and lay down. It was hot in the too-large, too-empty room. Hot and silent.

He sat up again, and aimed the flashlight toward the window. It was indeed open, but open only the width of his hand. He got out of bed, dropped the flashlight into the shirt pocket of his pajamas, and tried to raise the window farther. No effort he could put forth would budge it.

At last he lay down again, and the room felt hotter than ever.

When he had looked out through the window, it had seemed terribly high. How many flights of stairs had they climbed to get up here? He could remember only one, wide carpeted stairs that had curved as they climbed; but that one had been a long, long stair. From the window he had seen the tops of trees.

Treetops and stars. The moon had been out, lighting the lawn below and showing him the dark leaves of the treetops, although the moon itself had not been in sight from the window.

"It walks across the sky," he told himself. Dan, his father, had said that once.

"You could walk . . ." The voice seemed near, but faint and thin.

Robbie switched the flashlight back on. There was no one there.

Under the bed, he thought. They're under the bed.

But he dared not leave the bed to look, and lay down once more. An older person would have tried to persuade himself that he had imagined the voice, or would have left the bed to investigate. Robbie did neither. His line between palpable and imagined things was blurred and faint, and he had not the slightest desire to see the speaker, whether that speaker was real or make-believe.

There were no other windows that might be opened. He thought of going out. The hall would be dark, but Dan and Charity were sleeping in a room not very far away. The door of their room might be locked, though. They did that sometimes.

He would be scolded in any event. Scolded and perhaps spanked, too. It was not the pain he feared, but the humiliation. "I'll have to go back here," he whispered to himself. "Even if they don't spank me, I'll have to go back."

"You could walk away . . ." A girl's voice, very faint. From the ceiling? No, Robbie decided, from the side toward the door.

"No," he said. "They'd be mad."

"You'll die . . ."

"Like us . . ."

Robbie sat up, shaking.

Outside, the horror writer was hiking toward the old, rented truck he had parked more than a mile away. The ground was soft after yesterday's storm, and it was essential – absolutely essential – that there be tracks left by a strange vehicle.

A turn onto a side road, a walk of a hundred yards, and the beam of his big electric lantern picked out the truck among the trees. When he could set the lantern on its hood, he put on latex gloves. Soon, very soon, the clock would strike the children's hour and Edith with the golden hair would be his. Beautiful Kiara would be his. As for laughing Allegra, he neither knew nor cared who she might be.

"Wa' ish?" Kiara's voice was thick with vodka and sleep.

"It's only me," Robbie told her, and slipped under the covers. "I'm scared."

She put a protective arm around him.

"There are other kids in here. There are! They're gone when you turn on the light, but they come back. They do!"

"Uh huh." She hugged him tighter and went back to sleep.

In Scales Mound, the horror writer parked the truck and walked three blocks to his car. He had paid two weeks rent on the truck, he reminded himself. Had paid that rent only three days ago. It would

be eleven days at least before the rental agency began to worry about
it, and he could return it or send another check before then.

His gun, the only gun he owned, had been concealed in a piece of
nondescript luggage and locked in the car. He took it out and made
sure the safety was on before starting the engine. It was only a long-
barreled twenty-two; but it looked sinister, and should be sufficient
to make Kiara obey if the threat of force were needed.

Once she was down there . . . Once she was down there, she might
scream all she liked. It would not matter. As he drove back to the
house, he tried to decide whether he should hold it or put it into one
of the big side pockets of his barn coat.

Robbie, having escaped Kiara's warm embrace, decided that her
room was cooler than his. For one thing, she had two windows. For
another, both were open wider than his one window had been.
Besides, it was just cooler. He pulled the sheet up, hoping she would
not mind.

"Run . . ." whispered the faint, thin voices.

"Run . . . Run . . ."

"Get away while you can . . ."

"Go . . ."

Robbie shook his head and shut his eyes.

Outside Kiara's bedroom, the horror writer patted the long-barreled
pistol he had pushed into his belt. His coat pockets held rags, two
short lengths of quarter-inch rope, a small roll of duct tape, and a
large folding knife. He hoped to need none of them.

There was no provision for locking Kiara's door. He had been
careful to see to that. No key for the quaint old lock, no interior bolt;
and yet she might have blocked it with a chair. He opened it slowly,
finding no obstruction.

The old oak doors were thick and solid, the old walls thicker and
solider still. If Dan and his wife were sleeping soundly, it would take
a great deal of commotion in here to wake them.

Behind him, the door swung shut on well-oiled hinges. The click of
the latch was the only sound.

Moonlight coming through the windows rendered the penlight in
his shirt pocket unnecessary. She was there, lying on her side and
sound asleep, her lovely face turned toward him.

As he moved toward her, Robbie sat up, his mouth a dark circle,
his pale face a mask of terror. The horror writer pushed him down
again.

The muzzle of his pistol was tight against Robbie's head; this though the horror writer could not have said how it came to be there. His index finger squeezed even as he realized it was on the trigger.

There was a muffled bang, like the sound of a large book dropped. Something jerked under the horror writer's hand, and he whispered, "Die like my father. Like Alice and June. Die like me." He whispered it, but did not understand what he intended by it.

Kiara's eye were open. He struck her with the barrel, reversed the pistol and struck her again and again with the butt, stopping only when he realized he did not know how many times he had hit her already or where his blows had landed.

After pushing up the safety, he put the pistol back into his belt and stood listening. The room next to that in which he stood had been Robbie's. Presumably, there was no one there to hear.

The room beyond that one – the room nearest the front stair – was Dan's and Charity's. He would stand behind the door if they came in, shoot them both, run. Mexico. South America.

They did not.

The house was silent save for his own rapid breathing and Kiara's slow, labored breaths; beyond the open windows, the night-wind sobbed in the trees. Any other sound would have come, almost, as a relief.

There was none.

He had broken the cellar window, left tracks with the worn old shoes he had gotten from a recycle store, left tire tracks with the old truck. He smiled faintly when he recalled its mismatched tires. Let them work on that one.

He picked up Kiara and slung her over his shoulder, finding her soft, warm, and heavier than he had expected.

The back stairs were narrow and in poor repair; they creaked beneath his feet, but they were farther – much farther – from the room in which Dan and Charity slept. He descended them slowly, holding Kiara with his right arm while his left hand grasped the rail.

She stirred and moaned. He wondered whether he would have to hit her again, and decided he would not unless she screamed. If she screamed, he would drop her and do what had to be done.

She did not.

The grounds were extensive, and included a wood from which (long ago) firewood had been cut. It had grown back now, a tangle of larches and alders, firs and red cedars. Toward the back, not far from the property line, he had by merest chance stumbled upon the old well. There had been a cabin there once. No doubt it had burned. A cow or a child might have fallen into the abandoned well, and so some prudent person had covered it with a slab of limestone. Leaves and twigs on that stone had turned, in time, to soil. He had moved the stone away, leaving the soil on it largely undisturbed.

When he reached the abandoned well at last, panting and sweating, he laid Kiara down. His penlight showed that her eyes were open. Her bloodstained face seemed to him a mask of fear; seeing it, he felt himself stand straighter and grow stronger.

"You may listen to me or not," he told her. "What you do really doesn't matter, but I thought I ought to do you the kindness of explaining just what has happened and what will happen. What I plan, and your place in my plans."

She made an inarticulate sound that might have been a word or a moan.

"You're listening. Good. There's an old well here. Only I know that it exists. At the bottom – shall we say twelve feet down? At the bottom there's mud and a little water. You'll get dirty, in other words, but you won't die of thirst. There you will wait for me for as long as the police actively investigate. From time to time I may, or may not, come here and toss down a sandwich."

He smiled. "It won't hurt you in the least, my dear, to lose a little weight. When things have quieted down, I'll come and pull you out. You'll be grateful – oh, very grateful – for your rescue. Soiled and starved, but very grateful. Together we'll walk back to my home. You may need help, and if you do I'll provide it."

He bent and picked her up. "I'll bathe you, feed you, and nurse you."

Three strides brought him to the dark mouth of the well. "After that, you'll obey me in everything. Or you had better. And in time, perhaps, you'll come to like it."

He let her fall, smiled, and turned away.

There remained only the problem of the gun. Bullets could be matched to barrels, and there was an ejected shell somewhere. The gun would have to be destroyed; it was blued steel; running water should do the job, and do it swiftly.

Still smiling, he set off for the creek.

It was after four o'clock the following afternoon when Captain Barlowe of the Sheriff's Department explained the crime. Captain Barlowe was a middle-aged and heavy-limbed. He had a thick mustache. "What happened in this house last night is becoming pretty clear." His tone was weighty. "Why it happened . . ." He shook his head.

The horror writer said, "I know my house was broken into. One of your men showed me that. I know poor little Robbie's dead, and I know Kiara's missing. But that's all I know."

"Exactly." Captain Barlowe clasped his big hands and unclasped them. "It's pretty much all I know, too, sir. Other than that, all I can do is supply details. The gun that killed the boy was a twenty-two semi-automatic. It could have been a pistol or a rifle. It could even have been a sawn-off rifle. There's no more common caliber in the world."

The horror writer nodded.

"He was killed with one shot, a contact shot to the head, and he was probably killed for being in a room in which he had no business being. He'd left his own bed and crawled into his big sister's. Not for sex, sir. I could see what you were thinking. He was too young for that. He was just a little kid alone in a strange house. He got lonely and was murdered for it."

Captain Barlowe paused to clear his throat. "You told my men that there had been no cars in your driveway since the rain except your own and the boy's parents'. Is that right?"

The horror writer nodded. "I've racked my brain trying to think of somebody else, and come up empty. Dan and I are old friends. You ought to know that."

Captain Barlowe nodded. "I do, sir. He told me."

"We get together when we can, usually that's once or twice a year. This year he and Charity decided to vacation in this area. He's a golfer and a fisherman."

Captain Barlowe nodded again. "He should love our part of the state."

"That's what I thought, Captain. I don't play golf, but I checked out some of the courses here. I fish a bit, and I told him about that. He said he was coming, and I told him I had plenty of room. They were only going to stay for two nights."

"You kept your cellar door locked?"

"Usually? No. I locked it when I heard they were coming. The cellar's dirty and the steps are dangerous. You know how small boys are."

"Yes, sir. I used to be one. The killer jimmied it open."

The horror writer nodded. "I saw that."

"You sleep on the ground floor. You didn't hear anything?"

"No. I'm a sound sleeper."

"I understand. Here's my problem, sir, and I hope you can help me with it. Crime requires three things. They're motive, means, and opportunity. Know those, and you know a lot. I've got a murder case here. It's the murder of a kid. I hate the bastards who kill kids, and I've never had a case I wanted to solve more."

"I understand," the horror writer said.

"Means is no problem. He had a gun, a car, and tools. Maybe gloves, because we haven't found any fresh prints we can't identify. His motive may have been robbery, but it was probably of a sexual nature. Here's a young girl, a blonde. Very good-looking to judge by the only picture we've seen so far."

"She is." The horror writer nodded his agreement.

"He must have seen her somewhere. And not just that. He must have known that she was going to be in this house last night. Where did he see her? How did he know where she was going to be? If I can find the answers to those questions we'll get him."

"I wish I could help you." The horror writer's smile was inward only.

"You've had no visitors since your guests arrived?"

He shook his head. "None."

"Delivery men? A guy to fix the furnace? Something like that?"

"No, nobody. They got here late yesterday afternoon, Captain."

"I understand. Now think about this, please. I want to know everybody – and I mean everybody, no matter who it was – you told that they were coming."

"I've thought about it. I've thought about it a great deal, Captain. And I didn't tell anyone. When I went around to the golf courses, I told people I was expecting guests and they'd want to play golf. But I never said who those guests were. There was no reason to."

"That settles it." Captain Barlowe rose, looking grim. "It's somebody they told. The father's given us the names of three people and he's trying to come up with more. There may be more. He admits that. His wife . . ."

"Hadn't she told anyone?"

"That just it, sir. She did. She seems to have told quite a few people and says can't remember them all. She's lying because she doesn't want her friends bothered. Well, by God they're going to be bothered. My problem – one of my problems – is that all these people are out of state. I can't go after them myself, and I'd like to. I want have a good look at them. I want to see their faces change when they're asked certain questions."

He breathed deep, expanding a chest notably capacious, and let it out. "On the plus side, we're after a stranger. Some of the local people may have seen him and noticed him. He may – I said *may* – be driving a car with out-of-state plates."

"Couldn't he have rented a car at the airport?" the horror writer asked.

"Yes, sir. He could, and I hope to God he did. If he did, we'll get him sure. But his car had worn tires, and that's not characteristic of rentals."

"I see."

"If he did rent his car, it'll have bloodstains in it, and the rental people will notice. She was bleeding when she was carried out of her bedroom."

"I didn't know that."

"Not much, but some. We found blood in the hall and more on the back stairs. The bad thing is that if he flew in and plans to fly back out, he can't take her with him. He'll kill her. He may have killed her already."

Captain Barlowe left, Dan and Charity moved into a motel, and the day ended in quiet triumph. The experts who had visited the crime scene earlier reappeared and took more photographs and blood samples. The horror writer asked them no questions, and they volunteered nothing.

He drove to town the next morning and shopped at several stores. So far as he could judge, he was not followed. That afternoon he got out the binoculars he had acquired years before for bird-watching and scanned the surrounding woods and fields, seeing no one.

At sunrise the next morning he rescanned them, paying particular attention to areas he thought he might have slighted before. Selecting an apple from the previous day's purchases, he made his way through grass still wet with dew to the well and tossed it in.

He had hoped that she would thank him and plead for release; if she did either her voice was too faint for him to catch her words, this though it seemed to him there was a sound of some sort from the well, a faint, high humming. As he tramped back to the house, he decided that it had probably been an echo of the wind.

The rest of that day he spent preparing her cellar room.

He slept well that night and woke refreshed twenty minutes before his clock radio would have roused him. The three-eighths-inch rope he had brought two days earlier awaited him in the kitchen; he knotted it as soon as he had finished breakfast, spacing the knots about a foot apart.

When he had wound it around his waist and tied it securely, he discovered bloodstains – small but noticeable – on the back of his barn coat. Eventually it would have to be burned, but a fire at this season would be suspicious in itself; a long soak in a strong bleach solution would have to do the job – for the present, if not permanently. Pulled out, his shirt hid the rope, although not well.

When he reached the well, he tied one end of the rope to a convenient branch and called softly.

There was no reply.

A louder "Kiara!" brought no reply either. She was still asleep, the horror writer decided. Asleep or, just possibly, unconscious. He dropped the free end of the rope into the well, swung over the edge, and began the climb down.

He had expected the length of his rope to exceed the depth of the well by three feet at least; but there came a time when his feet could find no more rope below him – or find the muddy bottom either.

His pen light revealed it, eight inches, perhaps, below the soles of his shoes. Another knot down – this knot almost the last – brought his feet into contact with the mud.

He released the rope.

He had expected to sink into the mud, but had thought to sink to a depth of no more than three or four inches; he found himself floundering, instead, in mud up to his knees. It was difficult to retain his footing; bracing one hand against the stone side of the well, he managed to do it.

At the first step he attempted, the mud sucked his shoe from his foot. Groping the mud for it got his hands thoroughly filthy, but failed to locate it. Attempting a second step cost him his other shoe as well.

This time, however, his groping fingers found a large, soft thing in the mud. His pen light winked on – but in the space of twenty seconds or a little less its always-faint beam faded to darkness. His fingers told him of hair matted with mud, of an ear, and then of a small earring. When he took his hand from it, he stood among corpses, shadowy child-sized bodies his fingers could not locate. Shuddering, he looked up.

Above him, far above him, a small circle of blue was bisected by the dark limb to which he had tied his rope. The rope itself swayed gently in the air, its lower end not quite out of reach.

He caught it and tried to pull himself up; his hands were slippery with mud, and it escaped them.

Desperately, almost frantically, he strove to catch it again, but his struggles caused him to sink deeper into the mud.

He tried to climb the wall of the well; at his depth its rough stones were thick with slime.

At last he recalled Kiara's body, and by a struggle that seemed to him long managed to get both feet on it. With its support, his fingertips once more brushed the dangling end of the rope. Bracing his right foot on what felt like the head, he made a final all-out effort.

And caught the rope, grasping it a finger's breadth from its frayed end. The slight tension he exerted on it straightened it, and perhaps stretched it a trifle. Bent the limb above by a fraction of an inch. With his right arm straining almost out of its socket and his feet pressing hard against Kiara's corpse, the fingers of his left hand could just touch the final knot.

Something took hold of his right foot, pinning toes and transverse arch in jaws that might have been those of a trap.

The horror writer struggled then, and screamed again and again as he was drawn under – screamed and shrieked and begged until the stinking almost liquid mud stopped his mouth.

NICHOLAS ROYLE

Continuity Error

NICHOLAS ROYLE WAS BORN in Manchester in 1963. He is the author of five novels, *Counterparts*, *Saxophone Dreams*, *The Matter of the Heart*, *The Director's Cut* and *Antwerp*, and one short story collection, *Mortality* (Serpent's Tail). A novella, *The Enigma of Departure*, is forthcoming from PS Publishing.

Widely published as a journalist, with regular appearances in *Time Out* and the *Independent* newspaper, Royle has also edited twelve anthologies. He currently teaches creative writing at Manchester Metropolitan University.

"Much of what happens in the story did actually happen in so-called real life," confirms the author. "I would like to acknowledge Rebecca Healey's generous help with lip-reading and Michael Kemp's kind permission to quote from his poetry."

C HRISTINE RANG MADDOX on his mobile. A little accident, she said. A bump.

"Was anyone hurt?"

"No, no one was hurt."

He made his way to the side street in Shepherd's Bush where it had happened. A one-way street temporarily blocked off by roadworks at the junction with Goldhawk Road. Estate agent's on the corner. Christine had reversed away from the roadworks and at five miles an hour hit a silver Toyota coming out of the concealed exit from the sunken car park behind the estate agent's.

By the time Maddox arrived, the driver of the silver Toyota was in full magnanimous third-party mode, confident the insurance companies would find in his favour. Maddox hated him on sight. Too reasonable, too forthcoming. Like providing his address and insurance details was some kind of favour.

Maddox's son Jack had got out of the car and stood staring at the small pile of shattered glass on the road, seemingly transfixed by it. Christine was visibly upset, despite the unctuous affability of the Toyota driver and Maddox's own efforts to downplay the situation.

"It's only a couple of lights and a new wing. No one was hurt, that's the main thing."

Two days later, Maddox and Jack were walking past the top of the side street. The roadworks had been removed and a car was exiting into Goldhawk Road without any difficulty.

"Is that where the accident happened, Daddy?" asked the little boy.

"Yes."

Jack stopped, his big eyes taking in the details. The fresh asphalt by the junction, the concealed exit from the sunken car park behind the estate agent's.

"Is it still there?" the little boy asked.

"What? Is what still there?"

"The accident. Is the accident still there?"

Maddox didn't know what to say.

They were getting ready to go out. Christine was ready and Maddox was nearly ready, a too-familiar scenario. She waited by the front door, smart, made-up, tall in new boots and long coat, enveloped in a haze of expensive perfume.

"Are you nearly ready, Brian?"

That she added his name to the harmless query was a bad sign. It meant her patience was stretched too thin. But he'd lost his car key. He'd looked everywhere. Twice. And couldn't find it.

"Where did you last have it?" she shouted up the stairs.

The unhelpfulness of the question grated against his nerves.

"I don't know. That's the whole point."

He started again. Bedroom (bedside drawer, dressing gown). Jacket pockets. Kitchen.

"Have you looked in your box?"

"Yes, I've looked in my box."

They each had a box, like an in-tray, in the kitchen. Christine never used hers, but always knew where everything was. Maddox used his, but still managed to lose at least one important item every day. Wallet, phone, keys. Chequebook, bank card. Everything always turned up, sooner or later, but in this case, not soon enough.

"I can't find it. I've looked everywhere."

Heavy sigh.

If the atmosphere hadn't become tense he would jokingly accuse her of having hidden it, of trying to make him think he was losing his mind. But that wouldn't play now. They were beyond that.

"It's probably at the *flat*," she said, loading the word with her customary judgmental emphasis.

"How could it be at the flat when my car's outside?" he snapped before realising that *she* must have been joking.

"It's a pity you don't have a spare key," she said.

"It's a pity your car's in the garage," he retorted, "about to be declared uneconomical to repair. Look, Christine, it's very late. I can't find it and I certainly won't find it with you hovering, getting all wound up, so I suggest you get a cab and I'll follow."

"But what if you don't find it?'

"I'll find it. I'll be there, just a little late, that's all. You go. You'll easily pick up a black cab on the Green. You're only going to Ladbroke Grove."

Sweating, he listened as the front door was opened and shut – slammed. Gate clanged. Fading echo of footsteps receding. He felt the tension flow out of him and collapsed on to the nearest chair. He loosened his tie and reached for a glass.

In their bedroom he pressed the power button on his laptop. While waiting, he stared blankly at the framed poster on the wall. A production he'd been in more than twenty years ago. *Colossus*. Clive Barker's play about Goya. He allowed the faces of cast members to run through his mind, particularly those who'd gone on to other things. Lennie James – you saw him on television all the time now. A part in *Cold Feet*. A one-off drama, something he'd written himself. That prison series. *Buried*. Right. Buried in the schedules.

Aslie Pitter, the most naturally talented actor in the cast. He'd done one or two things – a Channel Four sitcom, guest appearance in *The Bill* – then disappeared. Maddox had last seen him working for a high-street chain. Security, demonstrating product – he couldn't remember which.

Elinore Vickery had turned up in something at the Waterman's. Maddox had liked her, tried to keep in touch, but there was an invisible barrier, as if she'd known him better than he knew himself.

Missing out on a couple of good parts because of his size (five foot

five in stocking feet, eight stone dead), Maddox had quit the theatre
and concentrated on writing. Barker had helped with one or two
contacts and Maddox sold a couple of horror stories. Over the years
he'd moved away from fiction into journalism and book-length non-
fiction. The current project, New Maps of Hell, hadn't found a home.
The publishers he'd offered it to hadn't been able to reject it quickly
enough. They didn't want it on their desks. It made them uncomfortable. That was fine by Maddox. He'd worry if it didn't. They'd want it
on their lists, though, when it was too late. He'd finish it first, then pick
one editor and let the others write their letters of resignation.

He read through the afternoon's work, then closed the laptop. He
opened his bedside drawer and there was his car key. He looked at it.
Had it been there before? Of course it had. How could it not have been?
But he'd not seen it, so it might as well not have been. It had effectively
disappeared. Hysterical blindness? Negative hallucination?

He pocketed the key and went downstairs. The door closed behind
him and the car started first time. He sneaked past White City – the
exhibition halls were gone, torn down for a future shopping centre –
and slipped on to the Westway. He didn't think of Christine as he
approached Ladbroke Grove, but of Christie, John Reginald Halli-
day. The former relief projectionist at the Electric, who had murdered at least six women, had lived at 10 Rillington Place, later
renamed Ruston Close before being demolished to make way for the
elevated motorway on which Maddox was now driving. The film,
starring Dickie Attenborough as the killer and John Hurt as his poor
dupe of an upstairs neighbour, who swung for at least one of
Christie's crimes, had been filmed in Rillington Place itself. Maddox
understood, from comments posted on ghoulish message boards on
the internet, that the interiors had been shot in No.8 and the exteriors
outside No.10. But when the police, acting on a tip-off from Timothy
Evans, yanked open a manhole cover outside No.10, Attenborough
could be seen peering out through the ground-floor window of the
end house in the terrace, No.10, where three of Christie's victims had
been walled up in the pantry, his wife Ethel being found under the
floorboards in the front room. For Maddox it was the key shot in the
film, the only clear evidence that they'd gained access to the charnel
house itself. The only other explanation being that they'd mocked up
the entire street in the studio, which he didn't buy.

The case accounted for five pages in Maddox's book. He concentrated mainly on the interweaving of fact and fiction, the merging
of film and reality. Attenborough as Christie. No.8 standing in for
No.10, if indeed it did. The internet also yielded a piece of Pathé film

footage of the demolition of Ruston Close. Two men with pickaxes. A third man speaking to camera. A burning house. Shots of the house at the end of the street with the white (replacement) door. Clearly the same house as that in the film. But there was no sound, the reporter mouthing inaudible commentary. Maddox lured a lip-reader to the flat, a junior editor from one of the publishers that had turned down his book. She reminded him of Linzi with her green eyes and shoulder-length streaked hair. Even in heels she didn't reach Maddox's height, but she had a confident, relaxed smile, She held his gaze when he spoke to her and appeared to be looking into his eyes, but must have been watching his lips, as she relied heavily on lip-reading.

Maddox was careful to make sure she was looking in his direction before speaking to her, probably over-careful. She must have spent a lifetime compensating for situations in which people wouldn't have made such allowances. Working backwards from the first words she managed to lip-read and then having to catch up. So much information assumed rather than known for certain, but Maddox could relate to that. In some areas of life he, too, knew nothing for certain. The deaf woman's name was Karen. He assumed the proposal for his book had been rejected by someone senior who had given Karen the unpleasant job of telling the author, but he didn't know *that* for certain. Possibly she'd read it and rejected it herself and only agreed to provide lip-reading services because she felt bad about it.

When she entered the flat, Maddox felt at ease. In control. He apologised for the loud, bass-heavy music coming from the downstairs flat, but she said she couldn't hear it.

"I thought you might be able to feel it," he said.

"It's a new building," she said. "Concrete floors. Otherwise . . ."

He showed her the footage. She said it wasn't straightforward. The quality was poor and the picture kept pixellating, plus the reporter unhelpfully turned his head to the side on several occasions.

Maddox asked her if she would come back and have another go if he was able to tidy the picture up a bit.

"I don't think I'll be able to get much off it for you," she said.

"If you wouldn't mind just trying one more time, perhaps when you're less tired," he said. "It's very important to me, for my book, you know."

Maddox pulled into one of the reserved spaces outside a block of purpose-built flats in the depressed residential trapezium bordered by Green Lanes and the roads of West Green, Seven Sisters and St Ann's. He listened to the ticking of the cooling engine for a few moments as he watched the darkened windows of the second-floor flat. The top flat.

The street door had been left open by one of his neighbours. He walked up.

Inside the flat, he left the light switched off, poured himself a drink and sat in the single armchair. He pulled out his phone and sent a short text message. Orange street-lighting cast a deathly glow over the cheap bookshelves stacked with pulp novels, true crime, horror anthologies and dystopian science fiction. His phone chimed. He opened it, read the return message and replied to it. When he'd lived here, the room had been dominated by a double bed. Moving into Christine's house had allowed him to turn the tiny flat into the dedicated office he'd always wanted by burning the bed on the waste ground out the back. He'd considered giving it away, since selling it had struck him as tiresome: placing an ad, answering calls, opening the door to strangers. Easier to burn the damn thing and all the memories associated with it. So then he'd moved his desk from the east end of the room, under the Velux window, to the west-facing windows overlooking the street.

Another text arrived. He read it and closed the phone without replying.

As usual, loud music was playing in the downstairs flat.

He drained his glass and let his head fall back against the soft cushion. The Artex ceiling had attracted cobwebs and grime, but he doubted he would ever feel the need to repaint or clean it. Very few people ever came here. Linzi had spent a lot of time in the flat, of course. He laughed bitterly, then chewed his lip and stared at the ceiling, sensitive to the slightest noise in spite of the thump of the bass from the downstairs flat. Christine had hardly stepped over the threshold. She'd been once or twice soon after they'd met, but not since. There was no reason to. It was clear from the odd comment that she resented his keeping the flat, since it was a drain on resources, but as he'd argued, there was no room in the house for all these books and tapes. Not to mention the stuff stored in the loft. He chewed his lip again.

He switched on the stereo and the ordered chaos of Paul Schütze's *New Maps of Hell* clattered into battle with the beat from below. Schütze's 1992 release was the constant soundtrack to any work he did on the book in the flat. (On the rare occasions that he worked on it at the house, he played the follow-up, *New Maps of Hell II: The Rapture of Metals*.) He believed it helped. *It started out as an aid to getting the mindset right*, he sometimes imagined telling Kirsty Wark or Verity Sharp in a television interview, *and soon became a habit, a routine. I simply couldn't work on the book without having the music playing in the background. It was about the creation of a hermetically sealed world. Which, I suppose you have to admit, Hell is. Although one that's expanding at an alarming rate, erupting in little pockets. North Kensington, Muswell Hill. London is going to Hell, Kirsty.*

He opened a file and did some work, tidied up some troublesome text. He saved it and opened another file, "Dollis Hill". Notes, a few stabs at an address, gaps, big gaps. He was going to have to go back.

He replayed the mental rushes. Autumn 1986. A fine day. Gusty, but dry, bright. Walking in an unfamiliar district of London. A long road, tree-lined. High up. View down over the city between detached houses and semis. Victorian, Edwardian.

The entryphone buzzed, bringing him back to the present with a start. He closed the file. He got to his feet, crossed to the hall and picked up the phone.

"The door's open. Come up," he said, before realising she couldn't hear him.

He remained standing in the hall, listening to footsteps climbing the interior staircase. When the footsteps stopped outside his door there was a pause before the knock came. He imagined her composing herself, perhaps straightening her clothes, removing a hair from her collar. Or looking at her watch and thinking of bolting. He opened the door as she knocked, which startled her.

"Come in," he said. "Thanks for coming."

All Maddox had done to improve the image on the video was change the size of the Media Player window so that the reporter's mouth, while slightly smaller, was less affected by picture break-up.

While Karen studied the footage, Maddox crossed to the far side of the room. He returned with a glass of red wine, which he placed beside the laptop. Karen raised a hand to decline, but Maddox simply pushed the glass slightly closer to her and left it there. Finally, while she was watching the footage for a third time, her hand reached out, perhaps involuntarily, to pick up the glass. She took a sip, then held the glass aloft while studying the image of the jaunty reporter: Michael Caine glasses, buttoned-up jacket, button-down shirt, hand alighting on hip like a butterfly.

Maddox watched as she replayed the footage again. Each time the reporter started speaking, she moved a little closer to the screen and seemed to angle her head slightly to the left in order to favour her right ear, in which she had a trace of hearing, despite the fact there was no sound at all on the film. Habit, Maddox decided.

Karen leaned back and looked at Maddox before speaking.

"He's saying something like *newspaper reports . . . of the investigation . . . into the discovery of the burned-out bodies of two women . . . Fifteen – or fifty – years ago . . . Something of the century*. I'm sorry, it's really hard."

Her speech was that of a person who had learned to talk the hard way, without being able to hear the sound of her own voice.

"That's great. That's very helpful, Karen. It would be fifteen, not fifty. I didn't even know for certain that he was talking about Christie's house. *Burned-out*, though, are you sure? That's strange."

"No, I'm not sure, but that's what it sounds like."

Karen's choice of expression – *sounds like* – reminded him of a blind man who had asked Maddox for help crossing the road as he was going to *see* the doctor.

Maddox went to fill up her glass, but she placed her hand over it.

"I've got to go," she said. "I said I could only stop by for a minute.'

Maddox stood his ground with the wine bottle, then stepped back.

"Another time," he said.

"Have you got something else you want me to look at?"

"I might have. If it's not too much of an imposition."

"Just let me know."

He showed her out, then switched the light off again and watched from the window as she regained the street. She stopped, looked one way, then went the other, as if deciding there and then which way to go. Hardly the action of a woman with an appointment. He watched as she walked south towards St Ann's Road and disappeared around the corner, then he sat down in the armchair and emptied her wine glass. His gaze roved across the bookshelves and climbed the walls before reaching the ceiling. He then sat without moving for half an hour, his eyes not leaving the ceiling, listening to the building's creaks and sighs, the music downstairs having been turned off.

He took a different route back, climbing the Harringay Ladder and going west past the top of Priory Park. He floored the pedal through the Cranley Gardens S-bend and allowed the gradient to slow the car so that he rolled to a stop outside No. 23. There he killed the engine and looked up at the second-floor flat where Dennis Nilsen had lived from October 1981 to February 1983. One of Nilsen's mistakes, which had led to his being caught, was to have left the window in the gable dormer wide open for long periods, attracting the attention of neighbours.

Maddox looked at his watch and started the engine. He got on to the North Circular, coming off at Staples Corner, heading south down Edgware Road and turning right into Dollis Hill Lane. He slowed to a crawl, leaning forward over the wheel, craning his neck at the houses on the south side. He was sure it would be on the south side. He definitely remembered a wide tree-lined avenue with views over central London. Land falling away behind the house. Long walk from the tube. Which tube? He didn't know.

He turned right, cruised the next street. He wasn't even sure of the street. Dollis Hill Lane sounded right, but as soon as he'd got the idea of Cricklewood Lane off the internet that had sounded right too. He'd gone there, to 108/110 Cricklewood Lane, after reading on the net that that was where they'd shot *Hellraiser*. When he got there and found it was a branch of Holmes Place Health Clubs, he worked out it must have been the former location of Cricklewood Production Village, where they'd done the studio work.

Some time in the autumn of 1986, Maddox had come here, to a house in Dollis Hill. A movie was being made. Clive Barker was directing his first film. *Hellraiser*. They were shooting in a rented house and Maddox had been invited to go on the set as an associate of Barker's. He was going to do a little interview, place it wherever possible. Could be his big break. It was good of Clive to have agreed to it. Maddox remembered the big white vans in the street outside the house, a surprising number of people hanging around doing nothing, a catering truck, a long table covered with polystyrene cups, a tea urn. He asked for Steve Jones, unit publicist. Jones talked to him about what was going on. They were filming a dinner party scene with Andrew Robinson and Clare Higgins and two young actors, the boy and the girl, and a bunch of extras. Maddox got to watch from behind the camera, trying to catch Barker's eye as he talked to the actors, telling them what he wanted them to do. Controlling everybody and everything. Maddox envied him, but admired him as well. A make-up girl applied powder to Robinson's forehead. A hairdresser fixed Ashley Laurence's hair. They did the scene and the air was filled with electricity. Everyone behind the camera held their breath, faces still and taut. The tension was palpable. The moment Barker called "Cut", it melted away. Smiles, laughter, everyone suddenly moving around. Maddox noticed the hairdresser, who looked lost for a moment, diminutive and vulnerable, but Steve Jones caught Maddox's arm in a light grip and cornered Barker. The director looked at Maddox and there was a fraction of a second's pause, no more, before he said, "Brian," in such a warm, sincere way that Maddox might have thought Clive had been looking forward to seeing him all morning.

They did a short interview over lunch, which they ate on the floor of a room at the back of the house.

"We're surrounded by images which are momentarily potent and carry no resonance whatsoever," Barker was saying in transatlantic Scouse. "Advertising, the pop video, a thing which seems to mean an awful lot and is in fact absolutely negligible."

Maddox noticed the hairdresser carrying a paper plate and a cup. She sat cross-legged on the floor next to another crew member and they talked as they ate.

"What frightens you?" he asked Barker.

"Unlit streets, flying, being stuck in the tube at rush hour. Places where you have to relinquish control."

Once they'd finished, Maddox hung around awkwardly, waiting for a chance to talk to the hairdresser. When it came – her companion rising to go – he seized it. She was getting up too and Maddox contrived to step in front of her, blocking her way. He apologised and introduced himself. "I was just interviewing Clive. We've known each other a couple of years. I was in one of his plays."

"Linzi," she said, offering her hand. "I'm only here for one day. The regular girl called in sick."

"Then I'm lucky I came today," he said, smiling shyly.

She was wearing a dark green top of soft cotton that was exactly the same shade as her eyes. Her hair, light brown with natural blonde streaks, was tied back in a knot pierced by a pencil.

"Are you going to stick around?" she asked.

"I've done my interview, but if no one kicks me out . . ."

"It's a pretty relaxed set."

He did stick around and most of the time he watched Linzi, promising himself he wouldn't leave until he'd got her number. It took him the rest of the afternoon, but he got it. She scribbled it on a blank page in her Filofax, then tore out the page and said, "Call me."

The chances of finding the house in darkness were even less than in daylight. He'd been up to Dollis Hill a couple of times in the last few weeks, once in the car and once on foot. Lately, he'd been thinking more about Linzi, and specifically about the early days, before it started to go wrong. He'd spent enough time going over the bad times and wanted to revisit the good. He wanted to see the house again, but couldn't. He needed to locate it for his book. He'd rewatched the film, which contained enough shots of the house's exterior that it should have been easy to locate it, but it didn't seem to matter how many times he trailed these suburban avenues, the house wasn't there. Or if it was, he couldn't see it. He'd begun to think it might have been knocked down, possibly even straight after the shoot. It could have been why the house had been available. In the film there was a No.55 on the porch, but that would be set dressing, like the renumbering of 25 Powis Square, in *Performance*, as No.81.

He looked at his watch and calculated that if he was quick he could get to Ladbroke Grove in time for coffee and to drive Christine home, thereby reducing the amount of grief she would give him. Negligibly, he realised, but still.

In the morning, he feigned sleep while she dressed. Her movements were businesslike, crisp. The night before had been a riot, as expected. When he had turned up at the dinner, two and a half hours late, she had contented herself with merely shooting him a look, but as soon as they left she started. And as soon as she started, he switched off.

It didn't let up even when they got home, but he wasn't listening. He marvelled at how closely he was able to mimic the condition with which Karen, his lip-reader, had been born. Thinking of Karen, moreover, relaxed him inside, while Christine kept on, even once they'd got into bed. Elective deafness – it beat hysterical blindness.

When he was sure Christine had left the house – the slammed door, the gate that clanged – he got up and showered. Within half an hour, having spent ten minutes pointing the DVD remote at the television, he was behind the wheel of the car with his son in the back seat. South Tottenham in twenty minutes was a bigger ask by day than by night, but he gave it his best shot. Rush hour was over (Christine, in common with everyone who worked on weekly magazines, finished earlier than she started), but skirting the congestion charge zone was still a challenge.

He parked where he had the night before and turned to see that Jack was asleep. He left him there, locked the car and walked up. He had decided, while lying in bed with his back to Christine, that it would be worth going up into the loft. Somewhere in the loft was a box containing old diaries, including one for 1986. He had never been a consistent diarist, but some years had seen him make more notes than others. It was worth a rummage among the spider's webs and desiccated wasps" nests. His size meant he didn't bang his head on the latticework of pine beams.

The loft still smelled faintly of formalin. He suspected it always would until he got rid of the suitcase at the far end. He shone the torch in its direction. Big old-fashioned brown leather case, rescued from a skip and cleaned up. Solid, sturdy, two catches and a strap with a buckle. Could take a fair weight.

He redirected the torch at the line of dusty boxes closer to the trap door. The first box contained T-shirts that he never wore any more but couldn't bear to throw away. The second was full of old typescripts stiff with Tipp-Ex. The diaries were in the third box along. He bent down and sorted through: 1974, a shiny black Pocket Diary filled mainly with notes on the history of the Crusades; 1976, the summer of the heatwave, *Angling Times* diary, roach and perch that should have been returned to the water left under stones to die; 1980, the deaths of his three remaining grandparents, three funerals in one year, coffins in the front room, all burials; 1982, his first term at university, meeting Martin, his best friend for a while. Martin was a year older, which had impressed Maddox. The age difference hadn't mattered. Everything was changing. Leaving school, leaving home. Living in halls. Martin was a medical student. They would stay up late drinking coffee and Martin would smoke cigarettes and tell Maddox about medicine, about anatomy and about the bodies he was learning to dissect.

Maddox could listen to Martin for hours. The later they stayed up, the more profound their discussions seemed to become. Maddox watched as Martin dragged on his cigarette and held the smoke in his lungs for an eternity, stretching the moment, before blowing it out in perfect rings. When Martin talked about the bodies in the anatomy lab, Maddox became entranced. He imagined Martin alone in the lab with a dozen flayed corpses. Bending over them, examining them, carefully removing a strip of muscle, severing a tendon. Getting up close to the secrets, the mysteries, of death. Martin said it didn't matter how long he spent washing his hands, they still smelled of formalin. He held them under Maddox's nose, then moved to cup his cheeks in an affectionate, stroking gesture.

"You don't mind, do you?" he said, as his hand landed on Maddox's knee.

"Could you get me in there? Into the lab?" Maddox asked, shaking his head, picturing himself among the bodies, as Martin's hand moved up his thigh.

"No. But I could bring you something out. Something you could keep."

Martin's hand had reached Maddox's lap and Maddox was mildly surprised to discover that far from objecting, he was aroused. If this was to be the downpayment on whatever Martin might fetch him back from the dissection table, so be it.

"I've got something for you," Martin said a couple of days later, "in my room."

Maddox followed Martin to his room.

"So where is it?" Maddox asked.

"Can't just leave that sort of thing lying about. But what's the rush?'

Martin lay down on the bed and unbuckled his belt.

Maddox hesitated, considered walking out, but he felt certain he'd always regret it if he left empty-handed. Instead, he knelt beside the bed and spat into his palm.

Afterwards, Martin pulled open his desk drawer.

"There you go," he said.

Maddox withdrew a strong-smelling package. He started to work at the knot in the outermost plastic bag, but it wouldn't come easily. He asked Martin what it contained.

"A piece of subcutaneous fat from the body of a middle-aged man. If anyone ever asks, you didn't get it from me."

Maddox returned to his own room on the seventh floor, washing his hands on the way. He cut open the bag and unwrapped his spoils. The gobbet of fat, four inches by two, looked like a piece of tripe, white and bloodless, and the stench of formalin made him feel sick and excited at the same time. Maddox was careful not to touch the fat as he wrapped it up again and secured the package with tape. He opened his wardrobe and pulled out the brown suitcase he'd liberated from a skip in Judd Street.

He saw less of Martin after that. At first he contrived subtly to avoid him and then started going out with Valerie, a girl with fat arms and wide hips he picked up in the union bar on cocktails night. He wasn't convinced they were a good match, but the opportunity was convenient, given the Martin situation.

The piece of fat remained wrapped up in its suitcase, which smelled so strongly that Maddox only had to open the case and take a sniff to re-experience how he had felt when Martin had given him the body part. As he lay in bed trying to get to sleep (alone. Valerie didn't last more than a few weeks) he sometimes thought about the man who had knowingly willed his cadaver to science. He wondered what his name might have been and what kind of man he was. What he might have been in life. He would hardly have been able to foresee what would happen to the small part of him that was now nestled inside Maddox's wardrobe.

When Maddox left the hall of residence for a flat in Holloway, the case went with him, still empty but for its human remains. He kept it

on top of a cupboard. It stayed there for two years. When he moved
into the flat in N15, he put the suitcase in the loft, where it had
remained ever since. The piece of fat was no longer in Maddox's
possession, but the suitcase was not free of the smell of formalin.

Maddox's 1986 diary was at the bottom of the box. It took only a
couple of minutes to find what he was looking for. "*Hellraiser*, 11:00
a.m." he'd written in the space reserved for Friday 10 October. A
little further down was an address: 187 Dollis Hill Lane.

He drove to Dollis Hill via Cranley Gardens, but on this occasion
didn't stop.

"Why didn't I think of checking my old diaries before, eh, Jack?"
he said, looking in the rear-view mirror.

His son was silent, staring out of the window.

Turning into Dollis Hill Lane from Edgware Road, he slowed to a
crawl, oblivious to the noisy rebuke of the driver immediately behind
him, who pulled out and swerved to overtake, engine racing, finger
given. Maddox brought the car to a halt on a slight incline outside
No.187. He looked at the house and felt an unsettling combination
of familiarity and non-recognition. Attraction and repulsion. He had
to stare at the house for two or three minutes before he realised why
he had driven past it so many times and failed to recognise it.

Like most things recalled from the past, it was smaller than the
version in his memory. But the main difference was the apparent age
of the building. He remembered a Victorian villa, possibly Edwardian. The house in front of him was new. The rendering on the front
gable end had gone up in the last few years. The wood-framed bay
windows on the first floor were of recent construction. The casement
window in the top flat, second floor, was obviously new. The
mansard roof was a familiar shape, but the clay Rosemarys were
all fresh from the tile shop. The materials were new, but the style was
not. The basic design was unchanged, from what he could remember
of the exterior shots in the film, which he'd looked at again before
coming out, but in spite of that the house looked new. As if a skeleton
had grown new muscle and flesh.

"Just like Frank," he said out loud.

"What, Daddy?"

"Just like Frank in the film."

"What film?"

"They made a film in this house and I came to see them make it.
You're too young to see it yet. One day, maybe."

"What's it about?"

"It's about a man who disappears and then comes back to life with the help of his girlfriend. It happened in that room up there." He pointed to the top flat. "Although, the windows are wrong," he said, trying to remember the second-floor window in the film. "I need to check it again."

The only part of the exterior that looked as if they'd taken care to try to match the original was the front door.

As he'd walked from the *Hellraiser* set back to the tube two decades earlier, he'd read and re-read Linzi's number on the torn-out piece of Filofax paper. He called her the next day and they arranged to meet for a drink.

"Why are you so interested in this house, Daddy?" Jack asked from the back seat.

"Because of what happened here. Because of the film. And because I met somebody here. Somebody I knew before I met your mother.'

Linzi lived in East Finchley. They went to see films at the Phoenix or met for drinks in Muswell Hill. Malaysian meals in Crouch End. He showed her the house in Hillfield Avenue where he had visited Clive Barker.

"Peter Straub used to live on the same road, just further up the hill," he told her.

"Who's Peter Straub?"

"Have you heard of Stephen King?"

"Of course."

"Straub and King wrote a book together. *The Talisman*. They wrote it here. Or part of it, anyway. King also wrote a story called 'Crouch End', which was interesting, not one of his best."

Maddox and Linzi started meeting during the day at the Wisteria Tea Rooms on Middle Lane and it was there, among the pot plants and mismatched crockery, that Maddox realised with a kind of slow, swooning surprise that he was happy. The realisation was so slow because the feeling was so unfamiliar. They took long walks through Highgate Cemetery and across Hampstead Heath.

Weeks became months. The cherry blossom came out in long straight lines down Cecile Park, and fell to the pavements, and came out again. Linzi often stayed at Maddox's flat in South Tottenham, but frowned distastefully at his true-crime books. One morning while she was still asleep, Maddox was dressing, looking for a particular T-shirt. Unable to find it, he climbed up the ladder into the loft. Searching through a box of old clothes, he didn't hear Linzi climbing the ladder or see her head and shoulders suddenly intrude into the loft space.

"What are you doing?" she said.

"Shit." He jumped, hitting his head. "Ow. That hurt. Shit. Nothing. Looking for something."

"What's that smell?"

"Nothing."

He urged her back down the ladder and made sure the trap door was fastened before pulling on the *Eraserhead* T-shirt he'd been looking for.

Whenever he went into the loft from then on, whether Linzi was around or not, he would pull the ladder up after him and close the trap door. The loft was private.

When he got back to the flat that evening, he went up into the loft again – duly covering his tracks, although he was alone – and took the small wrapped parcel from the suitcase. The lid fell shut, the old-fashioned clasps sliding home without his needing to fasten them. Quality craftsmanship.

When it was dark, he buried the slice of tissue in the waste ground behind the flats.

As the decade approached its end, the directionless lifestyle that Maddox and Linzi had drifted into seemed to become more expensive. The bills turned red. Maddox started working regular shifts on the subs' desk at the *Independent*. He hated it but it paid well. Linzi applied for a full-time job at a ladies' salon in Finsbury Park. They took a day trip to Brighton. They went to an art show in the Unitarian Church where Maddox bought Linzi a small watercolour and she picked out a booklet of poems by the artist's husband as a return gift. They had lunch in a vegetarian café. Maddox talked about the frustrations of cutting reviews to fit and coming up with snappy headlines, when what he'd rather be doing was writing the copy himself. Linzi had no complaints about the salon. "Gerry – he's the boss – he's a really lovely guy," she said. "Nicest boss I've ever had."

They spent the afternoon in the pubs and secondhand bookshops of the North Laines. Maddox found a Ramsey Campbell anthology, an M. John Harrison collection and *The New Murderers" Who's Who*. On the train waiting to leave Brighton station to return to London, with the sun throwing long dark shapes across the platforms, Linzi read to Maddox from the pamphlet of verse.

"'This is all I ever wanted / to meet you in the fast decaying shadows / on the outskirts of this or any city / alone and in exile.'"

As the train rattled through Sussex, Maddox pored over the photographs in his true-crime book.

"Look," he said, pointing to a caption: "Brighton Trunk Crime No.2: The trunk's contents."

"Very romantic," Linzi said as she turned to the window, but Maddox couldn't look away from the crumpled stockings on the legs of the victim, Violette Kaye. Her broken neck. The pinched scowl on her decomposed face. To Maddox the picture was as beautiful as it was terrible.

Over the next few days, Maddox read up on the Brighton Trunk Murders of 1934. He discovered that Tony Mancini, who had confessed to putting Violette Kay's body in the trunk but claimed she had died accidentally (only to retract that claim and accept responsibility for her murder more than forty years later), had lodged at 52 Kemp Street. He rooted around for the poetry pamphlet Linzi had bought him. He found it under a pile of magazines. The poet's name was Michael Kemp. He wanted to share his discovery of this coincidence with Linzi when she arrived at his flat with scissors and hairdressing cape.

"Why not save a bit of money?" she said, moving the chair from Maddox's desk into the middle of the room. As she worked on his hair, she talked about Gerry from the salon. "He's so funny," she said. "The customers love him. He certainly keeps me and the other girls entertained."

"Male hairdressers in women's salons are all puffs, surely?"

Linzi stopped cutting and looked at him.

"So?" she said. "So what if they are? And anyway, Gerry's not gay. No way."

"Really? How can you be so sure?"

"A girl knows. Okay?"

"Have you fucked him then or what?"

She took a step back. "What's the matter with you?"

"How else would you know? Gerry seems to be all you can talk about."

"Fuck you."

Maddox shot to his feet, tearing off the cape.

"You know what," he said, seizing the scissors, "I'll cut my own fucking hair and do a better job of it. At least I won't have to listen to you going on about *Gerry*."

He started to hack at his own hair, grabbing handfuls and cutting away. Linzi recoiled in horror, unable to look away, as if she were watching a road accident.

"Maybe I should tell you about all the women at the *Independent*?" he suggested. "Sheila Johnston, Sabine Durrant, Christine Healey . . . I don't know where to start."

It wasn't until he jabbed the scissors threateningly in her direction that she snatched up her bag and ran out.

The next day he sent flowers. He didn't call, didn't push it. Just flowers and a note: "Sorry."

Then he called. Told her he didn't know what had come over him. It wouldn't happen again. He knew he'd be lucky if she forgave him, but he hoped he'd be lucky. He hadn't felt like this about anyone before and he didn't want to lose her. The irony was, he told her, he'd been thinking his flat was getting a bit small and maybe they should look for a place together. He'd understand if she wanted to kick it into touch, but hoped she'd give him another chance.

She said to give her some time.

He shaved his head.

He drove down to Finsbury Park and watched from across the street as she worked on clients. Bobbing left and right. Holding their hair in her hands. Eye contact in the mirror. Gerry fussing around, sharing a joke, trailing an arm. As she'd implied, though, he was distributing his attentions equally among Linzi and the two other girls.

Mornings and evenings, he kept a watch on her flat in Finchley. She left and returned on her own. He chose a route between his flat and hers that took in Cranley Gardens in Muswell Hill. He parked outside No.23 and watched the darkened windows of the top flat. He wondered if any of the neighbours had been Nilsen's contemporaries. If this man passing by now with a tartan shopping trolley had ever nodded good morning to the mass murderer. If that woman leaving her house across the street had ever smiled at him. Maddox got out of the car and touched the low wall outside the property with the tips of his fingers.

Linzi agreed to meet up. Maddox suggested the Wisteria Tea Rooms. It was almost like starting over. Cautious steps. Shy smiles. His hair had grown back.

"What got into you?"

"I don't know. I thought we'd agreed to draw a line under it."

"Yes, you're right."

At the next table a woman was feeding a baby.

"Do you ever think about having children?" Linzi asked, out of the blue.

"A boy," Maddox said straightaway. "I'd call him Jack."

Maddox didn't mention Gerry. He took on extra shifts. Slowly, they built up trust again. One day, driving back to his place after dropping Linzi off at hers, he saw that a board had gone up outside

23 Cranley Gardens. For sale. He rang the agents. Yes, it was the top flat, second floor. It was on at £64,950, but when Maddox dropped by to pick up a copy of the details (DELIGHTFUL TOP FLOOR ONE BEDROOM CONVERSION FLAT), they'd reduced it to £59,950. He made an appointment, told Linzi he'd arranged a surprise. Picked her up early, drove to Cranley Gardens. He'd never brought her this way. She didn't know whose flat it had been.

A young lad met them outside. Loosely knotted tie, shiny shoes. Bright, eager.

Linzi turned to Maddox. "Are you thinking of moving?"

"It's bigger and it's cheap."

Linzi smiled stiffly. They followed the agent up the stairs. He unlocked the interior door and launched into his routine. Maddox nodded without listening as his eyes greedily took everything in, trying to make sense of the flat, to match what he saw to the published photographs. It didn't fit.

"The bathroom's gone," he said, interrupting the agent.

"There's a shower room," the boy said. "And a washbasin across the hall. An unusual arrangement."

Nilsen had dissected two bodies in the bathroom.

"This is a lovely room," the agent said, moving to the front of the flat.

Maddox entered the room at the back and checked the view from the window.

"At least this is unchanged," he said to Linzi, who had appeared alongside.

"What do you mean?"

He looked at her and realised what he'd said.

"This flat's all different. I've seen pictures of it."

The story came out later, back at Maddox's place.

"You took me round Dennis Nilsen's flat?"

He turned away.

"You didn't think to mention it first? You thought we might live there together? In the former home of a serial killer? What the fuck is wrong with you?"

"It's cheap," he said, to the closing door.

He watched from the window as she ran off towards West Green Road. He stayed at the window for a time and then pulled down the ladder and went up into the loft. He pulled up the ladder and closed the trap door. He opened the big brown suitcase. It was like getting a fix. He studied the dimensions of the suitcase. It was not much smaller than Tony Mancini's trunk.

*   *   *

Christine was at work. Maddox read a note she'd left in the kitchen: "We need milk and bread."

He went into the living room and took down the *Hellraiser* DVD from the shelf. Sitting in the car with Jack outside the house on Dollis Hill Lane, Maddox had noticed something not quite right about the windows on the second floor. They were new windows and set in two pairs with a gap between them, but that wasn't it. There was something else and he didn't know what. He fast-forwarded until the exterior shot of Julia leaving the house to go to the bar where she picks up the first victim. The second-floor window comprised six lights in a row. For some reason, when rebuilding the house, they'd left out two of the lights and gone with just four, in two pairs. But that wasn't what was bothering him.

He skipped forward. He kept watching.

Frank and Julia in the second-floor room, top of the house. She's just killed the guy from the bar and Frank has drained his body. Julia re-enters the room after cleaning herself up and as she walks towards the window we see it comprises four lights in a row. Four windows. Four windows in a row. Not six. Four.

Maddox wielded the remote.

Looking up at the house as Julia leaves it to go to the bar. Second floor, six windows. Inside the same room on the second floor, looking towards the windows. Four, not six.

So what? The transformation scenes, which take place in that second-floor room at the front of the house, weren't shot on Dollis Hill Lane. Big deal. That kind of stuff would have to be done in the studio. The arrival of the Cenobites, the transformation of Frank, his being torn apart. It wasn't the kind of stuff you could shoot on location. But how could they make such a glaring continuity error as the number of lights in a window? Six from outside, four from within. It couldn't be a mistake. It was supposed to mean something. But what?

"Daddy?"

Maddox jumped.

"What is it, Jack?"

"What are you watching?"

Maddox looked at the screen as he thought about his response.

"This film, the one shot in that house."

"The house with the windows?"

"Yes."

"Why is it important?"

"I don't know. No, I do know." His shoulders slumped. "I don't know. Maybe it's not."

He drove to the supermarket. Jack was quiet in the back. They got a trolley. Maddox stopped in front of the newspapers. He looked at the *Independent*. Although he'd first met Christine on the *Independent* arts desk, it wasn't until they bumped into each other some years later, when they were both freelancing on TV listings magazines at IPC, that they started going out. Although they were equals at IPC, Christine had routinely rewritten his headlines at the *Independent* and while he pretended it didn't still rankle, it did. Not the best basis for a relationship, perhaps. Then a permanent position came up on *TV Times*, and they both went for it, but Christine's experience counted. They decided it wouldn't affect things, but agreed that maybe Maddox should free himself of his commitments at IPC. He said he had a book he wanted to write. Together they negotiated an increasingly obstacle-strewn path towards making a life together. If they stopped and thought about it, it didn't seem like a very good idea, but neither of them had a better one.

Maddox looked around to check that Jack was still in tow, then moved on.

He stood silently in cold meats, swaying very gently.

"Gone," he said quietly. "All gone. Disappeared."

"What, Daddy? What's gone?"

"Wait there, Jack. I'll be back. Don't move."

He walked to the end of the aisle and turned the corner. He walked to the end of the next aisle and then the next, looking at the items on the shelves, familiar brands, labels he'd seen a thousand times. All meaningless. He recognised nothing. What was he looking for? Bread and milk? Where were they? He couldn't remember. He went back to where he'd left the trolley. It was there, but Jack wasn't.

He looked up and down the aisle. The brand names that had meant nothing to him a moment ago now leapt out at him, shouting, screaming for attention. It was as if the two sides of the aisle had suddenly shifted inward. Jack was nowhere to be seen.

"Jack!"

Maddox ran to the end of the aisle and looked both ways. He looked up the next aisle, then up the next and the one after. He kept calling Jack's name. Shoppers stopped and stared, but Maddox moved faster and shouted louder. He looked at the line of tills and wondered if Jack had gone that way. He could already be out of the store, wandering around the car park, about to be run over or abducted. He told himself to calm down, that he would find him, but at the same time another voice suggested that sometimes the worst thing imaginable did happen. It had before, after all. Would this be the next case heard about on the news? A half-page in the paper. London man loses child in supermarket. Brian Maddox, 42, took his eyes off his son for one moment and he was gone. But he hadn't taken his eyes off him for just one moment. He'd gone to the next aisle, or the one after. He'd gone away. He could have been gone five minutes. Ten, fifteen.

"Jack!"

"Sir?"

A young lad, a shelf stacker, was standing in front of him. Maddox told him his son had disappeared. The shelf stacker asked for a description. Maddox gave him one and the lad said he would start from the far end of the store and advised Maddox to start from the other. They would meet in the middle and most likely one of them would have found Jack. Maddox did as he was told and neither of them found Jack. Maddox was short of breath, dry in the mouth, his chest rising and falling, unbearable pressure being exerted on his temples. He could no longer call out Jack's name without his voice breaking. More staff were on hand now. They took Maddox's arms and led him to an office where he was sat down and given a drink of water.

"Maybe the boy's with his mother?" someone suggested.

Maddox shook his head.

"Do you have a number for her?"

Maddox produced Christine's number. He was dimly aware of a phone call being made. The office was full of people. Managers, security, cashiers. They swopped remarks, observations. Some expressions hardened. "What did she say?" a voice asked. "There is no son," another one answered. "No kids at all, apparently." A security guard replayed videotape on a monitor. Grainy, vivid. Maddox entering the store on his own with a trolley. Standing in front of the newspapers, on his own. Leaving the trolley in cold meats. No unattached children.

They gave Maddox another glass of water while waiting for the police to arrive. The store didn't want to press charges. "What would be the point?" Maddox was free to go. "Has this happened before?" Shake of the head. "If it were to happen again, the store would have to consider taking action . . . Very upsetting for other shoppers . . . You *will* see someone?"

Maddox sat in the car park, behind the wheel of the car. He hadn't got what he'd come for. The milk and the bread. Maybe it didn't matter any more. He sat in the car for a long time and only turned the key in the ignition when he realised the sky over central London was beginning to get dark.

He didn't go to the house. He didn't imagine Christine would be there, but it was kind of irrelevant either way. Instead, he drove to South Tottenham. He drove through the top of the congestion charge zone. It didn't matter any more. It was rush hour. It took an hour and a half to get to N15. The street door was open. He walked up, entered the flat. Thump-thump-thump from downstairs. He took out his phone and sent a text message, then stood by the window for a while watching the street. He left the phone on the window ledge and pulled down the ladder and climbed into the loft, retrieving the ladder and closing the trap door behind him. Stooping, he walked over to the suitcase, which smelled strongly of formalin. He knelt in front of it for several minutes, resting his hands on the lid, then touching the clasps.

He released the clasps and opened the case.

It was empty.

He frowned, then sat and stared at the empty case for some time, listening to the creaks of the beams and the muffled basslines from the downstairs flat. He wondered if Karen would come, how long she might be. He wasn't sure what he would do when she arrived.

Slowly, he rose, then lowered the upper half of his body into the case, folding his legs in afterwards. Inside the case, the smell of formalin was very strong. He stared at the pine beams, the cobwebs, the shadows clinging to the insulating material. He could still faintly hear his neighbour's loud music, which Karen had been unable to hear, and then, rising above it, the clear and unmistakeable chime of his phone, down in the flat, announcing the arrival of a text message. He started to uncurl his body and the lid of the case fell forward.

He had twisted his body far enough that the hump of his shoulder caught the closing lid.

He climbed out and lay down next to the suitcase.

A minute later his phone chimed a reminder.

He thought about Linzi. Linzi had been good for him, until things went bad. He wondered where she was. He looked at the empty suitcase again and plucked a long fine strand of fair hair from the lining. He thought about Karen and her need, unacknowledged, to be looked after. He remembered how vulnerable Linzi had seemed when he saw her for the first time.

Karen would be along soon. Probably. She hadn't let him down yet.

He still had options.

MICHAEL BISHOP

Dr Prida's Dream-Plagued Patient

MICHAEL BISHOP HAS PUBLISHED seventeen novels in his nearly thirty years as a freelance writer, including the Nebula Award-winning *No Enemy But Time*; *Unicorn Mountain*, winner of the Mythopoeic Fantasy Award; and *Brittle Innings*, an imaginative study of minor-league baseball in the Deep South during World War II and winner of the Locus Award for best fantasy novel.

His short-fiction collections include *Blooded on Arachne*, *One Winter in Eden*, *Close Encounters with the Deity*, *Emphatically Not SF Almost*, *At the City Limits of Fate*, *Blue Kansas Sky* and *Brighten to Incandescence: 17 Stories*, featuring an incandescent wraparound cover by his son, Jamie. His recent novelettes "The Door Gunner" and "Bears Discover Smut" have each won Southeastern Science Fiction Association awards for best short fiction.

He has published numerous essays and reviews, including a collection from PS Publishing, *A Reverie for Mister Ray*, also with an evocative wraparound cover by his son, and edited such anthologies as *Light Years and Dark*, winner of the Locus Award for best anthology, three *Nebula Award* volumes and, most recently, *A Cross of Centuries: Twenty-Five Imaginative Tales About the Christ*.

He lives in Pine Mountain, Georgia, with his wife Jeri, an elementary-school counsellor, and he is currently Writer in Residence at LaGrange College in LaGrange, Georgia.

"I'm not very keen on vampire fiction," Bishop admits, "although I recognise this bias as a form of bigotry, based on stereotypes, and know that any theme or subject matter admits of excellent work if the writer focuses, rethinks, and eschews cliché. Have I done that here? I hope so."

"My inspiration for the story was an invitation from the editors of a relatively new magazine, *Aberrant Dreams*, to submit to them and the fact that I'd come to the end of a semester of full-time teaching, with four writing classes that kept me so busy either preparing for each new session or grading essays that I wrote nothing of my own (beyond blood-red notes in the margins of student papers) for over four months.

"When January came, then, and I had my first free day in a long time, I wrote 'Dr Prida's Dream-Plagued Patient' at our kitchen table in longhand with a fine felt-tipped pen in four or five hours of concentrated work. Careful readers will note that I afflicted my narrator with a devilish horror of the mundane and conventional, and that aberrant dreams play a significant, moody role in my quasi-Lovecraftian piece because I was writing for a magazine with that provocative name."

WELL, OF COURSE, I sleep during the day, Dr Prida – in a storm pit or canning cellar (whichever term you prefer) beneath the pantry of a country Victorian home in an aggressively modernizing county in a Southern state whose denizens display little belief in and even less tolerance for creatures of my ilk. I lie in a rotting wooden johnboat on a slab of plywood atop a pair of stumpy-legged sawhorses, and my diurnal companions – in the clayey darkness beneath the prosaic brightness of day – include spiders of several species, spotted camel crickets, and bewildered moths. (The moths' wings often fleck my lips and forehead with their chalky powder.) The darkness attracts and soothes, I guess, not only these unlovely insects but also the rarely sated longings of my forfeited soul. Selah.

I'm here this evening, Dr Prida, at the urging of an early mentor and under protest, but must admit that your gracious couchside manner and delicate bone-china complexion – is that last observation sexist? – have considerably palliated my initial prejudice against this visit. Perhaps it will in fact lessen my anxiety, counteract my depression, and give me the necessary incentive to explore those perilous extremities of night – dawn and dusk – with a bravado heretofore alien to me. By the way, I like your chignon. And the flush at your throat derives, I feel sure, from the lamp beside your wing-back rather than from the somatic manifestations of a quickened pulse. After all, with that Chopin nocturne playing almost inaudibly in the background, your office has a truly calming ambience –

indeed, the security of my canning cellar without the attendant dankness.

Ah, how charmingly you chuckle. All right, then, *laugh*. By that descriptive verb, Dr Prida, I meant no derogation of your femininity. Willie Shakespeare had a character – was it Edgar in *King Lear*? – say that ripeness is all, but in another context. I place more value on specificity, whatever the circumstances, and am like to remark a person's looks and actions, not to mention speech, with more apprehensive detail than does your ordinary machine-stamped client. No offense, of course, to either you or those pitiable lockstep clones. Let me also note that you have decidedly appealing little wren tracks beside your eyes when you frown.

My dreams? You want to know what sort of aberrant dreams I have lying in my great-grandfather's johnboat in my great-grand-mother's canning cellar? What would any sane and cogent profes-sional expect? They appal me, my dreams. They make the plush beneath my fingernails engorge and the flesh of my scrotum tighten. My languid heart accelerates, my flaccid lungs assume the groaning liveliness of bellows, my back arches, and my agitated body balances on the sensitive points of my shoulder blades, coccyx, and heels. A low-level galvanic current crisscrosses my chest and abdomen and streams discontinuously, maddeningly, from a shifting locus in my brain to my fingertips and toes. An onlooker would no doubt suppose me electrified: an epileptic suffering a fit at once disruptive and shackling. If only I could awaken.

Their substance? Relate the substance of these dreams? Specificity? Of course. You want from me only what I pride myself on providing: namely, facts: namely, details; namely, the distillation of the synaptic impulses informing my visions into words that narrate and evoke. Very well. How can I deny you? How can I transgress against the eminence who made me this way – and who sent me to you – by withholding that which, fully aired and processed, could perhaps end my torment? But, Dr Prida, I hesitate – out of conscience as well as shame – to subject you, a respectable professional woman, to the specifics, to the dreadful aberrance of these subterranean sleep-engendered imaginings. I hesitate to alarm, repel, violate, and, ultimately, estrange you. I cringe from disclosing the heinous con-structs of my id, whose depravity only a god or a child could visit without life-altering damage.

You scoff? Well, go ahead. As young as you look, you claim to have practiced a decade and a half? You've heard – as confessions – the laments of anorexics, adulterers, pederasts, fools, bigots, self-mutilators, poltroons, traitors, murderers, and blasphemers? Nothing I can say – no shameful act I might reveal – could possibly dent your therapist's armor, much less pierce it and render you, the queen of unshakable aplomb, a gibbering parody of your degree-bearing self? Very well, then, I'll speak. Remember that I warned you. Remember that I hold in higher regard that kernel of innocence at your venerable core than you do yourself . . .

Three days ago, in my johnboat coffin amid the pseudo-foetuses of canned squash and tomatoes in their ill-shelved Mason jars, I had three devastatingly aberrant dreams in a row. That I survived even one of them – that I outlasted all three – even yet astonishes me, Dr Prida. The first alone would have unmanned nine-tenths of the diurnal sleepers of my unhappy persuasion – indeed, shocked them to utter insentience and left them the unresisting prey of brown recluses, camel crickets, and mice. Forgive what must sound like unmitigated boasting, but I know the Achilles' heels of my colleagues, as well as my own, and that first dream let fly its pernicious arrow at that highly vulnerable portion of my psychic anatomy, and struck it square on.

The dream: get to the dream. I'll recount it as starkly as it inflicted itself upon me: I awoke – not in reality, but in the washed-out opalescent landscape of my vision – and struggled out of bed into a chamber of undivided white: white ceiling, white floor, white walls, white bedstead, white clothes-tree, and, upon this clothes-tree, an assortment of white clothes for the ten-year-old boy that, in dreaming, I had become. I had to garb myself, for I had awakened naked and the stinging brightness of the chamber required an immediate adjustment on my part to prevent my going blind. Shuddering at the touch of each item, I donned a pair of schoolboy briefs, a ribbed white wife-beater undershirt, a pair of white-duck trousers, a starched white dress shirt, and a hooded white sweatshirt, whose hood allowed me some small shelter from the overweening brightness. Head down, I groped my way back to the bed, found a pair of white cotton sweat socks on the white feather pillow, and pulled one of these socks onto my pallid toes, over my albino's instep, and up and over my leprous left ankle. The sock had no end. It covered my calf, knee, thigh, groin, and, by some inexplicable geometric convolution, my midriff, torso, and neck, so that I was finally imprisoned in a snowy full-body strait-stocking that clung to nearly every square inch of me, mercilessly. When I screamed, still sleeping, this first dream unraveled – without, however, releasing me to the dank but comforting reality of my great-grandmother's canning cellar.

Ah, my recitation has left you speechless, Dr Prida. I understand.
What could more reliably silence a psychiatrist than the indelible
image of an ignorant child wrapped in a tenacious white strait-
stocking? You smile – no doubt to solace me, to convey by a
compassionate look that not even this horror estranges you, that I
may speak freely, with no inhibiting fear of your outrage or censure.
All right, then, my second dream, which followed the first after an
interval of chaotic blankness and erupted into my apprehensive
consciousness in the workaday vicinity of noon.

Not surprisingly, this daymare centered on eating.

As a young man of twenty-five or -six, I sat in a rustic Victorian
kitchen before an immense porcelain tureen of potato soup. Beside
this tureen resided a large white platter hosting a grilled sandwich of
mozzarella or possibly provolone cheese, a hardboiled egg, and a
scoop of macaroni pasta with almond slices, buttons of watercress,
and shards of sun-bleached celery. From the table's white Formica
surface a tumbler of skin milk rose up like a small Doric pillar.
Nauseated, I spooned soup, nibbled at the sandwich, bit off tatters of
egg, sampled the pasta, and sipped the milk in a predictably ceaseless
repeating sequence that my dream self had no power to halt. The
peristaltic action of my throat continued without hindrance or
interruption until white tears began falling into my soup and a
muffling lambency-shot fog filled the kitchen, putting a gauzy clamp
on both my esophagus and my second dream.

You smile again? More comfort for a troubled client? More
compassion for a deviant dreamer? Of course, of course. What else
do we pay you for, Dr Prida? Who else can we turn to? But you see
now why shame mantles me and my conscience gnaws. But if I've
gone this far, how may I refrain from unburdening myself of my final
dream, my third and most ruthlessly aberrant horror show?

Listen, then, Dr Prida. Listen as you have listened to the others,
and withhold your condemnation – your outrage and its inevitable
articulation – until I have wholly purged myself of this psychic
poison. Know, though, that it has a narrative arc absent from the
first two dreams and an additional character: a story as opposed to
the static imagery of those inchoate earlier visions. Know, too, that
had my mentor not found me in the throes of an abreactive post-
dream spasm and stepped in to help me, I might have died forever.
The word *forever*, at least in this hypothetical projection, has more
finality to it than I, or any of my anonymous half-, quarter-, or no-
blood siblings, can fully bear.

Listen:

As a man of forty or so (my apparent age this evening, Dr Prida), I stand at an altar in a white tuxedo and exchange vows with a woman twelve years my junior clad in a traditional white bridal gown. She gazes upon me with a nonjudgmental gentleness as rare as midsummer sleet. After the wedding and a grand reception in a country Victorian house appointed ivory and cream – from interior dome to transoms to louvered shutters to wainscoting to balusters – we ride in a bone-hued limousine to a marble villa on the crest of a mountain of quartz and milky chalcedony. Here, in the last light of the afternoon in a high-windowed room overlooking a valley carpeted with white mums and pale gardenias, we consummate with neither bites nor strangle marks the promise of our vows and lie in each other's arms until we move again in the same tender way and so traverse the entire self-negating night to the doorstep of morning . . . at which point my real body, the one in the pit, began to thrash in dread-stricken protest against the conventional harmoniousness of such a wholesome union. And, as I've already said, I might have died forever but for the timely intercession of Gregor, your undying father.

Yes, smile: smile wider. And approach me smiling in your black-velvet slippers. What big pretty teeth you have, such incisive incisors, my dear Dr Prida, and such a way with wordlessness that perhaps we need never speak again . . .

MARK CHADBOURN

The Ones We Leave Behind

A WINNER OF THE BRITISH FANTASY AWARD, Mark Chadbourn is the author of eleven novels and one non-fiction book. His current fantasy sequence, "Kingdom of the Serpent", continues with *The Burning Man* in early 2008.

A former journalist, he is now a screenwriter for BBC television drama. His other jobs have included running an independent record company, managing rock bands, working on a production line and as an engineer's "mate". He lives in a forest in the English Midlands.

"A few years ago," recalls Chadbourn, "I had the pleasure of spending time in several conversations with the acclaimed Vietnam War photographer Tim Page for a magazine article I was writing.

"Tim's pictures helped define that war, but his own personal story illustrated the horrors of the conflict just as clearly. Torn apart by an explosion, losing a significant part of his brain to shrapnel, he spent agonising years reclaiming his health and his life. His recovery was so amazing these days it's hard to tell how much he suffered.

"He is the inspiration behind 'The Ones We Leave Behind'."

T HE PAST CAN'T BE TRUSTED. Our memories play tricks with us, whispering lies to make us feel better or haunting us with images half-glimpsed in the shadows of our heads. I used to think photographs were different. They captured the moment so perfectly, more real than real because they saw things you never did. Subtle expressions barely noticed, a fugitive smile or nascent tear, rare light, odd juxtapositions, nature's secret ironies. In photographs, old friends lived forever, just as you always knew them.

Or so I thought.

Outside the sound of the shells hitting the suburbs are almost lost beneath the screams of panic. A woman, face contorted by grief, throws herself off the building opposite. One of those who fled the north twenty years ago. Better death at her own hand than the slow killing of an unforgiving revenge.

I never thought I would see Saigon like this. The City of Smiles. The eye of optimism and tranquillity at the heart of the Vietnam storm. Everyone is running. For escape, for shelter. For food, for drink, for love and money. No point. The city is encircled by sixteen divisions – 140,000 men. In his resignation speech, President Thieu blamed the US for paying for the war in money while the Vietnamese paid in blood. He tried to get his betrayal in first, but he'd missed the boat by several years.

Anyone with half a brain would be attempting to buy their way out on one of the Hercules transports leaving the airport. As a photo-journalist and integral part of the Imperialist propaganda machine, I should be first in the queue. Once the Communists get here, they'll have my head on a spike at the Presidential Palace faster than you can say Tan Son Nhut.

But in a way, I'm just like that poor woman committing suicide. Sometimes it's not just about life or death; there are occasions when worse things enter the equation. I have to find an old man with a bitter heart before the past catches up with me. Before I fall off the edge of existence and can't even claim a memory to my name.

The first time I saw Van Diemen was in the back of a tent, glowing with the seething light of a hissing lamp while shadows of jungle moths passed across his face. I remember the stickiness of the night, the way my shirt clung to my back, the sickening taste of fear that never left my dry mouth. You lived with all those things back then, and they are still as real as anything I know.

It was 7 January 1967, the evening before Operation Cedar Falls. The regular grunts had no idea they were on the brink of a KO punch into VC strongholds, designed to stop the Communists in their tracks and provide a springboard for US victory. At least that was the plan.

The Pack knew no more, cared even less. We saw ourselves as old-style adventurers, relishing the adrenaline rush of any danger zone. The scent of napalm or Agent Orange on the breeze was enough to get us grabbing our cameras. There were four of us, all in our twenties, young enough not to know the distinction between bravery and stupidity. Chet was from some dusty Arizona town; a lazy accent, a love of grass and a nice little commission from *Life*. Alain had given up documenting the tensions on the streets of Paris for what he saw as life on the edge in 'Nam.

And then there was Justin and myself, childhood friends from the same dorm in some second-rate public school no one had ever heard of, both with too-rich parents and no real need to earn a living. Brits abroad with Empire-borne arrogance that neither of us recognised. Justin was brash, revelling in his aristocrat links, however far removed. I was quieter. And in the arrogance of our youth and our background and our job, we thought nothing could touch us.

That night we'd been smoking some grass, drinking a little bourbon, talking about where we would go once the current mess had blown over. The Middle East, maybe. Always good for a little mayhem. Or Africa, a leaking steam pipe waiting to blow.

The sound of the chopper coming in low over the tree-tops stirred us from our debate. We watched with stoned fascination as it landed in the camp to release a flurry of wild activity, soldiers free of the sweat and grime of the jungle coalescing around a smaller group, at the core a shock of silver hair shimmering in the glare of the lights. They ducked low beneath the whirring blades and hurried as one into the heart of the camp.

"Something is afoot," Alain said.

"What do you say, Will?" Justin asked me. "Too high to creep down there to see if we've had a secret visit from the Prez himself?"

"Go yourself. I'm not your lackey." I felt obliged to offer the lip service protest, but we both knew it would be me. I was too curious by far and everyone else always took advantage of it.

"The Prez," Chet said dreamily. "Now that would be a picture. Maybe . . . maybe it's Ann-Margret." He drifted off into a reverie.

"Are we going to do this or not?" I said before I lost them further. With foul-mouthed protest, they shuffled into a seated position, Alain propping up Chet. I made Justin stop skinning up and then checked the camera. Through the lens they looked like a bunch of idiots on holiday. I set the timer and threw myself into the middle of them. In the white flash, the whole world disappeared.

I slipped away a few minutes later, past the stinking latrines, skirting the tent where Love were singing that "Seven and Seven Is", until I found myself at Ops, where the officers regularly pored over their maps, drinking beer and reminiscing about life before they went In Country and mutated into a different species.

The coterie of guards in pristine fatigues had melted away. Through the tent flaps I could see three officers, two men in civilian clothes – spooks, I guessed – and that shock of silver hair. It was on a man with a face like an Easter Island statue, impenetrable, mysterious, aloof. He must have been in his seventies, but he didn't look frail; there was a gravity to him that turned all the others into satellites. He wore small, wire-framed glasses that reflected the light like flares as he examined a map spread out on the trestle table.

"Where, exactly?" His voice had European precision, jarring to hear among all the lazy speech and expletives.

One of the spooks leaned over and tapped the map. "Intelligence says here. Whatever happened, they're scared."

"And you are certain my presence is justified?" The silver-haired guy didn't look up from the map.

"Absolutely Professor Van Diemen. If there's any truth at all to the reports we're getting back, you're probably the only one who could help," the spook replied.

"The Pentagon said you were the man for the job after you consulted the State Department on that San Francisco business." A general I'd never seen before.

"You know how serious things are, Professor," the spook continued. "If things fall apart here, the entire world will be next. We need to stamp our authority on the situation, and anything that can help us is absolutely justified."

Van Diemen nodded slowly. Finally he did look up at the faces turned towards him. "Tomorrow, then?"

"Operation Cedar Falls begins at eight hundred hours," the General said. "The 1st Infantry Division's 2nd Brigade will move into Ben Suc. It will distract the VC so we can fly you along the Saigon River to the heart of the triangle with the 242nd Chemical Detachment. There's a small window of opportunity before the 173rd Airborne move in from Ben Cat."

Back with the others I could barely conceal my excitement. "Who is it?" Justin had shaken off the dope haze with the speed of someone who always keeps his eye on the main chance.

"A professor. Sounded like he was from the Netherlands or Belgium."

"Not Ann-Marget?" Chet said wistfully.

"Come on, Will," Justin urged. His eyes had that hungry gleam he always developed when he sensed an opportunity – for good pictures, good sex or any kind of drugs.

"There's something big kicking off tomorrow." I hunkered in

among them, whispering. "A push into the Iron Triangle. Operation Cedar Falls. But that's not the interesting thing."

I proceeded to tell them what little I had overheard, but it was enough to get their news senses tingling. Not knowing what lay ahead, we were very excited.

Back then we'd never have imagined Saigon falling. Or a lot of things that happened since. I'm tempted to take out the photo from that night, but I know it's just a nervous habit, imbued with the desperate wishful thinking of a child. It's taken me weeks to get to this point, following a trail that was not only two years out of date but had also been obscured by the old man himself.

He didn't want to be found. Maybe he felt guilty.

From the outside the room looks non-descript. BLACKWALL IMPORTS-EXPORTS, the sign says. A front for the secret service and their employees. I never used to care about any of the grubby games the "adults" played; it had no bearing on my life. Now I'm building up a hard core of hatred in my heart for the lengths to which people will go. Yet I still can't decide if I want to save myself or if I just want revenge.

My first glimpse of the room is a shock. Religious symbols everywhere: crucifixes, Stars of David, a Buddha, a shrine, the Bible, the Koran. But no Van Diemen. I don't allow myself to get disappointed, not after everything I've been through.

I never took Van Diemen to be a spiritual man. Far from it. What I'd seen of him suggested he was completely mired in the stinking mud of the real world. *Realpolitik*, not prayer. He's a symbol of everything that's going wrong at the moment: frightened, old, white men trying to stop the world turning, going to any lengths to crush youth, hope, innocence at home, to eradicate different ways of thinking abroad. Men who see threats where there is only change. Men who want to seal the planet in a block of ice.

This is the room of someone obsessed. Beyond the religious artefacts are other, more disturbing items: occult books, signs scrawled on the walls in a frantic hand. The distant echoes of what we found that day in the Iron Triangle.

I remember, I remember . . . I spent a couple of hours that night developing the roll of film. The photo taken earlier that evening perfectly captured the moment, carefree grins, lazy, king-of-the-world expressions. Nature's secret ironies.

We woke to a dawn of fiery reds and hateful purples. Justin was already up, loading his camera bag, checking lenses and stashing film. Alain helped me drag Chet out of his crib; he was bad-tempered and sluggish and it took a shot of Jack in a stained mug to get him moving.

At a five-minute briefing, the captain told us we could accompany the troops into Ben Suc. It was a big day, the start of the war's turning, and we were there to capture the moment the US became the winning side.

We'd already made our plans, bribed the right people with a small sack of prized grass, and slipped into the back of the chopper just before it took off. Ben Suc was far behind us when we were discovered, and by then what could they do? We were threatened with losing our accreditation, told we'd be shipped out of 'Nam the minute we got back to camp, ordered to remain with the chopper ready for dust-off. We made the correct contrite noises and then laughed among ourselves when the Captain went back to his seat.

Van Diemen sat with the brass and the spooks as if they were afraid of allowing him contact with the regular grunts. I watched him carefully, thought how troubled he looked, how deeply sad; wondered what he had done in San Francisco that made him such a vital resource for the Government.

We came down in a clearing not far from the silver-gleaming river. The troops fanned out to clear the area; there were about twenty of them, with a further twenty Tunnel Rats from the 242nd Chemical Detachment, for whom I had the ultimate respect. In a country of nightmares, theirs was the worst, crawling into the Viet Cong tunnel system with nothing more than a hand gun, a knife and a flashlight to flush out the enemy.

Finally Van Diemen and his shiny, stiff shadows ventured out and we followed close behind. Nobody told us to get back, and we knew why the minute we were on solid ground and the chopper's engines were stifled.

When you'd been In Country for a while, you started to develop what the grunts called "Jungle Sense". You knew when danger was rolling towards you like a tropical storm on the horizon. This was worse than that feeling. I could see it in everyone's faces the same: an expression of distaste overlaying dread.

The air was dead. No birdsong. No animal sounds. No evidence of human life. It felt like we were trapped in a bubble.

"Is this part of it?" the spook said to Van Diemen ahead of us.

"I think it possibly is." Something odd had happened to the old man. Once he stepped into that disturbing atmosphere he appeared to come alive with strength and purpose in his movements.

The point man followed the Captain's directions deep into the trees. It was already growing hot and humid. Nobody spoke. All eyes remained on the green world pressing tight on every side.

After fifteen minutes we reached a makeshift shelter. Smoke drifted up from the embers of a small fire over which hung a pot of water. In the shelter a rifle lay on a blanket next to an oily rag as if it had been dropped in the process of cleaning. A dead radio stood on a splintered fruit crate.

"Where's the resistance?" The Captain looked like a surfer, sun-bleached blond hair, blue eyes, still younger but ageing faster than time allowed.

"Maybe they ran when they heard us coming," Chet ventured.

The spook whirled as if he'd only just realised we were there. "No pictures! Of anything! This is a top-secret mission! Any problems and you'll be shot for treason."

That sounded a little extreme, even for 'Nam. The Captain suggested we be escorted back to the chopper, but the spook's attention had already wandered uneasily back to the shelter.

"The entrance should be around here somewhere." He motioned to the zone around the shelter. The Captain ordered his men to scour the area and the trapdoor was found within a minute.

"How good is your intelligence?" Van Diemen peered into the hole despite the attempts of those around to drag him back.

"As good as can be expected from within the Iron Triangle," the spook said. "We have details . . . but there are gaps."

"So you are not sure if there is a degree of control?"

"We *believe* there to be."

"You *believe* it can be controlled?"

The spook's jaw tightened. "That's your area, not mine."

Van Diemen turned to the surfer. "Captain, you plan to have your men secure these tunnels?"

"That's the general idea."

"But what if the source of our mission is down there?"

The captain looked blank for a moment. "I'm not aware of the source of our mission, sir."

Van Diemen glanced at the spook. "Need to know basis," the spy replied.

"Then I suggest I go in with you," Van Diemen said to the captain.

You have to admire the professor's balls. Half the grunts in 'Nam wouldn't have willingly ventured into that hole with the Tunnel Rats.

They tried to talk him out of it with lots of gruesome descriptions of booby-traps and hidden snipers, but he was having none of it.

"If he's going in there, we should too," I whispered to Justin.
"Are you mad?"

"Will is right," Alain said. "Whatever they're looking for, must be down there."

"Well, why don't we just wait here until they bring it out?" Justin said as if we were both stupid.

"Under a blanket or in a box?" I replied. "Nice photo. Make the cover of *Life*, that will."

Two of the Tunnel Rats dropped down the hole before Van Diemen shouldered his way forward to go third. I steeled myself and jumped in immediately afterwards. It felt ludicrously dangerous, but I told myself that was what we were about.

A horizontal tunnel barely big enough for a dog ran out about six feet below ground level. I almost turned back then, but with another Tunnel Rat behind me I had no choice but to proceed. It was oppressively hot, the air thin and filled with the choking smell of soil and vegetation. Vermin scurried in the dark ahead of us.

Claustrophobia mounted quickly, fired by the knowledge that some booby trap could bring the whole thing down upon me. The tunnel roof pressed down against my back. My elbows were constricted against the walls on either side so that I had to drag myself along like an animal. With each foot I crawled, it felt like my throat constricted another half inch.

And then Van Diemen was pulling himself out and up. I followed so frantically I almost knocked the old man over. We were in an underground room big enough to stand, with a makeshift table, a stubby candle, still alight, and more guns.

"I don't get it," one of the Rats said uneasily. "They wouldn't leave their weapons lying around like this."

"Unless the whole place is a trap," the other Rat mused. He shrugged, did eeny-meeny between the two tunnels that ran off from the room, then ducked into the one he had selected, knife clenched between his teeth.

"What are we looking for, Professor?" I ventured.

He smiled, quite warmly I thought, but knew what I was attempting. "Secrets." He waved one long, delicate finger in my face. "And mysteries."

The tunnel system was a maze, switching back and forth and crosscutting, with room after room that looked exactly like the last one. We could have crawled for miles for all I knew. And the ever-present threat never lessened, so that by the end my chest burned and my muscles ached from the constant alertness. I felt queasy from the feeling that each movement could be my last. I thought about explosions in that confined area, the heat, the ripping shrapnel. I thought about the soil coming down hard, into my mouth, my throat. I thought about a gun emerging from a shadow to blast into my temple. Poison gas. Burning chemicals. I thought about everything. But I didn't believe the Professor considered any of them. He was calm and focused on the matter at hand, as though these things held no fear for him at all.

I don't quite know how it happened, but at some point the Professor and I got separated from the Tunnel Rats and the other snappers. We'd been warned against this happening and I thought we'd been taking special care. Maybe not; or maybe the Professor, who was ahead of me, wanted it that way.

We found ourselves in one of those rooms carved out of the earth. In the light of the Professor's torch it appeared empty, but I caught a glimpse of a doorway to other rooms beyond.

"We should wait." The pounding of the blood in my brain made me dizzy. "Let the experts clear the place out before we go stumbling around."

"They will not find anything." His voice was distracted.

"How can you be so sure?"

"It is my job to be certain."

"The Government must be paying you a lot of money to take these kinds of risks."

"I am not here for money."

"Love, then." I laughed, trying to ease my tension.

He moved ahead, the light dancing around. I caught sight of something white in the room beyond.

"Are you interested in politics . . . ?" He paused, waiting for me to fill in my name.

"Will Kennet. Politics is for old guys who've forgotten how to have fun."

"There are many your age – and younger – who would disagree, Mr Kennet. Across America, in Australia, Europe, protests against this war are growing. The season is changing. Polarities are coming into opposition."

"I don't know what you mean." We'd reach the doorway into the rooms beyond. There was that white shape again. And another. But he was moving the torch around too quickly for me to get a handle on it.

"The young and the old. The West and the East. Authority and the forces of rebellion."

He stopped in the doorway. The light fell on the white shapes fully, and I could see it was stone: blocks that appeared to have been exposed in the digging of the tunnels, twin columns, with a doorway between them.

"Order and chaos." He pointed the torch into my face, blinding me. "Which side are you on, Mr Kennet?"

I knocked his hand down, annoyed by his disrespect. "My own side. I told you, I'm not interested in any of that." I'd half started to like him, but now I could see something I'd come across before, in the politicians, and the generals, and all the ones fighting to maintain their place in the world. Not something that was bad, particularly, but a hardness. A recognition that if you wanted to keep the world the way you felt comfortable with, you'd have to go one step further than the next guy. I'd decided it came from fear. Some people just didn't like change.

"There is only one side or the other." He was moving again; the light painted a path to the door between the stone columns. "If you have not decided yet, you will be forced to do so soon. That is knowledge for you, Mr Kennet, given freely, earned by age. Take a short cut to wisdom and choose your path now."

I was more interested in the stone. I could see it carried on into a corridor beyond.

"What is this place?"

He carefully examined some carvings thrown up by the play of light and shade. They appeared to be illustrations of some kind, and writing; it didn't look like any Vietnamese script I recognised. "Great age," he mused to himself.

"Is this what you were sent to find?"

"I did not know what I was going to find. The reports were vague. But it appeared to be related to my particular sphere of expertise."

As we stepped into the corridor, the temperature dropped several degrees. Maybe it was the stone, but it didn't *feel* right.

"What is that?"

"Metaphysics. The imposition of the rules of logic and reason on the illogical and irrational."

"You see, Professor, this is why Americans think Europeans come from a different planet. Same words, different language. I come from there and I don't understand what you're saying."

He held an arm across my chest to stop me.

"What is it?"

He hushed me urgently. I peered into the dark ahead; for some reason he had covered the torch with his hand.

"Did you hear something?" I hissed.

"Go cautiously," he said, as if I was thinking of doing anything else.

I should have gone back. Every sense was telling me to do that; everything I knew about Vietnam warned me about venturing into the unknown. But I was in the grip of the moment and my own fabulous self-image.

We moved ahead together. Chambers lay on either side of the corridor, bare stone boxes that I would have taken for prison cells if they had any doors. Van Diemen placed the torch on the flags to half-light the whole area before proceeding to examine one of the small rooms. I carried on along the corridor and was disappointed to find it came up against a bare stone wall. That was all it was, a corridor with a few rooms on either side. No buried city from Vietnam's ancient past. No hidden "secrets and mysteries". As dull as the rest of the tunnel complex. The whole expedition was turning into a damp squib.

"There's nothing here," I said. "Let's get back to the others." Van Diemen mumbled some distracted reply from the depths of one of the chambers. And then my eyes fell on something out of the ordinary. Hanging from the lintel of the final chamber on the right was what at first looked like a wind-chime. It was a mixture of stones of varying sizes and hard wood, carved into unusual shapes, hung on pieces of wire that showed no signs of corrosion. I carefully lifted it down from its hook and carried it back to Van Diemen.

"What do you make of this?" I was surprised that it was quite robust despite its appearance of fragility.

Van Diemen emerged from the chamber, still distracted. But when he saw what I was holding he became animated. "For God's sake, put it back!"

"What's the big deal?"

He snatched it from me and attempted to push past, then stopped in his tracks, his face rigid.

At first I thought it was my eyes adjusting from the torchlight to the gloom, but pin-pricks of luminescence were coalescing in the dark, like fireflies coming together. A definite shape, its outline indistinct.

With surprising strength, Van Diemen grabbed my shirt and threw me behind him. I went down hard on the stone flags and as I hauled myself back to my feet he was already forcing me out of the corridor.

"Get away from here," he rasped. "Back to the helicopter. Tell the others."

The tiny, flickering lights were now moving towards us. I didn't know what I was seeing, but the Professor's anxiety was catching. I ran across the outer room and dived into the first tunnel.

In the hi-tension atmosphere my panic flared easily. Barely thinking, I scrambled, the claustrophobia fuelling my rising emotions. When I finally burst out into the light, I must have looked like some wild man.

Justin, Chet and Alain were sitting around drinking water from a canteen while a few of the grunts ensured the area remained secure. The spook, the General and the other officers stood to one side, talking conspiratorially. "Get out of here!" I yelled. "Back to the chopper!"

The Pack knew me well enough to heed my warning. Justin grabbed me and pulled me with him as we ran towards the tree-line.

The men surrounded the tunnel entrance, guns pointing into the dark hole. That was the last I saw of them.

We didn't stop until we made it back to the chopper, crashing to our knees breathless before breaking into anxious laughter.

"You idiot!" Justin roared. "I bet there was nothing down there!"

"There was!" I protested. "Some kind of . . . some kind . . ."

Justin laughed some more at my disorientation; to be honest, I really didn't know why I had run so hard. Imagination; or instinct?

Yet Chet was growing agitated. "What is wrong, brother?" Alain asked.

"It doesn't make any sense." Chet pointed a wavering finger at the chopper. "How could that get here if there weren't any pilots?"

As I stared into the empty chopper, I knew exactly what Chet meant, though it was only later when understanding came.

Justin ran his hand through his long hair, puzzled. "He's right. There were no pilots on board. Who was flying it?"

"I can't remember . . ." Alain tapped his temple. "How many came with us? Twenty-five?"

"Twenty-four," I corrected.

"Twenty-three," Justin said.

Chet collapsed into a seated position, holding his head in his hands.

"Definitely, twenty-two," I said. My head was hurting. Had I breathed in some gas? Had we all been affected? I stumbled away from the chopper, trying to get a hold of myself. The sound of running came from the tree-line and I hurried towards it to usher the others back to the chopper.

And that was when the blast stopped my world.

*　　*　　*

I've turned Van Diemen's room over, but there's no sign to suggest whether he was there today or a week ago. But as I sit amid the chaos of his Saigon life, a frightened young Vietnamese man appears at the door. I jump up, grab him by the shoulders.

"Professor Van Diemen?" I bark.

He shakes his head, his eyes wondering if it would be better if I killed him before the Communists get here.

"Old man, silver hair?"

"Mr Harker?"

"If that's what he's calling himself."

"Gone. To the airport."

Typical of his kind. Work their magic, stir up their brew of misery, and then get out when everything starts to fall apart rather than face the repercussions of their actions. I push my way out of the door and run into the crazed city.

Feeble memories. The illusion we construct with our consciousness is such a fragile thing, easily disrupted, altered, warped. But the body on the other hand is a remarkably hardy piece of engineering. One of the grunts coming back to the chopper had stepped on a mine; apparently there were hundreds in that area and it was a miracle we'd all avoided them on the way to the tunnel system.

Talking of miracles . . . Shrapnel took me apart. I was split open from groin to chest. Another piece hit me in the head and went straight out of the back, taking with it a third of my brain. Now you may think it's impossible to survive having lost that much grey matter, but I can assure you that is not the case. I could cite cases of people who led fulfilling lives only for an autopsy to discover they had malformed brains the size of a walnut, but suffice to say that I did survive, though it was touch and go for a long time.

Only fragments of the subsequent weeks come back to me. Lying on a bed in a field hospital with corpses stacked up all around, jazzed on pain and morphine. People saying, "He'll never make it," over and over in easy earshot as if I were already gone.

I remember Justin at the bedside, crying, saying something about being forced to go back home, but he'd keep in touch, check up on me.

And at one point I recall a wrinkled face leaning over me, a shock of silver hair. Van Diemen; I'm pretty sure I wasn't dreaming. He said he was sorry in a way that, too, suggested I was already dead. I think he sat by my bed for a while, just talking to himself. Snippets come back. Something about fighting chaos . . . winning the war . . . Who cares?

My recovery was a long, slow and agonising process. The drugs became a constant friend. I had to re-learn how to speak, how to hold a pen, write. The physical therapy was excruciating. My brain had to re-wire itself, shifting the functions from the part that was missing to what remained, nestled under the metal plate. Just to cap things, the nice zipper scar up my stomach itched like hell.

They let me leave the hospital two years later and it was another year before I could rejoin the world. Things had moved on – rockets on the moon, bands I'd loved long gone – but the Vietnam War ploughed on regardless. The Americans hadn't won. Nobody had as far as I could see. But I still had one thing to give me comfort: the photo of that happy, drugged-up night before I fell off the ride, reminding me of the best friends a man could ever have. It was time to look them up.

England was nothing like Vietnam: wet, cold, quiet, safe. I'd only heard from Justin once in all the time of my recovery. That upset me; we'd been so close for so long and when I really needed his support he was no longer around. The one letter I did get from him didn't sound like Justin at all. He told me he'd given up photojournalism and had gone back to living with his parents in their rambling old pile in Surrey, but there was an undercurrent to all the banal statements that suggested he was scared. I'm not stupid. Someone had got to him, and it had to be one of the spooks. The mission we'd muscled our way in on was top secret and those kind of people had long memories. I'd probably been written off because of my injuries – nobody expected me to be thinking never mind walking around. But Justin and the others had probably all been warned off.

I turned up at his parents' house late one Saturday night. It took a few seconds for his mother to recognise me – my injuries had made me haggard – but she welcomed me warmly.

She'd heard about what happened to me in 'Nam from my own family and I spent a few minutes making small talk about my recovery. Then I asked her if I could see Justin and she grew puzzled and then agitated.

"Who's Justin?" she said, kneading the palm of one hand insistently.

I laughed. "Justin. Come on! Your son!"

Her uneasy gaze ranged across my face. "I have no son, you know that Will. Derek and I never had children."

I laughed again, but it dried up when I saw she was deathly serious. You can tell when someone is pretending, especially if it's something

as big and obvious as that. My first thought was that she was
covering for him. He was hiding out after the spooks' threat, making
a new life for himself.

"Okay," I said, "I'll go along with you. But let me show you this."
I dipped into my worn backpack that had followed me halfway
round the world. The photo was crumpled after months of travelling.
I handed it over. "Far right."

She glanced at it, shook her head, handed it back. "That's you."

My stomach knotted when I looked at the picture. She was correct
– I was on the far right of the group. Of three young men. Chet, Alain
and me. No Justin. My head spun; I was still shaky after the injuries
and the sheer act of comprehending made me feel queasy.

"I have no son," she repeated in a strained voice. Another thought
broke on her face. "An old man was round here a few weeks ago
asking the same question. What is going on, Will?"

I looked around the antique-stuffed study. Photos were everywhere, on the sideboard, the mantelpiece, the wall. They showed Mr
and Mrs Glendenning, Justin's aunts and uncles, family gatherings.
But no Justin in any of them. There was one photo taken on our last
day of school; in it, I now stood alone. It made no sense that a photo
of me alone would be hanging on the Glendenning's study wall, but
when I pointed that out to Mrs Glendenning she became even more
agitated.

I went out into the rain with a shattering sense of dread and the
desperate feeling that my mind was falling apart.

I visited my father, but he didn't recall Justin at all. None of my own
photos showed him. Every reference to him in my childhood diaries no
longer existed. They hadn't been erased – the writing was mine, the
content too, but whenever I had done anything with Justin, I had now
experienced it alone. It was as though Justin had never existed.

Frantically, I booked a flight to Paris to see Alain. I held the photo in
sweating hands all the way, staring at it so hard my head hurt. If only
I could pierce the illusion and Justin would materialise in his familiar
place.

Just before we touched down in Paris-Orly, I looked out over the
rooftops of the City of Lights and when I looked back at the photo
Alain was gone too.

The story was the same. At Alain's flat and in every one of his
familiar haunts, no one had heard of him.

                    *   *   *

I slipped into a deep depression for a month during which I was convinced my so-called recovery had been a lie and my brain had been damaged irreparably. I tried not to think about what was happening, but it haunted my every moment. Finally, I could bear it no more. Chet was my last hope for some kind of understanding.

At least he was still on the photo: the two of us, arms around each other's shoulders. The best way to get to him was through his work, so I rang the Picture Editor on *Life* magazine, an irascible man with the hard-edged tones of a New Yorker. He said he had a number for Chet and disappeared from the phone, but when he came back with his contact book he asked me who I was after.

I mentioned Chet's name again, but this time I only got a blank silence. The Picture Editor had never commissioned Chet, had never even heard of him. I asked a secretary to check particular issues that I knew featured Chet's work, but all the pictures were now different to what I remembered, all by other photographers. And when I hung up and examined my snap, I saw only my own face staring back at me.

Beyond everything that was happening, one other thing disturbed me immensely: why was I the only one to remember these people? But that wasn't true, I realised. At least one other person knew. He had visited Justin's parents, and with a little digging around I found he'd asked questions in Paris and called *Life*. Van Diemen was the key, and I started to wonder if he wasn't perhaps the cause. The spooks had decided to tie up the loose ends, and their cat's-paw had been set the task.

Over time it came to me. Somehow it was linked to whatever had been uncovered in that mysterious stone corridor in the heart of the Iron Triangle. Van Diemen knew what it was: I think he had always known. When we ran from the tunnels for the chopper and we couldn't understand why there were no pilots . . . failed to get a handle on the number of troops that came with us . . . they had all been wiped out like Justin, Alain and Chet. We couldn't remember them because they never existed.

A sizeable portion of my US dollars buys me a trip to the airport in a ten-year-old car loaded with chicken coops. Somehow we make our way through streets packed with people carrying beds from the houses of the rich, or siphoning petrol, or making fluttering paper rain with their now-useless South Vietnamese money.

I fight my way through the crush at the airport gates – people screaming for blood, shouting for help, wanting to know why they're being abandoned. The MPs let me by when they see my press accreditation, and I run across the tarmac amid the stink of fuel and the hell of engine noise, wondering when I'll wink out like a star at dawn. Will I feel something coming for me? Cold talons on my neck? Will there be something beyond that instant? Or just a nothing and a never-having-been?

Searching back and forth along the ranks of men in short-sleeved white shirts and black ties and the very few women, make-up free and tear-stained, I start to think Van Diemen has already made good his escape. But then I see that silver hair shining in the sun and he turns and sees me as if I'd shouted him. But he doesn't run. Instead his face grows briefly bright, and he smiles before becoming deeply sad. He holds out his arms for me.

Away from the crowds, we face each other. I try to stop myself shaking. For some reason, the words won't come.

"My boy," he said with surprising gentleness. "They told me you were dying." He read my face and added quickly, "Of course. You want answers."

"I want to be saved." My voice sounded so pathetic, like a child's.

He rested a paternal hand on my shoulder. "I came to you to explain. Eventually I tracked down your friends too. For one I was too late. But I spoke to the Frenchman and the American before the end."

"You killed them."

"No. I tried to make amends." He looked away to a plane slowly filling with people; *desperate to get away*, I thought. When he looked back, his eyes were filled with tears. "The Vietnamese have a legend, of vampirical beasts that feed on life itself. Their name translates, very roughly, as *The Teeth of the Stars*, but the myths only hint at their true nature. Not vampires as you or I would understand them. These things are bound into the very fabric of this reality . . . silent shadows moving behind a painted scenery."

"They took Justin . . ." I gulped in air to stop myself shaking.

"They can remove a life from existence itself, so that not only does it not exist, it never existed, and never will exist."

"Then how can I remember them?"

"Your injuries . . ." He shrugged; we both knew it didn't matter. "And you?"

He dipped into his jacket and removed the charm I'd found hanging from the doorway of the stone cell. "It keeps me safe, and lets me see the truth. These hung from all the chambers. The Viet

Cong removed them when they found that place and freed what had been imprisoned within."

I recall the reports of how Operation Cedar Falls had failed so badly, because once the US troops went into the Iron Triangle for the climactic battle they found no enemy. It was as if they had melted away, retreated long before the assault began. But I could see now that wasn't true.

"When intelligence reported that something unbelievable and dangerous had been discovered by the Communists in the heart of the Iron Triangle it was decided to seize this potential weapon for the benefit of the West."

"A weapon?" I said, dumbfounded. "Something with the kind of power that you're talking about?"

"We are all for turning, given the right impetus," he continued in a flat voice. "I am not a stupid man. Yet I am affected by the weaknesses that shape us all. Petty fears make idiots of even the wisest. I wanted to see order imposed on the world. With youth in open rebellion in our homelands, with the forces of chaos sweeping across East Asia, I was prepared to go to great lengths to hold back the tide." He removed his glasses to wipe his eyes. "But I never realised there were others prepared to go to even greater lengths."

Another glance at the plane on the runway, nearly full now. I wanted to hit him for his heartlessness and insensitivity.

"Yes, I helped them contain the power. I thought I was doing the right thing, you see? But the use of it, that was down to them. In the end, they only needed so much of me." He took a deep juddering breath. "Did you know Kissinger planned to use nuclear weapons here? Can you imagine the loss of civilian life? Those things did not matter to the people I worked for. It was all about order, at any cost. Hard men." He shook his head as if he still couldn't quite comprehend. "I heard what happened at Kent State University in America. What was happening all over in the name of order. Hard, hard men. They didn't know how to direct the power. They had to learn to control it. They needed a test before time ran out here in Vietnam . . ."

Realisation dawned on me. We were the test.

"Once I learned what they planned, I attempted to stop it. Naturally, I became an unacceptable burden. I was forced to stay one step ahead."

"You changed sides?"

"You are talking about politics. I am speaking about moral absolutes. I did not go over to the *enemy*. I experienced one of those moments when the white light shines into the deep, shadowed parts of oneself. I did not like what I saw. Sometimes there are worse things than an absence of order, as there are worse things than death."

I eased a little. Perhaps there was hope after all. "So you're going to kill it? Drive a stake through its heart or something."

"It cannot be killed. It is part of the universe, beyond you or I or the things we see around us. It can be guided. A little. But not controlled how my former partners wanted to control it."

The plane was now taxiing up the runway. I could see he hadn't been anxious to get on board. He'd only come here to watch.

Van Diemen held up the mysterious charm once more. "The key," he said with smile. "They used to have it . . . and now they do not. Soon those who wanted to do terrible things in the names of their politics will be gone. Indeed, they will never have existed. And the world will be a better place. Yes, Vietnam will be lost. But in the end, is that such a bad thing?"

He was right – there are worse things than failing to impose order. When you confront all the horrors thrown up by reality, all the great spiritual questions, the terrors of the never-ending night, politics seems faintly ridiculous. Who cares about this territory or that? Who cares about money and taxes? Moral absolutes, he said. Rules of existence that should never be transgressed.

"What about me?" I could see the answer in his eyes, had known from the moment I'd spoken to him.

"I am sorry," he said. "Truly. There is no turning back what is set in motion. But know this: I will remember you. I will never forget."

He holds out his arms and I collapse into them, crying silently for what is about to happen, for what I have lost. My tears are insubstantial, moisture-ghosts that will soon fade and be gone. Like the past. Like the present.

Like the future.

JOEL LANE

Mine

JOEL LANE IS THE AUTHOR of two collections of supernatural horror stories, *The Earth Wire* (Egerton Press) and *The Lost District and Other Stories* (Night Shade Books), as well as two novels, *From Blue to Black* and *The Blue Mask* (both Serpent's Tail), and two collections of poems, *The Edge of the Screen* and *Trouble in the Heartland* (both Arc). He is currently working on a third novel, *Midnight Blue*.

"'Mine' was one of a batch of stories that I wrote for *The Lost District*," the author explains. "They all had to do with the myths surrounding death and the afterlife. One of Rainer Maria Rilke's poems influenced this story, which I'd been trying to write for years.

"I've been reassured by the amount of offence it has caused."

NIGHT WAS FALLING as he found the place. He'd have liked to wait until dark, but there wasn't time. He had a gig that evening. It was a ritual: the first night of every tour. Once that had meant small towns in the Black Country; now it meant cities scattered across Europe. But always, for him, it started with this visit. His songs needed it. His voice needed it. He supposed most punters told themselves something similar. And it was always the same time of year: late autumn, as the trees burnt themselves out like cigarettes and dropped traces of frost on the pavement.

It was the same in every town, in every inner-city district. A shuttered window with a sign above it, lit up so as to be visible from the road at night. Always on a main road, close to other shops: being discreet was less important than ease of parking and access. The front door open, leading to a short entry passage; then a hermetically sealed inner door with a bell. As Mark got out of the car, the fading daylight made the buildings seem older: a modern street became grey and close-built, like the terraces he'd grown up in. He shivered and pulled at the collar of his black jacket.

The door was opened by a thin, pale-faced woman in a mauve gown. "Come in, darling," she whispered. The sodium light caught her cheekbones for a moment before she turned away. Her hair was tied in a long pony-tail. Her feet made no sound on the vinyl floor of the hallway.

The reception lounge had two sofas, a table with a cash desk, and a blue mercury strip light that was just beginning to flicker. Another three men were waiting, their faces blank with a studied anonymity. "Have you been here before?" the receptionist said. Something in her voice and her blue-lit face made him realise that she was a man. He wondered if he'd come to the wrong kind of place.

"Yes." It was always easier to say that. He leaned forward. "Is Carole here tonight?"

The receptionist's sleeves rustled as he flicked through a leather-bound diary. "Yes, darling, she is. And she's free just now. That'll be ten pounds for the room." He tucked the note into the cash-box with a movement like striking a match. "I'll take you to her."

Beyond the fringed curtain of the reception room, stairs led down into a basement corridor with several doors. The thin man walked a pace ahead of him, his slipper-clad feet and long gown making him almost seem to float. It was evidently a bigger place than the frontage suggested. They walked on to the end of the corridor, and down another set of stairs. He could smell incense and smoke in the air. It was colder down here, and the wall-set lights were the dead white of a smile in a magazine. These places were rarely strong on ambience. A draught made the receptionist's sleeves tremble as he stopped at the last door.

The room inside was clearly not a bedroom. It had bare stone walls, and a ceiling that glistened with moisture. Mark couldn't see where the light was coming from. His own breath was a pale smoke in the air. He could hear a distant echo of a woman's voice crying out, only the rhythm allowing any distinction between pleasure and pain. So faint, it could have been an overdub from his own memory.

The receptionist gestured to an alcove on the left-hand side. Carole was sitting on a narrow white bed, wearing a silvery dress. She was brushing her long dark hair. The light of a smoky oil lamp picked out the individual strands like the strings inside a piano. The thin man went up to her and bent to whisper something in her ear. She smiled at Mark, then held out her left hand. "That'll be sixty pounds, please."

He fumbled with his wallet as the receptionist made himself scarce. As he placed the three twenties in her perfectly white palm, he noticed that the gash in her wrist was still open. Ice crystals were forming in it. He cupped his hands to his mouth and breathed into them. Carole stood up and pulled off her dress. He stared at her like a peeping Tom as she unfastened her bra and slipped off her black knickers. She smiled. "Are you going to undress as well?" His hands shook as he unbuttoned his shirt, unable to look away from her.

They lay on the bed and caressed each other. Mark remembered the first nights they'd spent together, in her basement flat on the edge of the park. She still looked about nineteen; only her eyes were older. The skin of her face was pale and neutral, like scar tissue. His mouth crept across her body, kissing the bony ridges of her shoulders, then moving down to touch her injuries. The cuts she'd made on herself, where the ice had formed like salt. The bruises he'd given her long ago, still blooming like ink blots on the white skin. His tongue made her shiver. She turned in his arms to face the wall, and he spread her legs gently. The voices in the wall cried out to him, trapped echoes of need and release. The rhythm track. His fingers probed her, stirred warmth in her passive flesh.

It was time for the bridge. Carole turned again, reached down by the lamp, tore open a foil packet. Her thin fingers sheathed him, then guided him into her. Just as it had always been. There'd be no need to change positions. He kissed her lightly on the mouth, then pressed his lips to the side of her neck. His fingers gripped her ribs, pressing hard where the bruises were. She cried out with pain. "Sorry," he whispered. There were tears in her eyes. He reached up and stroked her forehead, running his fingers through the soft dark hair. It felt dry, almost brittle. He bent over her and placed a slow kiss in the hollow of her throat. She moved against him and dug her nails into his back. The final chorus.

Submission wasn't enough for him: he needed her response. It always took time to get her warmed up. Her soft cries rang in his head, where all the lights were going out. His back arched, and he stared at the side of her face. She looked peaceful. She could almost have been asleep. He'd found her like this.

Still out of breath, Mark pulled on his clothes. The sweat glued him to his shirt; but it didn't matter, he'd be changing soon enough. Carole sat on the edge of the bed, putting on her underclothes, then stood up to pull on her dress. The flickering oil lamp made the silver fabric look grainy, like ash. He reached out to take her hand. "Come with me."

She stepped towards him, hesitantly. He looked into her eyes. "Will you follow me?" She nodded. He felt a quiet pang of joy, a tenderness mingled with the November ache of loss. Fire in the dead leaves. He gripped her hand, feeling the bones under the smooth skin. Then he let go and slowly walked towards the doorway. He thought he could hear footsteps behind him.

As he climbed the dark stairs, fatigue began to tug at him. It would be easier to stay down here, sleep for a while. Never mind the gig. But he kept walking. In the hallway, the cries of pleasure from behind the closed doors were a coda to accompany the two of them into the starlit night. He shivered. The moisture in his eyes blurred his vision. He stumbled up the second staircase to the lounge. There was no one there but the receptionist, who looked at Mark, then looked at the doorway behind him. He seemed about to say something, but instead just waved them on.

Mark took a deep breath and turned the handle on the inner door, then stepped through. The night was a blue-black curtain at the end of the passageway. He walked on until he could feel the cold air on his face, then turned around. His parting gesture was almost a wave. It could even have been a touch, if she'd been close enough to feel it. But she was already backing off, her face a mask the funeral parlour had been unable to make lifelike. The inner door closed behind her, and Mark was alone on the narrow street.

He waited to cross to where his car was parked. A line of vehicles was crawling past in both directions. Somewhere in the distance, a siren was caught up in the rush hour traffic. The air was stale with exhaust fumes. Mindful of the time, he began to walk between the slowly moving cars. It would be disastrous to be late on the first night of his tour. If you wanted to build a life in music, you had to observe these superstitions. They were part of what it meant to belong.

DAVID J. SCHOW

Obsequy

DAVID J. SCHOW IS A short story writer, novelist, screenwriter (teleplays and features), columnist, essayist, editor, photographer and winner of the World Fantasy and International Horror Guild awards (for short fiction and non-fiction, respectively).

His association with New Line Cinema began with horror icons Freddy Kreuger (*A Nightmare on Elm Street: Freddy's Nightmares*), Leatherface (*Leatherface: Texas Chainsaw Massacre III*) and the eponymous Critters (*Critters 3* and *Critters 4*). In 1994 he wrote the screenplay for *The Crow* and has since worked with such directors as Alex Proyas, James Cameron, E. Elias Merhige, Rupert Wainwright, Mick Garris and William Malone.

For the premiere season of Showtime Network's *Masters of Horror* he adapted his own short story "Pick Me Up" for director Larry Cohen, and for the second season he scripted "We All Scream for Ice Cream" (based on a John Farris story) for director Tom Holland.

Schow also wrote forty-one instalments of his popular "Raving & Drooling" column for *Fangoria* magazine, later collected in the book *Wild Hairs*. His many other books include his fourth novel, *Bullets of Rain*, and seventh story collection, *Havoc Swims Jaded*.

He is currently on the verge of his next book, script, or chaotic house renovation.

" 'Obsequy' was originally written to demonstrate the difference between a 'half-hour's worth of story' versus an hour for the benefit of several TV executives," reveals the author.

"Now, I know what you're thinking: *That would be like trying to train a dog to eat with a fork*. And you would be right. The good part is the story came to life on its own and didn't need TV for anything.

One indirect result was that I was asked to rewrite the 2004 French film *Les Revenants* (released in the US as *They Came Back*) for an American production company.

"As American re-takes of foreign horror movies are mandated to provide *lots of explanations* for everything going on, I had to invent these. The reaction I got on my somewhat anti-linear take was . . . horrifying.

"Horror fiction seems to spawn more dumbass 'rules' than any other kind of writing, and one of the dumbest is the assumed 'require-ment' of a twist ending, going all the way back to H. H. Munro. This story is also the result of a long rumination on how stories are sometimes scuttled or diminished by succumbing to such 'rules'.

"Another landmine is use of the zombie archetype, which has become polluted with extra-stupid assumptions derived from an end-less mudslide of movies featuring resurrected corpses who want to eat your brain. That's fine, but it's not what I wanted to explore here."

D OUG WALCOTT'S NEED for a change of perspective seemed simple: *Haul ass out of Triple Pines, pronto. Start the next chapter of my life. Before somebody else makes the decision for you, in spades.*

He grimly considered the shovel in his grasp, clotted with mulchy grave dirt. Spades, right. It was the moment Doug knew he could not go on digging up dead people, and it was only his first day on the job. Once he had been a teacher, with a teacher's penchant for seeing structure and symbols in everything. *Fuck all that,* he thought. *Time to get out. Time to bail, now.*

"I've got to go," he said, almost mumbling, his conviction still tentative.

Jacky Tynan had stepped down from his scoop-loader and ambled over, doffing his helmet and giving his brow a mop. Jacky was a simple, basically honest guy; a spear carrier in the lives of others with more personal color. Content with burgers and beer, satellite TV and dreams of a someday-girlfriend, Jacky was happy in Triple Pines.

"Yo, it's Douglas, right?" Jacky said. Everybody had been intro-duced shortly after sunrise. "What up?" He peeled his work gloves and rubbed his hands compulsively until tiny black sweatballs of grime dropped away like scattered grains of pepper.

"I've got to go," Doug repeated. "I think I just quit. I've got to tell Coggins I'm done. I've got to get out of here."

"Graves and stuff getting to ya, huh?" said Jacky. "You should give it another day, at least. It ain't so bad."

Doug did not meet Jacky's gaze. His evaluation of the younger man harshened, more in reaction against the locals, the natives, the people who fit into a white trash haven such as Triple Pines. They would hear the word "cemetery" and conclude "huge downer". They would wax prosaic about this job being perverse, therefore unhealthy. To them, digging up long-deceased residents would be that sick stuff. They all acted and reacted strictly according to the playbook of cliché. Their retinue of perception was so predictable that it was almost comically dull. Jacky's tone suggested that he was one of those people with an almost canine empathy to discord; he could smell when something had gone south.

Doug fought to frame some sort of answer. It was not the funereal atmosphere. The stone monuments, the graves, the loam were all exceptionally peaceful. Doug felt no connection to the dearly departed here . . . with one exception, and one was sufficient.

"It's not the work," Doug said. "It's me. I'm overdue to leave this place. The town, not the cemetery. And the money doesn't matter to me any more."

Jacky made a face as though he had whiffed a fart. "You don't want the money, man? Hell, this shit is easier than workin' the paper mill or doin' stamper time at the plant, dude." The Triple Pines aluminum plant had vanished into Chapter Eleven a decade ago, yet locals still talked about it as if it were still a functioning concern.

The people in Triple Pines never saw what was right in front of them. Or they refused to acknowledge anything strange. That was the reason Doug had to eject. He had to jump before he became one of them.

One of them . . .

A week ago, Doug had not been nearly so philosophical. Less than a week from now, and he would question his own sanity.

Craignotti, the job foreman, had seen Jacky and Doug not working – that is to say, not excavating – and already he was humping his trucker bulk over the hilltop to yell at them. Doug felt the urge to just pitch his tools and helmet and run, but his rational side admitted that there were protocols to be followed and channels to be taken. He would finish out his single day, then do some drinking with his workmates, then try to decide whether he could handle one more day. He was supposed to be a responsible adult, and responsible adults adhered to protocol and channels as a way of reinforcing the gentle myth of civilisation.

Whoa, dude, piss on all that, Jacky might say. *Just run.* But Jacky rarely wrestled with such complexities. Doug turned to meet Craignotti with the fatalism of a man who has to process a large pile of tax paperwork.

A week ago, things had been different. Less than a week from now, these exhumations would collide with every one of them, in ways they could not possibly predict.

Frank Craignotti was one of those guys who loved their beer, Doug had observed. The man had a *relationship* with his pilsner glass, and rituals to limn his interaction with it. Since Doug had started haunting Callahan's, he had seen Craignotti in there every night – same stool at the end of the bar, same three pitchers of tap beer, which he emptied down his neck in about an hour and a half. Word was that Craignotti had been a long-haul big-rig driver for a major nationwide chain of discount stores, until the company pushed him to the sidelines on account of his disability. He had stepped down from the cab of his sixteen-wheeler on a winding mountain road outside of Triple Pines (for reasons never explained; probably to relieve himself among Nature's bounty) and had been sideswiped by a car that never saw him standing there in the rain. Presently he walked with a metal cane because after his surgery one leg had come up shorter than the other. There were vague noises of lawsuits and settlements. That had all happened before Doug wound up inside Callahan's as a regular, and so it maintained the tenuous validity of small-town gossip. It was as good a story as any.

Callahan's presented a nondescript face to the main street of Triple Pines, its stature noted solely by a blue neon sign that said BAR filling up most of a window whose sill probably had not been dusted since 1972. There was a roadhouse fifteen miles to the north, technically "out of town", but its weak diversions were not worth the effort. Callahan's flavor was mostly clover-colored Irish horse apples designed to appeal to all the usual expectations. Sutter, the current owner and the barman on most weeknights, had bought the place when the original founders had wised up and gotten the hell out of Triple Pines. Sutter was easy to make up a story about. To Doug he looked like a career criminal on the run who had found his perfect hide in Triple Pines. The scar bisecting his lower lip had probably come from a knife fight. His skin was like mushrooms in the fridge the day before you decide to throw them out. His eyes were set back in his skull, socketed deep in bruise-colored shadow.

Nobody in Triple Pines really knew anything bona fide about anybody else, Doug reflected.

Doug's first time into the bar as a drinker was his first willful act after quitting his teaching job at the junior high school which Triple Pines shared with three other communities. All pupils were bussed in from rural route pickups. A year previously, he had effortlessly scored an emergency credential and touched down as a replacement instructor for History and Geography, though he took no interest in politics unless they were safely in the past. It was a rote gig that mostly required him to ramrod disinterested kids through memorising data that they forgot as soon as they puked it up on the next test. He had witnessed firsthand how the area, the towns, and the school system worked to crush initiative, abort insight, and nip talent. The model for the Triple Pines secondary educational system seemed to come from some early 1940s playbook, with no imperative to change anything. The kids here were all white and mostly poor to poverty level, disinterested and leavened to dullness. Helmets for the football team always superceded funds for updated texts. It was the usual, spirit-deflating story. Doug spent the term trying to kick against this corpse, hoping to provoke life signs. Past the semester break, he was just hanging on for the wage. Then, right as summer vacation loomed, Sheila Morgan had deposited herself in the teacher's lounge for a conference.

Doug had looked up from his newspaper. The local rag was called the *Pine Grove Messenger* (after the adjacent community). It came out three times weekly and was exactly four pages long. Today was Victoria Day in Canada. This week's Vocabulary Building Block was "ameliorate."

"Sheila," he said, acknowledging her, not really wanting to. She was one of the many hold-backs in his classes. Hell, many of Triple Pines' junior high schoolers already drove their own cars to battle against the citadel of learning.

"Don't call me that," Sheila said. "My name's *Brittany*."

Doug regarded her over the top of the paper. They were alone in the room. "Really."

"Totally," she said. "I can have my name legally changed. I looked it up: I'm gonna do it, too. I don't care what anybody says."

Pause, for bitter fulfillment: One of his charges had actually *looked something up*.

Further pause, for dismay: Sheila had presented herself to him wearing a shiny vinyl mini as tight as a surgeon's glove, big-heeled boots that laced to the knee, and a leopard top with some kind of boa-like fringe framing her breasts. There was a scatter of pimples between her collarbones. She had ratty black hair and too much eye kohl. Big lipstick that had tinted her teeth pink. She resembled a hillbilly's concept of a New York streetwalker, and she was all of 14 years old.

Mara Corday, Doug thought. *She looks like a goth-slut version of Mara Corday. I am a dead man.*

Chorus girl and pinup turned B-movie femme fatale, Mara Corday had decorated some drive-in low-budgeters of the late 1950s. *Tarantula. The Giant Claw. The Black Scorpion.* She had been a *Playboy* Playmate and familiar of Clint Eastwood. Sultry and sex-kittenish, she had signed her first studio contract while still a teenager. She, too, had changed her name.

Sheila wanted to be looked at, and Doug avoided looking. At least her presentation was a relief from the third-hand, Sears & Roebuck interpretation of banger and skatepunk styles that prevailed among most of Triple Pines' other adolescents. In that tilted moment, Doug realised what he disliked about the dunnage of rap and hip-hop: all those super-badasses looked like they were dressed in gigantic baby clothes. Sheila's ass was broader than the last time he had not-looked. Her thighs were chubbing. The trade-off was bigger tits. Doug's heartbeat began to accelerate. *Why am I looking?*

"Sheila—"

"Brittany." She threw him a pout, then softened it, to butter him up. "Lissen, I wanted to talk to you about that test, the one I missed? I wanna take it over. Like, not to cheat it or anything, but just to kinda . . . take it over, y'know? Pretend like that's the *first* time I took it?"

"None of the other students get that luxury, and you know that."

She fretted, shifting around in her seat, her skirt making squeaky noises against the school-issue plastic chair. "I know, I know, like, right? That's like, totally not usual, I know, so that's why I thought I'd ask you about it first?"

Sheila spent most of her schooling fighting to maintain a low C-average. She had won a few skirmishes, but the war was already a loss.

"I mean, like, you could totally do a new test, and I could like study for it, right?"

"You should have studied for the original test in the first place."

She wrung her hands. "I know, I know that, but . . . well let's just say it's a lot of bullshit, parents and home and alla that crap, right? I couldn't like do it then but I could now. My Mom finds out I blew off the test, she'll beat the shit outta me."

"Shouldn't you be talking to a counselor?"

"Yeah, right? No thanks. I thought I'd like go right to the source, right? I mean, you like me and stuff, right?" She glanced toward the door, revving up for some kind of Big Moment that Doug already dreaded. "I mean, I'm flexible; I thought that, y'know, just this one time. I'd do anything. Really. To fix it. Anything."

She uncrossed her legs, from left on right to right on left, taking enough time to make sure Doug could see she had neglected to factor undergarments into her abbreviated ensemble. The move was so studied that Doug knew exactly which movie she had gotten it from.

There are isolated moments in time that expand to gift you with a glimpse of the future, and in that moment Doug saw his tenure at Triple Pines take a big centrifugal swirl down the cosmic toilet. The end of life as he knew it was embodied in the bit of anatomy that Sheila referred to as her "cunny".

"You can touch it if you want. I won't mind." She sounded as though she was talking about a bizarre pet on a leash.

Doug had hastily excused himself and raced to the bathroom, his four-page newspaper folded up to conceal the fact that he was strolling the hallowed halls of the school, semi-erect. He rinsed his face in a basin and regarded himself in a scabrous mirror. *Time to get out. Time to bail. Now.*

He flunked Sheila, and jettisoned himself during summer break, never quite making it to the part where he actually *left* Triple Pines. Later he heard Sheila's mom had gone ballistic and put her daughter in the emergency ward at the company clinic for the paper mill, where her father had worked since he was her age. Local residual scuttlebutt had it that Sheila had gotten out of the hospital and mated with the first guy she could find who owned a car. They blew town like fugitives and were arrested several days later. Ultimately, she used her pregnancy to force the guy to sell his car to pay for her train fare to some relative's house in the Dakotas, end of story.

Which, naturally, was mostly hearsay anyway. Bar talk. Doug had become a regular at Callahan's sometime in early July of that year, and by mid-August he looked at himself in another mirror and thought, *you bagged your job and now you have a drinking problem, buddy. You need to get out of this place.*

That was when Craignotti had eyeballed him. Slow consideration at reptile brain-speed. He bombed his glass at a gulp and rose; he was a man who always squared his shoulders when he stood up, to advise the talent of the room just how broad his chest was. He stumped over to Doug without his walking stick, to prove he didn't really need it. He signaled Sutter, the cadaverous bartender, to deliver his next pitcher of brew to the stool next to Doug's.

After some preliminary byplay and chitchat, Craignotti beered himself to within spitting distance of having a point. "So, you was a teacher at the junior high?"

"Ex-teacher. Nothing bad. I just decided I had to relocate."

"Ain't what I heard." Every time Craignotti drank, his swallows were half-glass capacity. One glassful, two swallows, rinse and repeat. "I heard you porked one of your students. That little slut Sheila Morgan."

"Not true."

Craignotti poured Doug a glass of beer to balance out the Black Jack he was consuming, one slow finger at a time. "Naah, it ain't what you think. I ain't like that. Those little fucking whores are outta control anyway. They're fucking in goddamned grade school, if they're not all crackheads by then."

"The benefits of our educational system." Doug toasted the air. If you drank enough, you could see lost dreams and hopes, swirling there before your nose, demanding sacrifice and tribute.

"Anyhow, point is that you're not working, am I right?"

"That is a true fact." Doug tasted the beer. It chased smooth.

"You know Coggins, the undertaker here?"

"Yeah." Doug had to summon the image. Bald guy, ran the Triple Pines funeral home and maintained the Hollymount Cemetery on the outskirts of town. Walked around with his hands in front of him like a preying mantis.

"Well, I know something a lotta people around here don't know yet. Have you heard of the Marlboro Reservoir?" It was the local project that would not die. It had last been mentioned in the *Pine Grove Messenger* over a year previously.

"I didn't think that plan ever cleared channels."

"Yeah, well, it ain't for you or me to know. But they're gonna build it. And there's gonna be a lotta work. Maybe bring this shithole town back to life."

"But I'm leaving this shithole town," said Doug. "Soon. So you're telling me this because—?"

"Because you look like a guy can keep his trap shut. Here's the deal: this guy Coggins comes over and asks me to be a foreman. For what, I say. And he says – now get this – in order to build the reservoir, for some reason I don't know about, they're gonna have to move the cemetery to the other side of Pine Grove – six fucking *miles*. So he needs guys to dig up all the folks buried in the cemetery, and catalogue 'em, and bury 'em again on the other side of the valley. Starts next Monday. The pay is pretty damned good for the work, and almost nobody needs to know about it. I ain't about to hire these fucking deadbeats around here, these dicks with the muscle cars, 'cept for Jacky Tynan, 'cos he's a good worker and don't ask questions. So I thought, I gotta find me a few more guys that are, like, responsible, and since you're leaving anyhow . . ."

Long story short, that's how Doug wound up manning a shovel. The money was decent and frankly, he needed the bank. "Answer me one question, though," he said to Craignotti. "Where did you get all that shit about Sheila Morgan, I mean, why did you use that to approach me?"

"Oh, that," said Craignotti. "She told me. Was trying to trade some tight little puddy for a ride outta town." Craignotti had actually said *puddy,* like Sylvester the Cat. *I tot I taw* . . . "I laughed in her face; I said, what, d'you think I'm some kinda baby-raper? I woulda split her in half. She threw a fit and went off and fucked a bunch of guys who were less discriminating. Typical small-time town-pump *scheiss.* She musta lost her cherry when she was twelve. So I figured you and me had something in common – we're probably the only two men in town who haven't plumbed *that* hole. Shit, we're so fucking honest, folks around here will think we're queer."

Honor and ethics, thought Doug. Wonderful concepts, those were.

There were more than a thousand graves in Hollymount Cemetery, dating back to the turn of the 19th century. Stones so old that names had weathered to vague indentations in granite. Plots with no markers. Minor vandalism. The erosion of time and climate. Coggins, the undertaker, had collated a master name sheet and stapled it to a gridded map of the cemetery, presenting the crew picked by Craignotti with a problem rather akin to solving a huge crossword puzzle made out of dead people. Doug paged through the list until he found Michelle Farrier's name. He had attended her funeral, and sure enough – she was still here.

After his divorce from Marianne (the inevitable ex-wife), he had taken to the road, but had read enough Kerouac to know that the road held nothing for him. A stint as a blackjack dealer in Vegas. A teaching credential from LA; he was able to put that in his pocket and take it anywhere. Four months after his arrival in Triple Pines, he attended the funeral of the only friend he had sought to develop locally – Michelle Farrier, a runner just like him.

In the afterblast of an abusive and ill-advised marriage, Michelle had come equipped with a six-year-old daughter named Rochelle. Doug could easily see the face of the mother in the child, the younger face that had taken risks and sought adventure and brightened at the prospect of sleeping with rogues. Michelle had touched down in Triple Pines two months away from learning she was terminally ill. Doug had met them during a seriocomic bout of bathroom-sharing at Mrs Ives' rooming house, shortly before he had rented a two-bedroom that had come cheap because there were few people in town actively seeking better lodgings, and fewer who could afford to move up. Michelle remained game, as leery as Doug of getting involved, and their gradually kindling passion filled their evenings with a delicious promise. In her kiss lurked a hungry romantic on a short tether, and Doug was working up the nerve to invite her and Rochelle to share his new home when the first talk of doctor visits flattened all other concerns to secondary status. He watched her die. He tried his best to explain it to Rochelle. And Rochelle was removed, to grandparents somewhere in the Bay area. She wept when she said goodbye to Doug. So had Michelle.

Any grave but that one, thought Doug. *Don't make me dig that one up. Make that someone else's task.*

He knew enough about mortuary tradition to know it was unusual for an undertaker like Coggins to also be in charge of the cemetery. However, small, remote towns tend not to view such a monopoly on the death industry as a negative thing. Coggins was a single stranger for the populace to trust, instead of several. Closer to civilisation, the particulars of chemical supply, casket sales, and the mortician's craft congregated beneath the same few conglomerate umbrellas, bringing what had been correctly termed a "Tru-Value hardware" approach to what was being called the "death industry" by the early 1990s. Deceased Americans had become a cash crop at several billion dollars per annum . . . not counting the flower arrangements. Triple Pines still believed in the mom-and-pop market, the corner tavern, the one-trade-fits-all handyman.

Doug had been so appalled at Michelle's perfunctory service that he did a bit of investigative reading-up. He discovered that most of the traditional accoutrements of the modern funeral were aimed at one objective above all – keeping morticians and undertakers in business. Not, as most people supposed, because of obscure health imperatives, or a misplaced need for ceremony, or even that old favorite, religious ritual. It turned out to be one of the three or four most expensive costs a normal citizen could incur during the span of an average, conventional life – another reason weddings and funerals seemed bizarrely similar. It was amusing to think how simply the two could be confused. Michelle would have been amused, at least. She had rated one of each, neither very satisfying.

Doug would never forget Rochelle's face, either. He had gotten to play the role of father to her for about a week and change, and it had scarred him indelibly. Given time, her loss, too, was a strangely welcome kind of pain.

Legally, disinterment was a touchy process, since the casket containing the remains was supposed to be technically "undamaged" when removed from the earth. This meant Jacky and the other backhoe operators could only skim to a certain depth – the big scoops – before Doug or one of his co-workers had to jump in with a shovel. Some of the big concrete grave liners were stacked three deep to a plot; at least, Craignotti had said something about three being the limit. They looked like big, featureless refrigerators laid on end, and tended to crumble like plaster. Inside were the burial caskets. Funeral publicists had stopped calling them coffins about forty years ago. "Coffins" were boxes shaped to the human form, wide at the top, slim at the bottom, with the crown shaped like the top half of a hexagon. "Coffins" evoked morbid assumptions, and so were replaced in the vernacular with "caskets" – nice, straight angles, with no Dracula or Boot Hill associations. In much the same fashion, "cemeteries" had become "memorial parks". People did everything they could, it seemed, to deny the reality of death.

Which explained the grave liners. Interment in coffins, caskets, or anything else from a wax-coated cardboard box to a shroud generally left a concavity in the lawn, once the body began to decompose, and its container, to collapse. In the manner of a big, mass-produced, cheap sarcophagus, the concrete grave liners prevented the depressing sight of . . . er, depressions. Doug imagined them to be manufactured by the same place that turned out highway divider berms; the damned things weighed about the same.

Manning his shovel, Doug learned a few more firsthand things about graves. Like how it could take eight hours for a single digger, working alone, to excavate a plot to the proper dimensions. Which was why Craignotti had been forced to locate operators for no fewer than three backhoes on this job. Plus seven "scoopers" in Doug's range of ability. The first shift, they only cleared 50 final resting places. From then on, they would aim for a hundred stiffs per working day.

Working. Stiffs. Rampant, were the opportunities for gallows humor.

Headstones were stacked as names were checked off the master list. BEECHER, LEE, 1974-2002 – HE PROTECTED AND SERVED. GUDGELL, CONROY, 1938-2003 – DO NOT GO GENTLY. These were newer plots, more recent deaths. These were people who cared about things like national holidays or presidential elections, archetypal Americans from fly-over country. But in their midst, Doug was also a cliché – the drifter, the stranger. If the good folk of Triple Pines (the living ones, that is) sensed discord in their numbers, they would actively seek out mutants to scotch. Not One of Us.

He had to get out. Just this job, just a few days, and he could escape. It was better than being a mutant, and perhaps getting lynched. He moved on to STOWE, DORMAND R., 1940-1998 – LOVING HUSBAND, CARING FATHER. Not so recent. Doug felt a little bit better.

They broke after sunset. That was when Doug back-checked the dig list and found a large, red X next to Michelle Farrier's name.

"This job ain't so damned secret," said Joe Hopkins, later, at Callahan's. Their after-work table was five: Joe, Jacky, Doug, and two more guys from the shift, Miguel Ayala and Boyd Cooper. Craignotti sat away from them, at his accustomed roost near the end of the bar. The men were working on their third pitcher. Doug found that no amount of beer could get the taste of grave dirt out of the back of his throat. Tomorrow, he'd wear a bandana. *Maybe.*

"You working tomorrow, or not, or what?" said Craignotti. Doug gave him an if-come answer, and mentioned the bandana. Craignotti had shrugged. In that moment, it all seemed pretty optional, so Doug concentrated on becoming mildly drunk with a few of the crew working the – heh – graveyard shift.

Joe was a musclebound ex-biker type who always wore a leather vest and was rarely seen without a toothpick jutting from one corner of his mouth. He had cultivated elaborate moustaches which he waxed. He was going grey at the temples. His eyes were dark, putting Doug in mind of a gypsy. He continued: "What I mean is, nobody's supposed to know about this little relocation. But the guys in here know, even if they don't talk about it. The guys who run the Triple Pines bank sure as shit know. It's a public secret. Nobody talks about it, is all."

"I bet the mayor's in on it, too," said Miguel. "All in, who cares? I mean, I had to pick mushrooms once for a buck a day. This sure beats the shit out of that."

"Doesn't bother you?" said Boyd Cooper, another of the backhoe jockeys. Older, pattern baldness, big but not heavy. Bull neck and cleft chin. His hands had seen a lifetime of manual labor. It had been Boyd who showed them how to cable the lids off the heavy stone grave liners, instead of bringing in the crane rig used to emplace them originally. This group's unity as mutual outcasts gave them a basic common language, and Boyd always cut to the gristle. "Digging up dead people?"

"Nahh," said Jacky, tipping his beer. "We're doing them a favor. Just a kind of courtesy thing. Moving 'em so they won't be forgotten."

"I guess," said Joe, working his toothpick. He burnished his teeth a lot with it. Doug noticed one end was stained with a speck of blood, from his gums.

"You're the teacher," Boyd said to Doug. "You tell us. Good thing or bad thing?"

Doug did not want to play arbiter. "Just a job of work. Like resorting old files. You notice how virtually no one in Triple Pines got cremated? They were all buried. That's old-fashioned, but you have to respect the dead. Laws and traditions."

"And the point is . . . ?" Boyd was looking for validation.

"Well, not everybody is entitled to a piece of property when they die, six by three by seven. That's too much space. Eventually we're going to run out of room for all our dead people. Most plots in most cemeteries are rented, and there's a cap on the time limit, and if somebody doesn't pay up, they get mulched. End of story."

"Wow, is that true?" said Jacky. "I thought you got buried, it was like, forever."

"Stopped being that way about a hundred years ago," said Doug. "Land is worth too much. You don't process the dead and let them use up your real estate without turning a profit."

Miguel said, "That would be un-American." He tried for a chuckle but it died.

"Check it out if you don't believe me," said Doug. "Look it up. Behind all that patriotic rah-rah-rah about community brotherhood and peaceful gardens, it's all about capital gains. Most people don't like to think about funerals or cemeteries because, to them, it's morbid. That leaves funeral directors free to profiteer."

"You mean Coggins?" said Joe, giving himself a refill.

"Look, Coggins is a great example," said Doug. "In the outside world, big companies have incorporated most aspects of the funeral. Here, Coggins runs the mortuary, the cemetery, everything. He can charge whatever he wants, and people will pay for the privilege of shunting their grief and confusion onto him. You wouldn't believe the markup on some of this stuff. Caskets are three times wholesale. Even if they put you in a cardboard box – which is called an 'alternative container', by the way – the charge is a couple of hundred bucks."

"Okay, that settles it," said Miguel. When he smiled big, you could see his gold tooth. "We all get to live forever, because we can't afford to die."

"There used to be a riddle," said Doug. "What is it: the man who made it didn't want it, the man who bought it had no use for it, and the man who used it didn't know it. What is it?"

Jacky just looked confused.

His head honeycombed with domestic beer, Doug tried not to lurch or slosh as he navigated his way out of Callahan's. The voice coming at him out of the fogbound darkness might well have been an aural hallucination. Or a wish fulfillment.

"Hey stranger," it said. "Walk a lady home?"

The night yielded her to him. She came not as he had fantasised, nor as he had seen her in dreams. She wore a long-sleeved, black, lacy thing with a neck-wrap collar, and her hair was up. She looked different but her definitive jawline and frank, grey gaze were unmistakable.

"That's not you," he said. "I'm a tiny bit intoxicated, but not enough to believe it's you." *Yet.* There was no one else on the street to confirm or deny; no validation from fellow inebriates or corroboration from independent bystanders. Just Doug, the swirling night, and a woman who could not be the late Michelle Farrier, whom he had loved. He had only accepted that he loved her after she died. It was more tragic that way, more delusionally romanticist. Potent enough to wallow in. A weeper, produced by his brain while it was buzzing with hops and alcohol.

She bore down on him, moving into focus, and that made his grief worse. "Sure it's me," she said. "Look at me. Take a little bit of time to get used to the idea."

He drank her in as though craving a narcotic. Her hair had always been long, burnished sienna, deftly razor-thinned to layers that framed her face. Now it was pinned back to exhibit her gracile neck and bold features. He remembered the contour of her ears. She smiled, and he remembered exactly how her teeth set. She brought with her the scent of night-blooming jasmine. If she was a revenant, she had come freighted with none of the corruption of the tomb. If she was a mirage, the light touch of her hand on his wrist should not have felt so corporeal.

Her touch was not cold.

"No," said Doug. "You died. You're gone."

"Sure, darling – I don't deny that. But now I'm back, and you should be glad."

He was still shaking his head. "I *saw* you die. I helped *bury* you."

"And today, you helped *un*-bury me. Well, your buddies did."

She had both hands on him, now. This was the monster movie moment when her human visage melted away to reveal the slavering ghoul who wanted to eat his brain and wash it down with a glass of his blood. Her sheer *presence* almost buckled his knees.

"How?"

"Beats me," she said. "We're coming back all over town. I don't know exactly how it all works, yet. But that stuff I was buried in – those *cerements* – were sort of depressing. I checked myself out while I was cleaning up. Everything seems to be in place. Everything works. Except for the tumor; that kind of withered away to an inert little knot, in the grave. I know this is tough for you to swallow, but I'm here, and goddammit, I missed you, and I thought you'd want to see me."

"I think about you every day," he said. It was still difficult to meet her gaze, or to speed-shift from using the accustomed past tense.

"Come on," she said, linking arms with him.

"Where?" Without delay his guts leaped at the thought that she wanted to take him back to the cemetery.

"Wherever. Listen, do you recall kissing me? See if you can remember how we did that."

She kissed him with all the passion of the long-lost, regained unexpectedly. It was Michelle, all right – alive, breathing, returned to him whole.

No one had seen them. No one had come out of the bar. No pedestrians. Triple Pines tended to roll up the sidewalks at 7:00 p.m.

"This is . . . nuts," he said.

She chuckled. "As long as you don't say it's distasteful." She kissed him again. "And of course you remember that other thing we never got around to doing?"

"Antiquing that rolltop desk you liked, at the garage sale?" His humor was helping him balance. His mind still wanted to swoon, or explode.

"Ho, ho, very funny. I am so glad to see you right now that I'll spell it out for you, Doug." She drew a tiny breath of consideration, working up nerve, then puffed it out. "Okay: I want to hold your cock in my hand and feel you get hard, *for me*. That was the dream, right? That first attraction, where you always visualise the other person naked, fucking you, while your outer self pretends like none of that matters?"

"I didn't think that," Doug fibbed. Suddenly his breath would not draw.

"Yes you did," Michelle said. "I did, too. But I was too chicken to act. That's all in the past." She stopped and smacked him lightly on the arm. "Don't give me that lopsided look, like *I'm* the one that's crazy. Not now. Not after I died, thinking you were the best damned thing I'd found in a long time."

"Well, there was Rochelle," said Doug, remembering how cautiously they had behaved around her six-year-old daughter.

"My little darling is not here right now," she said. "I'd say it's time to fulfill the fantasy, Doug. Mine, if not yours. We've wasted enough life, and not everybody gets a bonus round."

"But—" Doug's words, his protests had bottlenecked between his lungs. (And for-crap-sake *why* did he feel the urge to *protest* this?)

"I know what you're trying to say. I *died*." Another impatient huff of breath – living breath. "I can't explain it. I don't know if it's temporary. But I'll tell you one thing I do know: All that shit about the 'peace' of the grave? It doesn't exist. It's not a release, and it's not oblivion. It's like a nightmare that doesn't conveniently end when you wake up, because you're not *supposed* to wake up, ever! And you know what else? When you're in the grave, you can hear every goddamned footfall of the living, above you. Trust me on that one."

"Jesus . . ." he said.

"Not Jesus. Neither Heaven nor Hell. Not God. Not Buddha, not Allah, not Yahweh. Nothing. That's what waits on the other side of that headstone. No pie in the sky by and by when you die. No Nirvana. No Valhalla. No Tetragrammaton. No Zeus or Jove or any of their buddies. Nothing. Maybe that's why we're coming back – there's nothing out there, beyond. Zero. Not even an echo. So kiss me again. I've been cold and I've been still, and I need to make love to you. Making love; that sounds like we're manufacturing something, doesn't it? Feel my hand. There's living blood in there. Feel my heart; it's pumping again. I've felt bad things moving around inside of me. That happens when you're well and truly dead. Now I'm back. And I want to feel *other* things moving around inside of me. You."

Tomorrow, Doug would get fired as a no-show after only one day on the job. Craignotti would replace him with some guy named Dormand R. Stowe, rumored to be a loving husband and a caring father.

One of the most famous foreign pistols used during the Civil War was the Le Mat Revolver, a cap and ball weapon developed by a French-born New Orleans doctor, unique in that it had two barrels – a cylinder which held nine .40 caliber rounds fired through the upper barrel, and revolved around the lower, .63 caliber barrel, which held a charge of 18 or 20-gauge buckshot. With a flick of the thumb, the shooter could realign the hammer to fall on the lower barrel, which was essentially a small shotgun, extremely deadly at close range, with a kick like an enraged mule. General J. E. B. Stuart had carried one. So had General P. G. T. Beauregard. As an antique firearm, such guns in good condition were highly prized. Conroy Gudgell cherished his; it was one of the stars of his modest home arsenal, which he always referred to as his "collection". His big mistake was showing his wife how to care for it. How to clean it. How to load it. How to fire it, you know, "just in case". No one was more surprised than Conroy when his loving wife, a respected first-grade teacher in Triple Pines, blew him straight down to Hell with his own collectible antique.

Ellen Gudgell became a widow at sixty-one years of age. She also became a Wiccan. She was naked, or "sky-clad", when she burned the braided horsehair whip in her fireplace after murdering Conroy. Firing the Le Mat had broken her right wrist; she'd had to make up a story about that. With her left hand she had poured herself a nice brandy, before working herself up into enough lather to phone the police, in tears, while most of Conroy's head and brains were cooling in various corners of his basement workshop. A terrible accident, oh my lord, it's horrible, please come. She kept all the stuff about Earth Mother religious revelations to herself.

She treated Constable Dickey (Triple Pines' head honcho of law enforcement) as she would one of her elementary school charges. Firm but fair. Matronly, but with just the right salting of manufactured hysteria. Conroy had been working with his gun collection in the basement when she heard a loud boom, she told the officer. She panicked and broke her wrist trying to move what was left of him, and now she did not know what to do, and she needed help.

And the local cops had quite neatly taken care of all the rest. Ellen never had to mention the beatings she had suffered under the now-incinerated whip, or that the last fifteen years of their sex life had consisted mostly of rape. When not teaching school, she used her free time – that is, her time free of Conroy's oppression – to study up on alternate philosophies, and when she found one that made sense to her, it wasn't long before she decided to assert her new self.

After that, the possibilities seemed endless. She felt as though she had shed a chrysalis and evolved to a form which made her happier with herself.

Therefore, no one was more surprised than Ellen when her husband Conroy thumped up the stairs, sundered head and all, to come a-calling more than a year after she thought she had definitively killed the rotten sonofabitch. His face looked exactly as it had when Coggins, the undertaker, had puttied and waxed it back into a semblance of human, dark sub-dermal lines inscribing puzzle pieces in rough assembly. The parts did not move in correct concert when Conroy spoke to her, however. His face was disjointed and broken, his eyes, oddly fixed.

"Time for some loving," is what Conroy said to her first.

Ellen ran for the gun cabinet, downstairs.

"Already thought of that," said Conroy, holding up the Le Mat. He did not shoot her in the head.

Despite the fact that Lee Beecher's death had been inadvertent, one of those Act of God things, Constable Lon Dickey had always felt responsible. Lee had been a hometown boy, Dickey had liked him, and made him his deputy; ergo, Lee had been acting as a representative of the law on Dickey's behalf, moving a dead deer out of the middle of the road during a storm. Some local asshole had piled into the animal and left it for dead, which constituted Triple Pines' only known form of hit and run. If you'd had to guess the rest of the story, Dickey thought, you'd say *and another speeding nitwit had hit Lee*. Nope. Struck by *lightning*, for christ's sake. Hit by a thunderbolt out of the ozone and killed deader than snakeshit on the spot, fried from the inside out, cooked and discarded out near the lumber yard which employed about a quarter of Triple Pines' blue-collar workforce.

Lee had been buried in his uniform. A go-getter, that kid. Good footballer. Instead of leaving Triple Pines in his rearward dust, as so many youngsters ached to do, Lee had stuck close to home, and enthusiastically sought his badge. It was worth it to him to be called an "officer", like Dickey. Death in Triple Pines was nearly always accidental, or predictable – no mystery. This was not the place where murderers or psychos lived. In this neck of the woods, the worst an officer might have to face would be the usual rowdiness – teenagers, or drunks, or drunk teenagers – and the edict to act all authoritative if there was a fire or flood or something naturally disastrous.

Beecher's replacement was a guy named James Trainor, shit-hot out of the academy in Seattle and fulminating to enforce. Too stormtrooper for Triple Pines; too ready to pull his sidearm for a traffic stop. Dickey still had not warmed up to him, smelling the moral pollution of citified paranoia.

Feeling like a lazy lion surveying his domain, Dickey had sauntered the two blocks back to the station from the Ready-Set Dinette, following feeling his usual cheeseburger late-lunch. (The food at Callahan's, a block further, was awful – the burgers as palatable as pucks sliced off a Duraflame log.) Time to trade some banter with RaeAnn, who ran the police station's desk, phones and radios. RaeAnn was a stocky chunk of bottle-blonde business with multiple chins and an underbite, whose choice of corrective eyewear did not de-emphasise her Jimmy Durante nose. In no way was RaeAnn a temptation, and Dickey preferred that. Strictly business. RaeAnn was fast, efficient, and did not bring her problems to work. Right now she was leaning back at her station with her mouth wide open, which seemed strange. She resembled a gross caricature of one of those mail-order blowjob dolls.

Before he could ask what the hell, Dickey saw the bullet hole in the center of her forehead. Oh.

"Sorry I'm a little bit late, Chief," said Lee Beecher. He had grave dirt all over his moldy uniform, and his face was the same flash-fried nightmare that had caused Coggins to recommend a closed-casket service. Beecher had always called Dickey "Chief".

Deputy Trainor was sprawled behind Dickey's desk, his cap over his eyes, his tongue sticking out, and a circlet of five .357 caliber holes in his chest. Bloodsmear on the bulletin board illustrated how gracelessly he had fallen, hit so hard one of his boots had flown off. The late Lee Beecher had been reloading his revolver when Dickey walked in.

"I had to shoot RaeAnn, she was making too much bother," said Beecher. His voice was off, dry and croaky, buzzing like a reed.

Dickey tried to contain his slow awe by muttering the names of assorted deities. His hand wanted to feel the comfort of his own gun.

"How come you replaced me, Chief?" said the late Lee Beecher. "Man, I didn't quit or nothing. You replaced me with some city boy. That wasn't our deal. I thought you liked me."

"I—" Dickey stammered. "Lee, I . . ." He just could not force out words. This was too wrong.

"You just put me in the dirt." The late Lee Beecher shook his charred skull with something akin to sadness. He snapped home the cylinder on his pistol, bringing the hammer back to full cock in the same smooth move. "Now I'm gonna have to return the favor. Sorry, Chief."

Constable Dickey was still trying to form a whole sentence when the late Lee Beecher gave him all six rounds. Up at RaeAnn's desk, the radio crackled and the switchboard lit up with an influx of weird emergency calls, but there was no one to pay any attention, or care.

*   *   *

Doug's current home barely fit the definition. It had no more character than a British row flat or a post-war saltbox. It was one of the basic, ticky-tacky clapboard units thrown up by the Triple Pines aluminum plant back when they sponsored company housing, and abandoned to fall apart on its own across slow years once the plant folded. It had a roof and indoor plumbing, which was all Doug had ever required of a residence, because addresses were disposable. It had storm shutters and a rudimentary version of heat, against rain and winter, but remained drafty. Its interior walls were bare and still the same vague green Doug had always associated with academia. The bedroom was sort of blue, in the same mood.

He regretted his cheap sheets, his second-hand bed, his milk-crate nightstand. He had strewn some candles around to soften the light, and fired up a portable, radiant oil heater. The heat and the light diffused the stark seediness of the room, just enough. They softened the harsh edges of reality.

There had been no seduction, no ritual libations, no teasing or flirting. Michelle had taken him the way the Allies took Normandy, and it was all he could muster to keep from gasping. His pelvis felt hammered and his legs seemed numb and far away. She was alive, with the warm, randy needs of the living, and she had plundered him with a greed that cleansed them both of any lingering recriminations.

No grave rot, no mummy dust. Was it still necrophilia when the dead person moved and talked back to you?

"I have another blanket," he said. His left leg was draped over her as their sweat cooled. He watched candle-shadows dance on the ceiling, making monster shapes.

"I'm fine," she said. "Really."

They bathed. Small bathtub, lime-encrusted shower head. It permitted Doug to refamiliarise himself with the geometry of her body, from a perspective different than that of the bedroom. He felt he could never see or touch *enough* of her; it was a fascination for him.

There was nothing to eat in the kitchen, and simply clicking on the TV seemed faintly ridiculous. They slept, wrapped up in each other. The circumstance was still too fragile to detour into lengthy, dissipate conversations about need, so they slept, and in sleeping, found a fundamental innocence that was already beyond logic – a *feeling* thing. It seemed right and correct.

Doug awoke, his feet and fingertips frigid, in the predawn. He added his second blanket and snuggled back into Michelle. She slept with a nearly beatific expression, her breath – real, living – coming in slow tidal measures.

The next afternoon Doug sortied to the market to stock up on some basics and find some decent food that could be prepared in his minimal kitchen. In the market, he encountered Joe Hopkins, from the digging crew. Doug tried unsuccessfully to duck him. He wanted to do nothing to break the spell he was under.

But Joe wanted to talk, and cornered him. He was holding a fifth of bourbon like he intended to make serious use of it, in due course.

"There was apparently a lot of activity in the cemetery last night," he said, working his toothpick from one corner of his mouth to the other. Both ends were wet and frayed. "I mean, after we left. We went back this morning, things were moved around. Some graves were disrupted. Some were partially refilled. It was a mess, like a storm had tossed everything. We had to spend two hours just to get back around to where we left off."

"You mean, like vandalism?" said Doug.

"Not exactly." Joe had another habit, that of continually smoothing his upper lip with his thumb and forefinger, as though to keep his moustache in line when he wasn't looking. To Doug, it signaled nervousness, agitation, and Joe was too brawny to be agitated about much for very long. "I tried to figure it, you know – what alla sudden makes the place not creepy, but threatening in a way it wasn't, yesterday. It's the feeling you'd have if you put on your clothes and alla sudden thought that, hey, somebody *else* has been wearing my clothes, right?"

Doug thought of what Michelle had said, about the dead hearing every footfall of the living above them.

"What I'm saying is, I don't blame you for quitting. After today, I'm thinking the same thing. Every instinct I have tells me to just jump on my bike and ride the fuck out of here as fast as I can go. And, something else? Jacky says he ran into a guy last night, a guy he went to high school with. They were on the football team together. Jacky says the guy died four years ago in a Jeep accident. But the he *saw* him, last night, right outside the bar after you left. Not a ghost. He wasn't that drunk. Then, this morning, Craignotti says something equally weird: That he saw a guy at the diner, you know the Ready-Set? Guy was a dead ringer for Aldus Champion, you know the mayor who died in 2003 and got replaced by that asshole selectman, whatsisname—?"

"Brad Ballinger," said Doug.

"Yeah. I been here long enough to remember that. But here's the thing: Craignotti checked, and today Ballinger was nowhere to be found, and he ain't on vacation or nothing. And Ballinger is in bed with Coggins, the undertaker, somehow. Notice how that whole

Marlboro Reservoir thing went into a coma when Champion was mayor? For a minute I thought Ballinger had, you know, had him whacked or something. But now Champion's back in town – a guy Craignotti swears isn't a lookalike, but *the* guy. So now I think there was some heavy-duty money changing hands under a lot of tables, and the reservoir is a go, except nobody is supposed to talk about it, and now we're out there, digging up the whole history of Triple Pines as a result."

"What does this all come to?" Doug really wanted to get back to Michelle. She might evaporate or something if left alone too long.

"I don't know, that's the fucked up thing." Joe tried to shove his busy hands into his vest pockets, then gave up. "I'm not smart enough to figure it out, whatever it is . . . so I give it to you, see if any lightbulbs come on. I'll tell you one thing. This afternoon I felt scared, and I ain't felt that way since I was paddy humping."

"We're both outsiders, here," said Doug.

"Everybody on the dig posse in an outsider, man. Check *that* out."

"Not Jacky."

"Jacky don't pose any threat because he don't know any better. And even him, he's having fucking hallucinations about his old school buddies. Listen: I ain't got a phone at my place, but I got a mobile. Do me a favor – I mean, I know we don't know each other that well – but if you figure something out, give me a holler?"

"No problem." They traded phone numbers and Joe hurried to pay for his evening's sedation. As he went, he said, "Watch your ass, cowboy."

"You, too."

Doug and Michelle cooked collaboratively. They made love. They watched a movie together both had seen separately. They made more love. They watched the evening sky for several hours until chilly rain began to sheet down from above, then they repaired inside and continued to make love. The Peyton Place antics of the rest of the Triple Pines community, light years away from their safe, centered union, could not have mattered less.

The trick, as near as Billy Morrison could wrassle it, was to find somebody and pitch them into your hole as soon as you woke up. Came back. Revived. Whatever.

So he finished fucking Vanessa Billings. "Bill-ing" her, as his cohort Vance Thompson would crack, heh. Billy had stopped "bill-ing" high school chicks three years ago, when he died. Now he was billing a Billings, wotta riot.

Billy, Vance, and Donna Christiansen had perished inside of Billy's Boss 302 rebuild, to the tune of Black Sabbath's "Mob Rules" on CD. The car was about half grey primer and fender-fill, on its way back to glory. The CD was a compilation of metal moldies. No one ever figured out how the car had crashed, up near a trailer suburbia known as Rimrock, and no one in authority gave much of a turd, since Billy and his fellow losers hailed from "that side" of town, rubbing shoulders an open-fire garbage dump, an auto wrecking yard, and (although Constable Dickey did not know it) a clandestine crack lab. The last sensation Billy experienced as a living human was the car sitting down hard on its left front as the wheel flew completely off. The speed was ticketable and the road, wet as usual, slick as mayonnaise. The car flipped and tumbled down an embankment. Billy dimly recalled seeing Donna snap in half and fly through the windshield before the steering column punched into his chest. The full tank ruptured and spewed a meandering piss-line of gasoline all the way down the hill. Vance's cigarette had probably touched it off, and the whole trash-compacted mess had burned for an hour before new rain finally doused it and a lumber yard worker spotted the smoke.

Their plan for the evening had been to destroy a bottle of vodka in the woods, then Billy and Vance would do Donna from both ends. Donna dug that sort of thing when she was sufficiently wasted. When they awoke several years later in their unearthed boxes, they renewed their pleasure as soon as they could scare up some more liquor. They wandered into a roadside outlet known as the 1-Stop Brew Shoppe and Vance broke bottles over the head of the proprietor until the guy stopping breathing. Then Donna lit out for the Yard, a quadrangle of trees and picnic benches near most of the churches in town. The Yard was Triple Pines' preferred salon for dropouts fond of cannabis, and Donna felt certain she could locate an old beau or two lingering among the waistoids there. Besides, she could bend in interesting new ways, now.

Billy had sought and duly targeted Vanessa Billings, one of those booster / cheerleader bitches who would never have anything to do with his like. She had graduated in '02 and was still – *still!* – living in her parents' house. It was a kick to see her jaw gape in astonishment at the sight of him. *Omigod, you like died!* It was even more of a kick to hold her by the throat and fuck her until she croaked, the stuck-up little cuntling. Getting Vanessa out of her parents' house caused a bit of ruckus, so Billy killed them, too.

Ultimately, the trio racked up so many new corpses to fill their vacant graves they needed to steal a pickup truck to ferry them all back to Hollymount. Their victims would all be back soon enough, and the fun could begin again.

None of them had a precise cognition of what they needed to do. It was more along the lines of an ingrained need – like a craving – to take the heat of the living to avoid reverting to the coldness of death. That, and the idea of refreshing their grave plots with new bodies. Billy had always had more cunning than intelligence, but the imperatives were not that daunting. Stupid dogs learned tricks in less time.

Best of all, after he finished billing Billings, Billy found he *still* had a boner. Death was apparently better than Viagra; he had an all-night hard-on. And since the night was still a toddler, he began to hunt for other chicks he could bill.

The sun came up. The sun went down. Billy thought of that rhyme about how the worms *play pinochle on your snout*. Fucking worms. How about the worms *eat your asshole inside-out*. For starters. Billy had been one super-sized organ smorgasbord, and had suffered every delicious bite. Now a whole fuckload of Triple Pines' good, upstanding citizens were going to pay, pay, pay.

As day and night blended and passed, Triple Pines continued to mutate.

Over at the Ready-Set Dinette, a pink neon sign continued to blink the word EAT, just as it had before things changed in Triple Pines.

Deputy Lee Beecher (the late) and RaeAnn (also the late) came in for lunch as usual. The next day, Constable Dickey (recently deceased) and the new deputy, James Trainor (ditto), joined them.

Vanessa Billings became Billy Morrison's main squeeze, and what with Vance and Donna's hangers-on, they had enough to form a new kind of gang. In the next few days, they would start breaking windows and setting fires.

Over at Callahan's, Craignotti continued to find fresh meat for the digging crew as the original members dropped out. Miguel Ayala had lasted three days before he claimed to have snagged a better job. Big Boyd Cooper stuck – he was a rationalist at heart, not predisposed to superstitious fears or anything else in the path of Getting the Job Done. Jacky Tynan had apparently taken sick.

Joe had packed his saddlebags and gunned his panhead straight out of town, without calling Doug, or anyone.

In the Gudgell household, every day, a pattern commenced. In the morning, Conroy Gudgell would horsewhip his treacherous wife's naked ass, and in the evening, Ellen Gudgell would murder her husband, again and again, over and over. The blood drenching the inside of their house was not ectoplasm. It continued to accrete, layer upon layer, as one day passed into another.

In the middle of the night, Doug felt askew on the inside, and made the mistake of taking his own temperature with a thermometer.

Eighty-seven point-five degrees.

"Yeah, you'll run a little cold," said Michelle, from behind him. "I'm sorry about that. It's sort of a downside. Or maybe you caught something. Do you feel sick?"

"No, I—" Doug faltered. "I just feel shagged. Weak."

"You're not a weak man."

"Stop it." He turned, confrontational. He did not want to do anything to alienate her. But. "This is serious. What if I start losing core heat? Four or five degrees is all it takes, then I'm as dead as a Healthy Choice entrée. What the hell is happening, Michelle? What haven't you told me?"

"I don't *know,*" she said. Her eyes brightened with tears. "I'm not *sure.* I didn't come back with a goddamned manual. I'm afraid that if I go ahead and do the *next* thing, the thing I feel I'm supposed to do . . . that I'll lose you."

Panic cinched his heart. "What's the next thing?!"

"I was avoiding it. I was afraid to bring it up. Maybe I was enjoying this too much, what we have right now, in this isolated bubble of time."

He held her. She wanted to reject simple comfort, but succumbed. "Just . . . tell me. Say it, whatever it is. Then it's out in the world and we can deal with it."

"It's about Rochelle."

Doug nodded, having prepared for this one. "You miss her. I know. But we can't do anything about it. There'd be no way to explain it."

"I want her back." Michelle's head was down, the tears coursing freely now.

"I know, baby, I know . . . I miss her, too. I wanted you guys to move in with me. Both of you. From here we could move anywhere, so long as it's out of this deathtrap of a town. Neither of us likes it here very much. I figured, in the course of time—"

She slumped on the bed, hands worrying each other atop her bare legs. "It was my dream, through all those hours, days, that things had happened differently, and we had hooked up, and we all got to escape. It would be great if you were just a means to an end; you know – just another male guy-person, to manipulate. Great if I didn't care about you; great if I didn't actually love you."

"I had to explain your death to Rochelle. There's no going back
from that one. Look at it this way: she's with your mother, and she
seemed like a nice lady."

When her gaze came up to meet his, her eyes were livid. "You
don't know anything," she said, the words constricted and bitter.
"Sweet, kindly old Grandma Farrier? She's a fucking sadist who has
probably shot pornos with Rochelle by now."

"What?!" Doug's jaw unhinged.

"She is one sick piece of shit, and her mission was always to get
Rochelle away from me, into her clutches. I ran away from home as
soon as I could. And when I had Rochelle, I swore that bitch would
never get her claws on my daughter. And you just . . . handed her
over."

"Now, wait a minute, Michelle . . ."

She overrode him. "No – it's not your fault. She always presented
one face to the world. Her fake face. Her human masque. Inside the
family with the doors closed, it was different. You saw the masque.
You dealt with the masque. So did Rochelle. Until Grandma could
actually strap the collar on, she had to play it sneaky. Her real face is
from a monster who needed to be inside a grave decades ago. I
should know – she broke me in with a heated glass dildo when I was
nine."

"Holy shit. Michelle, why didn't you tell me this before?"

"Which 'before?' Before now? Or before I died? Doug, I died not
knowing you were as good as you are. I thought I could never make
love to anybody, ever again. I concentrated on moving from place to
place to keep Rochelle off the radar."

Doug toweled his hands, which were awash in nervous perspira-
tion, yet irritatingly cold. Almost insensate. He needed to assuage her
terror, to fix the problem, however improbable; like Boyd Cooper, to
Get the Job Done. "Okay. Fine. I'll just go get her back. We'll figure
something out."

"I can't ask you to do that."

"Better yet, how about we *both* go get her? Seeing you ought to
make Grandma's brain hit the floor."

"That's the problem, Doug. It's been the problem all along. *I can't
leave here.* None of us can. If we do . . . if any of us goes outside of
Triple Pines . . ."

"You don't mean 'us' as in you-and-me. You're talking about us as
in the former occupants of Hollymount Cemetery, right?"

She nodded, more tears spilling. "I need you to fuck me. And I
need you to love me. And I was hoping that you could love me

enough so that I didn't have to force you to take my place in that hole in the ground, like all the rest of the goddamned losers and dim bulbs and fly-over people in Triple Pines. I want you to go to San Francisco, and get my daughter back. But if you stay here – if you go away and come back here – eventually I'll use you up anyway. I've been taking your heat, Doug, a degree at a time. And eventually you would die, and then resurrect, and then you would be stuck here too. An outsider, stuck here. And no matter what anyone's good intentions are, it would also happen to Rochelle. I can't kill my little girl. And I can't hurt you any more. It's killing me, but – what a joke – I can't die." She looked up, her face a raw, aching map of despair. "You see?"

Michelle had not been a local, either. But she had died here, and become a permanent resident in the Triple Pines boneyard. The population of the town was slowly shifting balance. The dead of Triple Pines were pushing out the living, seeking that stasis of small town stability where once again, everyone would be the same. What happened in Triple Pines had to stay in Triple Pines, and the Marlboro Reservoir was no boon to the community. It was going to service coastal cities; Doug knew this in his gut, now. In all ways, for all concerned, Triple Pines was the *perfect* place for this kind of thing to transpire, because the outside world would never notice, or never care.

With one grating exception. Which suggested one frightening solution.

Time to get out. Time to bail, now.

"Don't you see?" she said. "If you don't get out now, you'll never get out. Get out, Doug. Kiss me one last time and get out. Try to think of me fondly."

His heart smashed to pieces and burned to ashes, he kissed her. Her tears lingered on his lips, the utterly real *taste* of her. Without a word further, he made sure he had his wallet, got in his car, and drove. He could be in San Francisco in six hours, flat-out.

He could retrieve Rochelle, kidnap her if that was what was required. He could bring her back here to die, and be reunited with her mother. Then he could die, too. But at least he would be with them, in the end. Or he could put it behind him, and just keep on driving.

The further he got from Triple Pines, the warmer he felt.

DON TUMASONIS

Thrown

FRESH FROM AN EVENING of overindulgence on the island of Anafi some years ago, Don Tumasonis awoke with a story in his head, and immediately wrote it down.

Encouraged by fellow orgy survivors, to whom he shyly showed the fragment, he realised that honour, power, riches, fame, and the love of women were within his grasp. He acquired a Muse, as is recommended, having already been provided with that *sine non qua* of writers, a long-suffering wife. Two International Horror Guild awards, a film option and a Hawthornden Fellowship soon followed. He still awaits power and riches, but admits that three out of five is not too bad.

His longish tale "The Swing" was recently published in the Ash-Tree Press anthology *At Ease With the Dead*, edited by Barbara and Christopher Roden. Other projects are in the works.

"Once, I dreamed of becoming an anthropologist," Tumasonis recalls. "I had, after all, got stinking drunk on cheap plonk with Sir Edmund Leach, so I thought myself eminently qualified. Fired with explorers' tales, I fixated on northern Nepal. Months of struggle with Tibetan put paid to that fantasy and, suddenly more realistic, I settled for Crete.

"Field work in the glorious mountains of Sfakia produced little of academic value. Penitent, I vowed to cross the Great Island by foot, east to west. As may now be suspected, even that last project was somehow thwarted short of completion. Not all was lost – the narrative of 'Thrown' draws largely on events that occurred during several legs of that journey."

I T WAS STRANGE COUNTRY, cast into tumult by disaster.

Signs of this were everywhere, from the seaside city in the south where they first stayed, to the northern village from whence they would start their walk. Across the neck of the island, debris was visible all over, through the dusty windows of their ageing Mercedes bus, running late. The delay was a result of the massive flood of several days past, with traffic still detoured around the washed-out main highway bridge, to the old road a bit further inland.

When Martin and Marline had first come to Crete two days after the deluge, quasi-urban Ierapetra was drying out from the rampageous torrent that had wrecked its streets and invaded buildings. The branch Agricultural Bank's records and documents were spread out on sidewalks and streets, stones and bricks neatly pinning papers in place, the sun wrinkling and baking fibres. Nearby, a flower-filled Roman sarcophagus doubling as a sidewalk planter lent white Parian cachet to an adjacent telephone booth.

Floods came often enough on this island of canyons and gorges, but this one had been a monster, by every local estimation. It was the usual chain of events. Heavy autumn rains washed broken trees and branches down a ravine, compacting with clay and gravel at a pinched slot, forming a natural dam. Before anyone even knew, or had time to react, millions of tons of water had built up, until the sudden giving way, and catastrophic release.

A couple had been taken out to sea, drowned in their Volkswagen beetle. Excepting these, and one old woman at an isolated farm, there was no other loss of human life, amazing as that seemed in the aftermath.

But the water, gaining speed, spewing like a jet from the mouth of the deep cleft above the cultivated plain, took all else living with as it ripped through the countryside, crashing to the sea in a few calamitous minutes.

Some short hours after having checked into their room – the cheapest they could find, with a bare concrete floor, the two followed the lead of everyone else: they promenaded, taking in the chaos and damage, trying to assimilate the monstrous extent of the wreckage about them.

Crowds of foreigners from the large tourist complex near the shore mingled with the local Greeks, walking east out of town. Hundreds, clumped together in their scores, their pairs, were heading along the beach, where the detritus of the flooding was spread. All were silent and stunned, even two days after, and talked, if at all, in hushed voices, in the descending light of the sun.

Past the hotels, a new river channel had torn through the shore road, destroying it, and people waded across, past a parked bulldozer there for the clean-up. On the other side, all over the long broad beach, lay hundreds of animal corpses, wild and domestic. Lizards rotted promiscuously with goats. Pathetic lambs, wool matted and muddy, strewn broken amid snapped tree limbs. Snakes, and above all, chickens, were everywhere, half-buried in the sand. Let this their memorial be.

Back at their rundown hotel room, the couple made love. Rattled by what they had seen, they drank to excess, and things ran wilder than usual between them, married ten years.

Marline sat at an angle leaning forward, hands on Martin's ankles, facing his feet, as he lay on his back, in the *reverse cowgirl*, pornographic industrial standard pose, provider of unobstructed views. They had started prone, two layers, both face up, with her on top. Disembodied hands stroked her, leaving her too open and exposed, as if naked in public with some unspeakable object inside. She slid upright and forward, into the unpremeditated position, a natural extension of the first, really, looking upward as she rocked.

A single red light bulb, forming the sole illumination, bare, dangled on its brown plastic wire from the ceiling, casting a garish glow throughout the room. The double shutters were closed, and the chamber, already damp from their showering, became even more so, heating up.

The entire tawdriness of the situation inspired Marline to a totally uncharacteristic frenzy. Replying in the dialogue of the flesh, Martin grew enormous, larger than ever inside her, and imagined himself in the cheapest of houses of prostitution, some bold and promiscuous whore working him for all his money's worth. The red light added to the fantastic aspect, that of being in a Fellini film, or a Turkish camp of ill-fame, where poor young widows, respectable and married the one day, the next, with no one to protect them, are thrown headlong into the wildest of debaucheries, with no escape.

Marline's face was invisible as Martin clenched her smoothly sculpted, heaving buttocks. Perfectly rounded, they were starting to fleck with pigment from the hours in the Cretan sun, complementing the rest of her freckled body, now writhing like a snake, as she and he both gasped for breath. He held those nether spheres tightly from behind, as it seemed otherwise she would rocket off him in her now fierce motion.

Her short red hair was like a helmet, and under the crimson bulb, dark. At the moment of ecstasy, she turned for the first time to face him, from over her shoulder. Her sharp jaw was distended – *like a John dory*, the thought came to him from nowhere – and her eyes were wild. She was not looking at him. She saw beyond, to something else. He could not recognise her again; this was the face of an entirely different person: had he met this one in the street, he would not know her.

The more he looked at her frenzied eyes, the more strange she appeared, until he conceived her a demon, the devil itself, no woman, no wife he knew. At their mutual orgasm, a chill of irrational fright ran through him, but he closed his eyes, taking in air in huge gulping heaves, uncaring.

Flush fading, consciousness revived, Martin saw Marline collapsed forward across his legs. He was still inside her, the sticky wetness draining down from his crotch and then his buttocks, turning cold on the sheet beneath him. She rolled off, and resting on her side, eyes closed, a smile across her mouth, murmured something about going out again, a night-cap. Then she yawned.

"Napoleon slept here, did you know? Ierapetra's 'holy rock' in Greek," he said.

Marline was already putting on her clothes.

Dropped off past the lines of delayed traffic still waiting to cross the old narrow bridge, they had gone more or less straight up from the sea, from the small settlement clinging to steep slope above coastal highway.

At the upper end of the little hamlet, by the trailhead, they tipped their heads back to see the inland range hanging above. It had been his idea to go up it and explore its interior, part of a larger plan to walk the island from east to west. This day's march would link together sections done previous seasons, thus completing eastern Crete, an opportunity provided by doctor's orders, after a second, work-related breakdown.

Old women, bent nearly double and swathed in black, assured them they were on the right way, no guarantee in itself, as Greeks would rather die than admit to ignorance of any subject, no matter how far removed from their normal competence. Enormous cliff faces towered to the east; they had come down from there two years back, an epic struggle to find a disappearing track.

Village noise was soon below them, growing ever more faint and distant, replaced by the always present susurrant wind. The trail, an old respectable Cretan path, wound steadily upwards in large or smaller switches. After an hour's trudge or more in the expanding sunlight, they stopped on a shoulder, the site of some stronghold of Minoan refugees, driven to the heights after their civilisation had collapsed. While Marline put together a picnic, Martin puttered about on the partially excavated ruins above.

There was not much more to see than dry stone walls, crumbling remnants of some '20s dig, German or Italian, he did not remember what the guidebook said. The overwhelming vista looked north over the Ægean, with Thera somewhere volcanically looming, invisible in the slight haze, on the horizon distant before him.

Only one thing distinguished the fast decaying ruins from any modern wreckage of local revolution: a flat, carved stone bowl, cut into the living rock, like some small birdbath. Cracked in several places, stains covered one side of the interior.

They ate, and before wrapping up after their little meal, Martin looked out over the scene in front of them, and without preamble, spoke out.

"You know, when I grew up in Rochester, I never felt comfortable with the sky."

"How's that?"

"Well, there was always something, something about it that never *felt* quite right. D'you know what I mean?"

"Not really . . ."

"At first I thought it was the colour. Summers were warmer then, or so it seems now. I'd lie back, on the grass of a lawn in July, and stretch out, looking up at the sky. It would be cloudless, and the heavens so deep when I concentrated, I felt I was plunging into them.

"It was then I began to get a strange impression, that the vast inverted bowl I was falling into was somehow *wrong*."

"What do you mean?"

He paused, and all was silent but for the wind. "I'm not quite sure how to express it – alien, perhaps?" he continued.

"I thought perhaps it was just the flatness of hue the sky can attain on a clear day in the middle of the year. But with the notion established in my mind – I was only eleven or twelve the first time I conceived it – or rather, made it articulate, since I later realised it was a perception I had had all along, that I was only then putting into words – I came to the conclusion that the feeling was more general.

"It could come upon me other seasons of the year, when the sky had a different colour, under other conditions of time and temperature. For a while, I thought something was wrong with me.

"I developed the odd notion that I was *born* with an instinct of how a proper sky should look, I mean, in the old days people seldom moved from the districts where they were raised. Rooted in the soil, they might just in some way become attuned, after generations, to the *look* of a certain latitude and longitude, so that any variation in colour of air or position of sun from that imprinted on their bones, would somehow appear odd."

He paused. "I mean, some animals have iron in their brains, they've found out, onboard compasses that always point north, so . . ." His voice trailed off, and they were silent for a lingering moment.

"You've never mentioned that before. If you want to know," she said with a slight smile, "I think it's all a load of rubbish." She flicked out playfully with her foot at his leg, as they sat.

He smiled back weakly, and continued: "I began to think so too, especially after I got older, and started travelling about, first locally, then, around the Continent, and further. I suppose I was always, at some unconscious level, thinking that if I found the right spot, the sky would brighten, things would look up, and all would be right in God's world."

She gave him a friendly smirk, hearing that, but he did not react.

"Y'know, at one point the whole idea came back to me, and I started to think, what if we really came from somewhere else, even from off the planet? A spaceship crashes here eons ago, seeds the place with its offspring – it would explain our exceptional place in the world."

"But DNA."

"Right you are, dead on. Common kinship. Once the implications of *that* discovery had percolated through my thick skull, I abandoned the idea. We're here where we began, all right."

They set about packing the remains of their picnic lunch; he wrapped the water bottle in towelling to keep it cool, while she cleaned the knife and stowed the food in her sack. Gear ready, they hoisted their packs, and stood a moment in the boiling sun, adjusting their straps and buckles.

Martin rested on his walking stick, a *katsouni*, store-bought, but being made of rare local wood, some protected dwarf elm that grew here and there in the high mountains, a great conversation starter in the rural districts.

"It has to do with a feeling, more than anything else, a feeling of not belonging here at all. As if . . ."

"What?"

"As if I were some kind of object, something hurled here unwittingly, against its will, like that German philosopher used to claim. To a place not my true home."

"Oh."

Martin did not dare mention or even hint at the experience of the night before – that, during their making love, alienation had triggered this memory of an old idea, up to now all but half-forgotten.

They started up the hill.

They reached, an hour or two later, the upper verge of the cliff, a flat ridge separating two peaks. Stalky anisette plants, tall invaders from another dimension, stood all around. Martin and Marline stopped to rest and admire the tremendous view before them.

The sea was far below; ahead lay a vast bowl, surrounded by bare and rugged peaks. The depression was partly cultivated, and they could see a few tiny dark-clad figures taking in the harvest, and few more working the vines. A dirt track threaded through it.

Martin gave Marline a hug, spontaneously, and it felt like he was hugging the air.

The trail descended into the sere arena below, desiccate but for the few irrigated plots chequering its innermost concavities. Small lizards scurried off the path. Marline and Martin headed down, pointing themselves towards the biggest of the summer houses, a massive white-washed affair with a shaded porch.

There were huge rust-coloured plastic barrels with black lids in the shadows; commonly used for storing wine, these gave promise of a kafenion. This hope was bolstered by a few rucksacks, obviously alien, resting above the steps, the bright colours an evidence of foreign wanderers or customers nearby. A peasant woman, middle-aged, in black with a grubby grey apron, walked out from inside, her cheap plastic flip-flops slapping against the concrete floor of the patio. She smiled pleasantly, shaking her head from side to side, the Balkan gesture of query. A trace of concern was in her eyes.

"*Xeni. Katse, katse,*" she insisted.

Thus invited, the couple seated themselves on a couple of run-down chairs with worn-through wicker seats.

"*Nero thelete?*"

Martin nodded, and the woman shuffled off to get water, and glasses. While she was inside, Martin looked at the nearby packs leaning on a pillar, and recognised a German marque.

The woman came out again, bearing a tray loaded with pumpkin seeds and shelled hazelnuts, a few garishly wrapped boiled sweets mixed in. Two glasses filled with water completed the ensemble.

They were careful to toast the woman's health in Greek, before swallowing the cool water. There followed the inevitable questions: Where do you come from? What work do you do? Why are you here? Have you any children? followed by clucks of sympathy at the answer "none".

It was a formula, probably being repeated dozens of times that same moment across the island, wherever tourists and Greeks were meeting for the first time. Were a man the interrogator, topics would have drifted over to money earned, and yearly wages. A delicate little probing, performed with overt politeness, with always the under-current of gaining information, reaping some advantage; the pull, the tug, with little exception always towards: *how is this one useful to me?*

Her questions tapered off once it was established that the couple were ordinary people doing the familiar if incomprehensible act of travel for its own sake. Martin then took his opportunity, with his kitchen Greek.

No, there was no kafenion. No place to overnight. The mountain over there was Effendis Christos. The people here were all from the village below, and were up to tend their summer gardens and trees; they would go down in the evening. Yes, there were other strangers here, Germans, up on the mountain.

Marline, with better eyes, saw them first. A red spot, a yellow, and two blues – chemical colours of the jackets or jerseys, up near the summit, stretched out along a fairly vertiginous route.

They've been up there all day, the woman said.

At which point, as if to confirm her statement, the sounds of a distant yodel echoed from far up the hill. *Fun, up on the rocks*, Martin thought.

At length, having questioned the woman about the track to the next village, the two set off again, early evening approaching. They went uphill through the dry landscape, east, sun to their backs, up a low pass, then up to another and finally a third, the watershed. No one had been by, and the enveloping silence was profound.

They could see down, back to the brink crossed hours before, at the foot of the northern massif. On either side of the dusty way where they stood, two ranges, here close, ran parallel. To the right, the flat ridgeline of Effendis now sat low, a hundred metres above them. The road had climbed up almost level with the long spine of the peak; it would be an easy walk to the top from here.

Like a shadow-show, Martin thought, and he felt somehow cheated realising that what was so difficult from the one side, could be done so easily from the other. This brought to mind the automata of Descartes, gliding down the streets in cavalier cloaks hiding clockwork, indistinguishable from passersby.

"They are the passersby," Martin said aloud.

"What?"

"Oh, nothing, just a thought about the mountain."

Marline laughed, her voice echoing with a strange tinny tone.

"Effendis Christos – Jesus! They're probably all Turks here!" she giggled.

"She didn't even know the word is from her neighbours to the east, or is it maybe cousins?"

Still laughing, Marline suggested setting up camp. If they went on down a few minutes more, they could still see both ways, but would be shielded from the eyes of any loitering villagers behind them. The deep empty valley, next morning's walk, opened out long ahead before turning right; beyond, they could see a fair stretch of the south coast.

Going a few metres off the rutted track that now ran over patches of bare rock, they unfurled their sleeping mats and bags. Cooking up a brew on a small gas stove, they drank it with bread and cheese, sitting wordlessly on the inflated cushions.

The view was extraordinarily clear, with every object sharp and definite in the limpid air. Objects that must have been miles off seemed close enough to touch. Shadows were being magnified and thrown vast distances. Clarity imagined, but seldom seen.

Martin felt a gnawing unease, but unable to find words to express it, remained silent.

"What?"

"Nothing. It's just – I can't say it."

Another long pause, and then Martin said, "It's really nothing," and felt his eyes for no reason suddenly fill with tears. Standing up quickly, so Marline would not see, he turned to face the way they had come.

"I'm going up back a little bit," he said to her. "I just want to see how long the shadows actually are." She did not reply, so he began to slowly move through the low bushes, sole cover to the treeless earth, through the infinite symphonic tones of yellows and browns and black-greens that reeked of spice and animal excreta. The sky was absolutely cloudless.

Some paces uphill, back on the unmetalled track, he turned to look. The north slopes of Effendis to the right were now in shadow, but every object in the imperfect dark was still visible. He could almost hear the rocks, dusty purple in the shade, crack as they started to cool from the day's impartible heat.

The rest of the hills, ahead and to the left, and the valley between, were filled with light that tore the heart, obsidian sharp, crystalline, clear. Marline, small and distant below, had packed the few pieces of mess gear, and was now smoking a cigarette, seated arms around her knees, looking the same direction as Martin, setting sun to their backs.

And then he saw the shadow, his own. At first he was not sure, until he moved, and the shadow moved with him. It was enormous, occluding acres of hillside below the horizon up to the valley's end, beyond, miles away. He felt dizzy, and to steady himself, turned round and stumbled further up, hugging himself with his arms, gulping great breaths, gasping after air.

Coming to a halt, he slowly turned again.

His shadow, since he was higher, had of course moved upward with him. In the flat light, it was now taller than the lofty ridgeline of the farthest range, and covered a reasonably large part of the sky above, darkening the air, which still remained transparent.

Stunned, Martin slowly lifted an arm, and its umbra eclipsed the blue, almost to the zenith.

He began to hyperventilate sharply, and with vertigo and nausea washing over him, panic took hold. He ran down to his wife, stumbling once, falling, cutting open a pant leg at the knee, so he bled, but paid no heed.

She was waiting, with her arms stretched wide, waiting to catch him, to enfold him. He wept, eyes closed, as she held him, crooning, soothing her lost child.

"Don't be afraid, there's nothing wrong, you're here, with me, there now . . ." she said.

"But you saw it, didn't you?" he repeated over and over again, without her any reply, only the soft caress. Eventually, shaking still, he left her embrace, and stood up.

The shadows were gone now, the sun down at last behind them. At the spot where the world had turned to the dimensions of a shoe box minutes before, the sky was evenly shaded.

It must be my eyes, he thought, *the macular degeneration, those spots that float across.* He saw one now, thread-like in the air before him, and blinked to make it go away. When he opened his eyes, the hanging string, like a piece of thick shimmering cord, was larger, wriggling in front of him, a dark blue transparent plastic worm vibrating at an impossible rate. He blinked furiously; with each blink, the writhing blue rope gained in definition, and his breathing stopped.

Speechless, mouth hanging open in supplication, he looked back at Marline. But it was no longer her, but the grinning thrust-jawed demon of the night before who looked back at him. Teeth gleaming, this creature shook her head in quick small jerks from side to side, like someone palsied, and small, brilliant blade-like rays of green and blue outlined her silhouette, streaming off her.

Despairing, Martin turned round a last time, and faced the now motionless protuberance. Its hue, he noted on the abstract, complemented, but did not match, that of the air. He heard *Yes, yes,* come from behind him, but he did not know whose voice.

Reaching out, using his nails, he worried the limp thing loose, except for one solidly emplaced end, embedded in the air.

With a firm grip and a single wrap around his fist, using great force, he jerked the cool and wet object straight down, ripping open – to the applause of his wife behind him, with the satisfying roar of torn canvas and rock-broken waves in his ears – the mountains to their root, and the sky, the traitor sky he always knew was wrong.

CAITLÍN R. KIERNAN

Houses Under the Sea

CAITLÍN R. KIERNAN IS A FOUR-TIME recipient of the International Horror Guild Award and a World Fantasy Award finalist.

Her novels include *Silk, Threshold, Low Red Moon, Murder of Angels* and *Daughter of Hounds,* and her short fiction has been collected in *Tales of Pain and Wonder, From Weird and Distant Shores, Alabaster* and *To Charles Fort With Love.* She is currently working on her next novel, *Joey LaFaye,* and a collection of science-fiction stories, both of which will be released in 2008. The author lives in Atlanta, Georgia, with her partner, doll-maker Kathryn Pollnac.

" 'Houses Under the Sea' was written in February and March 2004, and was only my third attempt to write a short story as a first-person narrative," Kiernan reveals. "For many years, I'd avoided fp, for a number of reasons, some perfectly valid and some admittedly questionable. But beginning with 'Riding the White Bull' and *The Dry Salvages* in 2003, I finally became intrigued enough with its possibilities that I began to experiment.

"When I finished 'Houses Under the Sea' on March 5th, I was still somewhat sceptical, though, as evidenced by this comment from my online journal entry from March 6th regarding the difficulty I was having finding a title for the piece: 'If I had my druthers, it would have no title at all. In most cases, giving titles to first-person narratives only compounds the problems of disbelief. Not only am I to believe that Character X sat down and wrote this story for me to read, I'm to believe that she gave it a title.

" 'And if she didn't, then who did? The author? No, Character X *is* the "author"; to believe otherwise defeats the illusion.' Finally, I took a line from T. S. Eliot's 'East Coker' for the title, as it seemed appropriate and the poem had served as one of the story's central inspirations."

I

W HEN I CLOSE MY EYES, I see Jacova Angevine.

I close my eyes, and there she is, standing alone at the end of the breakwater, standing with the foghorn as the choppy sea shatters itself to foam against a jumble of grey boulders. The October wind is making something wild of her hair, and her back's turned to me. The boats are coming in.

I close my eyes, and she's standing in the surf at Moss Landing, gazing out into the bay, staring towards the place where the continental shelf narrows down to a sliver and drops away to the black abyss of Monterey Canyon. There are gulls, and her hair is tied back in a ponytail.

I close my eyes, and we're walking together down Cannery Row, heading south towards the aquarium. She's wearing a gingham dress and a battered pair of Doc Martens that she must have had for fifteen years. I say something inconsequential, but she doesn't hear me, too busy scowling at the tourists, at the sterile, cheery absurdities of the Bubba Gump Shrimp Company and Mackerel Jack's Trading Post.

"That used to be a whorehouse," she says, nodding in the direction of Mackerel Jack's. "The Lone Star Cafe, but Steinbeck called it the Bear Flag. Everything burned. Nothing here's the way it used to be."

She says that like she remembers, and I close my eyes.

And she's on television again, out on the old pier at Moss Point, the day they launched the ROV *Tiburon II*.

And she's at the Pierce Street warehouse in Monterey; men and women in white robes are listening to every word she says. They hang on every syllable, her every breath, their many eyes like the bulging eyes of deep-sea fish encountering sunlight for the first time. Dazed, terrified, enraptured, lost.

All of them lost.

I close my eyes, and she's leading them into the bay.

Those creatures jumped the barricades
And have headed for the sea

All these divided moments, disconnected, or connected so many different ways, that I'll never be able to pull them apart and find a coherent narrative. That's my folly, my conceit, that I can make a mere *story* of what has happened. Even if I could, it's nothing anyone would ever want to read, nothing I could sell. CNN and *Newsweek* and *The New York Times*, *Rolling Stone* and *Harper's*, everyone already knows what they think about Jacova Angevine. Everybody already knows as much as they want to know. Or as little. In those minds, she's already earned her spot in the death-cult hall of fame, sandwiched firmly in between Jim Jones and Heaven's Gate.

I close my eyes, and "Fire from the sky, fire on the water," she says and smiles; I know that this time she's talking about the fire of September 14, 1924, the day lightning struck one of the 55,000-gallon storage tanks belonging to the Associated Oil Company and a burning river flowed into the sea. Billowing black clouds hide the sun, and the fire has the voice of a hurricane as it bears down on the canneries, a voice of demons, and she stops to tie her shoes.

I sit here in this dark motel room, staring at the screen of my laptop, the clean liquid-crystal light, typing irrelevant words to build meandering sentences, waiting, waiting, waiting, and I don't know what it is that I'm waiting for. Or I'm only afraid to admit that I know exactly what I'm waiting for. She has become my ghost, my private haunting, and haunted things are forever waiting.

"In the mansions of Poseidon, she will prepare halls from coral and glass and the bones of whales," she says, and the crowd in the warehouse breathes in and out as a single, astonished organism, their assembled bodies lesser than the momentary whole they have made. "Down there, you will know nothing but peace, in her mansions, in the endless night of her coils."

"*Tiburon* is Spanish for shark," she says, and I tell her I didn't know that, that I had two years of Spanish in high school, but that was a thousand years ago, and all I remember is *si* and *por favor*.

What is that noise now? What is the wind doing?

I close my eyes again.

The sea has many voices.

Many gods and many voices.

"November 5, 1936," she says, and *this* is the first night we had sex, the long night we spent together in a seedy Moss Point hotel, the sort of place the fishermen take their hookers, the same place she was still staying when she died. "The Del Mar Canning Company burned to the ground. No one ever tried to blame lightning for that one."

There's moonlight through the drapes, and I imagine for a moment that her skin has become iridescent, mother-of-pearl, the shimmering motley of an oil slick. I reach out and touch her naked thigh, and she lights a cigarette. The smoke hangs thick in the air, like fog or forgetfulness.

My fingertips against her flesh, and she stands and walks to the window.

"Do you see something out there?" I ask, and she shakes her head very slowly.

I close my eyes.

In the moonlight, I can make out the puckered, circular scars on both her shoulder blades and running halfway down her spine. Two dozen or more of them, but I never bothered to count exactly. Some are no larger than a dime, but several are at least two inches across.

"When I'm gone," she says, "when I'm done here, they'll ask you questions about me. What will you tell them?"

"That depends what they ask," I reply and laugh, still thinking it was all one of her strange jokes, the talk of leaving, and I lie down and stare at the shadows on the ceiling.

"They'll ask you everything," she whispers. "Sooner or later, I expect they'll ask you everything."

Which they did.

I close my eyes, and I see her, Jacova Angevine, the lunatic prophet from Silinas, pearls that were her eyes, cockles and mussels, alive, alive-o, and she's kneeling in the sand. The sun is rising behind her and I hear people coming through the dunes.

"I'll tell them you were a good fuck," I say, and she takes another drag off her cigarette and continues staring at the night outside the motel windows.

"Yes," she says. "I expect you will."

II

The first time that I saw Jacova Angevine – I mean, the first time I saw her in *person* – I'd just come back from Pakistan and had flown up to Monterey to try and clear my head. A photographer friend had an apartment there and he was on assignment in Tokyo, so I figured I could lay low for a couple of weeks, a whole month maybe, stay drunk and decompress. My clothes, my luggage, my skin, everything about me still smelled like Islamabad. I'd spent more than six months overseas, ferreting about for real and imagined connections between Muslim extremists, European middlemen, and Pakistan's leaky nuclear arms program, trying to gauge the damage done by the enterprising Abdul Qadeer Khan, rogue father of the Pakistani bomb, trying to determine exactly what he'd sold and to whom. Everyone already knew – or at least thought they knew – about North Korea, Libya, and Iran, and American officials suspected that al Queda and other terrorist groups belonged somewhere on his list of customers, as well, despite assurances to the contrary from Major-General Shaukat Sultan. I'd come back with a head full of apocalypse and Urdu, anti-India propaganda and Mushaikh poetry, and I was determined to empty my mind of everything except scotch and the smell of the sea.

It was a bright Wednesday afternoon, a warm day for November in Monterey County, and I decided to come up for air. I showered for the first time in a week and had a late lunch at the Sardine Factory on Wave Street – Dungeness crab remoulade, fresh oysters with horseradish, and grilled sand-dabs in a lemon sauce that was a little heavy on the thyme – then decided to visit the aquarium and walk it all off. When I was a kid in Brooklyn, I spent a lot of my time at the aquarium on Coney Island, and, three decades later, there were few things a man could do sober that relaxed me as quickly and completely. I put the check on my MasterCard and followed Wave Street south and east to Prescott, then turned back down Cannery Row, the glittering bay on my right, the pale blue autumn sky stretched out overhead like oil on canvas.

I close my eyes, and that afternoon isn't something that happened three years ago, something I'm making sound like a goddamn travelogue. I close my eyes, and it's happening now, for the first time, and there she is, sitting alone on a long bench in front of the kelp forest exhibit, her thin face turned up to the high, swaying canopy behind the glass, the dapple of fish and seaweed shadows drifting back and forth across her features. I recognise her, and that surprises me, because I've only seen her face on television and in magazine photos and on the dust jacket of the book she wrote before she lost the job at Berkeley. She turns her head and smiles at me, the familiar way you smile at a friend, the way you smile at someone you've known all your life.

"You're in luck," she says. "It's almost time for them to feed the fish." And Jacova Angevine pats the bench next to her, indicating that I should sit down.

"I read your book," I say, taking a seat because I'm still too surprised to do anything else.

"Did you? Did you really?" and now she looks like she doesn't believe me, like I'm only saying that I've read her book to be polite, and from her expression I can tell that she thinks it's a little odd, that anyone would ever bother to try and flatter her.

"Yes," I tell her, trying too hard to sound sincere. "I did really. In fact, I read some of it twice."

"And why would you do a thing like that?"

"Truthfully?"

"Yes, truthfully."

Her eyes are the same color as the water trapped behind the thick panes of aquarium glass, the color of the November sunlight filtered through saltwater and kelp blades. There are fine lines at the corners of her mouth and beneath her eyes that make her look several years older than she is.

"Last summer, I was flying from New York to London, and there was a three-hour layover in Shannon. Your book was all I'd brought to read."

"That's terrible," she says, still smiling, and turns to face the big tank again. "Do you want your money back?"

"It was a gift," I reply, which isn't true and I have no idea why I'm lying to her. "An ex-girlfriend gave it to me for my birthday."

"Is that why you left her?"

"No, I left her because she thought I drank too much and I thought she drank too little."

"Are you an alcoholic?" Jacova Angevine asks, as casually as if she were asking me whether I liked milk in my coffee or if I took it black.

"Well, some people say I'm headed in that direction," I tell her. "But I did enjoy the book, honest. It's hard to believe they fired you for writing it. I mean, that people get fired for writing books." But I know that's a lie, too; I'm not half that naive, and it's not at all difficult to understand how or why *Waking Leviathan* ended Jacova Angevine's career as an academic. A reviewer for *Nature* called it "the most confused and preposterous example of bad history wedding bad science since the Velikovsky affair."

"They didn't fire me for writing it," she says. "They politely asked me to resign because I'd seen fit to publish it."

"Why didn't you fight them?"

Her smile fades a little, and the lines around her mouth seem to grow the slightest bit more pronounced. "I don't come here to talk about the book, or my unfortunate employment history," she says.

I apologise, and she tells me not to worry about it.

A diver enters the tank, matte-black neoprene trailing a rush of silver bubbles, and most of the fish rise expectantly to meet him or her, a riot of kelp bass and sleek leopard sharks, sheephead and rockfish and species I don't recognise. She doesn't say anything else, too busy watching the feeding, and I sit there beside her, at the bottom of a pretend ocean.

I open my eyes. There are only the words on the screen in front of me.

I didn't see her again for the better part of a year. During that time, as my work sent me back to Pakistan, and then to Germany and Israel, I reread her book. I also read some of the articles and reviews, and a brief online interview that she'd given Whitley Strieber's *Unknown Country* website. Then I tracked down an article on Inuit archaeology that she'd written for *Fate* and wondered at what point Jacova Angevine had decided that there was no going back, nothing left to lose and so no reason not to allow herself to become part of the murky, strident world of fringe believers and UFO buffs, conspiracy theorists and paranormal "investigators" that seemed so eager to embrace her as one of its own.

And I wondered, too, if perhaps she might have been one of them from the start.

III

I woke up this morning from a long dream of storms and drowning and lay in bed, very still, sizing up my hangover and staring at the sagging, water-stained ceiling of my motel room. And I finally admitted to myself that this isn't going to be what the paper has hired me to write. I don't think I'm even trying to write it for them any more. They want the dirt, of course, and I've never been shy about digging holes. I've spent the last twenty years as a shovel-for-hire. I don't think it matters that I may have loved her, or that a lot of this dirt is mine. I can't pretend that I'm acting out of nobility of soul or loyalty or even some selfish, belated concern for my own dingy reputation. I would write exactly what they want me to write if I could. If I knew how. I need the money. I haven't worked for the last five months and my savings are almost gone.

But if I'm not writing it for them, if I've abandoned all hope of a paycheck at the other end of this thing, why the hell then am I still sitting here typing? Am I making a confession? Bless me, Father, I can't forget? Do I believe it's something I can puke up like a sour belly full of whiskey, that writing it all down will make the nightmares stop or make it any easier for me to get through the days? I sincerely hope I'm not as big a fool as that. Whatever else I may be, I like to think that I'm not an idiot.

I don't know why I'm writing this, whatever this turns out to be. Maybe it's only a very long-winded suicide note.

Last night I watched the tape again.

I have all three versions with me – the cut that's still being hawked over the internet, the one that ends right after the ROV was hit, before the lights came back on; the cut that MBARI released to the press and the scientific community in response to the version circulating online; and I have the "raw" footage, the copy I bought from a robotics technician who claimed to have been aboard the *R/V Western Flyer* the day that the incident occurred. I paid him two thousand dollars for it and the kid swore to both its completeness and authenticity. I knew that I wasn't the first person to whom he'd sold the tape. I'd heard about it from a contact in the chemistry department at UC Irvine. I was never sure exactly how she'd caught wind of it, but I gathered that the tech was turning a handsome little profit peddling his contraband to anyone willing to pony up the cash.

We met at a Motel 6 in El Cajon, and I played it all the way through before I handed him the money. He sat with his back to the television while I watched the tape, rewound and started it over again.

"What the hell are you doing?" he asked, literally wringing his hands and gazing anxiously at the heavy drapes. I'd pulled them shut after hooking up the rented VCR that I'd brought with me, but a bright sliver of afternoon sunlight slipped in between them and divided his face down the middle. "Jesus, man. You think it's not gonna be the exact same thing every time? You think if you keep playing it over and over it's gonna come out any different?"

I've watched the tape more times than I can count, a couple hundred, at least, and I still think that's a good goddamned question.

"So why didn't MBARI release this?" I asked the kid, and he laughed and shook his head.

"Why the fuck do you think?" he replied.

He took my money, reminded me again that we'd never met and that he'd deny everything if I attempted to finger him as my source. Then he got back into his ancient, wheezy VW Microbus and drove off, leaving me sitting there with an hour and a half of unedited color video recorded somewhere along the bottom of the Monterey Canyon. Everything the ROV *Tiburon II*'s starboard camera had seen (the port pan-and-tilt unit was malfunctioning that day), twenty miles out and three kilometers down, and from the start I understood it was the closest I was ever likely to come to an answer, and that it was also only a different and far more terrible sort of question.

Last night I got drunk, more so than usual, a *lot* more so than usual, and watched it for the first time in almost a month. But I turned the sound on the television down all the way and left the lights burning.

Even drunk, I'm still a coward.

The ocean floor starkly illuminated by the ROV's six 480-watt HMI lights, revealing a velvet carpet of grey-brown sediment washed out from Elkhorn Slough and all the other sloughs and rivers emptying into the bay. And even at this depth, there are signs of life: brittlestars and crabs cling to the shit-coloured rocks, sponges and sea cucumbers, the sinuous, smooth bodies of big-eyed rattails. Here and there, dark outcroppings jut from the ooze like bone from the decaying flesh of a leper.

My asshole editor would laugh out loud at that last simile, would probably take one look at it and laugh and then say something like, "If I'd wanted fucking purple I'd have bought a goddamn pot of violets." But my asshole editor hasn't seen the tape I bought from the tech.

My asshole editor never met Jacova Angevine, never listened to her talk, never fucked her, never saw the scars on her back or the fear in her eyes.

The ROV comes to a rocky place where the seafloor drops away suddenly, and it hesitates, responding to commands from the control room of the *R/V Western Flyer*. A moment or two later, the steady fall of marine snow becomes so heavy that it's difficult to see much of anything through the light reflecting off the whitish particles of sinking detritus. And sitting there on the floor between the foot of the bed and the television, I almost reached out and touched the screen.

Almost.

"It's a little bit of everything," I heard Jacova say, though she never actually said anything of the sort to me. "Silt, phytoplankton and zooplankton, soot, mucus, diatoms, fecal pellets, dust, grains of sand and clay, radioactive fallout, pollen, sewage. Some of it's even interplanetary dust particles. Some of it fell from the stars."

And *Tiburon II* lurches and glides forward a few feet, then slips cautiously over the precipice, beginning the slow descent into this new and unexpected abyss.

"We'd been over that stretch more than a dozen times, at least," Natalie Billington, chief ROV pilot for *Tiburon II*, told a CNN correspondent after the internet version of the tape first made the news. "But that drop-off wasn't on any of the charts. We'd always missed it somehow. I know that isn't a very satisfying answer, but it's a big place down there. The canyon is over two hundred miles long. You miss things."

For a while – exactly 15.34 seconds – there's only the darkness and marine snow and a few curious or startled fish. According to

MBARI, the ROV's vertical speed during this part of the dive is about 35 meters per minute, so by the time it finds the bottom again, depth has increased by some five hundred and twenty-five feet. The seafloor comes into view again, and there's not so much loose sediment here, just a jumble of broken boulders, and it's startling how clean they are, almost completely free of the usual encrustations and muck. There are no sponges or sea cucumbers to be seen, no starfish, and even the omnipresent marine snow has tapered off to only a few stray, drifting flecks. And then the wide, flat rock that is usually referred to as "the Delta stone" comes into view. And this isn't like the face on Mars or Von Daniken seeing ancient astronauts on Mayan artifacts. The lowercase δ carved into the slab is unmistakable. The edges are so sharp, so clean that it might have been done yesterday.

The *Tiburon II* hovers above the Delta stone, spilling light into this lightless place, and I know what's coming next, so I sit very still and count off the seconds in my head. When I've counted to thirty-eight, the view from the ROV's camera pans violently to the right, signaling the portside impact, and an instant later there's only static, white noise, the twelve-second gap in the tape during which the camera was still running, but no longer recording.

I counted to eleven before I switched off the television, and then sat listening to the wind, and the waves breaking against the beach, waiting for my heart to stop racing and the sweat on my face and palms to dry. When I was sure that I wasn't going to be sick, I pressed EJECT and the VCR spat out the tape. I returned it to its navy-blue plastic case and sat smoking and drinking, helpless to think of anything but Jacova.

IV

Jacova Angevine was born and grew up in her father's big Victorian house in Salinas, only a couple of blocks from the birthplace of John Steinbeck. Her mother died when she was eight. Jacova had no siblings, and her closest kin, paternal and maternal, were all back east in New Jersey and Pennsylvania and Maryland. In 1960, her parents relocated to California, just a few months after they were married, and her father took a job teaching high-school English in Castroville. After six months, he quit that job and took another, with only slightly better pay, in the town of Soledad. Though he'd earned a doctorate in comparative literature from Columbia, Theo Angevine seemed to have no particular academic ambitions. He'd written several novels while in college, though none of them had managed to find a publisher. In 1969, his wife five months pregnant with their daughter, he resigned from his position at Soledad High and moved north to Salinas, where he bought the old house on Howard Street with a bank loan and the advance from his first book sale, a mystery novel titled *The Man Who Laughed at Funerals* (Random House; New York).

To date, none of the three books that have been published about Jacova, the Open Door of Night sect, and the mass drownings off Moss Landing State Beach, have made more than a passing mention of Theo Angevine's novels. Elenore Ellis-Lincoln, in *Closing the Door: Anatomy of Hysteria* (Simon and Schuster; New York), for example, devotes only a single paragraph to them, though she gives Jacova's childhood an entire chapter. "Mr Angevine's works received little critical attention, one way or the other, and his income from them was meager," Ellis-Lincoln writes. "Of the seventeen novels he published between 1969 and 1985, only two – *The Man Who Laughed for Funerals* [sic] and *Seven at Sunset* – are still in print. It is notable that the overall tone of the novels becomes significantly darker following his wife's death, but the books themselves never seem to have been more to the author than a sort of hobby. Upon his death, his daughter became the executor of his literary estate, such as it was."

Likewise, in *Lemming Cult* (The Overlook Press; New York), William L. West writes, "Her father's steady output of mystery and suspense potboilers must surely have been a curiosity of Jacova's childhood, but were never once mentioned in her own writings, including the five private journals found in a cardboard box in her bedroom closet. The books themselves were entirely unremarkable, so far as I've been able to ascertain. Almost all are out of print and very difficult to find today. Even the catalog of the Silinas Public Library includes only a single copy each of *The Man Who Laughed at Funerals*, *Pretoria*, and *Seven at Sunset*."

During the two years I knew her, Jacova only mentioned her father's writing once that I can recall, and then only in passing, but she had copies of all his novels, a fact that I've never seen mentioned anywhere in print. I suppose it doesn't seem very significant, if you haven't bothered to read Theo Angevine's books. Since Jacova's death, I've read every one of them. It took me less than a month to track down copies of all seventeen, thanks largely to online booksellers, and even less time to read them. While William West was certainly justified in calling the novels "entirely unremarkable," even a casual examination reveals some distinctly remarkable parallels between the fiction of the father and the reality of the daughter.

I've spent the whole afternoon, the better part of the past five hours, on the preceding four paragraphs, trying to fool myself into believing that I can actually write *about* her as a journalist would write about her. That I can bring any degree of detachment or objectivity to bear. Of course, I'm wasting my time. After seeing the tape again, after almost allowing myself to watch *all* of it again, I think I'm desperate to put distance between myself and the memory of her. I should call New York and tell them that I can't do this, that they should find someone else, but after the mess I made of the Musharraf story, the agency would probably never offer me another assignment. For the moment, that still matters. It might not in another day or two, but it does for now.

Her father wrote books, books that were never very popular, and though they're neither particularly accomplished nor enjoyable, they might hold clues to Jacova's motivation and to her fate. And they might not. It's as simple and contradictory as that. Like everything surrounding the "Lemming Cult" – as the Open Door of Night has come to be known, as it has been labeled by people who find it easier to deal with tragedy and horror if there is an attendant note of the absurd – like everything else about *her*, what seems meaningful one moment will seem irrelevant the next. Or maybe that's only the way it appears to me. Maybe I'm asking too much of the clues.

Excerpt from *Pretoria*, pp. 164–165; Ballantine Books, 1979:

Edward Horton smiled and tapped the ash from his cigar into the large glass ashtray on the table. "I don't like the sea," he said and nodded at the window. "Frankly, I can't even stand the sound of it. Gives me nightmares."

I listened to the breakers, not taking my eyes off the fat man and the thick grey curlicues of smoke arranging and rearranging themselves around his face. I'd always found the sound of waves to have a welcomed tranquilising effect upon my nerves and wondered which one of Horton's innumerable secrets was responsible for his loathing of the sea. I knew he'd done a stint in the Navy during Korea, but I was also pretty sure he'd never seen combat.

"How'd you sleep last night?" I asked, and he shook his head.

"For shit," he replied and sucked on his cigar.

"Then maybe you should think about getting a room farther inland."

Horton coughed and jabbed a pudgy finger at the window of the bungalow. "Don't think I wouldn't, if the choice were mine to make. But she wants me *here*. She wants me sitting right here, waiting on her, night and day. She knows I hate the ocean."

"What the hell," I said, reaching for my hat, tired of his company and the stink of his smoldering Macanudo. "You know where to reach me, if you change your mind. Don't let the bad dreams get you down. They ain't nothing but that, bad dreams."

"That's not enough?" he asked, and I could tell from his expression that Horton wished I'd stay a little longer, but I knew he'd never admit it. "Last night, goddamn people marching into the sea, marching over the sand in rows like the goddamn infantry. Must of been a million of them. What you think a dream like that means, anyway?"

"Horton, a dream like that don't mean jack shit," I replied. "Except maybe you need to lay off the spicy food before bedtime."

"You're always gonna be an asshole," he said, and I was forced to agree. He puffed his cigar, and I left the bungalow and stepped out into the salty Santa Barbara night.

Excerpt from *What the Cat Dragged In*, p. 231; Ballantine Books, 1980:

Vicky had never told anyone about the dreams, just like she'd never told anyone about Mr. Barker or the yellow Corvette. The dreams were her secret, whether she wanted them or not. Sometimes they seemed almost wicked, shameful, sinful, like something she'd done that was against God, or at least against the law. She'd almost told Mr. Barker once, a year or so before she left Los Angeles. She'd gone so far as to broach the subject of mermaids, and then he'd snorted and laughed, so she'd thought better of it.

"You got some strange notions in that head of yours," he'd said. "Someday, you're gonna have to grow out of crap like that, if you want people round here to start taking you seriously."

So she kept it all to herself. Whatever the dreams meant or didn't mean, it wasn't anything she would ever be able to explain or confess. Sometimes, nights when she couldn't sleep, she lay in bed staring at the ceiling, thinking about the ruined castles beneath the waves and beautiful, drowned girls with seaweed tangled in their hair.

Excerpt from *The Last Loan Shark of Bodega Bay*, pp. 57–59; Bantam Books, 1982:

"This was way the hell back in the fifties," Foster said and lit another cigarette. His hands were shaking and he kept looking over his shoulder. "Fifty-eight, right, or maybe early fifty-nine. I know Eisenhower was still president, though I ain't precisely sure of the year. But I was still stuck in Honolulu, right, still hauling lousy tourists around the islands in the *Saint Chris* so they could fish and snap pictures of goddamn Kilauea and what have you. The boat was on its last leg, but she'd still get you where you were goin', if you knew how to slap her around."

"What's this got to do with Winkie Anderson and the girl?" I asked, making no effort to hide my impatience.

"Jesus, Frank, I'm getting to it. You want to hear this thing or not? I swear, you come around here asking the big questions, expecting the what's-what, you can at least keep your trap shut and listen."

"I don't have all night, that's all."

"Yeah, well, who the hell does, why don't you tell me that? Anyway, like I was saying, back about fifty-nine, and we was out somewhere off the north shore of Molokai. Old Coop was fishing the thousand fathom line, and Jerry – you remember Jerry O'Neil, right?"

"No," I said, eyeing the clock above the bar.

"Well, whatever. Jerry O'Neil was mouthing off about a twelve-hundred-pounder, this big-ass marlin some Mexican businessman from Tijuana had up and hooked just a few weeks before. Fish even made the damn papers, right. Anyway, Jerry said the Mexican was bad news and we should keep a sharp eye out for him. Said he was a regular Jonah."

"But you just said he caught a twelve-hundred-pound marlin."

"Yeah, sure. He could haul in the fish, this chunt son of a bitch, but he was into some sort of Spanish voodoo shit and had these gold coins he'd toss over the side of the boat every five or ten minutes. Like goddamn clockwork, he'd check his watch and toss out a coin. Gold doubloons or some shit, I don't know what they were. It was driving Coop crazy, 'cause it wasn't enough the Mexican had to do this thing with the coins, he was mumbling some sort of shit non-stop. Coop kept telling him to shut the hell up, people was trying to fish, but this guy, he just keeps mumbling and tossing coins and pulling in the fish. I finally got a look at one of those doubloons, and it had something stamped on one side looked like a damn octopus, and on the other side was this star like a pentagram. You know, those things witches and warlocks use."

"Foster, this is crazy bullshit. I have to be in San Francisco at seven-thirty in the morning." I waved to the bartender and put two crumpled fives and a one on the bar in front of me.

"You ever head of the Momma Hydra, Frank? That's who this chunt said he was praying to."

"Call me when you run out of bullshit," I said. "And I don't have to tell you, Detective Burke won't be half as understanding as I am."

"Jesus, Frank. Hold up a goddamn second. It's just the way I tell stories, right. You know that. I start at the beginning. I don't leave stuff out."

These are only a few examples of what anyone will find, if he or she should take the time to look. There are many more, I assure you. The pages of my copies of Theo Angevine's novels are scarred throughout with yellow highlighter.

And everything leaves more questions than answers.

You make of it what you will. Or you don't. I suppose that a Freudian might have a proper field day with this stuff. Whatever I knew about Freud I forgot before I was even out of college. It would be comforting, I suppose, if I could dismiss Jacova's fate as the end result of some overwhelming Oedipal hysteria, the ocean cast here as that Great Ur-Mother savior-being who finally opens up to offer release and forgiveness in death and dissolution.

V

I begin to walk down some particular, perhaps promising, avenue and then, inevitably, I turn and run, tail tucked firmly between my legs. My memories. The MBARI video. Jacova and her father's whodunits. I scratch the surface and then pull my hand back to be sure that I haven't lost a fucking finger. I mix metaphors the way I've been mixing tequila and scotch.

If, as William Burroughs wrote, "Language is a virus from outer space," then what the holy hell were you supposed to be, Jacova?

An epidemic of the collective unconscious. The black plague of belief. A vaccine for cultural amnesia, she might have said. And so we're right back to Velikovsky, who wrote "Human beings, rising from some catastrophe, bereft of memory of what had happened, regarded themselves as created from the dust of the earth. All knowledge about the ancestors, who they were and in what inter-stellar space they lived, was wiped away from the memory of the few survivors."

I'm drunk, and I'm not making any sense at all. Or merely much too little sense to matter. Anyway, you'll want to pay attention to this part. It's sort of like the ghost story within the ghost story within the ghost story, the hard nugget at the unreachable heart of my heart's infinitely regressing babooshka, matryoshka, matrioska, matreshka, babushka. It might even be the final straw that breaks the camel of my mind.

Remember, I am wasted, and so that last inexcusable paragraph may be forgiven. Or it may not.

"When I become death, death is the seed from which I grow." Burroughs said that, too. Jacova, you will be an orchard. You will be a swaying kelp forest. There's a log in the hole in the bottom of the sea with your name on it.

Yesterday afternoon, puking sick of looking at these four dingy fucking walls, I drove down to Monterey, to the warehouse on Pierce Street. The last time I was there, the cops still hadn't taken down all the yellow CRIME SCENE–DO NOT CROSS tape. Now there's only a great big for-sale sign and an even bigger no-trespassing sign. I wrote the name and number of the realty company on the back of a book of matches. I want to ask them what they'll be telling pro-spective buyers about the building's history. Word is the whole block is due to be rezoned next year and soon those empty buildings will be converted to lofts and condos. Gentrification abhors a void.

I parked in an empty lot down the street from the warehouse, hoping that no one happening by would notice me, hoping, in particular, that any passing police would not notice me. I walked quickly, without running, because running is suspicious and inevi-tably draws the attention of those who *watch* for suspicious things. I was not so drunk as I might have been, not even so drunk as I *should* have been, and I tried to keep my mind occupied by noting the less significant details of the street, the sky, the weather. The litter caught in the weeds and gravel – cigarette butts, plastic soft-drink bottles (I recall Pepsi, Coke, and Mountain Dew), paper bags and cups from fast-food restaurants (McDonalds, Del Taco, KFC), broken glass, unrecognizable bits of metal, a rusted Oregon license plate. The sky was painfully blue, the blue of nausea, with only very high cirrus clouds to spoil that suffocating pastel heaven. There were no other cars parked along the street, and no living things that I noticed. There were a couple of garbage dumpsters, a stop sign, and a great pile of cardboard boxes that had been soaked by rain enough times it was difficult to tell exactly where one ended and another began. There was a hubcap.

When I finally reached the warehouse – the warehouse become a temple to half-remembered gods become a crime scene, now on its way to becoming something else – I ducked down the narrow alley that separates it from the abandoned Monterey Peninsula Shipping and Storage Building (established 1924). There'd been a door around that way with an unreliable lock. If I was lucky, I thought, no one would have noticed, or if they had noticed, wouldn't have bothered fixing it. My heart was racing and I was dizzy (I tried hard to blame that on the sickening color of the sky) and there was a metallic taste in the back of my mouth, like a freshly filled tooth.

It was colder in the alley than it had been out on Pierce, the sun having already dropped low enough in the west that the alley must have been in shadow for some time. Perhaps it is always in shadow and never truly warm there. I found the side door exactly as I'd hoped to find it, and three or four minutes of jiggling about with the wobbly brass knob was enough to coax it open. Inside, the warehouse was dark and even colder than the alley, and the air stank of mould and dust, bad memories and vacancy. I stood in the doorway a moment or two, thinking of hungry rats and drunken bums, delirious crack addicts wielding lead pipes, the webs of poisonous spiders. Then I took a deep breath and stepped across the threshold, out of the shadows and into a more decided blackness, a more definitive chill, and all those mundane threats dissolved. Everything slipped from my mind except Jacova Angevine, and her followers (if that's what you'd call them) dressed all in white, and the thing I'd seen on the altar the one time I'd come here when this had been a temple of the Open Door of Night.

I asked her about that thing once, a few weeks before the end, the last night that we spent together. I asked where it had come from, who had made it, and she lay very still for a while, listening to the surf or only trying to decide which answer would satisfy me. In the moonlight through the hotel window, I thought she might have been smiling, but I wasn't sure.

"It's very old," she said, eventually. By then I'd almost drifted off to sleep and had to shake myself awake again. "No one alive remembers who *made* it," Jacova continued. "But I don't think that matters, only that it was made."

"It's fucking hideous," I mumbled sleepily. "You know that, don't you?"

"Yeah, but so is the Crucifixion. So are bleeding statues of the Virgin Mary and images of Kali. So are the animal-headed gods of the Egyptians."

"Yeah, well, I don't bow down to any of them, either," I replied, or something to that effect.

"The divine is always abominable," she whispered and rolled over, turning her back to me.

Just a moment ago I was in the warehouse on Pierce Street, wasn't I? And now I'm in bed with the Prophet from Salinas. But I will not despair, for there is no need here to stay focused, to adhere to some restrictive illusion of the linear narrative. It's coming. It's been coming all along. As Job Foster said in Chapter Four of *The Last Loan Shark of Bodega Bay*, "It's just the way I tell stories, right. You know that. I start at the beginning. I don't leave stuff out."

That's horseshit, of course. I suspect luckless Job Foster knew it was horseshit, and I suspect that I know it's horseshit, too. It is not the task of the writer to "tell all," or even to decide what to leave in, but to decide what to leave *out*. Whatever remains, that meager sum of this profane division, that's the bastard chimera we call a "story." I am not building, but cutting away. And all stories, whether advertised as truth or admitted falsehoods, are fictions, cleft from any objective facts by the aforementioned action of cutting away. A pound of flesh. A pile of sawdust. Discarded chips of Carrara marble. And what's left over.

A damned man in an empty warehouse.

I left the door standing open, because I hadn't the nerve to shut myself up in that place. And I'd already taken a few steps inside, my shoes crunching loudly on shards of glass from a broken window, grinding glass to dust, when I remembered the Maglite hidden inside my jacket. But the glare of the flashlight did nothing much to make the darkness any less stifling, nothing much at all but remind me of the blinding white beam of *Tiburon II*'s big HMI rig, shining out across the silt at the bottom of the canyon. *Now*, I thought, *at least I can see anything, if there's anything to see*, and immediately some other, less familiar thought-voice demanded to know why the hell I'd want to. The door had opened into a narrow corridor, mint-green concrete walls and a low concrete ceiling, and I followed it a short distance to its end – no more than thirty feet, thirty feet at the most – past empty rooms that might once have been offices, to an unlocked steel door marked in faded orange letters, EMPLOYEES ONLY.

"It's an empty warehouse," I whispered, breathing the words aloud. "That's all, an empty warehouse." I knew it wasn't the truth, not anymore, not by a long sight, but I thought that maybe a lie could be more comforting than the comfortless illumination of the Maglite in my hand. Joseph Campbell wrote, "Draw a circle around a stone and the stone will become an incarnation of mystery." Something like that. Or it was someone else said it and I'm misremembering. The point is, I knew that Jacova had drawn a circle around that place, just as she'd drawn a circle about herself, just as her father had somehow drawn a circle about her—

Just as she'd drawn a circle around me.

The door wasn't locked, and beyond it lay the vast, deserted belly of the building, a flat plain of cement marked off with steel support beams. There was a little sunlight coming in through the many small windows along the east and west walls, though not as much as I'd expected, and it seemed weakened, diluted by the musty air. I played the Maglite back and forth across the floor at my feet and saw that someone had painted over all the elaborate, colorful designs put there by the Open Door of Night. A thick grey latex wash to cover the intricate interweave of lines, the lines that she believed would form a bridge, a *conduit* – that was the word that she'd used. Everyone's seen photographs of that floor, although I've yet to see any that do it justice. A *yantra*. A labyrinth. A writhing, tangled mass of sea creatures straining for a distant black sun. Hindi and Mayan and Chinook symbols. The precise contour lines of a topographic map of Monterey Canyon. Each of these things and *all* of these things, simultaneously. I've heard that there's an anthropologist at Berkeley who's writing a book about that floor. Perhaps she will publish photographs that manage to communicate its awful magnificence. Perhaps it would be better if she doesn't.

Perhaps someone should put a bullet through her head.

People said the same thing about Jacova Angevine. But assassination is almost always unthinkable to moral, thinking men until *after* a holocaust has come and gone.

I left that door open, as well, and walked slowly towards the center of the empty warehouse, towards the place where the altar had been, the spot where that divine abomination of Jacova's had rested on folds of velvet the colour of a massacre. I held the Maglite gripped so tightly that the fingers of my right hand had begun to go numb.

Behind me, there was a scuffling, gritty sort of noise that might have been footsteps, and I spun about, tangling my feet and almost falling on my ass, almost dropping the flashlight. The child was standing maybe ten or fifteen feet away from me, and I could see that the door leading back to the alley had been closed. She couldn't have been more than nine or ten years old, dressed in ragged jeans and a T-shirt smeared with mud, or what looked like mud in the half light of the warehouse. Her short hair might have been blonde, or light brown, it was hard to tell. Most of her face was lost in the shadows.

"You're too late," she said.

"Jesus *Christ*, kid, you almost scared the holy shit out of me."

"You're too late," she said again.

"Too late for what? Did you follow me in here?"

"The gates are shut now. They won't open again, for you or anyone else."

I looked past her at the door I'd left open, and she looked back that way, too.

"Did you close that door?" I asked her. "Did it ever occur to you that I might have left it open for a reason?"

"I waited as long I dared," she replied, as though that answered my question, and turned to face me again.

I took one step towards her, then, or maybe two, and stopped. And at that moment, I experienced the sensation or sensations that mystery and horror writers, from Poe on down to Theo Angevine, have labored to convey – the almost painful prickling as the hairs on the back of my neck and along my arms and legs stood erect, the cold knot in the pit of my stomach, the goose across my grave, a loosening in my bowels and bladder, the tightening of my scrotum. My blood ran cold. Drag out all the fucking clichés and there's still nothing that comes within a mile of what I felt standing there, looking down at that girl, her looking up at me, the feeble light from the windows glinting off her eyes.

Looking into her face, I felt *dread* as I'd never felt it before. Not in war zones with air-raid sirens blaring, not during interviews conducted with the muzzle of a pistol pressed to my temple or the small of my back. Not waiting for the results of a biopsy after the discovery of a peculiar mole. Not even the day she led them into the sea and I sat watching it all on fucking CNN from a bar in Brooklyn.

And suddenly I knew that the girl hadn't followed me in from the alley, or closed the door, that she'd been here all along. I also knew that a hundred coats of paint wouldn't be enough to undo Jacova's labyrinth.

"You shouldn't be here," the girl said, her minotaur's voice lost and faraway and regretful.

"Then where *should* I be?" I asked, and my breath fogged in air gone as frigid as the dead of winter, or the bottom of the sea.

"All the answers were here," she replied. "Everything that you're asking yourself, the things that keep you awake, that are driving you insane. All the questions you're putting into that computer of yours. I offered all of it to you."

And now there was a sound like water breaking against stone, and something heavy and soft and wet, dragging itself across the concrete floor, and I thought of the thing from the altar, Jacova's Mother Hydra, that corrupt and bloated Madonna of the abyss, its tentacles and anemone tendrils and black, bulging squid eyes, the tubeworm proboscis snaking from one of the holes where its face should have been. *Mighty, undying daughter of Typhaôn and serpentine Ecidna – Υδρα Λερναια, Urda Lernaia, gluttonous whore of all the lightless worlds, bitch bride and concubine of Father Dagon, Father Kraken —*

I smelled rot and mud, saltwater and dying fish.

"You have to go now," the child said urgently, and she held out a hand as though she meant to show me the way. Even in the gloom, I could see the barnacles and sea lice nestled in the raw flesh of her palm. "You are a splinter in my soul, always. And she would drag you down to finish my own darkness."

And then the girl was gone. She did not vanish, she was simply not *there* anymore. And those other sounds and odors had gone with her. There was nothing left behind but the silence and stink of any abandoned building, and the wind brushing against the windows and around the corners of the warehouse, and the traffic along roads in the world waiting somewhere beyond those walls.

VI

I know *exactly* how all this shit sounds. Don't think that I don't. It's just that I've finally ceased to care.

VII

Yesterday, two days after my trip to the warehouse, I watched the MBARI tape again. This time, when it reached the twelve-second gap, when I'd counted down to eleven, I continued on to twelve, and I didn't switch the television off, and I didn't look away. Surely, I've come too far to allow myself that luxury. I've seen so goddamn much – I've seen so much that there's no reasonable excuse for looking away, because there can't be anything left that's more terrible than what has come before.

And, besides, it was nothing that I hadn't seen already.

Orpheus' mistake wasn't that he turned and looked back towards Eurydice and Hell, but that he ever thought he could *escape*. Same with Lot's wife. Averting our eyes does not change the fact that we are marked.

After the static, the picture comes back and at first it's just those boulders, same as before, those boulders that ought to be covered with silt and living things – the remains of living things, at least – but aren't. Those strange, clean boulders. And the lines and angles carved deeply into them that cannot be the result of any natural geological or biological process, the lines and angles that can be nothing but what Jacova said they were. I think of fragments of the Parthenon, or some other shattered Greek or Roman temple, the chiseled ornament of an entablature or pediment. I'm seeing something that was *done*, something that was consciously fashioned, not something that simply happened. The *Tiburon II* moves forward very slowly, because the blow before the gap has taken out a couple of the port thrusters. It creeps forward tentatively, floating a few feet above the seafloor, and now the ROV's lights have begun to dim and flicker.

After the gap, I know that there's only 52.2 seconds of video remaining before the starboard camera shuts down for good. Less than a minute, and I sit there on the floor of my hotel room, counting – one-one thousand, two-two thousand – and I don't take my eyes off the screen.

The MBARI robotics tech is dead, the nervous man who sold me – and whoever else was buying – his black-market dub of the videotape. The story made the Channel 46 evening news last night and was second page in the *Monterey Herald* this morning. The coroner's office is calling it a suicide. I don't know what else they would call it. He was found hanging from the lowest limb of a sycamore tree, not far from the Moss Landing docks, both his wrists slashed nearly to the bone. He was wearing a necklace of *Loligo* squid strung on baling wire. A family member has told the press that he had a history of depression.

Twenty-three seconds to go.

Almost two miles down, *Tiburon II* is listing badly to starboard, and then the ROV bumps against one of the boulders and the lights stop flickering and seem to grow a little brighter. The vehicle appears to pause, as though considering its next move. The day he sold me the tape, the MBARI tech said that a part of the toolsled had wedged itself into the rubble. He told me it took the crew of the *R/V Western Flyer* more than two hours to maneuver the sub free. Two hours of total darkness at the bottom of the canyon, after the lights and the cameras died.

Eighteen seconds.

Sixteen.

This time it'll be different, I think, like a child trying to wish away a beating. *This time, I'll see the trick of it, the secret interplay of light and shadow, the hows and whys of a simple optical illusion—*

Twelve.

Ten.

And the first time, I thought that I was only seeing something carved into the stone or part of a broken sculpture. The gentle curve of a hip, the tapering line of a leg, the twin swellings of small breasts. A nipple the colour of granite.

Eight.

But there's her face – and there's no denying that it's *her* face – Jacova Angevine, her face at the bottom the sea, turned up towards the surface, towards the sky and Heaven beyond the weight of all that black, black water.

Four.

I bite my lip so hard that I taste blood. It doesn't taste so different from the ocean.

Two.

She opens her eyes, and they are *not* her eyes, but the eyes of some marine creature adapted to that perpetual night. The soulless eyes of an anglerfish or gulper eel, eyes like matching pools of ink, and something darts from her parted lips—

And then there's only static, and I sit staring into the salt-and-pepper roar.

All the answers were here. Everything that you're asking yourself . . . I offered all of it to you.

Later – an hour or only five minutes – I pressed EJECT and the cassette slid obediently from the VCR. I read the label, aloud, in case I'd read it wrong every single time before, in case the timestamp on the video might have been mistaken. But it was the same as always, the day before Jacova waited on the beach at Moss Landing for the supplicants of the Open Door of Night. The day before she led them into the sea. The day before she drowned.

VIII

I close my eyes.

And she's here again, as though she never left.

She whispers something dirty in my ear, and her breath smells like sage and toothpaste.

The protestors are demanding that the Monterey Bay Aquarium Research Institute (MBARI) end its ongoing exploration of the submarine canyon immediately. The twenty-five mile long canyon, they claim, is a sacred site that is being desecrated by scientists. Jacova Angevine, former Berkeley professor and leader of the controversial Open Door of Night cult, compares the launching of the new submersible Tiburon II *to the ransacking of the Egyptian pyramids by grave robbers. (San Francisco Chronicle)*

I tell her that I have to go to New York, that I have to take this assignment, and she replies that maybe it's for the best. I don't ask her what she means; I can't imagine that it's important.

And she kisses me.

Later, when we're done and I'm too exhausted to sleep, I lie awake, listening to the sea and the small, anxious sounds she makes in her dreams.

The bodies of fifty-three men and women, all of whom may have been part of a religious group known as the Open Door of Night, have been recovered following Wednesday's drownings near Moss Landing, CA. Deputies have described the deaths as a mass suicide. The victims were all reported to be between twenty-two and thirty-six years old. Authorities fear that at least two dozen more may have died in the bizarre episode and recovery efforts continue along the coast of Monterey County. (CNN.com)

I close my eyes, and I'm in the old warehouse on Pierce Street again; Jacova's voice thunders from the PA speakers mounted high on the walls around the cavernous room. I'm standing in the shadows all the way at the back, apart from the true believers, apart from the other reporters and photographers and camera men who have been invited here. Jacova leans into the microphone, angry and ecstatic and beautiful – *terrible*, I think – and that hideous carving is squatting there on its altar beside her. There are candles and smoldering incense and bouquets of dried seaweed, conch shells and dead fish, carefully arranged about the base of the statue.

"We can't remember where it began," she says, "where *we* began," and they all seem to lean into her words like small boats pushing against a violent wind. "We can't remember, of course we can't remember, and they don't want us to even *try*. They're afraid, and in their fear they cling desperately to the darkness of their ignorance. They would have us do the same, and then we would never recall the garden nor the gate, would never look upon the faces of the great fathers and mothers who have returned to the deep."

None of it seems the least bit real, not the ridiculous things that she's saying, or all the people dressed in white, or the television crews. This scene is not even as substantial as a nightmare. It's very hot in the warehouse, and I feel dizzy and sick and wonder if I can reach an exit before I vomit.

I close my eyes and I'm sitting in a bar in Brooklyn, watching them wade into the sea, and I'm thinking, *Some son of a bitch is standing right there taping this and no one's trying to stop them, no one's lifting a goddamn finger.*

I blink, and I'm sitting in an office in Manhattan, and the people who write my checks are asking me questions I can't answer.

"Good god, you were fucking the woman, for Christ's sake, and you're sitting there telling me you had no *idea* whatsoever that she was planning this?"

"Come on. You had to have known *something.*"

"They all worshipped some sort of prehistoric fish god, that's what I heard. No one's going to buy that you didn't see this coming—"

"People have a right to know. You still believe that, don't you?"

Answers are scarce in the mass suicide of a California cult, but investigators are finding clues to the deaths by logging onto the Internet and Web sites run by the cult's members. What they're finding is a dark and confusing side of the Internet, a place where bizarre ideas and beliefs are exchanged and gain currency. Police said they have gathered a considerable amount of information on the background of the group, known as the Open Door of Night, but that it may be many weeks before the true nature of the group is finally understood. (CNN.com)

And my clumsy hands move uncertainly across her bare shoulders, my fingertips brushing the chaos of scar tissue there, and she smiles for me.

On my knees in an alley, my head spinning, and the night air stinks of puke and saltwater.

"Okay, so I first heard about this from a woman I interviewed who knew the family," the man in the Radiohead T-shirt says. We're sitting on the patio of a bar in Pacific Grove, and the sun is hot and glimmers white off the bay. His name isn't important, and neither is the name of the bar. He's a student from LA, writing a book about the Open Door of Night, and he got my e-mail address from someone in New York. He has bad teeth and smiles too much.

"This happened back in '76, the year before Jacova's mother died. Her father, he'd take them down to the beach at Moss Landing two or three times every summer. He got a lot of his writing done out there. Anyway, apparently the kid was a great swimmer, like a duck to water, but her mother never let her to go very far out at that beach because there are these bad rip currents. Lots of people drown out there, surfers and shit."

He pauses and takes a couple of swallow of beer, then wipes the sweat from his forehead.

"One day, her mother's not watching and Jacova swims too far out and gets pulled down. By the time the lifeguards get her back to shore, she's stopped breathing. The kid's turning blue, but they keep up the mouth-to-mouth and CPR and she finally comes around. They get Jacova to the hospital up in Watsonville and the doctors say she's fine, but they keep her for a few days anyhow, just for observation."

"She drowned," I say, staring at my own beer. I haven't taken a single sip. Beads of condensation cling to the bottle and sparkle like diamonds.

"Technically, yeah. She wasn't breathing. Her heart had stopped. But *that's* not the fucked-up part. While she's in Watsonville, she keeps telling her mother some crazy story about mermaids and sea monsters and demons, about these things trying to drag her down to the bottom of the sea and drown her and how it wasn't an undertow at all. She's terrified, convinced that they're still after her, these monsters. Her mother wants to call in a shrink, but her father says no, fuck that, the kid's just had a bad shock, she'll be fine. Then, the second night she's in the hospital, these two nurses turn up dead. A janitor found them in a closet just down the hall from Jacova's room. And here's the thing you're not gonna believe, but I've seen the death certificates and the autopsy reports and I swear to you this is the God's honest truth."

Whatever's coming next, I don't want to hear it. I know that I don't *need* to hear it. I turn my head and watch a sailboat out on the bay, bobbing about like a toy.

"They'd drowned, both of them. Their lungs were full of saltwater. Five miles from the goddamn ocean, but these two women drowned right there in a *broom closet*."

"And you're going to put this in your book?" I ask him, not taking my eyes of the bay and the little boat.

"Hell yeah," he replies. "I am. It fucking happened, man, just like I said, and I can prove it."

I close my eyes, shutting out the dazzling, bright day, and wish I'd never agreed to meet with him.

I close my eyes.

"Down there," Jacova whispers, "you will know nothing but peace, in her mansions, in the endless night of her coils."

We would be warm below the storm

In our little hideaway beneath the waves

I close my eyes. Oh, God, I've closed my eyes.

She wraps her strong, suntanned arms tightly around me and takes me down, down, down, like the lifeless body of a child caught in an undertow. And I'd go with her, like a flash I'd go, if this were anything more than a dream, anything more than an infidel's sour regret, anything more than eleven thousand words cast like a handful of sand across the face of the ocean. I would go with her, because, like a stone that has become an incarnation of mystery, she has drawn a circle around me.

DAVID MORRELL

They

DAVID MORRELL IS THE AUTHOR of *First Blood*, the award-winning novel in which Rambo was created. He holds a Ph.D in American literature from the Pennsylvania State University and was a professor in the English department at the University of Iowa until he gave up his tenure to devote himself to a full-time writing career.

"The mild-mannered professor with the bloody-minded visions," as one reviewer called him, Morrell has written numerous best-selling thrillers that include *The Brotherhood of the Rose* (the basis for a highly rated NBC-TV mini-series), *The Fifth Profession* and *Extreme Denial* (set in Santa Fe, New Mexico, where he lives).

His short stories have appeared in many of the major horror and fantasy anthologies and periodicals, including the *Whispers, Shadows, Night Visions* and *Masters of Darkness* series, as well as *The Twilight Zone Magazine, The Dodd Mead Gallery of Horror, Psycho Paths, Prime Evil, Dark at Heart, MetaHorror, Revelations, 999: New Stories of Horror and Suspense* and *Redshift*.

Two of his novellas received Bram Stoker Awards from the Horror Writers Association, while his non-supernatural horror novel *The Totem*, which reinvents the werewolf myth, was included in *Horror: 100 Best Books*. His Stoker Award-winning novel *Creepers* has been called "genre defining" because of its unusual combination of thriller and horror elements. *Scavenger* is his latest book.

"A lot of my fiction deals with struggling to keep one's identity," observes Morrell, "about the fear of walking down the wrong corridor and entering the wrong room, only to discover a dangerously different version of reality. Often, these themes are dramatised against large landscapes.

"Years ago, reading a history book about the settlement of the American West, I learned that in spring, as the ground thawed, snakes sometimes fell from the sod roofs of farmhouses, landing inside, startling the inhabitants. That image stayed with me, insisting to be used in a story. The original text didn't specify what kind of snakes, but I knew they needed to be rattlesnakes, and I knew they'd appear at the beginning of the story, the prelude to something worse that the story's pioneer family would encounter. But what would that further horror be?

"As the decades passed, the answer kept eluding me until a recent December when a snow storm hit the New Mexico valley where I live. Normally, I see mountains in every direction. But on that blizzard-swept evening, visibility was reduced to almost nothing. With a fireplace crackling next to me, I peered out my living-room window. As dusk made the snowfall seem thicker, I suddenly saw quick movement outside, a fleeting shadow, then another and another. At once, the movement was gone.

"Perhaps I'd only imagined it. Even so, the experience unnerved me, and at that instant, a complex chain of association inspired me to imagine the further horror that my pioneer family – and especially a brave little girl – would face."

PAPA WAS CLEVER. In the spring, when the sod roof thawed and the snakes fell through, he hooked blankets to the ceiling and caught them. Usually, they were bull snakes, but sometimes, they were rattlers. They sounded like somebody shaking a package of seeds. Papa said they were still sleepy from hibernating, which was why he wasn't worried about going near them. He made a sack out of each blanket and carried their squirming weight to the far edge of the pasture, where he dumped them into our creek. The snowmelt from the mountains made the water high and swift and took them away. Just to be safe, papa warned us never to go downstream past where he dumped them. Mama wanted to kill them, but papa said they were too sleepy to mean us harm and we shouldn't kill what we didn't need to.

The snakes dropped from the ceiling because papa dug the back of the cabin into a slope. He piled the dirt over the sod on the roof beams. It kept us cool in the summer and warm in the winter, and shielded us from the wind that shrieked through the valley during bad weather. In time, grass grew up there, but while the dirt was soft, snakes burrowed into it. We always heard them moving before they fell, so we had warning, and it wasn't many, and it was only for a few weeks in the spring.

Papa was so clever, he made the best soap in the valley. Everybody knew how to make the soft kind. Pour water over wood ashes to dissolve the potash in them. Strain the water through a layer of straw to get rid of dirt. Add the potash water to boiling animal fat. Let the two of them cool and use the scummy stuff at the top. That was the soap. But we had an outcrop of salt on our property, and papa experimented by adding salt to the boiling water and fat. When the mixture cooled, it got hard. Papa also put sand in his soap, and everybody thought that was his secret, but they could never get their soap hard because his real secret was the salt, and he made us promise not to tell.

We had ten chickens, a horse, a cow, a sheep, a dog, and a cat. The dog was a collie. It and the cat showed up a day apart. We never knew where they came from. We planted lettuce, peas, carrots, beans, potatoes, tomatoes, corn, and squash. We had to build a solid fence around the garden to keep rabbits away. But birds kept trying to eat the seed, so papa traded his hard soap for sheets and tented them over the ground. The birds got discouraged. The rabbits that kept trying, papa shot them. He said they needed to be killed to save the garden and besides they made a good stew.

We were never hungry. Papa dug a root cellar under the cabin. It kept the carrots, potatoes, and squash through the winter. Mama made preserves of the peas and beans, using wax to seal the lids the way papa showed her. We even had an old apple tree that was there when we came, and mama made the best pies, and we stored the apples, too. All of us worked. Papa showed us what to do.

Hot summer nights, while he and mama taught us how to read from the Bible, we sometimes heard them howling in the hills. *Yip, yip, yip, yip.* Baying at the moon. God's dogs, papa said. That's what the Indians call them. Why? Judith asked. Because they're practically invisible, papa said. Only God can see them.

What do they look like? Daniel asked. Silly, I said. If only God can see them, how can anybody know what they look like? Well, a couple of times people have seen them, papa said. They're brown. They've got pointy ears and black tips on their tails.

How big are they? Judith asked, snuggling in his arms. A little bigger than Chester, papa said. Chester was our dog. They weigh about thirty pounds, papa said. They look a little like a dog, but you can tell them from a dog because they run with their tails down while a dog runs with its tail *up*.

Sure sounds like *somebody* got a good look at one, I said. Papa nodded. I saw one a long time ago, he said. Before I met your mother. I was alone at a campfire. It came out of the darkness and stared from the edge of the light. It must have smelled the rabbit I was cooking. After a while, it turned away. Just before it disappeared into the darkness, it looked over its shoulder, as if it blamed me for something.

Were you scared? Daniel asked. Time for you to go to sleep, mama said. She gave papa a look. No, papa said, I wasn't scared.

The harvest moon was full. They howled in the hills for several hours.

The next year, the rains held off. The other farmers lost their wells and had to move on. But the drainage from the snow in the mountains kept water in our creek, enough for the garden. The aspens on the slopes had it hard, though. They got so dry, lightning sparked fires. At night, parts of the hills shimmered. Smoke drifted into the valley. Judith had trouble breathing.

At last, we had a storm. God's mercy, mama said, watching the rain chase the smoke and put out the flames in the hills. The morning after the first hard freeze, Daniel ran into the cabin. His face was white. Papa, come quick, he said.

Our sheep lay in the middle of the pasture. Its neck was torn. Its stomach was chewed. Blood and chunks of wool lay everywhere. The other animals shivered, keeping a distance.

I saw the veins in papa's neck pulse as he stared toward the hills. At night, we'll fence the cow and the horse next to the cabin, he said. There's meat on the carcass. Ruth, he told me, get the axe and the knife. Daniel and I need to butcher the sheep. Get the shears, he told mama. We'll take the wool that's left.

The morning after that, papa made us stay inside while he went outside to check the rest of the animals. He was gone quite awhile. Mama kept walking to the only window we had. I heard papa digging. When he came back, his face looked tight. The chickens, he said. They're all killed. He turned toward mama. Heads and feathers. Nothing else left. Not enough meat for you even to make soup from. I buried it all. What about eggs? mama asked. No, he said.

That night, papa loaded his rifle, put on his coat, and went out to the shed beside where the horse and cow were fenced. *Yip, yip, yip, yip.* I stared at the ceiling and listened to them howl. But they were far away, their echo shifting from one part of the valley to another. When papa came inside the next morning, the breeze was cold. Snow dusted the ground. His eyes looked strained, but he sounded relieved. Seems they moved on, he said, putting his rifle on a shelf. We'll trade soap for more chickens, mama told him, and gave him a cup of coffee.

By noon, it was colder. Clouds capped the mountains. Looks like an early winter, papa said. Thank God, mama said. As dry as it's been, the mountains need moisture. The creek needs snowmelt, she said. At supper, we heard wood snapping outside, the horse whinnying. Papa dropped his fork and grabbed his rifle, which he hadn't unloaded. Mama handed him a lantern. From the window, we watched his light jerk this way and that as papa rushed toward the corral next to the shed.

He kept running. He passed the fence. The light from the lantern got smaller until I couldn't see it in the darkness. I listened to the wind. I flinched when I heard a shot. Then all I heard was the wind again. Snow was in the air. Mama whispered something as she stared through the window toward the night. I think she said, Please God. We waited. Ruth, get Daniel his coat and a lantern, mama told me. He needs to go out and see if papa wants help.

But Daniel didn't need to. Look, Judith said, standing on tiptoes, pointing. Through the window, we saw a speck of light. It got bigger, moving with the wind and papa's arm. Cold filled the room as he came in. Judith coughed. Papa locked the door and set down the lantern. Something scared the horse so bad it broke through the fence and tried to run off, he said. Tried? Daniel asked. Papa looked toward the window. Whatever scared the horse took it down. Didn't get much to eat, though. When I shot, they ran into the dark.

They? I asked. No need to alarm the children, mama told him. But everybody has to know so you can all be careful, papa said. We're already careful, mama said. Need to be even more, papa said. *They*, papa? I asked. I think I saw five, he said. Judith coughed. Five of *what*? Daniel asked. God's dogs? Did they run with their tails down? Papa nodded again. But now they're the *Devil's* dogs, he said. I think I hit one. I found a trail of blood, but maybe it was the horse's blood dripping from their mouths.

Nobody moved. Judith, get the axe and the knife, papa told me. Daniel and I need to butcher the horse before they come back. Butcher? Judith said. We're going to eat *horse* meat? Daniel asked. It's meat, papa said. When winter comes this early, we need all the food we can find.

With the dark around us, mama and I shivered and held lanterns that swung in the wind while papa and Daniel cut up the horse. Papa told us to keep staring toward the night, to watch in case *they* came back. He kept his rifle protected in a blanket beside him. Only Judith didn't work. She shivered too much to hold a lantern in the blowing snow.

Look at the paw prints in the snow, Daniel said. I know, papa said. Not natural. I took my gaze away from the darkness and frowned at the prints. I'd never seen anything like them. They were like huge blobs of melted wax, none of them the same size, all big and grotesque and misshapen. Ruth, keep watching the night, papa warned me.

We put big chunks of horsemeat in burlap bags and carried them to the storage pit papa had dug next to the cabin. That's where the meat from the sheep was. Papa set planks over the hole and put rocks on them. The cold will freeze the meat all winter, he said. At least, we won't starve. But what about the cow? mama asked. We'll put her in the shed at night, papa said.

In the cabin, we found Judith coughing in a chair by the fire. Even though the logs roared, she couldn't get warm. Her face was red. Has anybody seen Chester? she asked. I thought a moment. I hadn't seen the dog since the morning. And where's the cat? Judith asked. I looked at the others, who frowned. Did they smell what was out there and run off? mama asked. They'd need to be awfully scared to do that, Daniel said. Maybe they didn't run off, I thought.

Yip, yip, yip, yip. We turned toward snow blowing at the window and listened to the howls. They were close. I'll make coffee and warm us up, mama said. *Yip, yip, yip.* The howls sounded closer. Papa stopped unbuttoning his coat. I'd better stay with the cow in the shed.

Dawn was only a few hours away. The morning light was grey from the clouds and the blowing snow. As Judith coughed, I peered through the frosted window and saw papa step from the shed, which was large enough to hold him, the cow, and bales of alfalfa stacked at one end. He looked pale. Stiff. His shoulders were hunched. It was the first time I thought of him as old. He peered around, ready with his rifle. Then he motioned for me to come out and start my chores and milk the cow.

The day was busy as we raced against the night. Daniel went with papa to the woods at the edge of the valley, rigged ropes to logs, and dragged them back for more firewood. They had the rifle. I washed clothes and helped make mutton stew while mama used snow water for a sponge bath to try to lower Judith's fever.

The only smoke in the valley is from our chimney, papa said when he and Daniel got back. Through the window, I saw it snowing again, flakes hitting the pane. Mama turned from wiping Judith's brow. I guess more people moved on than we thought, she said.

Maybe that's why those things are coming here. After the drought
and the fires, there's no game in the mountains. And all the other
farms are deserted, papa said. There's no other livestock in the valley.

After supper, Daniel put on his coat. He took the rifle off the shelf.
You spent the last two nights in the shed, papa. Tonight, it's my turn.

Yip, yip, yip, yip. In the dark, I listened to them. Judith kept
coughing. Mama came in with tea from bark that papa said would
lower her fever. Maybe we should have moved on, I heard mama say
to herself.

Just before dawn, I jerked awake when I heard a shot.

I'm okay! Daniel yelled from the shed. The moon came out! I saw
them coming! Five like you said! One was limping! Probably the one
you shot, papa! I put a bullet into it! The others ran off!

In the morning, we all dressed warm, except for Judith, and went
out to see what Daniel shot. The sky was cold blue. The sun glinted
off the snow, making me squint. A breeze numbed my cheeks. We let
the cow into the pen next to the shed and fed her. Then we walked a
hundred yards, following more blobby, mis-shaped paw prints. We
came to something in the snow. Fine shot, papa said. At night, with
no sleep, at this distance. Daniel looked pleased. I had the moon to
help me, but thank you, papa, he said.

The snow was red. The thing was brown with pointy ears and a
black tip on its tail, just like papa described. Its sharp teeth were
bared, as if it died snarling. The cold wind blew snow across the
ground. Hard to tell, Daniel said, but that looks like a bullet wound
in its right front leg. Probably *my* shot, papa said. And that's *your*
shot through its chest. That's what brought it down.

The reason it was hard to tell is that the animal had been chewed
on. Its stomach was gnawed open. Its left flank was raw. Damned
things ate one of their own, papa said. That's how hungry they are,
mama said. I didn't know they got this big, papa said. It was five feet
from the tip of its nose to the end of its tail. Must have bred with
something else.

But the mutilation isn't just from being eaten, Daniel said. What
happened to its paws, its ears, and the snout? From the fires in the
mountains, papa said. I couldn't make myself look at it any longer. Its
paws had awful scars as if a fire had melted the pads. Its fur was singed.
Its ears had ragged edges. Its snout was deformed from having been
burned. This one got trapped up there in the flames, papa said.

Yip, yip, yip.

We turned toward the nearby hills. In daylight? papa asked.
They're howling in daylight? I never heard of that. *Yip, yip, yip.*

They're watching us, Daniel said. Yes, papa said. Ruth, get the knife so we can skin what's left of it, he told me. Even if it's scarred, we can use the pelt. There's no point in wasting anything, including this. Plus, I want them to see what we do to them. I want to put the fear of God into them. Mama said, You talk as if they're smart and can think. Oh, they're smart, all right, papa said. When I was a kid, a trapper told me these things hunt in packs better than wolves.

That night, as Judith coughed, I used the knife to scrape the last of the meat from the pelt. Then I stretched it on a frame, the way papa taught me, and put it just close enough to the fire so it would dry without shrinking. Mama gave Judith more of the bark tea. Daniel sharpened the knife and the axe. As their metal scraped on the stone, I went to the window and looked toward the lamplight in the shed, where papa guarded the cow.

Judith died in the night. She kept coughing, and her chest heaved, and she couldn't catch her breath. Her cheeks were scarlet, but she kept fighting to breathe. Then her lips got blue, and her face, and after two hours, she died. Mama held her, sobbing. Daniel kept looking at the floor. I stood at the window and stared at the dark of the shed.

A shadow ran between the cabin and the shed. Another shadow, dark against the snow on the ground. The howls were very close. I heard a shot, but mama didn't react. She just kept sobbing. I'm all right! Papa yelled. They're running away! But just in case, don't open the door!

Then the night was silent, except for a rising wind and mama's sobbing. We need to tell papa, I said. When it's light, Daniel said. It won't help Judith if we bring him in now. Mama started murmuring, In the valley of the shadow. I went over and took her hand. I'm sorry, mama, I said. Her eyes were red. Fear no evil, she murmured, holding Judith.

When papa came in at dawn, he stopped in the doorway and knew immediately what had happened. His face looked heavy. He closed the door and crossed the room. He knelt in front of mama, who was still holding Judith. Lord, give us strength, he said. Through the window, I saw more tracks in the snow. Papa sobbed. I wanted him to know I was brave. I'll do my chores, papa, I said. I'll take care of the cow.

My coat barely kept me warm as I milked the cow, then fed her in the pen. I took a pitchfork to the manure in the shed, throwing it in a pile at the side of the pen. Four brown specks watched from the rim of a hill.

Mama dressed Judith in her best clothes, her "church clothes", mama called them, although we hadn't see a church in two years. Papa set Judith on the kitchen table. We took turns reading from the Bible. About Job and Lazarus and Jesus on Easter morning. Except mama. She sobbed and couldn't bring herself to read. Then papa and Daniel put on their coats and went to the shed, where they got the shovel and the pickaxe. They spent the rest of the day digging. I was reminded of when they buried my other brother and sister when we lived in another valley. This grave was in a nice spot near the apple tree. Judith would like that. Judith loved apples. The ground was frozen hard, and Daniel and papa were soaked with sweat when they came back to the cabin.

Daniel spent the night in the shed with the cow. Papa and I stayed up with mama as she held Judith's hand. We prayed more. Eternal life, papa said. I expected to hear them howling, but there wasn't any sound, not even a wind. Daniel came in at dawn. I've never seen him look so exhausted. I went out and took care of the cow.

Then we said our last prayers. Judith's face was grey now. She seemed a little swollen. Papa carried her outside into the cold. The rest of us followed. Mama sobbed as Daniel and I guided her. When papa set Judith into the ground, mama murmured, Not even a coffin. Don't have the wood, papa said. She'll be so cold, mama said.

Papa and Daniel took turns shoveling dirt. Mama couldn't bear to look. I took her back to the cabin. Papa carried stones from a fence he was making and put them on the grave. Daniel went to the shed. I heard hammering, and Daniel came out with two branches nailed to form a cross. Papa pounded it into the ground.

Papa stayed in the shed that night. At dawn, we heard him wailing. Daniel and I ran to the window. No! papa screamed. He charged toward the apple tree. No! he kept screaming. Daniel and I raced out to see what was wrong. Dirt was scattered over the snow. Rocks were shoved aside. The grave was empty. Papa's voice broke. Fell asleep! No! Didn't mean to fall asleep!

Eternal life, mama said. I didn't hear her come up behind us. She wasn't wearing boots or a coat. Judith has risen, she said. A swath in the snow went across a field and into the woods. Monstrous paw prints were on each side. The sons of bitches dragged her that way, papa said. I never heard him speak that way before. Daniel hurried to the cabin to put on his coat. He and papa followed the tracks. Risen, mama said. I helped her back to the cabin. From the window, I saw papa and Daniel disappear into the woods.

It snowed again. I stood at the window, straining to see. I leaned against the wall and must have dozed. The gust woke me. The door was open. Snow blew in. Papa! I cried. Daniel! Thank God, you're back! You had me so worried! But no one came in. The wind blew more snow. Mama? I swung toward the chair by the fire. The chair was empty. Mama! I rushed to the open door and saw footprints going away. I grabbed my coat and hurried outside. The snow filled the footprints. I tugged the door shut. The quickly vanishing footprints led me toward the apple tree. They went past the apple tree. Then I couldn't see them any longer in the gusting snow. Mama! I screamed. But the wind shoved the word back into my mouth.

The snow swirled thicker. The air got darker. I stumbled forward but didn't know which direction to take. Then I realised that I didn't know how to go back even if I found her. I couldn't see the cabin. My tracks were almost full. I followed them as best I could. The wind seemed to push me to the ground. I thought I saw a low moving shadow. I struggled to my feet and ran, only to bang into the corral near the shed. But I knew where I was now and stumbled forward, whispering Thank God when I bumped into the cabin. Inside, I sank to the ground before the fire.

I woke in the dark and heard them. I heard the cow panicking. Then the only sound was the wind. In the morning, there was two feet of snow. It took me a long time to stamp through it to get to the shed. Somehow they got the latch open. The cow was all over the inside. Mostly blood, hide, and bones. Hooves. The head. Its eyes were wide with shock. I saw where the tracks went off in the snow in single file. The first one made it easier for the second, and the second made it easier for the third and fourth. Oh, they're smart, all right, papa had said.

They'll eat mama next, I thought. They're probably already eaten papa and Daniel. When there's nothing else left in the valley, they'll come for *me*? For a moment, I couldn't move. What am I going to do? I thought. What would papa do? Think like papa. I don't need to go out, I realised. I could stack wood in the cabin. I could bring meat from the storage pit. I had carrots, squash, potatoes, and apples in the root cellar. I could stay inside all winter. I'd need water, but if I was careful and I opened the door real quick and scooped a pail of snow, I could close the door before they got me.

I dug my way down through the snow to the boards across the storage pit. Unlike the rocks on Judith's grave, the ones on the boards were still there, maybe because they were heavier. I pried two parcels of horsemeat from the frozen pile. The rest was stuck together so solid, I couldn't get at the lamb meat under it. I stacked the parcels in a corner of the cabin. I planned to stuff myself on it before it rotted. I carried tools from the shed – the shovel, the pickaxe, the hammer, and the pitchfork. I spent the day bringing in wood. I kept looking over my shoulder as I split logs. My arms ached. Too soon, it was dark. I went in, cut away a slice of thawing meat, and cooked it over the fire. It was tough and bitter, but I didn't care. I ate it in a frenzy and fell asleep.

In the night, I needed to relieve myself. I used a pail in a corner. In the morning, the smell was so bad that I wanted to carry the pail outside and dump it. But it stormed in the night, and now there was three feet of snow. I was only a foot taller. Besides, I knew it wasn't safe to go out. There were animal tracks in the snow. Across from the cabin, eyes glared from the shed's open door. I was forced to relieve myself in the pail again, and the stench got worse. I knew I wouldn't be able to bear it for a whole winter.

What would papa do? I thought. I got the pickaxe, went to a corner, and chopped the dirt floor. I got the shovel and scooped out the dirt. I kept chopping and scooping. My arms ached worse. But eventually I had a hole deep enough. I dumped the pail of waste into it, covered the waste with dirt, and still had plenty of space to dump more.

I heard scratching on the other side of the wall. They must have heard me digging and burrowed down through the snow to the bottom of the wall. I put my ear against the logs. I heard them out there trying to dig under. But clever papa had built the wall with two logs below ground to guard against flooding. I listened to them working to claw through the frozen ground. But it was too deep. They clawed and clawed, and at last I no longer heard them.

Again it snowed. In the morning, the drifts were close to the window sill. Deformed paws scraped glass. One of the things stared through the window, its dark eyes, scarred ears, and teeth-bared, misshaped snout making me think of the devil. In a rush, I closed the inside shutter. I was frightened and sickened, yes, but I also closed the shutter because the thing was so smart I didn't want it to see what I was doing. I went to the shelf where papa kept the box of poison he used on prairie dogs. We need to kill them so our animals don't break a leg in one of their holes, he said. I cut off a slab of horse meat, sliced it open, filled the cavity with poison, and squeezed the meat together. As I went toward the door, I heard wood creaking above me. I saw that the beams were bent from the weight of the snow and dirt.

Need to be quick, I thought. While the thing scratched at the window, I went over to the door. I lifted the latch as quiet as could be. Then I said a prayer, jerked the door open, hurled the meat over the top of the snow, and slammed the door shut. Or tried to. Some of the snow fell, blocking the door. Panicking, I scooped frantically at the snow. I heard one of them straining to run through the drifts toward the open door. My heart beat so fast, I thought I'd be sick as I scooped the rest of the snow away and slammed the door. Something banged against the top and growled.

I trembled. Then I opened the shutter. Sunlight off snow almost blinded me as I saw three of them fighting over the meat. They had burn scars all over them. One didn't have a tail. Another didn't have lips on the left side of its jaw. The fourth, the biggest, was the most deformed of them all. Its scars made it seem it had huge warts all over its snout. It glared from the door to the shed. When it snarled, the others stopped fighting and turned to it. With another snarl, it moved forward, its mashed paws finding purchase in the snow. It sniffed the meat and growled for the others to leave the meat alone. Two stepped back. But the one without a tail took its chance, bit into the slab, and ran off. At a distance, it gobbled the meat and sat contentedly. In a while, it squirmed. In a while longer, it writhed, vomited blood, and died. This took a long time.

Gathering clouds brought darkness swiftly. As snowy wind shrieked past the cabin, I cooked horsemeat, but not before I used papa's soap to wash my hands. Make yourself clean, he often said. It's the difference between us and animals. I pushed the blanket from the wall at the back of the cabin and went down the sloped floor to the root cellar, from where I brought back potatoes and carrots. I set them on a clean spot next to the fire. I listened to the shriek of the wind and the creak of the roof beams.

After a while, I had an idea. I filled a lantern with coal oil and lit it. Certain that the storm was too fierce for the things to be prowling out there, I went to the door. I had a moment's doubt. Then I knew that papa would be proud of me for being so clever. Breathing quickly, I put on my coat, opened the door, closed it behind me, and crawled up through the snow to the top of the drift. The wind was so cold, it made my face feel burned. Shielding the lantern, I squirmed through the gusts. When I saw the dark outline of the shed, I hurled the lantern through the front door and raced toward the cabin. Glass broke. Behind me, flames whooshed as I slid down the trough I had made. I fumbled at the latch, shoved the door open, kicked fallen snow away, and slammed the door.

Outside, one of them wailed. So numb I didn't feel the cabin's warmth, I ran to the shutter, opened it, and saw the fiery shed. A thing raced from the door, its fur ablaze. Yelping in agony, it fled into the darkness. The flames on it got smaller in the distance as it raced away. The alfalfa in the shed ignited. The fire grew larger, the shed's walls and roof collapsing, sparks erupting. Soon, the wind and the snow killed the blaze. I closed the shutter and went to the fireplace, where I discovered the potatoes and carrots were getting soft. The horsemeat tasted better as I got used to it. I dozed on a blanket near the hearth. Sometimes, the creak of the roof beams wakened me.

Then silence wakened me. I raised my head and saw cracks of sunlight through the boards of the shutter. It was the first quiet morning in several days. I went to the pit in the corner, relieved myself, shoveled dirt down, and washed my hands with papa's soap. I nibbled on a piece of leftover potato, the skin crusty, the silence encouraging me that the fire had killed the remaining three. I went to the shutter, swung it open, and one of them charged through the window. The crash of glass, the rage in its eyes made me scream and stumble away, knocking against the table. The force of its attack carried it two-thirds through the window. Spit flying, it dangled, thrusting with its paws to get all the way through, and suddenly yelped, blood spurting, a shard of glass in its stomach holding it in place.

It squirmed, determined to reach me, the hate on its face giving it strength. Its snout had fresh blisters and burns. I grabbed the pitchfork. As the thing broke free from the window, landing on the floor, I charged with the pitchfork. A tine caught its throat. But the thing was as big as I was. Wrenching free, it snarled and lunged. I stabbed with the pitchfork, piercing one of its eyes. Twisting away, leaving a trail of blood, it braced itself, leapt, and caught the pitchfork straight in its chest. The force against the pitchfork's handle knocked me down. The handle twisted this way and that as the thing snarled and writhed and bled.

A noise brought me to my feet. I staggered and barely reached the shutter in time to slam it shut before something crashed against it, almost breaking the shutter's hinges. The thing out there growled like the devil's creature it was. Hearing a scrape behind me, I turned and saw the thing on the floor struggling to stand despite the pitchfork in it. I stepped back as it tried to crawl. Its eyes were red with fury, dimming, going blank. I vomited.

For a time, I didn't move. Then I went to the water pail, where I rinsed my mouth, spat into the fireplace, and drank. The water soothed my throat which was raw from screaming. Four dead, I thought. But I knew the last one was the smartest, and I decided it didn't want me only for food now. I'd killed its companions. I'd destroyed its den. It hated me.

Without shelter, it'll freeze out there, I thought. I seemed to hear papa say, No. It'll dig a cave in the snow.

But if I don't go out again, it'll need to move somewhere else to find food, I thought. Again, I heard papa say, The stench of the decaying carcass will poison you. You'll need to open the shutter to breathe. It'll charge in.

No, I told papa. I can stand anything. The shutter stays closed.

I cooked more horsemeat. It tasted delicious. As shadows gathered beyond the cracks in the shutter, I decided that the thing on the floor was truly dead. I lit the lantern on the table, edged toward the carcass, and tugged the pitchfork from its chest.

The roof creaked. Be clever, I heard papa say. I pushed away the rug on the wall and hurried to take the axe and the knife down the ramp to the root cellar. I carried down a pail of water. I rushed back to get the lamp and the rest of the tools, but I never got that far. With a massive *crack*, the roof collapsed. The crush of dirt and snow sent me rolling down the ramp. My head struck something hard.

For a moment, colors swirled inside my mind. Then my vision cleared, and I saw that the top of the ramp was almost entirely blocked by wood, dirt, and snow. Dust made me cough, but as it settled, I saw a gap behind which flames rose. The collapsed roof had knocked the lamp over. The table was on fire.

The flames will suck the air from the cellar, I thought. I climbed to the top. Because the shovel was still in the cabin, I had to use my hands to push dirt into the gap. As the space got small, I saw the flames grow brighter. Smoke filled the opening. Frantic, I pushed dirt until the space was closed. Surrounded by darkness, I retreated to the bottom, sat, and tried to calm myself. My breathing echoed. I shivered.

Hunger woke me. I had no way of telling how long I'd slept. I was slumped against potatoes. My back ached. The cellar, which was about five feet wide and high had wood across the top to keep earth from falling. It smelled damp and like rotted leaves. Darkness continued to surround me. My hunger insisted. Papa used to say that raw carrots were bad for digestion. But it was either them or raw potatoes or squash, so after waiting as long as I could, I felt for a carrot and bit into it, its hardness making my teeth hurt. I didn't choose the apples because they felt soft and wormy. I was afraid they would give me the runs. Continuing to shiver, I chewed until the piece of carrot was mush in my mouth. Only then did I swallow. I did that for a long time, hoping I wouldn't get sick.

I tried to count the passing seconds, but my mind drifted in the stale air. For all I knew, it was now day outside. I needed to relieve myself but forced myself to wait. Finally, I crawled up the ramp. About to dig through the blockade of dirt and snow, I heard noises beyond it. Where the gap had been, dirt began to shift. Stomach tightening, I backed away.

At once, I saw a speck of daylight. A snout poked through, clustered with whorls and outcrops of scars and blisters. The thing growled. As the light widened and the head thrust into view, its ears merely nubs, I grabbed a potato, hurling it as hard as I could. It thudded off the creature's snout. I threw a second potato and heard a snarl. The creature clawed to widen the hole, shoving its neck through as I grabbed the pail of water and threw its contents. Water splashed over the raging head but made no difference. Its eyes burned. I banged the empty pail against the head, but the creature was halfway through. The handle on the pail broke. The creature's hind legs were almost free. I raised the axe but didn't have room to swing, so I jabbed, but the thing kept coming, and abruptly it wailed.

It snapped its head to the side, staring wildly behind it. Its wail became a savage yelp as it whirled and bit at something. The fierce motion widened the hole, allowing it to turn and bite harder. Daylight blazed in. I heard a noise like someone shaking a package of seeds. As the creature spun, the snake came into view, flopping like a whip, rattling, its fangs buried in the creature's haunch. The snake must have fallen when the roof collapsed. The heat of the fire wakened it. It kept its fangs sunk in as the creature whirled and yelped. The poison made the creature falter. Breathing heavily, it steadied itself, as if it knew it was dying and had to concentrate on unfinished business. It took a step toward me. It opened its mouth to bite. I shoved the axe handle between its jaws and leaned forward, thrusting the handle down its throat.

Choking, the creature thrashed. I struggled with the axe, pressing harder, feeling vibrations through the handle. Gagging, the thing frothed, wavered, slumped, trembled, and after a while lay still. Only then did the snake stop rattling. It released its fangs and dropped to the ground. Papa said, Its poison sacks are empty. For a while, it can't hurt you. But I didn't believe papa. As the snake slithered down the ramp, I pressed against the wall, trying to keep a distance. The snake crawled over the pile of squash and disappeared behind it.

I edged around the carcass, fearing that any moment it would spring to life. The cold air smelled sweet. Wary of other snakes, I stood among the dirt and snow and surveyed the wreckage. Clouds hovered. Knowing I needed shelter before the next storm, I saw that beams had fallen on an angle in front of the fireplace, forming a kind of lean-to. I found the pelt that papa had cut from the creature he and Daniel shot. I secured the pelt over a hole between beams. I tugged down the scorched blanket from the entrance to the root cellar and hooked it over another hole between beams. I found other blankets and did more of the same.

But there were still holes, and the blankets wouldn't keep moisture out, so I clenched my teeth, went into the root cellar, found the knife, and skinned the creature. Damn you, I said all the time I cut away its pelt. I stuck it over other holes between beams. Then I skinned the carcass of the thing that had come through the window, and I crammed that pelt between beams. In time, I would look for the creature I had poisoned and use *its* pelt, but snow was falling, and I had to complete my shelter. A few embers glowed under charred wood in the fireplace. I layered kindling and logs and blew on the embers. I was almost out of breath before the kindling sparked and the logs began to burn.

As the snow thickened, I went down to the root cellar and carried as many potatoes and carrots as I could, all the time keeping a wary eye on the pile of squash. While a potato cooked next to the fire, I bit a chunk from a carrot. Papa was wrong that uncooked carrots would make me sick. Maybe papa was wrong about a lot of things. Darkness settled, but despite the falling snow, my shelter felt secure. Tomorrow, I planned to make it stronger. I chewed another carrot and watched the potato sizzle. I thought about papa, about the many valleys in which we lived and how he was never satisfied and we always had to move past every town. I thought of the brother and sister who were buried in one of those valleys. I thought about the bark tea papa gave Judith for her fever. Papa always told us how clever he was, but maybe he didn't know as much as he thought about bark, and it made her sicker. Maybe papa wasn't so clever when he and Daniel chased after the things that took Judith. Maybe he should have kept control and stayed home and mama wouldn't be dead and he and Daniel wouldn't be dead.

I think about that a lot. I sit in this tiny room and listen to motor cars rattling by outside. Eighty-eight years is a long time to remember back. You ask me what it was like living in the valley when I was twelve. The old days as you call them. For me, the young days, although I was never really young. Streets and houses and schools and churches are now where our farm was, where everyone died, where I spent the winter eating carrots, potatoes, and horsemeat. But never the squash. I never went near the squash. Damned stupid papa.

F. GWYNPLAINE MacINTYRE

The Clockwork Horror

F. GWYNPLAINE MacINTYRE IS A NATIVE of Perthshire, Scotland, but spent his formative years in the Outback as one of the thousands of "child migrants" who were expatriated from post-war Britain to rural Australia. He now divides his time between homes in New York City and in Gwynedd, North Wales.

MacIntyre is the author of several novels (some of them published under pseudonyms) and dozens of science fiction, horror and mystery stories published in British and American periodicals. An artist as well as an author, he has illustrated number of his own works as well as some of Ron Goulart's stories in *Analog* magazine.

He is currently working on the illustrations for his next science fiction novel, which has the intriguing title *The Lesbian Man*.

Although "The Clockwork Horror" is fiction, in writing the story MacIntyre made a genuine addition to the known facts of the life of Edgar Allan Poe, as he reveals: "In 1836, while editing the *Southern Literary Messenger* in Richmond, Virginia, Poe published an essay titled 'Maelzel's Chess-Player', describing his recent encounter with an Automaton – an ostensible mechanical man – that was capable of playing chess and even defeating most challengers.

"In his essay, Poe used observation and deduction to build a convincing case that the Automaton was a hoax, containing a human chess-player. Oddly, Poe's essay does not reveal precisely when and where he witnessed the performance of Maelzel's Automaton. His 1836 essay merely states that the machine was exhibited in Richmond 'a few weeks ago', giving neither a precise date nor an address for the exhibition.

"When I started the research for this story, I was astounded to discover that no existing biography of Edgar Allan Poe gave a date or a location for Poe's encounter with Maelzel's Automaton. Determined to solve this mystery, I went to Virginia in search of further clues. In the archives of the *Richmond Enquirer* – a newspaper of the 1830s, published twice-weekly – I discovered several contemporary references to the activities of 'Edgar Poe', denizen of Richmond.

"I also tracked down advertisements for Maelzel's touring exhibition, verifying that the Chess-Player was exhibited in Richmond's city museum from December 15th, 1835 through January 2nd, 1836. Somewhere within those eighteen days, the real Edgar Allan Poe encountered the authentic (fake) Automaton . . . although presumably not with the same results described in the story!"

JANUARY 6TH, 1836

RICHMOND! Unholy citadel, which both condemns me and exalts me! Grotesque city of the perverse, where black men's bodies are sold at auction in Capitol Square, and white men's souls are flung into the gutter. I am fettered to this Richmond: its destiny is enchained with my own, and both our fates are inescapable.

As my name opens no doors and purchases no ease, I render it for your inspection. I am Edgar A. Poe, latterly a native of Richmond, now returned once more within this city's gates. True! I was not born here, and I have been known to call myself a Bostonian. Yet it is Richmond, the resplendent carbuncle on Virginia's hindquarters, that holds the mortgage to my flesh. The city of Richmond holds the pawnbroker's ticket upon which I have pledged my immortal soul . . . and I no longer dare to hope that this pledge may be redeemed.

My mother was English by birth, and my father a Baltimore scoundrel: Richmond held no claim upon the one nor the other. Still, it was Richmond where my parents conjoined in holy wedlock, although my father clearly saw fit not to honour the nuptial vows. My sainted mother was the ingenue Elizabeth Arnold. My alleged father was David Poe: son of the war hero General Poe who was quartermaster to Lafayette in the late War of Independence. Improvident actors, my mother and father were "starring" respectively as the heroine Sophia Woodbine and the scapegrace Villars in "The Blind Bargain" at the Haymarket Theatre, here in Richmond. I will

show you their notices, if you like. The Easter weekend is always a
slow season for actors, so between engagements – on Easter Monday, the seventh of April, 1806 – my father and mother got married
in a Clay Street lodging-house.

My parents found no outlet for their thespian endeavours in
Richmond, so they soon joined Alexander Placide's touring company
in Boston, where I had the dubious privilege to be born. My actress
mother was renowned for her talent and beauty. My father, ag-
grieved that his own theatrick talents were vastily inferior, abandoned us in the spring of 1811, during a repertory season in
Philadelphia. Finding no compassion there, my mother returned
with me to Virginia's capital, where she briefly won acclaim at
the Richmond Theatre on Shockoe Hill at East Broad Street . . .
in a tragedian rôle as Angela in "The Castle Spectre", dancing a
hornpipe while disguised as a boy in "The Curfew", and displaying
her musical skills as the ingenue Letitia Hardy in "The Belle's
Stratagem".

Richmond murdered my mother. As she became too ill to travel
with the departing troupe of actors, my mother Elizabeth Poe gained
some meagre employment in the old Indian Queen tavern, at the
northwest corner of Ninth and Grace Streets, engaged as the assistant
to a Scots-born milliner. It was in this tavern's cellar that my mother
squandered her eyesight, stitching together the piecework of ladies'
shovel-bonnets by candelight. When I was scantly two years old – on
Sunday morning, the eighth of December 1811 – my half-blind
mother was carried off by an infectious fever, in the milliner's room.

Yet this dark city was not finished with me. My godparents, John
and Frances Allan, took me into their home in Richmond, in rooms
at Thirteenth and East Main Streets, abovestairs from the counting-
house of my foster father's business: the merchant firm Ellis & Allan.
My mother, meantime, was buried nearby, in an unmarked grave in
the eastern section of St John's Episcopal churchyard. It was in this
very church that Patrick Henry uttered his famous words – "Give me
liberty, or give me death!" – while neglecting to mention that he was
a slaveholder. I have visited this churchyard often, yet I cannot know
the sure location of my mother's grave.

Richmond baptised me. Three days after my mother's demise, with
my own beliefs never consulted, I was conscripted into the Protestant
faith in the Richmond home of Mr and Mrs John Richard. On this
same day, rumours arrived of my father's death in Baltimore.

By long tradition, the night after Christmas is when theatres are
most profusely attended. Eighteen nights after my mother's death –

December twenty-sixth, 1811 – the Richmond Theatre was utterly destroyed in a fire of unexplained source, while an audience of six hundred souls beheld Placide & Green's tragedians in a performance of "The Bleeding Nun". Seventy-three persons died, including Virginia's governor. The scene of my mother's greatest triumphs was burnt to ashes.

Richmond was the place of my breeching: I refer to the ritual transition of early boyhood, when a lad is deemed at last mature enough to exchange his childish skirts for honest trousers. In the inexorable torrent of my helpless boyhood years, my adoptive parents the Allans compelled me to attend services with them at Monumental Church. By a perverse whim of the fates, this church had been erected on the very site of the burning ruins of the Richmond Theatre. Where the stage had once been consecrated to the gods of drama, now stood an altar. Where bright lamps illumined in calcium carbonate gleamings had once served as footlights, now the guttering tongues of candelabra stood sentry-post. Oh! Sacred reader! I implore you to imagine the stark outline of my thoughts in 1815, as a sensitive lad of six years, huddled in Pew #80 of the Monumental Church, and aware that on this same spot – adjacent in space, separated in time – my mother had once danced upon the stage, singing her popular tune "Nobody Coming to Marry Me", scarcely a month before her tragic demise.

An exact *fac-simile* of the Richmond street directory could be transcribed from my life's ordeals. At age eleven, I attended school in the upper room of Doctor Leroy's store at Broad and Fifth Streets, where I learnt Ovid, Cicero and Xenophon. Aged thirteen, I played hoops and bandy in the gutters at Fourteenth Street and Tobacco Alley. After a quarrel with my foster father, I briefly lodged with his business partner Charles Ellis, in that gentleman's house on the linden square, at the south side of Franklin Street between First and Second.

Richmond clutches to me still, like a suckling leech that will not relinquish its prey. I have lived elsewhere – Baltimore, West Point, South Carolina, even London – yet it is incessantly to Richmond that my blood returns, drawing me along as if by Mesmer's animal magnetism.

In 1824 – when I was fifteen years of age – my paternal grandfather's distinguished war record fetched me a place in the junior Morgan Riflemen, where I served as a member of the honour guard at Richmond's Capitol Square, during the grand reception for the triumphal return of the Marquis de Lafayette. That noble Frenchman shook my hand before the vast assemblage, and in the presence of the throng he praised my grandfather whom I had never known: the war hero whose son was my cowardly father, the scoundrel who abandoned my mother.

I deem, then, that my credentials as a resident of Richmond are satisfactory. This city and I are in each other's pocket. If I unbosom myself in these pages, it is Richmond's dark soul as well as my own that gains the shrift of my confession.

Last summer, at twenty-six years of age and unable to sustain my mortal needs by the craft of my pen and inkwell, I took employment in a brickyard in West Fayette Street in Baltimore, at the firm of the partners Merryman & Young – although neither partner was a merry man, and most assuredly neither was young. During my unsupervised hours at the brickyard, while my employers thought me engaged in the urgent task of distinguishing one brick from another, I discreetly penned several poems and trifles which Mr Thomas Willis White of Richmond saw fit to publish in his *Southern Literary Messenger*. I make bold to say that my efforts were met with immoderate success. In October of last year, I returned to Richmond and took up my new position as chief reviewer, proof-reader and unofficial editor of the selfsame *Southern Literary Messenger*. I took lodgings at Mrs Yarrington's boarding-house, at the corner of Twelfth and Bank Streets, fronting the south side of Capitol Square. Mrs Yarrington keeps a most abstemious household, where intoxicating liquors are entirely forbidden. I have pledged to forsake all bottle-companions while I am her boarder.

Now the Automaton arrives. On a recent Tuesday morning – December 15, 1835 – I was at my editorial desk, reloading my inkwell for a fresh assault upon the barbarian squadrons, when Mr White came to my stool with that day's edition of the *Richmond Enquirer*. He thrust his forefinger at one portion of the newsprint, and challenged me: "What do you make of this, Eddy?"

In the extreme lower corner of the leftmost column of the front page, I discerned this tiny "squib" advertisement:

MAELZEL'S CONFLAGRATION OF MOSCOW, &c., – Now exhibiting at the Museum. – Exhibition every evening. Doors open at a quarter before 7 o'clock. Exhibition to commence at half past seven o'clock precisely.

And so forth. "Might be a few agate lines' worth of story here, Eddy," said White. "Saddle up Shank's mare this evening, and go fetch a look."

The Museum of Richmond stands at Franklin and Eighteenth Streets. I arrived promptly that evening, just lacking the quarter-hour of seven. The price of admission was fifty cents: one-twentieth of my weekly stipend at the *Messenger*. I paid this usury, and entered the portals.

The museum is gas-fitted, so the rooms were well-lighted. Most of the permanent exhibits are devoted to Richmond's history, especially this city's ordeals in the two British wars. In a glass bell-jar, a ragged headdress of turkey-cock's feathers summarised the advanced civilisation of Virginia's aboriginal inhabitants. A few keepsakes of Europe, China, and the slave-coast of Dahomey are exhibited as well.

The momentary chief attraction proved to be a sequence of tableaux and dioramas, crafted by one Johann Nepomuk Maelzel of Vienna, and now touring America. These images depicted the bloodied events of September 1812, when Russia's capital city was put to the firebrands to thwart its capture by Bonaparte's advancing legions. The singular architecturings of Moscow – Saint Basil's Cathedral, and so forth – were displayed here in exquisite miniature.

The front seats of the Museum's auditorium were reserved for children and their wet-nurses, although I have no notion as to why suckling babes would show interest in the atrocities of Bonaparte's hordes. I took care to seat myself out of pabulum's range, in the third row. A sheet of linen, as white and blank as foolscap, had been stretched upon the rear wall.

From behind a claret-coloured velvet curtain, Professor Maelzel stepped forth. He bowed, introducing himself to our assemblage and proclaiming his credentials. Speaking in stiff Teutonic accents, he announced himself as the inventor of the metronome and the panharmonicon, and vouched that he had been Beethoven's teacher. Now there was a strong odour of the new-fashioned paraffin oil, as one of the professor's attendants lighted a magic-lantern. The gas-jets were snuffed, and then the evening's revels commenced.

The audience gasped in astonishment as the room erupted in flames. Then, of a sudden, their cries transmuted into applause as it was discerned that this was a conjuror's illusion. By some ingenious means of projecting and amplification, Professor Maelzel had enlarged the image of a single candle-flame, and was projecting this upon the white screen confronting us. A further stage-effect made it appear that these flames were *within* the miniature buildings of Maezel's simulacrum, rather than behind them . . . so that indeed it seemed as if the city of Moscow, represented in miniature, was engulfed in fire. I perceived that mirrors were involved in the illusion:

flames are by nature asymmetrical in shape, and I saw at once that a certain asymmetry in the conflagration on the left side of the screen was precisely reversed, mirror-wise, in the conflagration to our right side.

In the darkness, a sound: *Doom! Doom!* An unseen war-drum began its mournful tattoo. (I had noticed a boy with a tom-tom lurking in the hall at my arrival.) There was a clangour of unseen bells. (I had noticed a second boy in the hallway as well.) To the steady impulse of the tocsin's throb, a sudden phalanx of homunculoids arose, and commenced marching through the burning streets of Moscow. They wore the dark blue uniforms of Bonaparte's army. These soldiers, I observed, were some ingenious regiment of mannikins: an army of *automata*, if you will, compelled by mainsprings and levers to parade in unison across the row of dioramas. A few other homunculi, dressed as Cossack peasants, emerged from the burning buildings and attempted to flee. The advancing rank of soldiers raised their miniature muskets and fired at these targets. There was a sharp sudden report, not precisely matching the instant of the gunfire. (No doubt due to a tardiness by the drummer-boy in the vestibule.) The miniature peasants fell. Behind them, the buildings of Moscow collapsed and were consumed in the flames.

In the flame-lit auditorium around me, the good citizens of Richmond applauded Moscow's death . . . for one city's tragedy is ever another city's entertainment.

In the seat at my left-hand side, a waistcoated gentleman nudged me. "This isn't in it, you know," he declared. "I've only come for the afterpiece, but that's a better show than this. Maelzel's brought his Chess-Player."

As the gentleman pronounced this phrase, it seemed to be typeset with its own capitalisations in the boldface font of his voice: MAELZEL'S CHESS-PLAYER. I nodded my comprehension. "A chess-master, you mean?" I asked.

"Well . . . some say it, and others suspect as much. Stay after with me, and see it yourself."

By now the principal audience had begun to disperse, for the burning of Moscow was completed. All the peasants had been slaughtered, and – as there would be no further atrocities – the entertainment was ended. A few *cognoscenti* lingered for the promised afterpiece, and I placed myself in the front row as the gas-jets were relighted. I observed two stagehands packing up the wreckage of Moscow: the miniature buildings had been cleverly designed to collapse at a chosen moment, to give the illusion of destruction by fire. These effects and the dioramas were now hustled away, as from behind the velvet curtain two men trundled forth a peculiar oblong box.

The thing was set on wheels, and these of such a height that a gap of several inches transpired between the auditorium's floor and the underside of the box. The box itself was carpentered of dark wood, three feet six inches in length, two feet four inches in depth, and two feet six inches in height. I will lay wager to those admeasurements. To be sure of them, I visually compared the proportions of the oblong box against the breadth and height of one of Maelzel's attendants. Afterwards, I took care to pass closely by this man, comparing his stature to my own. I am five feet eight inches tall – my height has not changed since my West Point days – and so by this ruse I divined the oblong box's dimensions. In the front of the cabinet were four cupboard panels with brass fittings: three tall vertical doors, and a long horizontal drawer beneath.

The peculiar feature of the oblong box was a large excrescence of irregular shape, rising from the cabinet's rear portion. I could not discern this thing properly, for it was draped in a shroud of red sailcloth.

Professor Maelzel greeted the surviving remnants of the audience, and thanked us for awaiting the afterpiece. "Before we inspect the Chess-Player," he said, "let us consider its cabinet." He rapped the top and sides of the oblong box, proclaiming these to be made of stoutest maple. By their soundings, I believed him.

A liveried attendant brought forth a small table, placing this between the cabinet and the audience, and to one side. A single candlestick was placed on this. A second attendant was affixing six more candlesticks to the top of the Chess-Player's cabinet: three either side, with an unlighted beeswax candle in each.

"Behold the Automaton," said Herr Professor Maelzel. With a flourish, he whisked away the shroud.

Once more, the audience gasped. Seated on the rear portion of the oblong box was a replica of a man. This was garbed in the likeness of a Turk, sitting cross-legged, with a large turban atop his counterfeit head, and a high plume rising from the turban. The turban and plume made it difficult – intentionally, I suspect – to reckon the figure's height, but my previous stratagem made clear that the Automaton was slightly larger than a typical man. The counterfeit Turk was dressed in a long coat of unknown cloth, in Oriental design. At its waist was a *cummerbund*, or sash, of some darkly-coloured fabric. It was beardless, yet the wooden face displayed thick black *mustachios*. Its eyes stared forth into the auditorium, lifeless and blind.

The Automaton's gloved hands were extended. The left hand brandished a long Turkish smoking-pipe. On the topmost surface of the cabinet was a chessboard.

Two attendants seized the upper corners of the cabinet, and trundled it around so that the audience could view its hindquarters. The rear side of the Turk was somewhat more crudely fashioned than the front portions. The cabinet's wheels, I repeat, were of sufficient diameter to raise the cabinet well clear of the floor, so there could be no suspicion of any human confederate entering or leaving the Automaton's box by means of a trap-door underneath.

"There is naturally much curiosity," said Herr Maelzel, "as to the clockwork mechanisms of the Automaton. These were crafted by Baron von Kempelen of Presbourg in 1769, and I have improved their design." By now the cabinet had completed its ambulation, and once more the Turk confronted the audience. "It will be observed," Maelzel resumed, "that both the cabinet, and the Automaton itself, are entirely filled with clockworks."

From his swallow-tail coat, Maelzel took a ring of keys. As an attendant lighted a taper, Maelzel with much ceremony unlocked the leftmost of the cupboard's three doors. He opened this fully. In the gaslight, and by the dint of one small candle, I beheld a mass of gears, pinions, levers and half-seen enginery. Leaving the cupboard door open, Maelzel went to the cabinet's rear and unlocked another panel. Stooping, he held the burning candle behind the unlocked panel, so that its glowing flame penetrated entirely through the cupboard's interior to the seated audience in front. Holding the candle quite near, Maelzel reached with his other hand into the cabinet and gripped one of the levers. He worked this back and forth, all the while propounding a lecture upon the history of the Automaton. The shifting lever in its turn rotated gears, which moved wheels, which turned pinions. I heard a clacketing noise, as the gears engaged at their tasks. I observed that the space between these mechanisms was too small to admit of any occupant much larger than a well-nourished rat.

Maelzel closed the rear panel, locked it, and came back to the front with his candle. The leftmost cupboard door beneath the Automaton was still wide open. Now Maelzel unlocked the long slender drawer at the base of the cabinet. Two attendants flung this drawer open to its full length. Within the drawer were a small green cushion, one chessboard, and four sets of chessmen: two white sets, two black.

These were fixed in a framework to support them perpendicularly. I could not anticipate why so many chessmen were required for a single game.

As Maelzel continued his lecture, he gently placed the cushion beneath the left-hand elbow of the Automaton. At the same time, he removed the long tobacco-pipe from the Automaton's left hand, and placed this pipe carefully in the drawer beneath the cabinet. "Is there any lady or gentleman here," Maelzel asked, "who is a superlative player of chess?"

I made ready to volunteer, but the waistcoated gentleman antici-pated me. "I am Mr Clarence Hall, proprietor of the Barque book-shop in Grace Street," he announced. "I am known throughout Virginia as an honest man and a tolerable chess-gamer. Perhaps I will serve." As he spoke, Mr Hall indicated a trinket on his watch-fob: the sign of the Freemason's compass. "There is a term, long used in the Masonic craft, which I have lately heard applied to chess-players of superior skill," Mr. Hall resumed. "Some of my opponents are pleased to call me a *grandmaster*."

A footman collected the chessboard and two sets of chessmen: one white, one black. As Maelzel gave sign, this board and chessmen were set up in regulation manner at the table to one side, where Mr Hall took a chair. An attendant lighted the candle at this table, some slight distance from the Automaton.

Surely, in any chess-match, the two antagonists ought to sit at the same board?

The leftmost of the three cupboard doors beneath the Automaton was still wide open. Maelzel now unlocked its two brethren, throw-ing these wide as well. The rightmost and the central door opened into a single compartment. This contained no enginery at all, save for two steel quadrants of uncertain utility. Beneath these, in the floor of the cabinet, was a pedestal about eight inches square, and covered in dark cloth. Such a pedestal might have served as an admirable stool for a human tenant. I could see no reason for its presence in a clockwork mechanism.

Maelzel's attendants now whirled the Automaton around once more, so that again its rear portions were afforded to us. All three of the front cupboard doors were still open. Maelzel unlocked another panel at the rear – not the one he had previously opened, which was now locked – and again we had a view of unknown gears and pinions. Again, the business with the candle was repeated, so that the light of the flame pierced the entire cabinet from front to back – or the other way, as the cabinet was now reversed – and again the light of the candle gave token that there was no hiding-space within for even a modest homunculus.

The wooden figure of the Turk was slightly larger than man-sized. Maelzel now lifted the Turk's coat, to reveal the replication's nether portions. A door about ten inches square was in the loins of the figure, and a smaller door in the left thigh. I perceived that the Turk's cummerbund was not genuine, for it did not truly encircle the Automaton's waist in the manner of such garments. The edges of the sash terminated at either side of the figure, so that the Turk's cummerbund was merely a false ornamentation on the front half of the likeness.

Unlocking and opening the doors within the Automaton, Professor Maelzel permitted the spectators to view what lurked within. I beheld a network of cogs, mainsprings, and enginery: all dormant and still. Maelzel rapped the upper portions of the figure, producing a solid heavy sounding with no rumours of hollowness.

Maelzel now closed and locked all the apertures, and the cabinet was trundled once more to its previous position, with the eyes of the Turk gazing outward, confronting the spectators. An attendant had set up the remaining chessmen on the board in front of the cross-legged Turk, with the black pieces facing the Automaton.

I have mentioned six candles upon the Automaton's board. These a footman now hastened to light, with a taper. No two of these six candles were of a like height. They varied in stature by as much as twelve inches. This is unremarkable, as candles consume their wax at differing rates, and so dwindle unequally. I assumed that, in pursuit of thrift, Herr Maelzel would save the stubs of candles previously lighted, and make use of them again until their wicks were spent.

With another flourish, Maelzel inserted one of his keys into an aperture in the left side of the cabinet: the Automaton's right side. I heard the snicketing sound of a mainspring winding taut within the clockwork engine.

Professor Maelzel withdrew the key, and bowed: "Let the chess-match begin."

Mr Hall, playing white, made the first move: a simple pawn's gambit. He was seated in profile, so that the spectators had a fair view of both the white and black positions at his chessboard. Professor Maelzel thanked him, then strode to the cabinet of the Automaton. Swiftly, Maelzel grasped the corresponding white pawn on the Automaton's chessboard, and copied Hall's move.

I saw no profit in this duplication. Surely it made more thrift for the machine and its antagonist to do battle across opposite ranks of the same chessboard. True, by seating Mr Hall to one side, Maelzel assured the spectators an unchallenged view of the Automaton and its chess pieces. And yet – by means of mirrors, during his makeshift conflagration of Moscow – Maelzel had already displayed his ingenuity in amplifying and translocating flames so that they burnt at one position in space while being perceived entirely elsewhere. Could not a man of such genius likewise project his Automaton's progress so that the chess-match was visible from all quarters of the room?

As I thought of this, there was a sharp intake of breath from several spectators.

The Automaton raised its left arm. The limb moved upward, forward, downward, jerking in stiff right-angled gesticulations. The Automaton's head moved slightly, the plumed turban shifting. The eyes rolled, in grotesque parody of human eyes.

The Automaton's hand lifted the black queen's pawn, advanced it slightly, and set it down in the square of the fourth rank. Then, releasing its prize, the Automaton's arm reversed its movements precisely, once more resting its elbow on the cushion.

Maelzel declaimed to the assemblage this movement of the queen's pawn, while he crossed to Mr Hall's board and advanced a black chessman in like fashion.

So the chess-match proceeded, each antagonist's move in duplicate.

The match, in fine, was a superior one: Mr Hall was an excellent gamer, yet the Automaton surpassed him. Several white chessmen were rapidly captured. The Automaton achieved this by lowering a black piece into the square already occupied by a white piece, clumsily knocking it askew. An attendant confiscated the taken piece. On the rarer occasions when Mr Hall captured a black piece, Maelzel removed its counterpart from the Automaton's display.

There was silence in the hall, utmost silence, as the game was prosecuted: this stillness being broken only by the audience's occasional cries of admiration at a clever gambit, or dismay at an ill-chosen manoeuvre.

The turbaned head of the Automaton shifted at intervals, yet these movements appeared to be random. More disconcerting were the mechanical eyes. The Turk was just above man-sized, and his eyes were slightly enlarged beyond that proportion, so they were perhaps twice as large as a living man's organs of sight. They appeared to be sightless, and ornamental, for the eyes of the Automaton never once bent towards the chessboard. Yet they moved. The eyelids blinked, the eyes shifted sidelong as if weighted with the guilt of unknown crimes. At the eleventh move, when Mr Hall made an especially maladroit gambit, the Automaton's eyes positively rolled in their sockets, arousing laughter from the spectators.

On the thirteenth move, the Automaton responded to Mr Hall's *en passant* with a bold assault by the black queen's rook. At this juncture, the Automaton's right hand – formerly idle – rapped the top of the cabinet, and the Automaton's jaws opened.

"*Echec*," said a voice within the Automaton's bosom.

Several spectators gasped as the machine spoke. I was less impressed. It is easy enough, by means of bellows, to equip a mechanism so as to voice a bird's call or a spoken word. One is put in mind of cuckoo-clocks. Indeed, the *cuckoo* seemed to be the appropriate bird flying over these proceedings, although there were clearly more than a few *gulls* within the premises as well. I prolonged this theme of birds by observing that the Automaton had played *a black rook*. Twenty years ago, when my stepfather brought me to England to be schooled at Stoke Newington, I learnt that the word "rook" signifies not merely a chessman and a black-plumed bird. It is also the London criminals' cant-word meaning *to cheat* . . .

I arose from my chair, and stepped into the avenue between the seats.

"I have unriddled this mystery," I said loudly. "The game is over, and it ends in a fool's mate. Maelzel's Automaton is a fraud."

There was a huzzbuzz, as the heads of spectators turned to confront my intrusion. Even the blind eyes of the Automaton seemed to swivel in their sockets, to behold me.

Herr Maelzel gestured for silence. "Who are you, sir?" he asked me.

"I am Edgar Poe, chief reviewer for the *Southern Literary Messenger*," I said, making so bold as to offer a half-bow. I fancied I saw the Automaton start in surprise as I rendered my name.

"I do not know you, Mr Poe," ventured Maelzel.

"The Automaton is a fraud whether you know me or not," I went on. "Five months ago, I might have hailed your clockwork Chess-Player as the greatest hoax of the century. But you have been outdistanced and out-hoaxed this past August by the *New York Sun*'s series of articles about bat-winged beaver-men allegedly observed upon the surface of the Moon. That hoax was exposed in September, and now your own diddling will be unhoaxed as well." I held up one hand to silence the clamouring spectators while

I confronted Maelzel. "I have unmasked your Chess-Player by means of observation and deduction. I ask everyone here to recall your demonstration, when you opened the Chess-Player's cabinet and moved the levers with your hand. There was a loud clacking noise, as we saw the gears engaged. Yet the Automaton has been waging chess-moves for several minutes now, and never once in that time have we heard the sound of those gears engaging! Further, we all heard you winding a mainspring within the Turk . . . yet there has been no consequent sound of an escapement, the tell-tale *tick-tick-tick* as the mainspring uncoils. I will wager that your Chess-Player's cupboard contains a ratchet, to counterfeit the sound of a mainspring turning, without an escapement."

The spectators' murmuring grew louder.

"Those gears were only stage-props," I continued, "to persuade us that the Automaton's cabinet is entirely filled with machinery, leaving no space for a man,. Yet why is Mr Hall obliged to distance himself from his opponent the Automaton, with the nuisance of two separate chessboards for a single game? The answer: if the Chess-Player's antagonist were to sit nearer the board, he would hear *breathing* from within the cabinet!"

The murmuring loudened, and some of the spectators began drumming their feet against the floorboards.

"Furthermore, look to the candles," I spoke. "One candle gives sufficient light for Mr Hall to distinguish his chessmen. The Automaton's eyes are sightless and ornamental, needing no light whatever . . . yet Herr Maelzel has set *six* candles by the board of his mechanical Chess-Player. That is because six candles are required to cast sufficient light so as to penetrate the thick gauze fabric of the Automaton's waistcloth. I deduce that there is a *human* confederate within the Automaton. He is seated upon the small pedestal which we all observed inside the cabinet. His head is of a height within the Turk's abdomen. And his eyes peer outward through the gauze of the Turkish sash."

I heard the shifting of chairs in the rows behind me, as several spectators now stood, to have a better vantage of the Automaton.

I gestured for silence. "Pray compare the six candles at the Automaton's chessboard. The four candles farthest from the Automaton burn steadily. There is no draught in this room. Yet the two candle-flames nearest the Turk are seen to flicker, as if caught in a current of air that oscillates back and forth. Only one manner of air current moves back and forth steadily: that of *respiration*. Good people, the porous cloth of the Chess-Player's sash affords two functions for the human agent concealed within the Automaton: he can see through it, and he can breathe through it."

By now, the spectators were demanding a chance to open the Automaton's casing. Once more, I bade them remain silent while I resumed:

"The gears and pinions in the Chess-Player's cabinet are merest stage-dressing. I will wager that among them are *mirrors*, casting reflections so as to make the gears and pinions inside the cabinet seem more numerous than they actually are, and so the cabinet more crowded. True, sir! You have opened all the cabinet's doors for our inspection, yet you were careful never to open all of them at once. The cupboard's human inhabitant must shift himself during your demonstration, so that there is always one shut door to conceal him. But I believe that *some* portion of your enginery is genuine, at least. Inside the Automaton, there must be an ingenious arrangement of levers, so that the human tenant can manipulate the Turk's arm from within the cabinet. The system probably involves a counterbalance. This would explain the cross-problem that had puzzled me: the operator within your cabinet is probably right-handed, yet the Automaton favours its *left* hand." I bowed again to the assemblage. "Good evening, ladies, gentlemen . . . and Automaton."

Then I turned and strode up the corridor, and made good my departure.

As I left the Museum's vestibule, and turned homeward for Mrs Yarrington's rooming-house, once more the grotesque image of *a large black-plumed rook* swooped through my fancy, its talons arousing my brain to preserve this stark image in a stanza of verse. But the black-winged rooks of England are unknown in America. Perhaps, for the sake of my readers, some other dark-plumed bird of carrion will serve the purpose . . .

My encounter with Maelzel's Chess-Player occurred three weeks ago. This afternoon – the sixth of January, 1836 – I was again busying myself at my desk in the *Messenger*'s offices at Fifteenth and Main Streets, when an apologetic messenger-boy brought me a folded length of foolscap. Opening this, it proved to be a scrawled letter. The author's handwriting was disarrayed, his capitals and cursives elbowing each other in confusion. There was no signature. In fine, the letter had plainly been written by someone in great distress, or by some paralytic who had only the vaguemost control of his own limbs. Here is the missive:

EDGAR POE. Maelzel's troupe have finished their
engagement in Richmond, and depart on the morrow for
their next booking. If you will come alone to the
Monumental Church tonight, after the vesper-service, you
will learn something to your advantage.

That was all. I flung the letter into a waste-paper receptacle, and
resumed my duties. But the missive, and its mysteries, held hostage
my curiosity. Thus, at eventide tonight, guided by a bright moon
nearly full, I made my way through Richmond's cobblestoned streets
to Shockoe Hill.

The Monumental Church is octagonal, surmounted by a dome of
peculiar shape and modest convexity. Within the front portico,
between the Doric pillars flanking the church's entrance, stands a
white marble tablet commemorating the unfortunates who were lost
in the fire of 1811. Stepping past this, I was surprised to find the
door-bolt of the entranceway set ajar . . . perhaps by someone
anticipating my arrival. Pushing the door open, I stepped within.

I have been here before. This was the church of my childhood. The
place was dark now, yet I have been here so often and so intimately
that I knew each detail of the church's interior by embittered
memory. Before me was the chancel. I knew by heart the inscription
carved in gilt uncial script above the chancel-frame: GIVE EAR, O
LORD.

My footsteps echoed on the tiling as I proceeded down the aisle
towards the altar. Two candle-frames stood there, either side. Some
few of the candles were lighted, and by their faint gleam I beheld a
dim shape placed in front of the altar, like some sacrificial offering. A
shape like an oblong box, surmounted by an effigied resemblance of
a man.

It was the chess-player. Maelzel's Automaton.

The unseeing eyes of the Turk were downturned, regarding me
silently. On top of the cabinet, a few chessmen stood vigil on the
gameboard in front of the cross-legged effigy. As I approached, I saw
that the chessmen on the board were positioned for the gambit
known as an *endgame*.

With a sudden right-angled convulsion, the Automaton's left hand
jerked sidelong, and nudged the black queen's rook to the bishop's
file.

I responded in kind, grasping the solitary white knight, and
placing this so as to endanger the Automaton's king.

"*Echec*," I declared.

"*You were wrong, Edgar Poe,*" spoke a muffled voice emerging from the Turk's abdomen. "*There is no man within Maelzel's Chess-Player.*"

I kept standfast. "I have proved through rational deduction that the cabinet is fashioned to contain a human operator."

"*Indeed. And it contains an operator, right enough. But the Chess-Player within the cabinet is no man . . . for I am no longer human.*"

There came a sound of gears meshing within the oblong box. The rightmost door of the cabinet swung faintly ajar. From within the cupboard of the Automaton, a hand emerged . . . beckoning.

By candlelight, I beheld the hand of the unseen Chess-Player. There was a discrepancy of fingers, three digits being entirely absent. The remaining thumb and forefinger were scarred and fractured, bent into appendages more nearly resembling claws than any human flesh.

"*I was a chess-gamer once, of no little ability,*" harshed a voice within the cabinet. The unseen speaker's voice, like his hand, seemed defective and bestial. "*My father, being of respectable Maryland stock, desired for me a career at law. If I had heeded his wishes instead of my own, I would never have come to this crossing.*"

I could just barely perceive, within the shadowed cabinet, a human face. *Human?* There was a hideous concavity within the face, as if some of its portions had been gnawed away, and the remainder twisted beyond recognition. The candlelight threw its faint gleam against a bright cicatrix of scar tissue, bordered by a single pale eye and a cavity where nostrils should have been. A man that was used up . . .

"*This church was built upon the wreckage of the Richmond Theatre,*" said the voice within Maelzel's Chess-Player. "*I was there that dread night, Edgar Poe. In the first act of the melodrama of 'The Bleeding Nun', in the stage-setting representing the house of Baptiste the Robber, a chandelier was employed to illumine the stage. At the second-act climax, a call-boy was ordered to raise the chandelier into the fly-lofts, where the candles could burn in safety.*"

The patchworked face within the cabinet paused, as if each word required immense effort. Then it spoke again: "*I stood watching, in the wings. I snatched the rope from the boy's hands, intentionally pulling the chandelier askew so that it went into the scenery flats. These were made of oiled canvas, and they burnt most industriously.*"

"You did this?" I asked. "Why?"

"*In the service of envy, and anger, and a few other sins. I was a disgraced gambler, a drunkard, a failed actor. My own inadequacy before the footlights was made more embittered by the envy I held for my wife's superlative talents on the stage."*

The Chess-Player moved within the cabinet. I beheld his face now from a fresh angle. The thick scarrings and disfigurements were less numerous here. In utter revulsion, I discerned in his mutilated countenance a grotesque parody of *my own face* . . .

"I was David Poe, your father," said the beckoning thing. *"When word reached me in Philadelphia of my wife's penniless death in a Richmond tavern, I came back here in mourning: to the Richmond Theatre, the scene of her triumphs. I could scarce contain my rage as I stood in the wings and I heard your mother's understudy speak her lines. How dare this actress live and breathe, when your mother could not? How dare the audience applaud?"*

"Wretch!" I said. "You speak concern for my mother, yet she might never have died in poverty if you had not abandoned her."

"True enough," said the remnants of my father. *"I had no right to live, and I hungered for death. I coveted my wife's safe passage out of the living world, and I decided to join her onstage in some other realm. When I set the theatre afire, eighteen nights after my wife's inglorious death, I resolved to immolate myself in the flames . . . and to take with me as many innocents as possible."*

"You succeeded in that last particular."

"True. The place went up like matchwood, and the entire Richmond Theatre was aflame in two minutes. The pit and the stalls were swiftly abandoned, as the patrons in the dollar seats fled quickly. The galleries upstairs were not so fortunate." The half-man in the cabinet gestured pathetically; I glimpsed the stub of an interrupted limb, bound in ragged bandagings.

"I was gravely maimed in the conflagration," moaned the voice of the patchworked half-man. *"The major portions of my limbs were amputated in a Richmond poor-ward, where I took care not to give my true name. I knew that my family in Baltimore would not welcome me, so I sent them false news of my death. I lived on such charity as I could find."* The half-man coughed. *"Charity came easier for me after August 1812, when I could claim I lost my limbs as a soldier in the siege of Detroit, in Madison's war against the British."* He coughed again. In the light of the church candles, I saw that the chess-player's disfigured mouth was coughing up blood.

"How does Herr Maelzel enter this conundrum?" I asked.

"Maelzel was my savior," said the maimed thing that alleged to be my father. *"Maelzel had need of a chess-master who could fit into a*

small cabinet." The half-man laughed mirthlessly, and brandished one of his stumps. *"In this one vocation, my abbreviated limbs give me an advantage over men more complete than myself. If only your mother . . ."*

The Automaton fell silent.

"What about my mother?" I asked.

A faint rustling within the oblong box.

"You spoke of my mother," I persisted.

The thing in the box uttered a profane oath.

From that instant, I found myself overcome by a grotesque phrensy. It felt precisely as if my arms and legs were suspended on wires, and I became a marionette whose movements were governed by an unseen puppet-master. Confronting me was a man who masqueraded as an Automaton. True! But now I became an Automaton in the guise of a man . . . for my soul no longer captained my flesh, and I found myself moving and gesticulating as if by clockwork: no more the master of my actions, but compelled as if by gears and levers unseen. As a puppet moves on jointed limbs, so I sprang to the altar.

Just as a chesspiece, with no soul of its own, is manipulated by a grandmaster who cares not for the pawn's ultimate fate, so I was controlled now by *a mind alien to myself.*

On the chancel's wall was a wrought-iron sconce, holding three lighted candles. My hands grasped it, obeying the whispered commands of some unseen clockmaker – perhaps it was Maelzel – as I seized this heavy implement, tore it loose of the wall and smashed it squarely into the carved wooden head of the Turkish chess-player, knocking aside the plumed turban and shattering the face. As the Automaton's face burst open, I saw the articulated eyes tumble forth; they were fashioned of Vienna-glass, and for one instant my own mind was freed from the clockmaker's grasp long enough for me to admire the workmanship of the counterfeit eyes. Then the mind of the clockmaker seized me again, bidding me to strike the hour. I brought the sconce down – again! again! – upon the cabinet of Maelzel.

The Automaton was headless, for I had decapitated the figure of the Turk. Now a low groan emerged from the figure's abdomen, and I recalled that the monstrous figure within the chess-player was concealed in that portion. I fractured this with the sconce. I had the fierce pleasure of seeing blood upon the wrought-iron flange in my grasp. I brought it down again . . .

There was an odour of burning cloth. I turned, and perceived that in my phrensy I had scattered the candles. One of these had ignited the drapes behind the altar. And now the chancel was afire.

Inside the cabinet of Maelzel, some scuttling thing – an abridged edition of a man – was struggling desperately to free itself. I brought the sconce down once more, full in the patch-quilt face of the inhuman occupant. The thing groaned, and went slack. I saw the two remaining fingers of its fragmented hand fall open. A single chessman – a carved wooden pawn – tumbled out of the maimed grasp, and it fell upon the burning altar-cloth.

The nameless grandmaster released my soul from the endgame. The unseen puppeteer unloosed my strings. I was no longer clock-worked.

I turned, and fled the Memorial Church as it burst into flame. In the portico, I was confronted by a tall white apparition. It was the marble tablet, commemorating the names of the dead who perished on this site amidst the burning Richmond Theatre. I was tempted to add one more soul to the death-list: the name of my father, David Poe.

I awoke to the strong vapours of distilled spirits. I found myself sprawled on the floor of my room in Mrs Yarrington's lodging-house The door is latched. The derangement of my clothes, and the spasmodic trembling of my limbs, give token that once more I have succumbed to intemperance. My shirtfront is soaked with bourbon, and a shattered bottle lies nearby.

On the table in front of me is an unproofed manuscript, its ink still wet. The handwriting I recognise as my own, but the penmanship is wild and abandoned, and the ink has spattered several passages where the pen-nibs have torn entirely through the paper.

Reading the pages, I find that they contain the above narrative . . . excepting these last paragraphs. But have I written fiction, or reportage? This manuscript is filled with incident, yet my memory is a blank page. I remember nothing of these recent hours.

Are these words on the page truth, or falsehood? Have I night-mared all of this, or some portion? Or is all of it real, in cold sanity? Did I go to Memorial Church tonight? Have I confronted Maelzel's Automaton? Is the man inside that clockwork hoax the unmourned David Poe? Have I murdered my father? *Did I set the church ablaze?*

There are shouts in the hall. Someone is pounding on the door, and there are voices.

I must see what they require of me.

RICHARD CHRISTIAN MATHESON

Making Cabinets

RICHARD CHRISTIAN MATHESON IS A NOVELIST, short story writer and screenwriter/producer. He has written and produced hundreds of episodes of television, for over thirty dramatic and comedic primetime network series and, at nineteen, was the youngest writer ever put under contract by Universal Studios.

He has written feature film and television projects for Richard Donner, Mel Brooks, Joel Silver, Ivan Reitman, Steven Spielberg and many others. To date, Matheson has written and sold twelve original, spec feature scripts; considered a record. He has also written over twenty pilots for comedy and dramatic series for Showtime, Fox, NBC, ABC, Spike and CBS.

Matheson recently wrote three scripts for Showtime's *Masters of Horror* (the first two directed by Tobe Hooper), while for TNT's *Nightmares & Dreamscapes* he wrote the critically acclaimed adaptation of Stephen King's short story "Battleground", a one-hour episode starring William Hurt. His decision to write the entire script with no dialogue amazed critics and *The New York Times* called the episode ". . . a minor masterpiece." He is currently scripting two feature films and an eight-hour mini-series for director Bryan Singer.

Thirty stories are collected in Matheson's *Scars and Other Distinguishing Marks*, with an introduction by Stephen King. *Dystopia*, a hardcover collection of sixty stories is introduced by Peter Straub. His debut novel, *Created By*, was Bantam's hardcover lead, a Bram Stoker Award winner and a Book-of-the-Month Club lead selection. It has been translated into several languages.

"In a culture intoxicated by extreme," observes Matheson, "serial killers, inevitably, are fabled. In their ghastly, photogenic wakes, are collateral victims; those, still living, who knew the killer as routine participant in life – children, co-workers, friends, wives. Once news coverage, funerals and death penalties are eclipsed by fresher abduction and atrocity, the serial killer's inner circle must continue, despite betrayal which inverts their world.

" 'Making Cabinets' spends time with such a person. Its first draft was fleshless outline. Details were added, though few. In all, I wanted the feelings of aftermath to be a traumatised void."

ICE WATER; a diamond stalk on white linen.

The clearness tastes warm, red. The thin woman chokes, covers mouth with napkin.

One table over, a boy eats pie, eyes unblinking. Watches her hold menu in pale hands.

She scans gourmet adjectives. Imagines soups, meats. Their dark succulence, piquant sauces.

All of it horror.

She searches more dishes, stomach a sick pit.

Maybe a salad, no dressing.

But the tomatoes; the cook would slice them open, their seeded flesh unprotected, seeping helplessly.

The waitress approaches. Perhaps the Special of the Day? Lamb. Unspiced; a meticulous blank.

The thin woman's stomach twists. She imagines the dead flesh using her mouth like a coffin; fights nausea.

Why hadn't she heard them?

The waitress tilts head. The thin woman needs another minute. The waitress nods; the same conversation everyday.

A couple, at the next table, excavate lobster, amused by lifeless claws. The busboy sweeps; a metronome.

The thin woman sees the boy eating pie, his lips berry-blue like a corpse.

Electric saws, pounding hammers.

Maybe the vermicelli. Plain.

But the long strands, like fine, blonde hair.

She tries to sip water, again. But the cubes have melted; water like dread-warm saliva.

His gentle smile, serving his recipes. The perfect husband.

The waitress reminds her she must eat. She loses more weight every day. She's so pretty. It was almost a year ago. She must move on. The thin woman listens, nods. Tries not to look at the boy.

Making cabinets, he'd said; basement door always locked.

The thin woman looks up at the waitress. The young woman's lipstick resembles a tortured mouth.

She runs between the red lips, down lightless corridor to the banned door. Inside, music deafens. She presses ear to door; hears blades severing. Pounds on door until it gives.

Finds two little boys, hanging upside down from ropes, screaming through gagged mouths, half peeled. He turns, goggles freckled red, black rubber apron stained. The stove behind him gurgles with spiced stews.

The thin woman tells the waitress she's lost her appetite.

Maybe tomorrow.

The boy's smile falls as he watches her leave, bones and veins visible through her starved skin.

GEOFF RYMAN

Pol Pot's Beautiful Daughter
(Fantasy)

GEOFF RYMAN WAS BORN in Canada, but he has lived most of his life in Britain. The author has won the British Science Fiction Award, the World Fantasy Award, the British Fantasy Award, the Arthur C. Clarke Award, the John W. Campbell Memorial Award, the James Tiptree, Jr. Award and the Nebula Award.

Ryman's science fiction and fantasy books include *The Warrior Who Carried Life, The Unconquered Country, The Child Garden, Was, Lust* and *Air*. His *253, or Tube Theatre* was initially published electronically before appearing in print, and his latest novel, *The King's Last Song*, is set in Cambodia's past and present.

"In 1975 I read a from-the-scene dispatch in *The Times* of the evacuation of Phnom Penh and that absolutely gripped my imagination," remembers Ryman. "In 2000 I was invited by an Australian friend to stay at an Australian archaeological dig. Returning to do research, I fell in love with Cambodia all over again, and the way it was healing. I still haven't managed to write about the healing, but two long short stories and one novel did follow."

One of those long stories was "Pol Pot's Beautiful Daughter (Fantasy)", which was nominated for a science fiction Hugo Award. "Didn't they realise it was a ghost story?" asks the author.

I N CAMBODIA PEOPLE ARE used to ghosts. Ghosts buy newspapers. They own property.

A few years ago, spirits owned a house in Phnom Penh, at the Tra

Bek end of Monivong Boulevard. Khmer Rouge had murdered the whole family and there was no one left alive to inherit it. People cycled past the building, leaving it boarded up. Sounds of weeping came from inside.

Then a professional inheritor arrived from America. She'd done her research and could claim to be the last surviving relative of no fewer than three families. She immediately sold the house to a Chinese businessman, who turned the ground floor into a photo-copying shop.

The copiers began to print pictures of the original owners.

At first, single black and white photos turned up in the copied dossiers of aid workers or government officials. The father of the murdered family had been a lawyer. He stared fiercely out of the photos as if demanding something. In other photocopies, his beautiful daugh-ters forlornly hugged each other. The background was hazy like fog.

One night the owner heard a noise and trundled downstairs to find all five photocopiers printing one picture after another of faces: young college men, old women, parents with a string of babies, or government soldiers in uniform. He pushed the big green off-buttons. Nothing happened.

He pulled out all the plugs, but the machines kept grinding out face after face. Women in beehive hairdos or clever children with glasses looked wistfully out of the photocopies. They seemed to be dreaming of home in the 1960s, when Phnom Penh was the most beautiful city in Southeast Asia.

News spread. People began to visit the shop to identify lost relatives. Women would cry, "That's my mother! I didn't have a photograph!" They would weep and press the flimsy A4 sheets to their breasts. The paper went limp from tears and humidity as if it too were crying.

Soon, a throng began to gather outside the shop every morning to view the latest batch of faces. In desperation, the owner announced that each morning's harvest would be delivered direct to *The Truth*, a magazine of remembrance.

Then one morning he tried to open the house-door to the shop and found it blocked. He went round to the front of the building and rolled open the metal shutters.

The shop was packed from floor to ceiling with photocopies. The ground floor had no windows – the room had been filled from the inside. The owner pulled out a sheet of paper and saw himself on the ground, his head beaten in by a hoe. The same image was on every single page.

He buried the photocopiers and sold the house at once. The new owner liked its haunted reputation; it kept people away. The FOR SALE sign was left hanging from the second floor.

In a sense, the house had been bought by another ghost.

This is a completely untrue story about someone who must exist.

Pol pot's only child, a daughter, was born in 1986. Her name was Sith, and in 2004, she was eighteen years old.

Sith liked air conditioning and luxury automobiles. Her hair was dressed in cornrows and she had a spiky piercing above one eye. Her jeans were elaborately slashed and embroidered. Her pink T-shirts bore slogans in English: CARE KOOKY. PINK MOLL.

Sith lived like a woman on Thai television, doing as she pleased in lip-gloss and Sunsilked hair. Nine simple rules helped her avoid all unpleasantness.

1. Never think about the past or politics.
2. Ignore ghosts. They cannot hurt you.
3. Do not go to school. Hire tutors. Don't do homework. It is disturbing.
4. Always be driven everywhere in either the Mercedes or the BMW.
5. Avoid all well-dressed Cambodian boys. They are the sons of the estimated 250,000 new generals created by the regime. Their sons can behave with impunity.
6. Avoid all men with potbellies. They eat too well and therefore must be corrupt.
7. Avoid anyone who drives a Toyota Viva or Honda Dream motorcycle.
8. Don't answer letters or phone calls.
9. Never make any friends.

There was also a tenth rule, but that went without saying.

Rotten fruit rinds and black mud never stained Sith's designer sports shoes. Disabled beggars never asked her for alms. Her life began yesterday, which was effectively the same as today.

Every day, her driver took her to the new Soriya Market. It was almost the only place that Sith went. The colour of silver, Soriya rose up in many floors to a round glass dome.

Sith preferred the 142nd Street entrance. Its green awning made everyone look as if they were made of jade. The doorway went directly into the ice-cold jewellery rotunda with its floor of polished black and white stone. The individual stalls were hung with glittering necklaces and earrings.

Sith liked tiny shiny things that had no memory. She hated politics. She refused to listen to the news. Pol Pot's beautiful daughter wished the current leadership would behave decently, like her dad always did. To her.

She remembered the sound of her father's gentle voice. She remembered sitting on his lap in a forest enclosure, being bitten by mosquitoes. Memories of malaria had sunk into her very bones. She now associated forests with nausea, fevers, and pain. A flicker of tree-shade on her skin made her want to throw up and the odour of soil or fallen leaves made her gag. She had never been to Angkor Wat. She read nothing.

Sith shopped. Her driver was paid by the government and always carried an AK-47, but his wife, the housekeeper, had no idea who Sith was. The house was full of swept marble, polished teak furniture, iPods, Xboxes, and plasma screens.

Please remember that every word of this story is a lie. Pol Pot was no doubt a dedicated communist who made no money from ruling Cambodia. Nevertheless, a hefty allowance arrived for Sith every month from an account in Switzerland.

Nothing touched Sith, until she fell in love with the salesman at Hello Phones.

Cambodian readers may know that in 2004 there was no mobile phone shop in Soriya Market. However, there was a branch of Hello Phone Cards that had a round blue sales counter with orange trim. This shop looked like that.

Every day Sith bought or exchanged a mobile phone there. She would sit and flick her hair at the salesman.

His name was Dara, which means Star. Dara knew about deals on call prices, sim cards, and the new phones that showed videos. He could get her any call tone she liked.

Talking to Dara broke none of Sith's rules. He wasn't fat, nor was he well dressed, and far from being a teenager, he was a comfortably mature twenty-four years old.

One day, Dara chuckled and said, "As a friend I advise you, you don't need another mobile phone."

Sith wrinkled her nose. "I don't like this one anymore. It's blue. I want something more feminine. But not frilly. And it should have better sound quality."

"Okay, but you could save your money and buy some more nice clothes."

Pol Pot's beautiful daughter lowered her chin, which she knew made her neck look long and graceful. "Do you like my clothes?"

"Why ask me?"

She shrugged. "I don't know. It's good to check out your look."

Dara nodded. "You look cool. What does your sister say?"

Sith let him know she had no family. "Ah," he said and quickly changed the subject. That was terrific. Secrecy and sympathy in one easy movement.

Sith came back the next day and said that she'd decided that the rose-coloured phone was too feminine. Dara laughed aloud and his eyes sparkled. Sith had come late in the morning just so that he could ask this question. "Are you hungry? Do you want to meet for lunch?"

Would he think she was cheap if she said yes? Would he say she was snobby if she said no?

"Just so long as we eat in Soriya Market," she said.

She was torn between BBWorld Burgers and Lucky7. BBWorld was big, round, and just two floors down from the dome. Lucky7 Burgers was part of the Lucky Supermarket, such a good store that a tiny jar of Maxwell House cost US$2.40.

They decided on BBWorld. It was full of light and they could see the town spread out through the wide clean windows. Sith sat in silence.

Pol Pot's daughter had nothing to say unless she was buying something.

Or rather she had only one thing to say, but she must never say it.

Dara did all the talking. He talked about how the guys on the third floor could get him a deal on original copies of *Grand Theft Auto*. He hinted that he could get Sith discounts from Bsfashion, the spotlit modern shop one floor down.

Suddenly he stopped. "You don't need to be afraid of me, you know." He said it in a kindly, grownup voice. "I can see, you're a properly brought up girl. I like that. It's nice."

Sith still couldn't find anything to say. She could only nod. She wanted to run away.

"Would you like to go to K-Four?"

K-Four, the big electronics shop, stocked all the reliable brand names: Hitachi, Sony, Panasonic, Philips, or Denon. It was so expensive that almost nobody shopped there, which is why Sith liked it. A crowd of people stood outside and stared through the window at a huge home entertainment centre showing a DVD of *Ice Age*. On the screen, a little animal was being chased by a glacier. It was so beautiful!

Sith finally found something to say. "If I had one of those, I would never need to leave the house."

Dara looked at her sideways and decided to laugh.

The next day Sith told him that all the phones she had were too big. Did he have one that she could wear around her neck like jewelry?

This time they went to Lucky7 Burgers, and sat across from the Revlon counter. They watched boys having their hair layered by Revlon's natural beauty specialists.

Dara told her more about himself. His father had died in the wars. His family now lived in the country. Sith's Coca-Cola suddenly tasted of anti-malarial drugs.

"But . . . you don't want to *live* in the country," she said.

"No. I have to live in Phnom Penh to make money. But my folks are good country people. Modest." He smiled, embarrassed.

They'll have hens and a cousin who shimmies up coconut trees. There will be trees all around but no shops anywhere. The earth will smell.

Sith couldn't finish her drink. She sighed and smiled and said abruptly, "I'm sorry. It's been cool. But I have to go." She slunk sideways out of her seat as slowly as molasses.

Walking back into the jewellery rotunda with nothing to do, she realised that Dara would think she didn't like him.

And that made the lower part of her eyes sting.

She went back the next day and didn't even pretend to buy a mobile phone. She told Dara that she'd left so suddenly the day before because she'd remembered a hair appointment.

He said that he could see she took a lot of trouble with her hair. Then he asked her out for a movie that night.

Sith spent all day shopping in K-Four.

They met at six. Dara was so considerate that he didn't even suggest the horror movie. He said he wanted to see *Buffalo Girl Hiding*, a movie about a country girl who lives on a farm. Sith said with great feeling that she would prefer the horror movie.

The cinema on the top floor opened out directly onto the roof of Soriya. Graffiti had been scratched into the green railings. Why would people want to ruin something new and beautiful? Sith put her arm through Dara's and knew that they were now boyfriend and girlfriend.

"Finally," he said.

"Finally what?"

"You've done something."

They leaned on the railings and looked out over other people's apartments. West toward the river was a building with one huge roof terrace. Women met there to gossip. Children were playing toss-the-sandal. From this distance, Sith was enchanted.

"I just love watching the children."

The movie, from Thailand, was about a woman whose face turns blue and spotty and who eats men. The blue woman was yucky, but not as scary as all the badly dubbed voices. The characters sounded possessed. It was though Thai people had been taken over by the spirits of dead Cambodians.

Whenever Sith got scared, she chuckled.

So she sat chuckling with terror. Dara thought she was laughing at a dumb movie and found such intelligence charming. He started to chuckle too. Sith thought he was as frightened as she was. Together in the dark, they took each other's hands.

Outside afterward, the air hung hot even in the dark and 142nd Street smelled of drains. Sith stood on tiptoe to avoid the oily deposits and cast-off fishbones.

Dara said, "I will drive you home."

"My driver can take us," said Sith, flipping open her Kermit-the-Frog mobile.

Her black Mercedes Benz edged to a halt, crunching old plastic bottles in the gutter. The seats were upholstered with tan leather and the driver was armed.

Dara's jaw dropped. "Who . . . *who* is your father?"

"He's dead."

Dara shook his head. "Who was he?"

Normally Sith used her mother's family name, but that would not answer this question. Flustered, she tried to think of someone who could be her father. She knew of nobody the right age. She remembered something about a politician who had died. His name came to her and she said it in panic. "My father was Kol Vireakboth." Had she got the name right? "Please don't tell anyone."

Dara covered his eyes. "We – my family, my father – we fought for the KPLA."

Sith had to stop herself asking what the KPLA was.

Kol Vireakboth had led a faction in the civil wars. It fought against the Khmer Rouge, the Vietnamese, the King, and corruption. It wanted a new way for Cambodia. Kol Vireakboth was a Cambodian leader who had never told a lie and or accepted a bribe.

Remember that this is an untrue story.

Dara started to back away from the car. "I don't think we should be doing this. I'm just a villager, really."

"That doesn't matter."

His eyes closed. "I would expect nothing less from the daughter of Kol Vireakboth."

Oh for gosh sake, she just picked the man's name out of the air, she didn't need more problems. "Please!" she said.

Dara sighed. "Okay. I said I would see you home safely. I will." Inside the Mercedes, he stroked the tan leather.

When they arrived, he craned his neck to look up at the building. "Which floor are you on?"

"All of them."

Colour drained from his face.

"My driver will take you back," she said to Dara. As the car pulled away, she stood outside the closed garage shutters, waving forlornly.

Then Sith panicked. Who was Kol Vireakboth? She went online and Googled. She had to read about the wars. Her skin started to creep. All those different factions swam in her head: ANS, NADK, KPR, and KPNLF. The very names seemed to come at her spoken by forgotten voices.

Soon she had all she could stand. She printed out Vireakboth's picture and decided to have it framed. In case Dara visited.

Kol Vireakboth had a round face and a fatherly smile. His eyes seemed to slant upward toward his nose, looking full of kindly insight. He'd been killed by a car bomb.

All that night, Sith heard whispering.

In the morning, there was another picture of someone else in the tray of her printer.

A long-faced, buck-toothed woman stared out at her in black and white. Sith noted the victim's fashion lapses. The woman's hair was a mess, all frizzy. She should have had it straightened and put in some nice highlights. The woman's eyes drilled into her.

"Can't touch me," said Sith. She left the photo in the tray. She went to see Dara, right away, no breakfast.

His eyes were circled with dark flesh and his blue Hello trousers and shirt were not properly ironed.

"Buy the whole shop," Dara said, looking deranged. "The guys in K-Four just told me some girl in blue jeans walked in yesterday and bought two home theatres. One for the salon, she said, and one for the roof terrace. She paid for both of them in full and had them delivered to the far end of Monivong."

Sith sighed. "I'm sending one back." She hoped that sounded abstemious. "It looked too metallic against my curtains."

Pause.

"She also bought an Aido robot dog for fifteen hundred dollars."

Sith would have preferred that Dara did not know about the dog. It was just a silly toy; it hadn't occurred to her that it might cost that much until she saw the bill. "They should not tell everyone about their customers' business or soon they will have no customers."

Dara was looking at her as if thinking: *This is not just a nice sweet girl.*

"I had fun last night," Sith said in a voice as thin as high clouds.

"So did I."

"We don't have to tell anyone about my family. Do we?" Sith was seriously scared of losing him.

"No. But Sith, it's stupid. Your family, my family, we are not equals."

"It doesn't make any difference."

"You lied to me. Your family is not dead. You have famous uncles."

She did indeed – Uncle Ieng Sary, Uncle Khieu Samphan, Uncle Ta Mok. All the Pol Pot clique had been called her uncles.

"I didn't know them that well," she said. That was true, too.

What would she do if she couldn't shop in Soriya Market anymore? What would she do without Dara?

She begged. "I am not a strong person. Sometimes I think I am not a person at all. I'm just a space."

Dara looked suddenly mean. "You're just a credit card." Then his face fell. "I'm sorry. That was an unkind thing to say. You are very young for your age and I'm older than you and I should have treated you with more care."

Sith was desperate. "All my money would be very nice."

"I'm not for sale."

He worked in a shop and would be sending money home to a fatherless family; of course he was for sale!

Sith had a small heart, but a big head for thinking. She knew that she had to do this delicately, like picking a flower, or she would spoil the bloom. "Let's . . . let's just go see a movie?"

After all, she was beautiful and well brought up and she knew her eyes were big and round. Her tiny heart was aching.

This time they saw *Tum Teav*, a remake of an old movie from the 1960s. If movies were not nightmares about ghosts, then they tried to preserve the past. *When*, thought Sith, *will they make a movie about*

Cambodia's future? Tum Teav was based on a classic tale of a young monk who falls in love with a properly brought up girl but her mother opposes the match. They commit suicide at the end, bringing a curse on their village. Sith sat through it stony-faced. *I am not going to be a dead heroine in a romance.*

Dara offered to drive her home again and that's when Sith found out that he drove a Honda Dream. He proudly presented to her the gleaming motorcycle of fast young men. Sith felt backed into a corner. She'd already offered to buy him. Showing off her car again might humiliate him.

So she broke rule number seven.

Dara hid her bag in the back and they went soaring down Monivong Boulevard at night, past homeless people, prostitutes, and chefs staggering home after work. It was late in the year, but it started to rain.

Sith loved it, the cool air brushing against her face, the cooler rain clinging to her eyelashes.

She remembered being five years old in the forest and dancing in the monsoon. She encircled Dara's waist to stay on the bike and suddenly found her cheek was pressed up against his back. She giggled in fear, not of the rain, but of what she felt.

He dropped her off at home. Inside, everything was dark except for the flickering green light on her printer. In the tray were two new photographs. One was of a child, a little boy, holding up a school prize certificate. The other was a tough, wise-looking old man, with a string of muscle down either side of his ironic, bitter smile. They looked directly at her.

They know who I am.

As she climbed the stairs to her bedroom, she heard someone sobbing, far away, as if the sound came from next door. She touched the walls of the staircase. They shivered slightly, constricting in time to the cries.

In her bedroom she extracted one of her many iPods from the tangle of wires and listened to *System of a Down*, as loud as she could. It helped her sleep. The sound of nu-metal guitars seemed to come roaring out of her own heart.

She was woken up in the sun-drenched morning by the sound of her doorbell many floors down. She heard the housekeeper Jorani call and the door open. Sith hesitated over choice of jeans and top. By the time she got downstairs she found the driver and the housemaid joking with Dara, giving him tea.

Like the sunshine, Dara seemed to disperse ghosts.

"Hi," he said. "It's my day off. I thought we could go on a motorcycle ride to the country."

But not to the country. Couldn't they just spend the day in Soriya? No, said Dara, there's lots of other places to see in Phnom Penh.

He drove her, twisting through back streets. How did the city get so poor? How did it get so dirty?

They went to a new and modern shop for CDs that was run by a record label. Dara knew all the cool new music, most of it influenced by Khmer-Americans returning from Long Beach and Compton: Sdey, Phnom Penh Bad Boys, Khmer Kid.

Sith bought twenty CDs.

They went to the National Museum and saw the beautiful Buddha-like head of King Jayavarman VII. Dara without thinking ducked and held up his hands in prayer. They had dinner in a French restaurant with candles and wine, and it was just like in a karaoke video, a boy, a girl, and her money all going out together. They saw the show at Sovanna Phum, and there was a wonderful dance piece with sampled 1940s music from an old French movie, with traditional Khmer choreography.

Sith went home, her heart singing, *Dara, Dara, Dara.*

In the bedroom, a mobile phone began to ring, over and over. CALL 1 said the screen, but gave no name or number, so the person was not on Sith's list of contacts.

She turned off the phone. It kept ringing. That's when she knew for certain.

She hid the phone in a pillow in the spare bedroom and put another pillow on top of it and then closed the door.

All forty-two of her mobile phones started to ring. They rang from inside closets, or from the bathroom where she had forgotten them. They rang from the roof terrace and even from inside a shoe under her bed.

"I am a very stubborn girl!" she shouted at the spirits. "You do not scare me."

She turned up her iPod and finally slept.

As soon as the sun was up, she roused her driver, slumped deep in his hammock.

"Come on, we're going to Soriya Market," she said.

The driver looked up at her dazed, then remembered to smile and lower his head in respect.

His face fell when she showed up in the garage with all forty-two of her mobile phones in one black bag.

It was too early for Soriya Market to open. They drove in circles with sunrise blazing directly into their eyes. On the streets, men pushed carts like beasts of burden, or carried cascades of belts into the old Central Market. The old market was domed, art deco, the colour of vomit, French. Sith never shopped there.

"Maybe you should go visit your Mom," said the driver. "You know, she loves you. Families are there for when you are in trouble."

Sith's mother lived in Thailand and they never spoke. Her mother's family kept asking for favours: money, introductions, or help with getting a job. Sith didn't speak to them any longer.

"My family is only trouble."

The driver shut up and drove.

Finally Soriya opened. Sith went straight to Dara's shop and dumped all the phones on the blue countertop. "Can you take these back?"

"We only do exchanges. I can give a new phone for an old one." Dara looked thoughtful. "Don't worry. Leave them here with me, I'll go sell them to a guy in the old market, and give you your money tomorrow." He smiled in approval. "This is very sensible."

He passed one phone back, the one with video and email. "This is the best one, keep this."

Dara was so competent. Sith wanted to sink down onto him like a pillow and stay there. She sat in the shop all day, watching him work. One of the guys from the games shop upstairs asked, "Who is this beautiful girl?"

Dara answered proudly, "My girlfriend."

Dara drove her back on the Dream and at the door to her house, he chuckled. "I don't want to go." She pressed a finger against his naughty lips, and smiled and spun back inside from happiness.

She was in the ground-floor garage. She heard something like a rat scuttle. In her bag, the telephone rang. Who were these people to importune her, even if they were dead? She wrenched the mobile phone out of her bag and pushed the green button and put the phone to her ear. She waited. There was a sound like wind.

A child spoke to her, his voice clogged as if he was crying. "They tied my thumbs together."

Sith demanded. "How did you get my number?"

"I'm all alone!"

"Then ring somebody else. Someone in your family."

"All my family are dead. I don't know where I am. My name is . . ."

Sith clicked the phone off. She opened the trunk of the car and tossed the phone inside it. Being telephoned by ghosts was so . . .

unmodern. How could Cambodia become a number one country if its cell phone network was haunted?

She stormed up into the salon. On top of a table, the $1500, no-mess dog stared at her from out of his packaging. Sith clumped up the stairs onto the roof terrace to sleep as far away as she could from everything in the house.

She woke up in the dark, to hear thumping from downstairs.

The sound was metallic and hollow, as if someone were locked in the car. Sith turned on her iPod. Something was making the sound of the music skip. She fought the tangle of wires, and wrenched out another player, a Xen, but it too skipped, burping the sound of speaking voices into the middle of the music.

Had she heard a ripping sound? She pulled out the earphones, and heard something climbing the stairs.

A sound of light, uneven lolloping. She thought of crippled children. Frost settled over her like a heavy blanket and she could not move.

The robot dog came whirring up onto the terrace. It paused at the top of the stairs, its camera nose pointing at her to see, its useless eyes glowing cherry red.

The robot dog said in a warm, friendly voice, "My name is Phalla. I tried to buy my sister medicine and they killed me for it."

Sith tried to say, "Go away," but her throat wouldn't open.

The dog tilted its head. "No one even knows I'm dead. What will you do for all the people who are not mourned?"

Laughter blurted out of her, and Sith saw it rise up as cold vapour into the air.

"We have no one to invite us to the feast," said the dog.

Sith giggled in terror. "Nothing. I can do nothing!" she said, shaking her head.

"You laugh?" The dog gathered itself and jumped up into the hammock with her. It turned and lifted up its clear plastic tail and laid a genuine turd alongside Sith. Short brown hair was wound up in it, a scalp actually, and a single flat white human tooth smiled out of it.

Sith squawked and overturned both herself and the dog out of the hammock and onto the floor. The dog pushed its nose up against hers and began to sing an old-fashioned children's song about birds.

Something heavy huffed its way up the stairwell toward her. Sith shivered with cold on the floor and could not move. The dog went on singing in a high, sweet voice. A large shadow loomed out over the top of the staircase, and Sith gargled, swallowing laughter, trying to speak.

"There was thumping in the car and no one in it," said the driver.

Sith sagged toward the floor with relief. "The ghosts," she said. "They're back." She thrust herself to her feet. "We're getting out now. Ring the Hilton. Find out if they have rooms."

She kicked the toy dog down the stairs ahead of her. "We're moving now!"

Together they all loaded the car, shaking. Once again, the house was left to ghosts. As they drove, the mobile phone rang over and over inside the trunk.

The new Hilton (which does not exist) rose up by the river across from the Department for Cults and Religious Affairs. Tall and marbled and pristine, it had crystal chandeliers and fountains, and wood and brass handles in the elevators.

In the middle of the night only the Bridal Suite was still available, but it had an extra parental chamber where the driver and his wife could sleep. High on the twenty-first floor, the night sparkled with lights and everything was hushed, as far away from Cambodia as it was possible to get.

Things were quiet after that, for a while.

Every day she and Dara went to movies, or went to a restaurant. They went shopping. She slipped him money and he bought himself a beautiful suit. He said, over a hamburger at Lucky7, "I've told my mother that I've met a girl."

Sith smiled and thought: and I bet you told her that I'm rich.

"I've decided to live in the Hilton," she told him.

Maybe we could live in the Hilton. A pretty smile could hint at that.

The rainy season ended. The last of the monsoons rose up dark grey with a froth of white cloud on top, looking exactly like a giant wave about to break.

Dry cooler air arrived.

After work was over Dara convinced her to go for a walk along the river in front of the Royal Palace. He went to the men's room to change into a new luxury suit and Sith thought: he's beginning to imagine life with all that money.

As they walked along the river, exposed to all those people, Sith shook inside. There were teenage boys everywhere. Some of them were in rags, which was reassuring, but some of them were very well dressed indeed, the sons of Impunity who could do anything. Sith swerved suddenly to avoid even seeing them. But Dara in his new beige suit looked like one of them, and the generals' sons nodded to him with quizzical eyebrows, perhaps wondering who he was.

In front of the palace, a pavilion reached out over the water. Next to it a traditional orchestra bashed and wailed out something old fashioned. Hundreds of people crowded around a tiny wat. Dara shook Sith's wrist and they stood up to see.

People held up bundles of lotus flowers and incense in prayer. They threw the bundles into the wat. Monks immediately shovelled the joss sticks and flowers out of the back.

Behind the wat, children wearing T-shirts and shorts black with filth rootled through the dead flowers, the smouldering incense, and old coconut shells.

Sith asked, "Why do they do that?"

"You are so innocent!" chuckled Dara and shook his head. The evening was blue and gold. Sith had time to think that she did not want to go back to a hotel and that the only place she really felt happy was next to Dara. All around that thought was something dark and tangled.

Dara suggested with affection that they should get married.

It was as if Sith had her answer ready. "No, absolutely not," she said at once. "How can you ask that? There is not even anyone for you to ask! Have you spoken to your family about me? Has your family made any checks about my background?"

Which was what she really wanted to know.

Dara shook his head. "I have explained that you are an orphan, but they are not concerned with that. We are modest people. They will be happy if I am happy."

"Of course they won't be! Of course they will need to do checks." Sith scowled. She saw her way to sudden advantage. "At least they must consult fortunetellers. They are not fools. I can help them. Ask them the names of the fortunetellers they trust."

Dara smiled shyly. "We have no money."

"I will give them money and you can tell them that you pay."

Dara's eyes searched her face. "I don't want that."

"How will we know if it is a good marriage? And your poor mother, how can you ask her to make a decision like this without information? So. You ask your family for the names of good professionals they trust, and I will pay them, and I will go to Prime Minister Hun Sen's own personal fortuneteller, and we can compare results."

Thus she established again both her propriety and her status.

In an old romance, the parents would not approve of the match and the fortuneteller would say that the marriage was ill-omened. Sith left nothing to romance.

She offered the family's fortunetellers whatever they wanted – a car, a farm – and in return demanded a written copy of their judgment. All of them agreed that the portents for the marriage were especially auspicious.

Then she secured an appointment with the Prime Minister's fortuneteller.

Hun Sen's *Kru Taey* was a lady in a black business suit. She had long fingernails like talons, but they were perfectly manicured and frosted white.

She was the kind of fortuneteller who is possessed by someone else's spirit. She sat at a desk and looked at Sith as unblinking as a fish, both her hands steepled together. After the most basic of hellos, she said. "Dollars only. Twenty-five thousand. I need to buy my son an apartment."

"That's a very high fee," said Sith.

"It's not a fee. It is a consideration for giving you the answer you want. My fee is another twenty-five thousand dollars."

They negotiated. Sith liked the Kru Taey's manner. It confirmed everything Sith believed about life.

The fee was reduced somewhat but not the consideration.

"Payment upfront now," the Kru Taey said. She wouldn't take a check. Like only the very best restaurants she accepted foreign credit cards. Sith's Swiss card worked immediately. It had unlimited credit in case she had to leave the country in a hurry.

The Kru Taey said, "I will tell the boy's family that the marriage will be particularly fortunate."

Sith realised that she had not yet said anything about a boy, his family, or a marriage.

The Kru Taey smiled. "I know you are not interested in your real fortune. But to be kind, I will tell you unpaid that this marriage really is particularly well favoured. All the other fortunetellers would have said the same thing without being bribed."

The Kru Taey's eyes glinted in the most unpleasant way. "So you needn't have bought them farms or paid me an extra twenty-five thousand dollars."

She looked down at her perfect fingernails. "You will be very happy indeed. But not before your entire life is overturned."

The back of Sith's arms prickled as if from cold. She should have been angry but she could feel herself smiling. Why?

And why waste politeness on the old witch? Sith turned to go without saying good-bye.

"Oh, and about your other problem," said the woman.

Sith turned back and waited.

"Enemies," said the Kru Taey, "can turn out to be friends."

Sith sighed. "What are you talking about?"

The Kru Taey's smile was a wide as a tiger-trap. "The million people your father killed."

Sith went hard. "Not a million," she said. "Somewhere between two hundred and fifty and five hundred thousand."

"Enough," smiled the Kru Taey. "My father was one of them." She smiled for a moment longer. "I will be sure to tell the Prime Minister that you visited me."

Sith snorted as if in scorn. "I will tell him myself."

But she ran back to her car.

That night, Sith looked down on all the lights like diamonds. She settled onto the giant mattress and turned on her iPod.

Someone started to yell at her. She pulled out the earpieces and jumped to the window. It wouldn't open. She shook it and wrenched its frame until it reluctantly slid an inch and she threw the iPod out of the twenty-first-floor window.

She woke up late the next morning, to hear the sound of the TV. She opened up the double doors into the salon and saw Jorani, pressed against the wall.

"The TV . . . ," Jorani said, her eyes wide with terror.

The driver waited by his packed bags. He stood up, looking as mournful as a bloodhound.

On the widescreen TV there was what looked like a pop music karaoke video. Except that the music was very old fashioned. Why would a pop video show a starving man eating raw maize in a field? He glanced over his shoulder in terror as he ate. The glowing singalong words were the song that the dog had sung at the top of the stairs. The starving man looked up at Sith and corn mash rolled out of his mouth.

"It's all like that," said the driver. "I unplugged the set, but it kept playing on every channel." He sompiahed but looked miserable. "My wife wants to leave."

Sith felt shame. It was miserable and dirty, being infested with ghosts. Of course they would want to go.

"It's okay. I can take taxis," she said.

The driver nodded, and went into the next room and whispered to his wife. With little scurrying sounds, they gathered up their things. They sompiahed, and apologised.

The door clicked almost silently behind them.

It will always be like this, thought Sith. Wherever I go. It would be like this with Dara.

The hotel telephone started to ring. Sith left it ringing. She covered the TV with a blanket, but the terrible, tinny old music kept wheedling and rattling its way out at her, and she sat on the edge of her bed, staring into space.

I'll have to leave Cambodia.

At the market, Dara looked even more cheerful than usual. The fortunetellers had pronounced the marriage as very favourable. His mother had invited Sith home for the Pchum Ben festival.

"We can take the bus tomorrow," he said.

"Does it smell? All those people in one place?"

"It smells of air freshener. Then we take a taxi, and then you will have to walk up the track." Dara suddenly doubled up in laughter. "Oh, it will be good for you."

"Will there be dirt?"

"Everywhere! Oh, your dirty Nikes will earn you much merit!"

But at least, thought Sith, there will be no TV or phones.

Two days later, Sith was walking down a dirt track, ducking tree branches. Dust billowed all over her shoes. Dara walked behind her, chuckling, which meant she thought he was scared too.

She heard a strange rattling sound. "What's that noise?"

"It's a goat," he said. "My mother bought it for me in April as a present."

A goat. How could they be any more rural? Sith had never seen a goat. She never even imagined that she would.

Dara explained. "I sell them to the Muslims. It is Agricultural Diversification."

There were trees everywhere, shadows crawling across the ground like snakes. Sith felt sick. *One mosquito*, she promised herself, *just one and I will squeal and run away*.

The house was tiny, on thin twisting stilts. She had pictured a big fine country house standing high over the ground on concrete pillars with a sunburst carving in the gable. The kitchen was a hut that sat directly on the ground, no stilts, and it was made of palm-leaf panels and there was no electricity. The strip light in the ceiling was attached to a car battery and they kept a live fire on top of the concrete table to cook. Everything smelled of burnt fish.

Sith loved it.

Inside the hut, the smoke from the fires kept the mosquitoes away. Dara's mother, Mrs Non Kunthea, greeted her with a smile. That triggered a respectful sompiah from Sith, the prayer-like gesture leaping out of her unbidden. On the platform table was a plastic sack full of dried prawns.

Without thinking, Sith sat on the table and began to pull the salty prawns out of their shells.

Why am I doing this?

Because it's what I did at home.

Sith suddenly remembered the enclosure in the forest, a circular fenced area. Daddy had slept in one house, and the women in another. Sith would talk to the cooks. For something to do, she would chop vegetables or shell prawns. Then Daddy would come to eat and he'd sit on the platform table and she, little Sith, would sit between his knees.

Dara's older brother Yuth came back for lunch. He was pot-bellied and drove a taxi for a living, and he moved in hard jabs like an angry old man. He reached too far for the rice and Sith could smell his armpits.

"You see how we live," Yuth said to Sith. "This is what we get for having the wrong patron. Sihanouk thought we were anti-monarchist. To Hun Sen, we were the enemy. Remember the Work for Money program?"

No.

"They didn't give any of those jobs to us. We might as well have been the Khmer Rouge!"

The past, thought Sith, *why don't they just let it go? Why do they keep boasting about their old wars?*

Mrs Non Kunthea chuckled with affection. "My eldest son was born angry," she said. "His slogan is 'ten years is not too late for revenge.'"

Yuth started up again. "They treat that old monster Pol Pot better than they treat us. But then, he was an important person. If you go to his *stupa* in Anlong Veng, you will see that people leave offerings! They ask him for lottery numbers!"

He crumpled his green, soft, old-fashioned hat back onto his head and said, "Nice to meet you, Sith. Dara, she's too high class for the likes of you." But he grinned as he said it. He left, swirling disruption in his wake.

The dishes were gathered. Again without thinking, Sith swept up the plastic tub and carried it to the blackened branches. They rested over puddles where the washing-up water drained.

"You shouldn't work," said Dara's mother. "You are a guest."

"I grew up in a refugee camp," said Sith. After all, it was true.

Dara looked at her with a mix of love, pride, and gratitude for the good fortune of a rich wife who works.

And that was the best Sith could hope for. This family would be fine for her.

In the late afternoon, all four brothers came with their wives for the end of Pchum Ben, when the ghosts of the dead can wander the Earth. People scatter rice on the temple floors to feed their families. Some ghosts have small mouths so special rice is used.

Sith never took part in Pchum Ben. How could she go the temple and scatter rice for Pol Pot?

The family settled in the kitchen chatting and joking, and it all passed in a blur for Sith. Everyone else had family they could honour. To Sith's surprise one of the uncles suggested that people should write names of the deceased and burn them, to transfer merit. It was nothing to do with Pchum Ben, but a lovely idea, so all the family wrote down names.

Sith sat with her hands jammed under her arms.

Dara's mother asked, "Isn't there a name you want to write, Sith?"

"No," said Sith in a tiny voice. How could she write the name Pol Pot? He was surely roaming the world let loose from hell. "There is no one."

Dara rubbed her hand. "Yes there is, Sith. A very special name."

"No, there's not."

Dara thought she didn't want them to know her father was Kol Vireakboth. He leant forward and whispered. "I promise. No one will see it."

Sith's breath shook. She took the paper and started to cry.

"Oh," said Dara's mother, stricken with sympathy. "Everyone in this country has a tragedy."

Sith wrote the name Kol Vireakboth.

Dara kept the paper folded and caught Sith's eyes. *You see?* he seemed to say. *I have kept your secret safe.* The paper burned.

Thunder slapped a clear sky about the face. It had been sunny, but now as suddenly as a curtain dropped down over a doorway, rain fell. A wind came from nowhere, tearing away a flap of palm-leaf wall, as if forcing entrance in a fury.

The family whooped and laughed and let the rain drench their shoulders as they stood up to push the wall back down, to keep out the rain.

But Sith knew. Her father's enemy was in the kitchen.

The rain passed; the sun came out. The family chuckled and sat back down around or on the table. They lowered dishes of food and ate, making parcels of rice and fish with their fingers. Sith sat rigidly erect, waiting for misfortune.

What would the spirit of Kol Vireakboth do to Pol Pot's daughter? Would he overturn the table, soiling her with food? Would he send mosquitoes to bite and make her sick? Would he suck away all her good fortune, leaving the marriage blighted, her new family estranged?

Or would a kindly spirit simply wish that the children of all Cambodians could escape, escape the past?

Suddenly, Sith felt at peace. The sunlight and shadows looked new to her and her senses started to work in magic ways.

She smelled a perfume of emotion, sweet and bracing at the same time. The music from a neighbour's cassette player touched her arm gently. Words took the form of sunlight on her skin.

No one is evil, the sunlight said. *But they can be false.*

False, how? Sith asked without speaking, genuinely baffled.

The sunlight smiled with an old man's stained teeth. *You know very well how.*

All the air swelled with the scent of the food, savoring it. The trees sighed with satisfaction.

Life is true. Sith saw steam from the rice curl up into the branches. *Death is false.*

The sunlight stood up to go. It whispered. *Tell him.*

The world faded back to its old self.

That night in a hammock in a room with the other women, Sith suddenly sat bolt upright. Clarity would not let her sleep. She saw that there was no way ahead. She couldn't marry Dara. How could she ask him to marry someone who was harassed by one million dead? How could she explain I am haunted because I am Pol Pot's daughter and I have lied about everything?

The dead would not let her marry; the dead would not let her have joy. So who could Pol Pot's daughter pray to? Where could she go for wisdom?

Loak kru Kol Vireakboth, she said under her breath. *Please show me a way ahead.*

The darkness was sterner than the sunlight.

To be as false as you are, it said, *you first have to lie to yourself.*

What lies had Sith told? She knew the facts. Her father had been the head of a government that tortured and killed hundreds of thousands of people and starved the nation through mismanagement. I know the truth.

I just never think about it.

I've never faced it.

Well, the truth is as dark as I am, and you live in me, the darkness.

She had read books – well, the first chapter of books – and then dropped them as if her fingers were scalded. There was no truth for her in books. The truth ahead of her would be loneliness, dreary adulthood, and penance.

Grow up.

The palm-leaf panels stirred like waiting ghosts.

All through the long bus ride back, she said nothing. Dara went silent too, and hung his head.

In the huge and empty hotel suite, darkness awaited her. She'd had the phone and the TV removed; her footsteps sounded hollow. Jorani and the driver had been her only friends.

The next day she did not go to Soriya Market. She went instead to the torture museum of Tuol Sleng.

A cadre of young motoboys waited outside the hotel in baseball caps and bling. Instead, Sith hailed a sweet-faced older motoboy with a battered, rusty bike.

As they drove she asked him about his family. He lived alone and had no one except for his mother in Kompong Thom.

Outside the gates of Tuol Sleng he said, "This was my old school."

In one wing there were rows of rooms with one iron bed in each with handcuffs and stains on the floor. Photos on the wall showed twisted bodies chained to those same beds as they were found on the day of liberation. In one photograph, a chair was overturned as if in a hurry.

Sith stepped outside and looked instead at a beautiful house over the wall across the street. It was a high white house like her own, with pillars and a roof terrace and bougainvillaea, a modern daughter's house. What do they think when they look out from that roof terrace? How can they live here?

The grass was tended and full of hopping birds. People were painting the shutters of the prison a fresh blue-grey.

In the middle wing, the rooms were galleries of photographed faces. They stared out at her like the faces from her printer. Were some of them the same?

"Who are they?" she found herself asking a Cambodian visitor.

"Their own," the woman replied. "This is where they sent Khmer Rouge cadres who had fallen out of favour. They would not waste such torture on ordinary Cambodians."

Some of the faces were young and beautiful men. Some were children or dignified old women.

The Cambodian lady kept pace with her. Company? Did she guess who Sith was? "They couldn't simply beat party cadres to death. They sent them and their entire families here. The children too, the grandmothers. They had different days of the week for killing children and wives."

An innocent looking man smiled out at the camera as sweetly as her aged motoboy, directly into the camera of his torturers. He seemed to expect kindness from them, and decency. *Comrades*, he seemed to say.

The face in the photograph moved. It smiled more broadly and was about to speak.

Sith eyes darted away. The next face sucked all her breath away.

It was not a stranger. It was Dara, her Dara, in black shirt and black cap. She gasped and looked back at the lady. Her pinched and solemn face nodded up and down. Was she a ghost too?

Sith reeled outside and hid her face and didn't know if she could go on standing. Tears slid down her face and she wanted to be sick and she turned her back so no one could see.

Then she walked to the motoboy, sitting in a shelter. In complete silence, she got on his bike feeling angry at the place, angry at the government for preserving it, angry at the foreigners who visited it like a tourist attraction, angry at everything.

That is not who we are! That is not what I am!

The motoboy slipped onto his bike, and Sith asked him: What happened to your family? It was a cruel question. He had to smile and look cheerful. His father had run a small shop; they went out into the country and never came back. He lived with his brother in a *jeum-room*, a refugee camp in Thailand. They came back to fight the Vietnamese and his brother was killed.

She was going to tell the motoboy, drive me back to the Hilton, but she felt ashamed. Of what? Just how far was she going to run?

She asked him to take her to the old house on Monivong Boulevard.

As the motorcycle wove through back streets, dodging red-earth ruts and pedestrians, she felt rage at her father. How dare he involve her in something like that! Sith had lived a small life and had no measure of things so she thought: *it's as if someone tinted my hair and it all fell out. It's as if someone pierced my ears and they got infected and my whole ear rotted away.*

She remembered that she had never felt any compassion for her father. She had been twelve years old when he stood trial, old and sick and making such a show of leaning on his stick. Everything he did was a show. She remembered rolling her eyes in constant embarrassment. Oh, he was fine in front of rooms full of adoring students. He could play the *bong thom* with them. They thought he was enlightened. He sounded good, using his false, soft and kindly little voice, as if he was dubbed. He had made Sith recite Verlaine,

Rimbaud, and Rilke. He killed thousands for having foreign influences.

I don't know what I did in a previous life to deserve you for a father. But you were not my father in a previous life and you won't be my father in the next. I reject you utterly. I will never burn your name. You can wander hungry out of hell every year for all eternity. I will pray to keep you in hell.

I am not your daughter!

If you were false, I have to be true.

Her old house looked abandoned in the stark afternoon light, closed and innocent. At the doorstep she turned and thrust a fistful of dollars into the motoboy's hand. She couldn't think straight; she couldn't even see straight, her vision blurred.

Back inside, she calmly put down her teddy-bear rucksack and walked upstairs to her office. Aido the robot dog whirred his way toward her. She had broken his back leg kicking him downstairs. He limped, whimpering like a dog, and lowered his head to have it stroked.

To her relief, there was only one picture waiting for her in the tray of the printer.

Kol Vireakboth looked out at her, middle-aged, handsome, worn, wise. Pity and kindness glowed in his eyes.

The land line began to ring.

"*Youl prom,*" she told the ghosts. Agreed.

She picked up the receiver and waited.

A man spoke. "My name was Yin Bora." His voice bubbled up brokenly as if from underwater.

A light blinked in the printer. A photograph slid out quickly. A young student stared out at her looking happy at a family feast. He had a Beatle haircut and a striped shirt.

"That's me," said the voice on the phone. "I played football."

Sith coughed. "What do you want me to do?"

"Write my name," said the ghost.

"Please hold the line," said Sith, in a hypnotised voice. She fumbled for a pen, and then wrote on the photograph *Yin Bora, footballer.* He looked so sweet and happy. "You have no one to mourn you," she realised.

"None of us have anyone left alive to mourn us," said the ghost.

Then there was a terrible sound down the telephone, as if a thousand voices moaned at once.

Sith involuntarily dropped the receiver into place. She listened to her heart thump and thought about what was needed. She fed the printer with the last of her paper. Immediately it began to roll out more photos, and the land line rang again.

She went outside and found the motoboy, waiting patiently for her. She asked him to go and buy two reams of copying paper. At the last moment she added pens and writing paper and matches. He bowed and smiled and bowed again, pleased to have found a patron.

She went back inside, and with just a tremor in her hand picked up the phone.

For the next half hour, she talked to the dead, and found photographs and wrote down names. A woman mourned her children. Sith found photos of them all, and united them, father, mother, three children, uncles, aunts, cousins and grandparents, taping their pictures to her wall. The idea of uniting families appealed. She began to stick the other photos onto her wall.

Someone called from outside and there on her doorstep was the motoboy, balancing paper and pens. "I bought you some soup." The broth came in neatly tied bags and was full of rice and prawns. She thanked him and paid him well and he beamed at her and bowed again and again.

All afternoon, the pictures kept coming. Darkness fell, the phone rang, the names were written, until Sith's hand, which was unused to writing anything, ached.

The doorbell rang, and on the doorstep, the motoboy sompiahed. "Excuse me, Lady, it is very late. I am worried for you. Can I get you dinner?"

Sith had to smile. He sounded motherly in his concern. They are so good at building a relationship with you, until you cannot do without them. In the old days she would have sent him away with a few rude words. Now she sent him away with an order.

And wrote.

And when he came back, the aged motoboy looked so happy. "I bought you fruit as well, Lady," he said, and added, shyly. "You do not need to pay me for that."

Something seemed to bump under Sith, as if she was on a motorcycle, and she heard herself say, "Come inside. Have some food too."

The motoboy sompiahed in gratitude and as soon as he entered, the phone stopped ringing.

They sat on the floor. He arched his neck and looked around at the walls.

"Are all these people your family?" he asked.

She whispered. "No. They're ghosts who no one mourns."

"Why do they come to you?" His mouth fell open in wonder.

"Because my father was Pol Pot," said Sith, without thinking.

The motoboy sompiahed. "Ah." He chewed and swallowed and arched his head back again. "That must be a terrible thing. Everybody hates you."

Sith had noticed that wherever she sat in the room, the eyes in the photographs were directly on her. "I haven't done anything," said Sith.

"You're doing something now," said the motoboy. He nodded and stood up, sighing with satisfaction. Life was good with a full stomach and a patron. "If you need me, Lady, I will be outside."

Photo after photo, name after name.

Youk Achariya: touring dancer

Proeung Chhay: school superintendent

Sar Kothida child, aged 7, died of "swelling disease"

Sar Makara, her mother, nurse

Nath Mittapheap, civil servant, from family of farmers

Chor Monirath: wife of award-winning engineer

Yin Sokunthea: Khmer Rouge commune leader

She looked at the faces and realised. *Dara, I'm doing this for Dara.*

The City around her went quiet and she became aware that it was now very late indeed. Perhaps she should just make sure the motoboy had gone home.

He was still waiting outside.

"It's okay. You can go home. Where do you live?"

He waved cheerfully north. "Oh, on Monivong, like you." He grinned at the absurdity of the comparison.

A new idea took sudden form. Sith said, "Tomorrow, can you come early, with a big feast? Fish and rice and greens and pork: curries and stir-fries and kebabs." She paid him handsomely, and finally asked him his name. His name meant Golden.

"Good night, Sovann."

For the rest of the night she worked quickly like an answering service. This is like a cleaning of the house before a festival, she thought. The voices of the dead became ordinary, familiar. Why are people afraid of the dead? The dead can't hurt you. The dead want what you want: justice.

The wall of faces became a staircase and a garage and a kitchen of faces, all named. She had found Jorani's coloured yarn, and linked family members into trees.

She wrote until the electric lights looked discoloured, like a headache. She asked the ghosts, "Please can I sleep now?" The phones fell silent and Sith slumped with relief onto the polished marble floor.

She woke up dazed, still on the marble floor. Sunlight flooded the room. The faces in the photographs no longer looked swollen and bruised. Their faces were not accusing or mournful. They smiled down on her. She was among friends.

With a whine, the printer started to print; the phone started to ring. Her doorbell chimed, and there was Sovann, white cardboard boxes piled up on the back of his motorcycle. He wore the same shirt as yesterday, a cheap blue copy of a Lacoste. A seam had parted under the arm. He only has one shirt, Sith realised. She imagined him washing it in a basin every night.

Sith and Sovann moved the big tables to the front windows. Sith took out her expensive tablecloths for the first time, and the bronze platters. The feast was laid out as if at New Year. Sovann had bought more paper and pens. He knew what they were for. "I can help, Lady."

He was old enough to have lived in a country with schools, and he could write in a beautiful, old-fashioned hand. Together he and Sith spelled out the names of the dead and burned them.

"I want to write the names of my family too," he said. He burnt them weeping.

The delicious vapours rose. The air was full of the sound of breathing in. Loose papers stirred with the breeze. The ash filled the basins, but even after working all day, Sith and the motoboy had only honoured half the names.

"Good night, Sovann," she told him.

"You have transferred a lot of merit," said Sovann, but only to be polite.

If I have any merit to transfer, thought Sith.

He left and the printers started, and the phone. She worked all night, and only stopped because the second ream of paper ran out.

The last picture printed was of Kol Vireakboth.

Dara, she promised herself. *Dara next.*

In the morning, she called him. "Can we meet at lunchtime for another walk by the river?"

Sith waited on top of the marble wall and watched an old man fish in the Tonlé Sap river and found that she loved her country. She loved its tough, smiling, uncomplaining people, who had never offered her harm, after all the harm her family had done them. Do you know you have the daughter of the monster sitting here among you?

Suddenly all Sith wanted was to be one of them. The monks in the pavilion, the white-shirted functionaries scurrying somewhere, the lazy bones dangling their legs, the young men who dress like American rappers and sold something dubious, drugs, or sex.

She saw Dara sauntering toward her. He wore his new shirt, and smiled at her but he didn't look relaxed. It had been two days since they'd met. He knew something was wrong, that she had something to tell him. He had bought them lunch in a little cardboard box. Maybe for the last time, thought Sith.

They exchanged greetings, almost like cousins. He sat next to her and smiled and Sith giggled in terror at what she was about to do.

Dara asked, "What's funny?"

She couldn't stop giggling. "Nothing is funny. Nothing." She sighed in order to stop and terror tickled her and she spurted out laughter again. "I lied to you. Kol Vireakboth is not my father. Another politician was my father. Someone you've heard of . . ."

The whole thing was so terrifying and absurd that the laughter squeezed her like a fist and she couldn't talk. She laughed and wept at the same time. Dara stared.

"My father was Saloth Sar. That was his real name." She couldn't make herself say it. She could tell a motoboy, but not Dara? She forced herself onward. "My father was Pol Pot."

Nothing happened.

Sitting next to her, Dara went completely still. People strolled past; boats bobbed on their moorings.

After a time Dara said, "I know what you are doing."

That didn't make sense. "Doing? What do you mean?"

Dara looked sour and angry. "Yeah, yeah, yeah, yeah." He sat, looking away from her. Sith's laughter had finally shuddered to a halt. She sat peering at him, waiting. "I told you my family were modest," he said quietly.

"Your family are lovely!" Sith exclaimed.

His jaw thrust out. "They had questions about you too, you know."

"I don't understand."

He rolled his eyes. He looked back round at her. "There are easier ways to break up with someone."

He jerked himself to his feet and strode away with swift determination, leaving her sitting on the wall.

Here on the riverfront, everyone was equal. The teenage boys lounged on the wall; poor mothers herded children; the foreigners walked briskly, trying to look as if they didn't carry moneybelts.

Three fat teenage girls nearly swerved into a cripple in a pedal chair and collapsed against each other with raucous laughter.

Sith did not know what to do. She could not move. Despair humbled her, made her hang her head.

I've lost him.

The sunlight seemed to settle next to her, washing up from its reflection on the wake of some passing boat.

No you haven't.

The river water smelled of kindly concern. The sounds of traffic throbbed with forbearance.

Not yet.

There is no forgiveness in Cambodia. But there are continual miracles of compassion and acceptance.

Sith appreciated for just a moment the miracles. The motoboy buying her soup. She decided to trust herself to the miracles.

Sith talked to the sunlight without making a sound. *Grandfather Vireakboth. Thank you. You have told me all I need to know.*

Sith stood up and from nowhere, the motoboy was there. He drove her to the Hello Phone shop.

Dara would not look at her. He bustled back and forth behind the counter, though there was nothing for him to do. Sith talked to him like a customer. "I want to buy a mobile phone," she said, but he would not answer. "There is someone I need to talk to."

Another customer came in. She was a beautiful daughter too, and he served her, making a great show of being polite. He complimented her on her appearance. "Really, you look cool." The girl looked pleased. Dara's eyes darted in Sith's direction.

Sith waited in the chair. This was home for her now. Dara ignored her. She picked up her phone and dialled his number. He put it to his ear and said, "Go home."

"You are my home," she said.

His thumb jabbed the C button.

She waited. Shadows lengthened.

"We're closing," he said, standing by the door without looking at her.

Shamefaced, Sith ducked away from him, through the door.

Outside Soriya, the motoboy played dice with his fellows. He stood up. "They say I am very lucky to have Pol Pot's daughter as a client."

There was no discretion in Cambodia, either. Everyone will know now, Sith realised.

At home, the piles of printed paper still waited for her. Sith ate the old, cold food. It tasted flat, all its savour sucked away. The phones began to ring. She fell asleep with the receiver propped against her ear.

The next day, Sith went back to Soriya with a box of the printed papers.

She dropped the box onto the blue plastic counter of Hello Phones.

"Because I am Pol Pot's daughter," she told Dara, holding out a sheaf of pictures toward him. "All the unmourned victims of my father are printing their pictures on my printer. Here. Look. These are the pictures of people who lost so many loved ones there is no one to remember them."

She found her cheeks were shaking and that she could not hold the sheaf of paper. It tumbled from her hands, but she stood back, arms folded.

Dara, quiet and solemn, knelt and picked up the papers. He looked at some of the faces. Sith pushed a softly crumpled green card at him. Her family ID card.

He read it. Carefully, with the greatest respect, he put the photographs on the countertop along with the ID card.

"Go home, Sith," he said, but not unkindly.

"I said," she had begun to speak with vehemence but could not continue. "I told you. My home is where you are."

"I believe you," he said, looking at his feet.

"Then . . ." Sith had no words.

"It can never be, Sith," he said. He gathered up the sheaf of photocopying paper. "What will you do with these?"

Something made her say, "What will *you* do with them?"

His face was crossed with puzzlement.

"It's your country too. What will you do with them? Oh, I know, you're such a poor boy from a poor family, who could expect anything from you? Well, you have your whole family and many people have no one. And you can buy new shirts and some people only have one."

Dara held out both hands and laughed. "Sith?" *You, Sith are accusing me of being selfish?*

"You own them too." Sith pointed to the papers, to the faces. "You think the dead don't try to talk to you, too?"

Their eyes latched. She told him what he could do. "I think you should make an exhibition. I think Hello Phones should sponsor it. You tell them that. You tell them Pol Pot's daughter wishes to make amends and has chosen them. Tell them the dead speak to me on their mobile phones."

She spun on her heel and walked out. She left the photographs with him.

That night she and the motoboy had another feast and burned the last of the unmourned names. There were many thousands.

The next day she went back to Hello Phones.

"I lied about something else," she told Dara. She took out all the reports from the fortunetellers. She told him what Hun Sen's fortuneteller had told her. "The marriage is particularly well favoured."

"Is that true?" He looked wistful.

"You should not believe anything I say. Not until I have earned your trust. Go consult the fortunetellers for yourself. This time you pay."

His face went still and his eyes focused somewhere far beneath the floor. Then he looked up, directly into her eyes. "I will do that."

For the first time in her life Sith wanted to laugh for something other than fear. She wanted to laugh for joy.

"Can we go to lunch at Lucky7?" she asked.

"Sure," he said.

All the telephones in the shop, all of them, hundreds all at once began to sing.

A waterfall of trills and warbles and buzzes, snatches of old songs or latest chart hits. Dara stood dumbfounded. Finally he picked one up and held it to his ear.

"It's for you," he said and held out the phone for her.

There was no name or number on the screen.

Congratulations, dear daughter, said a warm kind voice.

"Who is this?" Sith asked. The options were severely limited.

Your new father, said Kol Vireakboth. The sound of wind. *I adopt you*.

A thousand thousand voices said at once, *We adopt you*.

In Cambodia, you share your house with ghosts in the way you share it with dust. You hear the dead shuffling alongside your own footsteps. You can sweep, but the sound does not go away.

On the Tra Bek end of Monivong there is a house whose owner has given it over to ghosts. You can try to close the front door. But the next day you will find it hanging open. Indeed you can try, as the neighbours did, to nail the door shut. It opens again.

By day, there is always a queue of five or six people wanting to go in, or hanging back, out of fear. Outside are offerings of lotus or coconuts with embedded josh sticks.

The walls and floors and ceilings are covered with photographs. The salon, the kitchen, the stairs, the office, the empty bedrooms, are covered with photographs of Chinese-Khmers at weddings, Khmer civil servants on picnics, Chams outside their mosques, Vietnamese holding up prize catches of fish; little boys going to school in shorts; cyclopousse drivers in front of their odd, old-fashioned pedalled vehicles; wives in stalls stirring soup. All of them are happy and joyful, and the background is Phnom Penh when it was the most beautiful city in Southeast Asia.

All the photographs have names written on them in old-fashioned handwriting.

On the table is a printout of thousands of names on slips of paper. Next to the table are matches and basins of ash and water. The implication is plain. Burn the names and transfer merit to the unmourned dead.

Next to that is a small printed sign that says in English HELLO.

Every Pchum Ben, those names are delivered to temples throughout the city. Gold foil is pressed onto each slip of paper, and attached to it is a parcel of sticky rice. At 8:00 am food is delivered for the monks, steaming rice and fish, along with bolts of new cloth. At 10:00 a.m. more food is delivered, for the disabled and the poor.

And most mornings a beautiful daughter of Cambodia is seen walking beside the confluence of the Tonlé Sap and Mekong rivers. Like Cambodia, she plainly loves all things modern. She dresses in the latest fashion. Cambodian R&B whispers in her ear. She pauses in front of each new waterfront construction whether built by improvised scaffolding or erected with cranes. She buys noodles from the grumpy vendors with their tiny stoves. She carries a book or sits on the low marble wall to write letters and look at the boats, the monsoon clouds, and the dop-dops. She talks to the reflected sunlight on the river and calls it Father.

GLEN HIRSHBERG

Devil's Smile

GLEN HIRSHBERG'S MOST RECENT collection, *American Morons*, was published by Earthling in 2006. *The Two Sams*, his first collection, won the International Horror Guild Award and was selected by *Publishers Weekly* and *Locus* as one of the best books of 2003.

Hirshberg is also the author of the novels *The Snowman's Children* (published by Carroll & Graf in 2002) and *Sisters of Baikal* (forthcoming). With Dennis Etchison and Peter Atkins, he co-founded the Rolling Darkness Revue, a travelling ghost story performance troupe that tours the West Coast of the United States each October.

His fiction has appeared in numerous magazines and anthologies, including multiple appearances in *The Mammoth Book of Best New Horror* and *The Year's Best Fantasy and Horror*, *Dark Terrors 6*, *The Dark*, *Inferno*, *Trampoline*, *Cemetery Dance*, *Summer Chills* and *Alone on the Darkside*. He lives in the Los Angeles area with his wife and children.

"This story grew out of a delicious winter evening spent reading my children a book by Donald J. Sobol called *True Sea Adventures*," Hirshberg recalls, "in which we discovered the astonishing story of Charles F. Tallman, his boat the *Christina*, and the blizzard of January 7th, 1866.

"But the whole piece coalesced during my visit to New Bedford, Massachusetts, which still feels grim and blubber-soaked and strange even before you stick your head in the Whaling Museum and see the wall of implements for carving up whales at sea – as terrifying and poignant in their shapes as the gynaecological instruments for working on 'mutant women' in David Cronenberg's *Dead Ringers* – or the photographs of forests of baleen drying on the docks."

"In hollows of the liquid hills
Where the long Blue Ridges run
The flatter of no echo thrills
For echo the seas have none;
Nor aught that gives man back man's strain –
The hope of his heart, the dream in his brain."
                          – Herman Melville

TURNING IN HIS SADDLE, Selkirk peered behind him through the
flurrying snow, trying to determine which piece of debris had
lamed his horse. All along what had been the carriage road, bits of
driftwood, splintered sections of hull and harpoon handle, discarded
household goods – pans, candlesticks, broken-backed books, empty
lanterns – and at least one section of long, bleached-white jaw lay
half-buried in the sand. The jaw still had baleen attached, and bits of
blown snow had stuck in it, which made it look more recently alive
than it should have.

Selkirk rubbed his tired eyes against the grey December morning
and hunched deeper into his inadequate long coat as the wind
whistled off the whitecaps and sliced between the dunes. The straw
hat he wore more out of habit than hope of protection did nothing to
warm him, and stray blond curls kept whipping across his eyes.
Easing himself from the horse, Selkirk dropped to the sand.

He should have conducted his business here months ago. His
surveying route for the still-fledgling United States Lighthouse Service had taken him in a crisscrossing loop from the tip of the Cape all
the way up into Maine and back. He'd passed within fifty miles of
Cape Roby Light and its singular keeper twice this fall, and both
times had continued on. Why? Because Amalia had told him the
keeper's tale on the night he'd imagined she loved him? Or maybe he
just hated coming back here even more than he thought he would.
For all he knew, the keeper had long since moved on, dragging her
memories behind her. She might even have died. So many did,
around here. Setting his teeth against the wind, Selkirk wrapped
his frozen fingers in his horse's bridle and led her the last down-
sloping mile and a half into Winsett.

Entering from the east, he saw a scatter of stone and clapboard
homes and boarding houses hunched against the dunes, their windows dark. None of them looked familiar. Like so many of the little
whaling communities he'd visited during his survey, the town he'd
known had simply drained away into the burgeoning, bloody
industry centers at New Bedford and Nantuckett.

Selkirk had spent one miserable fall and winter here fourteen years ago, sent by his drunken father to learn candle-making from his drunken uncle. He'd accepted the nightly open-fisted beatings without comment, skulking afterward down to the Blubber Pike tavern to watch the whalers: the Portuguese swearing loudly at each other and the negroes – so many Negroes, most of them recently freed, more than a few newly escaped – clinging in clumps to the shadowy back tables and stealing fearful glances at every passing face, as though they expected at any moment to be spirited away.

Of course, there'd been his cousin, Amalia, for all the good that had ever done him. She'd just turned eighteen at the time, two years his senior. Despite her blond hair and startling fullness, the Winsett whalers had already learned to steer clear, but for some reason, she'd liked Selkirk. At least, she'd liked needling him about his outsized ears, his floppy hair, the crack in his voice he could not outgrow. Whatever the reason, she'd lured him away from the pub on several occasions to stare at the moon and drink beside him. And once, in a driving sleet, she'd led him on a midnight walk to Cape Roby Point. There, lurking uncomfortably close but never touching him, standing on the rocks with her dark eyes cocked like rifle sites at the rain, she'd told him the lighthouse keeper's story. At the end, without any explanation, she'd turned, opened her heavy coat and pulled him to her. He'd had no idea what she wanted him to do, and had wound up simply setting his ear against her slicked skin, all but tasting the water that rushed into the valley between her breasts, listening to her heart banging way down inside her.

After that, she'd stopped speaking to him entirely. He'd knocked on her door, chased her half out of the shop one morning and been stopped by a chop to the throat from his uncle, left notes he hoped she'd find peeking out from under the rug in the upstairs hallway. She'd responded to none of it, and hadn't even bothered to say goodbye when he left. And Selkirk had steered clear of all women for more than a decade afterward, except for the very occasional company he paid for near the docks where he slung cargo, until the Lighthouse Service offered him an unexpected escape.

Now, half-dragging his horse down the empty main street, Selkirk found he couldn't even remember which grim room the Blubber Pike had been. He passed no one. But at the western edge of the frozen, cracking main thoroughfare, less than a block from where his uncle had kept his establishment, he found a traveler's stable and entered.

The barn was lit by banks of horseshoe-shaped wall sconces – apparently, local whale oil or no, candles remained in ready supply –

and a coal fire glowed in the open iron stove at the rear of the barn. A dark-haired stable lad with a clam-shaped birthmark covering his left cheek and part of his forehead appeared from one of the stables in the back, *tsked* over Selkirk's injured mount and said he'd send for the horse doctor as soon as he'd got the animal dried and warmed and fed.

"Still a horse doctor here?" Selkirk asked.

The boy nodded. He was almost as tall as Selkirk, and spoke with a Scottish burr. "Still good business. Got to keep the means of getting out healthy."

"Not many staying in town anymore, then?"

"Just the dead ones. Lot of those."

Selkirk paid the boy and thanked him, then wandered toward the stove and stood with his hands extended to the heat, which turned them purplish red. If he got about doing what should have been done years ago, he'd be gone by nightfall, providing his horse could take him. From his memory of the midnight walk with Amalia, Cape Roby Point couldn't be more than three miles away. Once at the lighthouse, if its longtime occupant did indeed still live there, he'd brook no romantic nonsense – neither his own, nor the keeper's. The property did not belong to her, was barely suitable for habitation, and its lack of both updated equipment and experienced, capable attendant posed an undue and unacceptable threat to any ship unlucky enough to hazard past. Not that many bothered anymore with this particular stretch of abandoned, storm-battered coast.

Out he went into the snow. In a matter of minutes, he'd left Winsett behind. Head down, he burrowed through the gusts. With neither buildings nor dunes to block it, the wind raked him with bits of shell and sand that clung to his cheeks like the tips of fingernails and then ripped free. When he looked up, he saw beach pocked with snow and snarls of seaweed, then the ocean thrashing about between the shore and the sandbar a hundred yards or so out.

An hour passed. More. The tamped-down path, barely discernible during Winsett's heyday, had sunk completely into the shifting earth. Selkirk stepped through stands of beach heather and sand bur, pricking himself repeatedly about the ankles. Eventually, he felt blood beneath one heavy sock, but he didn't peel the sock back, simply yanked out the most accessible spines and kept moving. Far out to sea, bright, yellow sun flickered in the depths of the cloud cover and vanished as suddenly as it had appeared. Devil's smile, as the Portuguese sailors called it. At the time, it hadn't occurred to Selkirk to ask why the light would be the devil, instead of the dark or the gathering storm. Stepping from the V between two leaning dunes, he saw the lighthouse.

He'd read the report from the initial Lighthouse Service survey three years ago, and more than once. That document mentioned rot in every beam, chips and cracks in the bricks that made up the conical tower, erosion all around the foundation. As far as Selkirk could see, the report had been kind. The building seemed to be crumbling to nothing before his eyes, bleeding into the pool of shorewater churning at the rocks beneath it.

Staring into the black tide racing up the sand to meet him, Selkirk caught a sea-salt tang on his tongue and found himself murmuring a prayer he hadn't planned for Amalia, who'd reportedly wandered into the dunes and vanished one winter night, six years after Selkirk left. Her father had written Selkirk's father that the girl had never had friends, hated him, hated Winsett, and was probably happier wherever she was now. Then he'd said, "*Here's what I hope: that she's alive. And that she's somewhere far from anywhere I will ever be.*"

On another night than the one they'd spent out here, somewhere closer to town but similarly deserted, he and Amalia once found themselves beset by gulls that swept out of the moonlight all together, by the hundreds, as though storming the mainland. Amalia had pitched stones at them, laughing as they shrieked and swirled nearer. Finally, she'd hit one in the head and killed it. Then she'd bent over the body, calling Selkirk to her. He'd expected her to cradle it or cry. Instead, she'd dipped her finger in its blood and painted a streak down Selkirk's face. Not her own.

Looking down now, Selkirk watched the tide reach the tips of his boots again. How much time had he wasted during his dock-working years imagining – hoping – that Amalia might be hidden behind some stack of crates or in a nearby alley, having sought him out after leaving Winsett?

Angry now, Selkirk picked his way between rocks to the foot of the tower. A surge of whitewater caught him off guard and pasted his trousers to his legs, and the wind promptly froze them with a gust.

Up close, the tower looked even worse. Most of the bricks had crumbled and whitened, the salt air creating blotchy lesions like leper spots all over them. The main building still stood straight enough, but even from below, with the wind whipping the murky winter light around, Selkirk could see filth filming the windows that surrounded the lantern room, and cracks in the glass.

The keeper's quarters squatted to the left of the light tower, and looked, if possible, even more disheveled. Along the base, lime had taken hold, sprouting up the wooden walls like algae. Or maybe it was algae. This would not be somewhere the Service salvaged. Cape Roby Light would have to come down, or simply be abandoned to the sea.

Selkirk rapped hard on the heavy oak door of the tower. For answer, he got a blast of wind nearly powerful enough to tip him off the rocks. Grunting, he rapped harder. Behind him, the water gurgled, the way spermaceti oil sometimes did as it bubbled, and though he knew it wasn't possible, Selkirk would have sworn he could smell it, that faint but nauseating reek his uncle swore was imaginary, because that was the glory of spermaceti oil, the whole goddamn point: it had no significant odor. Every day of that dismal fall, though, Selkirk's nostrils had filled anyway. Blood, whale brain, desiccated fish. He began to pound.

Just before the door opened, he became aware of movement behind it, the slap of shoed feet descending stone steps. But he didn't stop knocking until the oak swung away from him, the light rushing not out from the lighthouse but in from the air.

He knew right away this was her, though he'd never actually seen her. Her black hair twisted over her shoulders and down her back in tangled strands like vines, just as Amalia had described. He'd expected a wild, white-haired, wind-ravaged thing, bent with age and the grief she could not shake. But of course, if Amalia's story had been accurate, this woman had been all of 20 during Selkirk's year here, and so barely over 18 when she'd been widowed. She gazed at him now through royal blue eyes that seemed set into the darkness behind her like the last sunlit patches in a blackening sky.

"Mrs Marchant," he said. "I'm Robert Selkirk from the Lighthouse Service. May I come in?"

For a moment, he thought she might shut the door in his face. Instead, she hovered, both arms lifting slightly from her sides, as though she were considering taking wing. Her skirt was long, her blouse pale yellow, clinging to her square and powerful shoulders.

"Selkirk," she said. "From Winsett?"

Astonished, Selkirk started to raise his hand. Then he shook his head. "From the lighthouse service. But yes, I was nephew to the Winsett Selkirks."

"Well," she said, the Portuguese tilt to her words stirring memories of the Blubber Pike whalers, the smoke and the smell in there. Abruptly, she grinned. "Then you're welcome here."

"You may not feel that way in a few minutes, Mrs Marchant. I'm afraid I've come to . . ."

But she'd stepped away from the door, starting back up the stairs and beckoning him without turning around. Over her shoulder, he heard her say, "You must be frozen. I have tea."

In he went, and stood still in the entryway, listening to the whistling in the walls, feeling drafts rushing at him from all directions. If it weren't for the roof, the place would hardly qualify as a dwelling anymore, let alone a lifesaving beacon and refuge. He started after the woman up the twisting stairs.

Inside, too, the walls had begun to flake and mold, and the air flapped overhead, as though the whole place were full of nesting birds. Four steps from the platform surrounding the lantern room, just at the edge of the spill of yellow candlelight from up there, Selkirk slowed, then stopped. His gaze swung to his right and down toward his feet.

Sitting against the wall with her little porcelain ankles sticking out of the bottom of her habit and crossed at the ankle, sat a doll of a nun. From beneath the hood of the doll's black veil, disconcertingly blue eyes peered from under long lashes. A silver crucifix lay in the doll's lap, and miniature rosary beads trailed back down the steps, winking pale yellow and pink in the flickering light like seashells underwater. And in fact, they were bits of shell.

Glancing behind him, Selkirk spotted the other dolls he'd somehow missed. One for every other stair, on alternating walls. These were made mostly from shell, as far as he could tell. Two of them were standing, while a third sat with her legs folded underneath her and a stone tucked against her ear, as though she were listening. At the top of the steps, still another nun dangled from her curved, seashell hands on the decaying wooden banister. Not only were her eyes blue, but she was grinning like a little girl. Momentarily baffled to silence, Selkirk stumbled the rest of the way up to the lantern room. This time, he froze completely.

Even on this dark day, even through the dust and salt that caked the window glass inside and out, light flooded the chamber. None of it came from the big lamp, which of course lay unlit. Assuming it still worked at all. Across the platform, a pair of white wicker chairs sat side by side, aimed out to sea. Over their backs, the keeper had draped blankets of bright red wool, and beneath them lay a rug of similar red. And on the rug stood a house.

Like most of the dolls, it had been assembled entirely from shells and seaweed and sand. From its peaked roof, tassels of purple flowers hung like feathers, and all around the eves, gull feathers hung like the decorative flourishes on some outrageous society

woman's hat. On the rug – clearly, it served as a yard – tiny nuns
prowled like cats. Some lay on their backs with their arms folded
across their crucifixes, soaking up the light. One was climbing the leg
of one of the wicker chairs. And a group – at least five – stood at the
base of the window, staring out to sea.

And that is what reminded Selkirk of his purpose, and brought him
at least part way back to himself. He glanced around the rest of the
room, noting half a dozen round wooden tables evenly spaced
around the perimeter. On each, yellow beeswax candles blazed in
their candlesticks, lending the air a misleading tint of yellow and
promising more heat than actually existed here. Mostly, the tables
held doll-making things. Tiny silver crosses, multi-colored rocks,
thousands of shells. The table directly to Selkirk's right had a single
place setting laid out neatly upon it. Clean white plate, fork, spoon,
one chipped teacup decorated with paintings of leaping silver fish.

Selkirk realised he was staring at a crude sort of living sundial.
Each day, Mrs Marchant began with her tea and breakfast, proceeded around the platform to assemble and place her nuns, spent far
too long sitting in one or the other of the wicker chairs and staring at
the place where it had all happened, and eventually retired, to do it
all over again when daybreak came. In spite of himself, he felt a
surprisingly strong twinge of pity.

"That hat can't have helped you much," Mrs Marchant said,
straightening from a bureau near her dining table where she apparently kept her tea things. The cup she brought matched the one on
her breakfast table, flying fish, chips and all, and chattered lightly on
its saucer as she handed it to him.

More grateful for its warmth than he realised, Selkirk rushed the
cup to his mouth and winced as the hot liquid scalded his tongue. The
woman stood a little too close to him. Loose strands of her hair
almost tickled the back of his hand like the fringe on a shawl. Her
blue eyes flicked over his face. Then she started laughing.

"What?" Selkirk took an uncertain half-step back.

"The fish," she said. When he stared, she laughed again and
gestured at the cup. "When you drank, it looked like they were
going to leap right into your teeth."

Selkirk glanced at the side of the cup, then back to the woman's
laughing face. Judging by the layout and contents of this room, he
couldn't imagine her venturing anywhere near town, but she clearly
got outside to collect supplies. As a result, her skin had retained its
dusky continental coloration. A beautiful creature, and no mistake.

"I am sorry," she said, meeting his eyes. "It's been a long time since anyone drank from my china but me. It's an unfamiliar sight. Come." She started around the left side of the platform. Selkirk watched, then took the opposite route, past the seaweed table, and met the woman in the center of the seaward side of the platform, at the wicker chairs. Without waiting for him, she bent, lifted a tiny nun whose bandeau hid most of her face like a bandit's mask off the rug, and settled in the right-hand chair. The nun wound up tucked against her hip like a rabbit.

For whom, Selkirk wondered, was the left-hand chair meant, on ordinary days? The obvious answer chilled and also saddened him, and he saw no point in wasting further time.

"Mrs Marchant—"

"Manners, Mr Selkirk," the woman said, and for the second time smiled at him. "The sisters do not approve of being lectured to."

It took him a moment to understand she was teasing him. And not like Amalia had, or not exactly like. Teasing him hadn't made Amalia any happier. He sat.

"Mrs Marchant, I have bad news. Actually, it isn't really bad news, but it may feel that way at first. I know – that is, I really think I have a sense – of what this place must mean to you. I did live in town here once, and I do know your story. But it's not good for you, staying here. And there are more important considerations than you or your grief here, anyway, aren't there? There are the sailors still out there braving the seas, and . . ."

Mrs Marchant cocked her head, and her eyes trailed over his face so slowly that he almost thought he could feel them, faintly, like the moisture in the air but warmer.

"Would you remove your hat, Mr Selkirk?"

Was she teasing now? She wasn't smiling at the moment. Increasingly flustered, Selkirk settled the teacup on the floor at his feet and pulled his sopping hat from his head. Instantly, his poodle's ruff of curls spilled onto his forehead and over his ears.

Mrs Marchant sat very still. "I'd forgotten," she finally said. "Isn't that funny?"

"Ma'am?"

Sighing, she leaned back. "Men's hair by daylight." Then she winked at him, and whispered, "The nuns are scandalised."

"Mrs Marchant. The time has come. The Lighthouse Service – perhaps you've heard of it – needs to—"

"We had a dog, then," Mrs Marchant said, and her eyes swung toward the windows.

Selkirk closed his eyes, feeling the warmth of the tea unfurling in his guts, hearing the longing underneath the play in the keeper's voice. When he opened his eyes again, he found Mrs Marchant still staring toward the horizon.

"We named the dog Luis. For my father, who died at sea while my mother and I were on our way here from Lisbon. Charlie gave him to me."

After that, Selkirk hardly moved. It wasn't the story, which Amalia had told him, and which he hadn't forgotten. It was the way this woman said her husband's name.

"He didn't have to work, you know. Charlie. His family built half the boats that ever left this place. He said he just wanted to make certain his friends got home. Also, I think he liked living in the lighthouse. Especially alone with me. And my girls."

"Smart fellow," Selkirk murmured, realised to his amazement that he'd said it aloud, and blushed.

But the keeper simply nodded. "Yes. He was. Also reckless, in a way. No, that is wrong. He liked . . . playing at recklessness. In storms, he used to lash himself to the railing out there." She gestured toward the thin band of metal that encircled the platform outside the windows. "Then he would lean into the rain. He said it was like sailing without having to hunt. And without leaving me."

"Was he religious like you?" Selkirk hadn't meant to ask anything. And Mrs Marchant looked completely baffled. "The . . ." Selkirk muttered, and gestured at the rug, the house. Sand-convent. Whatever it was.

"Oh," she said. "It is a habit, only." Again, she grinned, but unlike Amalia, she waited until she was certain he'd gotten the joke. Then she went on. "While my father lived here, my mother and I earned extra money making dolls for the Sacred Heart of Mary. They gave them to poor girls. Poorer than we were."

The glow from Mrs Marchant's eyes intensified on his cheek, as though he'd leaned nearer to a candle flame. Somehow, the feeling annoyed him, made him nervous.

"But he did leave you," he said, more harshly than he intended. "Your husband."

Mrs Marchant's lips flattened slowly. "He meant to take me. The Kendall brothers – Kit was his best and oldest friend, and he'd known Kevin since the day Kevin was born – wanted us both to come sail with them, on the only beautiful January weekend I have ever experienced here. 1837. The air was so warm, Mr Selkirk, and the whales gone for the winter. I didn't realise until then that Charlie had never once, in his whole life, been to sea. I'd never known until that weekend that he wanted to go. Of course I said yes. Then Luis twisted his foreleg in the rocks out there, and I stayed to be with him. And I made Charlie go anyway. He was blonde like you. Did you know that?"

Shifting in his seat, Selkirk stared over the water. The sky hung heavy and low, its color an unbroken blackish grey, so that he no longer had any idea what time it was. After noon, surely. If he failed to conclude his business here soon, he'd never make it out of Winsett before nightfall, horse or no. At his feet, the nuns watched the water.

"Mrs Marchant."

"He wasn't as tall as you are, of course. Happier, though."

Selkirk swung his head toward the woman. She took no notice.

"Of course, why wouldn't he be? He had so much luck in his short life. More than anyone deserves or has any right to expect. The Sacred Heart of Mary sisters always taught that it was bad luck to consort with the lucky. What do you make of that, Mr Selkirk?"

It took Selkirk several seconds to sort the question, and as he sat, Mrs Marchant stood abruptly and put her open palm on the window. For a crazy second, just because of the stillness of her posture and the oddly misdirected tilt of her head – toward land, away from the sea – Selkirk wondered if she were blind, like her dolls.

"I guess I've never been around enough luck to say," Selkirk finally said.

She'd been looking down the coast, but now she turned to him, beaming once more. "The sisters find you an honest man, sir. They invite you to more tea."

Returning to the bureau with his cup, she refilled it, then sat back down beside him. She'd left the nun she'd had before on the bureau, balancing in the center of a white plate like a tiny ice skater.

"The morning after they set sail," she said, "Luis woke me up." In the window, her eyes reflected against the grey. "He'd gotten better all through the day, and he'd been out all night. He loved to be. I often didn't see him until I came outside to hang the wash or do the chores. But that day, he scratched and whined against the door. I thought he'd fallen or hurt himself again and hurried to let him in. But when I did, he raced straight past me up the stairs. I hurried after, and found him whimpering against the light there. I was so worried that I didn't even look at the window for the longest time. And when I did . . ."

All the while, Mrs Marchant had kept her hands pressed together in the folds of her dress, but now she opened them. Selkirk half-expected a nun to flap free of them on starfish wings, but they were empty. "So much whiteness, Mr Selkirk. And yet it was dark. You wouldn't think that would be possible, would you?"

"I've lived by the sea all my life," Selkirk said.

"Well, then. That's what it was like. A wall of white that shed no light at all. I couldn't even see the water. I had the lamp lit, of course, but all that did was emphasise the difference between *in here* and *out there*."

Selkirk stood. If he were Charlie Marchant, he thought, he would never have left the Convent, as he'd begun to think of the whole place. Not to go to sea. Not even to town. He found himself remembering the letters he'd sent Amalia during his dock-working years. Pathetic, clumsy things. She'd never responded to those, either. Maybe she'd been trying, in her way, to be kind.

"I've often wondered if Luis somehow sensed the ship coming," Mrs Marchant said. "We'd trained him to bark in the fog, in case a passing captain could hear but not see us. But maybe that day Luis was just barking at the whiteness.

"The sound was unmistakable when it came. I heard wood splintering. Sails collapsing. A mast smashing into the water. But there wasn't any screaming. And I thought . . ."

"You thought maybe the crew had escaped to the lifeboats," Selkirk said, when it was clear Mrs Marchant was not going to finish her sentence.

For the first time in several minutes, Mrs Marchant turned her gaze on him. Abruptly, that luminous smile crept over her lips. "You would make the most marvelous stuffed giraffe," she said.

Selkirk stiffened. Was he going to have to carry this poor, gently raving woman out of here? "Mrs Marchant, it's already late. We need to be starting for town soon."

If she understood what he meant, she gave no sign. "I knew what ship it was." She sank back into her wicker chair, the smile gone, and crossed her legs. "What other vessel would be out there in the middle of winter? I started screaming, pounding the glass. It didn't take me long to realise they wouldn't have gone to the rowboats. In all likelihood, they'd had no idea where they were. The Kendall boys were experienced seamen, excellent sailors, Mr Selkirk. But that fog had dropped straight out of the heart of the sky, or maybe it had risen from the dead sea bottom, and it was solid as stone.

"And then – as if it were the fogbank itself, and not Charlie's boat, that had run aground on the sandbar out there – all that whiteness just shattered. The whole wall cracked apart into whistling, flying fragments. Just like that, the blizzard blew in. How does that happen, Mr Selkirk? How does the sea change its mind like that?"

Selkirk didn't answer. But for the first time, he thought he understood why the sailors in the Blubber Pike referred to those teasing, far-off flickers of light the way they did.

"I rushed downstairs, thinking I'd get the rowboat and haul myself out there and save them. But the waves . . . they were snarling and snapping all over themselves, and I knew I'd have to wait. My tears were freezing on my face. I was wearing only a dressing gown, and the wind whipped right through me. The door to the lighthouse was banging because I hadn't shut it properly, and I was so full of fury and panic I was ready to start screaming again. I looked out to sea, and all but fell to my knees in gratitude.

"It was there, Mr Selkirk. I could see the ship. Some of it, anyway. Enough, perhaps. I could just make it out. The prow, part of the foredeck, a stump of mast. I turned around and raced back inside for my clothes.

"Then I ran all the way to town. We never kept a horse here, Charlie didn't like them. The strangest thing was this sensation I kept having, this feeling that I'd gotten lost. It was impossible; that path out there was well-traveled in those days, and even now, you had no trouble, did you? But I couldn't feel my skin. Or . . . it was as though I had come out of it. There was snow and sand flying all around, wind in the dunes. So cold. My Charlie out there. I remember thinking, *This is what the Bruxsa feels like. This is why she torments travelers. This is why she feeds.* You know, at some point, I thought maybe I'd become her."

Pursing his lips, Selkirk stirred from the daze that had settled over him. "Brucka?"

"*Bruxsa.* It is like . . . a banshee? Do you know the word? A ghost, but not of anyone. A horrid thing all its own."

Was it his imagination, or had the dark outside deepened toward evening? If he didn't get this finished, neither one of them would make it out of here tonight. "Mrs Marchant, perhaps we could continue this on the way back to town."

Finally, as though he'd slapped her, Mrs Marchant blinked. "What?"

"Mrs Marchant, surely you understand the reason for my coming. We'll send for your things. You don't *have* to leave today, but wouldn't that be easiest? I'll walk with you. I'll make certain—"

"When I finally reached Winsett," Mrs Marchant said, her stare returning as that peculiar, distant smiled played across her mouth, "I went straight for the first lit window I saw. Selkirk's. The candle-maker. Your uncle."

Selkirk cringed, remembering those hard, overheated hands smashing against the side of his skull.

"He was so kind," she said, and his mouth quivered and fell open as she went on. "He rushed me inside. It was warm in his shop. At the time, it literally felt as though he'd saved my life. Returned me to my body. I sat by his fire, and he raced all over town through the blizzard and came back with whalers, sailing men. Charlie's father, and the Kendalls' older brother. There were fifteen of them, at least. Most set out immediately on horseback for the point. Your uncle wrapped me in two additional sweaters and an overcoat, and he walked all the way back out here with me, telling me it would be all right. By the time we reached the lighthouse, he said, the sailors would already have figured a way to get the boys off that sandbar and home."

To Selkirk, it seemed this woman had reached into his memories and daubed them with colors he knew couldn't have been there. His uncle had been kind to no one. His uncle had hardly spoken except to complete business. The very idea of his using his shop fire to warm somebody, risking himself to rouse the town to some wealthy playboy's rescue . . .

But of course, by the time Selkirk had come here, the town was well on its way to failing, and his aunt had died in some awful, silent way no one spoke about. Maybe his uncle had been different, before. Or maybe, he thought with a sick quivering deep in his stomach, he was just an old lecher, on top of being a drunk.

"By the time we got back here, it was nearly dusk," Mrs Marchant said. "The older Kendall and four of the sailors had already tried four different times to get the rowboat away from shore and into the waves. They were all tucked inside my house, now, trying to stave off pneumonia.

" 'Tomorrow,' one of the sailors told me. 'Tomorrow, please God, if they can just hold on. We'll find a way to them.'

"And right then, Mr Selkirk. Right as the light went out of that awful day for good, the snow cleared. For one moment. And there they were."

A single tear crept from the lashes of her right eye. She was almost whispering, now. "It was like a gift. Like a glimpse of him in heaven. I raced back outside, called out, leapt up and down, we all did, but of course they couldn't hear, and weren't paying attention. They were scrambling all over the deck. I knew right away which was Charlie. He was in the bow, all bundled up in a hat that wasn't his and what looked like three or four coats. He looked like one of my nuns, Mr Selkirk." She grinned again. "The one with the bandeau that hides her face? I was holding her in my lap before. I made her in memory of this one moment."

Selkirk stared. Was the woman actually celebrating this story?

"I could also see the Kendall boys' hair as they worked amidships. So red, like twin suns burning off the overcast.

" 'Bailing,' Charlie's father told me. 'The ship must be taking on water. They're trying to keep her where she is.' "

Again, Mrs Marchant's smile slid, but didn't vanish entirely. "I asked how long they could keep doing that. But what I really wondered was how long they'd already been at it. Those poor, beautiful boys.

"Our glimpse lasted two minutes. Maybe even less. I could see new clouds rising behind them. Like a sea-monster rearing right out of the waves. But at the last, just before the snow and the dark obliterated our sight of them, they all stopped as one, and turned around. I'm sorry, Mr Selkirk."

She didn't wipe her face, and there weren't any tears Selkirk could see. She simply sat in her chair, breathing softly. Selkirk watched her with some relief.

"I remember the older Kendall boy standing beside me," she finally said. "He was whispering. *'Aw, come on boys. Get your gear on.'* The Kendalls, you see . . . they'd removed their coats. And I finally realised what it meant, that I could see their hair. They hadn't bothered with their hats, even though they'd kept at the bailing. Remember, I've been around sailors all my life, Mr Selkirk. All the men in my family were sailors, long before they came to this country. My father had been whaling here when he sent for us. So I knew what I was seeing."

"And what was that?"

"The Kendalls had given up. Less than 100 yards from shore, they'd given up. Or decided that they weren't going to make it through the night. Either rescue would come before dawn, or it would no longer matter. The ship would not hold. Or the cold would overwhelm them. So they were hastening the end, one way or another.

"But not Charlie. Not my Charlie. He didn't jump in the air. He just slumped against the railing. But I know he saw me, Mr Selkirk. I could feel him. Even under all those hats. I could always feel him. Then the snow came back. And night fell.

"The next time we saw them, they were in the rigging."

Silently, Selkirk gave up the idea of escaping Winsett until morning. The network of functioning lights and functional keepers the Service had been toiling so hard to establish could wait one more winter evening.

"This was midday, the second day. That storm was a freak of nature. Or perhaps not natural at all. How can that much wind blow a storm nowhere? It was as though the blizzard itself had locked jaws on those boys – on my boy – and would not let go. The men who weren't already racked by coughs and fever made another five attempts with the rowboat, and never got more than fifteen feet from shore. The ice in the air was like arrows raining down.

"Not long after the last attempt, when almost everyone was indoors and I was rushing about making tea and caring for the sick and trying to shush Luis, who had been barking since dawn, I heard Charlie's father cry out and hurried outside.

"I'd never seen light like that, Mr Selkirk, and I haven't since. Neither snow nor wind had eased one bit, and the clouds hadn't lifted. But there was the ship again, and there were our boys. Up in the ropes, now. The Kendalls had their hats back on and their coats around them, tucked up tight together with their arms through the lines. Charlie had gone even higher, crouching by himself, looking down at the brothers or maybe the deck. I hoped they were talking to each other, or singing, anything to keep their spirits up and their breath in them. Because the ship . . . have you ever seen quicksand, Mr Selkirk? It was almost like that. This glimpse lasted a minute, maybe less. But in that time, the hull dropped what looked like another full foot underwater. And that was the only thing we saw move."

"I don't understand," Selkirk said. "The sandbar was right there. It's what they hit, right? Or the rocks right around it? Why not just climb down?"

"If they'd so much as put their feet in that water, after all they'd been exposed to, they would have frozen on the spot. All they could do was cling to the ropes.

"So they clung. The last healthy men came out behind Charlie's father and me to watch. And somehow, just the clear sight of the ship out there inspired us all. And the way the mast was tilting toward the surface got us all angry and active again.

"We got close once, just at dark. The snow hadn't cleared, but the wind had eased. It had been in our ears so long, I'm not sure we even realised it at first. The sickest men, including the older Kendall boy, had been run back to town on horseback, and we hoped other

Winsett whalers might be rigging up a brig in the harbor to try reaching Charlie's ship from the sea-side, rather than from land, the moment the weather permitted. I kept thinking I'd heard new sounds out there, caught a glimpse of the mast of a rescue vessel. But of course it was too soon, and we couldn't really hear or see anything but the storm, anyway. And in the midst of another round of crazy, useless running about, Charlie's father grabbed my wrist and whirled me around to face the water and said, 'Stop. Listen.'

"And I understood finally that I heard nothing. Sweet, beautiful nothing. Right away I imagined that I should be able to hear Charlie and the Kendalls through the quiet. Before anyone could stop me, I was racing for the shore, my feet flying into the frozen water and my dress freezing against my legs, but I could hardly feel it. I was already so cold, so numb. We all were. I started screaming my husband's name. It was too shadowy and snowy to see. But I went right on screaming, and everyone else that was left with us held still.

"But I got no answer. If it weren't for the swirling around my feet, I might have thought even the water had had its voice sucked from it.

"And then."

Finally, for the first time, Mrs Marchant's voice broke. In a horrible way, Selkirk realised he envied her this experience. No single hour, let alone day, had ever impressed itself on him the way these days had on her, except perhaps for those few fleeting, sleet-drenched moments with Amalia. And those had cast an uglier, darker shadow.

When Mrs Marchant continued, the quaver had gone, as though she'd swallowed it. "It was to be the last time I heard his real voice, Mr Selkirk. I think I already knew that. And when I remember it now, I'm not even certain I really did hear it. How could I have? It was a croak, barely even a whisper. But it was Charlie's voice. I'd still swear to it, in spite of everything, even though he said just the one word. '*Hurry.*'

"The last two remaining men from Winsett needed no further encouragement. In an instant, they had the rowboat in the water. Charlie's dad and I shoved off while they pulled with all their might against the crush of the surf. For a minute, no more, they hung up in that same spot that had devilled all our efforts for the past thirty-six hours, caught in waves that beat them back and back. Then they just sprung free. All of a sudden, they were in open water, heaving with all their might toward the sandbar. We were too exhausted to clap or cheer. But my heart leapt so hard in my chest I thought it might break my ribs.

"As soon as they were twenty feet from shore, we lost sight of them, and later, they said all they saw was blackness and water and snow, so none of us knows how close they actually got. They were gone six, maybe seven minutes. Then, as if a dyke had collapsed, sound came rushing over us. The wind roared in and brought a new, hard sleet. There was a one last, terrible pause that none of us mistook for calm. The water had simply risen up, you see, Mr Selkirk. It lifted our rescue rowboat in one giant black wave and hurled it halfway up the beach. The two men in the boat got slammed to the sand. Fortunately – miraculously, really – the wave hadn't crested until it was nearly on top of the shore, so neither man drowned. One broke both wrists, the other his nose and teeth. Meanwhile, the water poured up the beach, soaked us all, and retreated as instantaneously as it had come."

For the first time, Selkirk realised that the story he was hearing no longer quite matched the one Amalia had told him. Even more startling, Amalia's had been less cruel. No rescues had been attempted because none had been possible. No real hope had ever emerged. The ship had simply slid off the sandbar, and all aboard had drowned.

"Waves don't just rise up," he said.

Mrs Marchant tilted her head. "No? My father used to come home from half a year at sea and tell us stories. Waves riding the ghost of a wind two years gone and two thousand leagues distant, roaming alone like great, rogue beasts, devouring everything they encounter. Not an uncommon occurrence on the open ocean."

"But this isn't the open ocean."

"And you think the ocean knows, or cares? Though I will admit to you, Mr Selkirk. At the time, it seemed like the sea just didn't want us out there.

"By now, the only two healthy people at Cape Roby Point were Charlie's father and me. And when that new sleet kept coming and coming . . . well. We didn't talk about it. We made our wounded rowers as comfortable as we could by the fire on the rugs inside. Then we set about washing bedding, setting out candles. I began making this little sister here—" as she spoke, she toed the doll with the white bandeau, which leaned against her feet "—to keep him company in his coffin. Although both of us knew, I'm sure, that we weren't even likely to get the bodies back.

"My God, the sounds of that night. I can still hear the sleet drumming on the roof. The wind coiling around the tower. All I could think about was Charlie out there, clinging to the ropes for hope of reaching me. I knew he would be gone by morning. Around 2:00 a.m., Charlie's father fell asleep leaning against a wall, and I eased him into a chair and sank down on the floor beside him. I must have been so exhausted, so overwhelmed, that I slept, too, without meaning to, right there at his feet.

"And when I woke . . ."

The Kendalls, Selkirk thought, as he watched the woman purse her mouth and hold still. Had he known them? It seemed to him he'd at least known who they were. At that time, though, he'd had eyes only for Amalia. And after that, he'd kept to himself, and left everyone else alone.

"When I woke," Mrs Marchant murmured, "there was sunlight. I didn't wait to make sense of what I was seeing. I didn't think about what I'd find. I didn't wake Charlie's father, but he came roaring after me as I sprinted from the house.

"We didn't even know if our rowboat would float. We made straight for it anyway. I didn't look at the sandbar. Do you find that strange? I didn't want to see. Not yet. I looked at the dunes, and they were gold, Mr Selkirk. Even with the blown grass and seaweed strewn all over them, they looked newly born.

"The rowboat had landed on its side. The wood had begun to split all down one side, but Charlie's father thought it would hold. Anyway, it was all we had, our last chance. Without a word, we righted it and dragged it to the water, which was like glass. Absolutely flat, barely rolling over to touch the beach. Charlie's father wasn't waiting for me. He'd already got into the boat and begun to pull. But when I caught the back and dragged myself in, he held position just long enough, still not saying a single thing. Then he started rowing for all he was worth.

"For a few seconds longer, I kept my head down. I wanted to pray, but I couldn't. My mother was a Catholic, and we'd worked for the nuns. But somehow, making the dolls had turned God doll-like, for me. Does that make sense? I found it impossible to have faith in anything that took the face we made for it. I wanted some other face than the one I knew, then. So I closed my eyes and listened to the seagulls squealing around, skimming the surface for dead fish. Nothing came to me, except how badly I wanted Charlie back. Finally, I lifted my head.

"I didn't gasp, or cry out. I don't think I even felt anything.

"First off, there were only two of them. The highest was Charlie. He'd climbed almost to the very top of the main mast, which had tilted over so far that it couldn't have been more than twenty-five feet above the water. Even with that overcoat engulfing him and the hat pulled all the way down over his ears, I could tell by the arms and legs snarled in the rigging that it was him.

" 'Is he moving, girl?' Charlie's father asked, and I realised he hadn't been able to bring himself to look, either. We lurched closer.

"Then I did gasp, Mr Selkirk. Just once. Because he *was* moving. Or I thought he was. He seemed to be settling . . . resettling . . . I can't explain it. He was winding his arms and legs through the ropes, like a child trying to fit into a hiding place as you come for him. As if he'd just come back there. Or maybe the movement was wind. Even now, I don't know.

"Charlie's father swore at me and snarled his question again. When I didn't answer, he turned around. 'Lord Jesus,' I heard him say. After that, he just put his head down and rowed. And I kept my eyes on Charlie, and the empty blue sky beyond him. Anywhere but down the mast, where the other Kendall boy hung.

"By his ankles, Mr Selkirk. His ankles, and nothing more. God only knows what held him there. The wind had torn his clothes right off him. He had his eyes and his mouth open. He looked so pale, so thin, nothing like he had in life. His body had red slashes all over it, as though the storm had literally tried to rip him open. Just a boy, Mr Selkirk. His fingertips all but dancing on the water.

"Charlie's father gave one last heave, and our little boat knocked against the last showing bit of the Kendalls' ship's hull. The masts above us groaned, and I thought the whole thing was going to crash down on top of us. Charlie's father tried to wedge an oar in the wood, get us in close, and finally he just rowed around the ship and ran us aground on the sandbar. I leapt out after him, thinking I should be the one to climb the mast. I was lighter, less likely to sink the whole thing once and for all. Our home, our lighthouse, was so close it seemed I could have waded over and grabbed it. I probably could have. I leaned back, looked up again, and this time I was certain I saw Charlie move.

"His father saw it, too, and he started screaming. He wasn't even making words, but I was. I had my arms wide open, and I was calling my husband. 'Come down. Come home, my love.' I saw his arms disentangle themselves, his legs slide free. The ship sagged beneath him. If he so much as touched that water, I thought, it would be too much. The cold would have him at the last. He halted, and his father stopped screaming, and I went silent. He hung there so long I thought he'd died after all, now that he'd heard our voices one last time. Then, hand over hand, so painfully slowly, like a spider crawling down a web, he began to edge upside-down over the ropes. He reached the Kendall boy's poor, naked body and bumped it with his hip. It swung out and back, out and back. Charlie never even looked, and he didn't slow or alter his path. He kept coming.

"I don't even remember how he got over the rail. As he reached the deck, he disappeared a moment from our sight. We were trying to figure how to get up there to him. Then he just climbed over the edge and fell to the sand at our feet. The momentum from his body gave the wreck a final push, and it slid off the sandbar into the water and sank, taking the Kendall boy's body with it.

"The effort of getting down had taken everything Charlie had. His eyes were closed. His breaths were shallow, and he didn't respond when we shook him. So Charlie's father lifted him and dropped him in the rowboat. I hopped in the bow with my back to the shore, and Charlie's father began to pull desperately for the mainland. I was sitting calf-deep in water, cradling my husband's head facedown in my lap. I stroked his cheeks, and they were so cold. Impossibly cold, and bristly, and hard. Like rock. All my thoughts, all my energy, all the heat I had I was willing into my fingers, and I was cooing like a dove. Charlie's father had his back to us, pulling for everything he was worth. He never turned around. And so he didn't . . ."

Once more, Mrs Marchant's voice trailed away. Out the filthy windows, in the grey that had definitely darkened into full-blown dusk now, Selkirk could see a single trail of yellow-red, right at the horizon, like the glimpse of eye underneath a cat's closed lid. Tomorrow the weather would clear. And he would be gone, on his way home. Maybe he would stay there this time. Find somebody he didn't have to pay to keep him company.

"It's a brave thing you've done, Mrs Marchant," he said, and before he could think about what he was doing, he slid forward and took her chilly hand in his. He meant nothing by it but comfort, and was surprised to discover the sweet, transitory sadness of another person's fingers curled in his. A devil's smile of a feeling, if ever there was one. "He was a good man, your husband. You have mourned him properly and well."

"Just a boy," she whispered.

"A good boy, then. And he loved you. You have paid him the tribute he deserved, and more. And now it's time to do him the honor of living again. Come back to town. I'll see you somewhere safe and warm. I'll see you there myself, if you'll let me."

Very slowly, without removing her fingers, Mrs Marchant raised her eyes to his, and her mouth came open. "You . . . you silly man. You think . . . But you said you knew the story."

Confused, Selkirk squeezed her hand. "I know it now."

"You believe I have stayed here, cut off from all that is good in the world, shut up with my nuns all these years like an abbess, for love? For grief?"

Now Selkirk let go, watching as Mrs Marchant's hand fluttered before settling in her lap like a blown leaf. "There's no crime in that, surely. But now—"

"I've always wondered how the rowboat flipped," she said, in a completely new, expressionless tone devoid of all her half-sung tones, as he stuttered to silence. "All the times I've gone through it and over it, and I can't get it straight. I can't see how it happened."

Unsure what to do with his hands, Selkirk finally settled them on his knees. "The rowboat?"

"Dead calm. No ghost wave this time. We were twenty yards from shore. Less. We could have hopped out and walked. I was still cooing. Still stroking my husband's cheeks. But I knew already. And I think his father knew, too. Charlie had died before we even got him in the boat. He wasn't breathing. Wasn't moving. He hadn't during the whole, silent trip back to shore. I turned toward land to see exactly how close we were. And just like that I was in the water.

"If you had three men and were trying, you couldn't flip a boat that quickly. One of the oars banged me on the head. I don't know if it was that or the cold that stunned me. But I couldn't think. For a second, I had no idea which way was up, even in three feet of water, and then my feet found bottom, and I stood and staggered toward shore. The oar had caught me right on the scalp, and a stream of blood kept pouring into my eyes. I wasn't thinking about Charlie. I wasn't thinking anything except that I needed to be out of the cold before I became it. I could feel it in my bloodstream. I got to the beach, collapsed in the sun, remembered where I was and what I'd been doing, and spun around.

"There was the boat, floating right-side up, as though it hadn't flipped it all. Oars neatly shipped, like arms folded across a chest. Water still as a lagoon beneath it. And neither my husband nor his father *anywhere*.

"I almost laughed. It was impossible. Ridiculous. So cruel. I didn't scream. I waited, scanning the water, ready to lunge in and save Charlie's dad if I could only see him. But there was nothing. No trace. I sat down and stared at the horizon and didn't weep. It seemed perfectly possible that I might freeze to death right there, complete the event. I even opened the throat of my dress, thinking of the Kendall boys shedding their coats that first day. That's what I was doing when Charlie crawled out of the water."

Selkirk stood up. "But you said—"

"He'd lost his hat. And his coat had come open. He crawled right up the beach, sidewise, like a crab. Just the way he had down the rigging. Of course, my arms opened to him, and the cold dove down my dress. I was laughing, Mr Selkirk. Weeping and laughing and cooing, and his head swung up, and I saw."

With a single, determined wriggle of her shoulders, Mrs Marchant went completely still. She didn't speak again for several minutes. Helpless, Selkirk sat back down.

"The only question I had in the end, Mr Selkirk, was when it had happened."

For no reason he could name, Selkirk experienced a flash of Amalia's cruel, haunted face, and tried for the thousandth time to imagine where she'd gone. Then he thought of the dead town behind him, the debris disappearing piece by piece and bone by bone into the dunes, his aunt's silent death. His uncle. He'd never made any effort to determine what had happened to his uncle after Amalia vanished.

"I still think about those boys, you know," Mrs Marchant murmured. "Every day. The one suspended in the ropes, exposed like that, all torn up. And the one that disappeared. Do you think he jumped to get away, Mr Selkirk? I think he might have. I would have."

"What on earth are you—?"

"Even the dead's eyes reflect light," she said, turning her bright and living ones on him. "Did you know that? But Charlie's eyes . . . Of course, it wasn't really Charlie, but . . ."

Selkirk almost leapt to his feet again, wanted to, wished he could hurtle downstairs, flee into the dusk. And simultaneously he found that he couldn't.

"What do you mean?"

For answer, Mrs Marchant cocked her head at him, and the ghost of her smile hovered over her mouth and evaporated. "What do I mean? How do I know? Was it a ghost? Do you know how many hundreds of sailors have died within five miles of this point? Surely one or two of them might have been angry about it."

"Are you actually saying—?"

"Or maybe that's silly. Maybe ghosts are like gods, no? Familiar faces we have clamped on what comes for us? Maybe it was the sea. I can't tell you. What I can tell you is that there was no Charlie in the face before me, Mr Selkirk. None. I had no doubt. No question. My only hope was that whatever it was had come for him after he was gone, the way a hermit crab climbs inside a shell. Please God, whatever that is, let it be the wind and the cold that took him."

Staggering upright, Selkirk shook his head. "You said he was dead."

"So he was."

"You were mistaken."

"It killed the Kendall boy, Mr Selkirk. It crawled down and tore him to shreds. I'm fairly certain it killed its own father as well. Charlie's father, I mean. Luis took one look at him and vanished into the dunes. I never saw the dog again."

"Of course it was him. You're not yourself, Mrs Marchant. All these years alone . . . It spared you, didn't it? Didn't he?"

Mrs Marchant smiled one more time and broke down weeping, silently. "It had just eaten," she whispered. "Or whatever it is it does. Or maybe I had just lost my last loved ones, and stank of the sea, and appeared as dead to it as it did to me."

"Listen to me," Selkirk said, and on impulse he dropped to one knee and took her hands once more. God, but they were cold. So many years in this cold, with this weight on her shoulders. "That day was so full of tragedy. Whatever you think you . . ."

Very slowly, Selkirk stopped. His mind retreated down the stairs, out the lighthouse door to the mainland, over the disappearing path he'd walked between the dunes, and all the way back into Winsett. He saw anew the shuttered boarding houses and empty taverns, the grim smile of the stable-boy. He saw the street where his uncle's cabin had been. What had happened to his uncle? His aunt? *Amalia*? Where had they all gone? Just how long had it taken Winsett to die? His mind scrambled farther, out of town, up the track he had taken, between the discarded pots and decaying whale-bones toward the other silent, deserted towns all along this blasted section of the Cape.

"Mrs Marchant," he whispered, his hands tightening around hers, having finally understood why she had stayed. "Mrs Marchant, please. Where is Charlie now?"

She stood, then, and twined one gentle finger through the tops of his curls as she wiped at her tears. The gesture felt dispassionate, almost maternal, something a mother might do to a son who has just awoken. He looked up and found her gazing again not out to sea but over the dunes at the dark streaming inland.

"It's going to get even colder," she said. "I'll put the kettle on."

KIM NEWMAN

The Man Who
Got Off the Ghost Train

KIM NEWMAN IS A NOVELIST, critic and broadcaster. His published fiction includes *The Night Mayor, Bad Dreams, Jago,* the *Anno Dracula* novels and stories, *The Quorum, The Original Dr Shade and Other Stories, Famous Monsters, Seven Stars, Unforgivable Stories, Dead Travel Fast, Life's Lottery, Back in the USSA* (with Eugene Byrne), *Where the Bodies Are Buried, Doctor Who: Time and Relative, The Man from the Diogenes Club* and *Secret Files of the Diogenes Club* under his own name, and *The Vampire Genevieve* and *Orgy of the Blood Parasites* as "Jack Yeovil".

His non-fiction books include *Nightmare Movies, Ghastly Beyond Belief* (with Neil Gaiman), *Horror: 100 Best Books* and *Horror: Another 100 Best Books* (both with Stephen Jones), *Wild West Movies, The BFI Companion to Horror, Millennium Movies* and *BFI Classics* studies of *Cat People* and *Doctor Who.*

He is a contributing editor to *Sight & Sound* and *Empire* magazines and has written and broadcast widely on a range of topics. His short story "Week Woman" was adapted for the TV series *The Hunger* and he has directed and written a tiny short film, *Missing Girl.*

Newman has won the Bram Stoker Award, the International Horror Critics Award, the British Science Fiction Award and the British Fantasy Award. He was born in Brixton (London), grew up in the West Country, went to University near Brighton and now lives in Islington (London).

As the author reveals: " 'The Man Who Got Off the Ghost Train' was written for my collection *The Man from the Diogenes Club* –

mostly to fill in background for Richard Jeperson, the hero of those
stories (while keeping a few mysteries back for later).

"Also, I happen to like stories set on trains and wanted to do one. I
dimly remember being taken with a British TV *Sexton Blake* serial in
the 1960s set on a train, and I make a connection here with *Terror by
Night*, a 1946 Basil Rathbone Sherlock Holmes film that follows a
similar route.

"In *Throw Momma from the Train*, Billy Crystal's character
claims 'Every great mystery or romance has a train in it somewhere'."

Culler's Halt

"TEN HOURS, GUV'NOR," said Fred Regent. "That's what the
time-table says. Way this half-holiday is going, next train
mightn't come for ten *months*."

Richard Jeperson shrugged. A cheek-muscle twitched.

Pink-and-grey-streaked autumn skies hung over wet fields. Fred
had scouted around. No one home. Typical British Rail. He only
knew Culler's Halt was in use because of the uncollected rubbish.
Lumpy plastic sacks were piled on the station forecourt like wartime
sandbags. The bin-men's strike was settled, but maybe word hadn't
reached these parts. A signpost claimed CULLER 3m. If there were a
village at the end of the lane, it showed no lamps at the fag-end of this
drab afternoon.

Fred wasn't even sure which *country* Culler was in.

On the platform, Richard stood by their luggage, peering at the
dying sunlight through green-tinted granny glasses. He wore a floor-
length mauve travel coat with brocade frogging, shiny PVC bondage
trousers (a concession to the new decade) and a curly-brimmed
purple top hat.

Fred knew the Man From the Diogenes Club was worried about
Vanessa. When a *sensitive* worried about someone who could
famously take care of herself, it was probably time to panic.

At dawn, they'd been far South, after a nasty night's work in
Cornwall. They had been saddled with Alastair Garnett, a civil
servant carrying out a time-and-motion study. In a funk, the man
from the ministry had the bad habit of giving orders. If the local cops
had listened to Richard rather than the "advisor", there'd have been
fewer deaths. The hacked-off body parts found inside a stone circle

had to be sorted into two piles – goats and teenagers. An isolated family, twisted by decades of servitude to breakfast food corporations, had invented their own dark religion. Ceremonially masked in cornflakes packets with cut-out eyeholes, the Penrithwick Clan made hideous sacrifice to the goblins Snap, Crackle and Pop.

Bloody wastage like that put Richard in one of his moods, and no wonder. Fred would happily have booted Garnett up his pin-striped arse, but saw the way things were going in the 1980s.

Trudging back to seaside lodgings in Mevagissey, hardly up for cooked breakfast and sworn off cereal for life, they were met by the landlady and handed Vanessa's telegram, an urgent summons to Scotland.

Abandoning the Penrithwick shambles to Garnett, Richard and Fred took a fast train to Paddington. They crossed London by taxi without even stopping off at homes in Chelsea and Soho for a change of clothes or a hello to the girlfriends – who would of course be ticked off by that familiar development – and rattled out of Euston in a slam-door diesel.

The train stank of decades' worth of Benson & Hedges. Since giving up, Fred couldn't be in a fuggy train or pub without feeling queasily envious. At first, they shared their first-class compartment with a clear-complexioned girl whose T-shirt (sporting the word "GASH", with an Anarchy Symbol for the A) was safety-pinned together like a disassembled torso stitched up after autopsy. She quietly leafed through *Bunty* and *The Lady*, chain-smoking with a casual pleasure that made Fred wish a cartoon anvil would fall from the luggage rack onto her pink punk hairdo. At Peterborough, she was collected by a middle-aged gent with a Range Rover. Fred and Richard had the compartment to themselves.

Outside Lincoln, something mechanical got thrown. The train slowed to a snail's pace, overtaken by ancient cyclists, jeered at by small boys ("Get off and milk it!"), inching through miles-long tunnels. This went on for agonising hours. Scheduled connections were missed. The only alternative route the conductor could offer involved getting off at York, a stopping train to Culler's Halt, then a service to Inverdeith, changing there for Portnacreirann. In theory, it was doable. In practice, they were marooned. The conductor had been working from a time-table good only until September the 1st *of last year*. No one else had got off at Culler's Halt.

Beyond the rail-bed was a panoramic advertising hoarding. A once-glossy, now-weatherworn poster showed a lengthy dole queue and the slogan LABOUR ISN'T WORKING – VOTE CONSERVA-

TIVE. Over this was daubed NO FUTURE. A mimeographed sheet, wrinkled in the fly-posting, showed the Queen with a pin through her nose.

"There's something wrong, Frederick," said Richard.

"The country's going down the drain, and everyone's pulling the flush."

"Not just that. Think about it: 'God Save the Queen' came out for the Silver Jubilee, two years *before* the election. So why are ads for the single pasted *over* the Tory poster?"

"This is the wilds, guv. Can't expect them to be up with pop charts."

Richard shrugged again. The mystery wasn't significant enough to be worth considered thought.

They had more pressing troubles. Chiefly, Vanessa.

Their friend and colleague wasn't a panicky soul. She wouldn't have sent the telegram unless things were serious. A night's delay, and they might be too late.

"I'm not happy with this, Frederick," said Richard.

"Me neither, guv."

Richard chewed his moustache and looked at the time-table Fred had already checked. Always gaunt, he was starting to seem haggard. Deep shadow gathered in the seams under his eyes

"As you say, ten hours," said Richard. "*If* the train's on time."

"Might as well kip in the waiting room," suggested Fred. "Take shifts."

There were hard benches and a couple of chairs chained to pipes. A table was piled with magazines and comics from years ago: Patrick Mower grinned on the cover of *Tit-Bits*; Robot Archie was in the jungle in *Lion*. A tiny bookshelf was stocked with paperbacks: *Jaws*, *Mandingo*, *Sexploits of a Meter Maid*, *Zen and the Art of Motorcycle Maintenance*, Guy N. Smith's *The Sucking Pit*. Richard toggled a light-switch and nothing happened. Fred found a two-bar electric fire in working order and turned it on, raising the whiff of singed dust. As night set in, the contraption provided an orange glow but no appreciable heat.

Fred huddled in his pea-coat and scarf. Richard stretched out on a bench like a fakir on a bed of nails.

The new government wasn't mad keen on the Diogenes Club. Commissions of Inquiry empowered the likes of Alastair Garnett to take a watching brief. Number Ten was asking for "blue skies suggestions" as to what, if anything, might replace this "hold-over from an era when British intelligence was run by enthusiastic amateurs". Richard said the 1980s "would not be a comfortable decade for a *feeling* person". His chief asset was sensitivity, but when his nerves frayed he looked like a cuckoo with peacock feathers. Called up before a Select Committee, he made a bad impression.

Fred knew Richard was right to be paranoid. Wheels were grinding and the team was being broken up. He had been strongly advised to report back to New Scotland Yard, take a promotion to Detective Inspector and get on with "real police work". Rioters, terrorists and scroungers needed clouting. Task Forces and Patrol Groups were up and running. If he played along with the boot boys, he could have his own command, be a Professional. The decision couldn't be put off much longer.

He'd assumed Vanessa would stay with the Club, though. Richard could chair the Ruling Cabal, planning and *feeling*. She would handle field-work, training up new folk to tackle whatever crept from the lengthening shadows.

Now, he wasn't sure. If they didn't get to Vanessa in time . . .

"There used to be a through train to Portnacreirann," mused Richard. "The Scotch Streak. A sleeper. Steam until 1962, then diesel, then . . . well, helicopters took over."

"Helicopter?" queried Fred, distracted. "Who commutes by helicopter?"

"NATO. Defence considerations kept the Scotch Streak running long after its natural lifetime. Then they didn't. March of bloody progress."

Richard sat up. He took off and folded his glasses, then tucked them in his top pocket behind an emerald explosion of display handkerchief.

"It's where I started, Frederick," he said. "On the Scotch Streak. Everyone has a first time . . ."

"Not 'arf," Fred smiled.

Richard smiled too, perhaps ruefully. "As you so eloquently put it, 'not 'arf'. For you, it was that bad business at the end of the pier, in Seamouth. For your lovely Zarana, it was the Soho Golem. For Professor Corri it was the Curse of *The Northern Barstows*. For me, it was the Scotch Streak . . . the Ghost Train."

Fred's interest pricked. He'd worked with Richard Jeperson for more than ten years, but knew only scattered pieces about the man's earlier years. Richard himself didn't know about a swathe of his childhood. A foundling of war, he'd been pulled out of a refugee camp by Major Jeperson, a British officer who saw his *sensitivity*. Richard had been raised as much by the Diogenes Club as his adoptive father. He had no memory of any life before the camps. Even the tattoo on his arm was a mystery. The Nazis were appallingly meticulous about record-keeping, but Richard's serial number didn't match any name on lists of the interned or to-be-exterminated. The numbers weren't even in a configuration like those of other Holocaust survivors or known victims. Suspicion was that the Germans had seen the boy's qualities too and tried to make use of him in a facility destroyed, along with its records and presumably other inmates, before it could fall into Allied hands. The lad had slipped through the clean-up operation, scathed but alive. Major Geoffrey Jeperson named him Richard, after Richard Riddle – a boy detective who was his own childhood hero.

Of Richard's doings between the War and the Seamouth Case, Fred knew not much. After Geoffrey's death in 1954, Richard's sponsors at the Club had been Edwin Winthrop, now dead but well-remembered, and Sir Giles Gallant, now retired and semi-disgraced. Vanessa came into the picture well before the Seamouth Case. She had Richard's habit of being evasive without making a fuss about it. All Fred knew was that her first meeting with their patron was another horror story. Whenever it came up, she'd touch the almost-invisible scar through her eyebrow and change the subject with a shudder.

"Now we're near the end of the line," said Richard, "perhaps you should hear the tale."

They were here for the night. Time enough for a ghost story.

"Frederick," said Richard, "it was 195–, and I was down from Oxford . . ."

Act I: London Euston

I

. . . it was 195– and Richard Jeperson was down from Oxford. And the LSE. And Cambridge. And Manchester Poly. And RADA. And Harrow School of Art. And . . . well, suffice to say, many fine institutions, none of which felt obliged to award him any formal qualification.

Geoffrey Jeperson had sent him to St Cuthbert's, his old school. Richard hadn't lasted at "St Custard's", setting an unhappy precedent insofar as not lasting at schools went. After the Major's death, Edwin Winthrop took over *in loco parentis*. He encouraged Richard to regard schooling as a cold buffet, picking at whatever took his fancy. Winthrop called himself a graduate of Flanders and the Somme, though as it happened he had a Double First in Classics and Natural Philosophy from All Souls. Since Richard was known for his instincts – his *sensitivities*, everyone said – he was allowed to follow his nose. He became a "New Elizabethan renaissance man", though teachers tended to tut-tut as he acquired unsystematic tranches of unrelated expertise then got on with something else before he was properly finished.

Though the Diogenes Club supported him with a generous allowance, he took on jobs of work. He assisted with digs and explorations. He sleuthed through Europe in search of his past, and drew suspicious blanks – which persuaded him to pay more attention to his present. He spent a summer in a biscuit factory in Barnsley, making tea and enduring harassment from the female staff. He was a film extra in Italy, climbing out of the horse in *Helen of Troy*. He couriered documents between British Embassies in South America. He studied magic – *stage* magic, not yet the other stuff – with a veteran illusionist in Baltimore. He dug ditches, modelled for catalogues, worked fishing boats, wrote articles for manly magazines, and the like.

Between education and honest toil, he did his National Service. He was in the RAF but never saw an aeroplane. The Club placed him in a system of bunkers under the New Forest. He fetched and carried for boffins working on an oscillating wave device. After eighteen months, a coded message instructed him to sabotage an apparently routine experiment. Though he liked the backroom boys and had worked up enthusiasm for the project, he followed orders. The procedure failed and – he was later given to understand – an invasion of our plane of existence by malign extra-dimensional entities was prevented. That was how the Club worked under Edwin Winthrop: pre-emptive, unilateral, cutting out weeds before they sprouted, habitually secretive, pragmatically ruthless. A lid was kept on, though who knew whether the pot really had been boiling over?

After the RAF, Richard spear-carried for a season at the Old Vic, and played saxophone with The Frigidaires. The doo-wop group was on the point of signing with promoter Larry Parnes – of "parnes, shillings and pence" fame – when the girl singer married a quantity surveyor for the security. Though her rendition of 'Lipstick on Your Collar', lately a hit for Connie Francis, was acceptable, Richard couldn't really argue with her. Frankly, the Frigidaires were never very good.

Richard only knew within a year or so how old he actually was, but must be out of his teens. Edwin felt it was time the boy knuckled down and got on with the work for which he had been prepared. Richard moved into a Georgian house in Chelsea which was in the gift of the Club, occasionally looked after by an Irish housekeeper who kept going home to have more children. He meditated, never missed *Hancock's Half Hour* on the wireless and read William Morris and Hank Jansen. Edwin told him to wait for a summons to action.

Richard dressed in the "Edwardian" or "teddy boy" manner: scarlet velvet frock coat with midnight black lapels (straight-razor slipped into a special compartment in the sleeve), crepe-soled suede zip-up boots with winkle-picker toe-points, a conjurer's waistcoat with seventeen secret pockets, his father's watch and chain, bootlace tie with silver tips, navy-blue drainpipe jeans tighter than paint on his skinny legs. His thin moustache was only just established enough not to need augmentation with eyebrow pencil. A Brylcreem pompadour rose above his pale forehead like a constructivist sculpture in black candyfloss.

If he took his life to have begun when his memory did, his experience was limited. He had never seen a woman naked, except in *Health & Efficiency* magazine. He could not drive a car, though he intended to take lessons. He had never killed anything important. He had never had a broken bone. He had never eaten an avocado.

Within a year, all that would change.

One morning, a special messenger arrived on a motorbike, with instructions that he give himself over to a side-car and be conveyed to the Diogenes Club. This, he knew, was to be his debut.

The retired Royal Marine Sergeant who kept Door in the Mall went beet-coloured as Richard waltzed past his post. Outlandish folk must come and go from the Diogenes Club, but Richard's clothes and hair were red rag to a bull for anyone over twenty-five – especially a uniformed middle-aged man with a short back and sides and medal ribbons. There was talk about playwrights and poets who were "angry young men", but the older generation would not easily yield a monopoly on sputtering indignation.

He rather admired himself in the polished black marble of the hallway pillars. The whole look took hours to achieve. His face no longer erupted as it had done a few years earlier, but the odd plague-rose blemish surfaced, requiring attention.

Escorted by a silk-jacketed servant beyond the famously noiseless public rooms of the Club, he puffed with pride. Ordinary Members mimed *harrumphs*, seconding the Doorman's opinion of him. The servant opened an Inner Door, and stood aside to let Richard pass. He had not been this deep into the building since childhood. Then, he had almost been a possession, shown off by his father. Now, he was entitled to pass on his own merit. He could walk the corridors, consult the archives, visit the private collections, accept commissions. He was not merely a Life Member, inheriting that status from Major Jeperson, but an Asset, whose Talent suited him to act for the Club in Certain Circumstances.

He was treading in the footsteps of giants. Mycroft Holmes, the mid-Victorian civil servant who was instrumental in founding what was ostensibly a "club for the unclubbable" but actually an auxiliary extraordinary to British intelligence and the police. Charles Beauregard, the first Most Valued Member – the great puzzle-chaser of the 1880s and '90s and visionary chairman of the Ruling Cabal through the middle-years of the current century. Carnacki, the Ghost-Finder. Several terrifying individuals who operated covertly under the goggles of "Doctor Shade". Adam Llewellyn de Vere Adamant, the adventurer whose disappearance in 1903 remained listed on the books as an active, unsolved case. Catriona Kaye, Winthrop's life-long companion, the first woman to accept full membership in the Club. Flaxman Low. Sir Henry Merrivale. Robert Baldick. Cursitor Doom.

He was ushered upstairs. In an underlit Ante-Room, his coat was taken by a turbaned orderly. He had a moment before a two-way mirror to be awed by the great tradition, the honour to which he would ascend in the presence of the Ruling Cabal. He patted his pockets, checked his fly and adjusted his tie. The weight of the razor was gone from his sleeve. Somewhere between the street and the Ante-Room, he had been frisked and defanged.

A baize door opened, and a tiny shove from the silent Sikh was necessary to propel him along a short dark corridor. One door shut behind him and another opened in front. Richard stepped into the windowless Star Chamber of the Ruling Cabal.

"Good Gravy, Edwin," said someone sour, "is this what it's come to? A bloody teddy boy!"

Some of Richard's puff leaked out.

"I think he's *sweet*," purred a woman with a whisky-and-cigarettes voice, like Joan Greenwood or Fenella Fielding. "Winner of the Fourth Form fancy dress."

The last of his self-esteem pooled on the floor.

"Cool, man," said another commentator, snapping his fingers. "Straight from the fridge."

He didn't feel any better.

Edwin Winthrop sat at the big table that had been Mycroft's desk, occupying one of three places. He had slightly hooded eyes and an iron-grey moustache. Even if Richard weren't attuned to "vibrations", he'd have had no doubt who was in charge. Next to him was Catriona Kaye, a compact, pretty woman as old as the century. She wore a dove-grey dress and pearls. The only one of the Inner Circle who had treated him as a little boy, she was now the only one who treated him as a grown-up. She was the heart and conscience of the Diogenes Club. Edwin recognised his own tendency to high-handedness, and kept Catriona close – she was the reason why he wasn't a monster. To Edwin's right was an empty chair. Sir Giles Gallant, make-weight on the Ruling Cabal, was absent.

"If we've finished twitting the new boy," said Edwin, impatiently, "perhaps we can get on. Richard, welcome and all that. This is the group . . ."

Edwin introduced everyone. Richard put faces to names and resumés he already knew.

Dr Harry Cutley, the pipe-smoking, tweed-jacketed scowler held a chair of Physics at a provincial redbrick university. He had unexpectedly come under the Club's remit, as Quantum Mechanics led him to Parapsychology. When Edwin vacated the post of Most Valued Member to run the Ruling Cabal, Sir Giles recruited Cutley to fill his roomy shoes. The academic finally had funds and resources to mount the research programme of his dreams, but was sworn *not* to share findings with his peers, turning his papers over instead to the Cabal. They then had to root out others capable of *understanding* Cutley's work and determining what should leak onto the intellectual open market and what the world was not yet ready to know. In practice, Cutley had exchanged one set of grumbling resentments for another. He knew things no-one else on the planet did, but colleagues in the real world wrote him off as a dead-ended time-server whose students didn't like him and whose ex-wife slept with other faculty members. Cutley had a boozer's red-veined eyes, hair at all angles and a pulsing, hostile aura – the plainest Richard had ever sensed, as if inner thoughts were written on comic strip bubbles.

The husky-voiced blonde in the black leotard and pink chiffon scarf was Annette Amboise, of Fitzrovia and the Left Bank. She wore no lipstick but a lot of eye make-up and had hair cropped like Jean Seberg as Joan of Arc. She smoked Gauloises in a long, enamel holder. Of Anglo-French parentage, she'd spent her mid-teens in Vichy France, running messages for the Resistance and Allied

Intelligence. She came to the Club's notice after an unprecedented run of good fortune, which is to say she outlived all other agents in her district several times over. Catriona diagnosed an inbuilt ability to intuit random factors and predict immediate danger. Annette thought in knight moves – two hops forward, then a kink to the side. Since the War, she'd been doing other things. A retired interpretive dancer, past thirty with too many pulled muscles, she was authoress of a slim volume, *Ectoplasm and Existentialism*. Knowing what would probably happen next gave her a peculiarly cheerful fatalism. She had no accent, but showed an extremely French side in occasional "*ça va*" shrugs.

The tall, thin hipster was Danny Myles, whom Richard recognised as "Magic Fingers Myles", piano-player in a modern jazz combo famous for making "I Can't Get Started With You" last an entire set at Ronnie Scott's. He wore a green polo-neck and chinos, and had a neatly-trimmed goatee. His fingers continually moved as if on an infinite keyboard or reading a racy novel in Braille. Born blind, Myles developed extra senses as a child. Gaining sight in his teens, Myles found himself in a new visual world but retained other sharpnesses. Besides his acute ear, he had "the Touch". Richard and Annette took the psychic temperature of a room with invisible antennae (Catriona called them "mentacles"), but Myles had to lay hands on something to intuit its history, associations or true nature. The Magic Fingers Touch worked best on inanimate objects.

"This is Geoffrey's boy," explained Edwin. "We expect great things from him."

From Magic Fingers, Richard gathered non-verbal information: he understood how everyone related to each other, where the frictions were, whom he could trust to come through, when he'd be on his own. Cutley was like a football manager required to play a board member's nephew in goal. He hated "spook stuff" and wanted to haul paraphenomena back to measurable realities. Annette was emotionally off on another plane, but mildly amused. She had vague, not-related-by-blood auntie feelings for Richard and a nagging concern about his short-term future that did little for his confidence. Richard thanked Myles with a nod no one else noticed.

This is what it was like: Richard *knew* things most people had to guess at. A problem growing up, which he was not quite done with, was that he rarely appreciated few others felt and understood as he did. His first thought was that English people were too polite to mention things that were glaringly obvious to him. That had not gone down well at St Custard's. If he hadn't been able to a chuck a

KIM NEWMAN

cricket ball with a degree of devious accuracy, he'd likely have been burned at the stake behind the Prefects' Hut.

"Now we're acquainted," said Edwin, "let's get to why you've been brought together. Who's heard of the Scotch Streak?"

"It's a train, man," said Myles. "Euston to Edinburgh, overnight."

"Yes," said Edwin. "In point of fact, the service, which leaves London at seven o'clock every other evening, does not terminate in Edinburgh. It continues to Portnacreirann, on Loch Linnhe."

"Is this one of those *railway mysteries*?" asked Annette, squeezing her palms together. "I adore those."

Edwin nodded, and passed the conch to Catriona.

II

"In 1923, Locomotive Number 3473-S rolled out of foundry sheds in Egham," began Catriona Kaye, the Club's collector of ghost stories. "It was an A1 Atlantic Class engine. To the non-trainspotters among us, that means a shiny new chuff-chuff with all the bells and whistles. It was bred for speed, among the first British trains to break the hundred-mile-an-hour barrier. The London, Scotland and Isles Railway Company presented the debutante at the British Empire Exhibition in 1924, and christened 'the Scotch Streak'. A bottle of champagne was wasted on the cow-catcher by the odious Lady Lucinda Tregellis-d'Aulney. She mercifully passes out of the narrative. The LSIR got wind of a scheme by a rival to run a non-stop from London to Edinburgh, and added a further leg to their express, across Scotland to Portnacreirann. This sort of one-upmanship happened often before the railways were taken into public ownership. The Streak's original colours were royal purple and gold. Even in an era of ostentation in high-speed transport, it was considered showoffy.

"The Scotch Streak was quickly popular with drones who wanted to get sozzled in Piccadilly, have a wee small hours dram in Edinburgh, then walk off the hangover in Glen Wherever while shooting at something feathery or antlered. All very jolly, no doubt. Until the disaster of 1931.

"There are stories about Inverdeith. In the 18th century, fishermen on Loch Gaer often netted human bones. After some decades, this led to the capture of the cannibal crofter famed in song as 'Graysome Jock McGaer'. He was torn apart by a mob on his way to the scaffold. During the interregnum, the Scots God-botherer Samuel Druchan, fed up because England's Matthew Hopkins was hogging the headlines, presided over a mass witch-drowning. As you know, proper witches float when "swum", so the Druchan took the trouble to sew iron weights to his beldames' skirts. In 1601, a local diarist recorded that a 'stoon o' fire spat out frae hell' plopped into the waters with a mighty hiss. However, the railway bridge disaster really put Inverdeith on the tragedy map.

"What exactly happened remains a mystery, but . . . early one foggy morning in November, the Scotch Streak was crossing Inverdeith Bridge when – through human agency, gremlins, faulty iron or sheer ill-chance – 3473-S was decoupled from the rest of the train. The locomotive pulled away and steamed safely to the far side. The bridge collapsed, taking eight passenger carriages and a mail car with it. The rolling stock sank to the bottom of Loch Gaer with the loss of all hands, except one lucky little girl who floated.

"A board of inquiry exonerated Donald McRidley, the engine driver, though many thought he'd committed the unforgivable sin of cutting his passengers loose to save his own hide. Only Nicholas Bowler, the fireman, knew for sure. Rather than give testimony, Bowler laid on the tracks and was beheaded by an ordinary suburban service. McRidley was finished as an engineer. Some say that, like T. E. Lawrence re-enlisting as Aircraftman Ross, McRidley changed his name and became a navvy, working all weathers on a maintenance gang, looking over his shoulder at dusk, dreading the reproachful tread of the Headless Fireman.

"Whatever he might or might not have done, McRidley couldn't be blamed for the 'In-for-Death Bridge'. All manner of Scots legal inquiries boiled down to an unlovely squabble between Inverdeith Council and the LSIR. One set of lawyers claimed the sound structure wouldn't have collapsed were it not for the Scotch Streak rattling over it at speeds in excess of the recommendation. Another pack counter-claimed eighty-nine people wouldn't be dead if the bridge wasn't a rickety structure liable to be knocked down by a stiff breeze. This dragged on. A newspaperman dug up a local legend that one of Druchan's witches cursed her weights as she drowned, swearing no iron would ever safely span the loch. 'Local legend' is a Fleet Street synonym for 'something I've just made up'.

"The Streak ran only from London to Edinburgh until 1934, when a new bridge was erected and safety-tested. A fuss was made about the amount of steel used in the construction. Witches have nothing against steel, apparently. Then, full service to Portnacreirann resumed.

"Memories being what they were, folks who *didn't* have a financial interest in the venture were reluctant to board the 'In-for-Death Express'. Only grimly smiling directors and their perspiring wives and children were aboard for the accident-free re-inaugural run. You can imagine the sighs of relief when Inverdeith Bridge was safely behind them.

"Controlling interest in the LSIR was held by Douglas Gilclyde of Kilpartinger, who horsewhipped a secretary he thought misreferred to him as 'Lord Killpassengers'. It was a point of pride for His Lordship, a *parvenu* ennobled by Lloyd George, to make the Scotch Streak a roaring success again. He tarted 3473 up with a fresh coat of purple and replaced the gold trim with his own newly minted tartan – which the unkind said made the engine look like a novelty box of oatcakes.

"Kilpartinger lured back the hunting set by trading speed records for social cachet. From 1934, the Scotch Streak became famously, indeed *appallingly*, luxurious. Padding on padding, Carrera marble sinks, minions in Gilclyde kilts servicing every whim. The train gained a reputation as a social event on rails. 3473 pulled a ballroom carriage, a bar to rival the Criterion and sleeping cars with compartments like rooms at the Savoy. In addition to tweedy fowl-blasters, the Streak gained a following among the 'fast' crowd. Debutantes on the prowl booked up and down services for months on end, in the hope of snaring a suitable fiancé. One or two even got married before they were raped. When his disgusted *pater* kicked him out of the family pile, Viscount St John 'Buzzy' Maltrincham took a permanent lease on a compartment and made the Scotch Streak his address – until a pregnant Windmill Girl cut his throat somewhere between the Trossachs and Clianlarich.

"He wasn't the only casualty. The Streak's Incident Book ran to several spine-tingling volumes. People threw themselves under the train, got up on top and were swept off in tunnels, were decapitated when they disregarded DO NOT LEAN OUT OF THE WINDOW notices, opened doors and flung themselves across the landscape. Naturally, a number of fatalities occurred around Inverdeith. There was a craze for booking the up service on the Streak, naturally not bothering with the return. The procedure was to put a particular record on the wind-up Victrola as the train crossed the bridge, then take a graceful suicide leap as Bing Crosby crooned 'a golden goodbye'. Mistime it, and you smashed into a strut and rained down in pieces.

"Kilpartinger played up the Streak's glamour by engaging the likes of Noël Coward, Elsie and Doris Waters, Jessie Matthews and

Gracie Fields to entertain through the night. A discreet doctor prescribed pick-me-ups to keep the audience, and not a few performers, awake and sparkling. Houdini's less-famous brother escaped from a locked trunk in the mail van and popped out of the coal tender. The Palladium-on-Rails business soured when a popular ventriloquist was institutionalised after an argument with his dummy. His act started off with the usual banter, then the dummy began making passes at women in the carriage. The vent was besieged. His dummy jeered him as he was beaten up by angry escorts. He snatched a hatchet and chopped at the dummy's mocking head, taking off three of his own fingers.

"Of course, there were *whispers*. Among railwaymen, the Streak picked up a new nickname, 'the Ghost Train'. In 1938, I drafted a pamphlet for inclusion in my series, *Haunted High-Ways*. I got a look at the Incident Book. I conducted tactful interviews with passengers. They expressed a vague, unformed sense of *wrongness*. They *saw* things, *felt* things. Anecdotes piled up. The dirty dummy and the throat-cut bounder were the least of it. Several regulars dreaded trips on the Streak, but were unable to resist making them – as if afraid of what 3473 would do if they abandoned it. Real addicts use the serial number, never the name. Lord Kilpartinger issued writs and threats, then invited me to tea at Fortnum & Mason. With *some* justification, he pointed out that any train that carried as many passengers over as many years must collect horror stories and that I might as well investigate tragedies associated with the 5:12 from Paddington to Swindon. Besides, he had just bought a controlling interest in my publisher and wondered if I wouldn't rather write books on flower-arrangement or how to host a dinner party.

"As I left, in something approaching high dudgeon, His Lordship tried to reassure me about the train. After all, he said, he'd travelled more miles on the Streak than anyone else with no obvious ill-effects. A month later, for some anniversary run or other, he boarded at Euston, posing cheerfully in his tartan cummerbund for the newspapers, clouds of steam billowing all around. After retiring to his compartment, he disappeared and did *not* pop out of the coal tender. He didn't get off at Edinburgh or Portnacreirann. The general consensus was that he had contrived a fabulous exit to avoid the bankruptcy proceedings which, it turned out, were about to bring down the LSIR.

"Maybe Kilpartinger became another anonymous navvy on his beloved line, swinging a hammer next to the disgraced McRidley. Or perhaps he dissolved into a Scotch mist and seeped into the upholstery. If you run across him, give him my best.

"With the LSIR in ruins, it seemed likely the Streak had made its last run. It was saved by the War. Luxury took a back seat to pulling together, but the Streak was classified an essential service, supporting the Royal Navy Special Contingencies School at Portnacreirann. The Diogenes Club was busy on other fronts, but spared a young parapsychologist with a plum-bob and an anemometer to make a routine inspection. He ruled the train, the tracks and Inverdeith Bridge were perhaps *slightly* haunted. Had the Ruling Cabal listened to me rather than that bright lad, we would perhaps not be in this current pickle, but there's no use squalling about it now.

"Soon, there was another strange story about. Take the Streak to your Special Contingencies course, and you'd win a medal. I went over the records last week – an enormously tedious job – and can confirm this was, in fact, true. 'Special Contingencies', as you might guess, is a euphemism for 'Dirty Fighting', which goes a long way towards explaining things. Nevertheless, a high proportion of the Streak's sailors proved aggressive, valiant and effective in battle. A high proportion of that high proportion got their gongs posthumously. The more often a man rode the Scotch Streak, the more extreme his conduct. We don't publicise the British servicemen tried for war crimes, but out of fewer than a dozen bad apples in World War II, five were Streak regulars. Americans rode the Ghost Train too. We don't have official access to their records, but they have Alexanders and Caligulas too.

"After the War, the railways were nationalised. In *Thomas the Tank Engine*, the Fat Director became the Fat Controller. The LSIR was swallowed by British Rail. 3473-S steams still, purple faded to the colour of a weak Ribena, tartan trim buried under a coat of dull dun. No Noel, no Gert and Daisy, no Archie Andrews. Providing you don't mind changing trains at Edinburgh, there are cheaper, faster ways of getting to Loch Linnhe. But the Scotch Streak clings to its 'essential service' classification. Which saves it from the unsentimental axe taken to unprofitable branch-lines and quaint countryside stations.

"The haunting never stopped."

III

"We've reams of anecdotal evidence for ab-natural activity," said Edwin, taking over from Catriona. "Apparitions, apports, bilocation, sourceless sound, poltergeist nuisance, echoes from deep time, fits of precognition, possession, spontaneous combustion, disembodied clutching hands, phantoms, phantasms, pixies, nipsies, revelations, revenants, Old Uncle Tom Cobley and all. Few sleep well on the sleeper.

"A typical toff thinks he's slightly train-sick and decides to spend his next day out murdering English foxes rather than Scottish grouse. A percentage have much nastier turns. Outcomes range from severe ill-health and mental breakdown to disappearance and, well, death."

"What about the staff, Ed?" asked Cutley, who had been taking notes.

Richard saw Edwin calculate how to keep aces in his hole while seeming to lay his cards on the table. It was habitual in these circles.

"BR have trouble keeping guards, waiters and porters," Edwin admitted. "Even then, one see-no-evil conductor who's been on the Streak for yonks swears the shudder stories are all hogwash. Presumably, he's the opposite of *sensitive*."

"Why now?" asked Annette, pluming smoke. She drew a question mark in the air with her burning cigarette-end.

"That's the thing, Annie," said Edwin. "With fewer souls riding the Streak, the haunting isn't as noticeable as when Cat was on the case. But the Americans have expressed a *concern*. HM Government is under diplomatic pressure to sort things out, and you know where Ministers of the Crown call when ghoulies and ghosties rattle chains without permission."

Edwin opened his hands, indicating the whole room.

Richard had paid close attention to Catriona Kaye's story. Something in it jogged his mind.

"We've Miss Kaye's manuscript and the wartime report," said Harry Cutley, as if giving a tutorial. "Everyone is to read them by Thursday, then we'll start fresh. Those of you who were with me on the Edgley Vale Puma Cult know how I like things done. Those of you who weren't will find out soon enough. Annette, visit the newspaper library and go over all the cuttings on the Scotch Streak since the boiler was cast. Magic Fingers, get out in the yards, talk to railwaymen, choo-choo bores . . . pick up any more stories for the collection. You . . . ah, sorry . . . the Jeperson boy . . ."

Cutley knew very well what his name was, but waited for the prompt.

"Richard."

The Most Valued Member flashed a joyless smile.

"Thank you. I will remember. Not Greasy Herbert, but *Richard*. Richard Jeperson. Dick the Lad. Rickie the Roll-and-Rocker. Fixed in the mind's file, now. Anyway, *Richard*, you get your haircut down to Euston, trying not to slash cinema seats or terrorise old ladies *en route*, and book us on Thursday's Streak. Get me and Annette First Class sleeping compartments, a berth in Second for Magic Fingers, and the railway equivalent of steerage for you. We have to cover the whole train."

"I'll ride the mail car if you think it's a good idea."

Cutley considered it.

"The Club can spring for four compartments," put in Edwin, airily. "If you're all in First Class, no one will mind if you wander. With any other tickets, Richard and Danny wouldn't be allowed where interesting business might be going on."

"Whatever you think best," said Cutley. "If money's no object, we might as well all get the gold toilet seats and mints on the pillows. Dickie will qualify for a half-fare anyway."

The academic was used to working on the cheap, in fear of a redbrick budget review. He also wasn't happy to be given command of a group then undercut in front of them. Edwin had made Cutley "Most Valued Member", but was prone to step out from behind the desk and upstage his successor. Catriona laid a hand on Edwin's elbow, chiding with a gesture only the recipient and Richard noticed.

"Keep all the chits," said Cutley. "Bus tickets, and so forth. My procedure is big on chits, *comprenons-oui*?"

Now, Cutley was needling Richard because he couldn't afford to prick back at Edwin. Richard was getting a headache with the politics.

"This is a haunted house on wheels," Cutley told them. "There are boring procedures for haunted houses, which will be followed. Background check, on-the-spot investigation, listing of observable phenomena and effects. Once that's over, I will assess findings and make recommendations. If the haunting can be dispelled through scientific or spiritual efforts, no one will complain. Annette, I'd appreciate a run-down of possible rituals of exorcism or dispellment. Bell, book and railwayman's lamp? Of course, we can always advise the train be taken out of service and the line abandoned. If there are no passengers to be haunted, it doesn't matter if spectres drag their sorry shrouds along the rails."

Richard put his hand up, as if in class.

Cutley, annoyed, noticed. "What is it, boy?"

"A thought, sir. If the train could be put out of service, it already would have been. There must be a reason to keep it running."

Richard looked at Edwin. So did everyone else. Catriona massaged his arm.

At length, Edwin responded. "No use trying to keep secrets in a roomful of Talents, obviously."

Danny Myles whistled.

"What is it?" asked Cutley, catching up.

"The Scotch Streak must stay in service. The Special Contingencies School is now a submarine base. A vital component in our national deterrent."

"The gun we have to their heads while theirs is stuck into our tummy," put in Catriona.

"Cat goes on Aldermaston marches and wants to ban the Bomb," Edwin explained. "As a private individual, it is within her rights to hold such a position. In this Club, we do not decide government policy and can only advise . . ."

Annette almost snorted. She obviously knew Edwin Winthrop better.

"Every forty-eight hours," Edwin continued, "mathematicians convene in Washington DC and use a computer to generate number-strings which are fed into an electronic communications network accessible only from secure locations at the Pentagon and our own Ministry of War. There's another terminal in Paris, but it's a dummy – the French can fiddle all they want, but can't alter the workings of the big machine. We wouldn't want them getting offended by the creeping use of terms like 'le week-end' and kicking off World War Three in a fit of haughty pique. Annie, the French half of you didn't hear that.

"Once the numbers are in the net, they have to be conveyed to the President of the United States, the Prime Minister of Great Britain and selected officers on the front-lines of the Western Alliance. We don't use telephone, telegraph, telegram or passenger pigeon – we send couriers. The number-strings are known as the 'Go-Codes'. Unless they are keyed properly on special typewriters, orders cannot be given to arm a warhead, launch a missile or drop a bomb. Without the Go-Codes, we have no nuclear weapons."

"And *with* them, we can end the world," put in Catriona.

"So," said Myles, waving his hands for emphasis, "we've B-52s zooming over the Arctic, nuclear subs cruising the seven seas, ranks of computers the size of Jodrell Bank, and brave soldier boys in the trenches ready to respond to any dire threat from the godless commie horde . . . but it all depends on some git catching a seven o'clock steam train from Euston every other evening?"

"That's it, exactly," said Edwin

"Crazy, man," said Myles, snapping his fingers.

"As I said, matters of defence policy are beyond our remit. You understand now why governments are in a lather. If the Streak isn't secure, NATO wobbles. Quite apart from the haunting, they're worried about spies. One reason the Go-Codes are still carried by train is that our fiendish intelligence friends think the Russkies don't believe we'd *really* entrust so vital a duty to a couple of junior ratings on an overnight puff-puff."

"I hope I meet a spy," said Annette, posing languidly. "I always saw myself as Mata Hari. Can I lure young lieutenants to their doom?"

"Leave them alone, Annie," said Edwin. "They've enough on their plates, what with World Peace in their pockets. There's been a high turnover on that detail. One nervous collapse, one self-inflicted gunshot wound, one sudden convert off in a monastery somewhere. Do not let it be known outside this room, but in the past year there have been four separate blocks of up to eighteen hours when our defences were compromised because the Go-Codes didn't arrive without incident.

"Consider the poor general whose burdensome duty it is to inform the President of this situation, let alone the possibility the Other Side might get wind of a first-strike opportunity. If we do hold a gun to their head, they'd best not find out the firing pin is wonky."

Richard felt sickness in the pit of his stomach, as if he had washed down a half-pint of salted cockles with a strawberry milkshake. Despite Cutley's "boring procedures for haunted houses", this was a bigger deal than pottering around Borley Rectory feeling out cold spots. The nausea passed and, to his embarrassment, he found he was physically in a state of high excitement. He gathered this was common in the corridors of power – though, since his voice broke, it seemed the minutes of the day when he *wasn't* sporting a raging erection were more noteworthy. Tight trousers did not make him any more comfortable. He blushed as Annette, perhaps peeping indelicately into his immediate future, smiled at him.

"Will the Yanks know we're aboard?" asked Cutley.

"In theory, at the highest level. The boys on the train don't know anything. They've been encouraged to believe they're a decoy, and that their envelopes are to do with an inter-services gambling ring organised by a motor pool sergeant in Fort Baxter, Kansas. Spot the couriers if you must, but don't get too close. Come back with concrete intelligence about whatever threats are gathering in the dark. I've always wanted to end a briefing by saying 'this mission could shorten the War by six months'. The next best thing is 'the fate of the free world depends on you', which, I am sorry to say, it does. I'm sure you'll do us proud, Harry."

The lecturer shot glances at his group. Richard knew what Cutley thought of Annette, Magic Fingers and him. Two beatniks and a ted, not an elbow-patch between them, just the sorts Hard-Luck Harry hoped to get away from, *bloody students*!

"We'll make the best of it, Ed," said Cutley.

IV

Richard walked under the Doric arches of Euston Station at five o'clock, two hours before the Scotch Streak was due to depart. He was among crowds, streaming from city offices to commuter trains.

"*Star, News* and *Standard*!" shouted competing 60-year-old "boys", hawking the evening papers. Kruschev was in the headlines, shoe-banging at the UN. The Premier wouldn't be such a growling bear if he knew Uncle Sam's pants were down for up to 18 hours at a time. If his Sputnik spied a gap in the curtain, Old Nikita might well lob a couple of experimental hot ones just to see what happened.

"Don't even think about it, kiddo," said a voice close to his ear. "World's safe till midnight, at least. After that, it gets blurry . . . but Madame Amboise sees all. Worry not your pretty little head."

He recognised Annette from her perfume, Givenchy mingled with Gauloise, before he heard or saw her. She spun him round and kissed both his cheeks, not formally. Her wet little tongue dabbed the corners of his mouth.

For the trip, she had turned out in a black cocktail dress, elbow-length evening gloves, a shiny black hat with a folded-aside veil and a white fox-fur wrap with sewn-shut eyes. This evening, she wore lipstick – thin lines of severe scarlet. She posed like Audrey Hepburn, soliciting his approval, which was certainly forthcoming.

"That's the spirit," she said, patting his cheek.

He had a mental image of Annette in her underclothes – black, French and elaborate. It flustered him, and she giggled.

"I'm doing that," she said. "It's a trick."

She slipped off her shoulder strap to show black lace.

"And it's accurate," she added. "Sorry, I mustn't tease. You're so easy to get a rise out of. I don't get to play with anyone *in the know* very often."

She tapped the side of her head and made spooky conjuring gestures.

Under her brittle flirtatiousness, she ran a few degrees high, trying
to shake off a case of the scareds. That, in turn, worried him. Annette
Amboise might come on like the Other Woman in a West End farce,
but in the Diogenes Club's trade – not to mention actual war – she
was a battle-proved veteran. All he'd ever done was switch some
wires. If she knew enough to be frightened, he ought to be terrified.

"Aren't the arches magnificent?" she said. "They'll be knocked
down in a year or two. By idiots and philistines."

"You're seeing the future?"

"I'm reading the papers, darling. But I do see the future sometimes.
The *possible* future."

"What about . . . ?"

She puffed and opened a fist as if blowing a dandelion clock.
"Boom? Not this week, I think. Not if we have anything to do with it.
Of course, that'd bring down the arches too."

She touched the stone with a gloved hand, and shrugged.

"Nada, my love," she said. "Of course, that's Magic Fingers'
speciality, not mine. Laying on of hands. The Touch That Means So
Much."

Annette took him by the arm and steered him into the station. A
porter followed, shoving a trolley laden with a brassbound trunk,
matching pink suitcases, a vanity case and a hat-box. Richard had
one item of luggage, a Gladstone bag he'd found in a cupboard.

"There's our leader," said Annette, pointing.

Harry Cutley sat at a pie-stall, drinking tea. His own personal
cloud hung overhead. Richard wondered whether Edwin would
show up to see them off, then thought he probably wouldn't.

Annette stopped and held Richard back.

"Darling, promise me you'll be kind to Harry," she said, pouting,
adjusting his tie as if he were a present done up with a bow.

Richard shrugged. "I didn't have other plans."

"You don't need plans to be unkind. You're like me, a *feeler*. Try
to be a thinker too. Heaven knows, I won't be. You and Harry aren't
a match, but a mix. Don't be so quick to write him off. Now, let's go
and be nice."

Harry looked up and saw them coming. He waved his folded
newspaper.

"Where's Myles?" he asked.

Neither Richard nor Annette knew. Harry tutted, "Probably
puffing 'tea' in some jive dive."

"Tea would be lovely, thanks," said Annette.

Harry looked at the mug in his hand.

"Not this muck," he said, sourly. The woman behind the counter heard but didn't care.

"Supper on the train, then?" said Annette. "Sample that famous Scotch Streak luxury?"

"Just make sure to keep the chits," cautioned Harry.

"Don't be such a grumpy goose," said Annette, leaning close and kissing the lecturer, who didn't flinch. "This will be a great adventure."

"Like last time?"

"Well, let's hope not *that* great an adventure."

Harry pulled back the sleeve of his tweed jacket and showed a line of red weals leading into his cuff.

"Puma Cults," commented Annette, "*miaou*."

Richard gathered Harry and Annette had both come off the Edgley Vale case with scars. The Most Valued Member had put that successfully to bed. An Away Win for the Diogenes Club. No points for the Forces of Evil. Harry even smiled for a fraction of a second as Annette purred and stretched satirically.

At once, Richard understood the difference between his Talent and Annette's. He received, she sent. He picked up what others were feeling; she could make them feel what she felt. A useful knack, if she was in an "up" moment. Otherwise, she was a canary in a mineshaft.

Suddenly, Myles was there.

"Hey, cats," he said, raising an eyebrow as that set Annette off on more *miaous*. "Ready to locomote?"

"If we must," said Harry.

Magic Fingers dressed like a cartoon burglar – black jeans, tight jersey, beret, capacious carpet-bag. All he needed was a mask.

Passengers travelling First Class on the Scotch Streak had their own waiting room, adjacent to the platform where the train was readied. On presenting tickets, the party was admitted by a small, cherubic, bald, uniformed Scotsman.

"Good evening, lady and gentlemen," he said, like a head-waiter. "I'm Arnold, the Conductor. If there is any way I can be of service, please summon me at once."

"Arnold, the Conductor," said Harry, fixing the name in his mind.

Annette made arrangements to have her extensive luggage, and their three underweight bags, stowed on the train.

No extra-normal energies poured off Arnold, just polite deference. Considering his age and Richard's style, that was unusual. In the conductor's view, purchase of a First Class Sleeping Compartment ensured admission to the ranks of the elect. The passenger was always right, no matter what gaudy finery he wore or what gunk was slathered on his hair. Richard realised Arnold was the see-no-evil fellow Edwin had mentioned. The man who was not haunted. The conductor might be immune to ghosts, the way some people didn't catch colds. Or he could be a very, very good dissembler.

The waiting room wanted a thorough clean, but a residue of former glory remained. While Second and Third Class passengers made do with benches on the platform, First Class oiks could plump posteriors on divans upholstered in the Streak's "weeping bruise" purple. Complimentary tea was served from a hissing urn – which made Cutley mutter about wasting threepence (and collecting a chit) at the pie-stall.

Framed photographs hung like family portraits, commemorating the naming ceremony (there was that Lady Lucinda who Catriona disliked), the inaugural runs of 1928 and 1934 (Lord Kilpartinger in an engineer's hat) and broken speed records. Nothing about Inverdeith Bridge, of course.

Other passengers arrived. Two young men might as well have had "Secret Courier" stitched to their hankie pockets. They had adult-approved US navy crew-cuts and wore well-fitting civilian suits which didn't yet bend with their bodies. Matching leather briefcases must contain the vital envelopes. Annette cast a critical eye over the talent; one nudged the other, who cracked a toothy smile that dimpled in his corn-fed American cheek.

"So, where's the spy?" whispered Annette.

"*We're* the spies," said Richard. "Remember? Mata Hari."

Three sailors in whites looked like refugees from a road company of *On the Town*; one very drunk, his mates alert for the Shore Patrol. They'd be through for Portnacreirann too, though it would be a surprise if they really were travelling First Class. An allied uniform counted with Arnold. Mrs Sweet, an elderly lady in a checked ulster, was particular about her gun-cases. She issued Arnold with lengthy instructions for their storage. A clergyman swept in and Richard's first thought was that he was a disguised Chicago gangster. His ravaged cheeks and slicked-down widow's peak irresistibly suggested a rod in his armpit and brass knucks up his sleeve. However, he radiated saintly benevolence. Richard ought to know not to judge by appearances.

A fuss erupted at the door. Arnold and a guard were overwhelmed by a large, middle-aged woman. She wore a floral print dress and a hat rimmed with wax grapes and dry, dead roses.

"I've got me ticket somewhere, ducks," she said. "Give us a mo. Here we are. Me ticket, and me card."

The woman had a Bow Bells accent and one of those voices that could crack crystal. Something about her alerted Richard. Annette and Myles had the same reaction. Psychic alarm bells.

"What is it?" asked Harry, noticing his group's ears all pricked up at once.

"Calm," said Annette.

Richard realised his heart was racing. He breathed deliberately and it slowed. Myles let out a whistle.

"Me card," repeated the woman. "Elsa Nickles, Missus, Psychic Medium. I'm here to 'elp the spirits. The ones tevvered to this plane. The ones who cannot find the rest they need. The ones trapped on your Ghost Train."

Arnold was less interested in the woman's card than her ticket, which turned out to be Third Class. Not a sleeping compartment, but a seat in the carriage next to the baggage car. A trained contortionist with no feeling at all in her back or lower limbs might stretch out and snooze.

The conductor told her this waiting room was First Class only. She wasn't offended.

"I don't want to go in, ducks. Just wants a butcher's. The vibrations are strong in the room. No wonder your train's got so many presences."

The "Psychic Medium" craned over Arnold's head and scanned the room, more obviously than Richard had done. She frankly stared at everyone in turn.

"Evenin', vicar," she said to the saturnine clergyman, who smiled, showing rotten teeth. "Should have those fixed," she advised. "Pull 'em all on the National Health and get porcelain choppers, like me."

She grinned widely, showing a black hollow rim around her plates.

The vicar wasn't offended, though he looked even more terrifying when assembling a smile.

Mrs Nickles didn't give Harry, Richard or the US Navy a second glance, but fluttered around Annette – "Cor, wish I had the figure for that frock, girl" – and was taken with Magic Fingers.

"You've got the Gift, laddie. I can always tell. You see beyond the Visible Sphere."

Myles didn't contradict her.

"I sense a troubled soul 'ere, or soon to be 'ere," she announced. "Never mind, I can make it well. It's all we can do, ducks, make things well."

Mrs Sweet hid behind her *Times* and rigidly ignored everything. Harry muttered, unnoticed by Mrs Nickles.

The woman was a complication, not accounted for in Harry's "boring procedures". Richard sensed the Most Valued Member wonder idly if Mrs Nickles might step under rather than onto the train.

The first time he'd "eavesdropped" on a musing like that, he'd picked up a clear vision from the Latin master; the Third Form mowed down by a machine gun barrage. He'd been horrified and torn: keep quiet and share in the guilt, speak out and be reckoned a maniac. Even if he prevented slaughter, no one would ever *know*. For two days, he'd wrestled the problem, close to losing bowel control whenever he saw the master round the quad with an apparently distracted smile and mass murder in mind. Then, Richard picked up a *similar* stray thought, as the Captain of the Second Eleven contemplated the violent bludgeoning of a persistent catch-dropper. With nervy relief, he realised *everyone* contemplated atrocities on a daily basis. So far, he hadn't come across anyone who really meant it. Indeed, imagined violence seemed to take an edge off the homicidal urge – folks who *didn't* think about murder were more likely to commit one.

"Ahh, bless," said Mrs Nickles, standing aside so someone with a proper ticket could be let into the room.

A solemn child, very sleepy, had been entrusted by a guardian into the care of the Scotch Streak. She wore a blue, hooded coat and must be eight or nine. Richard, who had little experience with infants, hoped the girl wouldn't be too near on the long trip. Children were like time bombs, set to go off.

"What's your name?" asked Annette, bending over.

The girl said something inaudible and hid deeper in her hood.

"Don't know? That's nothing to be ashamed of."

Mrs Nickles and Annette were both smitten. Richard intuited neither woman had living children. If Mrs Nickles really was a medium, that was no surprise. Kids were attention sponges and sucked it all up – a lot of Talents faded when there was a pram in the house.

Annette found a large label, stiff brown paper, fastened around the girl's neck.

"Property of Lieut-Cdr Alexander Coates, RN," she read. "Is this your Daddy?"

The little girl shook her head. Only her freckled nose could be seen. In the hooded coat, she looked more like a dwarf than a child.

"Are you a parcel then?"

The hooded head nodded. Annette smiled.

"But you aren't for the baggage car?"

Another shake.

Arnold announced that the train was ready for boarding.

The Americans jammed around the door as the British passengers formed an orderly queue. Annette took the little girl's hand.

The Coates Parcel looked up and Richard saw the child's face. She had striking eyes – huge, emerald-green, ageless. The rest of her face hadn't fully grown around her eyes yet. A bar of freckles crossed her nose like Apache war paint. Two red braids snaked out of her hood and hung on her chest like bell-pulls.

"My name is Vanessa," she said, directly to him. "What's yours?"

The child was strange. He couldn't read her at all.

"This is Richard," said Annette. "Don't mind the way he looks. I'm sure you'll be chums."

Vanessa stuck out her little paw, which Richard found himself shaking.

"Good evening, Richard," she said. "I can say that in French. *Bon soir, Rishar*. And German. *Guten Abend, Richard*."

"Good evening to you, Vanessa."

She curtseyed, then hugged his waist, pressing her head against his middle. It was disconcerting – he was hugged like a pony, a pillow or a tree rather than a person.

"You've got a fan, man," said Magic Fingers. "Congrats."

Vanessa held onto him, for comfort. He still didn't know what to make of her.

Annette rescued him, detaching the girl.

"Try not to pick up waifs and strays, lad," said Harry.

Richard watched Annette lead Vanessa out of the waiting room. As the little girl held up her ticket to be clipped by Arnold, she looked back.

Those eyes!

V

Richard was last to get his ticket clipped. Everyone found their proper carriages. Mrs Nickles strode down the platform to Third Class, trailed by sailors.

He took in 3473-S. At a first impression, the engine was a powerful, massive presence. A huge contraption of working iron. Then, he saw it was weathered, once-proud purple marred and blotched, brass trim blackened and pitted. The great funnel belched mushroom clouds. He smelled coal, fire, grease, oil. Pressure built up in the boiler and heat radiated. A gush of steam was expelled, wet-blasting the platform.

"Bad beast, man," said Myles, fingertips to metal.

As Annette said, his talent was to read inanimate, or *supposedly* inanimate, objects. He was qualified to evaluate the locomotive.

"Got a jones in it, like a circus cat that's tasted blood, digs it, wants more."

"That's a comfort."

Myles clapped his shoulder, magic fingers lingering a moment. Briefly, Richard felt a chill. Myles took his hand away, carefully.

"Don't fret, man. I've known Number 73 buses go kill-crazy. Most machines are just two steps from the jungle. No wonder witches don't dig iron. Come on, Rich. 'All aboard for the Atchison, Topeka and the Santa Fe . . .'"

Arnold blew his whistle, a shrill night-bird screech. It was answered by a dinosaurian bellow from the locomotive. The steam-whoop rattled teeth and scattered a flock of pigeons roosting in the Euston arches.

"The train now standing at Platform 14," said an announcer over the Tannoy, sounding like a BBC newsreader fresh from an elocution lesson, "is the Scotch Streak, for Edinburgh, and Portnacreirann. It is due to depart at seven o'clock precisely."

Richard and Myles stepped up, into their carriage. The wide, plush-carpeted corridor afforded access to a row of sleeping compartments.

"You're next to me, Richard," said Annette, who had been installing Vanessa nearby. "How cosy."

He looked at Magic Fingers, who shrugged in sympathy – with a twinge of envy – and went to find his place.

Richard checked out his compartment. It was like a constricted hotel room, with built-in single bed, fixed desk (with complimentary stationery and inkwell) and chair, a cocktail cabinet with bottles cradled in metal clasps, wardrobe-sized en-suite "bathroom" with a sink (yes, marble) and toilet (no gold seat). A second bed could be pulled down from an upper shelf, but was presently stowed. From murder mysteries set on trains, he knew the upper berth was mostly used for hiding bodies. Richard's Gladstone bag rested at the foot of the bed like a faithful dog. His towel and toiletries were stowed in the bathroom.

At first look, everything in First Class was first class, then the starched white sheets showed a little fray, and that greyish, too-often-washed tinge; the blue-veined sink had orange, rusty splotches in the basin and a broken plug-chain; cigarette-burns pocked the cistern. KINDLY REFRAIN FROM USING THE WATER CLOSET WHILE THE TRAIN IS STANDING IN THE STATION said a framed card positioned above the toilet. In an elegant hand, someone had added TRESPASSERS WILL BE SHOT.

Richard thought he saw something in the mirror above the sink, and had to fight an instinct to turn. He knew there would be nothing there. He looked deeper into the mirror, peering past his pushed-out face, ignoring a fresh-ish blotch on his forehead, searching for patches where the silvering was thin. He exhaled, misting the mirror. Rune-like letters, written in reverse, stood out briefly. He deciphered DANGER, WARNING and FELL SPIRIT, then a heart, several Xs and a sigil with two "A"s hooked together.

"Made you look," said Annette, from the corridor. She giggled.

He couldn't help grinning. She was hatless now, languidly arranged against the doorframe, dress riding up a few inches to show a black stocking-top, shoulders back to display her fall of silky hair. She drew her "AA" in the air with her cigarette end, and puffed a perfect smoke ring.

She drew him along the corridor. They joined Harry and Myles in the next carriage. The ballroom in Lord Kilpartinger's day, it was now designated the First Class Lounge.

Magic Fingers found a piano, and extemporised on "The Runaway Train", which Annette found hilarious. She curled up in a scuttle-like leather seat.

At the far end of the carriage sat the vicar – probably working on a sermon, though his expression suggested he was writing death threats to be posted through the letter-boxes of nervous elderly ladies.

Arnold passed through the carriage, and informed them the bar would be open as soon as they were underway.

"Hoo-ray," said Annette. "Mine's a gimlet."

She screwed a fresh cigarette into her holder.

Arnold smiled indulgently and didn't tell Myles not to tinkle the ivories. They were First Class and could swing from the chandeliers – which were missing a few bulbs, but still glinted glamorously – if they wanted.

"Impressions?" asked Harry, who had a fresh folder open and a ball-point pen in his hand.

"All clear here," said Annette. "We'll live past Peterborough."

"This box has had its guts battered," said Magic Fingers, stuttering through a phrase, forcing the notes out, "but we're making friends, and I think he'll tell me the stories. 'The runaway train came over the hill, and she ble-e-ew . . .' "

Harry looked at him and prompted, "Jeperson? Anything to add?"

Richard thought about the little girl's ageless eyes.

"No, Harry. Nothing."

Harry bit the top of his pen. The plastic cap was already chewed.

"I hope this isn't a wasted journey," said the Most Valued Member. "Just smoke and mirror stories."

"It won't be that," said Annette. "I can tell."

The whistle gave out another long shriek, a Johnny Weissmuller Tarzan yell from the throat of a castrated giant.

" '. . . and she ble-ew-ew-ew-ew . . .' "

Without even a lurch, as smooth as slipping into a stream, the Scotch Streak moved out of the station. The train rapidly picked up speed. Richard sensed pistons working, big wheels turning, couplings stretching, the irresistible *pull* . . .

He had a thrill of anticipation. All boys loved trains. Every great mystery, romance or adventure must have a train in it.

" '. . . the engineer said the train must halt, he said it was all the fireman's—!' "

Myles's piano-playing was shut off by a crash. The lid had snapped shut like a bear-trap.

The jazzman swore and pulled back his hands. His knuckles were scraped. He flapped them about.

"Pain city, man," he yelped.

"First blood," said Annette.

"The beast's impatient," said Myles. "Antsy, itchy-pantsy. Out to get us, out to show who's top hand. Means to kill."

Harry examined the piano, lifting and dropping the lid. A catch should have held it open.

"Catch was caught, Haroldo," said Magic Fingers, pre-empting the accusing question. "No doubt about it."

Harry said the lid could easily have been jarred loose by the train in motion. Which was true. He did not make an entry in his folder.

Annette thought it was an attack.

"It knows we're here," she said. "It knows who we are."

They were on their way. Outside the window, dark shapes rushed by, lights in the distance. The train flashed through a suburban station, affording a glimpse of envious, pale-faced crowds. They were only waiting for a diesel to haul them home to "villas" in Hitchin or Haslemere and an evening with the wireless, but all must wish they were aboard the brightly-lit, fast-running, steam-puffing Streak. Bound for Scotland – mystery, romance and adventure!

Richard found he was shaking.

Act II: On the Scotch Streak

I

Over the train-rattle, Annette Amboise heard herself scream.

She was in the corridor. The lights were out. One of her heels was broken, and her ankle turned.

The train was being searched, papers demanded, faces slapped, children made to cry, bags opened, possessions strewn. She'd soon be caught and questioned. Then, hours of agony culminating in shameful release. She'd hold off as long as she could. But, in the end, she'd break.

She knew she'd *talk*.

Fingers slithered around her neck. A barbed thumb pressed into the soft flesh under her jaw.

Her scream shut off. She couldn't swallow her own spit. Air couldn't reach her lungs.

The grip lifted her off her feet. Her back pressed against a window that felt like an ice-sheet. She was wrung out, couldn't even kick.

She smelled foul breath, but saw only dark.

The train passed a searchlight. Bleaching light filled the corridor. Uniform highlights flashed: twin lightning-strike insignia, broken cross armband, jewel-eyed skull-badge, polished cap-peak like the bill of a carrion bird. No face under the cap, not even eyes. A featureless bone-white curve.

The *boche* had her!

She tried to forget things carried in her head. Names, code phrases, responses, locations, times, number-strings. But everything she knew glowed red, ready for the plucking.

Her captor held up his free hand, showing her a black, wet Luger. The barrel, cold as a scalpel, pressed to her cheek.

The light passed.

The pistol was pushed into her face. The gunsight tore her skin. Her cheek burst open like a peach. The barrel wormed between her teeth. Bitter metal filled her mouth.

The grip around her throat relaxed, a contemptuous signal.

She drew in breath and began to *talk*.

*   *   *

"Annie," said Harry Cutley, open hand cupped by her stinging cheek, "come back."

She had been slapped.

She was *talking*, giving up old names, old codes. "Dr Lachasse, Mady Holm, Moulin Vielle, La Vache, H-360 . . ."

She choked on her words.

Harry was bent over her. She was on a divan in the lounge carriage. Myles and Richard crowded around. Arnold the Conductor attended, white towel over his arm, bearing cocktails. Hers, she remembered, was a gimlet.

"Where were you?" asked Harry. "The War?"

She admitted it. Harry had been holding her down, as if she were throwing a fit. Suddenly self-conscious, he let her go and stood away. Annette sat up and tugged at her dress, fitting it properly. Nothing was torn, which was a mercy. She wondered about her face.

Her heart thumped. She could still feel the icy hand, taste oily gunmetal. When she blinked, SS scratches danced in the dark.

"Can we get you anything?" asked Harry. "Water? Tea?"

"I believe that's mine," she said, reaching out for her cocktail. She tossed it back at a single draught. Her head cleared at once. She replaced the empty glass on Arnold's tray. "Another would be greatly appreciated."

Arnold nodded. Everyone else had to take their drinks from the tray before he could see to her request. They sorted it out – a screwdriver for Myles, whisky and water for Harry, a virgin mary for Richard. Arnold, passing no comment on her funny turn, withdrew to mix a fresh gimlet.

"Case of the horrors?" diagnosed Myles.

She held her forehead. "In spades."

"A bad dream," said Harry, disappointed. His pen hovered over a blank sheet in his folder. "Hardly a *manifestation*."

"To dream, wouldn't she have to be asleep?" put in Richard. "She went into it standing up."

"A fugue, then. A fit."

Harry erred on the side of rational explanation. Normally, Annette admired that. Harry kept an investigation in balance, stopped her – and the rest of the spooks – from running off with themselves. Usually, ghosts were only smugglers in glow-in-the-dark skeleton masks. Flying saucers were weather balloons. Reanimated mummies were rag week medical students swathed in mouldy bandages. Now, his thinking was just blinkered. There *were* angry spirits on the

Scotch Streak. And, for all she knew, little green Martians and leg-dragging Ancient Egyptians.

"Have you had fits before?" asked Richard.

"No, Richard," she said patiently. "I have not."

"But you do get, ah, 'visions'?"

"Not like this," she said. "This was a new experience. Not a nice one. Trust me. *It* reached out and hit me."

" 'It'?" said Harry, frowning. "Please try to be more scientific, Annie! You must specify. What 'it'? Why an 'it' and not a 'them'?"

Her heartbeat was normal now. She knew what Harry – irritating man! – meant. She tried to be helpful.

"Just because it's an 'it' doesn't mean there's no 'them'? An army is an 'it', but has many soldiers, a 'them'."

Harry angry, at something Richard called him.

"What came for me wasn't one of my usuals," she continued. "I see what might happen. And not in 'visions', as Richard put it. I don't hear 'voices' either. I just know what's coming, or might be coming. As if I'd skipped ahead a few pages and skim-read what happens next."

Harry, Richard and Myles backing away from her. No, they were still close – they wouldn't back away for a few minutes.

"I see round corners. Into the future. This was from somewhere else."

"The past?" prompted Richard. "A ghost?"

"The past? Yes. A ghost? Not in the traditional sense. More like an *incarnation*, an embodiment. Not a personality. My idea of the Worst Thing. It reached into me, found out what my Worst Thing was, and played on it. But there was still the train. I was on the train. It lives here. The Worst Thing. The Worst Thing Ever. The Worst Thing in the World."

"Dramatic, Annie, but not terribly helpful."

Harry put the top back on his biro.

"Listen to her," said Richard, slipping an arm around her shoulder – a mature gesture for such a youth. "She's not hysterical. She's not imagining. She *is* giving you a report. Write down what she's said."

Harry was not inclined to pay attention to the Jeperson Boy.

"I can't," he said. "It's static. It'll cloud the issue. We need observable phenomena. Incidents that can be measured. Traced back to a source. I'll get the instruments."

"We *have* instruments," said Richard. "Better attuned than your doodads, Daddy-O. We have Annette and Magic Fingers."

He didn't include himself, but should have.

A burst of indignant fury belched from Harry as Richard called him "Daddy-O". She flinched at the psychic outpouring, but less than she would if she hadn't known it was coming.

The lad was pushing with Harry. He couldn't help himself.

Myles laid a hand on her forehead, nodded.

"Something's been at her," he said. She didn't like the sound of that. "Left clawmarks."

"Will everybody please stop talking as if this were my autopsy," she said. "I have been attacked, affronted, shaken. But I am not a fragile flower you need to protect. I can take care of myself."

Like she did in the War.

The curve under the SS cap came back to her. If questioned, she would have talked. Everyone did, eventually. It had never come to it, because of her trick, her way of putting her feet right, of avoiding situations. Others – the names that had come back to her – had been less fortunate. As far as she knew, they were dead or damaged beyond repair. Most had been caught – talking made no difference in the end, they were still killed.

Ever since, she had been putting her feet right. Walking near peril, not into it. Here, she was on a train – a row of linked boxes on wheels. There might be no right steps here. There might only be danger. Her gift was often knowing where not to be. Here, knowing where not to be did not mean she could avoid being there.

She trusted her instincts. Now, they were shouting: *pull the communication cord!* She could afford the fine for misusing the emergency stop signal. One swift tug, and brakes would be thrown. The Scotch Streak would scream to a halt. She could jump onto the tracks, head off over the fields.

Harry, Richard and Myles backed away from her. Just as she'd known they would. She ticked off the moment, grateful there wasn't anything more to it.

She was pulling the communication cord.

She suppressed the instincts. The red cord – a chain, actually – still hung above a window, unbothered in its recess. She would ignore it.

Would she pull the cord in the future or was she imagining what it would be like? No way to tell. She saw herself in the dock, being lectured, then paying five one-pound notes to a clerk of the court – but the clerk had no face. That usually meant she was imagining. If this was going to happen, she would see a face, and recognise it later.

Then, her brain buzzed. She couldn't mistake this for wandering imagination. Before the War, a child psychiatrist labelled Annette's puzzling malaise as "acute *déjà vu*". Catriona Kaye modified the diagnosis and coined the term "*jamais vu*". Annette did not have I-have-been-here-before memories of the present, but I-will-be-here-soon memories of the future.

An open exterior door, night-time countryside rushing past. Someone falling from the train, breaking against a gravel verge. And someone coming for her, from behind.

If that was a few pages ahead, she'd rather fold the corner at the end of this chapter, put the book on her bedside table and never open it again. But that wasn't how the world worked.

Arnold came with her second gimlet. This one she sipped.

"Perfect," she told the conductor, suppressing shivers.

II

Annette's recovery impressed Richard. Two gimlets and a nip to her compartment to fix her face, and she was set. Her strings were notches too tight, but so were anyone else's. She flirted, presumably on instinct, flitting among her colleagues, seeming to offer equal time. Only Richard noticed he was getting marginally more serious attention than Harry Cutley or Danny Myles. She already knew them but needed to puzzle out the new boy, fix him in her mind the way Harry fixed names, by rolling him around, pinching and fluffing, testing reactions. Which, as ever, were warm and, he thought, horribly obvious.

Harry sourly made shorthand notes in his folder.

The frightening vicar gently enquired as to the lady's condition. Annette said she was fine, and he retreated, satisfied. Richard still wondered if the man was faking his aura. His killer's hands seemed made to be gloved in someone else's blood.

Standing nearby, Annette was carefully not looking at the communication cord. Of course. Anyone who travelled by train knew that imp of the perverse which popped up at the sight of a PENALTY FOR IMPROPER USE – £5.00 notice – *pull the chain, see what happens, go on, you know you want to*. On the Scotch Streak, the imp was a bullying, nagging elemental.

Annette felt Richard's lapel between thumb and forefinger.

"Real," she said. "Sometimes I can't tell any more."

He didn't know where to put his hands.

"Put the boy down, Annie," said Harry. "Come fill in this Incident Form. Since you're convinced you were *assaulted*, we must have a first-person account before memories fade."

She shuddered and joined Harry. He gave her a sheet of paper and a pencil, which she proceeded to use as if sitting an exam, producing neat, concise notations in the spaces provided.

Danny Myles sat at the piano, fingers tapping the closed lid. His bruises were rising. He smiled, did a little two-finger Gene Krupa solo on the polished wood.

"Me next, you think?" Richard asked.

Myles lifted his shoulders.

"Watch your back, Jack."

The carriage windows were ebony mirrors. If Richard got close to the glass and strained, he could make out the rushing countryside. A late supper would soon be served in the dining carriage. The train didn't stop until Edinburgh, at half-past one; then, after a twenty-minute layover, it would continue to Portnacreirann, arriving with the dawn.

The overnight express felt more like an ocean liner than a train. Safe harbour was left behind and they were alone on the vast, deep sea.

Though they had compartments, none of them would sleep.

Richard took out his father's watch, checked it against the clock above the connecting door. He had ten past nine, the train clock had ten to. He'd wound the watch at Euston, setting the time against the big station clock.

Myles saw what he was doing, rolled his sleeve back and felt a glassless watch – a holdover from his blind days. "Stopped, man," he said. "Dead on the vine. Seven seven and seven seconds. That's a panic and a half."

"I won't have one of those things," said Annette, looking up from her form. "Little ticking tyrants."

"Prof?" Myles prompted Harry.

Harry pulled a travel clock out of a baggy pocket and held it next to his wrist-watch.

"Eight thirty-two. Ten-o'-six."

"Want to take a stab at which is the real deal?" asked Magic Fingers.

They all looked at the train clock, ticking towards supper time.

"What I thought," said the jazzman.

Harry Cutley riffled through his folder and dug out more forms. He handed them out. Myles got on with it, turning out a polished paragraph. Richard simply wrote down "WATCH FAST".

"Perhaps now you'll stay away from mechanical instruments and rely on people," said Annette. "You know clocks run irregularly in haunted places, so why do you trust thermometers, barometers, wire-recorders and cameras?"

"People run irregularly too," said Harry, reasonably. "Even – no, *especially* – Talents."

Richard was piqued. His watch was no ordinary timepiece. His father had inherited it from *his* grandfather, who had sat with Mycroft Holmes on the first Ruling Cabal. Geoffrey Jeperson had carried the watch all through the War. The Major, thinking his business done in a refugee camp, had been checking the time when he and a large-eyed, hollow-bellied child noticed one another. The watch brought them together. The boy who would become Richard Jeperson reached for the bauble, taking it reverentially when the Major, on instinct, trusted it to him. He had solemnly felt its weight, listened to its quiet tick, admired its Victorian intricacy through a panel in the face.

Inside, gears and wheels were tiny fragments of unknown crystal, which sparkled green or blue in certain light. The roman numerals were lost in tiny engravings of bearded satyrs and chubby nymphs.

Those first ticks were where Richard's memory began. Before now, the watch had never betrayed him.

If Jeperson's watch wasn't to be trusted, what else in the life furnished for him by the Diogenes Club was left? The watch wound with a tiny key, which was fixed to the chain – it could also stop the mechanism, and Richard did so. If the watch could not run true, it should not run at all. He felt as if a pet had died, and he'd never had pets. He unhooked the chain and wondered if he'd ever wear it again. He slipped watch and chain into a pocket and handed back the incident form.

Arnold, who obviously had no trouble with *his* watch – a railway watch, as much a part of the Scotch Streak as the wheels or the windows – announced that supper was served. According to the train clock, it was nine o'clock precisely.

Harry reset his watch and clock against the train time. He made a note in his folder.

"I foresee you'll be at that all night," said Annette. "Without using a flicker of Talent. It's Sod's Law."

Harry smiled without humour, not giving her an argument.

It hit Richard that something had gone on between Harry Cutley and Annette Amboise, not just an investigation into a Puma Cult. Harry took teasing from her he wouldn't from anyone else. He sulked like a boy when she paid attention elsewhere. She'd told Richard not to underestimate the Most Valued Member.

Now, in a way that annoyed him, he was jealous.

"Should we sample the Scotch Streak fare?" said Annette. "In

Kilpartinger's day, the cuisine was on a par with the finest continental restaurants."

"I doubt British Rail have kept up," said Harry. "It'll be beef and two veg, pie and chips or prehistoric bacon sarnies."

"Yum," said Magic Fingers. "My favourite."

"Come on, boys. Be brave. We can face angry spirits, fire demons, Druid curses and homicidal lunatics. A British Rail sandwich should hold no horrors for us. Besides, *I've* seen the menu. I rather fancy the quail's eggs."

Annette led them to the dining carriage. Wood-panel and frosted glass partitions made booths. Tables were laid for two or four.

As he passed under the lounge clock, Richard looked up. For a definite moment, he saw a face behind the glass, studded with bleeding numbers, clock-hands nailed to a flattened nose, cheeks distended, eyes wide, clockmaker's name tattooed on stretched lips.

"That's where you've got to," he mused, recognising Douglas Gilclyde. "Lord Killpassengers himself."

The face was gone. Richard thought he should mention the apparition, then realised he'd only have to fill in another form and opted to keep stum. There'd be plenty more where that came from.

III

They were all laughing at him, the bastards!

Harold Cutley tasted ash, bile and British Rail pork pie. He wanted to tell the bastards to shut up. The only noise he produced was a huffing bark that made the bastards laugh all the more.

"Gone down the wrong tube," said the insufferable Jeperson Boy.

The French tart slapped him on the back, not to clear the blockage – taking an excuse to give him a nasty thump.

"Get Prof a form to fill in," snarked the beatnik. "See how he likes it."

Cutley stood and staggered away from the table. He honked and breathed again. He could talk if so inclined. As it happened, he bloody well wasn't.

He knew they'd all gang up on him!

That was how it always was. At Brichester, no one understood his work and he was written off as "the Looney". Muriel hadn't helped, betraying him with all of them. Even Head of Physics, Cox-Foxe. Even bloody students! He was with the Diogenes Club toffs on the sufferance of Ed Winthrop, who habitually overruled and sidelined and superseded. Ed had saddled Harry with this shower so he couldn't get anywhere, would never have any findings to call his own.

No one was coming after him. He shot a glance back at the booth, where Annette was canoodling with the teddy boy. The bitch, the bastard! Magic Fingers was tapping the table, probably hopped up on "sneaky pete". If there were results to be had, he'd have to find them on his own.

He would show them. He would have to.

The conductor – what was his name? Why hadn't he fixed it? – was in his way, blocking the narrow aisle. Cutley got past the man, shrinking to avoid touching him, and strode towards the dark at the end of the carriage.

"Well, really," said the frumpy bat who was the only other diner, the old girl with the guns. She'd spilled claret on her gammon and pineapple and was going to blame Harold Cutley. "I must say. I never did."

Cutley thought of something devastating to snap back at the pinch-faced trout, but words got mixed up between his brain and his pie-and-bile-snarled tongue and came out as spittle and grunts.

The woman ignored him and forked a thin slice of reddened meat into her mouth.

He looked back. The carriage had stretched. The rest of his so-called group were dozens of booths away, in a pool of light, smiling and fondling, relieved he was gone, already forgetting he'd ever been there. The bastarding bastards! They had the only bright light. The rest of the carriage was dim.

Now there were other diners, in black and white and silent. One or two to every fifth or sixth booth. Shadows on frosted glass partitions. Starched collars and blurry faces. Some were missing eyes or mouths, some had too many.

Muriel was here somewhere, having her usual high old time while someone else brought home the bacon.

Bitch!

"May I see your ticket?"

It was the conductor. Or was it another official? This one looked the same, but the tone of voice was not so unctuous. He sounded deeper, stronger, potentially brutal. More like a prison warder than a servant.

What was the name again? Albert? Alfred? Angus? Ronald? Donald?

Arnold – like Matthew Arnold, Thomas Arnold, Arnie, Arnoldo, Arnold. That was it. *Arnold.*

"What is it, Arnold?" he snapped.

"Your ticket," he insisted. His collar insignia, like a police constable's, was a metal badge. LSIR. That was wrong, out of date. "You must have your ticket with you at all times and be prepared to surrender it for inspection."

"You clipped mine at Euston," said Cutley, patting his pockets.

Cutley searched himself. He found his bus ticket from Essex Road to Euston, a cinema stub (1s, 9d, *Naked as Nature Intended*, the Essoldo), a slip pinned inside his jacket since it was last dry-cleaned three years ago, a sheaf of shorthand notes for a lecture he'd never given, an invitation to Cox-Foxe's thirty-years-service sit-down dinner, a page torn out of the *Book of Common Prayer* with theorems pencilled in the margin, a linked chain of magician's handkerchiefs some bastard must have planted on him as a funny, a Hanged Man tarot card that had been slipped to him as a warning by that blasted Puma Cult, his primary school report card (FAIR ONLY), an expired ration book, a French postcard Muriel had once sent him, his divorce papers, a signed photograph of Sabrina, a Turkish bank-note, a card with spare buttons sewn onto it, a leaf torn out of a desk calendar for next week, and a first edition of Thomas Love Peacock's *Headlong Hall* he had once taken out of Brichester University Library and not got around to returning but which he could've sworn he'd left behind in the house Muriel had somehow wound up keeping when she walked out on him. But no ticket.

"Would this be yours?" said Arnold, holding up a strip of card.

Cutley was more annoyed. This was ridiculous.

"If you had it all the time, why didn't you say so, man?"

"We have to be sure of these things."

Cutley noticed that the conductor wasn't "sirring" him any more. Before he could take the proffered ticket, he had to return his various discoveries to his pockets. Even if he piled up the things he could afford to throw away, it was a devil of a job to fit everything back into his jacket, which was baggier and heavier by the minute.

Arnold watched, still holding out the ticket.

Beyond the conductor, the dining car was nearly empty again. Jeperson, Annette and Magic Fingers were in the far distance, merrily tucking into knickerbocker glory or some other elaborate, sickly-sweet pud. None of that on his old ration book, he remembered with a bitter twinge.

He was sorted out. Except he had put the Peacock with the used bus and cinema tickets. He slid the book into his side-pocket, tearing a seam with a loud rip. He had a paper of buttons but no needle and thread. Muriel always had a needle, ready threaded, pinned about her in case of emergencies. She wasn't in the dining carriage now – probably off in some fellow's compartment, on her knees, gagging for it, the cow, the harlot!

"Why are you still here?" he asked Arnold, snatching his ticket.

"To make sure," said the conductor. "This isn't your place. This is for First Class Passengers only."

Bloody typical! These jumped-up little Hitlers put on a blue serge uniform that looked *a bit* like a policeman's and thought they could order everyone else about, put them all in their proper and bloody places. One look at Harry Cutley was enough to tell them he didn't belong with silver cutlery and long-stemmed roses at every table. All the knickerbocker glory a fat girl could eat conveyed with the compliments of the chef to the table in crawling, grovelling deference! Only, just this once, Harry Cutley *did* belong. Baggy, torn, patched jacket and all, Cutley was in First Class. He had a First Class ticket, not bought with his own money, but *his* all the same. With angry pride, he brandished it at the conductor's nose.

"What does this say, my good man?"

"I beg your pardon," responded Arnold, with a tone Cutley didn't like at all. "What does what say?"

"This ticket, you bastard. What does this ticket say?"

"Third Class," said the conductor. "Which is where you should be, if you don't mind my saying. This is not the place for you. You would not be comfortable here. You would be conscious of your, ah, shortcomings."

Cutley looked at his ticket. It must be some sort of funny.

"This isn't mine," he said.

"You said it was. You recognised it. You would not want to make a scene in the First Class Dining Carriage."

"First Class! I don't call a stale pork pie first class dining!"

"The fare in Third Class might be more suited to your palate. More your taste. Rolls are available. Hard-tack biscuits. Powdered eggs, snoek, spam. Now, move along, there's a good fellow."

Arnold, seeming bigger, stood between him and the booth where the others were downing champagne cocktails. Cutley tried to get their attention but Arnold swayed and swelled to block him from their sight. Cutley tried to barge past. The conductor laid hands on him.

"I must ask you to go back to your place."

"Bastard," spat Cutley into the man's bland face.

Arnold had a two-handed grip on Cutley's lapels. So where did the fist that sank into Cutley's stomach come from?

Cutley reeled, hearing another long rip as a lapel tore in the conductor's hand. His gut clenched around pain. He knew when he was beaten. He slunk off, towards the connecting door. Beyond was Second Class, not his place either. He was supposed to be at the back of the train, with the baggage and the mail, probably with live chickens and families of untouchables sat on suitcases tied with string, lost in the crowd, one of the masses, trodden under by bastards and bitches. In his place.

There were things back there which he could use. He knew where they were. He had overheard, at Euston. He remembered the long cases.

Guns!

He limped out of the dining carriage, into the dark.

IV

"What's up with Harry?" Richard asked.

"Gyppy tummy?" suggested Magic Fingers.

"I should go after him," said Annette, folding her napkin. "We shouldn't be separated."

Richard touched her arm. His instincts tingled. So, he knew at once, did hers.

Harry had stumbled past Arnold, who was briefly bewildered, and charged out of the carriage.

"You stay here," said Richard. "I'll go."

He stood. Annette was supposed to admire his manly resolve. She radiated a certain mumsy pride as if he were a schoolboy striding to the crease to face the demon bowler of the Upper Sixth. Not quite what he intended.

Harry Cutley had been seized in the middle of a mouthful of pie. Not necessarily a phenomenon worth an Incident Form. Something in his eyes as he veered off, trying to staunch coughing, suggested he wasn't seeing what Richard was. The man had been touched. Attacked, even.

"Your friend, sir," said Arnold, with concern. "He seems taken poorly."

"What did he say?"

"Nothing repeatable, sir."

"I'll see to him, thank you, Arnold."

"Very good, sir."

Every time he spoke with Arnold, Richard had to quash an impulse to tip him. At the end of the journey, was it the done thing to palm a ten-bob note and pass it over with a handshake?

He walked the length of the carriage, rolling with the movement of the train. He had become accustomed to the Scotch Streak. He had to concentrate to hear the rattle of wheels, the chuff-chuff of the engine, the small clinkings of cutlery and crockery. Almost comforting. Catriona Kaye said the most dangerous haunted houses always feel like home.

Harry had barged past Mrs Sweet. Richard thought of talking with her, but she glared as he walked towards her. He was a duck's-arse-quiffed affront to everything she believed. Real killers wore respectable suits from Burton's and had faces like trustworthy babies. That was how they got close. Richard had a pang of worry that Mrs Sweet might have an extra gun about her – a hold-out derringer in her stocking-top or a pepperpot in her reticule – in case a wounded grouse flapped close enough to need its head dissolving with a single, deadly-accurate shot. This train gave people funny ideas. She might easily pot him on the offchance.

He got by Mrs Sweet unshot, looked over his shoulder at Annette and Myles, and stepped through the connecting door into the Second Class carriage. He checked the lavatory and didn't find Harry – though he caught sight of a cracked mirror and started, shocked at a glimpse of an antlered, fox-faced quarry with a target marked on his forehead in dribbling blood. How others see us.

The carriage was empty. The corridor was unlit. Second Class did not have sleeping berths, but there were regular compartments, suitable comfortably for six, which could take ten in a pinch. The dark made it easier to see out of the windows. This stretch of track ran though ancient forest. Branches twisted close, leaves reaching for the passing express.

Richard made his way down the carriage, checking each compartment. None of the privacy blinds were down. One seat supported a huddle of old clothes that might have been a sleeping Second Class passenger – though it was early to turn in for the night. On a second look, no one was there. He knew better than be caught out that way, and looked again. Whatever had been huddled was gone back to its hole. He trusted it would stay there.

It couldn't be the throat-cut spectre of "Buzzy" Maltrincham. The vicious Viscount wouldn't have been caught dead in Second Class. 3473 had many more ghosts than him. Would Lord Kilpartinger show up again? Disgraced old Donald McRidley – assuming he was dead. The Headless Fireman? The passengers of '31? The water-logged witches of Loch Gaer?

It got darker as he proceeded. Turning back, he saw the glass of the connecting door was now opaque – had someone drawn a blind? – and the dining carriage cut off from view.

"Harry?" he called out, feeling foolish.

Something pattered, near the toilet cubicle. Fast and light. Not clumsy Harry Cutley. It might be a large cat. They had railway cats, didn't they? There was one in *Old Mother Possum's*. But usually on stations, not on trains.

Another of Catriona Kaye's sayings was that sometimes observers brought their own ghosts and the haunted place merely fleshed them out. Was there a puma person still after Harry? Hadn't Annette been bothered by something from the War? Her "it", her Worst Thing? Some entities fished out your worst nightmare – your worst memory, your darkest secret – and threw it at you. But nothing dug for your happiest moments, your fondest wishes, your most thrilling dreams and wrapped them up as a present. What had Magic Fingers called it, Sod's Law?

Richard remembered his father's advice about how to see off a tiger if you were unarmed. Knock sharply on its snout, as if rapping on a front door. Just the once. Serve notice you are not to be bothered. The big cat would bolt like a doused kitten, leaving rending, clawing and devouring for another day. Pumas are just weedy imitation tigers, so the Major Jeperson treatment should send one chasing its tail. Of course, his father never claimed to have used his tiger-defying technique in the wild. It was wisdom passed down in the family – untested, but comforting.

"Harry?"

Now, Richard felt like an idiot. Plainly, lightfeet wasn't Harry Cutley.

He walked back, past the compartments – that huddle was still absent, thank you very much – towards the toilet and the connecting door. He moved with casual ease, controlling an urge to scream and run. The puma was Harry's Worst Thing. Not Richard Jeperson's.

The area between cubicle and door was untenanted. He thought. He held the door-handle, torn. He couldn't return to Annette and Myles with no news of Harry, but didn't want to venture further into the train without reporting back, even if he raised a fuss. Harry, technically, was in charge. He should have left instructions – not that Richard would have felt obliged to follow them. If it had been *Edwin Winthrop*, maybe. Catriona Kaye, certainly – though she never instructed. She provided useful information and a delicate nudge towards the wisest course.

The nagging imp came again – he was just a kid, he wasn't ready for this, he wasn't sure what *this* was. None of that nonsense, he told himself, sternly, trying to sound like Edwin or his father. You're a Diogenes Club man. Inner Sanctum material. Most Valued Member potential. Bred to it, *sensitive*, a Talent.

Click. He'd tell Annette that Harry had gone far afield, then co-opt Arnold and make a thorough search. This was a train, it was impossible to go missing (*Lord Kilpartinger did*) and Harry was simply puking his pie, not held by the Headless Fireman and clawed by a Phantom Puma.

He opened the connecting door.

And wasn't in the dining carriage, but the First Class Sleeping Compartments. Discreet overhead lights flickered.

At the end of the corridor, by an open compartment-door, stood a small figure in blue pyjamas decorated with space-rockets, satellites, moons and stars. Her label was tied loosely around her neck. Her unbound red hair fell to her waist, almost covering her face. Her single exposed eye fixed on him.

What was the girl's name? He was as bad as Harry.

"Vanessa?" it came to him. "Why are you up?"

Setting aside the Mystery of the Vanishing Carriage, he went to the child, and knelt, sweeping hair away from her face. She wasn't crying but something was wrong. He recognised emptiness in her, an absence he knew well – for he had it himself. He made a smile-face and she didn't cringe. At least she didn't see him as a werebeast whose head would fit the space over the mantelpiece. She also didn't laugh, no matter how he twisted his mouth and rolled his eyes.

"What's wrong?"

"Dreams," she said, hugging him around the neck, surprisingly heavy, lips close to his ear, "*bad* dreams."

V

". . . and then, chicklet, there were two."

Magic Fingers wished the Scotch Streak's famous facilities stretched to an espresso machine. He could use a java jolt to electrify the old grey sponge, get his extra-senses acting extra-sensible. Like most night-birds, he ran on coffee.

Annie pursed her lips at him and looked at the doorway through which Hard Luck Harry and now the Kid had disappeared.

"You said we shouldn't split the band and you were on the button," he told her. "We should have drawn the wagons in a circle."

"You're not helping," she said.

Was he picking up jitters from her? When Annie was discombobulated, everyone in the house came down with the sweats. It was a downside of her Talent.

"Chill, tomato, chill," he said. "Put some ice on it."

She nodded, knowing what he meant, and tried hard. There was a switch in her brain, which turned off the receptors in her fright centre. Otherwise she'd never have made it through the War.

Danny Myles had been blind during the War, evacuated from the East End to the wilds of Wales. He had learned his way around the sound-smell-touch-tastescape of Streatham in his first twelve years, but found the different environment – all cold wind-blasts, tongue-twisting language and lava bread – of Bedgellert a disorienting nightmare. He had run away from Mr and Mrs Jones the Farmers on his own, and *felt* his way back across two countries, turning up in his street to find it wasn't there any more and Mum was with Auntie Brid in Brixton. Lots of cockney kids ran away from yokels they were packed off to during the Blitz – some from exploitation or abuse far beyond lava bread every evening and tuneless chapel most of the weekend – but they weren't usually blind. It was a nine days' wonder. Mum wasn't sure whether to send him back to the Jones', with a label round his neck like that chick who took a shine to the Kid, or keep him in London, sheltering in the Underground during the raids.

Born without sight, it was hard for Danny to get his head around the *idea* of blindness or realise his extra-senses were out of the ordinary. Then, the switch in *his* brain was thrown. No miracle operation, no bump on the bonce, no faith healer – it was just like a door suddenly swinging open. There was a black-out, so there wasn't even much to see – until the sun came up. He didn't stop whooping for a week. At first, the bright new world in his eyes blotted out the patterns of sound and touch he had made do with, but when things settled, his ears were sharper than ever. Soon, he could channel music through anything with eighty-eight keys, really earning his "Magic Fingers" handle. Then Edwin Winthrop came into the scene and the Diogenes Club took an interest, labelling him a Talent.

He'd been doing these gigs for years. In '53, he'd unmasked the Phantom of the Festival of Britain. Then, he'd busted the Insane Gang. Defused the last of Goebbels' Psychic Propaganda Bombs. Rid London Zoo of the Ghost Gorilla and his Ape Armada. It was a sideline. Also, he knew, an addiction. Some jazzmen popped pills, mainlined horse, bombed out on booze, chased skirts – he went after spooks. Not just any old sheet-wearers, but haints which could turn about and bite. Heart-eaters. Like 3473-S. This was a bad one, worse than the Phantom, *worse than the Ghost Gorilla*. He knew it. Annie and the Kid knew it too, but they hadn't his extra-senses. They didn't know enough to be properly wary. Hell, not wary – *terrified*.

"You're doing it again," Annie chided him.

He realised he'd been drumming his fingers. "Stella By Starlight". A song about a ghost. He stopped.

His hands hurt. That snap from the piano-lid was coolly calculated to show him who was boss. The sides of his thumbs were numb. His knuckles were purple and blobby. He spread his fingers on the tablecloth.

"Like, ouch, man," he said.

Annie giggled.

"It hurts, y'know. How'd you like it if your face fell off?"

She was shocked for a moment.

"Not a lot," she said.

"These hands are my fortune, ought to be wrapped in cotton wool every night. If I could spring for payments, I'd insure them for lotsa lettuce. This . . . this *train* went for them, like a bird goes for the eyes. Dig?"

"The Worst Thing in the World."

"On the button, Mama."

"Less of the 'Mama'. I'm not that much older than you."

The Kid ought to be back by now. But he was a no-show. And Harry Cutley was far out there, drowning.

Magic Fingers cast his peepers over the dining car. There'd been an elderly frail strapping on the feed-bag down the way. She'd skedaddled, though he didn't recall her getting up. Arnold – the conductor-waiter-majordomo-high priest – was gonesville also. He and Annie were alone.

Man, the rattle and shake of the train was fraying his nerves with bring-down city jazz! It was syncopation without representation! All bum notes and missed melodies.

At first, movement had been smooth, like skimming over a glassy lake. Now, the waters were choppy. Knives and forks hopped on the tables. Windows thrummed in their frames. The cloth slid by fractions of an inch and had to be held down, lest it drag plates over the edge and into the aisle.

He felt it in his teeth, in his water, in his guts, in the back of his throat.

Speed, reckless speed. This beast could come off the rails at any time.

The windows were deep dark, as if the outsides were painted – or black-out curtains hung over them. Even if he got close to the cold glass, all he saw was a fish-eye-distorted, darked-up reflection.

They weren't in a tunnel. They could have been on a trestle stretched through a void, steaming on full-ahead, rails silently coming to pieces behind them. Alone in the night.

He raised his hand and fingertipped the glass, getting five distinct icy shocks. He'd been leery of using his touching, but now was the time.

"Anything?" asked Annie.

He provisionally shook his head, but felt into the glass. It was thick, like crystal, and veined. He felt the judder of pane in frame, and caught the train's music, a bebop with high notes, warning whistles and a thump of dangerous bass. 3473 had a heartbeat, a pulse.

A shock sparked into his fingers, pain outlining his hand-bones.

He was stuck to the window, palm flat against the glass, fingers splayed. Waves of hurt pulsed into him, jarring his wrist, his arm . . . up to the elbow, up to the shoulder.

Annie sat, mouth open, not moving. Frozen.

No, he felt her gloved fingers on his wrist, pulling. He scented her perfume, close. The brush of her hair, the warmth of her, near him.

But he saw her sitting still, across the table.

It was if his eyes had taken a photograph and kept showing it to him, while his extra-senses kept up with what was really happening. He moved his head: the picture in front of him didn't change.

Annie was speaking to him, but he couldn't make it out. Was she talking French? Or Welsh? He had the vile taste of lava bread in his mouth. He heard the train rattle, the music of 3473, louder and louder.

The picture changed. For another still image.

Annie was trying to help, one knee up on the table, both hands round his wrist, face twisted in concentration as she pulled.

But he couldn't feel her hands any more, couldn't smell her.

In his eyes, she was with him. But every other sense told him she'd left off.

His vision showed him still images, like slides in a church hall. It was as if he were in a cinema where the projector selected and held random frames every few seconds while the soundtrack ran normally.

A scream joined train noise.

Annie was in the aisle, arms by her sides, hands little fists, mouth open. Dark flurries in the air around her. Birds or bats, moving too fast to be captured by a single exposure.

The scream shut off, but Annie was still posed in her yell. Something broke.

In the next image, she was strewn among place-settings a few booths down, limbs twisted, dress awry. The frosted glass partition was cracked across.

The window let go of him. His hand felt skinless, wet.

Someone, not Annie, was talking, burbling words, scat-singing. No tune he could follow.

He waited for the next picture, to find out who was there. Instead the frame held, fixed and unmoving no matter how he shook his head. He stood and painfully caught his hip on the table-edge. He felt his way into the aisle, still seeing from his sat-by-the-window position. He tried to work out where he was in the picture before him, reaching out for chair-backs to make his way hand-over-hand to Annie, or to where Annie was in his frozen vision.

A heavy thump, and a hissing along with the gabble.

He stood still in the aisle, bobbing with the movement of the train, like the hipsters who didn't dance but nodded heads to the bop, shoulders and hands in movement, carried by jazz. He guesstimated he was three booths away from his original viewpoint.

Then the lights flared and faded.

The picture turned to sepia, as if there were an even flame behind the paper, and the brown darkened to blackness.

He shut and opened his sightless eyes.

His hands were on chair-backs and he had a better sense of things than when treacherous eyes were letting him down. He heard as acutely as before. The gabbling was a distraction. Just noise, sourceless. There was no body to it – nothing displacing air, raising or lowering temperature, smelling of cologne or ciggies. There was one breathing person in the carriage – Annette Amboise, asleep or unconscious. Otherwise, he was alone, inside the beast.

This was different; blindness, with the memory of sight. It was as if there had been white chalk marks around everything, just-erased but held in his mind as guide-lines.

It wasn't like seeing, but he knew what was where.

Tables, chairs, roses in sconces, windows, connecting doors, the aisle. Under him was carpet. Under that was the floor of the carriage. Under that hungry wheels and old, old rails.

Now there were shapes in the dark. Sitting at the tables. White clouds like human-sized eggs or beans, bent in the middle, limbless, faceless.

He heard the clatter of cutlery, grunts and smacks of swinish eating. In the next carriage, the piano was assaulted. Someone wearing mittens plunked through "Green Grow the Rushes-Oh", accompanied by a drunken chorus. This wasn't now. This was before the War.

This was the Scotch Streak of Lord Killpassengers.

How far off was the In-for-Death Bridge?

He couldn't smell anything. It was worse than being struck blind. He knew he could cope without eyes. He'd made it from Wales to London, once. He had the magic fingers.

Someone called him, from a long way away.

All he could taste was dry, unbuttered lava bread. Butter wasn't to be had in London, what with rationing – his Mum used some sort of grease that had to be mixed up in a bowl. In Wales, with farms all about, there was all the butter in the world and no questions asked, but Mr and Mrs Jones didn't believe in it. Like they didn't believe in hot water. Or sheets – thin blankets of horsehair that scratched like a net of tiny hooks would do. Or music, except the wheezing chapel organ. When Danny drummed his fingers, he'd get a slap across the hand to cure him of the habit. He was not to get up from the table, even if he needed to take the ten steps across the garden to the privy, until he'd cleared his plate and thanked the Good Lord for His Bounty.

Most nights, he'd sit, fighting his bladder and his tongue, struggling to swallow, trying not to have acute taste-buds, ignoring the hurt in his mouth until the lump was solid in his stomach. "There's lovely," Mrs Jones would say. "Bless the bread and bless the child."

In the dining carriage, there was lava bread on every table.

The communicating door opened. The racket rose by decibels, pouring in from the canvas-link between carriages where the din was loudest. A cold draught dashed into his face. Someone entered the dining car, someone who shifted a *lot* of air. The newcomer moved carefully, like a fat man who knows he's drunk but has to impress the Lord Mayor. A grey-white shape appeared in the dark and floated towards Danny, scraps of chalk-mark and neon squiggles like those sighted people have inside their eyelids coalescing into a huge belly constrained by vertically striped overalls, an outsize trainman's hat, a pitted moon-face. Danny saw the wide man as if he were spotlit on a shadowed stage, or cut out of a photograph and pasted on a black background.

He recognised the face.

A huge paw, grimy with engine dirt, stuck out.

"Gilclyde," boomed the voice, filling his skull. "Lord Kilpartinger."

Not knowing what else to do, Magic Fingers offered his hand to be shaken. Lord Killpassengers enveloped it with his banana-fingered ape-paws and squeezed with nerve-crushing, bone-crushing force.

Agony blotted out all else – he was in the dark again, feeling the vice-grip but not seeing His Lordship dressed up as Casey Jones. Burning pain smothered his hand.

It was a bad break. At the end of his wrist hung a limp, tangled dust-rag.

Then he felt nothing – no pain. No sound. No smell. No taste. No feeling.

For the first time in his life, he was completely cut off.

VI

Even beyond the usual assumption that quiet English children were aliens, there was *something* about Vanessa.

She made Richard feel the way grown-ups, even those inside the Diogenes Club, felt around him when he was a boy, the way a lot of people still felt when he was in the room. At first, they were on their guard because he dressed like the sort of youth the *Daily Mail* reckoned would smash your face in – though, in his experience, teds were as sweet or sour as anyone else, and the worst beatings he'd personally taken came from impeccably-uniformed school prefects. Once past that, people just got *spooked* – because he felt things, saw things, knew things.

Now he knew about Vanessa.

He was almost afraid of her. And this from someone who accepted the impossible without question.

Sherlock Holmes, brother of the Club's founder, said: "When you have eliminated the impossible, what remains, no matter how unlikely, must be the truth." Less frequently quoted was Mycroft's addendum, "And when you can *not* eliminate the impossible, refer the matter to the Diogenes Club." It was recorded in the Club's archives, though not in the writings of John Watson, that the Great Detective several times found himself stumped, and fielded the case to his contemporary Carnacki the Ghost-Finder.

It was *barely* possible that a gigantic conjuring trick could rearrange, or seem to rearrange, the carriages while the train was steaming through the darkened countryside. The archives weren't short of locked-room mysteries and like conundra. For some reason, especially from the 1920s and early '30s. The Scotch Streak dated from then, so it could have been built to allow baffling disappearances. However, an uncanny explanation required less of a stretch of belief. Richard couldn't see a *point* to the carriage substitution, and pointlessness was a frequent symptom of the supernatural. Haunted houses often had "treacherous" doors, opening to different rooms at different times. It should have been expected, by know-it-all Harry Cutley for instance, that a haunted train would have something along these lines. However, the switcheroo wasn't on the train's list of previously recorded phenomena.

Where was everybody? Harry was downwind, last seen heading towards Second and Third Class. Annette and Myles were in the misplaced dining car. Arnold the Conductor, omnipresent earlier, was nowhere to be seen.

Were the other passengers where they should be? Though it was easy to get distracted by fireworks, this investigation was supposed to be about protecting the American couriers.

Three compartments had blinds drawn and DO NOT DISTURB signs hung. One was Annette's and she wasn't there. Another was Vanessa's and she was with him.

That was a puzzle. Besides the couriers, Mrs Sweet and the sinister vicar (one of whom *must* be a spy) should be here. They couldn't all be crammed into one compartment playing whist with nuclear missiles. In theory, the British Government had *other* agents to deal with that sort of mess, kitted out with exploding cufflinks and licences to kill. In a pinch, Richard could muddle in. The Club had been dabbling in "ordinary" espionage since the Great Game of Victoria's reign. Edwin had served as an Intelligence Officer in the RFC during the First World War ("No, I *didn't* shoot down the Bloody Red Baron; what I shot was a lot of photographs from the back of a two-seater – if it matters, each exposure got more Huns killed than all the so-called flying aces put together.") before taking over Carnacki's ghost-finding practice.

"Have you seen any Americans?" he asked the child.

She solemnly shook her head and stuck out her lower lip. She wanted more attention paid to her.

He looked again at her label.

"Who *is* Lieutenant-Commander Coates?"

She gave a "don't know" shrug.

"Not your Dad, you said. Where are your parents?"

Another shrug.

"Lot of that about," he said, feeling it deeply. "Where do you live, usually?"

A small sound, inaudible – as if the girl weren't used to speech, like a well-bred, upper-middle-class Kaspar Hauser in spaceman pyjamas.

"Come again, love?"

"Can't remember," she said.

Richard had a chill, born of kinship. But he was also wary. This was too close to where he came from. If the train could come up with Worst Things to get under Annette's or Harry's skin, it could sidle up close to him and bite too.

"Vanessa What?"

Another "can't remember".

"It must be Vanessa Something. Not Coates, but Something."

She shook her head, braids whipping.

"Just Vanessa, then. It'll have to do. Nothing wrong with 'Vanessa'. Not a saint's name, so far. Not forged in antiquity and refined through passage from language to language like mine. Richard, from the Germanic for 'Rule-Hard', also 'Ricardo', 'Rickard', 'Dick', 'Dickie', 'Dickon', 'Rich', 'Richie', 'Clever Dick', 'Dick-Be-Quick', 'Crookback Dick'. Your name – like 'Pamela', 'Wendy' and 'Una' – was invented within recorded history. By Jonathan Swift, as it happens. Do you know who he was?"

"He wrote *Gulliver's Travels*."

So she remembered *some* things.

"Yes. He coined the name 'Vanessa' as a contraction – like 'Dick' for 'Richard' – for an Irish girl called 'Esther Vanhomrigh'."

"Who was she?"

"Ah, she was a fan of Dean Swift, you know, like girls today might be fans of Tommy Steele."

"Don't like Tommy Steele."

"Elvis Presley?"

Vanessa was keener on Elvis.

"Miss Vanhomrigh was Swift's biggest fan, so he invented a name for her. He preferred another woman called Esther, Esther Johnson, whom he called 'Stella'. I expect he made up the names so as not to get them mixed up. Stella and Vanessa didn't like each other."

"Did they fight?"

"In a way. They competed for Swift's attention."

"Did Vanessa win?"

"Not really, love. Both died before they could settle who got him, and he wasn't entirely in the business of being got."

Best not to mention the author might have married Stella.

How did they get into this? He didn't set out to be a lecturer, but he was recounting things he didn't think he remembered to this inquisitive, reticent child. Talking to her calmed him.

"Are we being got?" she asked.

"I'm afraid we might be."

"Please don't let me be got."

"Not if I can help it."

"Promise?"

"Promise."

Vanessa smiled up at him. Richard worried he had just given his word in the middle of a great unknown. He might not be in a position to keep his promise.

But he knew it was important.

Vanessa must not be got.

They were by the compartment with the DO NOT DISTURB sign. He saw a THROUGH TO PORTNACREIRANN notation. The blind wasn't pulled all the way down, and a spill of light wavered on the compartment floor. In that, Richard saw a pale hand dangling from the lower berth, thin chain fixed to the handle of a briefcase on the floor. It was one of the couriers.

At least they were safe.

Vanessa put her eye up to the gap and looked in, for a long while.

"Come away," he said. "Let the nice Americans sleep."

She turned and looked up at him. "Are you sure they're nice?"

"No, but they're important. And it's best to leave them alone. There are other people I want to find first."

"Your friends? The pretty lady. The scowly man. The blind person."

"Danny's not blind. Well, not now. How did you know he'd been blind?"

She shrugged.

"Just sensitive, I suppose," he prompted. "And, yes, them. I left them in the restaurant but I, ah, seem to have mislaid the carriage. It used to be there" – pointing at the connecting door – "but now it isn't."

"Silly," she said. "A restaurant can't get lost."

"You've got a lot to learn."

"No, I haven't," she declared, sticking up her freckled nose. "I've learned quite enough already."

Richard was slightly irked by her tone. He might have said Vanessa's education could hardly be considered complete since she'd omitted to learn her own full name. But that would be cruel. He understood too well how these situations came about.

"The supper carriage is through that door," she said. "I peeked, earlier."

She led him by the hand, back towards the connecting door.

"We should be careful," he said.

"Silly silly," she said. "Come on, Mr Richard, don't be scared . . ."

When anyone – even a little girl – told him not to be scared, his natural instinct was to wonder what there was not to be scared of, then whether the person giving the advice was as well up on the potential scariness or otherwise of the situation or entity in question as they might be.

The subdued lamps in the train corridor had dimmed to the point when everything seemed moonlit. The glass in the connecting door was black – he had a nasty thought that the carriages could have shifted about again, and there might be cold night air and a nasty fall to the tracks beyond.

He let Vanessa's hand go, and looked – trying to show more confidence than he felt – towards the door. He was over twice the girl's age, and should take the lead; then again, twice a single figure wasn't that much. He didn't really know how old he was, let alone how old he should act.

He hesitated. She gave him a little push.

The train noise was louder near the door, the floor shakier.

Richard told himself he was opening the door. Then he found he actually was.

Beyond was . . .

VII

Something had given her an almighty thump. And had got to Danny Myles.

Annette came to on a table. Forks were driven through her shoulder-straps, pinning her to Formica. She couldn't sit without ruining her Coco Chanel. Obviously, this was the work of a fiend from Hell. Or a jealous wife.

The table rattled. Was the Scotch Streak shaking to pieces?

A length of something spiny, like over-boiled stringy asparagus with teeth, stretched across her mouth. She clamped down, tasted bitter sap, and spat it away. It was the long-stemmed rose from the place-setting.

She carefully detached the forks, trying to inflict no more damage to her dress, and sat up. Wet, sticky blood pooled on the tablecloth. Then she noticed a paring-knife sticking out of her right thigh. Her stocking was torn. She gripped the handle, surprised not to feel anything but slight stiffness. Upon pulling out the knife, a gush of jagged pain came. She ignored it, and improvised a battlefield dressing – another useful trade learned in the War – with a napkin and cocktail sticks.

Sliding off the table, she looked up and down the dining carriage.

Danny Myles was backed into a space between the last booth and the door to the galley, hugging his knees, face hidden. He trembled, but she couldn't tell if it was with silent sobbing or the movement of the train.

She saw no one else, which didn't mean no one else was there.

Someone had forked and knifed her. The skewering had been too deliberate, too mocking, to be the result of a directionless phenomenon like the common-or-garden poltergeist. Something with a *personality* had skewered her. Something that thought itself a comedian. The worst kind of spook, in her opinion. Or maybe she'd been pinned by a mean person who wasn't here any more. Never neglect human agency. People could be wretched enough on their own, without calling in ghosts.

There were ghosts here, though.

"Danny," she said.

He didn't hear her. That tinkled a warning – Danny heard *everything*, even when you didn't want him to. He could probably smell or taste what was whispered in the next building in a room with taps running.

"Danny," she said, louder.

She went to him, feeling stabbed again with every step.

He wasn't dead, she saw, but in shock, crawled back into his shell. He looked up and around, seeing nothing.

Danny "Magic Fingers" Myles held up useless hands.

"Busted," he said. "Gone."

She knelt by him and examined his hands. No bones were broken. She found no wound of any kind. But they were dead, like sand-filled gloves.

"*Salauds boches,*" she swore. Nazi bastards!

She knew what the Worst Thing was for Danny Myles.

His head jerked and he flinched, as if he were being flapped at by a cloud of bats. He knew someone was near, but not that it was her. All his senses were gone. He was locked in his skull.

She took his arms and stood him up. He didn't fight her. She tried to reach him – not by talking or even touching, but with her inside self. She projected past the bony shields around his mind, to reassure, to promise help . . .

She didn't know if the damage was permanent – but she squashed the thought, screwing it into a tiny speck. He mustn't get that, mustn't catch despair from her, to compound his own.

It's Annie . . .

Because it was her way, she tried kissing him, but just smeared her lipstick. She held him tight, her forehead against his.

He wriggled, escaping from her. The napkin bandage came loose and her leg gave out. For support, she grabbed a tall trolley with shelves of dessert. It rolled down the aisle, dragging her. She bumped her head against the silvered frame. Cream and jam smeared the side of her face, matting in her hair. The trolley got away, and she was left, tottering, reaching out for something fixed . . .

Danny walked like a puppet, jerked past the galley, pulled towards the end of the carriage. Annette had seen people like that before, in shock or under the 'fluence.

"Danny!" she called out, frustrated. Nothing reached him.

She repaired her bandage. How much blood had she lost? Her foot was a mass of needles and pins. She wasn't sure her knee was working properly. Her fingers weren't managing too well knotting the napkin.

Danny was at the end of the carriage. The door slid open, not through his agency – the train had *tilted* to slam it aside. He vanished into shadow beyond, and fell down. She saw his trouser-cuffs and shoes slither into darkness as he pulled himself – or was pulled – out of the dining car.

This had gone far enough.

She reached out, slipped her hand into the alcove, and took a firm hold on the communication cord.

She had felt this coming. Now, here it was.

" 'Penalty for improper use – five pounds'," she read aloud. "Cheap at half the price."

She pulled, with her whole body. There was no resistance. She sprawled on the carpet. The red-painted metal chain was loose. Lengths rattled out of the alcove, yards falling in coils around her.

No whistle, no grinding of brakes, no sudden halt.

Nothing. The cord hadn't been fixed to anything. It was a con, like pictures of life-belts painted on the side of a ship.

The Scotch Streak streaked on.

If anything, the din was more terrific. Cold wind blew, riffling Annette's sticky hair.

Between the carriages, one of the exterior doors was open.

Another earlier flash-forward came back to her. An open door. Someone falling. Breaking.

"Danny!" she yelled.

She scrabbled, tripping over the bloody useless chain, got to her feet, one heel snapped. That had been in her Worst Thing vision. Slipping free of her pumps, she ran towards the end of the carriage, as light flared in the passage beyond. She saw the open door, had an impression of hedgerows flashing by, greenery turned grey in the scatter of light from the train. Danny Myles hung in the doorway, wrists against the frame, body flapping like a flag.

She grabbed for him. Her fingers brushed his jersey.

Then he was gone. She leaned out of the train, wind hammering her eyes, and saw him collide with a gravel incline. He bounced several times, then tangled with a fence-post, wrapping around it like a discarded scarecrow.

The train curved the wrong way and she couldn't see him. Magic Fingers was left behind.

Tears forced from her, she wrenched herself back into the train, pulling closed the door. It was as if she had taken several sudden punches in the gut, the prelude to questioning, to loosen up the prisoner.

She found herself sitting down, crying her heart out. For a long time.

"Why is your friend bawling?" asked a small voice.

Smearing tears out of her eyes with her wrist, Annette looked up.

Richard was back – from the wrong direction, she realised – with Vanessa. The little girl held out a handkerchief with an embroidered "V". Annette took it, wiped her eyes, and found she needed to blow her nose. Vanessa didn't mind.

"Danny's gone," she told Richard. "It got him."

She looked up at her colleague, the boy Edwin Winthrop had confidence in, the youth she'd entertained fantasies about. Recruited at an early age, educated and trained and brought up to become a Most Valued Member. Richard Jeperson was supposed to take care of things like this. Harry Cutley lead this group, but insiders tipped Richard as the man to take over, to defy the worst the dark had to offer.

She saw Richard had no idea what to do next. She saw only a black barrier in the future. And she swooned.

*   *   *

Act III: Inverdeith

I

He had nothing.

Annette was out cold. Harry was missing in action. Danny was finished. He was no use to them, they were no help to him.

Richard was at the sharp end, with no more to give.

Vanessa tugged his sleeve, insistent. She needed him, needed comfort, needed saving.

Nearby, in one of these shifting carriages, the NATO couriers slept. And others – Arnold the Conductor, the scary vicar, Mrs Sweet, that cockney medium, more passengers, the driver and fireman sealed off from the rest of the train in the cabin of the locomotive. Even if they didn't know it, they all counted on him. With the Go-Codes up for grabs, the whole world was on the table and the big dice rattled for the last throw.

The Diogenes Club expected him to do his duty.

He had the girl fetch chilled water in a jug from the galley, and sprinkled it on Annette's brow. The woman murmured, but stayed under. He looked at Vanessa, who shrugged and made a pouring motion. Richard resisted the notion – it seemed disrespectful to treat a grown-up lady like a comedy sidekick. Vanessa urged him, smiling as any child would at the idea of an adult getting a slosh in the face. With some delicacy, Richard tipped the jug, dripping fat bullets of water onto Annette's forehead. Her eyes fluttered and he tipped further. Ice-cubes bounced. Annette sat up, drenched and sputtering.

"Welcome back."

She looked at him as if she were about to faint again, but didn't. He shook her shoulders, to keep her attention.

"Yes, I understand," she said. "Now don't overdo it. And get me a napkin."

Like the perfect waiter – and where *was* Arnold? – he had one to hand. She dabbed her face dry and ran fingers through her short hair. She'd like to spend fifteen minutes on her make-up, but was willing to sacrifice for the Cause.

"You're lovely as you are," he said.

She shrugged it off, secretly pleased. She let him help her to her feet and slid into one of the booths. Vanessa monkeyed up and sat opposite. The child began to play, tracing scratch-lines on the tablecloth with a long-tined fork.

"I tried the communication cord," she said. "No joy."

He got up, found the loose loop of cord, examined it, sought out the next alcove, pulled experimentally. No effect whatsoever.

"Told you so," she said.

"Independent confirmation. Harry Cutley would approve. It counts as a finding if we fill in the forms properly."

Richard sat next to the little girl and looked at Annette, reaching out to catch a drip she had missed.

"Harry's gone?" she asked.

Richard thought about it. He calmed, reaching into his centre, and tried to feel out, along the length of the train.

"Not like Danny's gone," he concluded. "Harry's on board."

"What's he doing when he goes quiet like that?" Vanessa asked, interested. "Saying his prayers?"

"Being sensitive," said Annette.

"Is that like being polite, minding his 'P's and 'Q's?"

Richard broke off and paid attention to the people immediately around him.

"Something missing," he said. "Something's been taken."

"Time, for a start," said Annette. "How long have we been aboard?"

Richard reached for his watch-pocket, then remembered he'd retired the timepiece. There was a clock above the connecting door. The one in the ballroom carriage seemed to keep the right time when all others failed. The face of this clock was black – not painted over, but opaque glass. It still ticked.

"I won't carry a watch," said Annette, "but I've an excellent sense of time. And I've lost it. How long was I unconscious?"

"Ages," said Vanessa. "We thought you'd died."

"A few seconds," said Richard.

"See," said Annette. "No sense of time at all."

Richard looked at the nearest window. It was black glass, like the clock – a mirror in which he looked shockingly worn-out. Even when the overhead lights flickered, which they did more and more, he couldn't see out. He didn't know if they were rushing through England, Scotland or some other dark country. He felt the rattle-rhythm of the train – that, he knew, came from rolling over slight joins between lengths of rail, every ten or twenty feet. The Scotch Streak was still on tracks.

"Have we passed Edinburgh?" said Annette.

Edinburgh! That was a way out, a way off the Ghost Train!

From the station, he could phone Edwin, have the Club use its pull to cancel the rest of the journey, get everyone else out safely.

Danny's death was justification for calling off the whole jaunt, shutting down the line. The couriers could be sent across Scotland in a taxi. It would take longer, but they'd be surer to arrive intact. If anyone wanted to start World War III, they'd have to wait until after lunch.

Then, he could think of something else to do with his life.

What life?

"I have a picture of the station in my mind," said Annette, concentrating. "Passengers get off, coal is taken on. They try and do it quietly, so as not to wake the sleepers, but you can't pour tons of anything quietly. I can't tell if I'm seeing ahead or remembering. My Talent seems to be on the blink at the moment. 'Normal transmission will be resumed as soon as possible'. There's a black wall . . ."

"We've already stopped once," said Vanessa, in a small, scared voice. "In Scotland."

This was news. Richard couldn't imagine not noticing.

"Quite right, miss," said Arnold the Conductor, coming back from where the First Class Carriages should be. "I've clipped the ticket of the Edinburgh-to-Portnacreirann passenger. Just the one. Not what it used to be. Ah, someone's made a bit of a mess here. Don't worry. We'll get it cleaned up in a jiffy. Madame, might I bring you more water? This jug seems to be empty."

Richard, suddenly cool inside, saw Arnold was either mad or with the other side. Not *the other side* as in the Soviets (though that was possible) but *the other side* as in beyond the veil, the Great Old Whatevers. Maybe he'd been normal when he first boarded the Scotch Streak, who knows how many nights ago – now he was one of Them, aligned with Annette's "It". The conductor wore an old-fashioned uniform, a crimson cutaway jacket and high-waisted flyless matador trousers. His tie-pin was the crest of the long-gone London, Scotland and Isles Railway Company. His cap was oversize, a child's idea of railwayman's headgear.

He resisted an impulse to take Arnold by his antique lapels, smash him through a partition, throw a proper teddy boy scare into him, get the razor against his jugular, demand straight answers.

"Thank you," he told the conductor. "A refill would be appreciated."

Arnold took the jug and walked off. Annette, greatly upset, was about to speak, but Richard made a gesture and she bit her lip instead. She was up to speed. It wasn't just the train and the spooks. It was the people aboard, some of them at least.

"What is it?" said Vanessa, picking up on the wordless communication between grown-ups. "A secret? Tell me at once. You're not to have secrets. I say so."

Annette laughed indulgently, at the girl's directness. The corners of her eyes crinkled in a way she hated and tried to avoid, but which Richard saw was utterly adorable. She was far more beautiful as herself than the make-up mask she showed the world.

"No secrets from you, little thing," she said, pinching Vanessa's nose.

The little girl looked affronted by the impudence and stuck her fork into Annette's throat.

"Don't call me 'little thing'," she said, in a grown man's voice. "You French cow!"

II

Richard scythed a white china dinner-plate edge-first into the little girl's face. The plate broke, gashing Vanessa's eyebrow – it would leave a scar. Blood fountained out of the child-shaped thing.

She gave out a deep, roaring howl and held her face, kicking the underside of the table, twisting and writhing as if on fire.

Richard looked across the table at Annette.

She held her hand to her throat, fork stuck out between her fingers, blood dribbling down her arm. Her eyes were wide.

"Didn't see . . . that coming," she said, and slumped.

The light went out in her eyes.

Vanessa's hooked little fingers scrabbled at Richard's face, and he fell out of his seat. The child hopped onto his chest, pummelling, scratching and kicking. He slithered backwards, working his shoulders and feet, trying to throw the miniature dervish off him. Her blood poured into his face.

He caught hold of one of her braids and pulled.

A little girl yell came out of her, a *Mummy-he's-hurting-meee* scream. Was that the real Vanessa? Something else was in there with her, whoever she was, whatever *it* was.

The girl was possessed.

It had been hiding, deep in the blanks of her mind, but had peeped out once or twice. Richard hadn't paid enough attention.

And now another of the group was gone.

Annette Amboise. He'd only known her a few days, but they'd become close. It was as if they knew they would be close, had seen a future now cruelly revoked, had been rushing past this long night, speeding to get to a next leg of their journey, which they would take together.

All that was left of that was this *monster*.

As Vanessa shrieked, Richard hurled her off. He got to his feet, unsteady. He looked to Annette, hoping she was unconscious but knowing better. Slack-mouthed, like a fish, she toppled sideways, towards the window, slapping cheek-to-cheek with her equally dead reflection.

Arnold was back – not from the direction he had left. He carried a full jug.

"The lady won't be needing this now," he said.

The conductor ignored the frothing child-thing, who was crawling down the aisle, back seemingly triple-jointed, tongue extending six pink-and-blue inches, braids stood on end as if pulled by wires. It was like a giant gecko wearing a little girl suit, loose in some places and too tight in others. As its limbs moved, the suit almost tore.

One eye was blotted shut with blood. The other fixed on Richard. The girl hissed.

Then the Gecko became bipedal. The spine curved upwards, straining like a drawn bow. Forelegs lifted and became floppy arms, hands limp like paddles. The belly came unstuck from the aisle carpet. Snake-hips kinking, it hopped upright. It stood with feet apart and shoulders down, as if balancing an invisible tail.

"Vanessa," said Richard, "can you hear me? It's Richard."

Hot, obscene anger burst from whatever it was. He flinched. Annette might have been able to reach the girl inside, help her. That was her Talent. His left him open to emotional attack.

He stood his ground.

The label around the Gecko's neck was soggy with blood, words washed away, black shapes emerging.

He reached out and tore the label away. It left an angry weal around Vanessa's neck.

"Mine," she said, in her own voice. "Give it me back, you bastarrrd," in the thing's masculine, somehow Scots voice. "Mine," both voices together, blasting from her chest and mouth.

He rubbed his thumb over the bloody card. Scrapes came away. The label was actually an envelope, with a celluloid inner sleeve sealing strips of paper. He clawed with a nail, and saw number strings.

The couriers were decoys, after all.

"Give me those," said the Gecko.

Richard knew what he held. Not numbers, but a numerical key. Put in a slot, they could bring about Armageddon.

"Is that what you want?" he asked, talking to the thing.

The smile became cunning, wide. The unblotted eye winked.

"Give me back my numbers," it said, mimicking the girl's voice.

He could tell now when it was trying to fool him. Could tell how much she was Vanessa and how much the Gecko.

"Conductor," she said. "That man's got my ticket. Make him give it back to me."

"Sir," said Arnold. "This is a serious matter. May I see that ticket?"

Richard clutched the celluloid in his fist. He wouldn't let Arnold take the Go-Codes. He was with the Gecko.

Vanessa's eye closed and she crumpled. He had a stab of concern for the girl. If she fell badly, hit her head . . .

Arnold's gaze had a new firmness.

"Sir," he said, holding up his ticket-clippers. "The ticket."

By jumping from the girl to the conductor, the Gecko had got closer to him. But it wore a shape he was less concerned about damaging.

He stuck the Go-Codes into his top pocket, and launched a right cross at Arnold, connecting solidly with his chin, staggering him back a few steps. He'd perfectly hit the knock-out button, but the thing in Arnold didn't pay attention. It lashed out, clipper-jaws open, aiming for an ear or a lip, intent on squeezing out a chunk of face.

Richard ducked and the clippers closed on his sleeve, slicing through scarlet velvet, meeting in the fold. He hit Arnold a few more times, hearing school boxing instructors tell him he shouldn't get angry. In his bouts, he always lost on points or was disqualified, even if he pummelled his opponent insensible. What he did in a fight wasn't elegant or sporting, or remotely allowable under the Queensberry rules. He had learned something in the blanked portion of his childhood.

From a crouch, he launched an uppercut, smashing Arnold's face, feeling cartilage go in the conductor's nose. The clippers hung from Richard's underarm. They opened and fell to the juddering floor, leaving neat holes in his sleeve.

Not above booting a man while he was down, he put all his frustration into a hefty kick, reinforced toe sinking into Arnold's side, forcing out a Gecko-groan. The conductor emptied.

Then an arm was around Richard's neck. He was dragged to the floor.

Annette's elbow nut-crackered around his throat and her dead face flopped next to his, one eye rolling.

He felt a wave of disgust, not at physical contact with a corpse, but at the abuse of Annette's body. He couldn't fight her as he had Arnold, or even as he had Vanessa (he'd broken a plate on a child's face!) because of what had hung between them until moments ago.

The thing working Annette took the fork out of her throat and held it to Richard's eye.

"The codes," it said, voice rattling through her ruptured windpipe. "Now."

He pressed his hand over his top pocket. He blinked furiously as the fork got close. One jab, and there would be metal in his brain.

This trip was nearly over.

III

The Gecko inside Annette held Richard in a death-grip, fork-tines hugely out of focus against his eye. Beyond the blur, he saw Arnold watching with his habitual air of quizzical deference. Anything between the passengers was their own business.

Someone shouldered Arnold aside and levelled two double-barrelled shotguns at Richard and Annette.

It was Harry Cutley. Hard-Luck Harry to the Rescue!

"Ah-hah," declared Harry, a melodrama husband finding his wife in a clinch with her lover, "ah-bleedin'-hah! I knew Dickie-Boy was a wrong 'un from the first. Hold him steady, Annie and I'll save you!"

It wasn't easy to aim two shotguns at the same time, what with the swaying of the train. Harry couldn't keep them level.

"Annette's not home," Richard said. "Look at her eyes."

Harry ignored him.

He must have broken into the baggage car and requisitioned Mrs Sweet's guns. His pockets were lumpy with cartridges. He had a lifetime of resentments to work off, in addition to being under the influence of the Scotch Streak. Harry still couldn't hold the guns properly, but was close enough to Richard that aiming wouldn't make much difference.

At least, the fork went away.

The Gecko relaxed a little, holding Richard up as a shield and a target.

Harry saw Vanessa, half her face bruised and bloody.

"I see you can't be trusted on your own," he said to Richard. "There's a reason I'm Most Valued Member, Clever Dick. I observe at a glance, take in all the clues, puzzle out what has happened, make a snap decision, and act on it, promptly and severely."

He managed with an effort to get one gun half-cocked, but his left-hand gun twisted up and thumped his face. He flinched as if someone else had attacked him, and pointed the gun he had a better grip on.

Richard shrugged off Annette's dead fingers and stood.

The gun-barrel raised with him.

"Look at Annette, Harry," he said. "It got her. It got Danny. It had Vanessa. It's tried to have me. It is trying to get you. You can hear it, can't you? It's talking to you now."

Richard stood aside, to let Harry see Annette.

The Gecko couldn't get the corpse to stand properly. Her bloodied neck was a congealed ruin. Her bloodless face was slack, empty – only her eye mobile, twitching with alien intellect.

"Annie," said Harry, shocked, grieving.

"You see," said Richard, stepping forward. "We've got to fight it."

Both guns swung. The barrels jabbed against Richard's chest.

"Stay where you are, young feller-me-lad," said Harry, fury sparking again. "I *know* you're behind this. You may have Ed Winthrop fooled, but not Harry Cutley, oh no. Too clever by half, that's your bloody trouble. Went to a public school, didn't you?"

"Several," Richard admitted.

"Yes, I can tell. They're all like you, bright boys with no depth, no *backbone*. Had it too easy, all your lives. Silver spoons up your bums from Day One. Never had to work, never had to *think*. Reckon you can put one over on us all. Smarm out the posh accent and walk away from it."

Harry was off on his own. With the guns steady, he got all the cocks back.

Annette had pulled herself upright, assisted by Arnold. She puppet-walked towards them.

"Look behind you," whispered Richard, like a kid at a panto-mime.

Harry showed a toothy grin. "Won't fool me with that one, boy."

Annette's hands were out, thumbs barbed, nearing Harry's neck. When she gripped, his hands would clench – and four barrels-worth of whatever Mrs Sweet liked to load would discharge through Richard's torso.

"Just this once, do me a favour, Harry, and *listen*," said Richard.

The barrels jammed deeper. Richard shut up – he couldn't do anything about his educated accent, which set off Harry's class hatred.

Annette's hands landed, not around Harry's neck, but on his

shoulders. He shivered, in instinctive pleasure. He was enjoying himself. He had everyone where he wanted them. He angled his head and rubbed his cheek, like a cat's, on Annette's dead hand.

The Gecko used Annette's face to make a smile and kissed Harry's ear.

It was a miracle the guns didn't go off.

"See, just this once, bright boy, you lose."

The light in Annette's eyes went out and she was a corpse-weight against Harry's back. Harry was bothered, his eyes flickering.

"Don't do that," he said.

While Harry was distracted, Richard took hold of the barrels and tried to shift them. No dice. Harry shook his head as if trying to see off a buzzing wasp.

Annette fell away, collapsing on the floor.

Harry stepped backwards, his upper body jerking as if the wasps were now pestering in force. The guns slipped away from Richard's chest. He took the opportunity to get out of the way. Harry tripped over Annette's legs and went arse over teakettle.

One of the guns finally went off, blasting a plate-sized hole in the ceiling.

Night air rushed through. Up there somewhere were stars.

Harry, without even knowing what he was doing, resisted the Gecko. So it couldn't take anyone – only unformed minds, long-time Streak freaks, or the newly-dead. It could whisper, influence, mislead, work on weaknesses, but couldn't just move in and take over.

Richard sensed the thing's formless anger.

Then Vanessa, standing quietly a dozen feet away, was tagged and was "it" again. She ran, hopping past Annette, leap-frogging Harry, and soared at Richard, in defiance of gravity, a living missile.

Vanessa's head collided with Richard's stomach, and he was knocked over.

She snatched the celluloid from his pocket, and – with a girlish whoop of nasty triumph – was out of the carriage.

He heard her laugh dwindle as she got further away.

Harry stood, brushing a blood-smear on his jacket. He'd dropped one of the guns, but had the other under his arm. He flapped his wrung-out hand, still jarred from the discharge. The thumb, broken or dislocated, kinked stiffly.

Another person lumbered into the dining carriage, bulky in shawls, thick-ankled. Richard thought for a moment it was Mrs Sweet come to complain about the ill-treatment of her precious guns, but it was the old dear last seen at Euston. "Elsa Nickles, Missus, Psychic Medium."

Mrs Nickles eased past Arnold, who didn't tell her she was out of her class. She looked at the bloody ruins, the dead woman, the mad people.

"I knew no good would come of this," she said. "Them spirits is angered, *furious*. You can't be doin' anythin' wiv 'em when they're stirred up. Might just as well poke an umbrella into a nest of snakes. Or stick your dickybird in a mincer."

Mentally, Richard told Harry not to shoot the woman.

He could tell the Most Valued Member was thinking of it. Firing guns was addictive. The first time, you were afraid, worried about the noise, the danger, the mess. Then, you wanted to do it again. You wanted to do it *better*.

Didn't matter if it your finger was on the trigger of a .22 bird-blaster or the launch button of an Intercontinental Ballistic Missile, the principle was the same. Didn't even matter what you were aiming at. Pull . . . point and press! *Ka-pow*!

"Listen to her, Harry," he said.

Harry didn't know what Richard meant. Why should he pay attention to some unscientific loon? In Harry Cutley's parapsychology, cranks like Elsa Nickles were the enemy, dragging the field into disreputability, filler for the Sunday papers.

"Listen to her accent," Richard insisted.

"Oi don't know what 'e means," said Mrs Nickles, indignant.

Class solidarity in Harry. If Richard's manner got his back up, Elsie's plain talk – even when spouting nonsense – should soothe him. Of course, she was from London and he was a Northerner. He might hate her just for being Southern, in which case Richard would give up and let the world hang itself.

Harry put the gun down and held up his wonky thumb.

"Cor, that's shockin'," said Mrs Nickles. "Let me 'ave a butcher's. Raised seven kids an' never seen one of 'em do that to thesselves."

Harry let the woman examine his hand. She thought for a moment, then took a firm grip on the twisted digit and tugged it into place. Harry yelped, swore, but then flexed his thumb and blurted gratitude.

"That's better," said Mrs Nickles.

The pain had cleared Harry's mind, Richard hoped.

"We've met the thing behind the haunting," he told the Most Valued Member. "It was hiding in the little girl. It tried to possess you, but you fought it off. Do you remember?"

Harry nodded, grimly.

"Continue with the report, Jeperson," he said.

"It's some sort of discarnate entity . . ."

"A wicked spirit," said Mrs Nickles. "A frightful fiend."

"Not a ghost. Not the remnant of a human personality. Something bigger, nastier, more primal. But clever. It plucks things from inside you. It understands who we are, how we can be got at. It's simple, though. It does violence. That's its business. Feeds off pain, I think. Call it 'the Gecko'. When it's in people, they move in a lizardy way. Maybe it nestles in that reptile part of the brain, pulls nerve-strings from there. Or maybe it knows we don't like creepy-crawlies and puts on a horror show."

"'The Gecko'," said Harry, trying out the name. "I'll make a note of that. You found it, Jeperson. You're entitled to name it."

"Thank you."

"Now we know what we're up against, we should be better able to cage it. I'll write up the findings and, after a decent interval, we can come back with a larger, more specialist group. We can get your Gecko off the Ghost Train into a spirit box. In captivity, it can be properly studied."

Richard knew a spirit box wasn't necessarily of wood or metal. If 'sealed' properly, a little girl could be a spirit box.

Looking at Annette, who'd rolled under a table, Richard said, "If it's all the same, Harry, I'd rather kill it than catch it."

"We can still learn, Jeperson. How to deal with the *next* Gecko."

"Let's cope with this one first."

Richard's attention was called by the train's rattle. Something had changed.

A whistle-blast sounded. Had there been another ellipsis in time?

"Are we there yet?" asked Harry. "Portnacreirann?"

"Oh no, sir," said Arnold, who still didn't acknowledge anything unusual. "We're slowing to cross Inverdeith Bridge."

Richard felt the pace of the rattle.

"We're not slowing," he said. "We're speeding up."

IV

"It was on a night like this, in 1931," said Mrs Nickles, "Inverdeith Bridge fell . . ."

Richard understood why the Gecko had killed Annette. She'd have seen what was coming next.

"We're in no position to make a report and act later," he told Harry. "The Gecko's going to kill us *now*. It has what it wants."

Harry and Mrs Nickles both looked puzzled.

Richard had a familiar sensation, of *knowing* more than others, of the power that came with intuition. It was warm, seductive, pleasant – he had the urge to flirt with revelation, to hint that he was privy to mysteries beyond normal comprehension, to crow over his elders. No, that was a temptation – had it been left there to dangle by the Gecko, or some other "wicked spirit"? Or was it nestled in the reptile remnant of his own brain, a character trait he should keep in check?

"The Go-Codes," he said. "It has the number-strings."

Mrs Nickles nodded, as if she understood – Richard knew she was faking, just to stay in the game. Harry was white, genuinely understanding.

"It was lunacy to send the damned things by train," said Harry. "Ed advised against it, but the Club was overruled. By the *Americans*. Bloody Yanks."

"Bloody us too, though," said Richard. "This might have happened eventually, but it happened tonight because we were aboard. We *pushed* the Gecko. Which is what it wants. Us extraordinary people. We notice things, but things notice us too. We give it more fuel. If regular folks are lumps of coal, we're gallons of jet fuel. Annette, Danny, you, me."

"Not me," said Harry.

Richard shrugged, "Maybe not."

"But her?"

Harry looked at Elsa Nickles.

Richard did too, for the first time really. Psychic Medium. A Talent. But she had something else. Knowledge.

"Why are you on the Streak, Mrs Nickles?" he asked.

"I told you. To 'elp the good spirits and chase off the wicked."

"Fair enough. But there are many haunted places. Ruins you don't have to buy a ticket for. Why the Scotch Streak?"

She didn't want to explain. Harry helped her sit down in a booth. Arnold was eager to fetch her something.

"Gin and tonic, luv," she said.

The conductor busied himself. Richard hoped the Gecko hadn't left something in Arnold, to spy on them.

The whole carriage shook, from the speed. Crockery, cutlery, roses, anything not held down, bounced, slid, shifted. Air streamed through the hole in the roof, blasting tablecloths into screwed-up shrouds.

Arnold returned, dignified as a silent movie comedian before a pratfall, drink balanced on a tray balanced on his hand. Mrs Nickles drained the G and T.

"Hits the spot," she said.

"Why . . . this . . . train?" Richard asked.

"Because they're 'ere, still. Both of 'em. They're not what you call 'the Gecko', but they made it grow. What they did, what they didn't do, what they felt. That, and all the passengers who drownded. And all who come after, who were took by the train, bled their spirits into it. That's your blessed Gecko, all them spirits mixed up together and shook. It weren't born in 'ell. It were made. On the night when the bridge fell. Somethin' in the loch woke up, latched onto 'em."

"Them? Who do you mean?"

"Nick and Don," she said, a tear dribbling. "Me 'usband and . . . well, not me 'usband."

"Nick . . . Nickles?"

"Nickles is what you call me pseudernym, ducks. It's Elsa Bowler, really. I was married to Nick Bowler."

"The Headless Fireman," said Harry, snapping his fingers.

Mrs Nickles grimaced as about to collapse in sobs. The reminder of her husband's suicide was hardly tactful.

"Don would be the driver, Donald McRidley?" he prompted.

Arnold almost crossed himself at that disgraced name. The conductor fit into this story somewhere. He looked at Mrs Nickles as if he were a human being with real feelings, rather than an emotionless, efficient messenger of the railway Gods.

"Donald," spat Mrs Nickles. "Yes, blast 'is 'ide. The Shaggin' Scot, they used to call him. The girls in the canteen. We were all on the railways, on the LSIR. I was there when they named the Scotch Streak, serving drinks. I was Assistant Manager of the Staff Canteen in '31. Up the end of the line, in Portnacreirann. Don and Nick weren't usually on shift together, but someone was off sick. They were both speedin' towards me that night. I think it came out, while they were togevver in the cabin. About me. The bridge was comin' down, no matter what. But somethin' was goin' on in between Don and Nick. Afterwards, Don scarpered and Nick . . . well, Nick did what he did, poor lamb. So we'll never know. Don was a right basket. Don't know how I got in with him, though I was a stupid tart in them days and no mistake. Don weren't the only bloke who wasn't me 'usband. Even after all the mess. If you want to call anyone the Gecko's Mum, it's me."

"The driver and the fireman were arguing? Over you?"

Mrs Nickles nodded. Her false teeth jounced, distorting her mouth. Richard's fillings shook. Harry's face rippled. It was as if the Streak were breaking the sound barrier.

The train was going too fast!

"What about the uncoupling?"

"*That*! No human hand did that. It was your Gecko, come out of the loch and the fires in the 'earts of Don and Nick, reachin' out, like a baby after a first suck of milk. It killed all them passengers, let the carriages loose to go down with the bridge. That was a big meal for it, best it's ever had, gave it strength to live through its first hours. I've lost three kiddies, in hospital. That happened in them days. All the bloody time. One was Don's, I reckon. That little mite's in the Gecko too. It sucked in all the bad feelin', all the spirits, and it's still suckin'."

Richard understood.

But he saw where Mrs Nickles was lying. "No human hand." Maybe the Gecko was *partly* poltergeist. Using the shake, rattle and rock of the train to *nudge* inanimate objects. The piano-lid snapping at Danny was classic polter-pestering. But for the big things, the fork-stabbings and grabbing the Go-Codes, it needed human hands, a host, a body or bodies.

"It was both of them," he said. "It took them both. It made them do it, made them uncouple the train."

He *saw* it, vividly. Two men, in vintage LSIR uniform, crawling past the coal-tender, leaving the cabin unmanned, gripping like lizards, inhumanly tenacious. Four hands on the coupling, tugging the stiff lever which ought not be thrown while the train was in motion, disabling the inhibitor devices that should prevent this very act. Hands bleeding and nails torn, the hosts' pain receptors shut off by the new-made, already cunning, already murderous Gecko.

The coupling unlatched. A gap growing. Between engine and carriages. The awful noise of the bridge giving way. The train screaming as it plunged. Carriages coming apart among clanging girders and rails. Bursts of instantly-extinguished flame. Sparks falling to black waters. Breaking waves on the loch shores.

An outpouring of shock and agony. Gecko food.

"Jeperson," said Harry, snapping his fingers in front of his nose.

"I know what it did," he told the Most Valued Member. "What it wants to do. How it plans to do it. Another Inverdeith disaster, all of our deaths, and it can *get off the train*. Free of the iron of the Scotch Streak, it'll be strong enough to possess living, grown-up bodies. It can piggyback, get to the base, play pass the parcel between hosts, handing the Go-Codes on to itself. It can sit at a modified typewriter keyboard and use the numbers. It's a hophead, needing bigger and bigger fixes. The deaths of dozens don't cut it any more, so it needs to shoot up World War Three!"

Harry swore.

"We've got to stop the little girl," said Richard. "Pass me that shotgun."

V

At the connecting door, ready to barge after the Gecko, Richard caught himself.

"Fooled me once, shame on you, fooled me twice, shame on me."

He turned and walked deliberately to the other end of the dining carriage, past Harry, Mrs Nickles and Arnold.

"That's the wrong way, Jeperson."

"Is it?"

"I came from that way. Back there is, ah, Second and Third Class. And the baggage car."

Harry held up the other shotgun, left-handed.

"Things change. Haven't you noticed?"

Harry wasn't stupid or inexperienced. "Dislocation phenomena? Escher space?"

"Topsy-turvy," Richard said.

"How do you know the configuration won't switch back? The Gecko could keep us off balance, charging back and forth, always the wrong way? At Wroxley Parsonage in '52, there was a corridor like that, a man-trap. The MVM before me lost two of his group in it."

Jeperson was given pause.

He looked up through the hole in the ceiling, at telephone wires, clouds, the sky. He could tell which way the train was travelling but lost that certainty if he stepped too far away from the hole. The windows were no help. They might have been painted over or gooed on. A rifle-stock blow rattled but did not break the glass.

"There's a spirit 'ere 'oo wants to speak," said Mrs Nickles.

Harry was impatient. "There are too many spirits here."

"This is a new one, mate. I'm getting' . . . ah . . . fingers?"

"Magic Fingers?" said Harry, suddenly taking the woman seriously. "Danny Myles? What's happened to him?"

"Lost, Harry," said Richard. This was news to the Most Valued Member.

"Damn."

"'E says, don't think, *feel* . . . Does that make sense?"

To Richard, it did. He shut his eyes and in the dark inside his head sensed Danny, or something left behind by Danny. He stopped trying to work out which way the train was speeding, just let his body become aware of the movement, the rattle, the shifting. He had little thrills, like tugging hooks or pointing arrows.

"Spin me round," he said.

"Like the party game?" asked Mrs Nickles.

He nodded. Big hands took him and spun him. He went up on the points of his shoes, remembering two weeks of ballet training, and revolved like a human top.

He came to a stop without falling.

He knew which way to charge and did so, opening his eyes on the way. He didn't even know which end of the carriage he was exiting from. He opened the communication door and plunged on, as if Mrs Sweet's gun were a divining rod.

The others followed.

VI

Richard knew Danny was tied here, along with many others. Magic Fingers was fresh enough to have some independence, but soon he'd be sucked in and become another head of a collective pain-eating hydra. The Scotch Streak was home to a Bad Thing. Haunting a house, or a lonely road or public toilet or whatever, seldom meant more than floating sheets or clammy invisible touches. The worst haunters, the Bad Things, were monsters with *ambition*. They wanted to be free of the anchors that kept them earth-bound, not to ascend to a higher sphere or rest in peace or go into the light . . . but to wreak harm. Plague-and-Great-Fire-of-London harm. Japanese Radioactive Dinosaur Movie harm. End of all Things harm.

He was in a carriage he hadn't seen before but didn't doubt he was on the track of the Gecko.

There were no windows, not even black glass. Hunting trophies on shields – antlers and heads of antlered animals – stuck out of panelled walls, protruding as if bone were growing like wood, making the aisle as difficult to penetrate as a thick thorn forest. There were rhino-horns and elephant tusks, even what looked like a sabre-tooth tiger-head with still-angry eyes. Low-slung leather armchairs were spaced at intervals, between foot-high side-tables where dust-filled brandy snifter glasses were abandoned next to ashtrays with fat cigar grooves. Potent, manly musk stung Richard's nostrils.

"What's this?" he asked Arnold, appalled.

"The Club Car, sir. Reserved for friends of the Director, Lord Kilpartinger. It's not usually part of the rolling stock."

In one chair slumped a whiskered skeleton wearing a bullet-bandoleer, Sam Browne belt and puttees. It gripped a rifle-barrel with both hands, a loose toe-bone stuck in the trigger-guard, gun-mouth jammed between blasted-wide skull-jaws, the cranium exploded away.

"Any idea who that was?" Richard.

"He's in Catriona's pamphlet," put in Harry. " 'Basher' Moran, 1935. Some aged, leftover Victorian Colonel. Big-game hunter and gambling fiend. Stalked anything and everything, put holes in it and dragged hide, head or horns home to stick on the wall. Mixed up in extensive crookery, according to Catriona, wriggled out of a hanging more than once. He's here because he won his final bet. One of his jolly old pals wagered he couldn't find anything in the world he hadn't shot before. He proved his friend wrong, there and then."

An upturned pith helmet several feet away contained bone and dum-dum fragments.

"Case closed."

"Too true. They made a film about Moran and the train, *Terror by Night*."

Richard advanced carefully, between trophies, tapping too-persistent horns out of the way with the gun-barrel.

"Could do with a machete," he commented. "Careful of barbs."

The train took a series of snake-curve turns, swinging alarmingly from side to side. A narwhal horn dimpled Richard's velvet shoulder.

Richard heard Harry *ouch* as he speared himself on an antler-point.

"Just a scratch," he reported. "Doesn't hurt as much as my bloody hand."

"Shouldn't ought to be allowed," said Mrs Nickles. "Shootin' poor animals as never did no-one no harm."

"I rather agree with you," said Richard. "Hunting should be saved for man-killers."

Gingerly, they got through the club car without further casualties.

The next carriage was the dining car, again. Harry wanted to give up, but Richard pressed on.

"Table-settings here are the other way round," he said. "It's not the same."

"There ain't no bleedin' great 'ole in the roof neither," observed Mrs Nickles.

"That too."

"We shall be pleased to serve a light breakfast after Inverdeith," announced Arnold. "For those who wish to arrive at Portnacreirann refreshed and invigorated."

"Kippers later," said Richard. "After the world-saving."

Beyond this dining car was First Class. Richard led them past the sleeping compartments. Annette's door hung open: her night-gown was laid out on the counterpane, like a cast-off silk snakeskin. That was a thump to the heart.

The decoy couriers snored away. No need to bother them.

Another expedition was coming down the corridor towards them. Were they so turned around in time they were running into themselves? Or had evil duplicate ghost-finders emerged from the wrong-way-round dimension where knives and forks were right-to-left? No, there was a mirror at the end of the corridor. Score one for eliminating the impossible.

"Where's the connecting door?" Richard asked the Conductor.

"There's no need for one, sir," said Arnold. "Beyond is only the coal tender, and the locomotive. Passengers may not pass beyond this point."

The Gecko had managed, though.

One of the doors flapped, swinging open, banging back. Cold air streamed in, like water through a salmon's gills.

Richard pushed the door and leaned out of the carriage, keeping a firm grip on the frame.

Below, a gravel verge sped by. To the East, the scarlet rim of dawn outlined a black horizon. Up ahead, 3473-S rolled over the rails, pistons pumping, everything oiled and watered and fired.

An iron girder came up, horribly fast. Richard ducked back in.

"We're on the bridge," he said.

Before anyone could object, if they were going to, he threw himself out of the door.

VII

Clinging to the side of the carriage, it occurred to Richard that someone else might have volunteered to crawl – essentially one-handed, since shotguns don't have useful shoulder-slinging straps like field-rifles – along the side of a speeding steam train.

Harry had seniority and responsibility, but his injured hand disqualified him. Mrs Nickles was too hefty, overage and a woman besides. And the conductor was not entirely of their party. The Gecko had fit into him much too snugly. There was more mystery to

Arnold – a streak of sneakiness, of evasion, of tragedy. Richard had noticed a spark in his mild eyes as Mrs Nickles was talking about the good old days of the LSIR, about the Shagging Scot and the Headless Fireman and the In-for-Death Run of '31.

So, the train-crawling was down to him.

Once he'd swung out on the door, he eased himself around so he was hanging outside the train, blasted by the air-rush, deafened by the roar. About eight feet of carriage was left before the coupling. That was a mystery – a compartment not accessible to the passengers. No, it wasn't a mystery – it was a toilet and washroom for the driver and the fireman, reachable by a wide, safe running-board along the side of the coal tender, with guard-rails and hand-holds he would just now have greatly appreciated on *this* carriage.

Above him, however, were loops of red chain – the communication cord. Richard grabbed a loop and held tight. The whistle shrilled over the din of the train. Cold chain bit into his palm. He should have put gloves on.

He dangled one-handed, trusting the chain to take his weight, back against the carriage, and saw glints on the dark waters of Loch Gaer several hundred feet below. Down there were the angry spirits of Jock McGaer's "graysome" dinners, the drowned Inverdeith Witches and the cut-loose passengers of '31 – they must all be wrapped up in the Gecko too. Not to mention the "stoon o' fire spat out frae hell" of 1601. This had all started with that.

The flimsy-seeming bridge, he reminded himself, was the sturdy structure put up to *replace* the one that fell down. Girders flashed past, faster and faster. He used the stock of the gun to push himself along, and the barrel caught on a girder. The gun was wrenched out of his hand, twisted into a U-shape, and dropped into the loch. Mrs Sweet had made a special point of telling Arnold to look after her artillery. A stiff complaint would be made to British Rail in the next day or two, providing there *was* a next day or two.

With both hands free, it was easier to travel from loop to loop. He'd think about how to deal with the Gecko without a weapon when he got to it. A sound rap on the nose didn't seem likely to do the trick.

The door clanged shut behind him. Harry and Mrs Nickles hung out of the open window, fixed expressions of encouragement plastered on anxious faces.

He fought the harsh wind, cruel gravity, hot spits of steam and cinder, and his own clumsiness. Something shaped like a little girl had done this earlier, he knew. The Gecko could probably stick to the side of the train, like a real lizard.

Eight feet. A hard eight feet. The skirts of his frock coat lashed his thighs. He had no feeling in his hands, but blood dripped from weals across his palms. He reached out for the next loop, the last, and his fist closed on nothing, then locked. He had to force his hand open and look up, hooking nerveless, perhaps boneless fingers over the loop. He saw his grip, but couldn't feel it. He didn't want to let go of the hold he was sure of. But if he didn't, he was stuck. He reached out his leg, which didn't quite stretch enough to hook over the guard-rail. His boot-sole scraped tarnished brass. His cuff was sodden with his own blood. With a prayer to higher powers, he let go the sure hold, put all his weight on the unsure one, and swung towards the platform.

He made it and found his feet on a veranda-like platform at the end of the carriage. He shook with fear and weakness and relief. Feeling came back, unwelcome, to his bloodied hand.

Between the carriage and the locomotive was the big, heavy coupling. Black iron thickened with soot and grease.

On the coupling squatted the Gecko. Only the braids and oily pyjamas even suggested this was still Vanessa. It was goblin filth on a poison toadstool, a gremlin dismantling an aero-engine in flight, the imp in Fuseli's Nightmare hovering over a sleeping maiden.

With stubby-fingered, black hands, it picked at the coupling.

The Gecko looked up, eyes round, nostrils like slits. It hissed at Richard.

Blasts of steam came, surrounding them both with scalding fog. The whistle shrieked again.

In the coal tender, nearly empty this close to the destination, rolled two bodies, the driver and the engineer. They were sooty, with red torn-out throats. No one was at the open throttle.

Richard shook hot water off his face, which began to sting. He'd be red as a cooked lobster.

He grabbed the Gecko by the shoulders. He held folds of Vanessa's pyjama top and pulled.

It gnawed his wrists.

Things hadn't all gone the monster's way. In 1931, it had unhooked the coupling at this point on the bridge. Now, it was using one little girl's hands rather than two experienced men's. The Gecko could give its hosts strengths, ignore their injuries, distort their faces . . . but it couldn't increase a hand-span, or make tiny fingers work big catches.

The Gecko tried to take Richard and he shrugged it off.

They were more than halfway across the bridge.

"No room here," he told it. "No room anywhere for you. Why not quit?"

Vanessa slumped in his grip, hands relaxing on the coupling. Richard picked her up, pressed her face to his chest.

"Can't breathe," she said, in her own voice.

This was too easy.

In the coal tender, two bodies sat up and began to crawl towards Richard and Vanessa. The Gecko had found experienced railway-men's hands. This was where having a shotgun would have been useful – he doubted he could shoot Vanessa, even if he *had* smashed a plate in her face, but he'd have no compunction about blasting a couple of already dead fellows.

The Gecko had no trouble working both corpses at the same time, which meant there was probably still some of it in the child. It had been hatched in the driver's cabin of 3473, and was at its strongest here.

The fireman threw a lump of coal, which broke against the carriage behind Richard's head. The driver clambered off the tender, down to the coupling platform. There was a lever there, its restraints undone.

The bridge might not come down, but at this speed and gradient the uncoupled carriages would concertina, come off the rails, break through the girders, fall into the loch.

There was a lot of dawnlight in the sky now.

Holding Vanessa close, he felt something in the hankie pocket of her pyjamas. He shifted her weight to his left shoulder, freeing his right hand to pluck out the Go-Codes.

He held the celluloid up in the rush of air, then let it go, snatched away, up and over the lake, sailing towards Inverdeith. One of the most closely-guarded military secrets in the world was tossed into the wind.

"You should have committed the Go-Codes to memory," he told the monster.

The Gecko's corpse puppets opened throats and yelled, like the whistle. Then, the whistle itself sounded. The Gecko wasn't only in the driver and the fireman. It clothed itself in the iron of the locomotive, the brass-trim and scabby purple paint. Its fury burned in the furnace. Its frustration built up a seam-splitting head of steam. Its hunger ate up the rails.

Richard thought he'd saved the world, but not himself.

"What's keeping you here?" he asked.

Dead hands reached the uncoupling lever. Richard slid his cut-throat razor out of his sleeve and flicked it open. He drew the edge swiftly, six or seven times, across greasy, blackened meat, cutting muscle-strings.

The corpse's hands hung useless, fingers flopping against the lever like sausages. The corpse was suddenly untenanted, and crumpled, falling over the coupling, arms dangling.

The Scotch Streak was safely across Inverdeith Bridge.

VIII

The fireman lay dead, empty of the Gecko.

It was just in the train now. The Scotch Streak's lamps glowed a wicked red.

World War III was off, unless the Gecko could somehow let the Soviets know NATO's trousers were down. But everyone on the train could still be killed.

At this speed, slamming into the buffers at Portnacreirann would mean a horrific pile-up. Or the Scotch Streak might plough through the station, and steam down Portnacreirann High Street and over a cliff. Like Colonel Moran, the Gecko was intent on spiteful suicide. It could carry them all with it, in fire and broken metal.

Richard knew Diogenes Club procedure. Solve the problem, no matter the cost. His father had told him from the first this was a life of service, of sacrifice. Every Member, every Talent, gave up something. Danny and Annette weren't the first to lose their lives.

It might be a fair trade.

"Are we nearly there?" Vanessa asked, laying her head on his shoulder. "I'm very sleepy."

He felt the weight of the child in his arms. He had to carry the fight through. For her. He only had a half-life, snatched from a void. He should have been dead many times over. There was a reason he'd survived his childhood. Maybe it was Vanessa. She had to be saved, not sacrificed.

"There's one thing left to do," he told her. "Have you ever wanted to drive a choo-choo train?"

She laughed at him. "Only babies say 'choo-choo'!"

"Chuff-chuff, then."

Vanessa's giggle gave him the boost he needed, though he was still terrified. While facing demon-possessed zombies and nuclear holocaust, he'd misplaced his fear. Now, he was in charge of a runaway train, funk seeped back into his stomach. He found he was trembling.

He set the girl down safely and stepped over the dead driver, climbed the ladder to the coal tender, passed the dead fireman and got to the cabin. The furnace door clanked open. Levers and wheels swayed or rolled with the train's movement.

It occurred to him that he didn't know how to stop a train.

"Can I sound the whistle?" asked Vanessa. She had followed, monkeying over the coal tender, unfazed by dead folk. She found the whistle-pull, easily.

Richard absent-mindedly said she could and looked about for switches with useful labels like PULL TO SLOW DOWN or EMERGENCY BRAKES. He heard the Gecko's chuckle in the roll of coal in the furnace. It knew exactly the pickle he was in.

Vanessa blew the whistle, three long bursts, three short bursts, three long bursts. What every schoolchild knew in Morse code. SOS. Save Our Souls. Help! Mayday. *M'aidez!* Richard wasn't sure she even understood it was a distress signal, it was likely only Morse she knew.

The sun was almost up. The sky was the colour of blood.

Ahead, the rails curved across open space, towards Portnacreirann Station.

"I can see the sea," shouted Vanessa, from her perch.

Richard muttered that they might be making rather too close acquaintance with the sea – rather, Loch Linnhe – in a minute or two.

"Here comes someone," said Vanessa.

More trouble, no doubt! He looked back and couldn't see anything.

He was reluctant to leave the cabin, though he admitted he was useless at the throttle, but surrendered to an impulse. He was sensitive: he should trust his feelings while he had them. He made his way back past the tender.

The door to the staff toilet was open and Arnold stood with a fire-axe. He had smashed through the mirror. Mrs Nickles was behind him. And Harry Cutley. Richard kicked himself for not thinking of that, but hadn't known there was a door beyond the mirrored partition.

Arnold raised the axe and Richard knew the Gecko had its hook in him, had been reeling him in like trout. Mrs Nickles shouted something. They hadn't come in response to the SOS.

Now, in addition to the runaway train, he had an axe-wielding madman to deal with.

Richard dashed back to the cabin. Arnold leaped across the coupling, treading on his dead colleague, and followed.

The conductor was the full Gecko now. Richard had a razor against an axe.

He pulled the first lever that came to hand. Instinct paid off. A burst of steam pushed Arnold back, knocking him to his knees. Richard kicked at the axe-head and wrenched the weapon out of the conductor's hands. He took hold of the man's throat and held up his fist, enjoying the look of inhuman panic – the Gecko in terror! – in Arnold's eyes, then clipped him smartly, bang on the button. This time, fortune was with him. The Gecko's light went out. Arnold slumped in Richard's grip, blood creeping from his nose.

Mrs Nickles had followed Arnold. She clung to the hand-rail.

"It's Donald," she shouted. "Donald McRidley. I didn't recognise the blighter without 'is 'air. 'E were a ruddy woman about his blessed beautiful 'air when 'e were the Shaggin' Scot, an' now e's a bald-bonced old git."

Arnold's – Donald's! – eyes fluttered open.

So, he wasn't a navvy. Or not any more. He was back on his train. Unable to get away, Richard supposed. No wonder.

"Driver," he shouted. "Bring in the Streak!"

"Passengers aren't allowed in this part of the train, sir," he mumbled. "It's against regulations. The company can't be held responsible for accidents."

Richard saw the red glint, the Gecko creeping back. He slapped McRidley, hard. The eyes were clear for a moment.

"Time to stop the train," he told the man. "Do your duty, at last. Redeem your name."

"Do it for Else, ducks," said Mrs Nickles, cooing in McRidley's ear. "Do it for poor Nick. For the LSI-bloody-R."

McRidley broke free of the pair of them.

As if sleepwalking in a hurry, mind somewhere else, he pulled levers, rolled wheels, tapped gauges.

The station was dead ahead, sunlight flashing on its glass roof.

Wheels screamed on rails. Vanessa tooted the whistle, happily.

Harry was with them now, arm in a makeshift sling, hair awry. Every boy wanted to be in the cabin of a steam train.

They all had to hang onto something as McRidley braced himself.

Sparks showered the platform, startling an early-morning porter. The buffers loomed.

They did not crash. But there was a heavy jolt.

IX

Donald McRidley, Arnold the Conductor, was dead. When the train stopped, so did he – like grandfather and the clock in the song.

3473-S was decoupled now and shunted into a siding. The Gecko was still nestled in there, but its conduit to the train, to the passengers, was cut. Richard thought it might have been the communication cord, which had to be unhooked – but the monster had also been tied to the lifeline of the once-disgraced, now-redeemed driver.

"'E were a 'handsome devil," commented Mrs Nickles, putting her teeth back in. "Loved 'is train more than any girl, though."

Harry was on the telephone to Edwin Winthrop. He said the entity was in captivity, but Richard knew the Gecko was dying. As the fire went out in 3473's belly, the monster gasped its last. A bad beast, Danny had called it. The iron shell would just be a trophy. They should hang the cow-catcher in the Diogenes Club.

The decoy couriers were gone, off to the NATO base. Mrs Sweet was marching down to the baggage car, where a surprise awaited. The terrifying vicar looked even more ghastly in the light of day. Richard had brushed past the man several times, mind open for any ill-omen, to convince himself the Gecko wasn't sneaking off in this vessel to work its evil anew.

Police and ambulances were on their way. Edwin would have words in ears, to account for Danny, Annette and the crewmen, not to mention general damage. Richard found Annette rolled under a table, and carried her to her compartment, where he laid her out on her bed, over her night-gown, eyes closed.

A straight-backed American civilian, with teeth like Burt Lancaster and a chin-dent like Kirk Douglas, scouted along the platform.

"Buddy, have you seen a parcel?" he said. "For Coates?"

Richard tried to answer, but no words came.

The American looked further, walking past Vanessa.

Portnacreirann

The train finally came, as Richard finished telling the story.

They had been up all night. Cold Saturday dawn had broken.

Now, they sat in a carriage, not a compartment. Fred settled in, but Richard was restless.

"I used to love trains," he said. "Even after my Ghost Train ride. It was a nice way to travel. You had time and ease, to read or talk or look out the window. Now, it's all strikes and delays. This might as well be a motor-coach. *She* hates trains, you know. Mrs Thatcher. To her, anyone who travels on public transport is a failure, beneath contempt. She's going to bleed the railways. It'll be horrid. Like so much else."

Fred still had questions.

"So, guv, who *is* Vanessa?"

Richard shrugged. "Vanessa is Vanessa, Fred. Like me, she's no real memory of who she was, if she was anyone. In my case, there was a war, a decade of chaos. It was easy to get misplaced, left out of the records. With her . . . well, it shouldn't have been possible. Someone dropped her off at Euston with a label round her neck. A woman, she thought, but not her mother. Surely, she couldn't be a stray, she must belong to someone?"

"What about that Coates bloke? The Yank at Portnacreirann."

"That wasn't 'Lieutenant Commander Alexander Coates, RN'. That was a Colonel Christopher Conner, SAC 'Coates' wasn't an alias or a code – just a name on a label. Winthrop made enquiries. The only 'Alexander Coates' even remotely in the Navy was a 14-year-old sea-scout. We looked into the system of couriering the Go-Codes. The Americans had only given us the cover story even when they'd wanted help, so we threw a bit of a sulk. They eventually admitted – and this is how strange defence policy is – that they had, as they said, 'contracted out'. Hired a private firm to make delivery, not telling them what was being carried. The firm turned out to be a phone in an empty room with six weeks' rent in arrears. Maybe some semi-crook was hauling kids out of orphanages and bundling them up to Scotland under official cover, then selling them on or disposing of them. We'll never know and, in the end, it was beside the point."

"You *adopted* Vanessa?"

"No. No one adopted her, unless you count the Diogenes Club."

"Does she *have* a surname?"

"Not really. Where it's absolutely necessary, it's 'Kaye'. Catriona took an interest, as she did in me. Without her, we'd be complete freaks."

Fred kept quiet on that one.

"What about the Gecko? Harry Cutley?"

"The Gecko died, if it could be said to have lived. When 3473-S turned into cold scrap iron, it was gone. Puff. Harry poked around with his instruments before giving up. For a year or two, another old steamer pulled the Scotch Streak. Then it went diesel. Harry dropped out in 1967. Went to Nepal. And I became the Most Valued Member. There's a ceremony. Very arcane. Like the Masons. You know most of what's happened since."

Fred thought it through.

He did know most of the stories, but not all. Despite ten years' involvement with the Diogenes Club, with Richard and Vanessa, there were mysteries. They could both still surprise him. Once, in a close, tense, unexpected moment, before Fred met Zarana, he and Vanessa had kissed, deeply and urgently. She said, "You do know I'm a man," and, for dizzying seconds, he had believed her. Then she giggled, they were back in danger, and anything further between them cut off.

After a decade, he still didn't know if Richard and Vanessa had ever been a couple. Everyone else assumed, but he didn't. Now, knowing about the Ghost Train, he saw how complex their entanglement was: a kinship of siblings, raised under the aegis of a unique institution, but also guardianship, as Richard brought Vanessa into the circle the way his adoptive father had brought him. The only thing he really *knew* now that had been mystifying before was how Vanessa had got her eyebrow scar. Richard had given it to her.

Lately, Vanessa had been absent a great deal. So had Fred, of course – with Zarana, or at the Yard. But Vanessa had been on missions, cases, sealed-knot and under-the-rose business. A change was coming in the Club – when Richard took a seat on the Cabal, as seemed inevitable, Vanessa was in line to become Most Valued Member? There was a woman Prime Minister, so no reason why a woman couldn't hold that title. If she wanted it – which, Fred realised, he didn't know she did.

For three months, there'd been no word. While Richard and Fred were tracking cornflakes cultists, she was somewhere else, unavailable. Fred could tell Richard was concerned, though confident in the woman. She'd survived a lot since throwing off the Gecko. Now, this summons.

. . . to Portnacreirann.

"It's not over, is it?" said Fred. "It can't be coincidence that it's the same place."

Richard gave a non-committal *pfui*.

"We're at Inverdeith," he said. "And that's a Portnacreirann train on the other side of the platform."

They were off one train before it had completely stopped and on another already moving out.

And then Inverdeith Bridge. Sun glinted on the surface of Loch Gaer.

"This is where the Gecko was born," said Richard. "Between Nick Bowler and Donald McRidley and 3473-S. And that 'stoon o' fire spat out frae hell', if I'm any judge – which I am. The stoon was an egg, waiting for the right circumstances to hatch. All the other bloody business around the loch was influenced by the unborn thing. Maybe it was an alien, not a demon. The stoon was what we'd now call a meteorite, after all. From outer space. Witch-drownings and human haggis kept the embryo on a drip-feed for centuries, but it awaited a vehicle – literally. The shell-shards might still be down there. Maybe it was a clutch of eggs."

Fred looked at untroubled waters. This local train proceeded slowly over the bridge. He saw rust on the girders where paint had flaked away, missing rivets, spray-can INDEPENDENT SCOTLAND graffiti, scratched swear-words.

"In-for-Death," he said.

"Think calm thoughts, Frederick. And we'll be safe."

This was where it had happened. With that thought, Fred had a chill. He didn't only mean this was where the Gecko was born and defeated, but this was where *Richard and Vanessa* had started. When Richard got on the Ghost Train, he'd been a kid himself. When he got off . . .

Past the bridge, with Portnacreirann in sight and passengers taking luggage down from overhead racks, Fred's insides went tight. They had been delayed. What if they were too late? What was so urgent anyway? He had learned to be ready for anything. But what kind of anything was there at Portnacreirann?

"Did you bring your elephant gun, guv?"

Richard snorted at that.

They got off the train, carrying their bags.

They walked along the platform and into the station. It was busier than Culler's Halt, but emptied quickly.

A centrepiece of the station was an old steam engine, restored and polished, with a plaque and a little fence around it.

Richard froze. It was 3473-S, the locomotive that had pulled the Scotch Streak, the Ghost Train, the favoured physical form of the Gecko. Now, it was just a relic. No danger at all. A youth in naval dress uniform admired it. He turned and saw them.

"Mr Jeperson, Mr Regent," he said. "Glad you made it in time. Cutting it close, but we'll get you to the base by breaking petty road safety laws. Come on."

The officer trotted out of the station. Fred and Richard followed, without further thought for 3473-S.

A jeep and driver waited on the forecourt. The officer helped them up. Fred had a pang at being treated as if he were elderly when he was only just used to thinking of himself as "early middle aged". It happened more and more lately.

"I'm Jim," said the boy in uniform. "Al's cousin. We're a navy family. Put down for ships at birth like some brats are for schools. In the sea-scouts as soon as we're teething. I hope your lady knows what she's getting into."

Fred and Richard looked at each other, not saying anything.

"We all think she's rather super, you know. For her age."

"We admire her qualities, too," said Richard.

Fred had a brief fantasy of tossing Jim out of the jeep to watch him bounce on the road.

They travelled at speed down a winding lane. Three cyclists with beards and cagoules pedalling the other way wound up tangled in the verge, shaking fists as Jim blithely shouted out "sorry" at them. "Naval emergency," he explained, though they couldn't hear.

Whatever trouble Vanessa was in, Fred was ready to fight.

The jeep roared through a checkpoint. The ratings on duty barely lifted the barrier in time. Jim waved a pass at them, redundantly.

They were on the base.

It had been a fishing village once, Fred saw – the rows of stone cottages were old and distinctive. Prefab services buildings fit in around the original community. The submarine-launched "independent deterrent" was a Royal Navy show now. NATO – i.e. the Yanks – preferred intercontinental ballistic missiles they could lob at the Soviets from their own backyards in Kansas, or bombs dropped from the planes that could be scrambled from the pro-testor-fringed base at Greenham Common. There would still be Go-Codes, though.

The base was on alert. Sailors with guns rushed about. There were rumours of trouble in the South Atlantic. Naval budget cuts had withdrawn forces from the region so suddenly that a South American country, say Argentina, could easily get the wrong idea. It might be time to send a gun-boat to remind potential invaders that the Falk-lands remained British. If there were any gun-boats left.

The jeep did a tight turn to a halt, scattering gravel in front of a small building. Once the village church, it was now the base chapel.

"Just in time," said Jim, jumping down.

He opened the big door tactfully, so as not to disturb a service inside, and signalled for Fred and Richard to *yomp* in after him.

Fred remembered Richard leading him into a deconsecrated church at dead of midnight to stop a then-cabinet minister intent on slitting the throat of a virgin choirboy in a ritual supposed to revive the British moulded plastics industry. The Minister was resigned through ill-health and packed off to the House of Lords to do no further harm. The choirboy was now in the pop charts dressed as a pirate, singing as if his throat really had been cut. This wasn't like that, but a ritual was in progress.

No one in the congregation gave the newcomers a glance. Jim led Fred and Richard to places in a pew on the bride's side of the church. They found themselves sitting next to Catriona Kaye, and her nurse. All the others from her day – Edwin, Sir Giles – were gone. Barbara Corri was here too, in a cloud of *ylang-ylang* with her hair done like Lady Diana Spencer's. Even Inspector Price of the Yard, sporting a smart new mac. Fred looked around, knowing the other shoe would drop. Yes, Zarana, in some incredible dress, was at the front, clicking away with a spy camera lifted from Fred's stash of surveillance equipment.

"We got telegrams," whispered Professor Corri, fingers around Richard's arm.

Vanessa stood at the altar, red hair pinned up under the veil, in a white dress with a train. Beside her stood a navy officer Fred had never seen before. He couldn't focus on the groom's face for the glare of his uniform. He even had the dress-sword on his belt and plumed helmet under his arm.

"How did this happen?" Fred asked, to no one in particular.

"A loose end, long neglected," whispered Catriona. "Not that it explains *anything* . . ."

She dabbed a hankie to the corner of her eye.

Fred looked at Richard. The man was crying and Fred had absolutely no idea what he was feeling.

Fred looked at the altar, at the naval chaplain.

". . . Do you, Alexander Selkirk Coates take this woman, Vanessa, ah, No Surname Given, to be your lawfully wedded wife . . ."

Fred looked up at the vaulted ceiling, gob-smacked.

STEPHEN JONES
& KIM NEWMAN

Necrology: 2006

AS ALWAYS, we acknowledge the passing of writers, artists, performers and technicians who, during their lifetimes, made significant contributions to the horror, science fiction and fantasy genres (or left their mark on popular culture and music in other, often fascinating, ways) . . .

AUTHORS/ARTISTS/COMPOSERS

American TV scriptwriter **Arthur Browne, Jr** died on January 3rd, aged 82. Although best known for his Western credits, he also wrote episodes of *Voyage to the Bottom of the Sea*, *The Incredible Hulk* and *Planet of the Apes*, along with the Elvis Presley movie *Clambake*.

Playboy cartoonist **Eldon Dedini**, whose work was set in a world of nymphs and satyrs since the early 1960s, died of oesophageal cancer on January 12th, aged 84. He also worked for *Esquire*, *The New Yorker*, Universal Studios and Disney (where his credits include *Mickey and the Beanstalk*).

Prolific British children's book author **Jan Mark** (Janet Marjorie Brisland) died on January 15th, aged 62. A two-time winner of the Carnegie Medal, her short supernatural stories are collected in *Nothing to Be Afraid Of* and *In Black and White*, while her SF titles include *The Ennead*, its sequel *Divide and Rule*, *Aquarius*, *They Do Things Differently There*, *The Sighting* and *Riding Tycho*. In 1993 she edited *The Oxford Book of Chldren's Stories*.

British illustrator **John Stewart** died of liver failure in London's St. Thomas Hospital on January 18th. He was in his late fifties and had been ill for some time. During the 1970s and '80s he contributed to such small press magazines as *Whispers* and *Fantasy Tales*, producing a number of portfolios for the former (including one for the special Stephen King issue, inspired by *The Gunslinger*) and illustrating Clive Barker's story "The Forbidden" for the latter (later included in the anthology *The Best Horror from Fantasy Tales*). Stewart also illustrated the 1978 Whispers Press edition of Robert Bloch's Cthulhu Mythos novel *Strange Eons*, Michael Shea's 1987 collection *Polyphemus* for Arkham House, and contributed artwork to many European paperback books, including the 1982 Dutch anthology *Shangri-La*. More recently, Jerad Walters published an extensive retrospective of Stewart's art in the hardcover magazine *Chimera*, from Centipede Press. During the late 1980s to the mid-'90s, he was in a detox programme for drug and alcohol abuse, and it was during this period that a fire in his apartment reportedly destroyed much of his book collection and original artwork.

English-born animator and director **Norm McCabe** died the same day, aged 94. He began working at Warner Bros. in the mid-1930s, where his credits include a number of *Porky Pig* and *Daffy Duck* cartoons. He later contributed to such TV series and specials as *The Superman/Aquaman Hour*, *The Batman/Superman Hour*, *The Plastic Man Comedy/Adventure Show*, *The Grinch Grinches the Cat in the Hat*, *Daffy Duck's Movie: Fantastic Island*, *The Duxorcist*, *The Night of the Living Duck* and *Daffy Duck's Quackbusters*. McCabe's other credits include *Fritz the Cat* and *Transformers: The Movie*.

33-year-old American comic book artist **Seth Fisher** died on January 30th after falling seven stories from a roof in his adopted homeland of Japan. His credits include DC Comics' *Green Lantern: Willworld*, the Eisner Award-nominated *Flash: Time Flies*, *Batman: Snow*, and Marvel's *Fantastic Four/Iron Man: Big in Japan*.

British crime writer, actor and broadcaster **Ernest Dudley** (Vivian Ernest Coltman Allen), who created sinister BBC Radio detective "Dr. Morelle" in 1942, died on February 1st, aged 97. The character, inspired by Erich von Stroheim, who Dudley had met in Paris in the 1930s, was originally played by Cecil Parker. The 1949 Hammer film *The Case of the Missing Heiress* featured Valentine Dyall as Morelle, and Dudley himself portrayed the role in a 1951 film adaptation.

Veteran animator and illustrator **Myron Waldman** died of congestive heart failure on February 4th, aged 97. He was the last surviving animator from the Max Fleischer Studios, which he joined in 1930. There he helped develop such characters as Betty Boop (who started out as a dog), Popeye, Superman, Raggedy Ann, Baby Huey, Herman, Little Lulu and Casper the Friendly Ghost. In 1934 he began producing a number of "Color Classics" cartoons in response to Disney's series of "Silly Symphonies". He left the company in 1957 and moved to television (*Milton the Monster* and *Batfink*), before later touring on the lecture circuit.

The body of 76-year-old American TV writer and director **Alan Shalleck**, who collaborated with co-creator Margaret Rey to bring the *Curious George* series to the Disney Channel as more than 100 five-minute shorts, was found in Florida on February 7th. Two men were charged with his murder. Shalleck and Rey (who died in 1996) also collaborated on more that two dozen further books about the mischievous monkey after the death of artist H. A. Rey in 1977.

91-year-old Japanese composer **Akira Ifukube**, best known for his iconic *Godzilla* theme, died of multiple organ failure in Tokyo on February 8th. He later scored many other films in Toho's "Godzilla" series, along with such titles as *Rodan!*, *The Mysterians*, *Battle in Outer Space*, *Atragon*, *Dagora the Space Monster*, *Frankenstein Conquers the World*, *War of the Gargantuas*, *Majin* (and its sequels), *King Kong Escapes* and *Latitude Zero*. He came out of retirement in 1995 to score *Godzilla vs. Destroyer*, and his theme continued to be heard on the last series entry, *Godzilla: Final Wars* (2004). Ifukube also came up with Godzilla's trademark roar by running a resin-coated glove over the strings of a double bass.

British crime writer **Michael Gilbert** died the same day, aged 93. Named a Grand Master by the Mystery Writers of America in 1998, his ghost stories appeared in *Argosy* and *The After Midnight Ghost Book*.

Peter [Bradford] **Benchley**, the grandson of humorist Robert Benchley and best-selling author of *Jaws*, died of complications from idiopathic pulmonary fibrosis at his New Jersey home on February 11th, aged 65. *Jaws*, which has sold more than twenty million copies world-wide since its first publication in 1974, was successfully filmed by Steven Spielberg the following year from a script co-written by Benchley (who also had a cameo). It became the first film to gross more than $100 million and spawned a series of sequels and imitators. Benchley's other novels, *The Deep*, *The Island* and *Beast* were also filmed, but with less success, while his 1994 novel *White Shark*, about a Nazi-engineered man/shark hybrid, was made into the 1998 TV movie *Creature*. Although Benchley's *Jaws* did much to demonise sharks, the writer became a passionate conservationist and advocate for the species.

British-born film and television executive and author **James Hardi-man** died in San Francisco on February 19th, aged 86. He moved to Hollywood in 1956, where he worked for Walt Disney Productions, CBS-TV, Screen Gems and Columbia Pictures Television. He spent a number of years in Tokyo as a correspondent for *Daily Variety*, and his supernatural novel *The House Where Evil Dwells* was filmed in Japan in 1982 starring Edward Albert, Susan George and Doug McClure.

58-year-old African-American SF author **Octavia E.** (Estelle) **But-ler** died of a stroke on February 24th after striking her head during a fall on the sidewalk outside her Seattle home. She was reportedly on high blood pressure medication at the time. Inspired by the movie *Devil Girl from Mars*, she began writing at age twelve and her first story, "Crossover", appeared in the 1971 anthology of the Clarion Science Fiction Writers Workshop. She went on to publish nearly twenty books, including *Patternmaster*, *Kindred*, *Wild Seed*, *Parable of the Talents* and the 2005 vampire novel *Fledgling*. Butler received the Nebula Award, two Hugo Awards and the PEN Center West Lifetime Achievement Award. In 1995 she was the first SF writer granted a "genius" award from the John D. and Catherine T. MacArthur Foundation, receiving $295,000 over five years.

American artist **Ronald Clyne** died of a heart attack on February 26th, aged 80. He sold his first illustration to *Fantastic Stories* at the age of fifteen, and in 1945 he was commissioned to illustrate the dust-jacket for August Derleth's collection *Something Near*. This began a long association with Derleth's Arkham House imprint, and during the 1940s he produced numerous covers for the small press, including *The Opener of the Way* by Robert Bloch, *Night's Black Agents* by Fritz Leiber, Jr, *The Clock Strikes Twelve* by H. Russell Wakefield (his personal favourite) and *The Lurker at the Threshold* by H. P. Lovecraft and Derleth. He also contributed illustrations to the pulp magazines, including *Weird Tales*. Clyne occasionally returned to work for Arkham in the 1950s and '60s, but was by then a prolific and successful artist employed by all the major New York publishing houses. Between 1951 and 1981 he also created more than 500 distinctive album covers for Folkways Records, which he considered his best work.

American fantasy author **Ronald Anthony Cross** died from a stroke on March 1st, aged 68. His first story appeared in *New Worlds 6* in 1973, and since 1994 he published four volumes in the "Eternal Guardians" series.

Richard [Patrick] **Terra**, who published non-fiction in *Analog*, *The*

New York Review of Science Fiction and other publications, died of a pulmonary embolism on March 4th, aged 46.

Dutch-born SF writer **Nancy Ann Dibble** (Ansen Dibell) died on March 7th, aged 63. Her "King of Katmorie" series ran over five books (1978-85), and as "Nan Dibble" she wrote *Beyond Words, Beyond Silence*, a 1992 tie-in to the *Beauty and the Beast* TV series.

Former attorney, antiques dealer and science fiction author **David Feintuch** [Mason] died of a heart attack on March 16th, aged 61. He had a long history of cardiac troubles and suffered from Type II Diabetes. Mason won the John W. Campbell Award for best new writer in 1996 for his military SF novel *Midshipman's Hope*, and continued the Hornblower-like "Seafort Saga" over a further eight books. He also wrote the fantasy novels *The Still* and *The King*.

US academic and humorous fantasy author **John Morressy** died of a massive heart attack on March 20th, aged 75. He made his debut in *The Magazine of Fantasy and Science Fiction* with "Accuracy" in 1971, and his novels include *Starbrat, Frostworld and Dreamfire, The Juggler, Ironbrand, Graymantle* and *Kingsbane*. In 1986 he created the humorous "Kedrigern" series, which includes *A Voice for Princess, The Questing of Kedrigern* and *Kedrigern and the Dragon Comme Il Faut*.

SF author **Kurt von Trojan** died of bone and kidney cancer in Australia on March 22nd, aged 69. Born in Vienna, his books include the novels *The Transing Syndrome* and *The Atrocity Shop* and the collection *When I Close My Eyes*.

Jane Yolen's husband of more than forty years, poet **David W.** (William) **Stemple**, died in his sleep after a long battle with cancer the same day, aged 68.

Polish SF author and critic **Stanislaw Lem** died of heart failure on March 27th, aged 84. The author of *Solaris* (filmed twice), his more than seventy books sold over twenty-seven million copies worldwide and were translated into more than forty languages. Lem's other books include *Man from Mars, The Astronauts, Hospital of the Transfiguration, The Star Diaries, The Chain of Chance, Memoirs Found in a Bathtub, The Invincible, The Cyberiad, Scene of the Crime* and *One Human Minute*. He was made an honorary member of the SFWA in 1973, but that status was revoked when Lem published a controversial essay decrying the poor state of science fiction writing. He stopped writing fiction in 1989.

Typographical designer **Ruari McLean** died the same day, aged 88. During the 1950s and '60s he supervised the design of such iconic British children's comics as *Eagle, Girl, Swift* and *Robin*.

American author and screenwriter **Henry Farrell** (Charles Henry Myers), whose fiction was filmed as *What Ever Happened to Baby Jane?*, *Hush Hush Sweet Charlotte*, *How Awful About Allan* and *What's the Matter With Helen?*, died on March 29th, aged 85.

Australian fan **Diane Marchant** died of pancreatic cancer on April 5th. In 1972 she created the Aussie *Star Trek* Welcommitte with Jacqueline Lichtenberg, and is credited with publishing the first sexually explicit "slash" fan fiction two years later.

TV writer and producer **Burt Pearl** died of lymphoma on April 6th, aged 49. He scripted episodes of *The Highwayman*, *Something is Out There* and *Touched by an Angel*, also executive producing the latter series until 2003.

63-year-old British SF and fantasy author and editor **Angus Wells** died in an accidental fire at his home on April 11th. While working at Sphere Books in the 1970s he edited a number of "Best of" collections based around individual authors. His own books include the TV tie-in *Star Maidens* (as by "Ian Evans") and *Swordsmistress of Chaos* and *A Time of Ghosts* both with Robert Holdstock (as "Richard Kirk"), the first two volumes in the "Raven" series to which he contributed a further three solo novels. Wells' other fantasy novels, published under his own name, include the "Book of the Kingdoms", "Godwars" and "Exiles" series. He was also a prolific author of Westerns and adventure novels under a variety of house names.

88-year-old Scottish novelist Dame **Muriel Spark** (Muriel Sarah Camberg), whose novels *The Comforters*, *Memento Mori*, *The Ballad of Peckham Rye* and *The Hothouse by the East River* all contain elements of the supernatural, died in Florence, Italy, on April 13th. Best known for her 1961 book *The Prime of Miss Jean Brodie*, *The Ghost Stories of Muriel Spark* was published in 2003. Her revisionist 1951 biography, *Child of Light*, won a HWA Bram Stoker Award when expanded in 1987 as *Mary Shelley: A Biography*.

Scriptwriter, producer and director **David Peckinpah**, the nephew of film director Sam Peckinpah, died of a heart attack on April 23rd, aged 54. He scripted episodes of *Beauty and the Beast* and *Farscape*, produced *Silk Stalkings*, and produced and directed episodes of *Sliders*.

Screenwriter, dramatist and novelist **Jay Presson Allen** (Jacqueline Presson) died of a stroke on May 1st, aged 84. She adapted *Marnie* for Alfred Hitchcock, scripted the 1973 TV film *The Borrowers* and also wrote the screenplay for Ira Levin's *Deathtrap*.

47-year-old American fantasy author **Lisa A.** (Anne) **Barnett** died in her sleep of a brain tumor caused by metastatic breast cancer on May 2nd. She collaborated with her partner, Melissa Scott, on the novels *Point of Hopes, Point of Dreams* and *The Armor of Light*, while their novella "The Carmen Miranda Gambit" appeared in *Carmen Miranda's Ghost is Haunting Space Station Three*.

Music composer and conductor **Andre Brummer** died of pneumonia on May 6th, aged 89. His many credits include Roger Corman's *Monster from the Ocean Floor, Love Slaves of the Amazon, Eegah!, The Incredibly Strange Creatures Who Stopped Living and Became Mixed-Up Zombies!!?, Rat Pfink and Boo Boo, Sinthia the Devil's Doll* and *The Hollywood Strangler Meets the Skid Row Slasher*.

British editor and ghost story author **Elizabeth M.** (Margaret) **Walter** died on May 8th. Although she refused to divulge her age, she was believed to be around 78 or 79. Her stories are collected in *Snowfall and Other Chilling Events, The Sin-Eater and Other Scientific Impossibilities, Davy Jones's Tale and Other Supernatural Stories, Come and Get Me and Other Uncanny Invitations* and *The Dead Woman and Other Haunting Experiences*. James Turner compiled some of her best tales for the 1979 Arkham House collection *In the Mist and Other Uncanny Encounters*. Her story "The Spider" was filmed as "A Fear of Spiders" for *Rod Serling's Night Gallery*, and she also contributed to the 1972-73 TV series *Ghost Story*. Between 1961-93 Walter was chief editor of the Collins Crime Club at publisher William Collins.

George Lutz, whose claims in 1975 that his Long Island home was possessed by evil spirits became the basis of *The Amityville Horror*, died of heart disease the same day, aged 59. When the family moved out of their house after twenty-eight days following numerous bizarre occurrences, Lutz and his then wife Kathy (who died in 2004) collaborated with author Jay Anson on the 1977 best-seller. The story was filmed in 1977 and 2005, and inspired various sequels and spin-offs.

Russian philosopher and author **Alexander Zinoviev** died of cancer on May 10th, aged 83. His 1976 novel *The Yawning Heights* is a dystopian satire on the USSR.

American mathematics teacher and author **Arthur Porges** died after a long illness on May 12th, a couple of months short of his 91st birthday. He began his fiction career in the early 1950s, selling consistently to *The Magazine of Fantasy and Science Fiction*, and within a few years he had branched out with sales to *Galaxy, Amazing Stories, Startling Stories, Fantastic Universe* and other

SF digests. By the late 1960s Porges had moved into the mystery genre, with many memorable tales appearing in *Alfred Hitchcock's*, *Ellery Queen's* and *Mike Shayne's* magazines. A collection of horror stories, *The Mirror and Other Strange Reflections*, was edited by Mike Ashley and published by Ash-Tree Press in 2002.

44-year-old Bay Area fan, folk singer and author **Leigh Ann Hussey** was killed in a motorcycle accident on May 16th. She had stories in the anthologies *Werewolves* and *Vampires*, both edited by Jane Yolen and Martin H. Greenberg, and was a regular contributor to *Marion Zimmer Bradley's Fantasy Magazine*.

Tony Award-winning Broadway producer, director and composer **Cy Feuer** died on May 17th, aged 95. During the late 1930s he began working at Republic Pictures as a composer and head of the studio's music department. Over the next two decades he worked on *Fighting Devil Dogs*, *Hawk of the Wilderness*, *S.O.S. Tidal Wave*, *Daredevils of the Red Circle*, *Zorro's Fighting Legion*, *Drums of Fu Manchu*, *Mysterious Doctor Satan*, *Adventures of Captain Marvel*, *Dick Tracy vs. Crime Inc.*, *Spy Smasher* and *The Crimson Ghost*. He later produced such hit stage musicals as *The Boy Friend*, *Can-Can* and *Silk Stockings*.

British folk-singer **Gytha North** died of cancer on May 24th, aged 55. Terry Pratchett borrowed her name for his character Gytha (Nanny) Ogg, the witch in the popular "Discworld" novels.

American comics artist **Alex** (Alexander) **Toth** died at his drawing board on May 27th, aged 77. He joined DC Comics in 1947, where he illustrated such characters as Dr Mid-Nite, the Atom and Green Lantern for $30 per page. He went on to work on a number of Dell comics based on popular TV shows (*Zorro*, *Twilight Zone* etc.), as well as titles for Archie, Charlton, Marvel and Warren's horror and war magazines. A year after art directing the animated TV series *Space Angels* in 1964, Toth joined Hanna-Barbera Studios, where he designed many cartoon series, including *Jonny Quest*, *Battle of the Planets*, *Challenge of the Superfriends*, *The Herculoids*, *Shazzam*, *Birdman and the Galaxy Trio*, *The Fantastic Four*, *Scooby-Doo* and *Space Ghost*. He was also a storyboard artist on the SF film *Angry Red Planet* and worked as a sequence production designer on *Project X*.

Television writer **Robert Bielak**, who was supervising producer for *Hercules: The Legendary Journeys*, died on May 30th, aged 85. He also scripted episodes of *MacGyver* and *Kung Fu: The Legend Continues*.

"Seamus Cullen", the pseudonymous American-born author of the erotic 1976 novel *Astra and Flondrix* and other fantasies, including *A Noose of Light* and *Sultan's Turret*, was reported to have died of cancer when mail to his address in Ireland was returned in May marked "Deceased".

British playwright, novelist and prolific TV scriptwriter **Allan Prior** died on June 1st, aged 84. In the 1970s he scripted five episodes of BBC-TV's *Blakes 7*.

George Kashdan, who worked as an editor and writer at DC Comics from 1946 until 1968, died of complications from a stroke on June 3rd, aged 78. Among the characters he worked on were Green Arrow, Congo Bill and Johnny Quick. He wrote and often edited such titles as *House of Mystery*, *House of Secrets*, *Secrets of Haunted House*, *Tales of the Unexpected*, *Rip Hunter Time Master*, *Aquaman*, *Teen Titans*, *Metamorpho*, *Ghosts*, *Bomba the Jungle Boy*, *Hawkman*, *Weird War Tales* and *Blackhawk* (where he turned the World War II heroes into superheroes in the mid-1960s). After leaving DC, Kashdan moved to Dell/Gold Key, where he contributed to *Boris Karloff Tales of Mystery*, *Grimm's Ghost Stories*, *Flash Gordon*, *Star Trek* and *Twilight Zone*.

Former CIA intelligence agent and author **Karl T. Pflock**, whose 2001 book *Roswell: Inconvenient Facts and the Will to Believe* debunked the UFO conspiracy theory, died of Lou Gehrig's disease (ALS) on June 5th, aged 63.

67-year-old American fantasy artist **Tim Hildebrandt** (Timothy Allen Mark Hildebrant), one-half of the successful Brothers Hildebrandt team, died of complications from diabetes on June 11th. With his identical twin brother Greg he created the original *Star Wars* poster, a series of J. R. R. Tolkien calendars and numerous book covers, posters and collectibles. Since 1981 the two brothers had worked separately until they were reconciled in the early 1990s. Tim Hildebrandt executive produced and appeared in the 1983 film *Return of the Aliens: The Deadly Spawn*, which starred his son, Charles George Hildebrandt. With his wife Rita, he wrote the 1983 novel *Merlin and the Dragons of Atlantis* and the non-fiction *Fantasy Cookbook*. In 1992 he won a World Fantasy Award for Best Artist.

Austrian-Hungarian-born literary agent and film producer **Ingo Preminger**, the brother of director Otto, died in Los Angeles on June 7th, aged 95. Preminger represented a number of writers who were blacklisted during the McCarthy era, including Dalton Trumbo and Ring Lardner, Jr, along with such actors as Paul Henreid and Ralph Meeker. His film credits include *M*A*S*H* and *The Salzburg Connection*.

83-year-old Hungarian avant-garde composer **György Ligeti** died after a long illness in Vienna, Austria, on June 12th. The creator of a pioneering sound technique called "micropolyphony", he is best known for his work on the soundtrack for Stanley Kubrick's *2001: A Space Odyssey*.

Controversial American book publisher **Lyle Stuart** (Lionel Simon) died on June 24th following a heart attack. He was 83. After working as business manager for *Mad* magazine, he founded the investigative newspapers *Exposé* and *The Independent*. He launched his own publishing imprint, Lyle Stuart Inc., in 1956 with money won in a libel case. When he sold the publishing house in 1990, he founded Barricade Books.

62-year-old **Jim Baen** (James Patrick Baen), American editor and publisher and founder of the Baen Books imprint, died on June 28th after suffering a massive stroke two weeks earlier. He never regained consciousness. Baen began his career at Ace Books in 1972, and went on to edit the SF magazines *Galaxy* and *If*, and the paperback anthology *Destinies*, before forming Baen Books in 1983. He is credited as an innovator in using free e-texts and book extracts to publicise Baen's print titles.

American radio and TV broadcaster **Roderick MacLeish**, who wrote the 1982 fantasy novel *Prince Ombra*, died on July 1st, aged 80.

Bookseller and author **Martin** [Arthur] **Last** died on July 6th, aged 76. With his long-time partner Baird Searles (who died in 1993) he co-founded The Science Fiction Shop in New York City's West Village from 1973-86. Last also wrote fiction, poetry and reviews, and co-authored the 1979 study *A Reader's Guide to Science Fiction* with Searles, Beth Meacham and Michael Franklin. From 1975-76 he edited *The Science Fiction Review Monthly*.

Tough-guy crime writer **Mickey Spillane** (Frank Morrison Spillane), who created PI Mike Hammer in his first novel, *I, the Jury* (1947), died of cancer on July 17th after a long illness. He was 88. The author began his career writing for the pulp magazines and the comics, including *Batman*, *Captain America*, *Sub-mariner* and *The Human Torch*, and he returned to the medium in the 1990s with the SF detective series *Mickey Spillane's Mike Danger*. Many of his books and stories have been turned into films or TV series – including Robert Aldrich's classic *Kiss Me Deadly* (1955) – and Spillane himself portrayed Hammer in the low budget 1963 movie *The Girl Hunters*. He received a Grand Master Award from the Mystery Writers of America in 1995.

Best-selling British fantasy writer **David [Andrew] Gemmell** died at his computer on July 28th. Just over a week earlier, the 57-year-old author had undergone a quadruple heart bypass and appeared to be recovering well. Best known for his heroic fantasy "Drenai" series, which he began in 1984 with *Legend* (aka *Against the Horde*) and continued through ten further volumes, his other books include *Sword in the Storm*, *Wolf in Shadow* (aka *The Jerusalem Man*), *Ironhand's Daughter*, *Knights of Dark Renown*, *Lion of Macedon* and *The Lord of the Silver Bow*. Random House UK's SF and fantasy list was renamed "Legend" in the late 1980s in honour of Gemmell's debut novel, which has never been out of print.

Susan E. Michaud (Susan E. Roberts), who helped run small press imprint Necronomicon Press with her husband, Marc Michaud, died on August 3rd, aged 41.

Nebula-nominated American author **Bob** (Robert J.) **Leman** died of congestive heart failure on August 8th, aged 84. During the 1950s and '60s he produced the fanzine *The Vinegar Worm* (aka *Nematode*) and between 1967 and 2002 he published fifteen stories, all but one in *The Magazine of Fantasy and Science Fiction*. These later appeared in the 2002 collection *Feesters in the Lake & Other Stories*, which was included in *Horror: Another 100 Best Books*. His Nebula nominated story "Window" was adapted as an episode of the 2001 TV series *Night Visions*.

British SF author **Philip E.** (Empson) **High** died of respiratory failure on August 9th, aged 92. He had been admitted to hospital a week earlier following a heart attack. A contributor to such magazines as *Authentic Science Fiction*, *Nebula Science Fiction* and *Vision of Tomorrow*, he wrote fourteen novels between 1964 and 1979, including *The Prodigal Son*, *No Truce with Terra*, *The Mad Metropolis*, *Come Hunt an Earthman*, *Speaking of Dinosaurs* and *Blindfold the Stars*. His short fiction appeared in two collections, *The Best of Philip E. High* and *A Step to the Stars*.

79-year-old ghost hunter and author **Ed Warren** who, with his wife Lorraine, investigated more than 10,000 suspected hauntings, died on August 23rd of complications from a stroke. Having investigated the Amityville house in New York, the couple worked as consultants on *Amityville II: The Possession*. The TV movies *The Demon Murder Case* and *The Haunted* were based on books written by the Warrens.

American scriptwriter/producer **Joseph [William] Stefano**, who co-created and produced the TV show *The Outer Limits* (1963-65) with Leslie Stevens, died of a heart attack on August 24th, aged 84.

Best remembered as the writer of Alfred Hitchcock's *Psycho* and the 1998 remake, his other credits include *Eye of the Cat*, *The Kindred*, the TV movies *Psycho IV the Beginning*, *Revenge*, *Home for the Holidays* and *Snowbeast*, the 1990 series *Swamp Thing* and an episode of *Star Trek: The Next Generation*. In 1964, Stefano directed the "lost" TV pilot *The Ghost of Sierra de Cobre* (aka *The Haunted*).

Pioneering TV animation designer **Ed Benedict**, who created such iconic cartoon characters as The Flintstones, Quick Draw McGraw, Huckleberry Hound, Yogi Bear and The Jetsons, died on August 28th, aged 94. After working at the Walt Disney studio, with Oswald Lantz at Universal and with Tex Avery at MGM, he became the main character designer for Hanna-Barbera from the late 1950s until his retirement in the mid-1970s.

American songwriter **Paul Vance** (Paul Van Valkenburgh), whose cult hit "Itsy Bitsy Teenie Weenie Yellow Polka Dot Bikini" went to #1 for 16-year-old Brian Hyland in August 1960, died of lung cancer on September 6th, aged 68. With Lee Pockriss he also co-wrote "Catch a Falling Star", which was a #1 hit for Perry Como in 1958. Vance sold the rights to all his songs when he was younger.

Animator **Berny Wolf** died on September 7th, aged 95. After working on the *Betty Boop* cartoons at the Fleischer Studios, he moved to the Ub Iwerks Studio and then on to Disney Studios, where he contributed to *Snow White and the Seven Dwarfs*, *Fantasia*, *Dumbo* and many other titles. With Ward Kimball he worked on the design of *Pinocchio*'s Jiminy Cricket, and came up with the design for the costumes of the characters who still walk around Disney theme parks. Later, he worked in Tex Avery's unit at MGM, for Film Roman Studios, and at Hanna-Barbera, where he was involved with *Scooby-Doo and the Reluctant Werewolf*, *Scooby-Doo and the Ghoul School* and such TV series as *The Jetsons*, *Jonny Quest* and *The Flintstones*.

French screenwriter and director **Gérard Brach** died of cancer on September 9th, aged 79. Best known for his many collaborations with director Roman Polanski (including *Repulsion*, *Cul-de-sac*, *Dance of the Vampires*, *What?* and *The Tenant*), he also scripted *Bye Bye Monkey*, *Quest for Fire*, *The Name of the Rose* and *Renegade*.

American horror author and editor **Charles L. (Lewis) Grant** died of a heart attack in front of the television on September 15th, aged 64. He had been suffering from chronic obstructive pulmonary disease and emphysema from some years, and had returned from a care facility ten days earlier to his home in New Jersey to celebrate his birthday (and that of his wife of almost twenty-five years, editor and novelist Kathryn Ptacek) on September 12th. A prolific short story writer and novelist, Grant's career spanned more than thirty-five years. During that time he cultivated his unique style of "quiet horror" in many novels and collections, including *The Curse, The Hour of the Oxrun Dead, The Sound of Midnight, The Grave, The Bloodwind, The Soft Whisper of the Dead, The Nestling, The Tea Party, The Orchard, The Pet, For Fear of the Night, In a Dark Dream, Dialing the Wind, Stunts, Something Stirs, Jackals, The Black Carousel, Tales from the Nightside, A Glow of Candles* and *Nightmare Seasons*. More recent titles include the first two *X Files* novelisations, *Goblin* and *Whirlwind*, the "Millennium Quartet" inspired by the Four Horsemen of the Apocalypse, and the "Black Oak" series about a security team of paranormal investigators. Grant also published a variety of books under the pseudonyms "Felicia Andrews", "Deborah Lewis", "Geoffrey Marsh", "Lionel Fenn", "Steven Charles" and "Simon Lake". As an editor he was responsible for two dozen anthologies, including the influential *Shadows* series (twelve volumes) along with *Nightmares, Midnight, After Midnight, Greystone Bay, Doom City, The Dodd Mead Gallery of Horror, Night Visions: Dead Image* and *Gothic Ghosts* (with Wendy Webb). He won three World Fantasy Awards and two Nebulas for his fiction. A recipient of the of the British Fantasy Society's Special Award, the International Horror Guild Living Legend Award and the Horror Writers Association's Lifetime Achievement Award, he was also named a Grand Master at the 2002 World Horror Convention.

British TV scriptwriter **Peter** [George Derek] **Ling**, best-known as the co-creator of the soap opera *Crossroads*, died of a heart attack on September 14th, aged 80. He wrote for *Eagle* comic at an early age, and his other TV credits include the children's puppet series *Whirligig* and episodes of *The Avengers, Sexton Blake* and *Doctor Who* ("The Mind Robber").

American socialite **Patricia Kennedy Lawford**, the sister of John and Robert Kennedy and the widow of actor Peter Lawford, died of complications from pneumonia on September 17th, aged 82. She was believed to be the last person alive to know the truth behind the mysterious suicide of Marilyn Monroe in 1962.

Author and fan **Darrell C.** (Coleman) **Richardson** (aka "D. Coleman Rich") died after a long illness on September 19th, aged 88. He wrote more than forty books, several about the pulps that include

J. Allen St. John: An Illustrated Bibliography, "King of the Pulps": *The Life and Writings of H. Bedford-Jones* (with Victor A. Berch and Peter Ruber) and *Those Macabre Pulps*. Richardson was a co-founder of the FAX small press imprint in the 1970s and was a winner of the Big Heart Award and the Lamont Award.

British sculptor **Allister Bowtell** died of cancer on September 20th, aged 66. As well as creating the original Cybermen for *Doctor Who*, he also designed Rod Hull's "Emu" and created props for *Monty Python's Flying Circus*, *The Goodies*, Jonathan Miller's *Alice* and *Sir Henry at Rawlinson's End*.

Sir **Malcolm** [Henry] **Arnold** died of a chest infection on September 23rd, aged 84. Best known as the first British composer to win an Academy Award, for his score for *The Bridge Over the River Kwai*, his other credits include several of the *St Trinian's* movies, Hammer's *Stolen Face* and *Four Sided Triangle*, *The Sound Barrier*, *1984* (1956) and *Suddenly Last Summer*. When the classical music establishment ignored his symphonies, he suffered a number of violent episodes and was sanctioned in a mental asylum.

American science fiction and fantasy writer and poet **John M.** (Milo) "Mike" **Ford** (aka "Michael J. Dodge"/"Milo Dennison") died on September 25th, aged 49. He was diabetic and had undergone a kidney transplant in 2000. The winner of two World Fantasy Awards for his 1983 novel *The Dragon Waiting* and his narrative poem "Winter Solstice, Camelot Station", Ford's other books include *Web of Angels*, *The Princes of the Air*, *The Scholars of Night* and the *Star Trek* novels *The Final Reflection* and *How Much for Just the Planet?*. He was also an award-winning writer of role-playing games. Reportedly, the headline in the *St. Paul Pioneer* newspaper for his memorial event read: "Crafters of Sci-Fi Attend Obscure Writer's Eulogy".

French writer, editor and translator **Michel Demuth** died of liver failure on September 30th, aged 67. He translated the French editions of Arthur C. Clarke's *2001: A Space Odyssey* and Frank Herbert's *Dune*, and was the editor of *Galaxie* (the French edition of *Galaxy*).

American biographer and book collector **Virgil S.** (Starbuck) **Utter, Jr** died of congestive heart failure on October 3rd, aged 81. His published biographies of C. L. Moore and Henry Kuttner, Raymond King Cummings, Grant Allen and George Allen England, often in collaboration with Phil Stephensen-Payne and others.

Multiple Award-winning American SF author and fanzine writer [Arthur] **Wilson** "Bob" **Tucker**, credited with coining the term "space opera", died after a short illness on October 6th, aged 91. His most famous fanzine was *Le Zombie* (1938-2001), and he was Fan Guest of Honor at the 1948 and 1967 World Science Fiction Conventions. The author of sixty short stories (in *Super Science Stories*, *The Best of Wilson Tucker* etc.) and novels (*The City in the Sea*, *The Long Loud Silence*, *The Time Masters*, *The Year of the Quiet Sun* etc.), Tucker's many honours include three Hugo Awards (two retro), the First Fandom Hall of Fame Award, E. E. Smith Memorial Award and SFWA Author Emeritus. He was a 2003 inductee in the Science Fiction and Fantasy Hall of Fame.

British film critic **Philip Strick**, a regular contributor to the BFI's *Sight & Sound* magazine, died on October 7th, aged 67. He also taught Britain's first adult SF evening class, edited the humorous SF anthology *Antigrav* and was the author of the 1976 study *Science Fiction Movies*.

Emmy Award-winning scriptwriter, producer and director **Jerry Belson**, co-creator of TV's *The Odd Couple* (1970-75) with Garry Marshall, died of prostate cancer on October 10th, aged 68. His film credits include *Student Bodies*, *Jekyll and Hyde . . . Together Again* (which he also directed), *Close Encounters of the Third Kind* (uncredited) and *Always*.

Belgium writer **Jacques Sternberg** died of lung cancer on October 11th, aged 83. He is credited with publishing the first French SF Fanzine, *Le Petit Silence illustré*, edited many anthologies and wrote several hundred short stories, many of them fantastic. Sternberg also scripted Alain Resnais' 1968 film *Je t'aime, je t'aime*.

British children's author and illustrator **Ursula Moray Williams** died on October 17th, aged 95. Her more than seventy books include *The Adventures of the Little Wooden Horse* and *Gobbolino the Witch's Cat*. Her uncle was Sir Stanley Unwin, founder of the publishing imprint Allen & Unwin.

Animator and cartoonist **Don R. Christensen** (aka "Don Arr") died on October 18th, aged 90. He was a sketch artist at Disney from 1937 to 1941, working on such films as *Pinocchio* and *Dumbo*. After a brief stint with Bob Clampett's animation unit at Warner Bros., where he scripted several *Looney Tunes* shorts, Christensen moved to Dell/Gold Key, where he contributed to such comic books as *Magnus Robot Fighter* and *Scooby Doo*.

British playwright and YA author **John Symonds** died on October 21st, aged 92. He was also Aleister Crowley's literary executor.

British playwright and author **Paul** [Victor] **Ableman**, whose SF novel *The Twilight of the Vilp* was published in 1969, died on

October 25th, aged 79. He also scripted episodes of TV's *Tales of the Unexpected*.

British author and screenwriter [Thomas] **Nigel Kneale**, best remembered for his pioneering *Quatermass* trilogy for BBC-TV, died after a long illness and a series of strokes on October 29th, aged 84. When *The Quatermass Experiment* was first broadcast in 1953, it emptied the streets and pubs for the six weeks it ran. Hammer produced the film version in 1955 (aka *The Creeping Unknown*) and the studio went on to film the two sequels as well, *Quatermass 2* (aka *Enemy from Space*) and *Quatermass and the Pit* (aka *Five Million Years to Earth*). A fourth and final episode, *Quatermass* (aka *The Quatermass Conclusion*), was shown in 1979. There was a radio version, *The Quatermass Memoirs*, broadcast on BBC Radio 3 in 1996, and the original show was remade as a live broadcast by the BBC in 2005. The live broadcast of Kneale's adaptation on *Nineteen Eighty Four* (starring Peter Cushing and Donald Pleasence) in 1954 prompted questions in the British parliament. His other TV work includes such dramas as *The Creature* (filmed by Hammer as *The Abominable Snowman*), *Wuthering Heights* (1962), *The Road*, *The Year of the Sex Olympics*, *The Chopper*, *The Stone Tape*, *The Woman in Black* and the series *Beasts* (1976) and *Kinvig* (1981), although he turned down a request to contribute to *The X Files* in the 1990s. He also wrote the scripts for *First Men in the Moon*, Hammer's *The Witches* (aka *The Devil's Own*) and the original draft of *Halloween III: Season of the Witch*. Kneale's best short stories are collected in *Tomato Cain and Other Stories* (1949).

Leonard Schrader, the Oscar-nominated screenwriter of *Kiss of the Spider Woman*, died of heart failure on November 2nd, aged 62.

American pulp author and rare book dealer **Nelson S.** (Slade) **Bond** died of complications from heart problems on November 4th, just short of his 98th birthday. After making his SF debut in *Astounding* in 1937 with "Down the Dimensions", his work appeared in *Weird Tales*, *Unknown*, *Fantastic Adventures*, *Planet Stories* and such mainstream magazines as *Esquire*, *Blue Book* and *Argosy*. His books include the 1949 novel, *Exiles of Time*, and the short story collections *Mr Mergenthwirker's Lobblies and Other Fantastic Tales*, *The Thirty-first of February*, *The Remarkable Exploits of Lancelot Biggs Spaceman*, *Nightmares and Daydreams*, *The Far Side of Nowhere* and *Other Worlds Than Ours* (the last three titles from Arkham House). A scriptwriter for radio and TV, he wrote the 1957 teleplay *The Night America Trembled*, about Orson

Welles' *War of the Worlds* radio broadcast. He was honoured by the SFWA in 1998 as Author Emeritus.

British SF fan and book dealer **Ron Bennett**, whose fanzine newsletter *Skyrack* ran from 1959-71, died of leukaemia on November 5th, aged 73.

American composer **Basil Poledouris** died of cancer on November 8th, aged 61. His many film scores include *Tintorera*, *Conan the Barbarian*, *Conan the Destroyer*, *Red Dawn*, *Flesh+Blood*, *Robo-Cop*, *Cherry 2000*, *Spellbinder*, *The Hunt for Red October*, *Harley Davidson and the Marlboro Man*, *RoboCop 3*, *Serial Mom*, *The Jungle Book* (1994), *Starship Troopers* and *The Touch*. Poledouris also contributed music to the 1980s TV series *Alfred Hitchcock Presents*, *The Twilight Zone*, *Misfits of Science* and the mini-series *Amerika*, as well as the 3-D computer game *Conan* (2004).

American SF cover artist **Stanley Meltzoff** died on November 9th, aged 89. In the 1950s he painted a number of influential covers for Signet/NAL paperbacks for books by Isaac Asimov, Alfred Bester, Edmond Hamilton, Robert A. Heinlein and A. E. van Vogt, amongst others. He also did the covers for *Science Fiction Terror Tales* edited by Groff Conklin and the Gold Medal paperback of Richard Matheson's *I Am Legend*. Meltzoff illustrated the May 1955 issue of *The Magazine of Fantasy and Science Fiction*.

Jack (John Stewart) **Williamson** (aka "Will Stewart"), the oldest surviving author from *Weird Tales* and the early pulp magazines, died at his home in New Mexico on November 10th, aged 98. Widely regarded as "the Father of American Science Fiction", he began his career with "The Metal Man" in *Amazing Stories* in 1928 (three years before the term "science fiction" was actually coined). In a career that spanned an incredible nine decades, he contributed to most of the major magazines, including *Science Wonder Stories* and *Astounding*, and his novels include *The Girl from Mars* (with Miles J. Breuer, 1929) published by Hugo Gernsback, *The Legion of Space*, *Darker Than You Think*, *The Humanoids* and its sequel *The Humanoid Touch*, *Seetee Shock* and *Seetee Ship*, the "Undersea Quest" and "Starchild" trilogies (both with Frederik Pohl), *Manseed*, *Firechild* and *The Stonehenge Gate* (2005). In the 1990s, Haffner Press began collecting all Williamson's short fiction in handsome limited editions, and *Seventy-Five: The Diamond Anniversary of a Science Fiction Pioneer* was published in 2004. The annual Jack Williamson Lectureship Series began at Eastern New Mexico University in 1977, and The Jack Williamson Science Fiction Library at the university contains some 30,000 books and magazines. A winner

STEPHEN JONES & KIM NEWMAN

of both the Hugo and Nebula Awards for his fiction, he was also a recipient of the SFWA Grand Master Award, the World Fantasy Life Achievement Award, and the World Horror Convention Grand Master Award. His 1984 Hugo Award-winning autobiography, *Wonder Child: My Life in Science Fiction*, was updated in 2005.

Ken Ishikawa, who co-created the 1970s giant robot *anime Getter Robo*, died on November 15th, aged 58.

British literary agent **Maggie** (Margaret) [Irene] **Noach** died on November 17th, aged 57. She was admitted to hospital complaining of back pains. Diagnosed with a broken vertebra, she developed breathing problems during an operation on her spine that led to massive heart failure. After beginning her career at A. P. Watt, Noach established her own literary agency in 1982 and represented such SF authors as Brian Aldiss, Geoff Ryman, Stephen Baxter, Garry Kilworth, Michael Scott Rohan and Colin Greenland. With her second husband, Alan Williams (the son of actor and playwright Emlyn), she complied *The Dictionary of Disgusting Facts* (1986).

American-born writer **Guy Mariner Tucker**, author of the 1996 study, *Age of the Gods: The History of Japanese Fantasy Film*, died of heart failure in Tokyo the same day. He contributed many articles on Japanese fantasy films to such magazines as *G-Fan*, *Cult Movies* and *Kaiju-Fan*.

American television writer **Chris Hayward**, who co-created *The Munsters* and also worked on *Rocky and Bullwinkle*, died on November 20th, aged 81.

Russian-born Broadway lyricist and screenwriter **Betty Comden** (Basya Cohen), whose credits include the Mary Martin stage version of *Peter Pan*, *On the Town*, *Singin' in the Rain* and *The Band Wagon* with songwriter Adolph Green (who died in 2002), died of heart failure on November 23rd, following a long illness. She was aged around 90. Comden's lyrics were also heard in *What a Way to Go!*, *Blue Sunshine*, *The Addams Family*, *Dr Giggles* and TV's *Star Trek Deep Space Nine*.

Jerry G. (Gwin) **Bails**, regarded as "the father of American comic book fandom", died of a heart attack the same day, aged 73. He began publishing his influential fanzine, *Alter Ego*, in 1961 and his books include *Collector's Guide: The First Heroic Age*, *Who's Who in American Comic Books*, *Fifty Who Made DC Great*, *Golden Age of Comic Fandom* and *Alter Ego: The Best of the Legendary Fanzine*.

Prolific British author **Sydney J.** (James) **Bounds** died of cancer on November 24th, aged 86. He joined the Science Fiction Association in 1937, where he met writers Arthur C. Clarke, William F. Temple and

John Christopher (Sam Youd). Bounds founded the SF fan group, the Cosmos Club, during World War II, and his early fiction appeared in the club's fanzine, *Cosmic Cuts*. His first professional sale never appeared, but by the late 1940s he was contributing "spicy" stories to the monthly magazines published by Utopia Press. His early novels include *Dimension of Horror*, *The Moon Raiders*, *The World Wrecker* and *The Robot Brains*. Writing under a wide number of pseudonyms, he became a regular contributor to such SF magazines as *Tales of Tomorrow*, *Worlds of Fantasy*, *New Worlds Science Fiction*, *Other Worlds Science Stories* and *Fantastic Universe*, amongst other titles. When the magazine markets began to dry up, Bounds became a reliable contributor to such anthology series as *New Writings in SF*, *The Fontana Book of Great Ghost Stories*, *The Fontana Book of Great Horror Stories*, *The Armada Monster Book* and *The Armada Ghost Book*. His story "The Circus" was adapted by George A. Romero for a 1986 episode of the TV series *Tales of the Darkside*. Other anthologies to feature his stories include *Tales of Terror from Outer Space*, *Gaslight Tales of Terror*, *Frighteners*, *Keep Out the Night*, *The Mammoth Book of Vampires*, *The Mammoth Book of New Terror*, *Great Ghost Stories*, *Tales to Freeze the Blood* and Philip Harbottle's *Fantasy Adventure* series. In 2002, Harbottle edited the first-ever collections of Bounds' work, *The Best of Sydney J. Bounds: Strange Portrait and Other Stories* and *The Best of Sydney J. Bounds: The Wayward Ship and Other Stories*, for Cosmos Books.

90-year-old actress and author **Phyllis Fraser** (Helen Brown Nichols/Phyllis Cerf Wagner) died of complications from a fall the same day. The cousin of Ginger Rogers, she appeared in a handful of 1930s films, including *Thirteen Women* and *The Black Room* (with Boris Karloff). She married publisher and co-founder of Random House, Bennett Cerf, in 1940. With Herbert A. Wise she co-edited the seminal anthology *Great Tales of Terror and the Supernatural* in 1944 for her husband's The Modern Library imprint. Following Cerf's death in 1971, she married New York City Mayor Robert Wagner four years later. In the late 1950s she started collaborating with her friend Theodore Geisel ("Dr. Seuss") on a number of children's books, including *Green Eggs and Ham* and *The Cat in the Hat Comes Back*.

American academic **Leon E.** (Eugene) **Stover**, who collaborated with Harry Harrison on the 1968 anthology *Apeman, Spaceman* and the 1972 novel *Stonehenge*, died of complications from diabetes on November 25th, aged 77. Stover also wrote non-fiction studies about Harrison, H. G. Wells and Robert A. Heinlein.

American comic book illustrator **Dave** [Emmett] **Cockrum**, best-known for his work with Len Wein on Marvel's *X-Men* title during the mid-1970s, died after a long battle with diabetes on November 26th, aged 63. Many of the *X-Men* characters Cockrum co-created and designed, including Storm, Mystique, Nightcrawler and Colossus, went on to appear in the popular film franchise. His other credits include drawing the Legion of Super-Heroes for DC Comics before he moved to Marvel. He reportedly died wearing Superman pyjamas and was cremated in a Green Lantern shirt.

Film music composer and conductor **Shirley Walker** died of a brain aneurysm on November 29th, aged 61. Her many credits include *The Dungeonmaster*, *Ghoulies*, *Memoirs of an Invisible Man*, *Batman: Mask of the Phantasm*, *The Haunting of Seacliff Inn*, *The Adventures of Zoom in Outer Space*, *Escape from L.A.*, *It Came from Outer Space 2*, *Asteroid*, *The Love Bug* (1997), all three *Final Destination* films and the remakes of *Willard* (2003) and *Black Christmas* (2006). She also scored many animated TV series, including *Batman* (1992-95).

51-year-old American author [John] **Pierce Askegren** was found dead at his home from a massive heart attack the same day. He wrote the "Inconstant Moons" trilogy (*Human Resource*, *Fall Girl* and *Exit Strategy*) along with comic books and TV and gaming tie-ins.

42-year-old British writer **Craig Hinton**, whose credits include five *Doctor Who* spin-off novels, was found dead at his London home on December 3rd.

Romance writer **Patricia** [Anne] **Matthews** died of respiratory failure and congestive heart failure on December 7th, aged 79. Her 1991 novel *The Unquiet* was an occult romantic thriller, and as "Laura Wylie" she wrote the 1970s horror novel *The Night Visitor*. She was also the author of a number of Gothic romances, often in collaboration with her husband Clayton Hartley Matthews, under the pen name "Patty Brisco".

American comics artist **Martin Nodell**, who co-created and illustrated the original 1940s Green Lantern under the name "Matt Dellon", died on December 9th, aged 91. Nodell reportedly got the idea for Green Lantern's magic ring while waiting for a New York subway and seeing a train operator waving his green light. The character soon got his own comic book, which ran until 1947. He was revived in 1959 and has appeared in various incarnations since. Nodell eventually left the comics industry in the early 1950s and moved on to a career in advertising, where he was part of the original team who created the Pillsbury Doughboy.

TV scriptwriter **Robert Schaefer** died of emphysema on December 14th, aged 80. He wrote for numerous shows, including *Science Fiction Theater* and *Highway to Heaven*, and scripted the 1958 feature *The Lone Ranger and the Lost City of Gold*.

American comics artist **Hardin "Jack" Burnley**, who was the first person other than their creators to draw Superman, Batman and Robin during the Golden Age of comics, died of complications from a broken hip on December 19th, aged 95. Burnley drew the cover for *New York's World Fair* in 1940, featuring the heroic trio, and he continued at DC, assisted by his sister Betty as letterer and brother Ray as background inker, where he co-created Starman (with Gardner Fox) for *Adventure Comics* and *All-Star Comics*. He retired in 1976.

American SF author **Jayge Carr** (Margery Ruth Krueger), whose books include *Leviathan's Deep*, died on December 20th, aged 66. A contributor to *Omni*, *Analog*, *The Magazine of Fantasy & Science Fiction* and *Amazing*, she also wrote the "Rabelais" series of novels: *Navigator's Sindrome*, *The Treasure in the Heart of the Maze* and *Rabelaisian Reprise*.

86-year-old British children's author [Ann] **Philippa Pearce**, whose Carnegie medal-winning time-slip novel *Tom's Midnight Garden* was published in 1958, died of a stroke on December 21st while visiting an exhibition of her work at the Seven Stories children's book museum in Newcastle-upon-Tyne. Her other books include *What the Neighbours Did and Other Stories* and *Who's Afraid? and Other Strange Stories*, and she edited *Dread and Delight: A Century of Children's Ghost Stories*.

American SF fan **Dick** (Richard Harris) **Eney** died of a stroke on December 22nd, aged 74. He published the *Fancyclopedia II* in 1959 and was Fan Guest of Honor at the 1984 World Science Fiction Convention.

PERFORMERS/PERSONALITIES

49-year-old **Bryan Harvey**, the former singer and guitarist with folk/rock duo House of Freaks, was found dead with his family in the basement of his burning home in Richmond, Virginia, on New Year's Day. Along with his wife and two young daughters, he had been bound with tape and had his throat cut before the house was set ablaze. With drummer Johnny Hott, Harvey released five acclaimed albums between 1987 and 1995, including *Tantilla* (1989), *Cakewalk* (1991) and *Invisible Jewel* (1994).

Stuntman and actor **Jerry Summers** died the same day, aged 74. The movies he worked on include *Surf Party*, *Dr. Goldfoot and the Bikini Machine*, *The Phynx*, *Diamonds Are Forever*, *99 & 44/100% Dead*, *Charlie Chan and the Curse of the Dragon Queen*, *D.A.R.Y.L.*, *The Monster Squad* and *Alien Nation*.

Danish-born actress **Osa Massen** died in Santa Monica on January 2nd, aged 91. She went to Hollywood in the late 1930s, where she appeared in such films as *Cry of the Werewolf*, *Night Unto Night* and *Rocketship X-M*. She was also in a 1955 episode of TV's *Science Fiction Theatre*. After retiring from acting, she served on the foreign film selection committee for the Academy of Motion Picture Arts & Sciences.

Puerto Rican-born actor and television producer **Raul Davila**, who played a voodoo priest in *The Believers* (1987), died of a heart attack in New Jersey the same day, aged 74.

British character actor **John Woodnutt** died on January 3rd, aged 81. His film credits include *The Scarlet Blade*, *All Neat in Black Stockings*, *Lifeforce* and *Dragonheart: A New Beginning*. On TV Woodnutt appeared in *Children of the Stones*, as "Merlin" in *Knightmare* (1987-90) and in episodes of *Suspense*, *The Saint*, *Sherlock Holmes*, *The Avengers*, *Adam Adamant Lives!*, *Out of the Unknown*, *The Tomorrow People*, *Doctor Who* and *The Adventures of Sherlock Holmes*.

Phyllis [Lucille] Gates, the former wife of Rock Hudson (who died of AIDS in 1985), died of complications from lung cancer on January 4th, aged 80. She met Hudson in 1954 while working as a secretary for his agent. They married a year later but divorced in 1958. She later discovered that the romance had been arranged to dispel rumours that the actor was gay. Gates became an interior designer and never saw Hudson again.

Soul singer **Lou Rawls** died of lung and brain cancer on January 5th, aged 72. During a forty-year career, Rawls released more than sixty albums and won three Grammy Awards. His biggest hit was "You'll Never Find (Another Love Like Mine)" in 1976. During the 1960s he branched into acting, appearing in such films as *Angel Angel Down We Go* (aka *Cult of the Damned*), *Morella*, *Blues Brothers 2000* and episodes of *Fantasy Island*, *The Fall Guy*, *Early Edition* and *Baywatch Nights* (as regular "Lou Raymond"). As a voice artist he also contributed to *Garfield* and *The Rugrats Movie*.

Stage and screen actress **Anne Meacham** died on January 12th, aged 80. After earning an Obie Award for creating the role of "Catherine Holly" in the 1958 Off Broadway production of Tennessee Williams' *Suddenly Last Summer*, she appeared in such films as *Lilith*, *Dear Dead Delilah*, *Seizure* and *Seeds of Evil* (aka *The Gardener*).

Two-time Academy Award-winning Hollywood star **Shelley Winters** (Shirley Schrift) died of heart failure on January 14th, aged 85. She had been in poor health since suffering a massive heart attack the previous October. After working as a chorus girl on Broadway, Winters moved to Los Angeles in the early 1940s where she shared an apartment with a then unknown Marilyn Monroe. Initially cast for her curvaceous 37-26-36 figure, she later reinvented herself as a capable character actress with more than 130 films to her credit, including *A Thousand and One Nights*, *A Double Life* (she also appeared in the TV remake), *The Night of the Hunter*, *Wild in the Streets*, *The Mad Room*, Roger Corman's *Bloody Mama*, *What's the Matter with Helen?*, *Whoever Slew Auntie Roo?* (aka *Who Slew Auntie Roo?*), *Revenge*, *The Poseidon Adventure* (1972), *The Devil's Daughter* (1972), *Cleopatra Jones*, *The Tenant*, *Pete's Dragon*, *Tentacles*, *The Initiation of Sarah*, *The Visitor*, *Witchfire*, *Déjà Vu*, *Alice in Wonderland* (1985), *The Purple People Eater* and *Rudolph and Frosty's Christmas in July*. The actress also played "Ma Barker" on the 1960s *Batman* TV show. She was married and divorced three times, including to actors Vittorio Gassman and Anthony Franciosa, and in two biographies (1981 and 1989) claimed romances with Burt Lancaster, Erroll Flynn, Clark Gable, William Holden, Marlon Brando and Elvis Presley.

American leading man **Anthony** (Tony) **Franciosa** (Anthony Papaleo) died of a massive stroke on January 19th, less than a week after the death of his former wife (1957-60), actress Shelley Winters. He was 77. The actor, who went to Hollywood in the mid-1950s, had a reputation for being "difficult" on movie sets. His credits include Antonio Margheriti's *Web of the Spider*, *Earth II*, *Curse of the Black Widow*, Dario Argento's *Tenebrae* (aka *Unsane*), *Daughter of Death*, *Ghost Writer*, *La Morte e di Moda* and a TV remake of *The Night of the Hunter* (1991). In 1957 he served ten days in the Los Angeles County jail for punching a press photographer, and two years later went to prison for thirty days for possession of marijuana. Universal fired him from the 1968-71 TV series *The Name of the Game*, accusing of him of "erratic behaviour". He also co-starred in the 1972-73 series *Search* (as "Nick Bianco"), but his sci-spy show *Matt Helm* was cancelled after half a season in 1976.

American soul singer "Wicked" **Wilson Pickett** died of a heart attack on January 20th, aged 64. His 1960s hits include "Mustang

Sally" and "The Midnight Hour". His career enjoyed a renaissance in 1991 with the release of the film *The Commitments*, about a Dublin band that idolised him, and his last album, the Grammy-nominated *It's Harder Now*, was released in 1999.

43-year-old American character actor **Chris** (Christopher) **Penn**, the burly younger brother of actor Sean and son of director Leo (who died in 1998), was found dead on January 24th in his Santa Monica apartment. According to the coroner's office, the main cause of death was an oversized heart and the effects of multiple medication intake. Best remembered for his role as "Nice Guy Eddie Cabot" in Quentin Tarantino's *Reservoir Dogs*, his other credits include *Pale Rider*, *Future Kick* and *Fist of the North Star*.

91-year-old **Fayard Nicholas**, who performed with his younger brother Harold (who died in 2000) as the tap dancing Nicholas Brothers, died of pneumonia and complications from a stroke the same day. The team made their film debut in 1932 and later headlined at the Cotton Club in Harlem.

Benny Hill's straight man, comedian and actor **Henry McGee**, died of complications from Alzheimer's disease on January 28th, aged 77. Early in his career he appeared in the 1950 SF thriller *Seven Days to Noon*, and he was also in Hammer's *Fanatic* (aka *Die! Die! My Darling*), *Digby the Biggest Dog in the World*, *Come Play With Me*, *Revenge of the Pink Panther*, *Carry On Emmannuelle* and TV's *The Avengers*.

Scottish-born ballerina and actress **Moira Shearer** [King] (Lady Kennedy) died on January 31st, aged 80. She had been ill for some time. The flame-haired dancer first rose to prominence as the lead in Michael Powell's *The Red Shoes* (1948), and continued the collaboration with Powell in *The Tales of Hoffman* and *Peeping Tom*. She was married to author and broadcaster Ludovic Kennedy and hosted the 1972 Eurovision Song Contest in Edinburgh.

Brooklyn-born **Al Lewis** (Albert or Alexander Meister, sources vary), best remembered as the 378-year-old Grandpa Munster (actually Count Dracula) on the CBS-TV show *The Munsters* (1964-66), died after a long illness on February 3rd, aged 95 (although some sources claimed 82). In recent years, the cigar-chomping actor had undergone three angioplasty procedures and, in 2003, surgeons were forced to amputate his right leg below the knee and all five toes on his left foot. Lewis appeared in such films as *The Devil's Commandment* (aka *I Vampiri*), *They Might Be Giants*, *Fright House*, *My Grandpa is a Vampire* (aka *Moonrise*), *Night Terror*, the 1988 video compilation *Grampa's Monster Movies* and the spin-off movies *Munster Go Home*, *The Munster's Revenge* and *Here Come the Munsters*. He also played Officer Leo Schnauser on the 1961-63 series *Car 54, Where Are You?*, and his other TV appearances include *The Night Strangler* and episodes of *Lost in Space* and *Rod Serling's Night Gallery*. In a varied career, Lewis also worked as a circus clown, salesman, waiter, children's book author, basketball scout, successful restaurateur, poolroom owner, store detective and the Green Party's political candidate for the governorship of New York state in 1998 (he lost against incumbent Governor George Pataki, but still polled 52,000 votes).

American actress **Jean Byron** (Imogene Burkhart) died the same day, aged 80. A radio singer before being put under contract by Columbia Pictures, she starred opposite Johnny Weismuller in *Voodoo Tiger* and *Jungle Moon Men*. Her other credits include *The Magnetic Monster*, *Invisible Invaders* and episodes of *Science Fiction Theater* and *Batman* (as the Mayor's wife). Byron was briefly married to actor Michael Ansara in the 1950s.

Film and TV actor **Franklin Cover**, whose credits include *The Stepford Wives* (1975), died of pneumonia on February 5th, aged 77.

American character actor **Phil Brown**, best remembered for his role as Luke Skywalker's doomed "Uncle Owen" in *Star Wars* (1977), died of pneumonia on February 9th, aged 89. Blacklisted during the communist witch-hunts of the 1950s, he moved to London to work in films and on the stage. Brown's other credits include Universal's *Weird Woman* and *Jungle Captive*, *The Luck of the Irish*, *Superman* (1978) and *Twilight's Last Gleaming*. He also played a council elder in *Battlestar Galactica: The Second Coming*, a 1990 short inspired by the 1970s TV series, and appeared in episodes of *Colonel March of Scotland Yard* (with Boris Karloff), Hammer's *Journey Into the Unknown*, *Roald Dahl's Tales of the Unexpected* and *Tucker's Witch*.

American actor **Andreas Katsulas**, who played Ambassador G'Kar of Narn in the *Babylon 5* TV series and films (1993-2001), died of lung cancer on February 13th, aged 59. He also portrayed the one-armed man in the 1993 big-screen version of *The Fugitive* and appeared in *Seduction: Three Tales from the Inner Sanctum*, *The Death of the Incredible Hulk* and episodes of *Max Headroom*, *Alien Nation* and *Star Trek: The Next Generation* (in a recurring role as Romulan commander Tomalak).

72-year-old actor **Paul Carr** died of lung cancer in Los Angeles on February 17th. He played Lt. Lee Kelso in the pilot for *Star Trek* and was Lt Devlin on TV's *Buck Rogers*. Carr also appeared in episodes of *One Step Beyond*, *Men Into Space*, *Voyage to the Bottom of the Sea*, *Time Tunnel*, *The Green Hornet*, *Land of the Giants*, *Circle of Fear*, *The Six Million Dollar Man*, *Spider-Man*, *The Incredible Hulk* and *Highway to Heaven*. The actor's movie credits include *Ben*, *The Severed Arm*, *The Bat People*, *Sisters of Death*, *The Killings at Outpost Zeta* and *Solar Crisis*.

Billy Cowsill, lead singer of the 1960s family group The Cowsills, died of emphysema and osteoporosis on February 18th, aged 58. Reportedly the inspiration for TV's *The Partridge Family* (with David Cassidy in the lead), the band's hits included "We Can Fly", "Hair" and the theme for the 1969 TV series *Love, American Style*. The body of Cowsill's brother Barry was found in late December 2005, four months after he went missing from his New Orleans home in the wake of hurricane Katrina.

Emmy Award-winning American comedian and actor **Don Knotts** died of pulmonary and respiratory complications on February 24th, aged 81. Best remembered for his role as Deputy Barney Fife in *The Andy Griffith Show* (1960-68), the bug-eyed Knotts' other credits include *The Incredible Mr. Limpet*, *The Ghost and Mr. Chicken*, *The Reluctant Astronaut*, *I Love a Mystery* (1973), *Herbie Goes to Monte Carlo*, *Pleasantville* and Disney's *Chicken Little*.

Emmy Award-winning American actor and environmental activist **Dennis Weaver** died of complications from cancer the same day, also aged 81. Best remembered for his roles as limping sidekick Chester Goode in the CBS-TV Western *Gunsmoke* (1955-63) and later as fish-out-of-water Marshall Sam McCloud in a long-running series of 1970s NBC Mystery Movies (including *McCloud Meets Dracula* in 1977), his other credits include *Touch of Evil*, *Way . . . Way Out*, *What's the Matter With Helen?*, Steven Spielberg's *Duel*, *Don't Go to Sleep* and episodes of *Alfred Hitchcock Presents*, *Twilight Zone* and *The Hardy Boys/Nancy Drew Mysteries* ("The Mystery of the Hollywood Phantom").

American actor **Darren McGavin**, who starred as investigative reporter Carl Kolchak in the TV movies *The Night Stalker* (1971) and *The Night Strangler* (1972), as well as the spin-off series *Kolchak: The Night Stalker* (1974-75), died on February 25th, aged 83. His many other credits include *Mission Mars*, *The Challenge*, Steven Spielberg's *Something Evil*, *The Six Million Dollar Man* pilot, *The Martian Chronicles* mini-series, *Hangar 18*, *Firebird 2015*, *The Natural*, *Dead Heat* (with Vincent Price), *Captain America* and *By Dawn's Early Light*. On TV he played private eye Mike Hammer in the 1950s TV series of the same name, and appeared in episodes of

Suspense, Tales of Tomorrow, Alfred Hitchcock Presents, Alfred Hitchcock Hour, The Man from U.N.C.L.E., The Evil Touch, Fantasy Island, Tales from the Darkside, Roald Dahl's Tales of the Unexpected, Highway to Heaven and *Monsters*. He also made two guest appearances on *The X Files*, a show that acknowledged its debt to the *Kolchak* series.

Jackson 5 drummer **Johnny Jackson, Jr** (no relation) was stabbed to death on March 1st. He was 55. A woman was arrested for his murder.

Former British child actor **Jack Wild** died after a long illness on March 2nd, aged 53. After receiving an Academy Award nomination for his debut as the Artful Dodger in the 1968 musical *Oliver!*, his career never really took off. He starred in the American TV series *H. R. Pufnstuff* (1969) and the 1970 spin-off movie, but other film roles were sparse. He appeared in *The Pied Piper* (1971) opposite singer Donovan, and made a belated return to the screen twenty years later in *Robin Hood Prince of Thieves*. A heavy smoker and alcoholic since the age of twenty-one, he was diagnosed with oral cancer in 2000 and had an operation three years later to remove part of his tongue and vocal cords. Although he lost his voice, following the surgery he appeared on stage in a pantomime miming his role. When Daniel Radcliffe got the role of Harry Potter, Wild wrote an open letter to the teenage actor warning him of the dangers of becoming a child star.

Scottish writer and singer **Ivor Cutler** died on March 3rd, aged 83. He played Buster Bloodvessel in the Beatles TV movie *Magical Mystery Tour*.

44-year-old singer and former actress **Dana Reeve**, the widow of *Superman* actor Christopher Reeve (who died in 2004), died of lung cancer on March 6th, despite being a non-smoker.

British character actor, comedian, and radio and TV scriptwriter **John Junkin** died of lung cancer, emphysema and asthma on March 7th, aged 76. He appeared with the Beatles in *A Hard Day's Night*, and his other credits include *Vengeance* (aka *The Brain*), *How I Won the War, Wombling Free, Licensed to Love and Kill* (aka *The Man from S.E.X.*), plus episodes of *The Avengers* ("Never, Never Say Die" with Christopher Lee) and *Catweazle*.

Character actor **Kort Falkenberg**, who was featured as Cadet Farren in the 1950s TV series *Tom Corbett, Space Cadet*, died on March 13th, aged 88. He also appeared in episodes of *Men Into Space, One Step Beyond, Voyage to the Bottom of the Sea, Quantum Leap* and *The Adventures of Brisco County Jr*.

Oscar-winning American character actress **Maureen Stapleton** died of chronic pulmonary disease on March 14th, aged 80. Her many credits include *The Fan*, *Cocoon* and *Cocoon: The Return*, *Made in Heaven* and *Doin' Time on Planet Earth*. She also appeared as the eponymous character in a 1982 TV adaptation of Ray Bradbury's *The Electric Grandmother*.

80-year-old American actor and fencing expert **Britt Lomond** died after a long illness on March 22nd. Best remembered as the villainous Captain Monastario on the 1957 Walt Disney TV series *Zorro* and the spin-off feature *The Sign of Zorro*, he later worked behind the camera on such films as *Somewhere in Time*. In 2004, his Monastario character was featured on a US postage stamp.

Country music singer and guitarist **"Buck" Owens** [Alvis Edgar Owens, Jr] died in his sleep of an apparent heart attack on March 25th, aged 76. A pioneer of the "Bakersfield Sound", he co-hosted (1969-86) TV's *Hee-Haw* with Roy Clark. The Beatles covered his song "Act Naturally" in 1965. Owens' first wife, country singer **Bonnie Owens**, died on April 24th, also aged 76.

American character actor **Julian Burton** died on March 27th, aged 73. He appeared in Roger Corman's *Bucket of Blood* and *The Masque of the Red Death*, as well as episodes of TV's *Science Fiction Theatre*, *Thriller*, *The Outer Limits* and *Get Smart*.

55-year-old cult 1970s drive-in actress **Candice Rialson** died of liver disease on March 31st, although her death was not announced for another five months. She appeared in *Pets*, *Candy Stripe Nurses*, *Logan's Run*, *Hollywood Boulevard* (as "Candy Hope"), *Chatterbox* and *Winter Kills*.

Child actor **Gary Gray**, who appeared in MGM's final "Lassie" movie, *The Painted Hills*, died of cancer on April 4th, aged 69. Gray also appeared in *The Next Voice You Hear* as the son of Nancy Davis and James Whitmore.

65-year-old American singer/songwriter **Gene Pitney** died on April 5th, following a concert in Wales. The writer of such classic pop songs as "Hello, Mary Lou", "Rubber Ball" and "He's a Rebel", Pitney launched his own singing career in 1961. His distinctive falsetto voice could be heard on such hits as "Town Without Pity", "(The Man Who Shot) Liberty Valance", "Only Love Can Break a Heart", "24 Hours from Tulsa", "I'm Gonna Be Strong" and "Something's Gotten Hold of My Heart".

American actress **Amanda Duff** [Dunne] died of cancer on April 6th, aged 92. Married to screenwriter and film director Philip Dunne (who died in 1992), she appeared in *Mr Moto in Danger Island* with

Peter Lorre and *The Devil Commands* with Boris Karloff. Duff retired from acting in the early 1940s and became a successful photographer.

American country musician **Gordon Terry**, who appeared in Ron Ormond's 1968 movie *The Monster and the Stripper* (aka *The Exotic Ones*), died after a long illness on April 9th, aged 74.

Singer **June Pointer**, the youngest member of the Grammy-winning Pointer Sisters, died of cancer on April 11th, aged 52. With her sisters Ruth and Anita, she sang on such 1970s and '80s hits as "I'm So Excited", "Slow Hand" and "Jump (For My Love)". June Pointer was arrested for cocaine possession two years before her death and was sentenced to a rehabilitation centre.

German actress **Christiane Maybach**, who played the disembodied head in the 1959 horror film *The Head* (*Die Nackte und der Satan*), died of cancer on April 12th, aged 74. She also appeared in *The Thousand Eyes of Dr Mabuse*, *A Study in Terror* (as "Polly Nichols"), *Satan's Brew* and *Just a Gigolo*.

Indian producer, singer and mega-star **Rajkumer** (Muthuraj Singanalluru Puttaswamayya) died the same day, aged 76. A champion of Kannada language films, he made more than 200 mostly historical and mythological movies and was worshipped by millions. Five people died in demonstrations following his death. In July 2000 Rajkumer and four relatives were kidnapped by the Tamil bandit, Veerappan. He was eventually released 108 days later, after a secret deal was negotiated with the authorities.

American character actor **Henderson Forsythe**, who portrayed Dr David Stewart on the daytime soap opera *As the World Turns* for more than thirty years, died on April 17th, aged 88. He also appeared in the films *Dead of Night* (aka *Deathdream*), *The Cabinet of Dr Ramirez* and *Species II*.

Italian actress **Alida Valli** (Baroness Alida Maria Laura Altenburger von Marckenstein Freunberg), whose career spanned more than sixty years, died in Rome on April 22nd, aged 84. Born in Pula, Italy (in what is now Croatia), she began her film career at the age of nine and made her Hollywood debut in Alfred Hitchcock's *The Paradine Case* (1947). Her other credits include *Eyes Without a Face* (aka *The Horror Chamber of Dr Faustus*), *Antichristo*, *Tender Dracula* (with Peter Cushing), Mario Bava's *Lisa and the Devil* (aka *House of Exorcism*), and Dario Argento's *Suspiria* and *Inferno*.

British film and TV actress **Jennifer Jayne** (Jennifer Jones) died on April 23rd, aged 73. She appeared in *The Trollenberg Terror* (aka *The Crawling Eye*), Hammer's *Hysteria*, *Dr Terror's House of*

Horrors, *They Came from Beyond Space* and *The Medusa Touch*, as well as episodes of TV's *Invisible Man* and *Adam Adamant Lives!* Under the pseudonym "Jay Fairbank" she reportedly scripted the anthology movie *Tales That Witness Madness* and the offbeat musical *Son of Dracula* (1974). Her last screen appearance was as a barmaid in *The Doctor and the Devils*.

Elma G. "Pem" Farnsworth, reputedly the first person to appear on television, died in Utah on April 27th, aged 98. Often called "The Mother of Television", she was the wife of Philo T. Farnsworth and part of the technical team when he demonstrated his invention in San Francisco on September 7th, 1927.

Actress **Alberta Nelson** died of cancer on April 29th, aged 68. She was cast as the leather-clad blonde biker girlfriend of Eric Von Zipper (Harvey Lembeck) in a number of AIP's "Beach Party" movies in the 1960s, including *How to Stuff a Wild Bikini*, *Dr Goldfoot and the Bikini Machine* and *The Ghost in the Invisible Bikini*. Nelson also appeared in an episode of *Thriller* before retiring from the screen in the early 1970s.

British magician **Billy McComb**, who appeared in Clive Barker's *Lord of Illusions*, died on April 30th, aged 84.

American "B" movie actress **Betsy Jones-Moreland** died of cancer after a long illness on May 1st, aged 76. She is best known for her roles in Roger Corman's *The Saga of the Viking Women and Their Voyage to the Waters of the Great Sea Serpent*, *Last Woman on Earth* and *Creature from the Haunted Sea*. She was also in the "Lizard's Leg and Owlet's Wing" episode of TV's *Route 66* which teamed Boris Karloff, Lon Chaney, Jr and Peter Lorre, and her other credits include TV's *My Favorite Martian*, *The Outer Limits* and *The Ghost and Mrs Muir*.

Test pilot and NASA engineer **Bruce A. Peterson** died the same day, aged 72. In 1967, he survived a plane crash at the Dryden Flight Research Center thanks to extensive surgery. He became the model for TV's *The Six Million Dollar Man* (1973-78), the opening credits of which featured the crash of Peterson's wingless M2-F2 test aircraft.

Pro-football player turned actor **Michael "Bear" Taliferro**, who played with the Washington Redskins in the NFL, died of a stroke on May 10th, aged 45. His film credits include *Witch Hunt* and *Armageddon*.

Colombian-American singer **Soraya** died of breast cancer the same day, aged 37. She won a Latin Grammy Award for female album in 2004.

Frankie Thomas, Jr (Frank M. Thomas), who starred on live TV from 1950-55 as *Tom Corbett, Space Cadet*, died of respiratory failure following a stroke on May 11th, aged 85. A juvenile actor on stage and screen since the 1930s, he appeared in the serial *Tim Tyler's Luck*, and played Nancy Drew's boyfriend Ted Nickerson in the series of films made between 1938-39. He later became a recreational bridge instructor and the author of a string of mystery novels, including *Sherlock Holmes Bridge Detective, Sherlock Holmes and the Golden Bird* and *Sherlock Holmes and the Masquerade Murders*. Thomas was set to be a special guest at the 2006 World Science Fiction Convention in Los Angeles and, according to his wishes, he was buried in his Tom Corbett dress uniform on May 16th.

Prolific American character actor **Byron Morrow** died the same day, aged 94. Often cast as a military officer, police chief and other authority figures, he appeared in *The Mysterians, Atlantis the Lost Continent* (uncredited), *Panic in Year Zero!, King Kong vs. Godzilla, Black Zoo, The Strangler, Cyborg 2087, The Wrecking Crew* (uncredited), Disney's *The Computer Wore Tennis Shoes* (uncredited), *Colossus: The Forbin Project, Johnny Got His Gun, The Resurrection of Zachary Wheeler, The Ghost of Flight 401, Fantasy Island, The Golden Gate Murders, Dark Mansions* and episodes of TV's *Men Into Space, The Twilight Zone, The Man from U.N.C.L.E., I Dream of Jeannie, Get Smart, The Invaders, Lost in Space, Bewitched, Star Trek, The Wild Wild West, Night Gallery, Search, Kolchak: The Night Stalker, The Bionic Woman, The Greatest American Hero, Otherworld, Highway to Heaven* and *Beauty and the Beast*.

Actor **Paul Marco**, whose most famous role was Kelton the Cop in Edward D. Wood, Jr's infamous *Plan 9 from Outer Space* and *Night of the Ghouls*, died on May 14th. He was believed to have been around 80. A former child performer alongside Shirley Temple, Judy Garland and Mickey Rooney, Marco also appeared in Wood's *Bride of the Monster* and he was played by actor Max Casella in Tim Burton's biopic *Ed Wood*. Marco also contributed to such documentaries as *Flying Saucers Over Hollywood: The Plan 9 Companion* and *The Haunted World of Edward D. Wood, Jr*, and more recently he recreated his Patrolman Kelton character for the direct-to-DVD movie *Kelton's Dark Corner*.

Music arranger and composer **Lew Anderson**, who was the third person to play silent sidekick Clarabell the Clown on the popular 1950s children's TV show *Howdy Doody*, died of prostate cancer the same day, aged 84.

62-year-old Norwegian-born actress **Eva Norvind** (Eva Johanne Chegodayeva Sakonskaya), who appeared in a number of Mexican films during the 1960s, including *Pacto de Sangre* and *Santo versus the Martian Invasion*, drowned on May 14th off the coast of Zipolite, Oaxaca, when she was dragged under by a wave and thrown against the rocks. After a controversial statement over birth control ended her film career in Mexico in the late 1960s, she relocated to New York in the 1980s and developed the persona of dominatrix "Ava Taurel" in a number of short films and erotic role-playing documentaries. Her daughter, Naqilea Norvind, is an actress in Mexico.

69-year-old former milkman **Freddie Garrity**, lead singer with the 1960s Manchester group Freddie & the Dreamers, died in Wales of complications from emphysema on May 19th. The band's hits include "I'm Telling You Now", "You Were Made for Me" and "If You Gotta Make a Fool of Somebody".

Zoe Rae (Zoë Rae Bech), one of the earliest child stars of the silent film era, died on May 20th, aged 95. She made her screen debut at the age of three in 1914, and two years later Carl Laemmle signed her to a five-year contract at Universal for $100.00 per week. Billed as "Little Zoe, the Universal Baby", she worked with John Ford, Rupert Julian and Lon Chaney (*The Kaiser: The Beast of Berlin*, 1918). "I was just fascinated by him," she later recalled. "He was a very pleasant gentleman, in my eyes, and very dedicated."

64-year-old Jamaican ska and reggae singer **Desmond Dekker** (Desmond Adolphus Dacres) died of a heart attack on May 25th in Surrey, England. As Desmond Dekker and the Aces he had such hits in the 1960s as "Israelites" and "It Mek".

American actor **Paul Gleason**, usually seen in supporting roles as authority figures, died of a rare form of lung cancer on May 27th, aged 67. He had only been diagnosed three weeks earlier. A former professional baseball player and drinking companion of writer Jack Kerouac, Gleason's many credits include *Doc Savage: The Man of Bronze*, *He Knows You're Alone*, *Arthur*, *Ghost Chase*, *Maniac Cop 3: Badge of Silence*, *Abominable*, the 1985 *Star Wars* spin-off *Ewoks: The Battle for Endor*, and episodes of TV's *The Green Hornet* ("Alias the Scarf", with John Carradine), *Beauty and the Beast*, *Tales from the Crypt* ("The Reluctant Vampire"), *Lois & Clark: The New Adventures of Superman* and *Dark Skies*.

British actor and film and TV writer **David Butler** died the same day, aged 78. He appeared in the 1970 horror thriller *Crucible of Horror*.

British musical entertainer **Derek Scott** died on May 27th, aged 84. Following World War II, he formed a comedy duo with Tony Hancock, and he later composed the music for Hancock's 1960s TV series and the film *The Punch and Judy Man*. Scott also composed many songs for *The Muppet Show* and was the voice of the piano-playing dog, Rolfe.

American leading man **Robert Sterling** (William John Hart), best remembered for his role as the ghostly George Kirby in the 1953-56 TV series *Topper*, died on May 30th, aged 88. He had suffered from shingles for a decade. The son of baseball star William S. Hart (not to be confused with the silent screen actor), Sterling appeared in *Mandrake the Magician, Beware Spooks!*, and the 1961 film version of *Voyage to the Bottom of the Sea* as Captain Lee Crane, along with episodes of TV's *Lights Out, Suspense, Alfred Hitchcock Presents, Twilight Zone* and *Fantasy Island*. He was married to actresses Ann Sothern from 1943-49 and Anne Jeffreys (who he co-starred with in *Topper*) from 1951 until his death.

Johnny Grande, who played piano for Bill Haley and His Comets on their 1954 hit "Rock Around the Clock", died on June 2nd, aged 76. He also played on "See You Later, Alligator" and "Rockin' Through the Rye".

Grateful Dead and The Tubes keyboard player **Vince Welnick** apparently committed suicide the same day, aged 55.

75-year-old radio actor **James Barrett**, who voiced the part of Dan Reid, the young nephew of *The Lone Ranger*, died on June 4th. He also worked on *The Green Hornet* and *Sergeant Preston of the Yukon*.

59-year-old Texas-born singer, songwriter and musician **Billy Preston**, best known for playing keyboards on the Beatles' 1970 album *Let it Be*, died of a heart infection and kidney failure on June 6th. He had been in a coma since November the previous year. Often referred to as "the Fifth Beatle" after he was credited on "Get Back", Preston was the first musical guest to appear on TV's *Saturday Night Live* when the show premiered in 1975.

American character actor **Robert Donner**, a founding member of Harvey Lembec's comedy-improv group The Crazy Quilt Comedy Company, died of a heart attack on June 8th, aged 75. After his friend and neighbour, Clint Eastwood, encouraged him to try drama, Donner appeared in more than 100 films and TV shows. Best known for his recurring role as Exidor on *Mork and Mindy* (1978-82), he also appeared in *Agent for H.A.R.M., The Spirit is Willing, The Horror at 37,000 Feet, High Plains Drifter, Damnation Alley,*

Hysterical, *Alan Quatermain and the Lost City of Gold*, *Alien Nation: Dark Horizon* and episodes of TV's *Ghost Story*, *The Six Million Dollar Man*, *The Incredible Hulk*, *Voyagers!*, *Blue Thunder*, *Starman* and *Early Edition*.

Former model and exploitation actress **Audrey Campbell** (aka "Audrey Theile") died after a long illness the same day, aged 76. She suffered from kidney and respiratory problems for many years. Best remembered for her role as Madame Olga in the 1964 sexploitation trilogy *White Slaves of Chinatown*, *Olga's House of Shame* and *Olga's Girls*, she also appeared in *50,000 B.C. (Before Clothing)* and TV's original *Dark Shadows*.

Hollywood leading man **Arthur Franz** died of heart failure and emphysema on June 17th, aged 86. His film credits include *Abbott and Costello Meet the Invisible Man*, *Flight to Mars*, *Invaders from Mars* (1953), *Back from the Dead*, *The Flame Barrier*, *Monster on the Campus*, *The Atomic Submarine*, *Sisters of Death* and *Dream No Evil*. On TV he starred as Bill Winters in the 1959 series *World of the Giants* and appeared in episodes of *Science Fiction Theatre*, *Man Into Space*, *One Step Beyond*, *Voyage to the Bottom of the Sea*, *The Invaders*, *Land of the Giants* and *The Six Million Dollar Man*.

American character actor **Richard Stahl** (aka "Dick Stahl") died on June 18th, aged 74. His numerous credits include *The Student Nurses*, *Billy Jack*, *Slaughterhouse-Five*, *Beware the Blob*, *Terminal Island*, *Good Against Evil*, *High Anxiety*, *Hi Honey – I'm Dead*, plus episodes of TV's *Search*, *Struck by Lightning*, *Highway to Heaven* and *Lois & Clark: The New Adventures of Superman*.

Claydes "Charles" Smith, co-founder and lead guitarist with the 1970s jazz funk group Kool & the Gang, died after a long illness on June 20th, aged 57. Smith wrote the hits "Joanna" and "Take My Heart".

Welsh-born character actor and anti-establishment film-maker **Kenneth Griffith** (Kenneth Griffiths) died on June 25th, aged 84. He made his film debut in the early 1940s, and his credits include *Helter Skelter* (1947), *1984* (1956), *Expresso Bongo*, *Circus of Horrors*, *Jane Eyre* (1970), *Revenge* and *The House in Nightmare Park* (aka *Crazy House*). On TV he is best remembered for appearing in two episodes of the 1960s cult classic *The Prisoner*, including the series finale, "Fall Out".

71-year-old **Lennie Weinrib** (aka "Len Weinrib"), who supplied the voice of the title character on the 1969 TV series *H. R. Pufnstuff* (which he also wrote), died in Santiago, Chile, of a stroke on June 28th. As a prolific voice actor, he worked on numerous cartoons featuring the Addams Family, Flintstones, Charlie Chan, Batman and Scooby-Doo (he was the original voice of Scrappy-Doo), as well as Disney's *Bedknobs and Broomsticks*. Weinrib also appeared in Roger Corman's *Tales of Terror*, *The Strongest Man in the World* and episodes of TV's *The Twilight Zone*, *My Favorite Martian*, *The Munsters* and *The Man from U.N.C.L.E.*

55-year-old American actor **Benjamin Hendrickson**, who won a Daytime Emmy Award for playing police chief Hal Munson on the soap opera *As the World Turns*, committed suicide on July 1st by shooting himself in the head. He had apparently been depressed since his mother's death from cancer in 2003. Hendrickson also appeared in *The Demon Murder Case* and *Manhunter*.

80-year-old American actress **Kasey Rogers** (Josie Imogene Rogers, aka "Laura Elliot"), who played Louise Tate on TV's *Bewitched*, died of a stroke on July 6th after a long battle with cancer. She portrayed the murder victim in Alfred Hitchcock's *Strangers on a Train*, and her other film credits include *Two Lost Worlds*, *When Worlds Collide* and *My Favorite Spy*. A regular on *Peyton Place* (as "Julie Anderson"), she left the show in 1968 and was cast as the wife of advertising executive Larry Tate in *Bewitched*. After retiring from acting, she became a motor racing promoter.

Syd Barrett (Roger Keith Barrett), founder of the rock group Pink Floyd, died of diabetes-related symptoms on July 7th, aged 60. Barrett was the lead singer and guitarist of the group until 1968, when an LSD-induced mental breakdown led to him living as a recluse for more than thirty years. He wrote such early hits for the group as "Arnold Layne" and "See Emily Play", while the Floyd's songs "Wish You Were Here" and "Shine On You Crazy Diamond" celebrated Barrett's genius.

1940s Hollywood star **June Allyson** (Ella Geisman) died after a long illness from pulmonary respiratory failure and acute bronchitis on July 8th, aged 88. A former Broadway chorus dancer, late in her career she appeared in such TV movies as *Curse of the Black Widow* and *The Kid with the Broken Halo*, as well as episodes of *The Sixth Sense*, *The Incredible Hulk*, *Misfits of Science* and *Airwolf*. The first of her three marriages was to actor-director Dick Powell, which lasted from 1945 until his death in 1963.

Tony and Emmy Award-winning stage and screen actor **Barnard Hughes** died after a short illness on July 11th, aged 90. His film credits include *Sisters*, *Rage*, *Oh God!*, Disney's *Tron*, *Maxie*, *The Lost Boys* and such TV movies as *Dr. Cook's Garden*, *The Bor-*

rowers (1973) and *The UFO Incident*. He also appeared in episodes of *Way Out* and *Tales from the Darkside*.

Swiss-German actor **Kurt Kreuger** (aka "Knud Kreuger") often cast as Nazi officers in movies, died of a stroke in Los Angeles on July 12th, aged 89. He appeared in such films as *Secret Service in Darkest Africa* and *The Spider* (1945), and during the 1950s he was Twentieth Century-Fox's third most requested male pin-up. He moved to TV in the 1960s, appearing in episodes of *The Man from U.N.C.L.E.*, *The Wild Wild West*, *Get Smart* ("House of Max") and *Wonder Woman*, before later becoming a hugely successful Beverly Hills realtor.

American burlesque comedian and Oscar-winning supporting actor **Red Buttons** (Aaron Chwatt) died of vascular disease on July 13th, aged 87. In a career that spanned seven decades, his credits include *Five Weeks in a Balloon*, *Gay Purr-ee*, *The Poseidon Adventure* (1972), Disney's *Pete's Dragon*, *C.H.O.M.P.S.*, *When Time Ran Out*, *18 Again!*, *The Ambulance*, the TV movies *The New Original Wonder Woman* and *Alice in Wonderland* (1985), and episodes of *Suspense* and *Fantasy Island*. Buttons was onstage the night in 1942 New York mayor Fiorello La Guardia ordered the police to close down comedian Billy Minsky's club, the city's last burlesque show.

American stage and screen actress **Carrie Nye** (Carolyn Nye McGeoy) died of lung cancer on July 14th, aged 69. The wife of US talk show host Dick Cavett, she appeared in *Creepshow*, *Too Scared to Scream*, *Hello Again* and the TV movie *Screaming Skull*.

Veteran character actor **Jack Warden** (John H. Lebzelter) died on July 19th, aged 85. A former teenage boxer (under the name "Johnny Costello"), he appeared in *The White Buffalo*, *Heaven Can Wait* (1978, for which he was nominated for an Oscar), *Topper* (1979), *The Great Muppet Caper*, *Alice in Wonderland* (1985) and episodes of TV's *The Twilight Zone*, *Bewitched* and *The Invaders*.

Veteran character actor **Robert Cornthwaite** died on July 20th, aged 89. Best remembered for his roles as various doctors in *The Thing from Another World*, *Monkey Business*, *The War of the Worlds* (1953) and *What Ever Happened to Baby Jane?*, he also appeared in *Kiss Me Deadly* (uncredited), *The Ghost and Mr. Chicken*, *Colossus: The Forbin Project*, *The Devil's Daughter*, *The Six Million Dollar Man*, *Futureworld*, *Time Trackers*, *Matinee* (uncredited), *The Naked Monster* and episodes of TV's *Men Into Space*, *Thriller*, *The Twilight Zone*, *The Alfred Hitchcock Hour*, *The Munsters*, *Voyage to the Bottom of the Sea*, *Get Smart*, *Batman* (as villain "Alan A. Dale"), *Kolchak: The Night Stalker*, *Buck Rogers in the 25th Century*, *Beauty and the Beast* and *The Pretender*.

Oscar-nominated Japanese-American film and TV actor **Mako** (Makoto Iwamatsu) died of oesophageal cancer on July 21st, aged 72. He appeared in *The Island at the Top of the World*, *Conan the Barbarian*, *Conan the Destroyer*, *RoboCop 3*, *Highlander III the Sorcerer*, *Bulletproof Monk* and episodes of TV's *I Dream of Jeannie*, *The Green Hornet*, *The Time Tunnel*, *Wonder Woman*, *Supertrain*, *The Incredible Hulk*, *A Man Called Sloane*, *Fantasy Island*, *Voyagers!*, *The Greatest American Hero*, *Faerie Tale Theatre*, *The Secret Adventures of Jules Verne* and *Charmed*. In 1965 Mako co-founded East West Players, the United States' first Asian-American theatre company.

Former child actress and model **J. Madison Wright** [Morris] died of a heart attack the same day, aged 21. She had just returned from her honeymoon. Mostly known for her TV work, her first major role was playing True Danziger in the NBC-TV series *Earth 2* (1994-95). After an X-ray revealed she had an enlarged heart and she was diagnosed with restrictive cardiomyopathy, Morris had a heart transplant in 2000.

Classical music composer and teacher **Dika Newlin**, who later became an actress and unlikely punk rock performer, died on July 22nd, aged 82. A singer and keyboard player with the alternative rock band Apocowlypso in the 1980s, she composed the music for the horror film *Mark of the Devil 666: The Moralist* and appeared in the 1995 movie *Creep*.

British professional jockey turned film stuntman **Mick Dillon** died on July 23rd, aged 80. In 1961, Dillon and two other stuntmen took turns wearing the monster suit for *Gorgo*. He also played one of the deadly plants in *The Day of the Triffids* (1963) and was inside a Dalek for *Dr Who and the Daleks*.

52-year-old **Michael Sellers**, the son of British actor Peter, died of a heart attack on July 24th, twenty-six years to the day after his father died of the same condition at the age of 54. The first child of the actor's marriage to actress Anne Howe, Michael Sellers was left virtually penniless following his father's death and he subsequently wrote the biographies *PS I Love You* (1981) and *Sellers On Sellers* (with Gary Morecambe, 2000).

Johnny Weissmuller, Jr, the son of the Olympic swimmer famous for his movie portrayal of Tarzan in the 1930s and '40s, died of cancer on July 27th, aged 65. A former US Navy underwater demolition expert, the six-foot, six-inch actor appeared in a number of TV shows and movies, including George Lucas' *THX 1138* and *Ewoks: The Battle for Endor*. He co-authored the biography *Tarzan: My Father* with Bill Reed.

Square-jawed leading British actor and "King of the Voice-Overs" **Patrick Allen** (John Keith Patrick Allen) died on July 28th, aged 79. Born in the British protectorate of Nyasaland (now Malawi), he grew up in Canada and America before arriving back in the UK in 1953, where he got a small role in Alfred Hitchcock's *Dial M for Murder*. He starred as the eponymous adventurer in the 1963 TV series *Crane*, and his other film credits include *1984* (1956), Hammer's *Never Take Sweets from a Stranger*, *Captain Clegg* (aka *Night Creatures*) and *When Dinosaurs Ruled the Earth*, *The Night of the Generals*, *Night of the Big Heat* (aka *Island of the Burning Damned*), *The Body Stealers* (aka *Thin Air*) and *Persecution* (aka *The Terror of Sheba*). His also re-voiced Leon Greene's character "Rex" in Hammer's *The Devil Rides Out*. On TV Allen appeared in episodes of *Out of This World*, *The Avengers*, *Journey Into Darkness*, *The Champions*, *Journey to the Unknown*, *U.F.O.*, *Thriller* and *The Return of Sherlock Holmes* (as "Colonel Sebastian Moran"). His distinctive gravel-voice was used by the Ministry of Defence on twenty "Protect and Survive" videos, to be shown on TV in the event of a nuclear attack, and these were sampled by Frankie Goes to Hollywood for their #1 single "Two Tribes". He was married to actress Sarah Lawson since 1960.

57-year-old **Kim McLagan** (Patsy Kerrigan, aka "Kim Kerrigan"), a swinging '60s London fashion model and the former wife (1966-75) of The Who drummer Keith Moon (who died of a drug overdose in 1978), was killed in Texas on August 2nd when she apparently jumped a stop sign in her car and was hit by a truck. In 1978 she married Small Faces keyboard player Ian McLagan.

British wrestler turned actor **Ken Richmond** died on August 3rd, aged 80. From the mid-1950s he was the fourth bare-chested strongman to strike the giant gong for J. Arthur Rank film productions. He also had small roles in *Blithe Spirit* and *Mad About Men*.

Arthur Lee (Arthur Taylor Porter), lead singer with the 1960s Los Angeles band Love, died of lymphoblastic leukaemia the same day, aged 61. Such albums as *Forever Changes* (1967) are said to have influenced Led Zeppelin, Pink Floyd and others. Lee was jailed in 1995 for five years for firing a handgun in the air outside a neighbour's house.

British-born character actor **John** "Basher" **Alderson** died in California on August 4th, aged 90. His numerous credits include

Fritz Lang's *Moonfleet*, the Disney comedy *The Cat from Outer Space*, *Riders of the Storm* and episodes of TV's *Space Patrol*, *Alfred Hitchcock Presents*, *Alfred Hitchcock Hour*, *Voyage to the Bottom of the Sea*, *The Man from U.N.C.L.E.*, *Doctor Who*, *The Time Tunnel*, *The Wild Wild West*, *Rod Serling's Night Gallery* and *Automan*.

Japanese *anime* voice actor **Hirotaka Suzuoki** died of lung cancer on August 6th, aged 56.

Hollywood "B" movie actress [Laura] **Lois January** died of Alzheimer's disease on August 7th, aged 93. The heroine of countless Westerns, she also appeared in *The Black Cat* (1934) and *The Man Who Reclaimed His Head* (both uncredited), *Life Returns*, *Night Life of the Gods*, *The Wizard of Oz* (uncredited as the Emerald City's singing salon operator) and an episode of TV's *Kolchak: The Night Stalker* ("Bad Medicine").

American TV talk show host **Mike Douglas** (Michael Delaney Dowd, Jr) died on August 11th, aged 81. In the late 1940s he sang with Kay Kyser's band, and he was the singing voice of Prince Charming in Walt Disney's 1950 animated feature *Sleeping Beauty*.

73-year-old British-born character actor and prolific voice performer **Tony Jay**, best known as the voice of the scheming Judge Frollo in Disney's animated *The Hunchback of Notre Dame*, died in Los Angeles on August 13th following complications from surgery to remove a non-cancerous tumour from his lungs in April. A member of the Royal Shakespeare Company, he moved to America in 1986 and became a naturalised citizen. His many credits include *Time Bandits* (as the voice of the "Supreme Being"), *Warriors of the Wind*, *Twins*, *My Stepmother is an Alien*, *Beasties*, *Scooby-Doo in Arabian Nights*, *All Dogs Go to Heaven 2*, *Austin Powers: The Spy Who Shagged Me*, *Treasure Planet*, *The Jungle Book 2* and numerous others. The Emmy Award-nominated Jay had recurring roles as the villainous Paracelcus in the TV series *Beauty and the Beast*, Dougie Milford in *Twin Peaks* and Nigel St. John in *Lois & Clark: The New Adventures of Superman*, and appeared in episodes of *Eerie Indiana*, *Star Trek the Next Generation*, *The Adventures of Brisco County Jr* and *The Burning Zone*.

American character actor **Bruno Kirby** (Bruno Giovanni Quidaciolu, aka "B. Kirby, Jr") died of complications from leukaemia on August 14th, aged 57. His credits include *Flesh + Blood*, *Stuart Little*, *Helter Skelter* (2004) and an episode of HBO's *Tales from the Crypt* ("The Trap").

Singer and musician **Buck Page**, who founded the original Western band Riders of the Purple Sage in 1936, died on August 21st, aged 84.

Bruce Gary, drummer for The Knack ("My Sharona") died of non-Hodgkin's lymphoma on August 22nd, aged 55.

British character actor **Bill Stewart** died of complications from motor neurone disease on August 29th, aged 63. He appeared in such films as *Morons from Outer Space*, *101 Dalmatians* (1996) and *Fairy Tale: A True Story*.

Rockabilly singer and songwriter **Jumpin' Gene Simmons**, who had a novelty hit in 1964 with "Haunted House", died after a long illness the same day, aged 69.

90-year-old Canadian-born Hollywood star **Glenn Ford** (Gwyllyn Samuel Newton Ford) was found dead at his home on August 30th. He had suffered a series of strokes over the previous decade. Best known for his many Western roles, Ford also appeared in *The Visitor* (*Stridulum*), *Virus* (*Fukkatsu no hi*), *Happy Birthday to Me*, *Raw Nerve*, the TV movies *The Brotherhood of the Bell* and *The Disappearance of Flight 412*, and his final film appearance was as Jonathan Kent in *Superman* (1978). In 1958 Ford was voted the #1 male box-office attraction. Despite being romantically linked to Rita Hayworth for four decades, the first of his four wives was actress/dancer Eleanor Powell.

1948 and 1952 American Olympic decathlon champion **Bob Mathias**, who later became an actor and Republican Member of Congress, died of cancer on September 2nd, aged 75. He portrayed Prince Theseus in *The Minotaur* (1961).

Actor, radio singer/announcer and television station owner **John Conte** died on September 4th, aged 90. From 1955-58 he hosted more than 600 segments of the NBC-TV daytime anthology series *Matinee Theater*, which included adaptations of *Dracula* (with John Carradine), *Dr. Jekyll and Mr. Hyde* (with Robert Montgomery) and *Frankenstein* (with Primo Carnera). Conte founded the NBC affiliate KMIR-TV in California's Palm Springs-Rancho Mirage area in 1968 and ran the station until he sold it in 1999.

Crikey! Australian "Crocodile Hunter" **Steve Irwin** was killed the same day by a freak stingray strike in the heart during underwater filming for a show called *Ocean's Deadliest* at the Great Barrier Reef. He was only the third person in Australian history to die from a stingray attack. The 44-year-old TV personality and conservationist appeared in *Dr Dolittle 2* and starred in the 2002 movie *The Crocodile Hunter: Collision Course*.

Welsh-born actor **Bill Meilen**, who played Dr Egas Gottreich in *Stephen King's Kingdom Hospital*, died of cancer in Canada on September 4th, aged 74. He also appeared in *Scooby-Doo 2: Monsters Unleashed* and episodes of TV's *The Ray Bradbury Theater*, *The Outer Limits*, *Mysterious Ways*, *Dead Like Me* and *Battlestar Galactica*.

British actress **Hilary** [Lavender] **Mason**, best known for her role as the blind psychic Heather in Nicolas Roeg's *Don't Look Now* (1973), died on September 5th, the day after her 89th birthday. She also appeared in the films *I Don't Want to be Born* (aka *The Devil Within Her*), *Dolls*, *RobotJox*, *Meridian* (aka *Phantoms*), *Afraid of the Dark* and *Haunted*. Her TV credits include *The Secret Garden* (1960), *The Phoenix and the Carpet* (1976), the 1977 *Ripping Yarns* episode "The Curse of the Claw", *The Casebook of Sherlock Holmes: The Last Vampyre*, and episodes of *Out of the Unknown* and *Tales of the Unexpected*.

Broadway actor **Robert Earl Jones**, the father of actor James, died of heart failure on September 7th, aged 95. Blacklisted for refusing to testify before the House of Un-American Activities Committee in the 1950s, his relatively few film credits include *Sleepaway Camp* and *Maniac Cop 2*.

British character actor **Frank Middlemass** died on September 8th, aged 87. His credits include Hammer's *Frankenstein Must Be Destroyed*, *Madame Sin*, *The Island*, *Dreamchild*, *Sherlock Holmes and the Leading Lady* and episodes of *The Avengers*, *Sherlock Holmes* (1968), *The Adventures of Sherlock Holmes*, *The Invisible Man* (1984), *Highlander* and the mini-series *The 10th Kingdom*. In the mid-1960s, needing somewhere to stay in London, Middlemass asked actor Geoffrey Toone (who died in 2005) if he could borrow a spare room for a couple of weeks. Forty years later, he was still there.

American character actor **S. John Launer** died the same day, aged 86. He began his film career in *Creature with the Atom Brain* (1955) and went on to appear in *The Werewolf*, *I Was a Teenage Werewolf* and *Jailhouse Rock* (uncredited, as the judge who sends Elvis to prison), along with episodes of TV's *The Twilight Zone*, *The Alfred Hitchcock Hour*, *The Wild Wild West* and *Batman*. He retired in the late 1970s.

Herbert Rudley, who co-starred with Basil Rathbone, Lon Chaney, Jr, Bela Lugosi, John Carradine, Akim Tamiroff and Tor Johnson in *The Black Sleep* (1956), died of a heart attack on September 9th, aged 96. He also played Ira Gershwin in *Rhapsody in Blue* (1945), and his TV credits include episodes of *Lights Out*, *Science Fiction Theater*, *Suspicion*, *Men Into Space*, *Thriller*, *My*

Favorite Martian, My Living Doll, The Munsters, I Dream of Jeannie and *Project UFO*.

20-year-old **Daniel Smith**, the son of former *Playboy* model Anna Nicole Smith, died in Nassau, Bahamas, on September 10th. He had been visiting his mother in hospital after she had given birth to a daughter three days earlier. A pathologist later attributed his death to a heart attack caused by drugs.

American-born singer **Peter Tevis** died of Parkinson's disease on September 13th, aged 69. Tevis spent most of his early career in Italy, where he was instrumental in creating the distinctive themes for Spaghetti Westerns. After returning to America in the late 1960s, he was credited as music producer on *Flesh Gordon* (1974).

Hungarian-born champion bodybuilder turned actor **Mickey Hargitay** (Miklós Hargitay), the father of Emmy Award-winning actress Mariska, died after a long illness on September 14th, aged 80. Inspired by a magazine cover of muscleman Steve Reeves, Hargitay won the "Mr. Universe", "Mr America" and "Mr Olympia" contests in 1955 and went on to become an ensemble cast member of Mae West's night-club stage show. He was married to actress Jayne Mansfield from 1958 until three years before her untimely death in a car crash in 1967. The couple appeared together in *Will Success Spoil Rock Hunter?*, *Promises! Promises!* and the Italian films *The Loves of Hercules* and *Primitive Love*. Hargitay's other European movies include *Revenge of the Gladiators*, *Lady Frankenstein*, *Delirium*, *The Reincarnation of Isabel* and, most famously, as the "Crimson Executioner" in *Bloody Pit of Horror*. On TV he appeared in an episode of *The Wild Wild West*, and Arnold Schwarzenegger played Hargitay in the 1982 TV movie *The Jayne Mansfield Story*.

Senegal-born British actor **Johnny Sekka** (Lamine Secka) died of lung cancer in California the same day, aged 72. After stowing away on a ship to Europe in the 1950s, he initially worked on the British stage before appearing in such films and TV shows as *Incense for the Damned* (aka *Bloodsuckers*), *Charlie Chan and the Curse of the Dragon Queen*, *Babylon 5: The Gathering*, *The Avengers*, *The Hardy Boys/Nancy Drew Mysteries* ("Voodoo Doll") and *Tales of the Gold Monkey*.

Saxophone player **Danny Flores** (aka "Chuck Rio"), who shouted the word "Tequila!" on the Champs' 1958 hit song of the same name (which he wrote), died of pneumonia on September 19th, aged 77. A heavy drinker during the early days of the band, he reportedly signed away US royalties to the song (which was featured in such films as *Pee-wee's Big Adventure*) for a pittance.

59-year-old actor and voice-over artist **Tim** (Timothy) [Hayes] **Rooney**, the son of veteran Mickey Rooney, died on September 21st after a five-year battle with the muscle disease dermatomyositis. His credits include *Riot of Sunset Strip*, *Village of the Giants* and episodes of TV's *Bewitched* and *The Jetsons*.

Christopher Crawford, the second child adopted by film star Joan Crawford, died of cancer on September 22nd, aged 62. He apparently supported his adoptive sister Christina's account of their upbringing in her 1979 memoir *Mommy Dearest*.

American leading man **Edward** [Laurence] **Albert** (Jr), the only son of actor Eddie Albert (who died in 2005) and Mexican actress/dancer Margo, died of lung cancer the same day, aged 55. His credits include *The Fool Killer* (at the age of eleven), *Killer Bees*, *Death Cruise*, *When Time Ran Out . . .*, *Galaxy of Terror*, *The House Where Evil Dwells*, *Accidents*, *The Girl from Mars*, *Demon Keeper*, *Sorceress* (aka *Temptress II*), *Space Marines*, *Stageghost*, *Mimic 2* and *Sea of Fear*. He voiced Daredevil/Matt Murdock on the 1996 *Spider-Man* cartoon series and the Silver Surfer on *Fantastic Four* the same year. His other TV credits include episodes of *Orson Welles' Great Mysteries* ("A Terribly Strange Bed"), *Tales of the Unexpected*, *The Hitchhiker*, *Star Trek Deep Space Nine*, *Time Trax*, *Profiler*, *The Sentinel*, *Conan*, *Extreme Ghostbusters*, *Sabrina the Teenage Witch*, *Invasion America* and *She Spies*. He had recurring roles as Elliot Burch on *Beauty and the Beast*, Bennett Devlin in the supernatural soap opera *Port Charles* and Mr. Collins on *Power Rangers: Time Force*. Albert was married to British-born actress Katherine Woodville. A dedicated environmentalist, like his father, Malibu's Escondido Canyon was renamed in his honour as the Edward Albert Escondido Trail & Waterfalls.

Influential blues guitarist **Etta Baker**, who recorded with Taj Mahal, died on September 23rd, aged 93. She worked in a textile mill for twenty-six years before starting her professional career in the late 1950s.

Prolific Japanese actor **Tetsuro Tamba** (Shozaburo Tanba), who portrayed Tiger Tanaka in the James Bond movie *You Only Live Twice*, died of pneumonia on September 24th, aged 84. His more than 300 credits (he reportedly never turned down a role) include *The Depths*, *Kwaidan*, *Japan Sinks* (both 1973 and 2006 versions), *The Last Days of Planet Earth*, *Message from Space*, *Peking Man* (1997), *Jigoku*, *Blind Beast vs. Dwarf*, *The Happiness of the Katakuris*, *Gozu* and the popular *anime The Cat Returns*. He later became a spiritual cult leader in Japan.

Iva Toguri D'Aquino, who may have been better known as World War II propagandist "Tokyo Rose", died in Chicago on September 26th, aged 90. An American citizen, D'Aquino had been visiting relatives in Japan when war broke out and she reportedly began broadcasting anti-American propaganda to US troops in the Pacific. She was convicted of treason and jailed for six years in 1949 but, after doubts about guilt, she was pardoned by President Gerald Ford in 1977.

British-born actor, scriptwriter and author **Alan Caillou** (Alan Lyle-Smythe) died in Arizona on October 1st, aged 92. Following World War II, he worked as a police chief in Ethiopa and a district officer in Somalia before moving to Canada and then the United States. Usually cast a British "major" types in Hollywood, Caillou appeared in the 1959 *Journey to the Center the Earth* (uncredited), *Five Weeks in a Balloon, Sole Survivor, The Hound of the Baskervilles* (1972, as Inspector Lestrade), *Everything You Always Wanted to Know About Sex* *And Were Afraid to Ask, The Questor Tapes, Herbie Goes to Monte Carlo, Beyond Evil, The Sword and the Sorcerer* and *Ice Pirates*, along with episodes of TV's *One Step Beyond, Thriller, Tarzan, The Man from U.N.C.L.E.* and *The Girl from U.N.C.L.E.* He also had a recurring role as "The Head" in the SF comedy series *Quark* (1977-78). Among Caillou's scripting credits are the movies *Village of the Giants* and *Kingdom the Spiders*, plus episodes of *Thriller, Voyage to the Bottom of the Sea, The Man from U.N.C.L.E.* and *The Six Million Dollar Man*.

Six-foot, two-inch tall fashion model-turned-actress **Tamara Dobson** died of complications from pneumonia and multiple sclerosis on October 2nd, aged 59. In the 1970s she portrayed the eponymous kung-fu fighting government agent in *Cleopatra Jones* and its sequel, *Cleopatra Jones and the Casino of Gold*. Listed in the *Guinness Book of Records* as the tallest leading actress in films, her other credits include *Chained Heat* and the TV movie *Amazons*. She appeared in an episode of *Buck Rogers in the 25th Century* ("Happy Birthday, Buck") and played "Samantha" on the 1980-81 season of *Jason of Star Command*.

Actress and former model **Frances Bergen** (Frances Westerman), the widow of ventriloquist Edgar Bergen (who died in 1978) and mother of Candice Bergen, died after a long illness the same day, aged 84.

British character actor **Tom Bell** died after a short illness on October 4th, aged 73. Best known for his recurring role in the *Prime Suspect* TV movies, in an acting career dating back to 1948 his other credits include *Quest for Love* (based on a short SF story by John Wyndham), Hammer's *Straight on Till Morning*, an adaptation of Angela Carter's *The Magic Toyshop*, *Prospero's Books*, *Angels*, *Long Time Dead* and episodes of TV's *The Young Indiana Jones Chronicles* ("Young Indiana Jones and the Phantom Train of Doom") and *Dr Terrible's House of Horrible* ("Voodoo Feet of Death").

69-year-old Mexican-American singer **Freddy Fender** died of lung cancer at his home in Texas on October 14th. He had suffered numerous health problems for years due to drug and alcohol abuse. After recording a Spanish-language version of Elvis Presley's "Don't Be Cruel" in the 1950s, he later had hits with "Before the Next Teardrop Falls" and "Wasted Days and Wasted Nights" following a three-year prison sentence for possession of marijuana.

Scottish-born leading man **Derek** [William Douglas] **Bond** died on October 15th, aged 86. His film credits include *Uncle Silas* (aka *The Inheritance*) based on the novel by J. Sheridan Le Fanu, *The Hour of 13*, *Stranger from Venus* (aka *Immediate Disaster*), *Svengali* (1954) and *Visions*. He was one of the first reputable actors to appear in sexploitation films in the 1960s. Bond made his TV debut as a robot in a 1938 adaptation of Karel Capek's *R.U.R.*, and also appeared in episodes of *The New Adventures of Charlie Chan*, *Invisible Man* (1959), *Thriller* (1974) and *Sherlock Holmes and Doctor Watson*.

American actor **Jack DeLeon** died on October 16th. As well as appearing in such films as *Linda Lovelace for President* and *Train Ride to Hollywood*, as a TV voice performer he contributed to *Halloween is Grinch Night*, *The Hobbit*, *Scooby-Doo and Scrappy-Doo* and *Spider-Man* (1981).

Tuba player **Tommy Johnson**, who played the opening notes of the ominous shark theme in Steven Spielberg's *Jaws*, died of complications from cancer and kidney failure the same day, aged 71. Johnson also played on the soundtracks for *Close Encounters of the Third Kind*, *Raiders of the Lost Ark*, *Indiana Jones and the Temple of Doom*, *The Lion King* and various *Star Trek* movies.

Distinctive French character actor **Daniel Emilfork** [Berenstein] died on October 17th, aged 82. Born in Chile of Ukrainian parents, his film credits include *The Hunchback of Notre-Dame* (1956), *OSS 117*, *The Devil's Nightmare* (as the Devil), *The Thief of Baghdad* (1978) and *The City of Lost Children*.

Hollywood actress and former model **Phyllis Kirk** (Phyllis Kirkegaard) who co-starred with Vincent Price in the 1953 3-D movie *House of Wax*, died of a post-cerebral aneurysm on October 19th, aged 79. On TV she appeared in episodes of *Tales of Tomorrow*, *Suspense* ("The Moonstone"), *Climax!* and *The Twilight Zone*, and she played Nora Charles in the 1959 TV series *The Thin Man*, opposite Peter Lawford. She eventually became a publicist for CBS-TV and retired in 1992.

Emmy Award-winning actress **Jane [Waddington] Wyatt**, who co-starred with Ronald Coleman in *Lost Horizon* (1937), died on October 20th, aged 95. Her other film credits include *Great Expectations* (1934) and *Amityville: The Evil Escapes*. On TV she appeared in episodes of *Lights Out*, *The Alfred Hitchcock Hour* ("The Monkey's Paw – A Retelling"), *Fantasy Island*, *Starman* and *The Young Indiana Jones Chronicles*. She played Mr. Spock's mother Amanda in an episode of the original *Star Trek* series ("Journey to Babel"), and the actress later recreated the role in the 1986 film *Star Trek IV The Voyage Home*. She was blacklisted for several years for participating in communist-friendly cultural activities.

77-year-old British character actor **Peter Barkworth** died of broncho-pneumonia following a stroke on October 21st. A mainstay of British television during the 1960s, '70s and '80s, he appeared in episodes of *Doctor Who* ("The Ice Warriors"), *The Avengers*, *Shadows of Fear*, *Out of the Unknown*, *The Rivals of Sherlock Holmes*, *Dead of Night*, *Tales of the Unexpected* and *The Return of Sherlock Holmes*.

Sandy West, drummer with the all-female band The Runaways, died of lung cancer the same day, aged 47. She was only sixteen years old in 1975 when she founded the group with singer and guitarist Joan Jett. Their hits include "Cherry Bomb" and "Born to Be Bad".

84-year-old Canadian-born actor **Arthur Hill** died in a Los Angeles care facility on October 22nd after a long battle with Alzheimer's disease. He made his uncredited film debut in 1949, and went on to appear in *Mr Drake's Duck*, *The Chairman* (aka *The Most Dangerous Man in the World*), *The Andromeda Strain*, *Futureworld*, *Revenge of the Stepford Wives*, Disney's *Something Wicked This Way Comes* (as the Narrator), *Prototype*, *The Murder of Sherlock Holmes*, *Murder in Space* and *One Magic Christmas*, along with episodes of TV's *Colonel March of Scotland Yard* (with Boris Karloff), *Dow Hour of Great Mysteries* ("The Woman in White"), *Alfred Hitchcock Presents*, *Great Ghost Tales*, *Voyage to the Bottom of the Sea*, *The Invaders* and *Tales of the Unexpected*.

Acknowledged as the world's smallest actor, two-feet, four-inch tall **Nelson de la Rosa** died of a heart attack the same day, aged 38.

As well as being the good-luck charm for the Boston Redsox during the baseball team's victorious 2004 World Series run, the Dominican Republic national, who was born with the genetic syndrome microcephalic osteodysplastic primordial dwarfism type II, was the eponymous creature in *Ratman* (*Quella villa in fondo al parco*), portrayed a demon in *Fuoco incrociato* and appeared alongside Marlon Brando in the 1996 version of *The Island of Dr. Moreau* (a role that reportedly became the inspiration for the "Mini-Me" character in the *Austin Powers* films). He subsequently became a circus performer.

Freddie Marsden, the drummer for Liverpool band Gerry and the Pacemakers, which he co-founded with his younger brother in the early 1960s, died on October 23rd, aged 66. He played on such hits as "How Do You Do It", "I Like It", "You'll Never Walk Alone" and "I'm the One".

French actress **Tina Aumont** (Maria Christina Aumont), the daughter of actors Jean-Pierre Aumont and Maria Montez, died of a pulmonary embolism on October 26th, aged 60. After making her screen debut under the name "Tina Marquand" in the 1966 version of *Modesty Blaise*, her credits include Fellini's *Satyricon*, *Necropolis*, *Torso*, *Dinosaur from the Deep* and Jean Rollin's *Two Orphan Vampires*. She married director Christian Marquand in 1963.

66-year-old professional American footballer turned actor **Marlin McKeever** died of complications from injuries received at his home on October 27th. For thirteen years he played with the Los Angeles Rams, the Minnesota Vikings, the Washington Redskins and the Philadelphia Eagles. McKeever and his twin brother Mike (who died in 1967) played the Siamese Cyclops' Ajax and Argo in *The Three Stooges Meet Hercules* (1962). He also appeared in Disney's *The Absent Minded Professor* (1961).

Smooth-voiced British actor **William Franklyn** died of prostate cancer on Halloween, aged 81. His films include Roman Polanski's *Cul-de-sac*, plus Hammer's *Quatermass 2*, *The Snorkel* and *The Satanic Rites of Dracula* (aka *Count Dracula and His Vampire Bride*). On TV, Franklyn appeared in episodes of *The New Adventures of Charlie Chan*, *The Avengers*, *The Champions* and *The New Avengers*, and he took over the role of the Book from the late Peter Jones for the 2004 Radio 4 presentation of *Hitchhiker's Guide to the Galaxy*.

American actress **Bettye Ackerman** [Jaffe] died of complications from Alzheimer's disease on November 1st, aged 82. The widow of actor Sam Jaffe (who died in 1984 and was more than thirty years her senior), her film credits include *Face of Fire* and *Prehysteria! 2*, plus episodes of TV's *Alfred Hitchcock Presents* ("Speciality of the House"), *The Alfred Hitchcock Hour*, *The Sixth Sense*, *Wonder Woman* and *Tales of the Unexpected*.

40-year-old independent New York film actress **Adrienne Shelly** (Adrienne Levine) was found hanged in her office the same day. A 19-year-old construction worker was arrested several days later and charged with second-degree murder in connection with her death (apparently the result of an argument over noise). Shelly wrote and directed the 1994 horror film *Urban Legend*.

Trinidad-born Hollywood actress **Marian Marsh** [Henderson] (Violet Ethelred Krauth) died on November 9th, aged 93. Best known as the teenage Trilby O'Farrell under the mesmeric influence of John Barrymore in the 1931 *Svengali*, based on George du Maurier's 1894 novel, her other credits include *The Mad Genius* (again with Barrymore), *The Black Room* (with Boris Karloff), *Crime and Punishment* (with Peter Lorre), *The Man Who Lived Twice* and *Murder by Invitation*. After retiring in the late 1950s, she married her second husband, pioneer aviator Clifford Henderson, who founded the California community of Palm Desert in the 1940s.

Academy Award-winning "tough guy" actor **Jack Palance** (Vladimir Palahniuk, aka "Walter Jack Palance") died on November 10th, aged 87. Best known for his Westerns (including the classic *Shane*), Palance's more than 125 film appearances also included *Man in the Attic* (as Jack the Ripper), *The Silver Chalice*, Amicus' *Torture Garden*, *Dr Jekyll and Mr Hyde* (1968), Jess Franco's *Justine* (aka *Deadly Sanctuary*), *Craze*, *Dracula* (1973, as the Count), *Welcome to Blood City*, H. G. Wells' *The Shape of Things to Come*, *Hawk the Slayer*, *Without Warning*, *Evil Stalks This House* (aka *Tales of the Haunted*), *Alone in the Dark*, *Gor* and *Outlaws of Gor*, *Batman* (1989), *Solar Crisis*, *Cyborg 2*, *Twilight Zone: Rod Serling's Lost Classics*, *The Swan Princess*, *Ebenezer*, *The Incredible Adventures of Marco Polo* and *Living With the Dead* (aka *Talking to Heaven*). On TV he hosted the documentary series *Unknown Powers* (1978) and ABC's *Ripley's Believe It or Not!* (1980-85), the 1997 special *Monster Mania*, and narrated *The Omen Legacy* (2001). Palance also appeared in episodes of TV's *Lights Out*, *Suspense*, *The Man from U.N.C.L.E.*, *Buck Rogers in the 25th Century* and *Night Visions*.

76-year-old British character actress **Diana Coupland** died the same day after failing to recover from heart surgery. Her first husband was composer Monty Norman and, in 1962, she supplied the voice for Ursula Andress' Honey Ryder singing "Underneath the Mango Tree" in the first James Bond movie, *Dr. No*.

R&B singer **Gerald Levert**, son of The O'Jays' lead singer Eddie Levert, died on November 10th, aged 40. He suffered from a heart condition and died from an apparently accidental mixture of over-the counter and prescription drugs.

British character actor **Ronnie Stevens** died on November 12th, aged 81. For the 1963 puppet TV series *Space Patrol* (aka *Planet Patrol*) he voiced the characters Slim, Husky and Professor Haggarty. Other television work included narrating the children's series *Noggin the Nog* and appearing in episodes of *The Avengers*, *Tales of the Unexpected* and *Goodnight Sweetheart*. Stevens also appeared in the movies *Some Girls Do* and *Morons from Outer Space*.

Busy British character actor **John** [William Francis] **Hallam** died on November 14th, aged 65. Best known as the tyrannical 19th-century squire Thomas Mallen in the 1979 TV series of Catherine Cookson's *The Mallens*, he also appeared in the films *Quest for Love*, *Trial by Combat* (aka *Dirty Knight's Work*), *The People That Time Forgot*, *Flash Gordon* (1980), *Dragonslayer*, *Lifeforce*, *Santa Claus*, *Kull the Conqueror* and *The Incredible Adventures of Marco Polo*. His role as PC McTaggart in the opening scenes of *The Wicker Man* (1973) were cut from the original theatrical release of the cult movie. Hallam's TV credits include *The Chronicles of Narnia* (1989), *The 10th Kingdom*, *Arabian Knights* and episodes of *Randall and Hopkirk (Deceased)*, *Moonbase 3*, *Doctor Who* ("Ghost Light") and *She-Wolf of London*.

R&B singer **Ruth Brown** died of complications from a stroke and heart attack on November 17th, aged 78. Between 1949 and 1961 she had more than two dozen hits, including "(Mama) He Treats Your Daughter Mean". Brown also appeared in such films as *Under the Rainbow* and *Hairspray* (1988).

80-year-old American character actor **Jeremy Slate** died of complications following oesophageal cancer surgery on November 19th. His many films include Hitchcock's *North by Northwest* (uncredited), *Born Losers*, *Hell's Angels '69* (he also wrote the original story), *Hell's Belles*, the obscure *Curse of the Moon Child*, Wes Craven's *Stranger in Our House* (aka *Summer of Fear*), *The Dead Pit* and *The Lawnmower Man*. He also appeared in episodes of TV's *Men Into Space*, *One Step Beyond*, *Alfred Hitchcock Presents*, *The Man from U.N.C.L.E.*, *The Alfred Hitchcock Hour*, *Bewitched*, *Tarzan*, *Ghost Story*, *Wonder Woman* and *Starman*.

South African-born **Vonne Shelley**, who as a teenager appeared in a small number of films under the name "Yvonne Severn", including *Tower of London* (1939), died on November 22nd, aged 79.

76-year-old French actor **Philippe Noiret** died on November 23rd after a long battle with cancer. The two-time Cesar Award-winner's more than 125 film credits include *The Night of the Generals*, Hitchcock's *Topaz* and the supernatural comedy *Fantôme avec chauffeur*.

Veteran American jazz and big-band vocalist **Anita O'Day** (Anita Belle Colton) died of cardiac arrest the same day, aged 87. She recorded around thirty albums and wrote candidly of her battles with heroin addiction and alcoholism in her 1981 biography, *Hard Times, Hard Times*.

British actor **Anthony Jackson**, who played the ghostly Fred Mumford in the children's TV series *Rentaghost* (1976-78), died on November 26th, aged 62. As a voice artist, he contributed to *Labyrinth* and *Watership Down*.

"Greetings, pop-pickers!" After being diagnosed with arthritis in 1991, Australian-born British disc jockey **Alan** "Fluff" [Leslie] **Freeman** MBE died on November 27th, aged 79. He was a pioneering presenter for BBC Radio since the early 1960s and, later, TV's *Top of the Pops*. In 1965 he starred in the carnivorous vine episode of the anthology film *Dr Terror's House of Horrors* and appeared as God in two episodes of TV's *The Young Ones* (1984). "Not arf!"

French actress **Claude Jade** (Claude Marcelle Jorré) died of complications from eye cancer on December 1st, aged 58. A discovery of François Truffaut, who fell in love with her, she appeared in Hitchcock's *Topaz* and such TV productions as *A Midsummer Night's Dream* (1969), the mini-series *Coffin Island* and a 1990 episode of *The Hitchhiker*.

Actor and voice artist **Sid Raymond** (Raymond Silverstein) died of a stroke the same day, aged 97. Best remembered as the voice of such cartoon characters as Baby Huey and Katnip, he also appeared in *Fright* (aka *Spell of the Hypnotist*, 1957) and Tobe Hooper's *The Funhouse*.

84-year-old American supporting actor **Adam Williams** (Adam Berg) died of lymphoma on December 4th. His many credits include *The Day the Earth Stood Still*, *The Space Children*, and episodes of TV's *Science Fiction Theater*, *The Twilight Zone*, *Thriller*, *Alfred Hitchcock Presents* and *Voyage to the Bottom of the Sea*.

American stuntman turned actor **Michael Gilden** died on December 5th, aged 44. Best known for playing Finnegan and Liam on several episodes of TV's *Charmed*, he also appeared in *Star Wars IV: Return of the Jedi* (as an Ewok), *Freaked*, *Pulp Fiction*, *Snow White* (2001) and *Twice Upon Christmas*.

Actor **Russell Wade** died on December 9th, aged 89. Best remembered for his roles in Val Lewton's *The Leopard Man*, *The Ghost Ship* and *The Body Snatcher*, he also appeared in *The Falcon in Danger* and *A Game of Death*. He retired from the screen in the late 1940s for a career as a realtor.

American character actor **Peter Boyle** died of multiple myeloma and heart disease on December 12th, aged 71. A former member of the Christian Brothers religious order, he spent three years living in a monastery before he turned to acting. After working as a production manager on the offbeat science fiction comedy *The Monitors* (1968), Boyle's acting credits include *Young Frankenstein* (as a singing and dancing Monster), *Taxi Driver*, *Beyond the Poseidon Adventure*, *Outland*, *Solar Crisis*, *The Shadow* (1994), *The Santa Clause*, *A Deadly Vision*, *Species II*, *Doctor Dolittle* (1998), *The Adventures of Pluto Nash*, *The Santa Claus 2* (uncredited), *Scooby-Doo 2 Monsters Unleashed* and *The Santa Claus 3: The Escape Claus*. He also appeared in two episodes of TV's *Lois & Clark: The New Adventures of Superman*, and he won an Emmy Award for his guest-starring role in *The X Files* episode "Clyde Bruckman's Final Repose" (1995). John Lennon was the Best Man at Boyle's wedding to *Rolling Stone* journalist Loraine Alterman.

Mike Evans, who played Lionel Jefferson in the American TV sitcoms *All in the Family* and *The Jeffersons*, died of throat cancer on December 14th, aged 57. He also appeared in the films *Now You See Him Now You Don't* and *The House on Skull Mountain*.

Former model **Kimberly [Ann] Ross**, who starred in the 1989 horror film *Pumpkinhead*, died on December 19th, aged 47. She also appeared in *The Last Starfighter*.

Republic Pictures leading lady **Lois Hall** died of a heart attack on December 21st. The 80-year-old actress had earlier been taken ill on the set of David Fincher's *The Curious Case of Benjamin Button* filming in New Orleans. Although best known for appearing in Westerns, her many other credits include playing a low budget female Tarzan in *Daughter of the Jungle*, the 1949 serial *The Adventures of Sir Galahad* (as the Lady of the Lake) and Kenneth Branagh's *Dead Again*. On TV she appeared in episodes of *Dick Tracy* (1950), *Fireside Theatre* ("The Canterville Ghost"), *Adventures of Superman*, *Star Trek: The Next Generation*, *Miracles* and *Lost*.

Peter G. Spelson, who produced, scripted and starred in the 1980 horror/SF film *The Psychotronic Man,* died the same day, aged 75.

"Hello, my darlings." 81-year-old British TV and film comedian **Charlie Drake** (Charles Edward Springall) died in his sleep at a London nursing home on December 23rd following a long illness caused by two strokes in the late 1990s. In 1974 he starred in the Children's Film Foundation movie *Professor Popper's Problem,* in which he was shrunken down to miniature size. His novelty pop song "My Boomerang Won't Come Back" stayed at the #1 slot for four weeks in the Australian music charts in December 1961.

"The Godfather of Soul", influential American singer **James Brown,** died of pneumonia in Atlanta, Georgia, on Christmas Day, aged 73. Best known for such hits as "I Got You (I Feel Good)", "It's a Man's World" and "Get Up (I Feel Like Being a Sex Machine)", he appeared in *Ski Party, The Phynx, The Tuxedo, The Blues Brothers* and *Blues Brothers 2000.* Brown's funky music can also be heard on the soundtracks for *The Fan, Android, Jacob's Ladder, Hudson Hawk, Ghost in the Machine, Demon Knight, The Nutty Professor* (1996), *Face/Off, Kiss the Girls, Doctor Dolittle* (1996), *My Favorite Martian, Muppets from Space, Nutty Professor II: The Klumps, Osmosis Jones, Black Knight, Garfield, Blade Trinity* and Disney's *Robots.*

Tough guy character actor **Frank Campanella** died on December 30th, aged 87. One of his first roles was as Mook the Moon Man in an episode of TV's *Captain Video and His Video Rangers,* and Campanella's other credits include *Seconds, Matt Helm* (1975), *High Anxiety, Heaven Can Wait* (1978), *Angel on My Shoulder* (1980), *Dick Tracy* (1990) and episodes of TV's *Wild Wild West, Kolchak: The Night Stalker* and *Salvage 1.*

FILM/TV TECHNICIANS

American cinematographer **Leonard J. South** died of pneumonia and complications from Alzheimer's disease on January 6th, aged 92. Best known for his nearly a dozen collaborations with Alfred Hitchcock, including *Dial M for Murder, North by Northwest, Rear Window, The Trouble with Harry, The Man Who Knew Too Much, Vertigo, The Birds* and *Family Plot,* his other films include *Hang 'em High, Herbie Goes to Monte Carlo, Home for the Holidays, A Cold Night's Death, Scream Pretty Peggy, Satan's Triangle, The Ghosts of Buxley Hall* and the TV series *Rod Serling's Night Gallery* and *Buck Rogers in the 25th Century.*

74-year-old Academy Award-winning film editor **Stu Linder** died of a heart attack while on location on January 12th. His credits include *Seconds*, *Catch-22*, *The Day of the Dolphin*, *Young Sherlock Holmes* and *Sphere*.

British production designer **Norris Spencer**, a frequent collaborator with Ridley and Tony Scott, died of pneumonia the same day, aged 62. He worked on *Britannia Hospital*, *Hannibal* and *National Treasure*.

Oscar-winning German film producer **Franz Seitz** died after a long illness on January 19th, aged 84. In 1979 he directed a version of Thomas Mann's *Doctor Faustus*.

Austrian-Hungarian-born film and TV director **Otto Lang** died of complications from heart disease on January 30th, aged 98. Arriving in America in the mid-1930s, he worked on such TV series as *World of Giants* (which he also produced), *Men Into Space* and *The Man from U.N.C.L.E.*

Polish-born film director, animator, sculptor and photographer **Walerian Borowczyk** died in Paris on February 3rd, aged 82. His 1974 film *Immoral Tales* featured Paloma Picasso as Countess Bathory bathing in the blood of virgins, *The Beast* (1975) was an erotic retelling of "Beauty and the Beast", and *Bloodlust* (aka *Dr Jekyll and His Women*, 1979) marked the final screen appearance of actor Patrick Magee.

Writer, television director and drama professor **Luther James** died on February 5th, aged 76. He directed episodes of *Bewitched* and was a production executive on such CBS-TV shows as *Mission Impossible*, *The Wild Wild West*, *The Man from U.N.C.L.E.* and *The Girl from U.N.C.L.E.*

British animator **Eddie** (Edric) **Radage** died in early February. His many credits include *Animal Farm* (1954), *Yellow Submarine*, *Watership Down*, *The Lion the Witch and the Wardrobe* (1979), *The Snowman* and the 1967 TV series *The Beatles*.

Scriptwriter, producer and director **Frank Q. Dobbs** died of cancer on February 15th, aged 66. Although best-known for his many Western TV series, his credits also include *Enter the Devil* and the recent mini-series of *King Solomon's Mines*, *Mysterious Island* and *The Poseidon Adventure*.

Australian-born film director **Peter Sykes** died on March 1st, aged around 66. In the early 1970s he brought some class to a flagging Hammer Films with *Demons of the Mind* and *To the Devil a Daughter*. His other credits include *Venom* (aka *The Legend of Spider Forest*), the Frankie Howerd comedy *The House on Night-*

mare Park and several episodes of TV's *The Avengers* and *Orson Welles' Great Mysteries*.

Canadian-born director **Lindsay Shonteff** died in England on March 11th, aged 70. In the 1960s he filmed two low budget British horrors, *Devil Doll* and *Curse of Simba* (aka *Curse of the Voodoo*). His other credits include *Licensed to Kill* (aka *The Second Best Secret Agent in the Whole Wide World*), *The Million Eyes of Sumuru*, *Night After Night After Night* (as "Lewis J. Force"), *No.1 of the Secret Service* and *Licensed to Love and Kill*.

Animation director **Brad Case** died on March 19th, aged 93. He began his career as an animator on Disney's *Bambi* and also worked on *Song of the South* and *Make Mine Music*. In the 1960s he moved to television, where he directed episodes of *The Dick Tracy Show*, *The Pink Panther and Friends* and *The Fantastic Four*. His other credits include *Frankenstein Jr and the Impossibles*, *Birdman and the Galaxy Trio*, *Goober and the Ghost-Chasers*, *Shinbone Alley* and *Daffy Duck's Movie: Fantastic Island*.

66-year-old Spanish film director and scriptwriter **Eloy German de la Iglesia** died on March 23rd, following an operation for renal cancer. His films include *Fantasia . . . 3*, *Cannibal Man*, *Clockwork Terror* and *No One Heard the Scream*.

Australian film producer **Barbi Taylor** died on March 24th, aged 59. Her credits in various production capacities include *Patrick*, *Snapshot*, *Thirst*, *Road Games*, *Frog Dreaming* and Jackie Chan's *First Strike*.

Veteran Hollywood director **Richard Fleischer** died on March 25th, aged 89. The son of 1930s animator Max Fleischer, his numerous films include Disney's classic *20,000 Leagues Under the Sea*, *The Vikings*, *Fantastic Voyage*, *Doctor Dolittle* (1967), *The Boston Strangler*, *Blind Terror* (aka *See No Evil*), *10 Rillington Place*, *Soylent Green*, *Amityville 3-D*, *Conan the Destroyer* and *Red Sonja*.

Emmy Award-winning producer-director **Dan Curtis** died of brain cancer on March 27th, aged 77. Creator of the Gothic daytime soap opera *Dark Shadows* (1966-71 and 1991), which initially ran for 1,225 episodes on ABC-TV, his movies and TV films include *The Strange Case of Dr. Jekyll and Mr. Hyde* (1968), *House of Dark Shadows* and *Night of Dark Shadows*, *The Night Stalker* and *The Night Strangler*, *The Norliss Tapes*, *The Picture of Dorian Gray* (1973), *Dracula* (1973), *The Turn of the Screw*, *Scream of the Wolf*, *Trilogy of Terror*, *Burnt Offerings*, *Curse of the Black Widow*, *Dead of Night* (1977) and *Intruders* (1992). His wife Norma died of heart failure two weeks earlier.

Mechanical special effects technician **Gerald Endler** died the same day, aged 94. His many films include *Voyage to the Bottom of the Sea*, *Silent Running*, *Battle for the Planet of the Apes*, *Sleeper*, *The Towering Inferno*, *Apocalypse Now* and episodes of TV's *The Ghost and Mrs. Muir*, *Lost in Space*, *Land of the Giants* and *Time Tunnel*.

Gloria Monty, who executive produced ABC-TV's daytime soap opera *General Hospital* for more than a decade, died of cancer on March 30th, aged 84. She took over the struggling show in 1978, introducing more fantasy-orientated plots to attract a new audience. More recently, Monty produced a number of TV movies based on books by Mary Higgins Clark, including *Remember Me*, *While My Pretty One Sleeps* and *Let Me Call You Sweetheart*.

American cinematographer **Paul Hipp**, who began his career working on such exploitation films as *Sweet Trash* and *Trader Hornee*, died on April 10th, aged 68. His other credits include *Blood and Lace*, *The Incredible 2-Headed Transplant*, *Garden of the Dead*, *Grave of the Vampire*, *Psycho from Texas*, *Hanger 18*, *The Legend of Sleepy Hollow* (1980), *Earthbound*, *The Boogens* and *The Fall of the House of Usher* (1982).

Korean director **Shin Sang-Ok** died in Seoul on April 11th, aged 79. In the 1970s, both he and his actress wife were separately abducted and transported to North Korea, where they completed seven films before seeking asylum in the West in 1986. His 1985 socialist monster movie *Pulgasari* featured a metal-eating creature, while the horror film *The Gardener* (1998), directed under the name "Simon Sheen", starred Malcolm McDowell, Angie Everhart and Olivia Hussey.

50-year-old TV producer and director **Scott Brazil** died of respiratory failure due to complications from Lou Gehrig's disease (ALS) and lyme disease on April 17th. He directed episodes of TV's *Strange Luck*, *The Burning Zone* and *Buffy the Vampire Slayer* and served as a producer on the series *Space Rangers* and the 1993 TV movie *Lifepod*.

British-born TV director **Peter Ellis** died in California on April 24th. He relocated to the US in the 1980s, where he directed episodes of *Hercules: The Legendary Journeys*, *Highlander*, *Lois & Clark: The New Adventures of Superman*, *Highlander: The Raven*, *Mortal Combat: Conquest*, *Sliders*, *Tarzan*, *Smallville* and *Supernatural*.

Hollywood talent manager and publicist **Jay Bernstein** died of a stroke on April 30th, aged 69. His clients included Farrah Fawcett, Suzanne Somers and Kristy McNichol. He produced the TV films *The Wild Wild West Revisited* and *More Wild Wild West*.

Austrian-born Alpine cameraman **Herbert Raditschnig**, who shot specialist scenes for the James Bond movies *For Your Eyes Only* and *GoldenEye*, died of a stroke on May 6th, aged 72. He was also the cinematographer on the 1987 horror film *The Outing*.

American special effects technician **Philip Barberio** died of multiple myeloma on May 8th, aged 60. He worked on *Star Trek: The Motion Picture*, *Blade Runner*, *Return of the Jedi*, *Ghostbusters*, *The Blob* (1988), *The Abyss*, *Waxwork II: Lost in Time* and such TV series as *The Flash*, *Star Trek: Voyager* and *The Sentinel*.

Veteran British film director, screenwriter and producer **Val Guest** (Valmond Guest) died of prostate cancer in Palm Springs on May 10th, aged 94. A former film journalist, he worked on a number of comedy scripts, including *Alf's Button Afloat*, *Ask a Policeman*, *The Ghost Train* (1941) and *Back Room Boy* before becoming a director in the early 1940s. His numerous credits include Hammer's *The Quatermass Experiment* (aka *The Creeping Unknown*), *Quatermass 2* (aka *Enemy from Space*), *The Abominable Snowman* (aka *The Abominable Snowman of the Himalayas*), *Camp on Blood Island* and *When Dinosaurs Ruled the Earth*, along with *Mr Drake's Duck*, *Expresso Bongo* (with Cliff Richard), *The Day the Earth Caught Fire*, *Where the Spies Are*, *Casino Royale* and the "lost" SF musical *Toomorrow*. He also directed episodes of the TV series *Space: 1999* and *Hammer House of Mystery and Suspense*. Guest was married to actress Yolande Donlan.

Former actor turned BBC-TV producer **Peter Bryant** died on May 19th, aged 82. From 1967-69 he produced and/or story-edited *Doctor Who* starring Patrick Troughton, including such shows as "The Evil of the Daleks", "The Tomb of the Cybermen", "The Abominable Snowmen" and "The Web of Fear".

Two-time Academy Award-winning production designer and art director [Lloyd] **Henry Bumstead** died of prostate cancer on May 24th, aged 91. He worked on more than 100 films in a career than spanned nearly seventy years, including Hitchcock's *The Man Who Knew Too Much* (1956), *Vertigo* and *Family Plot*, *I Married a Monster from Outer Space*, *The Brass Bottle*, *The War Lord*, *Slaughterhouse-Five* (in which he also appeared), *The Concorde – Airport '79*, *The World According to Garp*, *Psycho III*, *Ghost Dad*, *Cape Fear* (1991) and thirteen collaborations with Clint Eastwood.

British documentary film-maker **Michael Croucher**, who produced and directed the 1973 ghost story TV series *Leap in the Dark*, died on May 26th, aged 76.

American special effects pioneer **Arthur Widmer**, who created the

Ulta Violet Travelling Matte (a forerunner of the bluescreen optical process), died on May 28th, aged 91.

Oscar-winning computer animation pioneer **Bill Kovacs** died of complications of a stroke and cerebral haemorrhage on May 30th, aged 56. Having helped develop animation software at Robert Abel and Associates in the 1970s, he used the technology on Disney's 1982 film *Tron*.

Bernard Loomis, one of the first people to successfully market toys through the entertainment industry, died of heart disease on June 2nd, aged 82. From the late 1950s into the 1990s, while working for Mattel, Kenner Toys and other companies, he turned various franchises (including *Star Wars*, *The Six Million Dollar Man* and *The Bionic Woman*) into greeting cards, TV movies and cartoon series. He famously rejected *Close Encounters of the Third Kind* for not being "toyetic" enough.

Pioneering scuba diver **Dick Anderson**, who served as diving equipment technician in Nassau for Disney's *20,000 Leagues Under the Sea*, died of Lou Gehrig's disease (ALS) on June 3rd, aged 73. He was also the dive master on *Jaws: The Revenge*.

Veteran Hollywood director **Vincent Sherman** (Abram Orovitz) died on June 18th, one month short of his 100th birthday. A former stage and screen actor, he made his directorial debut in 1939 with *The Return of Dr X* starring Humphrey Bogart in his only horror film role. In the 1950s Sherman was "greylisted" by the House Un-American Activities Committee, while his 1996 autobiography *Studio Affairs: My Life as a Film Director* revealed that his lovers included Joan Crawford, Bette Davis and Rita Hayworth.

British film producer, director and cinematographer **Monty Berman** (Nestor Montague "Monty" Berman), died on June 20th, aged 93. Born in London's Whitechapel, he worked with Michael Powell and Carol Reed before teaming up with Robert S. Baker in the late 1940s to turn out a string of low budget "B" movies, including *Blood of the Vampire*, *The Trollenberg Terror* (aka *The Crawling Eye*), *Jack the Ripper* (1959), *The Flesh and the Fiends* (aka *Mania*), *The Hellfire Club* and *What a Carve Up!* (aka *No Place Like Homicide*). In the early 1960s, Baker and Berman moved into TV with such popular ITC series as *The Saint* (starring Roger Moore) and *The Baron* (with Steve Forrest), and Berman was paired with writer Dennis Spooner for such shows as *The Champions*, *Randall and Hopkirk (Deceased)*, *Department S* and *Jason King*.

Aaron Spelling, who began his career as a character actor in the 1950s and went on to become one of the most powerful and influential independent producers in television, died after suffering a stroke on June 23rd, aged 83. His long list of credits include Rod Serling's short-lived series *The New People, Charlie's Angels, Fantasy Island, Kindred: The Embraced, Charmed* and the TV movies *How Awful About Allan, The House That Would Not Die, Crowhaven Farm, Five Desperate Women, The Last Child, A Taste of Evil, Home for the Holidays, Satan's School for Girls* (1973 and 2000 versions), *Death Cruise, Death at Love House, Cruise Into Terror, The Power Within,* and *Massarati and the Brain.* Credited with almost 4,000 hours of television and estimated to be worth $300 million, he is listed in the *Guinness Book of Records* as the most prolific producer of TV drama. His first wife was *The Addams Family* actress Carolyn Jones.

Kathy Wood, the widow of cult director Edward D. Wood, Jr (who died in 1978), died of cancer on June 26th, aged 84. She met and married the struggling film-maker in 1955, and worked closely with her husband as an editor and writer on a number of his projects (apparently coming up with the term "solarnite bomb" for *Plan 9 from Outer Space*). She was portrayed by Patricia Arquette in Tim Burton's 1994 biopic *Ed Wood.*

Italian author and film-maker **Stanis(lao) Nievo,** credited as one of the creators of the "mondo" genre of outrageous film documentaries with *Mondo Cane* (1962), died on July 12th, aged 78.

Former vaudeville comedian and country music producer **June Carr Ormond** died in Nashville of complications from a stroke on July 14th, aged 94. With her husband Ron (who died in 1981), she produced a number of poverty-row Western serials starring Lash LaRue and Fuzzy St. John as well as the 1952 cult classic *Mesa of Lost Women, Teenage Bride, White Lightnin' Road* and *Girl from Tobacco Row.* Following a plane crash in 1967, the couple turned to making religious exploitation movies, including *The Monster and the Stripper, The Burning Hell* and *Grim Reaper* (in which she played the witch, "Endor").

Film producer, screenwriter and publicist **Sam X. Abarbanel** died on August 9th, aged 92. A former publicist for Republic Pictures, he wrote and produced the 1950 cult favourite *Prehistoric Women* and scripted the Spanish horror film *Sound of Horror,* featuring Ingrid Pitt and an invisible dinosaur.

Emmy Award-nominated TV documentary writer, producer and director **Nicholas Webster** died after a long illness on August 12th, aged 94. A bit player in *All Quiet on the Western Front* (1930), he directed the feature films *Santa Claus Conquers the Martians, Mission Mars* and the documentary *Manbeast! Myth or Monster?*, plus episodes of TV's *Get Smart*, *The New People*, *The Immortal* and the Leonard Nimoy hosted *In Search of* . . . (including *In Search of Bigfoot*).

75-year-old British TV producer and director **Kim Mills** died after a long illness on August 28th. After working as an assistant director on such films as *Behemoth the Sea Monster* (aka *The Giant Behemoth*), he moved into television in 1960, working on such series as *Plateau of Fear*, *City Beneath the Sea* and *Secret Beneath the Sea*. Two years later he joined the drama team at ABC-TV, where he directed several episodes of *The Avengers*. His other credits include three episodes of *Mystery and Imagination*, *Zodiac* and *The Rivals of Sherlock Holmes*.

Hollywood producer **William M. Aldrich**, the son of director Robert Aldrich, died of cancer on August 31st, aged 62. He began his career as an actor in his father's films *What Ever Happened to Baby Jane?* and *Hush . . . Hush, Sweet Charlotte*, and he has associate producer credits on *What Ever Happened to Aunt Alice* and the 1991 TV version of *What Ever Happened to Baby Jane?*

Belgian director **Remy Belvaux** died in northern France on September 4th, aged 38. He co-directed and acted in the 1992 cult film *Man Bites Dog*, about a camera crew making a documentary about a serial killer. In 1998 he threw a custard pie at Microsoft founder Bill Gates and was found guilty of "mild violence" and fined.

Italian production manager **Armando Govoni** died on September 17th, aged 79. After working in the wardrobe department for Mario Bava's *Giant of Marathon*, he was the production assistant on the director's *Black Sunday* (aka *Revenge of the Vampire*) and *The Evil Eye*.

83-year-old Swedish-born cinematographer **Sven Nykvist** died of complications from the rare brain disease primary progressive aphasia and Alzheimer's disease on September 20th. In a career in which he worked with such directors as Ingmar Bergman, Roman Polanski, Woody Allen, Bob Fosse and Andrei Tarkovsky, the two-time Oscar winner's more than 120 film credits include *Hour of the Wolf*, *The Magic Flute* (1975), *Black Moon*, *The Tenant*, *Dream Lover* and *Curtain Call*.

American director, writer and producer **Stanley Z. Cherry** died of cancer on September 27th, aged 74. His various credits include *The Addams Family*, *The Monkees* and *The Kids from C.A.P.E.R.*

Italian director **Renato Polselli** (aka "Ralph Brown") died on October 1st, aged 84. His many credits include *The Vampire and the Ballerina* (which was reportedly the first Italian horror film to show a profit), *Il Monstro dell'opera*, *La Verità secondo Satana*, *Delirium*, *The Reincarnation of Isabel* and *Mania*.

Veteran film and TV producer **Herbert B.** [Breiter] **Leonard** died of cancer on October 14th, aged 84. He worked in various production capacities on numerous serials and low budget movies, including *Batman and Robin*, *Atom Man vs. Superman*, *Mysterious Island* (1951), *The Magic Carpet*, *Captain Video*, *King of the Congo*, *Blackhawk* and *Adventures of Captain Africa*, along with such "Jungle Jim" adventures as *Mark of the Gorilla*, *Captive Girl*, *Jungle Jim in Pygmy Island*, *Fury of the Congo*, *Killer Ape* and *Jungle Man-Eaters*. His TV credits include the series *The Adventures of Rin Tin Tin*, *Circus Boy* and *Route 66*.

Indian entrepreneur **Spoony Singh** [Sundher], who founded the world-famous Hollywood Wax Museum in 1965, died of congestive heart failure on October 18th, aged 83.

64-year-old Emmy Award-winning cinematographer **James M. Glennon** died from a blood clot following surgery for prostate cancer on October 19th. As well as working as a camera operator on such films as *Altered States* and *Star Wars Episode IV: Return of the Jedi*, and contributing additional photography to *Weird Science*, he shot *Jaws of Death*, *Flight of the Navigator*, *In the Deep Woods*, the 1995 TV drama/documentary *Edgar Allan Poe: Terror of the Soul*, *Invader*, *Carnivàle* and *Return to the Batcave: The Misadventures of Adam and Burt*.

Canadian film and TV director **Daryl Duke** died of pulmonary fribosis on October 21st, aged 77. His credits include *The Return of Charlie Chan* (aka *Happiness is a Warm Clue*) and episodes of *Rod Serling's Night Gallery* and *Ghost Story*.

American set designer and art director **Roy Barnes** died of lung and bone cancer on October 29th, aged 70. His many credits include *Buck Rogers in the 25th Century*, *Red Dawn*, *Poltergeist II: The Other Side*, *Deadly Friend*, *Who Framed Roger Rabbit*, *Nutty Professor II: The Klumps*, *Jurassic Park III*, *The Scorpion King*, *Hulk*, *Big Fish*, *Lemony Snicket's A Series of Unfortunate Events*, *War of the Worlds* (2005) and *Serenity*.

Film producer and composer **Edward L. Alperson, Jr** died on Halloween, aged 81. He received an associate producer credit on the 1986 remake of his father's classic *Invaders from Mars*.

Exploitation cinematographer, director, producer, film editor and actor **Gary Graver** died of cancer on November 16th, aged 68. He collaborated with Orson Welles on such unfinished projects as *The Other Side of the Wind*, *The Dreamers*, *King Lear*, *The Magic Show* and *Moby Dick*, plus the documentaries *F for Fake*, *Filming Othello* and *It's All True*. However, among Graver's more than 300 credits, he is better known for photographing such low-budget titles as *The Mighty Gorga*, *Satan's Sadists*, *Horror of the Blood Monsters* (with John Carradine), *Dracula vs. Frankenstein* (with Lon Chaney, Jr), *Invasion of the Bee Girls*, *The Clones*, *I Spit on Your Corpse!*, *Naughty Stewardesses*, *The Toolbox Murders*, *Doctor Dracula* (again with Carradine), *Deathsport*, *Death Dimension*, *The Glove*, the US footage for *Screamers*, *The Attic*, *Mortuary*, *The Phantom Empire*, *Ancient Evil*, *Deep Space*, *B.O.R.N.*, *Alienator*, *Wizards of the Demon Sword*, *Bad Girls from Mars*, *Haunting Fear*, *Merlin* (1992), *Evil Toons*, *Witch Academy*, *Time Wars*, *Dinosaur Island*, *Possessed by the Night*, *Star Hunter*, *Attack of the 60 Foot Centerfolds*, *Sorceress* and *Sorceress II The Temptress*, *Invisible Dad*, *Alien Escape*, *Femalien II*, *Timegate: Tales of the Saddle Tramps*, *Shandra: The Jungle Girl*, Curtis Harrington's *Usher*, *13 Erotic Ghosts*, *Leeches!*, *Haunting Desires*, *Tomb of the Werewolf* (with Paul Naschy), *Countess Dracula's Orgy of Blood* and *The Mummy's Kiss: 2nd Dynasty*. He also shot (uncredited) the Edward D. Wood, Jr-scripted *One Million AC/DC*. As a director/cinematographer, Graver's credits include *Trick or Treats*, *Moon in Scorpio*, *Evil Spirits* and *Veronica 2030*, while as "Robert McCallum" he directed numerous adult films to support his other projects.

Maverick American writer, producer and director **Robert** [Bernard] **Altman** died of cancer on November 20th, aged 81. After briefly trying acting (*The Secret Life of Walter Mitty*), he turned to writing and directing. His credits include *Countdown*, *Brewster McCloud*, *Images*, *The Long Goodbye*, *Quintet*, the live-action *Popeye*, *The Player*, *Gosford Park*, *A Prairie Home Companion* and episodes of TV's *Alfred Hitchcock Presents*. He received an honorary Oscar at the 2006 Academy Awards.

Japanese director **Akio Jissoji** died of stomach cancer on November 29th, aged 69. In the mid-1960s, while working for Tokyo Broadcasting System, he created the TV series *Ultraman* and *Ultra Seven* with special effects expert Eiji Tsuburaya. He later formed his own production company, and his films include *Ultraman* (1979), *Tokyo: The Last Megalopolis*, *Silver Mask*, *A Watcher in the Attic*, *Murder on D Street* and the omnibus *Rampo Noir* (the latter three titles based on stories by Edogawa Rampo).

Independent American writer, producer and director **Don Dohler** died of cancer on December 2nd, aged 60. Inspired by reading *Famous Monsters of Filmland*, he started making his own films at the age of twelve. His later credits include *The Alien Factor*, *Fiend*, *Nightbeast*, *The Galaxy Invader*, *Blood Massacre* and *The Alien Factor 2: Alien Rampage*. Dohler also scripted and produced *Harvesters*, *Stakes*, *Crawler* and *Vampire Sisters*. He was the founding editor of *Cinemagic* magazine, which published eleven issues between 1972-79.

83-year-old record producer **Ahmet Ertegun**, founder of the Atlantic Records label, died on December 14th, after falling and injuring his head at a Rolling Stones concert at New York's Beacon Theatre on October 29th. In 1947 he borrowed $10,000 to start Atlantic Records, whose artists included Dizzy Gillespie, The Drifters, Bill Haley and the Comets, Ray Charles, Aretha Franklin, Led Zeppelin, Buffalo Springfield and Bobby Darin (Ertegun produced his recording of "Mack the Knife").

Joseph Barbera, who co-founded the animation studio Hanna-Barbera with William Hanna (who died in 2001), died on December 18th, aged 90. Joining forces at MGM in 1937, the team won seven Academy Awards for their work on *Tom and Jerry* cartoons before setting up their own production company in 1957 to cater for television. Starting with *Ruff and Ready* that same year, they churned out around 300 cartoon series, including *The Huckleberry Hound Show*, *The Yogi Bear Show*, *The Flintstones*, *Top Cat*, *The Jetsons*, *The Adventures of Jonny Quest*, *Abbott & Costello*, *Space Ghost*, *Frankenstein Jr and the Impossibles*, *Scooby-Doo Where Are You!*, *The Funky Phantom*, *Sealab 2020* and numerous others, eventually winning eight Emmy Awards. In recent years, many shows originally created by Hanna-Barbera have been turned into big-budget movies with varying success. Barbera's autobiography, *My Life in Toons*, was published in 1994.

USEFUL ADDRESSES

THE FOLLOWING LISTING OF organisations, publications, dealers and individuals is designed to present readers and authors with further avenues to explore. Although I can personally recommend most of those listed on the following pages, neither the publisher nor myself can take any responsibility for the services they offer. Please also note that the information below is only a guide and is subject to change without notice.

—The Editor

ORGANISATIONS

The British Fantasy Society (*www.britishfantasysociety.org*) was founded in 1971 and publishes the bi-monthly newsletter *Prism* and the magazine *Dark Horizons*, featuring articles, interviews and fiction, along with occasional special booklets. The BFS also enjoys a lively online community – there is an e-mail news-feed, a discussion board with numerous links, and a CyberStore selling various publications. FantasyCon is one of the UK's friendliest conventions and there are social gatherings and meet-the-author events organised around Britain. For yearly membership details, e-mail: *secretary@britishfantasysociety.org.uk*. You can also join on-line through the Cyberstore.

The Friends of Arthur Machen (*www.machensoc.demon.co.uk*) is a group whose objectives include encouraging a wider recognition of Machen's work and providing a focus for critical debate. Members get a hardbound journal, *Faunus*, twice a year, and also the informative newsletter *Machenalia*. For membership details, contact Jeremy Cantwell, FOAM Treasurer, Apt.5, 26 Hervey Road, Blackheath, London SE3 8BS, UK.

The Ghost Story Society (*www.ash-tree.bc.ca/GSS.html*) is organised by Barbara and Christopher Roden. They publish the superb

All Hallows three times a year. For more information contact PO Box 1360, Ashcroft, British Columbia, Canada VOK 1A0. E-mail: *nebuly@telus.net*.

The Horror Writers Association (*www.horror.org*) is a world-wide organisation of writers and publishing professionals dedicated to promoting the interests of writers of Horror and Dark Fantasy. It was formed in the early 1980s. Interested individuals may apply for Active, Affiliate or Associate membership. Active membership is limited to professional writers. HWA publishes a monthly *Newsletter*, and its annual Bram Stoker Awards ceremony is now held in conjunction with World Horror Convention. Apply online or write to HWA Membership, PO Box 50577, Palo Alto, CA 94303, USA.

World Fantasy Convention (*www.worldfantasy.org*) is an annual convention held in a different (usually American) city each year, oriented particularly towards serious readers and genre professionals.

World Horror Convention (*www.worldhorrorsociety.org*) is a smaller, more relaxed, event. It is aimed specifically at horror fans and professionals, and held in a different city each year. The annual HWA Bram Stoker Awards ceremony is currently included as part of the events.

SELECTED SMALL PRESS PUBLISHERS

Bloody Books (*www.beautiful-books.o.uk*), 117 Sugden Road, London SW11 5ED, UK. E-mail: *office@beautiful-books.co.uk*

Cemetery Dance Publications (*www.cemeterydance.com*), 132-B Industry Lane, Unit 7, Forest Hill, MD 21050, USA.

Crowswing Books (*www.crowswingbooks.co.uk*), PO Box 301, King's Lynn, Norfolk PE33 OXW, UK.

Earthling Publications (*www.earthlingpub.com*), PO Box 413, Northborough, MA 01532, USA. E-mail: *earthlingpub@yahoo.com*

Fantagraphics Books (*www.fantagraphics.com*), 7563 Lake City Way N.E., Seattle, WA 98115, USA.

Gauntlet Press (*www.gauntletpress.com*), 5307 Arroyo Street, Colorado Springs, CO 80922, USA. E-mail: *info@gauntletpress.com*

Gray Friar Press (*www.grayfriarpress.com*), 19 Ruffield Side, Delph Hill, Wyke, Bradford, West Yorkshire, UK. E-mail: *g.fry@blueyonder.co.uk*

Hadesgate Publications (*www.hadesgate.co.uk*), PO Box 167, Selby, YO8 4WP, UK. E-mail: *hadesgate@hotmail.co.uk*

Hill House, Publishers (*www.hillhousepublishers.com*), 491 Illington Road, Ossining, NY 10562, USA. E-mail: *peter.hillhouse@gmail.com*

Kerlak Publishing (*www.kerlak.com*), 1779-1 Kirby Parkway, Suite 373, Memphis, TN 38138, USA.

Medusa Press (*www.medusapress.com*), PO Box 458, San Carlos, CA 94070, USA. E-mail: *info@medusapress.com*

MonkeyBrain Books (*www.monkeybrainbooks.com*), 11204 Crossland Drive, Austin, TX 78726, USA. E-mail: *info@monkeybrainbooks.com*.

Night Shade Books (*www.nightshadebooks.com*), 1423 33 rd Avenue, San Francisco, CA 94122, USA. E-mail: *night@.nightshadebooks.com*

Nocturne Press (*www.noctpress.com*), PO Box 226, Pacific, Washington 98047-0226, USA.

Pendragon Press (*www.pendragonpress.co.uk*), PO Box 12, Maesteg, Mid Glamorgan, South Wales CF34 0XG, UK.

PS Publishing (*www.pspublishing.co.uk*), Grosvenor House, 1 New Road, Hornsea, East Yorkshire HU18 1PG, UK. E-mail: *editor@pspublishing.co.uk*

Raw Dog Screaming Press (*www.rawdogscreaming.com*), 5103 72nd Place, Hyattsville, MD 20784, USA.

Sarob Press (*www.home.freeuk.net/sarobpress*), "Ty Newydd", Four Roads, Kidwelly, Carmarthenshire SA17 4SF, Wales, UK. E-mail: *sarobpress@freeuk.com*.

Savoy Books (*www.savoy.abel.co.uk*), 446 Wilmslow Road, Withington, Manchester M20 3BW, UK. E-mail: *office@savoy.abel.co.uk*

Solitude Publications, 9356 Lamont, Livonia, MI 48150, USA. E-mail: *jade0319@twmi.rr.com*

Subterranean Press (*www.subterraneanpress.com*), PO Box 190106, Burton, MI 48519, USA. E-mail: *subpress@earthlink.net*

Tachyon Publications (*www.tachyonpublications.com*), 1459 18th Street #139, San Francisco, CA 94107, USA. E-mail: *jw@tachyonpublications.com*

Telos Publishing Ltd (*www.telos.co.uk*), 61 Elgar Avenue, Tolworth, Surrey KT5 9JP, UK. E-mail: *feedback@telos.co.uk*

Twilight Tales (*www.TwilightTales.com*), PO Box 817, Chicago, IL 60614, USA. E-mail: *sales@twilighttales.com*

Wormhole Books (*www.wormholebooks.com*), 413 High Street, Fort Wayne, IN 46808, USA. E-mail: *info@wormholebooks.com*

* * *

SELECTED MAGAZINES

Alan K's Inhuman Magazine is an attractive digest fiction publication with an old-time pulp feel. For more information (no unsolicited manuscripts) e-mail: *outreart@aol.com*

Apex Science Fiction & Horror Digest (*www.apexdigest.com*) is a quarterly digest magazine edited by Jason B. Sizemore. Subscriptions are available from: Apex Digest, PO Box 2223, Lexington, KY 40588-2223, USA. E-mail: *jason@apexdigest.com*

Cemetery Dance Magazine (*www.cemeterydance.com*) is edited by Richard Chizmar and Robert Morrish and includes fiction up to 5,000 words, interviews, articles and columns by many of the biggest names in horror. For subscription information contact: Cemetery Dance Publications, PO Box 623, Forest Hill, MD 21050, USA. E-mail: *info@cemeterydance.com*

Locus (*www.locusmag.com*) is the monthly newspaper of the SF/fantasy/horror field. Contact: Locus Publications, PO Box 13305, Oakland, CA 94661, USA. Subscription information with other rates and order forms are also available on the website. Sterling equivalent cheques can be sent to: Fantast (Medway) Ltd, PO Box 23, Upwell Wisbech, Cambs PE14 9BU, UK. E-mail: *locus@locusmag.com*

The Magazine of Fantasy & Science Fiction (*www.fsfmag.com*) has been publishing some of the best imaginative fiction for more than fifty years. Edited by Gordon Van Gelder, single copies or an annual subscription (which includes the double October/November anniversary issue) are available by US cheques or credit card from: Fantasy & Science Fiction, PO Box 3447, Hoboken, NJ 07030, USA, or you can subscribe online.

New Genre (*www.new-genre.com*) is published annually in softcover book format by editors Adam Golaski (horror) and Jeff Paris (science fiction). Unsolicited submissions are welcomed up to 14,000 words. Unpublished works only, no electronic submissions. Enclose a SAE for reply. Back issues also available. New Genre, PO Box 270092, West Hartford, CT 06127, USA. E-mail: *info@new-genre.com*

PostScripts: The A to Z of Fantastic Fiction (*www.pspublishing.co.uk*) is an excellent hardcover magazine from PS Publishing. Each issue features approximately 60,000 words of fiction (SF, fantasy, horror and crime/suspense), plus a guest editorial, interviews and occasional non-fiction. Issues are also available as a signed, limited edition. For more information contact: PS Publishing Ltd., Grosvenor House, 1 New Road, Hornsea, East Yorkshire HU18 1PG, UK. E-mail: *editor@pspublishing.co*

Rue Morgue (*www.rue-morgue.com*), is a glossy bi-monthly magazine edited by Jovanka Vuckovic and subtitled "Horror in Culture & Entertainment". Packed with full colour features and reviews of new films, books, comics, music and game releases. Subscriptions are available from: Marrs Media Inc., 2926 Dundas Street West, Toronto, ON M6P 1Y8, Canada, or by credit card on the web site. E-mail: *info@rue-morgue.co*m. *Rue Morgue* also runs the Festival of Fear: Canadian National Horror Expo in Toronto. Every Friday you can log on to a new show at Rue Morgue Radio at *www.icebergradio .com* and your horror shopping online source, The Rue Morgue Marketplace, is at *www.ruemorguemarketplace.com*

SF Site (*www.sfsite.com*) has been posted twice each month since 1997. Presently, it publishes around thirty to fifty reviews of SF, fantasy and horror from mass-market publishers and some small press. They also maintain link pages for Author and Fan Tribute Sites and other facets including pages for Interviews, Fiction, Science Fact, Bookstores, Small Press, Publishers, E-zines and Magazines, Artists, Audio, Art Galleries, Newsgroups and Writers' Resources. Periodically, they add features such as author and publisher reading lists.

Talebones (*www.talebones.com*) is an attractive digest magazine of science fiction and dark fantasy edited and published 2-3 times a year by Patrick and Honna Swenson. For one and two year subscriptions (US funds only or credit card) write to: 5203 Quincy Avenue S.E., Auburn, WA 98092, USA. E-mail: *info@talebones.com*

Video Watchdog (*www.videowatchdog.com*) is a full colour monthly review of horror, fantasy and cult cinema on tape and disc, published by Tim and Donna Lucas. Described as "The Perfectionist's Guide to Fantastic Video", an annual twelve-issue subscription is available in US funds only or VISA/MasterCard to: Video Watchdog, PO Box 5283, Cincinnati, OH 45205-0283, USA. E-mail: *orders@videowatchdog.com*

Weird Tales (*www.weirdtalesmagazine.com*) is the latest large-size incarnation of "The Unique Magazine", recently revamped with a new logo. Published by Wildside Press LLC, in association with Terminus Publishing Co., Inc. Single copies or a six-issue subscription is available (in US funds only) from: Wildside Press, 9710 Traville Gateway Drive #234, Rockville, MD 20850, USA. Submissions should be sent to *weirdtales@gmail.com* or sent to PO Box 38190, Tallahassee, FL 32315, USA. Writers' guidelines are available from the website. For subscriptions in the UK contact: Cold Tonnage Books, 22 Kings Lane, Windlesham, Surrey, GU20 6JQ, UK (*andy@coldtonnage.co.uk*).

BOOK DEALERS

Bookfellows/Mystery and Imagination Books (*www.mystery andimagination.com*) is owned and operated by Malcolm and Christine Bell, who have been selling fine and rare books since 1975. This clean and neatly organised store includes SF/fantasy/horror/mystery, along with all other areas of popular literature. Many editions are signed, and catalogues are issued regularly. Credit cards accepted. Open seven days a week at 238 N. Brand Blvd., Glendale, California 91203, USA. Tel: (818) 545-0206. Fax: (818) 545-0094. E-mail: *bookfellows@gowebway.com*

Borderlands Books (*www.borderlands-books.com*) is a nicely designed store with friendly staff and an impressive stock of new and used books from both sides of the Atlantic. 866 Valencia Street (at 19th), San Francisco, CA 94110, USA. Tel: (415) 824-8203 or (888) 893-4008 (toll free in the US). Credit cards accepted. Worldwide shipping. E-mail: *office@borderlands-books.com*

Cold Tonnage Books (*www.coldtonnage.com*) offers excellent mail order new and used SF/fantasy/horror, art, reference, limited editions etc. Write to: Andy & Angela Richards, Cold Tonnage Books, 22 Kings Lane, Windlesham, Surrey GU20 6JQ, UK. Credit cards accepted. Tel: +44 (0)1276-475388. E-mail: *andy@coldtonnage.com*

Ken Cowley offers mostly used SF/fantasy/horror/crime/supernatural, collectibles, pulps, videos etc. by mail order at very reasonable prices. Write to: Trinity Cottage, 153 Old Church Road, Clevedon, North Somerset, BS21 7TU, UK. Tel: +44 (0)1275-872247. E-mail: *kencowley@blueyonder.co.uk*

Dark Delicacies (*www.darkdel.com*) is a friendly Burbank, California, store specialising in horror books, toys, vampire merchandise and signings. They also do mail order and run money-saving book club and membership discount deals. 4213 West Burbank Blvd., Burbank, CA 91505, USA. Tel: (818) 556-6660. Credit cards accepted. E-mail: *darkdel@darkdel.com*

DreamHaven Books & Comics (*www.dreamhavenbooks.com*) store and mail order offers new and used SF/fantasy/horror/art and illustrated etc. with regular catalogues (both print and e-mail). Write to: 912 West Lake Street, Minneapolis, MN 55408, USA. Credit cards accepted. Tel: (612) 823-6070. E-mail: *dream@dreamhavenbooks.com*

Fantastic Literature (*www.fantasticliterature.com*) mail order offers the UK's biggest online out-of-print SF/fantasy/horror genre bookshop. Fanzines, pulps and vintage paperbacks as well. Write to: Simon and Laraine Gosden, Fantastic Literature, 35 The Ramparts, Rayleigh, Essex SS6 8PY, UK. Credit cards and Pay Pal accepted. Tel/Fax: +44 (0)1268-747564. E-mail: *sgosden@netcomuk.co.uk*

Fantasy Centre (*www.fantasycentre.biz*) shop (open 10:00am-6:00pm, Monday to Saturday) and mail order has used SF/fantasy/horror, art, reference, pulps etc. at reasonable prices with regular bi-monthly catalogues. They also stock a wide range of new books from small, specialist publishers. Write to: 157 Holloway Road, London N7 8LX, UK. Credit cards accepted. Tel/Fax: +44 (0)20-7607 9433. E-mail: *books@fantasycentre.biz*

Ferret Fantasy, 27 Beechcroft Road, Upper Tooting, London SW17 7BX. George Locke's legendary mail-order business now shares retail premises at Greening Burland, 27 Cecil Court, London WC2N 4EZ, UK (10:00am-6:00pm weedays; 10:00am-5:00pm Sundays). Used SF/fantasy/horror, antiquarian, modern first editions. Catalogues issued. Tel: +44 (0)20-8767-0029. E-mail: *george_locke@hotmail.com*

Ghost Stories run by Richard Dalby issues semi-regular mail order lists of used ghost and supernatural volumes at very reasonable prices. Write to: 4 Westbourne Park, Scarborough, North Yorkshire YO12 4AT, UK. Tel: +44 (0)1723 377049.

Kayo Books (*www.kayobooks.com*) is a bright, clean treasure-trove of used SF/fantasy/horror/mystery/pulps spread over two floors. Titles are stacked alphabetically by subject, and there are many bargains to be had. Credit cards accepted. Visit the store (Wednesday-Saturday, 11:00am to 6:00pm) at 814 Post Street, San Francisco, CA 94109, USA or order off their website. Tel: (415) 749 0554. *E-mail: kayo@kayobooks.com*

Porcupine Books offers regular catalogues and extensive mail order lists of used fantasy/horror/SF titles via e-mail *brian@porcupine.demon.co.uk* or write to: 37 Coventry Road, Ilford, Essex IG1 4QR, UK. Tel: +44 (0)20 8554-3799.

Kirk Ruebotham (*www.abebooks.com/home/kirk61/*) is a mail-order only dealer, who sells out-of-print and used horror/SF/fantasy/crime and related non-fiction at very good prices, with regular catalogues. Write to: 16 Beaconsfield Road, Runcorn, Cheshire WA7 4BX, UK. Tel: +44 (0)1928-560540 (10:00am-8:00pm). E-mail: *kirk.ruebotham@ntlworld.com*

The Talking Dead is run by Bob and Julie Wardzinski and offers reasonably priced paperbacks, rare pulps and hardcovers, with catalogues issued regularly. They accept wants lists and are also the exclusive supplier of back issues of *Interzone*. Credit cards accepted. Contact them at: 12 Rosamund Avenue, Merley, Wimborne, Dorset BH21 1TE, UK. Tel: +44 (0)1202-849212 (9:00am-9:00pm). E-mail: *books@thetalkingdead.fsnet.co.uk*

Ygor's Books specialises in out-of-print science fiction, fantasy and horror titles, including British, signed, speciality press and limited editions. They also buy books, letters and original art in these fields. E-mail: *ygorsbooks@earthlink.net*

Other titles available from Constable and Robinson Ltd

The Mammoth Book of Haunted House Stories Ed. Peter Haining £7.99 [   ]
The biggest and best anthology of hauntings ever. More than 40 tales of visitations
from vengeful and violent spirits. There are also selections by famously spooky screen
stars such as Boris Karloff and Christopher Lee. These eerie tales will cast a chill in
your bones. Be sure to leave the hall light on when you go to bed!

The Mammoth Book of Monsters Ed. Stephen Jones £7.99 [   ]
A mammoth line-up of the most memorable monsters – vampires, werewolves, zombies, mad scientists' hideous creations – along with some frighteningly new surprises
– Medusa-like gargoyles and shape-changing selkies to name but a few. The pleasure
of making their acquaintance is dubious, but nonetheless, a thrilling one.

The Mammoth Book of Modern Ghost Stories Ed. Peter Haining £7.99 [   ]
Some of the finest writers of the twentieth and twenty-first centuries turn their hand
to the supernatural, from Algernon Blackwood and Daphne du Maurier to Philip
Pullman and Joyce Carol Oates. This superb selection of ghostly stories by masters of
the form will appeal to lovers of literature, as well as lovers of spectres and spooks.

The Mammoth Book of New Terror Ed. Stephen Jones £7.99 [   ]
A bumper crop of fantastically creepy writing that will hurtle you into a twilight
world. This fantastic anthology contains contemporary classics of unease by popular
authors such as Karl Edward Wagner, Brian Lumley and David Case, and brand-new
stories from Christopher Fowler, Graham Masterton, Tanith Lee and others.

*Constable and Robinson books are available from all good bookshops, or may be
ordered directly from the publisher. Just tick the boxes for the title you want (and
the quantity required if more than one copy of the title) and complete the form
below.*

TBS Direct
FREEPOST RLUL-SJGC-SGKJ, Cash Sales/Direct Mail Dept., The Book Service,
Colchester Road, Frating, Colchester, CO7 7DW
Tel: +44 (0) 1206 255 800
Fax: +44 (0) 1206 255 930
Email: sales@tbs-ltd.co.uk

UK/BFPO customers: please allow £1.00 p&p for the first book, plus 50p for the second, and
an additional 30p for each book thereafter, up to a maximum charge of £3.00. Overseas customers (incl. Ireland): please allow £2.00 p&p for the first book, plus £1.00 for the second,
plus 50p for each additional book.

Please send me the titles ticked above.

NAME (block letters) . . . .

ADDRESS . . . .

. . . .

. . . . POSTCODE . . . .

I enclose a cheque/PO (payable to 'TBS Direct') for the amount of £ . . . .

I wish to pay by Switch/Credit card

Card number: . . . .

Expiry date: . . . . Switch issue number: . . . .